MORPHIDS

THE TALES OF CERAHYA

KERRY ALEXANDER-HALL

This is a work of fiction. Names, characters, organisations, places, incidents and events are the product of the author's imagination; or are used fictitiously. Any resemblance to establishments or actual persons- living or dead are entirely coincidental.

No part of this book may be produced, or stored in a retrieval system or transmitted in any form or by means electronic, mechanical, photocopying, recording or otherwise, without express written permission of the author.

Acknowledgements

I had always believed I had no imagination; that I was a product of my academic career. Hence, this journey took me by surprise. It was only with encouragement and support from friends and family, could I begin to realise my dream. I have had the most amazing support from my darling husband Ken. His belief in me helped me to work through my insecurities and to realise; dreams can come true. That illness is no barrier to your passion in life; just take it one small step at a time. My frequent badgering of please read this chapter; I am sure tested his sanity.

A big kiss for my sweet fur-baby Molly; she was my constant companion and sounding board. Her sweet eyes looking lovingly into mine at all hours of the night for me meant, wow that sounds great mamma, but in reality it was can I please have another nummy.

A big thank you to the friends I have made on the Fantasy Sci-Fi-Network. They have kept me grounded and encouraged me to keep writing, even on my worst days.

I could not have completed this tale without the wonderful beta-reading skills and constructive feedback from Karen, Leisl, Wayne, Renee and Jill. I do hope you will forgive me for the length of this book.

I have had amazing support from my extended family. You will always remain in my heart; thank you Marina, my mother Miriam, Deb, Michelle and Naomi.

Renee and Garth, thank you for your insightful wisdom with the forms, exercises and sword dance instruction and Jason for your word-myster brain.

Karen, Leisl and Amanda, you ladies have been my rock; the most amazing friends throughout this wonderful journey. Your never faulting friendship, guidance and support have meant the world to me.

Teresa and Ken your artistic skills leave me breathless, Thank you so much.

For Ken

The love of my life

Table of Contents

The Last Prophecy: i
Map: iii
Chapter 1 The Academy of Magic-Ashmourne Island: 1
Chapter 2 The Journey Begins: 9
Chapter 3 The Game Master: Mist-Wick Island: 21
Chapter 4 The Camp of a Thousand Hells: 29
Chapter 5 What Lies Behind? 41
Chapter 6 Janlin Village: 49
Chapter 7 Meet and Greet: 59
Chapter 8 A Fine Mess: 73
Chapter 9 Strength to Strength: 81
Chapter 10 Flight or Fight: 89
Chapter 11 Show and Tell: 97
Chapter 12 Beaumont Castle: 107
Chapter 13 All in a Day's Work: 119
Chapter 14 Never a Dull Moment: 133
Chapter 15 True Lies: 143
Chapter 16 Some Secrets Revealed: 151
Chapter 17 The New Apprentice: 167
Chapter 18 Boys to Men: 175
Chapter 19 Games under Foot: 187
Chapter 20 No pain…No gain: 195
Chapter 21 Betha: 203
Chapter 22 Clagged: 213
Chapter 23 Preparations: 225
Chapter 24 The Turnings: 239
Chapter 25 The Alliance: 249
Chapter 26 The Cube: 257
Chapter 27 Bricks and Mortar: 271
Chapter 28 Reality Check: 281
Chapter 29 Northern Mission: 287
Chapter 30 Dilemmas: 295
Chapter 31 The Plateau & Ridgeways: 303
Chapter 32 Eggcitement: 313

Chapter 33 Escape from Mere Town:.....................................321
Chapter 34 Barron:...333
Chapter 35 The Mountain Rescue: 347
Chapter 36 The Ways that Time Forgot:.................................355
Chapter 37 This Way to the Cave-in 363
Chapter 38 The Wrong Road 375
Chapter 39 The Ancient Catacombs 383
Chapter 40 North Mede:...395
Chapter 41 The Exchange:...409
Chapter 42 Never a Dull Moment:......................................419
Chapter 43 A Father's Fury: 429
Chapter 44 The King's Dilemma:..437
Chapter 45 The Wizard's Nemi: 451
Chapter 46 Revelations:...463
Chapter 47 The Return:...475
Chapter 48 Memories: 483
Chapter 49 The Choice:...495
Chapter 50 The Last Goodbye:...509
Chapter 51 The Cube 11:..521
Chapter 52 Battle-lust:...531
Chapter 53 The Battle for Mist-Wick Island:............................553
Chapter 54 The Un-dead:..567
Chapter 55 The Aftermath:..581
Glossary l 595
Glossary lb 605
Glossary ll: 609
Thank you 613
About Author 614

The Last Prophecy:

Time, he knew was prophecy's mistress, ever self-possessed, in control, yet temperamental as nature itself. Could it also be its enemy; opposing and fickle? As the elders sat around and inhaled the eerie smoke emanating from the fire pit; The Prophet Lailoken sighed. This would be his last vision to share. The last words he would speak. The vice like grip tightened around his heart. *Wait a little longer, they must know; remember and prepare.*

Lailoken gazed at each of the elders. They swayed to the flame's inherent rhythm. Eyes closed, hearing words that were not spoken aloud. He realised that this prophecy would unfold in its own measure; over several millennium. As with most visions; their tales told around camp fires at night will change. Memories fade, generations renew and time twists and turns, ever the mistress again. History would be forgotten. Thus, the continuum of life events for the inhabitants moves along. Their indefinable progress of existence shall lead them unknowing; towards their destined fate.

THE LAST PROPHECY:

In times yet to pass, in a world out of reach;
Three Masters of all will sunder a breach.
The test they will fail; the power be too grand.
Sucked into a vortex and thrown on new land.
In time they shall Reign, many wars to be fought.
Their bloodlines to mingle and peace will be sought.

When days start to cool; from the bleaching hot sun;
Two souls will be born; instead of just one.
Far in the west, three blood lines of old.
Will converge bright in one; the second behold.

The first will be strong, a friend to the King.
The second shall dance; the blue flame she will sing.
A struggle to live; her will shall be strong.
Her mantra, her soul shall not falter or wrong.

A leader of men, for peace she will fight.
The evil that chides, then steals in the night.
The ancients of old will know when they see;
The one that's foretold will set the world free.
Three gifts she shall find, to help with her quest;
But to win, play the game; may cleave her heart yet.

The Prophet Lailoken:

SOFALA

Endless
Sea
North-Mede
Northern Boundary
Mist-Wick Island
Meder River
Billabong
Burning
Sea
Sanctuary
Beaumont
Gatlyn
Ashmourne Village
Mere Town
Jangly River
Ashmourne Island
Janlin Village
Trent Village
Strobe Village
Lyster
Southern Outpost
N
W
E
S

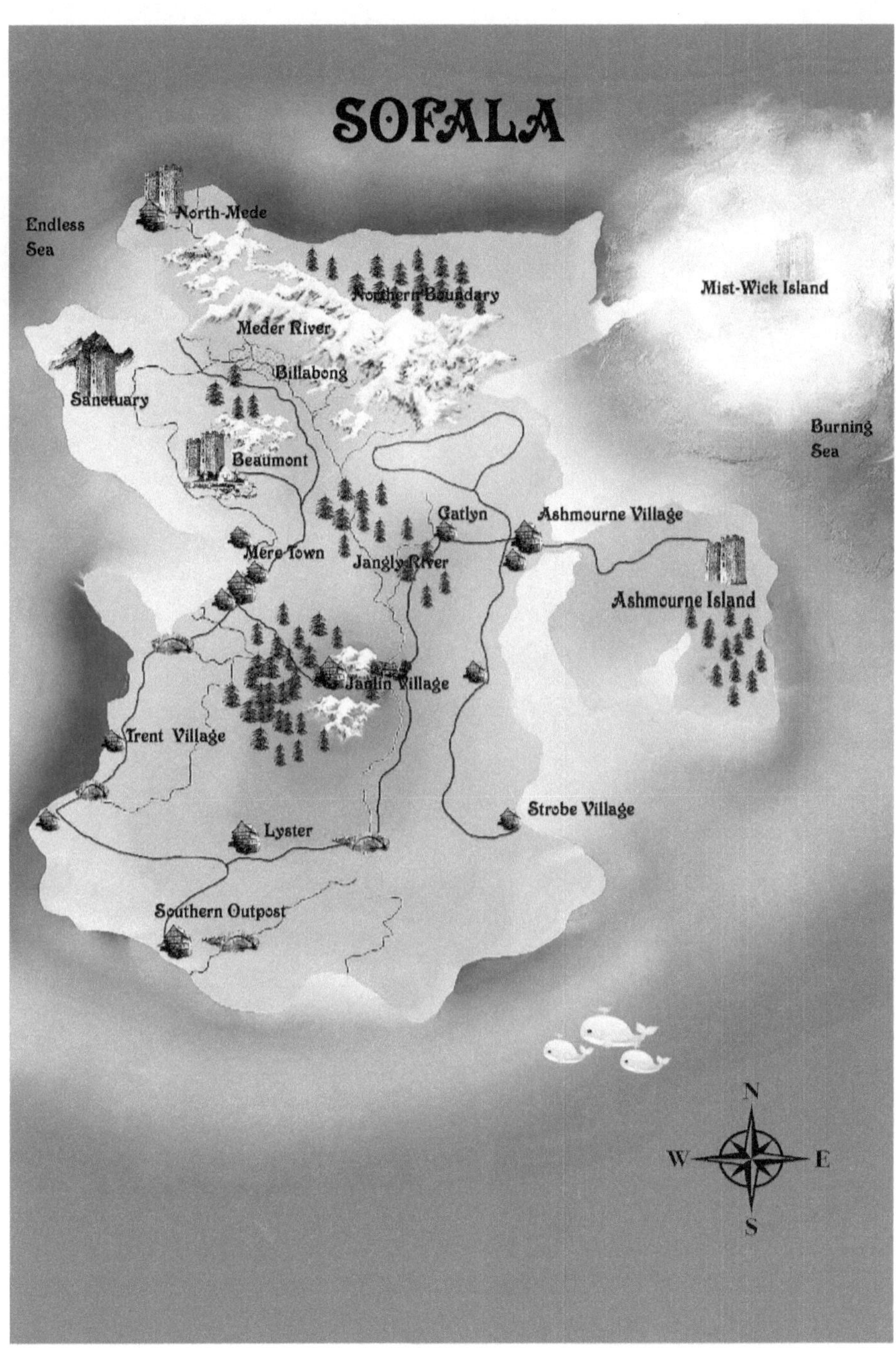

Chapter 1

The Academy
of Magic-Ashmourne Island:

In the far future: The prophecy awakens from its slumber.

"Ballard, watch out behind you." Commander Atesh yelled as she leapt off her war stallion. She somersaulted over Captain Ballard to thrust her scimitars into the large hairy neck, of an angry beast. They fell to the ground together with a deafening thud. Atesh then rolled away to avoid being crushed by the massive dead weight. She bounced up onto her feet and ran to assist the other men of her unit; Ballard in step beside her. Frowning together at the scene unfolding before them, they dove into the fray.

A pack of fierce corpulent grey wolves with gleaming eyes battled the unit of *Pace Knights* as they made ready to return home from the northern border. The creatures had sprung up and over the mounted knights; dragging several off their steeds. Cries rang out, as large fetid claws raked with ease through human flesh. Snarling cavernous maws, generous enough to fit a human head; kept on tearing, biting and gnashing. The rancid breath and drooling gore that hung like tendrils from the creature's jagged canines, often had the knights gagging; as they fought up close and personal.

"By the ancients that stink is worse than your feet Ballard. Who or what did they have for breakfast?"

Ballard smiled at his Commander, rolled his eyes and nodded as he sliced into the hide of the creature beside him. Atesh and her unit had never experienced such wild, blood lust ferocity before. She noted numerous wounds on her men, oozing through shredded leather uniforms, pooling the blood onto the rocky ground below. The knights however, fought on resolute. They slipped and slid alongside their foe, as they struggled for their lives. Atesh knew her first battalion was well trained. Their daily exercise routines gave them an advantage of flexibility, agility and speed; which may have been the only advantage they possessed. Or so Atesh believed. Perhaps it was the scent of the knights' terror that encouraged such selfless acts of bravery, or the possibility of losing a loved companion. With no thought to the consequences, Atesh watched in awe, as the knights' muscled war steeds joined in to protect their riders. They kicked with their powerful back legs and bit into the creatures' hairy flesh. This gave the knights the distraction they looked for; to take the lead in the lethal fight. It turned into quite a melee. Many of the dead and dying creatures enhanced the gore fest, covering all in the vicinity with their living essence. It was a jacket bloodbath with their spilt foul smelling innards and green body fluids. Many hours later the knights acquired the upper hand. By mid-morning the last of the 'doggies' were defeated.

Atesh was relieved that no knight sustained mortal wounds, as she watched the injured taken to a grassed area, where Healer Jenner performed her duties. Sage the horse handler, attended to his charges that were bitten, scored and bruised. With tears cascading down his reddened cheeks, he spoke kind words to these wonderful creatures thanking them for assisting their riders; in their time of need. The remainder of the first battalion sat down with caution; beside their injured fellows. Heads hung from sheer exhaustion as they inhaled deep, allowing the fresh air to revitalise them. Their swords lay at the ready across their bloodied laps. No words were later spoken as they watched with pride in their hearts, for their Supreme Commander and Captain. With quiet reverence, these two exceptional officers checked each and every creature; to ensure it had passed. Even abominations such as these, deserve to die with the least suffering; the Commander had explained to them. After the pyre was set ablaze, the knights moved on for a few hours and then set up camp beside the free flowing Jangly River to rest for the remainder of the day.

Arriving home to Ashmourne Island from their eight day mission up at the northern border, the Commander and her unit were greeted by the two bridge guards. They were the height of three grown men, both created from magic infused crystal and stone. Their weapons, the largest swords ever crafted in the known world; were held balanced before their enormous frames. Atesh often wondered if ever, the guards had cause to use them. Though she would not like to find out the hard way; how fast they would be.

"Good evening Commander Atesh." Their voices reverberated around the stone bridge loud and soulless. Observing the state of the tired unit and noticing the wounded. "Anything interesting come to pass on your tour?" As one they bent down to eye the knights.

Atesh arched her neck back, as far as nature allowed. Her eyes squinted to see up at the two rock faces. *It is so eerie how they always speak in unison.*

"You know I cannot divulge my mission; nice try though." *Boy for stone soldiers they're so nosey. I wonder when they will give up asking me. Perhaps it is a test…before we are allowed to cross.* "I believe Captain Ballard has some gossip for you ." Atesh turned to face her Captain , a mischievous grin adorned her face as she winked at her second in charge.

Ballard's face paled. "Damn you caught me again. You owe me a great favour Commander. No wait…that makes two." Pinching his nose between his fingers, head bowed in deep thought, he chastised himself for again falling into one of Atesh's traps. He turned to the fellows behind him. "Think men think, or you are all going to be stuck here with me at this gate for hours."

Groans and curses were mumbled. Ballard had them ensnared.

"The Master wants to see you as soon as possible Commander. He has been in quite a dizzy mood of late." The guard's booming voice seemed to bounce inside her skull.

"Oh no not again, thanks for the warning gentlemen."

Turning to address her unit, she noticed by their roving eyes and nodding gestures they were wracking their tired brains for a piece of gossip to satisfy the guards. Though, knowing Berend and his merry group of troublemakers they would be devising a plan, payback for Ballard and herself. *Well…it keeps their minds active and challenged.* Still Atesh had difficulty containing her mirth. "I will meet you back at the stables Captain. The usual applies men; the injured, your horses then home. Well done to you all, you have again made me proud to be your leader."

With a *whoop* Atesh leant forward over Kayne's withers and both moved off over the stone bridge in a synergistic rhythm; one that only they could hear.

Ciaran was perched atop Atesh's head; wings unfurled, but arced to allow the air to glide smooth over their surfaces. His snout, face and scaly body buffeted by the racing wind were in no danger. He had both claws secure; imbedded in a head of sun kissed coloured hair. "Ach this is the only way to fly lassie, woo-hoo."

Atesh surveyed her surroundings as she moved towards the Ashmourne academy of magic. It was known also as the Wizards' compound; housed within a large island off the east coast of Sofala. She marvelled at the majestic flow of the energy it produced. She felt unfettered, free.

The Wizard Master of the academy, Elias Freymore sat in his sparse office; he contemplated the island's surroundings in quiet solitude. Utilising his third eye; he watched the unit return from the northern border; the elite and famous knights, *'the Pace Alastriona '. Ah Atesh is back.* He decided to push his boundary further, seeking a sign of any disturbance. He had felt restless of late, had snatches of visions, felt uneasiness; something distant, yet familiar had been disrupting his sleep. *A signature of magic thought lost to time.* "I…wonder?" He whispered into the void; whilst he tapped his fingers rhythmically on the wooden table. *No, it definitely cannot be; memories resurfacing to haunt me. Yes, that must be the answer.* Another portion of his partitioned mind was aware that what he felt may be true.

He had listened to the bridge guards greet the Commander. *In a mood am I?* A rare smile creased his lips up at the corners, head bobbed in time with his laughs. *Those two stonies are too darn smart for their own good…yes; I suppose I have been a bit dizzy.* Breaking his whispered musings, he was just in time for Atesh, as she knocked on his opened door and entered.

"Commander Atesh, Ah…so nice to have you and your unit back home safe. What be the state of the Northern Border?"

"Sir, there was a threatening, eerie feeling, affecting all the animals in close proximity to the boundary. Birds silent, animals hidden and our horses were restless and skittish. There have been more sightings of unusual creatures from farmers; livestock missing or mauled. We were attacked on our last day, by unusual creatures. We sustained some injuries, nothing fatal, but there was enough evidence to show the wild creatures were venturing through the border. There must be a weakness in the barrier we have not yet seen."

Master Freymore sat and stared into space and stroked his unruly white beard.

Atesh shifted her feet, unsure if he had even listened. "Once we have resupplied, I would like to return to the border with my unit for a closer, more detailed inspection sir?"

Master Freymore turned his head to look at the Commander. "Atesh, we have maintained the barrier for close to two centuries. With very few incidents I might add; until now. This news bodes ill…very disturbing indeed. That mountain range was raised for a specific purpose, to keep those blasted destructive creatures behind it, away from the local inhabitants; we could then all live in peace. The activation crystals were still in place, I gather?"

Atesh nodded, "Of course sir."

"Atesh, there is a different mission for you. Rather a delicate matter, I want you and your unit to attend. Please rest up tonight and I will brief you in the morning after forms."

"What shall be done about the border issue sir?"

"I will send Captain Danurel and two units to do a closer and perhaps a more in-depth inspection. Yes! We definitely need to pursue that."

Commander Atesh marched out of the main building, fists clenched and knuckles turned ashen. She returned to the livery stables to attend to her beloved war steed Kayne. He measured sixteen hands in height, ready with a nip if he felt ignored or bored; his quirky sense of self-righteousness was undeniable. She leant on Kayne; half buried her face into his dusty mane.

"I cannot believe Master Freymore wants to send that poor excuse for a man, Captain painful out to the boundaries. If I am lucky, something large and hairy might eat him."

Ciaran her familiar sat upon her head. He nodded and cooed to Atesh and stroked her golden hair with his tiny paws. His love for her infused her mind and body. He often cuddled around her neck, such were his dimensions. Atesh smiled when she envisioned how Ciaran could breathe smoke rings in all amazing shapes and sizes; though never a flame was seen. He downed large amounts of ale with the best of the men and loved apples to excess. She often wondered why he never flew. There was no other physical reason why he couldn't; though in a remarkable twist of irony; Ciaran a dragonelle, she discovered was afraid of heights. These little quirks made him all the more unique and lovable.

The brief with Master Elias Freymore the next morning was not what Atesh expected. She listened with her hands clenched tight by her side. The Wizard Master outlined her orders.

"Atesh there are two parts to your mission. First, deliver this package to the Wizard Master at Beaumont Castle. You can contact him through the bar-keep at the Anvil Inn. It is located within the castle village."

At the end of her first set of orders Atesh's cheeks felt warm indeed. *I am to be an errand boy?*

"Second, I would like your unit to assist the King's First Regiment. They have been investigating the increase in disappearances, throughout the kingdom." He placed a kerchief up to his mouth, and then cleared his throat with a little cough, before continuing. "It seems the King's favourite cook had gone missing, right in the middle of a banquet; if you please." Winking at Atesh, an almost smile could be seen through his long unkempt beard; he grimaced as he tried to keep a straight face. "He was quite put out, poor sweetums…huhmmm; you can gather further information from Commander Marcus."

As Atesh prepared to leave his office, she noticed the Master's eyes had glazed over, pupils dilated, his posture upright, a *premonition now?*

Turning to look at Atesh, his head tilted on a slight angle. Master Elias spoke in an unnatural spine-chilling voice. The eerie tone sent shivers throughout Atesh's body.

> "Watch your back brave one, the game is in play.
> Find the answer, the truth; the spell to decay.
> Seek the mountain that's blind and sways to a beat.
> Use the dance you have learned; this time to defeat.
> Find a tear from afar, the tool you shall be.
> Hide inside for the strength; your mind must be free."

Chapter 2

The Journey Begins:

Exiting the island a few days later, Atesh could feel the buzz of excitement within the unit. There were smiles all around, eyes steady and eager. The knights seated astride their war steeds, had a slight forward lean to their posture. The barrier skirmish had whet their warrior appetite and they hoped for some more. The knights fought hard to be included in the First Battalion. Of the 1,000 warrior knights, only one hundred qualified for the first; these were further divided into four sub-units. On a mission such as this, only the primary would travel with Atesh. These were her most trusted and experienced fighters. They were more than comrades in arms to her, they were family. Atesh felt for the amethyst-crystal amulet, strung on a golden chain around her neck. The Master had given her this after his vision, whilst she prepared to leave. Added to the rings she already wore, Atesh felt the magical energy that coursed throughout her body and soul. It was very empowering.

What had he seen to give me such a gift?

Once past the gates, Atesh set the unit in motion. They raced past the ocean, where the seas myriad of twinkled sun beams bounced off and illuminated her deep cerulean eyes. She felt her golden hair which had plaited coloured side streaks; ride on the wind behind her. It flowed in rhythm with Kayne's reaching stride. The men looked at Atesh with fixed adoring eyes. Her face was set to the task at hand, committed and true. A small portion of their souls were lost to their Commander, she knew this and felt each and every one; all different in their own way. Their love and loyalty went deep; beyond understanding. Over the past twelve years, she had proven herself many times with her courage and fearlessness. The men could all feel the energy of an adventure looming and set their horses to race each other to the main road away from the salt air and sea winds.

Each morning before sunrise, the unit performed their forms; the sword dancing routines. Atesh led the morning sessions and Captain Ballard the evening exercises and remembrance. It would be a rare occurrence for a knight to miss these. Atesh believed with her whole heart that it kept them centred. Physically it gave them their acute sense of balance, precision in close combat, defence and attack. It maintained and built up their body core and limb muscle strength. It assisted with absolute trust, ensuring team work and synergy. Every now and again Atesh added a challenging movement and they would practice till they mastered each portion. They would speed up gradually till they were whirling and slashing so fast; it became a blur of extreme beauty and deadly precision.

Atesh knew the men sat alert for the first couple of days then settled into a comfortable pace. They often daydreamed, reliving past events. Their voices however, quiet as they tried to be, sounded like ants running amok in her head. She had still to perfect blocking of unwarranted voices; intruding into her mind. Her powers she felt were gaining.

It was good fortune that on the fifth day of travel, they had to pass by the town of Gatlyn. The local inhabitants were out in force and maneuvering through the narrow roadway towards the town, became a nightmare. Upon entry all were stopped at a wooden gateway by the local guards. Slowly the hoard moved forward as they were admitted entrance. Four guards walked around and checked the unit, noting their similar black outfits. Their eyes widened at the sight of the fierce weaponry carried and the Ashmourne academy motif on their sleeves and saddlebags.

"G…g…good day Commander, what be your reason to travel this way on this wonderous day; b…b…business or pleasure?"

"Atesh rolled her eyes at this; she was in no mood for such triviality. We are travelling through, on our way to Beaumont castle. We have business with the King."

Ballard maneuvered up next to Atesh. "What is happening to cause such a crowd?"

"Our town Lord, Lachlan Marshall is wedded this day. He's decreed that all visitors be invited to join in the merriment, of feasting, drink and games."

"Well thank you for the offer ah…Sergeant, but we must be on our way."

"It be seen as impolite if you do no' toast to his Lordship's happy day."

"Ballard what do you think?"

Looking behind at the unit, he smiled and nodded. "A short stop may be what we need Commander."

"Fine, we would be honoured to stay for a while and enjoy the festivities."

"All arms are to be left at the sheriff's office C…Commander."

Atesh's raptor eyes stared at the nervous Sergeant and his men. "Not likely: my men do not, under any circumstance remove their arms. Will this be a problem to you all here?"

"No, no I am sure his lordship would be happy with this." The guards all nodded in agreement. The knight's warrior reputation was well known throughout Sofala and they knew the Supreme Commander was not to be trifled with. She was considered fair, but tough.

As they passed through the checkpoint, Ballard leant over to Atesh. "Did you see their knees knocking? I thought that young one would faint, he was so ashen. You have a terrible habit of scaring the pants off the average soldier."

They locked eyes and burst into laughter. "I know…I am horrid. I promise to try and be nicer in future."

The men all enjoyed the enormous amount of food laid out on trestle tables throughout the town. Drinks flowed from casks at every corner. There were jugglers, fiddlers, acrobats, fire breathers, a tight rope walker, singers and an old gypsy telling fortunes. Atesh walked around in half a daze; noise, laughter and music, seemed to reverberate inside her head today.

The gypsy looked up as Atesh passed and she beckoned to her. "Please my lady, come, come and Stella will tell you your future."

"No thank you. I do not need to know."

Stella stared at Atesh. "Oh I think you will need to hear what I have to say Commander."

Atesh stood still, her neck hairs stood up on end. She turned and observed the Gypsy.

"Come, come and sit down."

Moving over to the coloured tent with the flaps hitched up. "How do you know who I am? Do I know you?"

"I know all. I see all. I am Stella, the gypsy, I am."

Atesh sat and placed her hands on the table. Stella looked them over and smiled when she touched the rings they held. Her eyes rolled up and her face blanched. She breathed slow and quiet, as in a trance.

"You are troubled I see, but all is not what it seems. You must know who you are, where you belong, before you can accept what life has to offer. Look inside for the truth." Stella drew in a breath. "Those that should…do not, those that should not…do. Be-careful, treachery is all around you, dangerous times ahead. There is darkness, foul stench, so much darkness. You will come to a fork in the road; one hand sends you left the other hand right. Combine them to find your way."

Stella's eyes returned to normal and her breathing quickened. "That is all I will say to ye Commander, the rest is not for me to tell." She then turned her head and creased her forehead, as she looked at Atesh's collar. A large smile then adorned her face as she shook her head in amazement. "You go now and leave this town before the night birds' sing."

"What do I owe you for this message Stella?"

"Oh this be free to you Commander. I am honoured to be of service."

As Atesh stood up and turned to leave, Stella the Gypsy called out to her.

"Oh Commander, the apple and toffee store is down on the next corner. Your friend's stomach is rumbling like thunder."

Atesh stifled a laugh and nodded to Stella, though she felt uneasy as she walked away. *Well that made a lot of sense. Why do they speak in riddles? Always—danger lies around the corner. Tell me something, I don't know.*

Loud noises caught her attention as it echoed around the town. After she purchased a small apple covered in sticky green toffee for Ciaran, she hastened over to where a crowd had formed. They cheered, booed and screamed with laughter. Atesh squeezed her way through the throng to where her men stood and watched. To her horror and amazement a few of the locals were trying their hand at horse acrobats. Ballard and a few of the unit's men had their heads together whispering.

"What is this all about Ballard?"

"These are the Lord's games. The best manoeuvre on horseback wins a heavy purse."

Atesh glanced up at her Captain and noticed the gleam in his eyes. "You are not thinking of trying this, are you?"

"Well how hard could it be, really…look how bad they are…I am sure we can beat them."

"Well, who am I to stop you making a fool of yourself."

"Nah, just watch us, this will be easy pickings. Come on lads; let us show them what real men can do, eh."

Ballard and Renny decided to join forces. They rode out on two local horses. Renny sat on the left horse behind Ballard. Ballard bounced up onto his feet and straddled the two horses, one foot balanced on the back of each, as he held both sets of reins tight. Renny then climbed up and sat on his captain's shoulders. The crowd clapped, whistled and cheered. Atesh cringed as Renny tried to climb up and stand on his Captain's shoulders. His feet kicked Ballard in the head and his hands and fingers ended up in all Ballard's facial orifices. Ballard's concentration was fierce, his jaw was set and eyes narrowed and focused. The only indication that this adventure was taking its toll, were the droplets of perspiration cascading down his forehead; interrupting his vision. He had managed to stay upright straddling two horses, with Renny now standing on his shoulders. Renny held his arms out wide to maintain balance, as the wind pummelled them; tossing their hair around unruly. The crowd turned wild and rowdy, laughing and jeering. Unbeknown to Renny as they cantered around the large arena, the horses slowly moved apart. He decided to try and perform a handstand from Ballard's head. He positioned his hands, lifted his feet off…then Ballard's legs stretched apart beyond comprehension and gave way. Atesh covered her eyes, she couldn't watch. She heard the thump as one landed with an abrupt suddenness onto his backside between the horses in the dirt, legs splayed. Renny however, got one foot caught in a stirrup as he fell and he was dragged around the circle screaming. Ballard bounced to his feet, bowed to the crowd and exited the arena. Once away from the crowd he sunk to his knees, tears welled in his eyes. Renny waddled in a little later and they laughed and cried tears of pain and joy.

Wyart thought to outdo his Captain; he managed to turn a few tricks. A handstand and back flip at a trot and then he tried a double flip at a canter and missed the horse completely and landed in a pile of fresh horse manure. Shreds of horse dung were flung in all directions, covering many spectators as they surged backwards away from the arena.

Berend and Vykter, the older men in the group, teamed up and performed horse jumping. Single then Tandem. Not too bad an effort, they pulled off a few easier jumps then tried to somersault whilst in the air moving from one horse to the other, their landing was a bit uncoordinated, arms and legs hanging from the saddles in all directions. They received a rousing applause from the crowd.

The last to try was Kerwin, the battalion's youngest and newest recruit. He rode bareback, facing the rear of the horse and smiling at the crowd. He launched up into a single somersault to land on his hands . He maneuvered one hand off the horse , holding his body perfect aligned ; his feet reaching for the sky . Then he twisted and rolled off the horse to the side. The crowd became restless ; they scanned the entire arena looking for his splayed carcass. Kerwin's body however, was pressed up close to the horse. He hung on to the bridle by his hands , his body and legs held up straight behind , by sheer muscle strength. The rider had vanished. The crowd gasped as Kerwin reappeared ; again he somersaulted up on top of the horse's back. He then vaulted from one side of the horse to the other all the way around the arena, alternating the vaults with a handstand. On the last vault he landed on the back of the horse and performed a double somersault over the horse's head to land facing the horse. He hung on by his feet curled around the neck. The crowd went into hysterics, laughed, whistled and threw hats and flowers into the ring as Kerwin kissed and snuggled the horse's face.

He back flipped under the horse's body. Atesh looked on in abject horror. From the rear Kerwin appeared, his head poked through the thick brushed tail. The horse took objection to this rather personal intrusion, her ears folded back, and her top lip turned up and twisted. Atesh was not sure if it was a laugh or a sneer, though she did hear some unladylike cussing in her head. She was sure it was not a good sign for her knight. Then the horse lifted her tail and covered Kerwin in fresh, hot steaming urine and green dung. He yelped, shook his head, coughed and spat out some wet manure and flipped up onto the rump, holding the horse's tail. Then he somersaulted to a perfect dismount on the ground and bowed to the crowd. His smiled and waved his arms in the air as he ran around the outer edge of the arena. This caused the crowd to surge back again. Not only did he smell like fresh horse pee, but bits of dung crud were flung from his hands into the onlookers. What brought the audience to their knees, bent over in agony from laughter was the innocent look of Kerwin's face. He did not realise his teeth were covered in green straw like manure and he looked heinous. He was later presented with the trophy for the acrobat games. The only criteria the Lord stipulated was that Kerwin had to be bathed and changed before presenting himself to the podium.

Later that afternoon the group left weary and sore, but they wore their wounds with pride and humour. It was an experience to remember and made all the better when Kerwin shared the booty with his entire unit. Atesh pushed the group on, taking heed of the gypsy woman's warning. The campfire that night became a quiet affair. Jesper struck up tunes on his handmade wooden pipes; rather haunting melodies that had the men gazing into the fire pit, reflecting on their lives and home. Jenner was kept busy treating the brave acrobats. Ballard thought he would never walk properly again or have children. Renny limped around being a total sook.

So to keep the men busy on this long ride and out of her head, Atesh set up practices. She had thought about the manoeuvres the men performed at the fair and how some could be adapted to benefit them in a fight situation. She named it horse forming. The knights of the first battalion would be the only military group to trial these techniques. Kerwin was asked to assist in tweaking the manoeuvres to suit a strategic advantage in combat and enhance their balance skills. He would teach them how to maintain balance and control the horse. They utilised what they had learned in their form dance routines and transferred the skills to the back of their trusted steeds. There would be single, double and triple tricks. There was the Kerwin whirly bird, then Ballard's nutcracker. The last was the side winder, leaning over to one side, so the horse looks rider-less. The only one that was rejected was the infamous Renny manoeuvre , being dragged along behind a horse by one foot entangled in a stirrup.

Atesh had led them for two long weeks travelling on the dusty roads; the scenery changed between mountains and flat dry grassy lands. The only company they passed was a few noisy merchant caravans or a lone rider herding a group of cattle to the nearest market. Tonight, Jesper decided they needed more energetic songs; where the men joined in and sang. He played a particular tune written for his Commander. He had written a few for Atesh, but some were too close to his heart to reveal just yet. The men made up the words, about their fearless Commander , not one for the general public ; but a typical fighting man's dirty ditty. This brought tears to all their eyes with raucous laughter. Atesh's cheeks warmed and reddened at first, then she joined in to the chorus and thought how sweet it was she had her own song; albeit a bawdy one.

It was with regret there was always one, to the dismay of all others that sang the loudest and was altogether motherless, tone deaf. This was Renny, a fine knight…but to be honest; apart from fighting, he could be a real klutz. He was a reservist, one that replaced a sick or injured knight. He usually rode with the secondary unit, but for this mission, Renny replaced one injured up at the northern boundary. Tune after tune was played, louder and louder Renny became. The noise was so horrific; Ciaran the dragonelle could not take this abuse to his ears any longer and clambered up onto Renny's head. He started hitting him, with his tiny appendages; yelling obscenities the whole time. When he stopped and looked around, there was dead silence; all the men had their mouths and eyes wide open; astonishment written all over their faces.

"Ciaran can speak out loud? All this time...." The men stammered in unison.

Another first for the men as they watched in silent wonder as Ciaran became embarrassed. He slowly turned flame red; from the top of his head to the end of his tail. He gathered his tiny body up as tall as possible, chest pushed out, nose in the air, and hopped down off Renny's head. Spitting out a few stray hairs lodged between his teeth, he stood resolute, then sauntered over to the tent and scampered inside. All eyes looked to Atesh and Ballard. She raised her shoulders in a shrug, looked away from any eye contact, laughed and resumed her beverage. Ciaran remained hidden for the next couple of days, his secret was out. He often heard the men murmuring as they walked past his tent.

Reaching the Jangly River after travelling another week, Atesh called for camp earlier than usual. She noticed the gentle motion of the water within the river, as it lapped up onto the sandy edges, kissing it with tenderness. The camp area was a carpet of fine soft grasses, semi-enclosed with trees and scrubs. It would give privacy and peace to the tired, dusty group.

It would be nice to have a tub and scrub, the water looks so inviting. "Break out the soap Captain . Some of the men are getting a bit high; if you know what I mean."

Laughing; " Yes Commander, I concur with that assessment." He pulled a sour face as he smelt under his own arm pits. "Yes a definite time for a tub."

Sniggers could be heard close by. As Captain Ballard turned around, only serious faces could be found. "Cheeky buggers, I'll teach ya some respect. Make camp over to the right at that clearing." Ballard with an enigmatic smile and raised eyebrow pointed to the three men close behind. "Chale, Wyart you two on latrine pit duty. Renny you have kitchen duty tonight."

Groans from all the men could be heard. They enjoyed their one hot meal of the day, and if Renny had a hand in it; anything could and would happen to it.

After a short time, Commander Atesh called out. "Sage can you make sure the horses do not wander too far tonight." *What is that feeling?* Turning around, she searched for any hint of danger. Atesh felt more than the hint of unease. Menacing shivers assaulted her body. All the hairs on her arms and neck were standing up. *I wonder if we should move on.*

Ciaran sensed her indecision. He knew that Atesh outwardly was decisive and thoughtful. Unbeknown to most, Atesh too, had inner fears. Making a wrong decision; failing the men and her duty. Worst of all she had a deep seated gnawing in her gut; wondering if anyone could really love her.

Some of the men also felt audible shivers; each had a certain amount of innate magic, which was a basic requirement to be a knight. This assisted the activation of their rings. They looked around at each other; but not a word was spoken. The breeze caressed their sweaty bodies as they continued to make camp. They all decided with an instinctive nature to keep their swords and bows handy; in-case. They had learnt from the past, to trust their Commander's intuition, it was always right.

Atesh whispered to her dragonelle. "What do you think Ciaran? Can you sense anything unusual?"

"Ach…I am feeling a wee somthing but, I dinna knows what t'is."

"So I am not just being paranoid."

"Ach nae lassie, ye are nor."

Atesh kept her armoury on as well; A Duel Rapier and Scimitar in the softened black leather sheath strapped on her back. A Kopis adorned her right hip and battle sword on her left. Many knives were sequestered around her body, hidden from all. She wandered through the tall straight trees; her senses were on full alert for any unusual noise, whilst she collected kindling and branches of wood for the large blaze, in their fire-pit tonight. Fire always gave Atesh comfort. She often sat and stared at the flames and would drift off into amazing dreams; of far off lands, with exotic and strange creatures, friendly folk, and a song sung from the face of an angel.

Twilight came around all too soon now, the white cool season approached. Soaking her tired and sore body in the mild warm river,

Atesh started to relax into the movement of the waves. A voice interrupted her musings inside her head, Ciaran called her for supper.

"Okay lassie, time ye stop wid ye dreamin; come on now, back to da camp with ye."

Atesh opened her eyes to watch the darkening clouds meander by.

"Boy, you are a nagger sometimes old man, but I still love you, Ciaran. Why don't you come in and I will give you a scrub?"

"Ach, nae lassie, the water is too deeps for da likes of me. A big fishy would eats me as soon as swim by. What ye mean old man, huh?"

The only sound to be heard came from a merchant caravan that had settled for the night a little further along the river's edge.

Odd really, the horses and night birds were all quiet. Atesh pondered on this while she redressed, then returned to the fire. The men were on guard duty or polished and sharpened their gear in hushed solitude.

Chapter 3

The Game Master: Mist-Wick Island:

"Damn…maggot munching, blood sucking, cat pissing, pig wallowing, boil popping, nert herders. Can't anyone follow simple instructions anymore? Indescribable idiots…." Mutterings were heard, leaking from under the closed door. Master Grey was in a foul mood again today.

"I would wait before going in there, if I were you." Mason tried to brush off the visitor to another time. *Ha…a few new ones today. Normally it was crud crunching, scum sucking, and son of a motherless goat. Ooooh…guess he woke up at his desk again.*

Pacing back and forth in front of the Wizard Master's door, Abi the Abomination created many years earlier; was the leader of the Gatherers. They were a group of unusual, ferocious beasts. Abi's black coat glistened as the sun kissed his tuffs of fur and scales. He looked somewhat like a dragon/ panther with wings. His large oval shaped golden eyes with black piercing irises narrowed at Mason. A low growl escaped his lips as they peeled back, showing sharp, brown stained elongated canines.

"I must explain to my Mathter. I am not like yous; I am not afraid."

With a great sigh and an evil smirk on his face, Mason proceeded to open the door. He bowed and flicked his hand in a gesture to enter. "Please yourself, you go on then; oh brave and mighty invincible one." Announcing Abi's arrival, Mason retreated back down the steps, away from imminent danger. *How ingenious. I would like to see someone herding those carnivorous little reptilian monstrosities that would be an interesting sight. I have heard they taste a lot like chicken.*

Wizard Master Grey had his back to the creature as it entered. "So what is your excuse this time abomination…I can't hear you. Cat got your tongue?" He sat down discordant in his chair, massaged his temples and then twisted around to face Abi.

"I…SAID…UNICORN! Not a blasted two headed horse. How did you manage to mix that one up?"

"I could not find the horthe with the horn, s-so I found a two headed horthe for you, very rare, one of a kind."

"Well yes, I suppose that may be correct Abi. But, I needed a Unicorn to complete this latest request. I will have to make adjustments."

Abi hated to admit how he adored and feared Master Grey, bowed in reverence as his body trembled.

"Abi, this was your last mistake, no more chances. Do you really want to have your wings clipped?"

"No Mathter, but thir, I have only made th-tmall mithtakes in all these years. I will make this upth to you, I promith, you will thee."

"No…You are wrong Abi; every mistake is costly to me, to our end result. Hours of work wasted, materials thrown out, money not received from buyers. They were not ever small, oh no. All were errors in judgement, lack of patience. They should never have occurred. You need to take more care, think things through. Did I err…in making you the leader of the gatherers, I wonder? Perhaps I should replace you."

"No Mathter I will do better, another chanthe pleathe?"

"Do I need to remind you of our little incident here on this very island?" His mind wandered back to many years previous. "Quite a disaster if you remember? You not only brought back the child, you killed the nanny which we could have used. Then to add insult to injury you failed to save that sweet child in her time of need. I still cannot fathom why you let her go? Do you not have any tolerance for pain? You let her fall to her death into the swirling ocean. Ruined years of work, she had such potential for a wee thing, not to mention, near destroyed poor Miss Maisie…."

Abi crawled on his stomach, pleading to the Master.

"Oh fine, stop grovelling; it's giving me a headache."

Master Grey stared with his piercing ebony coloured eyes, boring into his minion's head. "I have another assignment for you; don't be careless with this one. This will take a lot of thought and planning. Do you think you can handle it? I need a soldier, young, tall, strong. Oh and with his war horse; the whole package; got it?"

Turning away from Abi, Master Grey's eyes became glazed; he began stroking his long multi coloured unruly beard, lost in thought. He went back to mumbling and writing feverish scribbles in his journal.

Noticing that he was ignored and still alive, Abi retreated away in stealth.

Many hours later, The Master was yelling from the top of the stairs. "Mason, Bring me the Troldwite leader if you please; I need to know how they are progressing. Oh and some dinner if you don't mind, a man could starve to death here, you know?" He returned to mumbling again to the void. "So much work to do, so much to do, so little time. I have been too long." He sat back, rubbed his tired eyes and pondered over his latest journal entry. A lopsided smile adorned his face. He laughed out loud, to no one in particular. "If they could only see what I have accomplished. Oh, superior ones. What would they say if they only knew?" *The design this time will be unique. I will have the best with this for sure. Success is so close, I can almost taste it.*

Mason strode in haste in search of the Troldwites. They were nasty hairy, odoriferous creatures, living in the cold dark, dank caves down by the sea. Not wanting to find these creatures himself, he pointed to two young men, working the fields.

"You two, run and find the Troldwite leader Kroll. The Master wants to see him now."

"Y…y…yes sir." Eyes widened at the thought. Then they took off and ran at top speed. While sweat was beading on their foreheads; breathless and frightened to the point of near collapse, they headed for the caves at the far side of the island.

A short time later only one man returned, shaking, pale and covered in mud and blood. "Mister Mason sir, the Troldwite leader has received the message sir. But…they attacked us and ate the other worker sir."

"Yes they tend to do that." He drew one side of his mouth up in a sneer. "Go back to work now boy, no slacking off." Glancing at the floor around the man's feet, "Oh and clean that mess up before you go; you have dripped on Mistress Maisey's floor. She'll have your hide for that. I hear her coming now, hurry and make haste, lest she catch you."

Moving into the extra-large kitchen, Mistress Maisey's body bounced along as she walked. Being the chief cook, she enjoyed tasting all the meals before they were distributed, adding extra inches to her already expanding waist line. She insisted on a clean house and perfect kitchen. She had a soft spot for the two main men in her life, Mason and the Master. Spoiling them with treats was her second favourite past time.

"Do you have the Master's dinner ready Mistress Maisey? We all know what he is like when he forgets to eat." Both battered their eyes at the same time and laughed.

"Here ye go meh sweet cheeks." She stuffed a savoury bun into Mason's mouth, before he gave her lip. "Please try and keep dem filthy workers out' o my kitchen, de mess up the floor; I keep a clean place ye know."

As Mason watched Maisey waddle off, he had a fleeting thought of times gone by. They have been bantering like this for near to fifty years and had the odd tryst in their younger days. With a large grin only ever reserved for his secret love, Mason strode off with a tray of gravy meat, vegetables, biscuit, cheeses, sweet buns and a large tankard of warm mead.

Mason watched as the Troldwite Leader named Kroll, slowly navigated his way up the stairs. These creatures were a cross between the wild mountain/rock troll and an ancient dark dwarf; very hairy, long razor sharp teeth, protruding forehead, thick long body with short powerful arms and legs. Mason disliked these creatures, though he mused, *they had their uses.* They enjoyed the troll appetite for meat raw or cooked, loved ale and dark cold places. The power in their limbs was extraordinary; they could lift the equivalent of their weight many times over. They had what the Master thought were their best features. He instilled in them a severe lack of general ethics and morals for their undertakings, as well as fierce loyalty to his higher power.

The Master explained the need for the Troldwites when Mason assisted with their formation. He described how he happened to come across an ancient tome hidden in the Academy library when he was a youth. Inside were descriptions of creatures from a time before the second age, the landing of the first three on Sofala. What the population believe now to be nothing but tales, stories and folk lore, to tell around the fire at night; all magical and exciting. They really had existed thousands of years ago, but then overnight most of the exotic and mystical creatures disappeared. This led to an extraordinary adventure lasting many years searching and hunting down clues to find old tomes and relics in the lands beyond the great divide. Lands forbidden to all but the bravest, as traversing the rent in the ocean was impossible for most. Master Grey had found a way through. After returning with a fierce hunger to experiment and a hatred for certain civilisations he inhabited his island sanctuary. He set about trying to recreate some of these creatures; but added extra benefits or combined a few species. Some were successful others, not so much.

The Troldwites job was to dig underground in caves and retrieve treasures; rare crystals that harness and hold energy for use with the Master's work. For most, crystals would be found on rocky islands, or beneath volcanic mountains. The ones on Mist-Wick Island had been near depleted over the last two centuries, so the Troldwites were searching the large mountain range called the Northern Border. Many unusual creatures lived above the northern border; it had been a good dumping ground for Master Grey's failed experiments or uncontrolled creatures that had lost their usefulness.

"Ahhh, Kroll, what have you to report to me, good news I hope?"

"Master, we dig plenty, many crystals we see, but they are deeper, the rock starts to shake, move and fall in on us, so we run away." Grovelling on his knees, "Please sir, I will take braver with me, we will bring you these treasures."

"Yes you will, I need them NOW. Take some of the field workers to assist you, but hear me." Master Grey looked down at the Troldwite still on his knees. "You-will-not eat-the help…understand. Not a mark or a sniff on them at all."

"Yes Master, no eat fresh man meat."

"Now, get out of my sight and do not fail me again."

Why can't I find decent help anymore? What I need is an apprentice; yes, yes, yes, I will definitely look into this.

Day dreaming again, he sat in his favourite soft chair, eyes fixed, staring out his window mesmerised. He watched the waves kiss the rocks, in an eternal rhythmical embrace of ebb and flow. His mind wandered to his island of Mist-Wick, his home for near to two hundred years. His castle squatted in the middle, with many towers reaching towards the sky. Beneath are dank cold underground caverns, some house his birthing rooms, others containment areas, quarters for special guests and main workshops.

The fields yield all the food requirements they would ever need, whilst a fresh water spring irrigated the crops. The weather he maintained warm and sunny all year round as the cold affected him so. The inhabitants were from all walks of life, some natural others not. The two legs (Humans) had no names, apart from what they called each other and often disappeared to be replaced by another. Their faces were blank and they worked in a routine fashion. Food, basic clothes and lodging were all they required, though they were treated well enough. Mason was in charge of them, he ensured tasks were completed and the island ran smoothly. The island was surrounded by a dense impenetrable magical fog; safe and secure, for the many unusual creatures, subjects and human inhabitants.

A loud knock on his door drew the Master back to reality, braking this intimate moment of man and his environment. Mason announced the delivery of his meal. *MMMM, it smells wonderful as usual. Ahhh, that Mistress Maisey, she sure knows a way to a man's heart.* He smiled with tender thoughts for a brief time.

As Mason turned to leave Master Grey's office, he was beckoned closer.

"Do you think you can find me an apprentice; a young impressionable one, with a good deal of innate magic. Maybe a reject from that blasted academy, the high and mighty Wizard Compound. What do you think Mason?"

"Sir, I could make enquiries for you."

"That would be splendid, thank you Mason; you have been my eyes and ears for all these years. You have been a good friend. Yes…one like you would do fine."

As always the meal stayed untouched for many hours, it is no inconvenience really; being a Wizard Master had its perks.

Chapter 4

The Camp of a Thousand Hells:

As Atesh sat on a log and stared into the flickering fire, she was dragged out of her dream like state by a shout and a groan. Alert, she bolted upright; in unison with the men that lounged nearby. With pupils dilated, spine erect, she whipped her head around to identify the swift moving object that raced off into the bushes behind her. At the exact same time, she had unleashed her swords from their leather sheathes.

"OH NO, Damn it to hell!" Berend raced for his life towards the latrine pit. He fumbled with desperate haste to unfasten his trousers as he vaulted the logs into spiky bracken. His drink and swords flung in all directions.

"What's got into…?" Atesh tilted her head to hear further groans and loud gurgled noises. Knights from all directions ran past, bending over in apparent distress; they clutched their stomachs with one hand, whilst also performing the same latrine jiggle.

Ciaran emerged out of the tent, arms crossed. "What's wid all da ruckus. Can a dragon nae get som sleep?" Looking around Ciaran had to scramble out of the way of trampling feet. "By da heavens," He crinkled up his snout and narrowed his eyes. "What be that awful smell?"

Atesh watched in fascination as yet more of her unit were stricken with debilitating stomach cramps and latrine sprinting. Cursing and swearing came from the bushes as loud explosive sounds were heard. And yes, plumes of a powerful, overwhelming, horrifying, hair curling, breathe catching stench; that brought tears to the strongest eyes, wafted around all those in the near vicinity. Ballard, Jenner and Sage whom had that moment sat down to their meal started to gag; they looked in horror at their food bowls, then at their Commander.

"Geeze, whatever you do. . .don't-touch-that-food." With her right hand held up to cover her nose, Atesh wiped the tears from her eyes with the back of the left shirt sleeve. "Vykter and Renny report at once."

The two men ran when the Commander yelled, as it was a rare occurrence.

"What was in the food men?"

Both shrugged their shoulders. They watched the parade before them in horrified silence. The death glares conveyed from the afflicted men could even be felt beyond the bushes.

"Jenner where are you? Please tell me you have not eaten?"

"No Commander, I'm fine." The healer gasped, while trying not to breathe.

"Can you go back and have a look at the ingredients these men have used tonight and maybe fix a potion or two for the dying princesses over there…thanks."

I don't like being left so short-handed. Not tonight anyway.

It was to be a long night of assisting the men to and from their bedrolls by the fire to the bush latrine pits. Then assisting Jenner; administer her potions and fluids to combat pain and dehydration.

Jenner ran up to the fire pit. "Commander, I believe I have found the offending item. This container had been labelled Salt, but it contains Salzen and another item I cannot identify."

Noticing Atesh's furrowed brow and grimaced face; Jenner further explained.

"Salzen is for purging poisons from the body. It is usually a fine powder; whereas salt is used for seasoning and is in small crystal like form or blocks. I believe foul play has been at work sir."

"Foul play, what makes you suspect something as devious as that?" Atesh looked around at her un-well unit and she raised her eyebrows to Jenner.

"Well Commander, I know the stores are meticulously kept and checked. The medicinal potions were always measured and stored separate to food additives. There was no-way they would get mixed up sir, and it looked like it had been relabelled."

Commander pursed her lips and bowed her head in thought. "Right…Vykter, throw the rest of tonight's food into the latrine pits and deal out cheese and biscuits for anyone hungry." She turned to eye her second in command, "Who Ballard?"

Ballard knew full well the animosity between Atesh and the offending officer. "That would be…well…I believe it was…Captain Danurel."

The Commander's heart missed a beat; fists clenched, eyes narrowed, bearing her teeth she took a deep breath, nodded to Ballard and walked off to the other side of the fire.

He put all our lives at risk. I will run him through when I get home. He is a sore loser; with an overinflated ego. He is a pathetic, flea-ridden dog sniffer.

Ciaran bolted up onto Atesh's shoulder and whispered into her ear. "Dat's some mighty strong thoughts lassie, but I canna says I blame ye. Would ye be requiring som dragon cuddles then?"

Atesh gave the smallest grin at the thought of her men witnessing a dragon cuddle. "Maybe later thank you, Ciaran."

It was a few hours till sunrise when all the affected men were sleeping peacefully.

"I believe Ballard we will be waylaid another day. How many do we have left standing?"

He performed a swift head count. "It looks like, there be Vykter, Jenner, Sage and the two of us. Renny had only a mild dose, he only spoon licked."

"We will take hour rotations for standing watch. That way we will have at least a couple of hours sleep each."

"Sounds fair to me Commander, it will be light soon anyway and I am beat."

"Fine, I will take first watch then Captain."

Atesh and Ballard whipped their heads around to the sounds of blood curdling screams. Goose bumps travelled down both their spines. Adrenaline pumped into their vital organs and limbs. A clash of steel, twangs of arrows unleashed and further yelling were heard mixed with loud beast growls. It had originated from the Merchant Caravan Camp a little way through the bushes to their left.

Turning around fast, Atesh surveyed her unit; she then grabbed Ballard and yelled out to the others. "Sage, wake some of the sleeping beauties to protect the rest if needed. Jenner, Vykter grab your weapons and follow us; let's go Captain."

Energy coursed through their bodies. Atesh and Ballard sped through the thinned out trees. Legs leapt over logs as though possessed by their own thoughts; spurred on by the sounds of the calamity ahead. Blades whipped out of their secure havens, this was what they lived for. In no time at all they were in the middle of a blood bath. Two large sabre toothed tiger-bear abominations had attacked the merchant camp and were devouring the caravan guards.

"Oh dear Ancients, what are those?"

"No idea Captain, but let's see if we can redirect their focus. Watch out for those fangs, they were crunching into flesh and bone like soft butter. Righto play time kitties."

Ballard yelled out to the closest creature "Hey…ugly…over here." *Hmmm no response, well name calling isn't working; maybe if I poke it a bit, I can get its attention.*

While Ballard was playing with his prey, Atesh worked her way around the other side. She noticed Vykter had arrived behind in silence. Atesh pointed to his bow and held up two fingers to her eyes. Two arrows were loosened in quick succession; they hit the creature and lodged deep in the soft areas beneath the eye balls.

Wow that made the creature madder, if that was even possible.

Vykter then noticed Ballard in a bit of difficulty. He dropped his bow and raced over with his scimitar and dagger. He attacked the first creature head on. His sword glanced of its hide without a scratch. He did manage however to distract the creature, giving Ballard time to slide underneath. Long fangs brushed past Vykter by a breath. Then, with tree trunk sized front paws, ending with razor sharp claws, it swatted him like an annoying insect. This sent Vykter spiralling into a nearby caravan. Falling to the ground, he lay unmoving. Ballard raised his swords and with all his might cleaved the creature's soft unprotected abdomen.

Meanwhile nearby, Atesh stepped quiet and true. She dodged claws and fangs from the second creature. She grabbed and held onto its shoulder spikes and somersaulted up onto its back. With split second timing, Atesh had her two swords buried into the nape of the creature's neck; she pulled back as hard as possible. This caused the creature's head to pivot upwards. Though not as strong as the men in her unit she was well aware of the most vulnerable spots to attack. Jenner who had now arrived loosened two arrows and they travelled up into the creature's oversized nostrils. As the arrows entered the brain the calamity they caused was fatal. Atesh jumped clear as it slammed into the ground at her feet. Jenner then noticed Vykter lying in a heap on the ground ran over to render assistance. Vykter was dazed and bruised, but essentially uninjured.

"Ballard, where are you man?" Atesh looked around as she frowned and bit her bottom lip. All she could see were parts of the caravan guards' bodies and the two dead creatures. A small muffled sound was then heard. She traced the faint noise to where Ballard was last seen fighting the first creature. The sound was near but, barely audible. Atesh bent down next to the dead animal where she heard a strained voice.

"Someone get me out, before I suffocate."

Both Jenner and Atesh knelt down and used their hands and daggers in firm decisive movements. They dug through the viscera, gore and green blood. After the longest moments they found Ballard. He was penned down by the weight of the creature's innards that had spilled onto him, after he disembowelled it. Both grabbed hold of his slime coated arms. They tugged and pulled with all their might. Their feet scrambled and struggled to find hard earth for traction. Their efforts however were soon rewarded, as they wrenched him free; out into the fresh air. Ballard laid gasping, pain surged through him as he tried to draw in large deep breaths. Atesh and Jenner slumped down on the ground beside him, looked at each other and burst into laughter.

The Caravan Master and his family emerged from their hiding. Tears streamed down dirt encrusted faces, their bodies visibly shaken and eyes widened in fear. They surveyed the carnage around them. The caravan master wrung his hands and mumbled to himself. "How can we ever repay you for saving us? Never in my life…"

Atesh looked up from where she sat. "It's fine Master…"

"It is Master Briens; of Briens Fine Grade Silks and Rare Wines."

Master Briens tone changed completely when he noticed the Academy Pace Knight Insignia, on Atesh's Uniform sleeve. "May I ask where you were headed Commander. I have lost all our guards…Ooooh, what are we to do?"

A rustling of tree limbs and a commotion of voices was heard behind them.

"I believe these two belong to you Caravan Master." Renny and Sage appeared with wide broad smiles as they held tight two guards that had ran off into the bushes.

"Well Master Briens, looks like you still have two guards to take you home safe. We will say goodnight to you now and will clean up these creatures at daylight."

The Commander, Sage and Jenner assisted Ballard and Vykter back to their camp grounds. They still burst forth every now and again with sniggers and fits of laughter. The sight of Ballard wedged under the gizzards would not be forgotten for quite some time.

The men were awake, what with all the commotion going on close by. They were feeling rather solemn missing all the excitement, yet still too ill to assist, even if they wanted to. Ciaran had worn a path in the dirt waiting for his best friend to return. He spotted Renny, Atesh, Jenner, and Sage with Ballard and Vykter a little worse for wear. He raced over and scrambled up onto Atesh's shoulder.

"Oh, glad to see ye be fine lassie. Ye had me worried for da minute." He jumped down just as quick, wrinkling his snout, but saying naught.

The six of them sat down by the roaring fire and stared into it for a while. Not a sound could be heard as the men waited with anticipation. They stared at them; leant forward eager, waiting for the tale to be told.

With arms waving in exaggerated movements, Renny demonstrat-ed the gruesome details of the fight. Ballard held his head between his hands, elbows rested on entrails encrusted on his knees and stared into the flames. He didn't need the fire's warmth; his embarrassment warmed his entire body. He knew he shone bright red from nose to toes. Laughter and groans roared from the men. Atesh was unsure if they doubled over from too much laughter or the resultant pains of their earlier bouts of jelly belly. Their noise echoed into the darkness for miles. Ballard knew it; a new nickname was bound to come out of the night's events.

The rising of the sun witnessed a sad and sorry sight, as all the knights struggled to perform their stretch routines. They looked pale and washed out. Dance forms would be cancelled as precision movement with fine sharpened swords was deadly, if participants were not in top shape and alert. So they headed for breakfast which consisted of watery bland porridge for most, cheese and biscuits for those that could tolerate food.

Jenner continued to perform her usual magic. She had made many pots of chamomile tea, red clover tea and nettle infusions; these eased the men's stomach cramps and restored their hydration. A rest day was intended for most , but for those standing , a trip to the merchant caravan site was forthcoming.

"Captain Gizzard…umm…I mean Ballard, you up to a little inspection?"

The men fell about, holding their tender stomachs whilst either laughing or snortling. Renny was the worst offender for the latter, a sort of laugh, snort combination. This was often accompanied by a spray of fine boogie mist over the nearest unfortunate companion. Ballard's cheeks turned a rosy red and he sighed and shook his head.

"I feel we need to look at these creatures; Ciaran, Jenner."
Looking around the men that sat by the fire, "Anyone else want a look at the ugly critters?"

A line of all sixteen knights made their way slow and gentle through the trees to the merchant encampment; the location of the previous night's fiasco.

The Merchant and his caravan had left as soon as morning broke over the horizon. All that was left was the mess from the altercation.

Atesh was aghast that they had not even buried the dead guards or their bits.

"Geeze, you are kidding me right. What sort of man would leave his employees for the buzzards?"

The men nodded their heads in agreement. They looked a little closer at the two creatures and marvelled at their size and unusual features.

"Phew, they don't smell so good now eh, all this green goo. Is that supposed to be blood?"

"Ummm Commander, you three are covered in that stuff too."

Berend and the twelve knights moved back in unison from Atesh, Ballard and Jenner. They wrinkled and held their noses in disgust. Vykter and Renny had bathed earlier, before they made breakfast. Sage washed before the horses would allow him near them.

Atesh ran her fine fingers through her dirt, blood and innard covered locks and then gestured with wild exaggerated arm movements. This dislodged some small green gloop throughout the crowd. The men moved back with speed in all directions.

"Oh damn it all, I had just washed my hair, such a waste of good soap that."

Sniggers were heard all around.

"Right men; let's get this disgusting business over with. Burial detail over to the left, pyre detail here, we can burn these creatures back to wherever they came from. Jesper, can you do a quick drawing of these before we set them alight, I would like to send it to Master Elias."

"Certainly Commander, I will go and fetch my journal and pencils."

Once all the tasks were completed, they took it in turns for a rewash; a very unusual event for a warrior unit, but a necessary evil this day. It was around lunchtime when they again settled in around their fire pit for the afternoon for a deserved rest, after the previous night. Now the entire unit was beyond exhaustion. Snoring could be heard for miles, this time no one bothered to tape Kerwin's mouth shut, as they were all guilty of a snort or two.

It was a few hours later some of the men stirred.

"Renny, where are you hiding? You know yous has to help me with dinner tonight." Vykter searched all over camp. "Commander have you seen Renny?"

"No, I'm sorry. I haven't laid eyes on him for a while. Ballard have you seen our spoon licker anywhere?" They all looked around, at the latrine pits, by the river; he was not to be seen.

"Berend is unaccounted for as well Commander."

Two men missing, if Berend and Renny were involved it had to be trouble; what's going on here?

Being more than a little concerned, Atesh wandered between the tall smoke trees, their long limbs and pink blossoms extended out to capture and move with the gentle breeze. She pushed her way through small thick scrubby bushes, spiky prickle thickets and berry patches to wander further downstream for quite a way. She noticed again all the forest and river animals were strangely quiet. For this time of afternoon would be their busiest, scurrying for insects and fruits to feed their families, before the night descended. Atesh noticed the darkening clouds high above moved with a swifter breeze; indicating a change in weather or a possible shower later in the evening. She found Berend sitting hard up against a gnarled; bore eaten, poor excuse for a tree. He had been sharpening his blades, whistling quiet to himself, with a strange lopsided smile on his face. He noticed a pair of shiny black leather boots leading up to the finest pair of legs in the kingdom, or so he thought, standing in front of him. He raised his face to meet his Commander. Atesh looked deep into his emerald coloured eyes; knowing Berend as she did, he certainly was up to no good.

"Did you not hear us calling out to you Bear?" This was his nickname when he was in one of those stubborn ass moods; by the look in his eyes he was just that. He stared back at Atesh and grinned, more devilish, if that was even possible.

"Have you seen Renny around Berend?"

"I-I-I is h-here sir,"

"Where is here, Renny?"

"U…up here, sir."

Atesh's eyes followed the tree trunk up to a high branch and there perched on a thin outer limb, overhanging the river was Renny.

"Why are you up there like a blasted bird Renny?"

"Well sir, I was trying to keep my head on my shoulders. You see, they blame me for last night, and it wasn't my fault. The men have taken it rather bad, sir."

Shaking so hard the limb started to splinter. A look of resignation was on his face, eyes enlarged, as he shrugged his shoulders and looked into the river below. Berend at the base of the tree made sense now. Atesh stayed calm, but with the strength of her resolve and designation. She bent down to whisper into Berend's ear.

"Enough now Bear, move it or lose it. You have had your fun." Looking around with a frown, a shiver travelled up her spine again. "I need you both back to camp now; we will be going on full alert tonight. I do not need missing men."

The men remained vigilant and watchful throughout the night. The silence from man, birds and animals was deafening; which gave them all a feeling of impending doom.

Towards dawn a voice was heard in the Commander's head.

"Commander Atesh, can you hear me?"

"Master Elias is that you, how is this possible?"

"Atesh listen carefully to me. I do not have time to explain it all right now. Just know the amulet amplifies our essence. Another vision, you must leave that area immediately."

"Master, what is wrong?"

"You are in DANGER. Atesh leave NOW!"

The voice disappeared as quickly as it appeared. A feeling of dread was left ringing in the Commander's ears. Her body became adrenaline infused, her heart pounded through her chest wall and her mind raced with scenarios. She strode in a firm and precise manner towards the fire pit; this gave Atesh the air of authority that the knights knew was not to be messed with. She scanned the area, and noted where all the men were stationed, then shouted out loud for all to hear.

"Captain Ballard, men mount up; we need to leave now."

Having been on alert had its advantages; everything was packed and ready to move at a moment's notice. Horses had been left saddled and waited nearby. The men asleep around the fire, huddled up from the cool night air, awoke at the commotion. They shook their heads clear, ran to their horses, tightened the girths and leapt upon their steeds. Ciaran was asleep in Kayne's mane when Atesh bolted up behind him. Atesh became anxious as she moved to the front of the line. She then turned her head and with her right arm extended, signalled the unit to move out.

Chapter 5

What Lies Behind?

"Make for the bridge; we need to cross the river before dawn."

The men all followed their Commander's orders without delay, as they glanced around with faces set. The unit took off at a gallop and raced down the dark dirt track. Atesh held out her left hand with the clear crystal ring she adorned as part of her designation. It cast a beacon of light out in front; in case a surprise waited. Not long after their initial flight, a slight continuous tremble far below the surface was felt. Then the ground swayed left and right. The horses did not like the strange feeling under their feet and balked at times, almost sending their riders flying into the dark cool morning air.

"Faster men," Ballard indicated as he brought up the rear. "Move those nags you're on…Commander we must use our rings."

Atesh nodded her head. "NO, we need to keep an eye on each other; I don't like this earth shaking. If we blend into the environs, I may not be able to keep account of you all."

Ballard knew that not only do the rings allow for blending into the surrounding environment but, it can also enhance endurance and speed for the war steeds. This way they can cover long distances in a fraction of the time. He felt this may be their only saviour at this point.

The rumbling increased in volume and intensity. The groaning of the land being stretched beyond its normal limitations, grated on the entire units' ears and nerves; it seemed to radiate all around them. The horses were faring no better. They frothed at the mouth. Their eyes were wide with fear and their ears were turned back to listen to their riders' instructions. The knights' foreheads soon broke out in beads of sweat as they leant forward and urged their mounts to go faster. As dawn broke through the night's darkness, the bridge over the Jangly River was spotted up ahead. Now at least a dim light filtered the way.

Without warning the immediate surroundings to their right exploded. The entire unit faltered as their heads were whipped backwards with the force of the vibrations. Hot steam vents burst through cracks and crevices. In the smallest period of time the heat began to build up; in concentration and strength. The ground groaned and bulged now to the left of the riders. As it ruptured, plumes of heated vapour sent large earth projectiles spearing high into the air. Then sizeable fissures had cleaved open the land behind the riders egging them on faster; if that was possible. A small river of molten lava spewed forth from the earth, heading in the same direction as the knights. This flung small clumps of hot lava and ash all over the riders, their mounts and the surrounding grasses. It fuelled fires and inflicted nasty burns on contact.

At the bridge Atesh stopped. She faced a singular width, poorly maintained wooden overpass. The larger bridge the wagons and caravans used was further along the river; too far to reach safely. In no time at all the river had turned into a raging mass of turbulent brown foaming and frothing water; full of dirt, burning tree limbs, ash and debris.

"Ballard, take the men across first. I will bring up the rear. Be careful, it doesn't look that sturdy." Atesh shouted now over the noise.

A horrifying screech assaulted all within its vicinity. All the knights in the unit froze. They turned as one, with eyes widened to their fullest, mouths agape as they pointed back to where they had been.

"What in all the pirates' pox was that?" Berend, who would stand up to a dragon, looked aghast.

Atesh and Ballard turned around.

Atesh leaned over and grabbed Ballard by the arm, she bent over close to his ear. "Get them across now!"

Ballard started to cross the bridge slower than he would have liked. He was followed by the men one at a time. Once safe on the other side he shouted to Atesh; he pointed for her to turn around, his eyes were literally bulging out of their sockets.

"Oh dear ancients," He pointed again with animated vigour. His face showed abject terror. Ballard cupped his hands around his mouth and yelled as loud as possible.

"What did you say? I can't hear you?" Atesh placed her hands to her ears; she shook her head to acknowledge she had not heard him.

"Turn…around," Ballard used exaggerated hand movements to indicate turning.

Atesh whipped her head around and saw a swarm of giant, red hairy ant creatures. They had enormous gnashing pincers and spilled forth from the bowels of the earth. They were headed her way; racing alongside the lava.

Peeking out from his hiding spot in the saddle bag, Ciaran noticed they would be in a pickle shortly. "Ach Lassie, I think it's time to maybe get a move along. I dinna want to end up as dinner for those there critters. I'd always planned on a much more peaceful deeth."

"Ciaran, what be those?"

"They be flesh eating fire ants lassie, tis not good at all."

"Come on men move it." Atesh now became agitated; Renny was taking his time traversing the bridge.

The bridge was beginning to burn and buckle under the weight and movement of the knights. Atesh was almost onto the bridge whilst two other men were in the process of crossing when the bridge collapsed. Kayne leapt into the water as the earth they had been standing on erupted in flames and opened into a chasm. This enveloped most of the ants behind her, but scattered the remainder in all directions. Their death screams and burning flesh odour, was something no knight ever wanted to hear, smell or witness ever again in their lives. Lava flowed into the stream bed emitting thick grey steam.

Atesh and the last two knights were tumbled around in the raging foamed waters and taken down stream with the debris. Ciaran was perched on top of Atesh's head, hanging on for his life. His small extra weight was enough to submerge her head. She clung to the reins of Kayne's halter and gasped for breath whenever the opportunity came;

the majority of the time she gulped down mouthfuls of the dirt tasting putrid muck.

"Ciaran will you get off my blasted head, you are drowning me."

"Ach, sorry lassie, but I dinna think I canna swim in dis here water, it's too rough."

"I…am sorry Ciaran; I am caught on a branch from a fallen tree. I don't think I can hold on much longer. It's dragging me under and away from Kayne."

"Come on lassie, focus and swim for ye life. Don't give up on me; remember what I promised ya, when ye were a wee scrawny bairn?"

Ciaran leapt onto Kayne's wet, stringy mane and clung on desperately as the horse was swirled and taken further down the river. A mighty jolt hit Kayne side on and Ciaran near lost his balance. Renny and Kerwin had tumbled into one another and then were slammed against Kayne; they were the last two to cross the bridge when it collapsed under them. This motion dislodged Atesh and she was carried away at an alarming speed along with the tree branch. This also knocked the large portion of the branch into Atesh's forehead opening up a wide gash and rendering her unconscious. The boys were in far better shape than their Commander.

Kerwin threw his steed's reins at Renny. "Renny grab hold of Charlie and Kayne's reins when you can. Try and make your way to the bank. The men are not far away, they will help you. I am going after Atesh; wish me luck." With that Kerwin dove into the swirling water and climbed up onto the large branch Atesh was tangled in. Catching his breath and spitting out some foul bits of crud; he set about keeping her head above the water and tried to free her from the mess. Her wound oozed free, mixing with the foul water. He desperately tried to slash the small branches away with his dagger, and in the end he resorted to actually cutting some of her clothes to release the branch. The cold water started to make his muscles spasm and hanging onto Atesh was becoming difficult. The branch Kerwin held onto broke and sent the both of them swirling back into the raging river. They were taken by the swift current downstream away from any chance of rescue.

Renny's name was shouted out. When he looked up he saw Ballard and Berend had jumped into the river from the bank and swam to reach him and the horses. Ropes were tied around their waists, held at the other end by their fellow knights. They grabbed Renny, Tempest's reins, and then Kayne's. They dragged them onto the sandbank just before the bend. Charlie was pulled away from Renny's grip by a passing swirling mass of debris. It snagged on one of his stirrups and the steed disappeared around the bend to be carried along by the river.

"Glad to see you fellows decided to show up to the party." Renny choked out. Then he faded into the darkness from sheer exhaustion. The rest of the men soon caught up and carried the unconscious beauty to high, dry safe ground. Jenner attended to him and they moved away from any further danger.

Ballard had kept the unit moving till they made camp in a clearing on a plateau overlooking the small village of Janlin. Large bushman trees surrounded the clearing and these trees were large enough to keep weather out and build a warm fire within. The branches actually reached to the ground with their foliage, a hidden refuge for any traveller. Renny came around once he was warmed up as he lay beside the fire pit. After organising camp the men were anxious to search for their two missing team mates. Ballard knew however, that the horses and men required rest.

"We will set out first thing in the morning. We need to be fresh and alert in case we meet more of those ant creatures."

Kerwin and Atesh were taken many miles down the stream. Kerwin managed to manoeuvre their position closer to the bank, once they became wedged in a built up area of debris; forming a dam of sorts. He realised it would not be long before a larger pile would push its way through and they may not be able to extricate themselves to safety. He dragged Atesh along the branches and crawled up onto the bank; although taller than the average female, she was lithe and easy to be carried. Not long after they reached the bank, Kerwin spotted his steed Charlie floating past. He could see his head bobbing above the waterline. Kerwin summoned the last of his energy and rescued his beloved war horse and pulled Charlie up to safety. The three then collapsed up on the dry grassed area.

Atesh came around through the afternoon and released all the putrid water she had previously swallowed, in rather an explosive gush. Her focus came back slow and she smiled when she noticed Kerwin had built a small fire. He and Charlie were curled up together beside it; sound asleep. *Man and horse, how life should be.*

When Kerwin awoke a little while later, he noted Atesh had moved closer to the fire. This was a good sign, her head bandage was still in place and the bleeding stopped. His stomach growled informing him it was time for food. He placed water from his canteen on to boil and made some soup. It was a good thing the magic enhanced saddle bags had remained on Charlie. They were water proof and held all the rations and equipment they ever needed for a mission and survival.

Atesh opened her eyes, smiled up at him and spoke in a harsh croaky whisper. "I believe you saved my life." She took hold of his warmed hand, "Thank you kind sir." She again drifted off into sleep. As the dreams took over the day's excitement, she heard a faint reply.

"We do all we can for family Commander."

As evening approached the river had quietened down. Bush animals were once again rummaging around the forest floor and birds called out to each other before settling in for the night.

"Wake up sleepy, food is on the table."

Atesh woke to the smell of cooking. It stirred the feeling of hunger within her, but it also bought on the nausea as well. *All that mud, water and ash I swallowed-ugh.* Atesh looked up to the sky and smiled. She was delighted in the fact she survived to see this amazing array of colours that streaked across it. She marvelled at the balance of nature. One minute all was broken and then life rights itself to be reborn as new. She watched as the last of the red hues faded and descended below the horizon. The ash cloud that had turned day to night had stopped falling to blanket the surrounds. The air still held a dusty thickness to it; though a fresh burst of untainted air eddied around them from time to time.

Kerwin had put together some rations and made a concoction, a sort of soup-stew. "Here I have made you this nice cup of dandelion tea…you may find it refreshing."

"Thanks Kerwin." She placed her hands up to her throat as she forced a swallow of the hot beverage. She hurt all over and winched at any movement. "Where are we?"

"Well that I cannot say Commander, but we are safe and alive; that is the main thing. We are well hidden from any creatures; I believe these large trees and bushes should protect us tonight. I'm not sure, but I think we have travelled quite a ways down the river."

They sat by the fire for hours. Kerwin told tales of his childhood, how he dreamed of becoming a knight. He looked into the blaze of the fire and recalled the memories. He was slow to mature, a trial he had to endure. The other boys his age were much taller and stronger then he, so they bullied him day and night, every opportunity they could find. It made him more determined to be the knight he knew he could be. He practiced with homemade weights and ran twice a day for miles He begged the local aged, retired knight for lessons and soon enough, he had a growth spurt and muscled out. He knew he had strong innate magic most of his life. Water was his gift and he had Atesh smiling with the tricks he had played on his siblings, and the bullies; often it involved someone looking like a wrung out dish cloth. Funny he thought, how not one of those other boys ever made the grade; they were farmers or hands for hire now. He spoke of his wife Annabelle and his unborn child.

Atesh tried not to say too much, it would end up raspy and incoherent. She learnt a lot about her youngest and newest recruit and she liked what she saw.

The following morning they set off on Charlie. Atesh riding on the back, they took it slow and steady and headed North West. Towards the early afternoon they saw a plume of dust to their right, the cavalry had arrived. Atesh slid off Charlie and sat on the hard ground and waited. She looked up at the sky, blue with a hint of red on the horizon now. There was no hint of the calamity from the previous day. Once they were spotted by the knights, the unit galloped their horses across the plains; smiles could be seen for miles from the men.

A short way off a small creature jumped from the back of a galloping black, unmanned stallion and raced as fast as his legs would carry him. His small hops accelerated his speed and he surged onward, leaving the others behind in his dust. Ciaran launched himself at Atesh's chest and flew into her open arms. This knocked her backwards and a laughing dragon cuddle ensued.

Ballard nodded his head at Kerwin, smiled and placed his right arm across his chest to his heart. The men all surrounded Kerwin in a circle and followed suit. This was their way of applauding one of their own. He now felt like a true member of the Knights First Battalion family; a high honour indeed.

Chapter 6

Janlin Village:

Atesh and her company kept a measured pace towards the Village of Janlin. When they stopped for a rest, Atesh walked off and sat alone on a lush carpet of green grass. She crossed her legs, closed her eyes and cleared her mind. She slowed her breathing in an attempt to reach out to Master Elias Freymore. The purple amulet clutched between her hands, started to warm up and glow. *"Master Elias can you hear me?"*

"Atesh, oh my goodness yes, but not very clear, are you alright my dear?"

"We were all saved, thanks to you Master. It felt like hell had opened its gates Sir. The land awoke in a furious mood and tore apart, sending a river of lava and steam spearing into the sky. A swarm of fire ants ascended from the bowels of this rent and chased us to the river. The small wooden Jangly Bridge is no more."

"Oh my, make your way to the Beaumont castle as quick as you can Atesh. I will contact my brother and inform him you will not be long. Be safe."

Feeling refreshed after some meditation, Atesh re-joined the unit. They remounted and headed off. It took the best part of the following day to wind their way down to the Janlin Village.

Little did the knights know a large number of the fire ants had managed to cross the debris filled river. They regrouped behind their Queen and travelled slow as they shadowed the knights. Two young male ants had other ideas. They departed from this company of survivors and decided to show their mettle; flex their muscles. They followed closer and watched and assessed this small unit of fresh meat, till they were sure they could attack and win against those they believed caused their home to be destroyed.

Janlin was normally a busy stopover for the southern and eastern trade routes. For some reason the gates were shut and guards were on the battlement with weapons drawn. Atesh's voice was still hoarse from her dunking. So Captain Ballard performed the honours.

"Good evening Janlin Village, may we enter to resupply and seek a safe haven for the night?"

"Who are you to want entry at this foul time? We do not open our gates to strangers. There are peculiar happenings here about. Did you not feel the earth shake, the sky fill with a dark red glow? All these are bad omens, so move along to Mere town; quick now."

"This is Commander Atesh of the *'Pace Knights'* and we are the primary unit from the Ashmourne academy. I am Captain Ballard and we are on a mission to the King and must reach Beaumont Castle as soon as possible. But as you can see, we ran into some misfortune and unfriendlies."

"Ballard is that you…you old dog," A loud voice boomed from behind the front soldier.

"Tred, Tredenick what are you doing here? Will you please open up?"

Captain Tredenick bellowed at his soldiers. "Open the gates now men, don't dilly dally. These are the Wizard Compound Knights and their Supreme Commander."

Once inside the men all dismounted, they put on their bravest face and toughest straight posture. Atesh dismounted with Ciaran on her shoulder.

"Welcome to our humble village. How may we assist you?"
Captain Tredenick made an exaggerated bow to Ballard.

"Nice one. We are in need of a safe haven for the night and then we must move along. How is it, you are stationed here Tred? I thought you were retired?"

"Well once a soldier…you know, I couldn't settle. Don't get me wrong. I loved Ashmourne Village, but became restless. I wanted an adventure, travelled around for a while then I was offered a job I couldn't refuse, so here I am, Captain of a deserted village." Tredenick turned to the knight's Commander. "Atesh is that really you? I am feeling old if you are now the Supreme Commander."

Atesh grinned and gave Tred a huge cuddle and croaked out, "Hi there handsome, I have missed your visits and stories."

Tred gave Ciaran a scratch as he looked over the company. "Sounds like you all need some of my special brew."

"Oh that would be kind of you Sir Tred." Atesh placed her hand over her heart.

"Why were the gates shut to travellers?"

"Well Ballard, the village has been barren for two weeks now. There were strange earth shakes and villagers disappearing without sight or sound of a tussle. At night you would hear horrid screeches, growls that would twist the Master's bloomers. Beggin your pardon Commander; the villagers became spooked. They talked of bad omens, the end of days. So they all packed up and left for Mere town."

A shout from one of the city guards brought them out of their peaceful state. "Captain Tredenick, there are…t…t… creatures approaching sir."

The two captains and Atesh leapt up the steps to gaze over the gate. Atesh had a weird feeling in the pit of her stomach. It came as no surprise when she spied the creatures that approached. On the horizon two large fire ants charged towards the village.

"Ach nae again," Ciaran hid under Atesh's collar.

"Did they follow us Ballard?"

"That's possible Atesh. Though, I would suspect quite unusual behaviour for an ant."

"We must assume these are not normal ants then, eh." Atesh crossed her arms and rolled her eyes at her Captain.

"What in all Sofala are they Ballard? Was this, what did you call them…your unfriendlies…and you led them here?" Captain Tredenick eyes stared at the horror that raced toward them.

More of the village guards had assembled up on the walkway. They looked out at the abominations; then to the knights. It did not stop them from shaking with fear.

"We thought most of them had perished. We would never intentionally endanger your village Tred. Damn them, don't they ever die?" Ballard looked down at the knights whom had already organised themselves into battle form. *I love working with these men, so in tune.*

"Archers ready your selves on the wall. Two swords with me and two with the Commander, four spears to the rear; Tred all non-essential personnel to be inside if you please."

"There are only soldiers and essential army support personnel left, Ballard."

"Atesh, are you sure you are up to this?"

"Yes Ballard though, I will need the added energy from the crystals this time." She sat up on the battlement and placed her hands on her knees; head bowed, eyes closed as she centred herself with deep controlled breaths. It seemed to take no time at all for the warmth to spread throughout her body. As she stood upright, blue flames leapt out from her eyes . Her face was set in a mask of anger and determination . All the rings on her fingers gave off a gentle glow, as did the amulet around her neck. She drew her scimitars out from their black leather sheaths and somersaulted into the air. She performed the smoothest, graceful motion anyone had ever witnessed. She came to land in a crouch without disturbing any dust, down beside the knights.

Ballard whistled and all the men in the vicinity stared at the Commander. "Well that's a first; blue flames." He turned to Captain Tred. "I wonder what other surprises she has for us. I knew she was special, but wow…glad she is on our side." Ballard looked down and met the men's questioning looks . He raised his right eyebrow , shrugged his shoulders and smiled.

The men acknowledged this with a knowing smile of their own. They turned as one to face the gate; poetry of synergistic cadence. Now they were ready to do battle. They felt whole again. All had an overwhelming feeling of pride and blood lust pounding throughout their veins.

The two ant creatures stopped a short way before the wooden gate and staged an unusual dual routine of musical clicking noises. They opened and shut their enlarged sharp pincers, in a consistent snapping motion, their mandibles grinding in time to their music.

"Is that a challenge?" Ballard wondered.

The creatures bent down and sprang off the ground in unison. Folded underneath their overly bloated abdomens were tear shaped points that aimed forward towards the gate. These held elongated stingers. As they leapt in the air they sprayed out an amber coloured liquid. This thick fluid clung to the wooden structure and sizzled. It smoked and corroded; burning holes into the wood and metal pins that held the gate in place.

"Well that's new." Berend shook his head in disbelief as he watched from atop the walkway; the strange events unfolding before his eyes. "Commander be careful of their rear ends sir, them stingers, they squirt burning liquid."

"Thanks for the warning, Berend. Swords ready, Spears up. Archers fire as soon as the gates open and men…keep firing. Ballard you go left, we will take the right. Remember your training men. Swift, light and take no unnecessary chances."

This was not their normal approach to an attacking force. They would not run out and meet an adversary face to face at first instance. But Ballard and Atesh felt they had placed the village in imminent danger. The gates opened and the knights ran out amidst the raining down of arrows above them. Atesh knew her men had perfect aim; well most of the time. They kept to the off side of the creatures, taking no chances the village guards could aim as well. Most of the arrows however bounced off the hardened exteriors of the ant's thorax and abdomen. The lack of damage they caused frustrated the archers; so Berend decided on a new tactic.

Meanwhile, Kerwin fighting swords with pincers was swatted down flat on his back. He was held down by an enormous claw. Pincers edged closer for a decapitation. An arrow, a one in a million shot went straight into the ant's right eye. Berend let out a "whoop" from the top of the gate. The creature loosened its hold on Kerwin and he rolled out from beneath thrashing claws and twisting abdomen.

The ant started to rear on its hind legs and both Ballard and Renny drove their long blades into its soft unprotected underbelly, piercing its vital organs. It collapsed dying in slow motion. It sent mounds of dirt and green blood up into the air, as it unceremoniously hit the ground. The knights scrambled away as fast as possible. They knew that parts of the creature would envelop them if they did not clear the sheer size of it. In all the dust and confusion, Renny tripped over a mass on the ground and pushed it back away with his feet as he scrambled forward as fast as possible; into the fresh air.

Atesh and her two knights fought and ducked as the stinger sent burning liquid droplets raining down upon them. Wyart stuck his sword in between the hard shell of the thorax and its soft underside. The ant in a movement of extraordinary speed grabbed Wyart by his shirt and tossed him in the air to be swallowed whole. Atesh held her breath as she somersaulted over the ant's head. She knocked Wyart out of danger and landed beside him on the ground. Her reward from the angry creature was to be squirted with the burning fluid. Her right side and arm were aflame with a horrific burning sensation.

This has to end now, monstrosity. Atesh was beyond anger. She pivoted, ran and sprung up in the air from the balls of her feet. Arms flung out in front for balance. Then she somersaulted onto the ant's head in a quick fluid motion. Atesh bent over the ant's forehead upside down; her legs wrapped around its feelers. She stared with vicious intent into its left eye. With her teeth bared she hissed, "ENOUGH NOW." She held out her right hand into the air, "Jesper spear." A spear was instantly forced into her hand and she thrust it with all her pent up anger into the eye of the ant. It arced straight up into the brain, imploding the tissue on impact. It crumbled to the ground and threw itself into a death roll to dislodge the intruder. It squirted the last of its burning liquid in all directions; even covering its own body. The men scattered out of the way and Atesh unravelling her legs was thrown clear. She lay still for a moment, to gain her breath.

Ballard raced over and held out his hand to her. "Well done Atesh…well done. That was a new move. I didn't know you could conjure out of thin air?"

"What are you talking about; did you get hit on the head?"

"Atesh, a spear magically appeared in your right hand"

"No, I yelled to Jesper to throw me one."

Ballard held her by the shoulders and turned her towards Jesper.

"Commander, I still have my spear." Jesper held it up for all to see. "I was ready to throw it to you; when one appeared in your hand."

Atesh, Ballard and Jesper all looked at her hands. Then his spear; they frowned and shook their heads in unison.

"Wow really?" Atesh rotated her hands again and stared in disbelief. "No not possible?"

Ballard and Jesper stood still and nodded their heads up and down in unison.

After the initial burn to her right side and arm. Atesh had felt no further pain till now. She turned to examine the formed blisters and reddened areas, *Nasty critters.*

"Let Jenner have a look and treat these burns, Atesh."

Ballard and Atesh whipped their heads around as a commotion was heard a short distance away.

"I need help over here Commander." Renny was trying to dislodge Kerwin from the first ant. He was pinned from the waist down. As Atesh and Ballard ran closer, they yelled out in unison.

"STOP, DO NOT MOVE HIM."

Atesh could see the red blood pooling from beneath the ant. "Men this is a crush injury. If you move him out too quick; he will die from the trauma. The body shuts down."

"Ciaran we need Jenner now, please hurry."

All the rest of the knights and village guards poured out to see what was happening and to inspect the creatures. Jenner raced over to Kerwin. She placed a clear crystal on his forehead and closed her eyes.

Ballard and Berend held Renny back; he had become hysterical.

Berend whispered into Renny's ear. "Renny get a grip. You are a knight, act like it. They know what they are doing. I have seen this before many times in battle. You move him the shock will kill him in an instant. The Commander is right, trust in her judgement."

When Jenner reopened her eyes, a look of concern creased her face. With a soft voice she spoke to Atesh.

Atesh leant next to her youngest recruit. "Kerwin can you hear me, it is Atesh. You are in a spot of trouble my friend. The ant fell on you when he died. But his sharp pincer was folded under him and it has given you a nasty slice to your leg and crushed some of your bones; do you understand what I am saying?"

Kerwin opened his blood shot eyes. "Yes Commander. A little flesh wound?"

"Yes something like that; nothing we can't handle. I owe you…remember? Jenner is here and she will give you some poppy milk to dull your pain. Then we will lift the creature off you in small movements. Your blood will return gradually to where it should be. We cannot move this creature off you with any quick motion, without killing you in an instant."

Atesh nodded to Jenner who dosed Kerwin with the potion. Jenner placed a leather strap between his teeth and told him to bite down.

"We do not want you to bite your tongue off. I will not lie to you Kerwin. It is going to be painful; but the medicine will dull some of it."

Whispering between gritted teeth, Kerwin held onto Atesh's hand. "I believe in you Commander."

Oh Geeze, no pressure then.

Kerwin smiled at Atesh and closed his eyes.

Ballard had arranged men to lift the huge carcass off their comrade. Ten either side of Kerwin to progress in slow, steady movements. Wide wooden planks would be placed underneath the carcass to help keep the weight off. Then when Jenner declares it is safe, they will slide him out to safety.

Atesh watched in wonder as the men expertly worked as a team. Even the soldiers from the village pushed and lifted with all their might. Beads of sweat covered all their foreheads and muscles bulged with the strain, but not a sound was spoken. Kerwin tried to stifle the scream that eventually escaped from around the leather strap. This made the men only stronger in their resolve. After what seemed like a life time for poor Kerwin the knights dragged him out and away from the ant. The blood was oozing free now from his wounds. Jenner shook her head as she noticed the leg had almost been severed. They removed his boots and sockets to see his circulation returning to the last toe.

"Geeze man your feet stink. Near as bad as the Captains. Don't you wash em?" Berend held his nose. "Well we know what your nickname is going to be from now on eh; pinkie?"

This released the tension as sniggers echoed from the men. Kerwin was carried into the village infirmary by stretcher. The men then all waited outside the healers' quarters, refusing to move till they knew Kerwin would survive. Jenner had administered healing to the best of her abilities. But there was still a way to go before Kerwin was out of danger. He sustained severe injuries to his right leg, with a crush fracture to the pelvis. Jenner assured Kerwin and the men he would heal in time, given rest and more care from the Academy Masters. He may have a slight limp and a large scar to show off to the ladies. Atesh and Jenner decided to take him to Mere town on the way to Beaumont Castle. There were crystal healers from the academy at their hospice.

After all the discussions and recent events Atesh walked away from the crowd, she needed to be alone. Ciaran scooted after her and bounced up onto her head. He spoke quiet to her as she wandered off into the nearby scrub. She sat down on a patch of weathered grass, looked around at the peaceful surroundings and tears welled in her eyes. She was exhausted and not afraid to admit, she had been a little scared. A noise behind shook her out of her berating and self-reflection. She recognised Ballard from his purposeful stride. She stood and wiped her reddened eyes on her dirt ridden sleeve and turned to face him. Atesh noticed, he too had tears which also threatened to spill down his cheeks and a slight tremble emanated from his body. They had both been on an emotional ride the last couple of days. He stepped up to Atesh and encircled her into his arms like he used to when she was a child; she buried her face into his chest and he rested his cheek on her head.

Ballard broke the silence. "I thought…I had lost you at the river."

"I am sorry."

Ciaran climbed onto Ballard's shoulder and cooed to both while caressing them.

Chapter 7

Meet and Greet:

Most of the village guards elected to stay on at Janlin. They felt the dangers were past for now, but they would leave the moment any more creatures found their way to the area. The knights and four of the village guards set out for Mere Town. Kerwin too injured to ride was laid out in the back of an open farm cart. Jenner the healer sat close by the injured knight and tried her best to keep him sedated, warm and comfortable. The terrain was rough on the over used track. It had been a long and tiresome time for Kerwin as he lay dozing in and out of the forced sleep.

After two weeks of slow travel they reached their first destination, Mere Town. This was the largest of all the western settlements on the continent of Sofala. Rich farming land unfolded from the right side of the town boundary; dotted around small streams and undulating wooded hills. This stretched far back to the Jangly River and broadened up into the ice capped mountain ranges. The left held white sandy beaches and a large sheltered bay offering sanctuary to all; from the vast ill-tempered ocean. Once Jenner deposited her charge to the healers she caught up with her unit. They waited beyond the town's outer wall and watched in awe at the unusual hive of activity in and around the fish markets, food and tinker stalls and busy docks.

The salty ocean breeze stirred the knight's blood, reminding them of home. It eddied around the myriad of colourful sails which adorned the moored merchant vessels. It caressed them with its fine loving tendrils, whispering of adventures waiting for them in far off lands.

The ships waited in line with impatient fervour, for their chance at the unloading docks. The King's naval vessels always assumed priority and the sailors took their time with their unloading chores; they seemed to enjoy upsetting the greedy merchants any chance they could get. The King's personal standard noticed the mighty warriors and waved to the knights as they passed, or so it seemed. They then skirted around the main hub of the town and headed north-east towards Beaumont castle and its surrounding village a few miles further on.

"We will camp by the stream tonight Captain, left of the castle outer wall." Atesh led them off the main road and headed for a tree lined meandering stream. A large oval shaped grassed area spread out neatly next to their camp site. *This would be superb for our workouts. Good view from the castle windows as well, cannot hurt to show off a bit.*

Captain Ballard organised the camp and placed the 'Pace Alastriona' standard out the front. He watched the breeze stroke the material back and forth. It was a striking design, he mused. The three large yellow circles represented truth, honesty and integrity all encased on a background of purple for peace. Around the edges the intricate design for the Wizards Academy was in gold and red. The men noticed the guards up on the outer castle walls; as they pointed and stared down at the strangers that made camp with little fuss and expertise.

"Hey Vykter, do you think they are wondering if we be friend or foe?"

"I bet they are wondering where we keep all our wagons and supplies. Will ya look at that fancy kitchen? Ooooh, we are so jealous; would you be apt to sharing a keg or two with us poor country folk, eh Berend?"

This caused loud laughter from all those within hearing range and further interesting banter as to what they have or haven't got hidden in their saddle bags. Vykter was down on his knees, holding his stomach; it ached so much from laughing.

Ballard smiled and walked into view. "All right men enough. We don't want to give all our secrets away now, do we?"

This only made the men worse. Not only raucous laughter, but snortling again was heard from Renny. Atesh turned her head and smiled as she listened to their mirth. This was music to her ears. Over the last few weeks there had been such a diverse range of emotions running deep within their entire psyche, she feared it may have ended up tearing into the very fabric of their souls. Never had this unit before experienced such calamity in a short space of time. That they all remained alive was perhaps more to do with luck, rather than her leadership skills. Yes…her character as their Commander had been sorely tested. They may be the mighty 'Pace Knights' but, each and every one of them was human with a heart, a soul and an individual fragility or breaking point. There was nothing in their contract about fighting giant, hungry, meat eating, fire liquid squirting, vile, ugly…*the ugliest*…creatures ever to grace this planet. Or that they had to brave the extremes of nature's elements in a race to cheat death. *Perchance a raise is in order.* It was all surreal and quite bizarre. *Now that I am presentable, I shall go and deliver the Master's package; like a good errand boy.*

Ciaran meandered in the tent and whistled. "Wow goin on a date me bonny lassie, huhmmm; I meant your Highness." He bowed his head in mockery.

"Oh shut it, or maybe you want to stay here and play with the boys? Be nice now, what do you really think? Is it overdone?"

Ciaran circled Atesh a few times umming and ahhing. "Well da tight black leather trous, purple belt, wid d' matching boots is a nice touch; impressive, purrrrr. The long white shirt and black vest looks nae so bad. Oh and the blue flowing cape, showing our motif with hood a definite. Perfect, I would say lassie, if ye want all the lads in the castle eating out of ye hand and droolin. I noticed ye have kept ya hair the golden colour, so you dinna want anyone to know ye moods, eh?"

"Well, dear friend. I prefer this colour. I suppose when I am really mad I will let it change to flame red, so they can all run for the hills. Yes, we must use what we have been given." Then she struck an unlady like pose and they started to laugh too; definitely the mood was infectious.

As she exited the tent the men stopped, stared and whistled at their commander. Atesh knew she would blush. Her cheeks reddened, warm to the touch and her heart pounded fierce. She pulled her thoughts together and looked around for her escort. *Payback eh, they know how to embarrass me. Hurry up Ballard, before I burst into flame.*

"Ballard, are you decent yet?" Frustrated with waiting for his lordship to finish preening himself, she turned to eyeball the men surrounding her. "Hagan you are in charge while I'm gone. Good luck with this rabble and men…behave and you get to go and play with the big boys tonight." Atesh smiled as she leapt onto her gleaming four legged transport with Ciaran tucked away cosy under her hood. Her heart skipped a beat when she thought of how Sage had braided small beads of crystals into Kayne's mane and polished the saddle.

Ballard's misty grey monster of a stallion Caesar sparkled with tiny jewels and looked formidable.

Atesh laughed when she spied Ballard all dressed up, *so unnatural.* "Oh we do make a handsome pair."

Ballard's face felt warm too, he knew he blushed scarlet like a girl, *oh damn, another reason for the men to rib me later.*

Woof whistles loud and shrill were heard as the two beauties passed by. They looked at each other, grinned, shook their heads and cantered off to the castle gates. Riding up to the dirt road towards the castle, Atesh's eyes wandered up to the enormous looming curtain ashlar walls. Overlooking them was the largest castle she had ever laid eyes on; there were many turrets, spearing up into the clouds.

"Wow, the High King's Palace. It is so enormous and sounds so regal, eh Ciaran?"

"Ach it does that lassie. Bet they are all in their la de da finest too."

From a window high up in the castle, a face watched the visitors arrive. Master Thaddeus Freymore, High Wizard and Councillor to the King looked out from his sitting room. He lived in one of the large suites, designated for the royal family members. The sun's rays warmed the interior during the daytime. At night a large fireplace roared, warming his sitting room, study and library. His opened doors and terrace overlooked the grassed area, stream and of course the knight's camp site. *Ah, at last they are here. Finally, I get to meet the infamous Atesh. I wonder if what my brother suspects are true.* He sat down in his comfy chair by the fireplace and thought on what he might say to this young lady. *Well I better get myself organised, shouldn't keep her waiting now.*

At the entrance to Beaumont Village sat the large wooden gates and the raised spiked metal portcullis. They were stopped by a sliding wooden barrier strung across from the gate house.

"State your name, occupation and purpose for visiting Beaumont Castle." A guard rattled off, without even looking up from his ledger.

Atesh and Ballard looked at each other, raised their eyebrows, then with his best authoritative voice.

"Supreme Commander Atesh and Captain Ballard from Ashmourne Island wish to visit your wonderful establishment."

The guard stood up in haste, knocking his stool over backwards. He snapped to attention. His right arm thumped across his chest to his heart. His whole body trembled and his eyes widened in wonder as he looked up at the gleaming pair. He squinted as he tried to get a decent look at them. The sun's rays shone off their horses' riding gear, buckles and the like; making the riders almost invisible. He did notice a mature aged gentleman, obviously the Commander and his younger Captain with a hooded cloak.

"Where might we find the Anvil Inn, Ahhh Sergeant? We have travelled a great distance and are parched. We would like to taste a mug or two of your hospitality?"

"Follow the road to the right sir, and you will not miss it. Mighty glad to have you here sir, we have heard so much about you and the Knights sir. May I enquire if that is your camp down yonder; near the stream sir?"

"Yes that is correct; they may wander up here tonight. Be a good fellow and let them pass. It's been a journey to test the best of us."

With that, the barrier was lifted and Atesh and Ballard entered the Beaumont castle village. The road was paved with stone, so their quiet entrance was not as they had hoped. Kayne pranced around, throwing his head up and chest out. He felt frisky and important.

Caesar looked over at Kayne's performance and rolled his eyes, *I am too old for his rot.*

Atesh sniggered as she heard Caesar's admonishment of Kayne's self-indulgent behaviour.

Passers-by stopped and stared at the two strangers. A majestic black stallion strutting with the mysterious hooded rider and the regal looking grey horse with a rather large warrior seated astride with many years of experience etched into his features. What they didn't notice was a dragonelle that peeked out from under the hood to watch the surrounds. Arriving at the Anvil Inn they swung their right leg over the low pommel in one swift elegant movement and dismounted in unison. They walked their charges to the stable beside the Inn.

A young boy ran up and bowed to them. "I would love to take care of your wonderful horses' sirs."

In silence they all walked into the stables where privacy was assured. Ciaran jumped out from under the hood and sat on Kayne's back. The young lad stood still in fear; his large eyes never left the dragonelle.

"What's your name little master."

"I am known as Binji sir. Is that a dragon sir?"

Atesh removed her hood and with the largest smile, she picked up Ciaran, gave him a great big cuddle and kiss, and then looked at Binji. "I am Atesh; you may pat him if you like. His name is Ciaran and he is a Dragonelle."

Binji came over hesitant at first and gave Ciaran a gentle pat; Ciaran enjoyed the lads touch very much.

"I would love a scratch if ye could manage it wee laddie."

Binji stared at Ciaran, smiled and then held out his arms. They became instant friends.

"Binji look after our precious men and we will reward you well." With that Atesh tossed him a gold coin. Binji nodded as he was soon engrossed with his scratching task.

Both Atesh and Ballard laughed as they entered the Inn. *Keep an eye out for us Ciaran; don't get to comfy, eh. Is that you purring like a cat? I never realised a dragonelle could do that?*

They chose a table with four seats in the far back corner, their view of all exits assured. A message was given to the Barkeep; who nodded and walked into his back room. In no time at all, a waitress carried two mugs of ale and placed them on their table. Now it was a waiting game. They talked quiet amongst themselves and kept their observation skills on high alert. They noticed the inn was frequented by the village palace guards; constant in their coming and going as their shifts were commencing and completed. They were the centre of speculation as heads were melded together in close whispers. Often all eyes would be turned in their direction, some with frowns, and others with smiles. The waitress was even questioned by one particular guard with a shiny uniform and precision cut hair. He had a constant irritating habit of stroking his insignificant chin growth. She shook her head to him. It was in her own best interest to not ever tell on another patron. This she kept to.

"I believe that scowling pretty boy over to the right must be the Captain of the guard. He has an arrogant look about him. I don't like the way he frowns up at us."

"It will be fine Ballard; we are pissing on his turf…that is all. By the way he is preening himself; I would surmise he feels rather important. Then we come along in our finest la-de-da outfits and the conversations are not about him anymore. Maybe he feels threatened."

"When did you get so darn smart eh?" Ballard smiled in his ale.

A gleaming black, red and gold carriage pulled up outside the Inn. It had the palace insignia; a fire breathing dragon on the door. Out jumped a tall, aged looking gent. He was dressed in the academy black trousers and shirt, a wizard cloak with blue trim trailed behind him. He carried a long jewelled staff and stepped sprightly for a two century plus year old man. He nodded to the attendant, the waitress, barkeep and the guards. He headed over to where Atesh and Ballard sat, smiled then settled into the third chair.

Atesh and Ballard stared at the visitor to their table. Both took a sharp short intake of breath, eyes widened. Wizard Thaddeus Freymore noticed the shocked expression on their faces and lack of speech.

"Well I had better introduce myself. Yes…I am Master Thaddeus Freymore and as you can see; my dear brother and I are identical twins. Though I do believe, I am the handsomer of the two."

Atesh near chocked on her spit. "We had heard you were his brother Master Thaddeus, but this was a surprise. He likes to do that to us. A crafty one if I may say sir. I am Commander Atesh and this is Captain Ballard. My mentor, guardian and right arm sir."

"Nice to meet you Captain Ballard," He held out his hand to shake, grasping just below Ballard's elbow as academy tradition indicates.

"Ah now, my dear Atesh, I have waited many years to meet you. My brother had spoken so much about you. I thought you may be a figment of his imagination."

Atesh placed out her hand to shake, but instead Thaddeus held it ever so gentle and raised it to his lips. She received a tender kiss to the back of her hand instead. *Oh no; another smoothy.* Atesh not being as some would say market smart, didn't know what to say. She knew any minute she would go red as a tomato. *A distraction that is what I need.* Reaching under her cape she withdrew the concealed package and handed it over to Master Thaddeus.

"Thank you my dear. I appreciate this fine gesture. My brother tells me you have had a difficult time finding your way here."

"Yes sir, it was like all the demons of past tales rose up from the bowels of the earth, determined to stop our travels. That we are all alive is beyond belief, though we came too close to losing one man at Janlin. We have left Knight Kerwin in the care of the Mere Town hospice."

"Oh, my dear that is terrible news to hear. Well if I know Elias, Kerwin's family will be well looked after." He took a sip of ale that appeared at the table, with refills for Atesh and Ballard. "Ahhh, the best ale in town I say. Ben keeps it at the right temperature. Now you are camped down by the stream I see. The King extends to you all, his invitation to stay at the castle barracks. I will have an attendant meet you at the inner gates around noon tomorrow."

A pair of darkened eyes observed the package exchange and his frown deepened. The Captain of the Guard, Prince Kyle Beaumont was disturbed by what he had seen. He turned to an insignificant soldier at a nearby table. He lent back and whispered into his ear." Find the guard on duty at the front gate. I want to speak to him right away. Do you understand me?"

In a short space of time outside the inn, the gate sergeant fidgeted in nervous anticipation. He wondered what he had done to deserve this unwarranted attention. Standing to attention as Captain Kyle sauntered out. He walked right up to the sweating guard; and stood toe to toe. "You allowed two riders in with blue capes, one with the hood up. Who might they be Sergeant?"

"Oh sir, that is Commander Atesh and Captain Ballard of the Wizard's Compound sir; *the Pace Knights.*"

"What, are you sure?"

"Oh yes sir. I saw their papers and they had the motif on their saddles. Their unit is camped down by the stream, flying their standard sir."

"Thank you Sergeant, good job." *What are they doing here and with my grandfather? I must discuss this with father.* Captain Kyle raced back to the castle and stormed into the King's study . "Father why are the *Pace Knights* here?"

"Ah, they have arrived." The King sighed as he looked at his son, strutting around like a peacock.

"What…you knew they were to come here? Why wasn't I notified?"

"Oh, keep your pants on. I sent for them. They are to help Marcus with the increase in disappearances. It took me months to broker this deal. So don't you go and stick your nose in where it's not wanted…hear-me-son." Gareth shook his head trying hard not to think how he went wrong with this one. "I hear this Commander Atesh is amazing to see in action. Keep your eyes open son. You might learn a thing or two. One can only hope."

Kyle turned on his heels, his face and neck warmed in seething anger. He then turned his top lip up, contorted into a grimace and strutted out of the room. The wooden door slammed on his way out. As he returned to the Inn, Captain Kyle heard loud noises emanating from within. "What in the blazes is going on in there?" He stormed in pushing past a multitude of patrons. His temper flared to extreme.

Atesh and Master Thaddeus Freymore were in the middle of the strategic war game called 'Chances'.

The Barkeep Ben standing behind the players was trying to explain the game to his customers. "The players work together as a team to beat the game. You can have up to four players. In this instance they must sack and take control of the castle to win. Anyone can purchase a game and play, if they possess enough innate magic. Most of the nobility, academy wizards and the like have em. Some are played in the military to teach strategy to the junior officers. Each game is somehow unique to all the others made. The Game Master who makes these is known as the best strategist in the known world. But no one knows who the Game Master is. It's all very mysterious. The rules are; there are no rules. It should simulate a real, dirty, blood lusting battle. The games arrive with a strange rhyme attached; goes something like this.

> A ame of chance; the strategist call,
> You make your move, the players fall.
> To win the game, you must attest.
> Outplay, be smart, beat me the best."

"But how does the game play?" A patron yelled from the rear of the crowd.

"Well the castle has its own army of men and creatures. As to how they know what to do? I am not so sure. Remember it's a magical game, so anything goes. In days gone by, the players moved the pieces themselves, played against each other. They were made out of wood or stone, then a type of white crystal. Then after a few years the game master made the games more interesting, requiring greater tactical skills and battle knowledge. Now with this new version, all game pieces are interactive; as you will see. As a piece is taken captive or killed they move to the side of the board and wait for the conclusion. They don't really die of course, as they are not real people; just game pieces. Though, if you look at them, they are marvellous the way he has made them to look and act like us. A magical gift he has indeed.

"Now the players inform their army how they want them to move. What battle tactics to use and the types of weapons they wish them to hold. They can say it out loud or use mind speech, depending on how much innate magic the players have. Then the pieces move themselves as directed. It is very realistic. Now…let me get back to pilfering you scum of all your money." He laughed as he sauntered back to the bar.

The patrons gathered around close and noticed that indeed the characters were not the normal static board pieces. They talked and interacted with not only the actual players, but once killed and taken from the game, they yammered with anyone that would listen. Tales were told and songs were sung. Tears were even shed from some of the creatures, when they were marked as killed. What had caused most of the ruckus this day, was the singing Bard. He had been captured hiding in an orange bin. He made the mistake of throwing fruit at the attacking soldiers, hitting one on the side of the face. A sword ended his life and he was moved out from the castle grounds to wait on the sidelines.

He soon became bored, so he sang seafaring dirty ditties which sent the patrons into hysterics. The louder the crowd hollered the dirtier the songs became. What added the extra hysteria was the bard incorporating the soldiers from the attacking side into his songs. They would turn and sneer at the bard; some even became distracted and killed. Then one soldier chased him around the outer edge of the board game threatening to do all sorts of unmentionable acts to him. The bard had secreted a few oranges within his shirt and often turned and pelted the soldier as he ran. A direct hit covered the pursuer with sticky juice and pith. Bets were taken between the patrons as who would stick the bard first and the ale flowed without restraint. Then the bard performed 'a bare pear'. Something you would only see on a drunk in a whorehouse. He pulled down his trousers and exposed his disproportionate hairy backside to the crowd; he waggled it left and right in time with his song. Then he let an enormous bugle resonate out loud and clear. A plume of foul odour with tiny brown particles wafted up to surround the crowd. The patrons surged back a few steps, each holding their nose in amused horror; this pushed other patrons outside the inn doors into the street.

"I have never seen them act up like this before today." Master Thaddeus wiped the tears from his eyes with the back of his sleeve.

Atesh was laughing so hard she came close to falling off her seat. That was until the odour stung her eyes. She coughed as tears spilled down her warm, flamed cheeks from the fumes. It brought back memories of a recent event; *Damn, It's near the same odour.*

The crowd continued to grow wilder and louder.

"It's rather interesting. Quite entertaining for the crowd and Ben's pockets, I must say. Your turn my dear. I am having trouble thinking with all this noise and dare I say it…the fumes."

"Well, Master Thaddeus let's attack the buttress now, we are on the verge of a win."

"Butt, Butt, did you say you wanted to see my butt." The bard again waggled his bottom to the onlookers.

"Noooooooooooooooooo," All the patrons shouted in unison. Hysterical laughter continued unchecked. Even the off duty palace guards were in the midst of the hilarity.

Atesh stared at the castle for a minute as the light shone on it a certain way. She turned her head to the left, eyes glazed over. *I've seen this castle before somewhere, a memory?*

"Atesh your move, come now, stop day dreaming. We are close."

The castle had kept its prize winning master stroke till near the end. At the last possible moment to salvage their soon to be battle loss, a fire breathing, two headed dragon roared out from the deep enlarged well. He incinerated all the opponent's fighters, even those climbing up the exterior wall.

"Well I never." Master Thaddeus looked on astounded. "We must have a rematch Atesh that was the closest I have come to beating the blasted castle in near to one hundred years. Well played. You are as good as my brother indicates. You know, I still have all the original games in my work room; it is amazing how they have changed over the years. Maybe you would like to challenge me or even Marcus to one of the original strategy games. They are not interactive, but I found them real enough for battle training the officers here."

Atesh smiled at Master Thaddeus. "That would be great sir, any time." *I certainly will not tell them, I am the Academy's master player of the older games, an unbeaten record.*

"Oh Atesh I almost forgot…I am waiting for a new game to arrive; it is the most recent updated version. I have been told the pieces will be more advanced. I believe that will make this game even more interesting."

Ballard sat across from the game and enjoyed watching the whole spectacle. As the game completed the pieces disappeared and rearranged themselves into their relevant containers. They once again became inanimate pieces of crystallised rock. The patrons dispersed and quietened down. Still now and again a burst of laughter would echo throughout the inn, as villagers relived the antics of the game.

"Excuse me, may I sit and join you?"

Ballard looked up to see the Captain of the Palace Guards standing as straight as an arrow. He noticed how he wore a false smile; attached to a pristine baby face. Ballard smiled and gestured with his hand for the Captain to sit.

"I assume I am speaking with Commander Atesh. I am Captain Kyle Beaumont of the Palace Guards. It is a pleasure to finally meet the infamous Commander of the 'Pace Knights'. What brings you to our part of the Kingdom sir?"

Ballard locked eyes with the Captain; he raised one side of his mouth into a smirk. "I am sorry Captain, our mission parameters are only to be discussed with Commander Marcus."

"Then what were you doing meeting with the king's counsellor, in an inn of all places and what was in the parcel that the young officer passed to him?"

"Both of those questions are within our mission parameters, so again I cannot discuss them with you Captain."

"I am the Captain of the Guards here and I demand to know what you are doing here in my village."

"I am sorry Captain, but I cannot comply with that demand."

Ballard slammed down his ale. He was getting fed up with this dandy.

"Commander, I demand to know what you are doing in this establishment."

"First point; Captain Kyle Beaumont, I am trying to have a quiet drink. Secondly; what makes you believe I am the Commander?"

Captain Kyle frowned at Ballard then looked across to the young soldier sitting with his grandfather Master Thaddeus. "You are having a joke with me, right? Are you saying you are not the Supreme Commander Sir?"

You are as slow as you look, "That is correct Captain." He held out his hand to shake. "I am Captain Ballard of the Pace Knight's First Battalion. Commander Atesh is over at that table with the King's Counsellor. I believe they were trying to win a battle."

The Captain turned and glared at Atesh, eyes opened wide. Kyle was speechless with shock, and then he returned his gaze to Ballard. "But he is so young to command the knights. Only the best can do that, no; you are making a jest at my expense." Captain Kyle began to fidget and stroke his non-existent baby fluff of a beard.

"Oh, no doubt sir, Commander Atesh is the best. I can guarantee that." His smile went from creasing his face to bursting into outright guffaws. *Oh this is too good, oh my gut hurts, please stop now or I may disgrace myself.* He looked at the Captain's face and laughed even harder.

Chapter 8

A Fine Mess:

"Thank you for the entertaining game Atesh. Do not forget...tomorrow at the inner gates around noon." Back inside the carriage Master Thaddeus mumbled to himself. "Yes that was terrific, such raw talent. She is fare on her way to becoming a great and powerful wizard that is for sure."

"Brother can you hear me? Are you able to speak?"

"Thaddeus how are you going, have you met our Atesh yet?"

"Oh Elias yes, she is everything and more, than you conveyed to me. I believe she may surpass us in power. She must be taught how to control this before it corrupts her. She has no idea, does she?"

"No, Thaddeus, that's why I sent her to you. Can you test her and convince her to take the wizard's trial? She is devoted to the knights, but we must change that or at least combine them."

"Well that's a damn fine idea Elias; a Warrior Wizard or is it, Wizard Warrior. Oh never mind...We never had one of those before. Oh, I near forgot. Some disturbing news for your Academy, I am afraid. Young Kerwin had a nasty incident in a battle; he is alive though badly injured. Atesh can give you all the details."

"Oh dear me, not more excitement, was it creatures again? I am worried that everything that's happened ; the ground shakes and the creatures are somehow connected to the disappearances, though I cannot find the link Thaddeus."

"Yes, that could be possible, I suppose. Any way Atesh said something about having been stalked and chased all the way to Janlin village."

"Such times as I have never seen before. Thank you for this news Thaddeus, I have been concerned for their safety. I will contact Atesh tonight and get a full report, then inform Kerwin's wife."

"Talk to you soon Elias, I will let you know how we go."

"Goodbye dear brother, stay safe."

Looking at the empty box on his lap Thaddeus burst into laughter. *Oh brother you are the most horrid man. Atesh would be so mad at you if she realised; she was the package.*

Back at the Inn, Captain Kyle was called out to disperse the rowdy drunken crowd that had spilled out onto the roadway. Atesh and Ballard took this chance and snuck out the back to the stables.

"What's with that look? You are bursting at the seams?"

Ballard bent over laughing till tears fell down his cheeks unchecked. He held his girth from jiggling and curdling his overabundance of ale. "Oh no, it's too choice. I cannot bring myself…."

"Come on man. What has got your bloomer's twisted so?"

Binji came in with Ciaran curled up asleep in the crook of his neck; a large smile adorned his face. Ciaran awoke to the loud guffaws from Ballard. He jumped down and sauntered over and looked between them.

"What be going on here lassie, too much of the bonny stuff."

"I don't rightly know Ciaran, but something has tickled the old boy's fancy."

"Oh, it is just…" Ballard gasped, as he launched into another bout of laughing which sent him to his knees.

This had Binji and Ciaran laughing with the antics displayed. Atesh shook her head and brought the horses over. "When you have finished disgracing yourself, you can go on ahead and get the men organised for tonight. Maybe ask a couple of them to see if there are any fish in the nearby stream."

"Yes Commander, on my way…hahaha." Ballard's laughter echoed all the way down the road till he was out of sight.

"Honestly Ciaran I have no idea. When he has calmed down I will beat it out of him."

Checking her gear, she thanked Binji for his excellent care and handed him another gold coin.

His eyes widened. "Commander you already paid me more than enough before."

"That's fine Binji. It is not often we find one so young that can handle a war steed and they seem to like you. So buy something nice with it. We will be staying up at the castle barracks, if you would like to see Ciaran again. Just ask at the gate for me."

"Wow, thank you so much Commander." He bent down and gave the dragonelle a little man hug, "Bye Ciaran."

"Kayne are you ready to go back to the crazy men?"

The stallion turned his head around, rolled his eyes and bowed his head in acknowledgement, then stood ready to go. Binji watched in awe, he had never seen a horse answer its rider before. Atesh thought this was normal behaviour. She never gave it a second thought till now. A movement next to the wooden pole caught her eye. Someone stood there watching her. Frozen in place; she reached for her sword as the mysterious voice spoke.

"So you are the infamous Supreme Commander Atesh of the *'Pace Knights'*. I was curious to see for myself what all the fuss was about. You certainly play a good strategy game; I will give you that. But you know, we here in this part of the civilised world, abide by the rules of common courtesy. I do believe it is considered rude to stand with your back to a person, when they are addressing you. Are you afraid to show me your face? Are you that hideous or ashamed that you must hide beneath that hood?"

His speech and mannerisms crawled up her spine like a slimy snake; laced with an inflection of hidden venom and a sprinkle of sarcasm. Atesh steadied her breathing; her heart pounded as her adrenaline kicked in. Her fists were clenched tight in anger. She slowly turned around; her blue eyes sparkled when they found the intruder and pierced the man in the dark. "It is also considered rude to sneak up on another and stay hidden in the dark. What is it that you want?"

"Oh, only to meet you, to see who I am supposed to model myself by."

"What did you say?" Atesh was stunned for a moment, as the pristine officer walked out from the dark recess into the light. She gathered her wits and slowed her breathing and heart rate. "Oh, you must be the Captain of the Palace Guards. Nice to meet you, but I am sorry, I am in rather a hurry, if you will excuse me."

Standing now in front of Kayne, Captain Beaumont blocked them from passing. "Can you not let me see whom it is I am addressing?"

Atesh pulled down her hood and shook out her golden waves of hair and looked at the pristine soldier. They locked eyes; Atesh glanced with her strong piercing crystal blue sparkles, showing the decorum of her rank. While Captain Beaumont stared in contempt with his deep chocolate brownies; his eyes widened with shock as he stepped back in abject horror, shaking his head.

"You are a girl…a girl…this cannot be so? Is this some sort of despicable jest?"

"Yes…I believe a cruel one on you I suppose." Atesh replaced her hood and leapt up onto Kayne in one smooth gliding action.

Kyle stepped closer to the side of Kayne and placed one hand on his halter. He noticed there was not a bit in the horse's mouth to yank on and control. At that moment Ciaran appeared from underneath Atesh's hood. He climbed up onto her head, looked down at the Captain and hissed. Smoke emanated from his nostrils as he spread his wings and sharp claws extended from his paws; ready to attack this intruder and defend his soul mate if need be.

Captain Beaumont released the halter and stepped back in alarm.

"Oh I don't believe in bits, Captain. They are cruel and unnecessary. Goodbye Captain. It was almost a pleasure meeting you."

Kyle stood and watched Atesh and her war steed move off as one, it was pure perfection; symmetry in motion. His heart faulted for the briefest of moments.

Atesh could see in one look that Captain Kyle was used to having women fall at his feet; he would be always in charge. But in his eyes she saw a cruelty behind those baby browns. A cold hearted, dangerous man that would stop at nothing to own what he could not have. A feeling of foreboding overtook her senses, a challenge was looming; Atesh felt it in the very core of her being. She heard him snigger as he turned and strode back to the inn, perhaps to drown his wounded pride.

Back at the camp Ballard had everything organised as usual. It was obvious he had spoken to the men about his amusing story. When Atesh cantered up through the camp, she heard sniggers as she passed them. Looking around with her brows creased she stopped and called out. "Ballard where are you? Face me you coward. Either tell me or I will beat it out of you."

The men closest fell about holding their sides, laughing and crying at the same time.

Now Atesh became embarrassed, she felt her cheeks heat up again; she knew they would be rosy red. *There must be herbs I can take to stop my face from flaming red all the time.* She looked at her clothes, smelt under her armpits; she couldn't fathom it out. Ballard remained hidden. As she continued to look around the men roared harder.

"Please stop Commander. We can't take it anymore, the stitches, oh they hurt too much."

She looked around confused. *Well I best wear this for now, but he is going to pay later.* She shrugged her shoulders and walked over to her tent with a straight back. *"Ciaran can you please snoop and find out what this is all about. I have done something wrong or stupid. I do not want to lose face in front of the men."*

"Aye lassie I will do this for ye, but dinna be worrying about that, I ken the lads all love ye."

Meanwhile Jesper and Wyart were off downstream fishing. The brightness of the day's sun slowly ebbed its way behind the horizon to slumber for the night. The clouds were gathering together to form large patches in preparation for a near, moonless sky.

"We had better get back soon Jesper; it will be forms time before we know it."

"I will get this last one Wyart; he is nibbling around, the biggest one yet."

"Right-o then, I will take what I can carry and you come along soon, or Vykter will have us on his spit."

High up in the tree tops waited two dark winged creatures; the gatherers watched their prey.

"A tholdier the Mathter wants; a tholdier he will get." Abi showed his large fangs as he thought how proud the Mathter would be when he delivered this prize. "We must be quick and quiet. Yous grab the horthey and I will get the tholdier boy…NOW."

Like lightning the two gatherers swooped down on the unsuspecting pair and snatched Jesper and his war steed, Badges. They were squeezed enough to render them unconscious without uttering a sound. The creatures flew high up in the sky and hurried back the way they had arrived. They headed for the northern boundary, then east to the Island and their Master. Their captives lay limp and pale between their claws.

Ballard called for the evening's forms. He smiled as he glanced over the unit standing before him. *There are no others I would trust more with my life than this bunch of misfits.* Ballard again announced the forms were about to commence. "Jesper, you are holding us up from our ale time."

Atesh looked around and became concerned; her gut had twisted into a knot. "Where did you both go Wyart?"

"We were down the creek a short ways Commander. Jesper said he would not be too far behind me."

"Ballard, why don't you start the exercises and I will go and see what has kept him."

As Atesh walked away from the unit a shiver travelled up her spine. She hastened her stride and looked up at the fading light. She wondered if the moon was going to show her face tonight. For a split second the clouds parted and the moon shone in all her glory. An unusual shape cast a shadow and crossed in front of the light. *I wonder what that was. All the hairs on my arms stood up in unison. Oh, there is that shiver again.* Atesh grabbed a fire stick and lit it with a snap of her fingers. She secretly hoped that Jesper was caught up in a line tangle or something simple. A little distance from the camp she found the area the two men had been fishing. Fresh caught fish lay on a large rock gutted and scaled and then she noticed the fishing line bobbing gently in the shallows of the water. There was no sign of either Jesper or his steed Badges. Those two had a special connection and were often seen to sleep close by each other. Badgers a deep grey in colour had an unusual streak of white down his right foreleg and over his right eye. He was a gentle soul, with a warrior's heart. *"Ciaran, can you assist me please down by the stream?"*

"I am on me way lassie." Rushing through the grasses and brush Ciaran came upon Atesh squatting down to retrieve a fishing line from the water, as it made its way slow down stream with the current. "What is da problem here lassie?"

"We are missing Jesper and Badges. Can you sense them any-where? I will look further downstream in case the fool has fallen in. He can swim, can't he Ciaran?"

"I dinna be kenning that lassie. I thought all ye two legs could swim, excepting of course high wizards, they tend ta sink like a rock."

"Really, is that true?"

"Ach, lassie that be true, all dem wizards ken this." Ciaran scram-bled around the stumpy bushes. "Atesh, I am not sensing Jesper or his horsey anywhere. Oh look here, aren't dem his pipes?"

She picked up the broken pipe pieces; they looked like they had fallen from a great height to smash like that. Atesh once again looked upward to the sky; she had bitten her bottom lip as she does, when worried or confused. She scanned all around. "This place is giving me the creeps."

Ciaran was over by the water's edge and noticed a gigantic paw print embedded in the sand. "Lassie I dinna like this feeling I am getting, somthing not be right here. This smells wrong."

Atesh strode over to the sandy water's edge and froze when she saw the paw print. Close by she also found a piece of black fur caught in some bushes. She fell down to her knees and bowed her head. She then turned her head to the sky with the moon's smiling face fading in and out as dark clouds sauntered past her. *Oh Jesper, I am so sorry, hang on there. Do what you must to survive, we will find you, I promise.*

Chapter 9

Strength to Strength:

As Atesh strode back towards the camp, she became agitated and fiddled with the pipes in her hand. A thought was working its way forward from the locked and partitioned recesses of her mind. A memory was trying to emerge, screaming to be heard from her childhood long ago, something forgotten; familiar. She placed the piece of fur up to her nose again. *I remember this smell, but from where?*

The men had completed their evening ritual and turned as Atesh and Ciaran entered the camp. Atesh looked around at all the expectant faces as she clutched the pipes and fur harder. The fishing line with its catch still ensnared was dropped next to Vykter. She then went and sat on a log beside the fire pit and gazed into its mesmerising colours. Ciaran had climbed up onto her shoulder and had his head bowed. Crystal tears dropped like tiny jewels from his eyes into the fire coals, sparking little bursts of flame. The men all sat nearby, awaiting words from their Commander.

Ballard decided to speak first. "Atesh where be Jesper and Badges?"

She raised her head and spoke in a hushed tone. "I don't know where they are." She then handed the broken pipes and piece of black fur to Ballard.

He gasped when he inspected the held items. Near silent cursing could be heard as he passed them around from one man to the next. Some shook their heads in denial.

"Commander what does this mean?"

"Ciaran and I found the fishing rod and line afloat in the stream Berend; the pipes lay broken in the grasses nearby. We found that piece of fur and…" She choked at this point; not able to finish her sentence.

"And what else?" They all seemed to say in unison, as they leant forward.

Ciaran answered for Atesh, so she could hold it together. "Imprinted in the soft sand nearby the water was the biggest paw print you will ever see in ye life laddies, with claws longer den me wee body."

"What creature would take a soldier and his horse without noise or a fight?"

"Ach laddies, there be evil work at hand here. I'm feeling powerful magic. The smelling be nor natural, do I tell ye."

Atesh looked up to the sky again. The men all followed her gaze and then all said their own silent words for Jesper. Atesh swallowed the nausea rising from the pits of her stomach as she snapped out of her numbness for a moment and assumed her role.

"Men, if you are going anywhere tonight, even if it's to the privy, please ensure you stay in pairs whilst we are camped here. We will pack up in the morning and check out the stream and nearby land in daylight. We have been given an invitation…well, sort of an order to stay at the King's barracks from noon tomorrow. So that is what we shall do. The village is open for your enjoyment tonight, so have the night off; I will stay and guard our belongings. Ciaran will be with me. So eat up, have a tub and be careful; no fights. I do not want to have to explain to the King why my men are in the stocks." With that Atesh stood up and strode into her tent.

Jenner and Ryna decided to stay in camp as well. Drinking in an inn with hot, sweaty, inebriated men was not their idea of a great night off.

Ballard decided Atesh may need some fatherly advice. He walked in after Atesh and sat down beside her. "I can see you are struggling with this. You are a brave and smart Commander Atesh; it is only natural that this has unsettled you. By the ancients, this whole trip has been one crisis after another. You know I have been with the knights since I was a small boy and I have never faced so many obstacles as we have had to do of late. You do not always have to be so brave you know, you are allowed to have feelings, a heart and soul." Ballard placed his arm around her shoulder as she leaned into him. "These men out there will follow you to the ends of the earth. Your quick and decisive actions rescued the Merchant and his family and kept us alive to cross the river. Young Kerwin believed in you to get him through his ordeal. You keep Bear in check, which no other Commander has ever done before. You think forward, always two moves ahead of the rest of us. It was your leadership that saved Janlin village from destruction and damned if that wasn't the best game of 'Chances' I have ever seen today.

"Losing Jesper was not something any other Commander could have prevented; there is something unnatural at work here, I can feel it too. Is that not why we were assigned this duty? To find out what in blazes is going on with these weird abductions. The only difference now, is that it has become personal. You need to step back sometimes and allow us to take some of the responsibility. We are all proud of you, remember that?"

Atesh smiled and nodded. "You read me so well. I am unsure of myself at times like this, so overwhelmed; nothing prepares you for losing one of your men in such peculiar circumstances. Thank you for the pep talk; you are my voice of reason. I could never do this without your belief in me. So, go and take the men for some time out, they deserve it. I will be fine, I have Ciaran with me."

Ballard was about to exit the tent when he heard Atesh whisper behind him.

"Do you think he is still alive?"

"Oh, I have no doubt that he is. Jesper will be somewhere giving that monster a piece of his mind. But at the same time, I think he will be memorising a new song about his heroics."

It was a short time later Ballard and ten of the knights wandered past the gate guards and entered the Beaumont village. They headed for the Anvil Inn and seated themselves at the back of the hall and ordered their ale. They whispered amongst themselves about the evening's event and what, if anything could be done about it.

The barkeep Ben overheard their conversation and with a quiet word to them he leaned in. "Have you a missing lad? That is very bad, if they are now taking knights."

"What do you mean by that?"

"Well…Renny is it? These abductions have been happening since before I was born. They used to occur now and again, now it's like, people all the time and it doesn't matter who or what you are. I remember they even took the King's niece, a tiny babe she was. The nanny was killed trying to save her, but that was…let me think; about fourteen years ago if I recall." He took a stool and squeezed in between them. "Not one has ever been seen again. They say a black cat like creature with wings that does it; as big as a house. That's why you are here isn't it; to put a stop to this. Find out what is going on?"

Ballard eyed the barkeep. "We haven't been briefed on our mission yet. So how do you know why we are here Ben?"

"I overheard the snooty Captain of the guards telling his officers. He is not happy with his father for brokering the deal with the Academy. He doesn't want you here interfering in what he calls…his village. Be careful of that one my friends, he may be a prince, but there is something wired up wrong in his head; if you know what I mean. Anyways, I best keep working. I am sorry about your friend; this is not good news at all. The next rounds are on the house. I made a lot of coin today with that game your Commander played. Best day I have had in a long while."

"Ballard is all this true? Is this why we are here?"

Ballard gazed at Berend then the men seated around the tables. "I am sorry men; Atesh and I are to be briefed tomorrow. We have no idea what this is all about. We will let you know when we are told."

Vykter raised his mug, "To our friend Jesper, give that kitty misery boy."

The group all raised their mugs in salute to their brave comrade.

"We will find you Jesper. Don't give up, fight with all you have."

"True that Renny. Don't give up." They all said in unison and skulled their ale.

After many more free mugs of ale, the men pestered Ballard to relay the story of his afternoon here at the inn with Atesh.

Ballard spoke as low as possible, so the men all leaned in. They didn't want any of the palace guards to overhear their conversation. "He came over all shiny boots and buckles. He had neatly trimmed his baby fluff on his chin; you know the type you grow when you are trying to look like a man on your first date. Then in a deep toffy voice he stated, I presume you are the infamous Commander Atesh. I am Captain Fancy Pants."

Loud guffaws started and this became infectious.

"And then I said. What makes you think I am this Commander Atesh? I believe the Commander is over in the middle of a battle with the King's Counsellor. Well his eyeballs bugged out of their sockets, and his face started to twitch." Ballard embellished the story somewhat, making the faces in exaggerated motions, after his many drinks.

The knight's laughter grew out of control, as they bounced in their seats.

"I laughed so much I was crying and neared disgraced myself. Took a lot of control, I can tell you. Ciaran told me later that the prissy Captain found Atesh in the stables and the poor wee babe near pissed his bloomers with shock when she pulled down her hood. What is this a...a...girl? Who is playing this jest on me? I am the Prince Fancy Pants. I own you all. This is my village. Then Ciaran ran up on top of Atesh's head, hissed and puffed smoke at him."

The laughing became fierce and loud, Berend held onto his stomach and leaned back so far, his chair fell over backwards. "Please stop, this is killing me." He lay on the floor with his legs still kicking in the air, laughing his head off.

The other men all screamed in laughter and started hitting the table and bouncing harder on their wooden chairs.

A couple of the off duty palace guards watched this behaviour get out of hand. They considered these large men thugs and walked over in their stiff manner to order them out of the inn. "Men, we do not like your type here. You are disturbing the other patrons, shut it down now and leave this premises by order of the Palace Guards."

As Ballard stood his chair fell back and silence enveloped the entire inn. Being a large brute of a man, he towered over the snivelling starched uniforms. The guard looked up at the hulking, enormous Ballard; with his bulging muscles rippling beneath his white shirt. "What rank might I ask are you, Sir Guard?"

"I…I am Sergeant Philips. Not that it is any business of yours. Who allowed rabble like yourselves past the gates?" He stood taller, chest thrust out as he noted he had back up from four other guards standing behind him. "The gate guard will be punished for this lack of judgement."

Ballard bowed with a gesture of politeness. "Excuse us, Sir Sergeant. We meant no offense, just visiting your fine establishment to ease our sorrow. We will certainly leave now before we upset these fine patrons any further."

With a nod the men leapt to their feet and calmly stumbled out of the inn and made their way back to camp; laughing all the way. Before they reached the border of the camp, Ballard stopped and turned back to look at the village.

"Oh…he is mine tomorrow boys…all mine." Laughter resumed even harder.

Back at camp Atesh and Jenner made rounds together. Ryna would take her shift later on in the night. All seemed quiet when a strange feeling overcame Atesh. She stood, turned to stare over past the stream and her eyes glazed over.

Jenner called out to her and it took a few moments for her voice to register. "Atesh are you all right? You had zoned out."

"I had the weirdest feeling we were being watched. All the hairs on my body stood up on end and I thought I heard noises…like whisperings."

Atesh and Jenner both took their weapons out and looked around for any intruders; creatures or two legged. They even scanned the skies, watching for any shadows. The horses were slightly agitated and restless, but all else was quiet.

"I cannot hear or see anything Atesh, but I do know you are more in-tune to energies than I am. Now I have the creeps."

"Ciaran, can you feel anything strange here about?"

"Lassies, I would say be on ye guard. Ach, I be knowing that odour on the wind, T'is strange, but not, if ye know what I mean?" Ciaran scrambled up on to Atesh's shoulder. He whispered quiet into her ear. "Watched definitely, hunted possible; I don't think we have seen the last of our large fire squirting friends."

The knights came home far happier than when they had left. At the entrance to the camp the men each greeted Atesh. They bowed low in mock reverence with an over exaggerated sway of their arm. Then, as they passed by copious amounts of ale vapour wafted up, threatening to overwhelm her senses. In unison, inebriated knights bellowed as they swayed in front of their bed rolls, "By your leave, oh great and mighty warrior, sir." Then fell into their bed rolls by the fire pit. They were asleep before their heads touched the ground.

Ballard had followed at the rear herding them like sheep. He sat by the fire and explained their evening with exaggerated hand gestures. Raucous laughter could be heard from Jenner, Ryna, Ciaran and Atesh. Their one wish was to have been a fly on the wall witnessing the night's charade.

Atesh could not help herself; she pretended to stroke her non-existent beard. "You did well not to have punched him out, oh infamous Commander Ballard."

Ballard looked to Jenner then Ciaran and began to warm up again to turn bright red around the neck and cheeks. "Who told on me?"

Innocent eyes were his only reply.

"Ballard, I have a feeling tomorrow is going to be another one of 'those' days. But we will give them a right good show in the morning, eh? Till then, sleep well and dream of all the horrid things you can do to your Sergeant Philips, when next you meet."

Atesh and the girls stayed up talking the rest of the night.

Across the stream a pair of enormous red eye's lay, watched and waited.

Chapter 10

Flight or Fight:

Jesper roused to a painful tightening around his chest. He was able to take breaths albeit very shallow ones. His limbs had lost near all sensation from the frigid cold air biting at his flesh. His nose and ears fared no better. Trying to clear the fog from his mind, there seemed only the depths of confusion. He raised his head a small way, though it seemed an impossible task. *Why can I not stop my head from swinging…oh-I-feel-sick.* Jesper steadied himself and surveyed his surroundings. A large black paw was the offending chest crusher. His eyes travelled up the furry limb, where his heart almost missed a beat and eyes near burst out of their sockets. He was clutched and dangled by the largest, flying winged creature ever seen.

I am flying? Damn it all, man was not supposed to fly…lest he be born with wings. How did I come to be this creature's midnight snack? Jesper tried again to clear his muddled mind. His head was pounding fierce now. *C'mon, now gather your wits man; plan what to do next. Slow quiet movements without this creature being aware…that's it.*

Jesper started working on his toes and fingers to gather warmth and feeling into them. Then with tentative, minimal stretching; finger lengths at a time. He moved his head up onto his chest. This had the desired effect of un-pooling the blood within his head which lessened the thumping pains and memory fog. *I remember standing by the stream, dragging in my line with the last fish; oh and she was a beauty. Vykter would have been so proud of me. I was enjoying the moment…the air was fresh and crisp.*

There was a new song, in my head, another for dear brave, wondrous Atesh. She would have loved it.

Jesper's mind wandered back to the academy days. He had been sweet on his Commander from the moment he first laid eyes on her. He loved the way her hair bounced as she walked, the way it changed colour depending on her moods, and the tri coloured flame streaks; braided down one side. They were the most unusual and sensual features he had ever known on a woman. It enhanced her exotic, intoxicating and addictive azure eyes. He had even witnessed her dragonelle cuddles when she thought they were alone. Tears burst forth from his eyes and travelled down his cheeks, they glistened in the moonlight; when the clouds parted for the briefest of moments.

Drawn back from silent musings, Jesper's senses harkened to be heard. He screwed up his face as he became aware of the horrid and putrefying stench of his captor. The unfortunate side effect doubled, as he regained not only smell, but touch sensation. He now felt the straw like fur that nestled up close and personal to his body. They poked and tickled his nose, stretching up into open places; where they had no right to be. Jesper wanted to; no, he 'NEEDED' to sneeze. Horrified at the thought, he put his head to the side and buried it into the furry limb to snuff out the urgent demand. That didn't work and beads of sweat trickled down from his forehead to further annoy his offended nostrils. "Ah-ah-ah," *hold it man, don't…please…don't.*

At that moment the creature banked to the right over a large mountain range. The wind was fierce this close to the summit, so they were buffeted and jostled around quite a bit. The creature turned his head away from his captive and spoke in harsh tones to his companion. With all that noise, Abi the abomination did not hear the squeak of desperation in the ensuring, "Ah-choooo," from his captive. The creature's head movement caught Jesper's field vision, so he closed his eyes and pretended to be limp and unconscious again. He felt the whiskers of the large protruding snout brush past his head. One yellow eye flamed, piercing through Jesper's enclosed eyelids with painful ferocity; as it scrutinised its charge.

"We will lands over there for a rest. The human is stilths out."

The Laughter, lisping and spitting were horrendous sounds to Jesper's ears and he began to shake. His mind felt scattered. *No, quiet down now. Do not alert them. Plan, I need a plan. What would Atesh do? Yes, when they land, make an escape. Badges, where is my handsome boy? We are not going to be this kitty's dinner.*

The two creatures landed down onto a small clearing beside the rugged mountain range. Jesper was dropped unceremoniously onto the dirt and weedy grass patch. He rolled a few times and lay still. His war steed Badges fared no better. In fact it looked as though the beautiful stallion breathed not at all.

Abi scanned the area and positioned his snout to sniff in the fresh night air. He had hoped to scent out game. He curled his lip up exposing enormous fangs and sneered with disappointment. "There is nothing edible in the immediate vithinity. I will go and find foods to eat; you watch these two." Abi the panther creature flew off again into the night. The other gatherer known only as Fives received no other name from the Master. Abi the first to be designed was the only one to be adorned with the gift of a real name ; thus he was revered and became the leader of the other fifty. Fives was the next largest and trusted of the gatherers and Abi felt he was the best for this mission. *A last chance the Mathter had warned him.* Abi shook his head as he thought how the Mathter spoke to him. He was designed to be fearless in the field, to show no doubt; but this had unnerved him. He knew all too well the reputation of the Mathter when he was angry; he had seen it before many years ago. It was not a pretty sight. Plus, the wants of the Mathter was all that was important. Though blind obedience had been instilled in all his creations , Abi actually adored and respected the Mathter, but above all else; he worshipped his creator.

Back at the clearing, growls and yips were heard from within the surrounding woods. Fives became surrounded by a pack of enormous grey, hungry wolves. Their eyes were glowing, red and piercing. As they closed in to the overwhelming smell of fresh meat, Fives roared and retracted down on his hind legs. He sprung upon the first of the dogs, meeting their challenge head on. The fighting was fierce, bloody and noisy.

Jesper assessed the situation as his knight's precision training set in. He peered through slitted eyes and took the first opportunity to sneak away from all the action. He hobbled as fast as his cold legs would carry him. Thankful his swords were still strapped onto his back, snuggled tight within their black leather sheath. Jesper knew sooner or later the wolves would follow his trail and hunt him down. He ran along the edge of the mountain range and hoped to find a cave to hide in or at least a path that would lead up to the top. *I've got to get out of here. Geeze my heart's gonna burst…alright now, calm down, deep breaths…that's it.*

The landscape was unfamiliar and he felt confused. *I am so turned around. Where in all Sofala could I be?* The mountain was a sheer cliff with no available access; so Jesper ran on. He needed as much distance as possible between himself and all those hungry creatures. He turned towards the trees and used every bit of his warrior training to remain quiet and elusive. He vaulted over small bushes and fallen logs, he ran in the middle of the fast flowing creeks; always he kept the sight of the mountain cliff in view. Towards morning, the darkened night faded to reveal a dull sunrise; awakening from its slumber. Grey clouds moved overhead with a torrential downpour, quietening the forest creatures for a while. Jesper exhausted from his escape climbed a sturdy, tall tree with many branches and thick, large leaf cover. He would remain hidden for the rest of the daylight hours. He drank his fill from the captured raindrops within the nearest fronds, soothing his parched and sore throat. Jesper hoped the rain washed away his scent and tracks. For the first time since his abduction he felt secure, not quite safe, but the best he could do for the moment. He whispered a solemn goodbye to his steed Badges; closed his eyes and slept.

Meanwhile: Fives had performed admirably against the pack of wolves when Abi flew down, noticed the melee and joined in with gusto and glee. He destroyed the remaining wolves as he ripped, tore and shredded all within his reach. Badges the War horse had been dragged a short distance away where Jesper's padded leather saddle and bags had been shredded with deep rents. The wolves used claws and pointed teeth to try and breach the leather and vent their frustration and insatiable appetite on the downed horse flesh. Although unconscious from shock; Badges was still alive. The knight however, was nowhere to be seen. The rain had washed away all tracks, so Abi and Fives decided he must have been taken and was now dead. They ate a meal of deer and wolf and then flew back to the island with their single prize. The Mathter was not so upset which confused Abi. Later he was informed by Mason of a new and revised plan that he was ordered to complete, a way to redeem himself for the loss of the knight.

Jesper awoke with a start as the morning sun shone through the branches above. He realised he had slept the rest of the previous day and the entire night. He moved along now at a steady pace, each day blurring into the next. He now climbed up a sturdy, full leafed tree at night for safety, fearing the winged creatures or the wolves would still search for him during these hours. Berries and wild fruits had been his only sustenance and the early morning rain added fresh water. He had skirted a few strange looking creatures and by now he figured he was behind the Northern Barrier; no other explanation for it.

On the third day after his escape a large bear creature with horns had caught Jesper's scent. He tracked the lone human through the forest for hours in a deadly game of seek and stalk. Jesper this day chose poorly and took a wrong turn; he ended in a small dead end canyon with sheer cliffs on three sides. He turned and whipped out his swords as he heard footfalls behind. He stared open mouthed, eyes widened as the bear creature closed in. It rose on his hind legs and walked like a human towards its prey. His thick set, brown hairy paws ended with long razor sharp claws that arced in a downward fashion. The teeth were of equal size and shape, eyes beady and cruel, one brown and one green in colour.

Jesper sized the creature up as adrenaline began to race through-out his body. Eyes dilated and blood surged to his vital organs. Roaring, the creature charged straight for him. It seethed with anger, eager for the kill and a feed. Jesper however was light on his feet and managed to be creative, though he was only able to graze, not penetrate the thick fur at first. The metallic sounds of steel against razor sharp teeth and claws reverberated off the cliff rocks. The noise rose in volume with angry roars and high pitched screams.

Jesper lost concentration for a split second; he overbalanced and slipped in the blood soaked grasses. Before he could regain his stance, a large paw swatted the small morsel of walking meat. He tumbled across the dirt and rocks landing within a thorny bush. The razor claws had dug deep into Jesper's chest to open him from midline across the breast bone to the left side. Any deeper would have been a kill stroke. *Damn it, that was too close.*

Hours later both became weakened from blood loss and exhaustion. Even the creature had sustained multiple deep rents. His blood trickled down in continuous thick droplets to matt its fur. Neither would forfeit nor step away, so the fight continued on through the evening. Clumsy steps were taken and mistakes were made.

Jesper realised he was spent. He gathered the last of his innate energy and leapt up at the bear's head. As he sailed past he wrenched with both swords. Screaming to the world with pent up ferocity. This was it. *Do or die.* He used the last ounce of his being. The unexpected move confused the bear, resulting with its head landing a short way on the dirt and bloodied ground. The huge body toppled backwards, landing next to where Jesper stood on shaken legs. Jesper slumped to the ground, chest heaving, tears cascading down his cheeks. With trembling fingers he tore off the bottom of what was left of his shirt. He fashioned bandages to support his chest and the plethora of claw gashes to stop the ooze of his life force. He moved on at a slower and awkward pace. He backtracked away from the canyon, lest more predators decided to investigate the fresh blood smell.

Jesper was tired beyond exhaustion, with his stomach gurgling enough to wake the dead; his heart and soul however, still wanted to survive. *Never have I seen such a mixed up creature before. Any wonder there is a barrier, if this is the type of monstrosity to be found here. Oh, what a song that would make.*

As he hummed a few notes in hushed tones, he smiled for a brief moment. Then as the surrounding noises became louder, closer; he feared the hunters had ventured out for their usual night feast. The forest came alive at night. Roars, growls, screeches and screams of creatures fighting for their lives, or dying in agony surrounded him. It was deliberate and a measured attempt by the inhabitants to nibble and fray at one's nerves. Jesper stayed awake during these times, he often huddled with his hands over both ears or around his trembling legs pulled up to his chest for security and comfort. As he dozed off to sleep when the noises abated, he would roll up into a ball as tight as possible; unheard and unseen. His wound pained him, though he cleaned it with rain water from the daily down pour. It was inevitable considering his surroundings and the offending dirt encrusted claw that one morning Jesper noticed the wound had become infected. His mother's words ran around in his head. *Ill humours have spread throughout your body. Open it up and clean out the putrid flesh with the salty ocean waters.* He looked about. *Which way to go? Where did the sun set? He must head east to the sea.* He wore no shirt now, his trousers torn off at the knee. He had utilised all he could afford to; he had ripped the cloth up for the necessary bandages.

As he wandered and staggered his way towards the sea, the sharp spiked branches and leaves slashed and grooved his naked, battered torso. To add insult to injury, the nasty blood sucking, biting insects became troublesome the further east he travelled. He had to find civilisation soon, sweat beaded his forehead and his face and body became warm to the touch. A fever had accompanied the infected chest wound and he feared the worst. Towards mid sun, he came across a large unnatural opening in the side of the mountain border. He climbed a tree nearby when he heard voices emanating from within the darkened cavern. There was digging and unusual sounds from an unknown creature mixed with human voices. *Maybe this is my one and only chance to get help.* As he pondered on whether to jump down and investigate, a rumbling noise and earth shaking shocked him to the point of near letting go the tree branch. Then out ran a handful of short, hairy, gruesome and muscled creatures that pushed four young lithe men in front of them. They were manhandled into dragging and heaving large hessian bags out from within the mountain fissure, to be placed onto the back of a waiting wagon. The creatures jumped onto the wagon and the men ran along beside it, as they set off down a well-worn track to the east.

Jesper decided to follow the wagon, slow and careful for the rest of the day. Eventually they came to white undulating sand dunes. Upon hearing the waves break over the rocks and shore, he lifted his head to the east and breathed in the wonderful smell of salt air. *I am at the east coast of Sofala; I found the sea, now I will be saved.* When he rounded the next corner the wagon had disappeared from view. Only the sparkling sea to the right beckoned to him. Straight ahead was a long low fog bank obscuring all view to the distance? *That's odd, never have I ever encountered a low fog bank this time of day before.*

There were no tracks to follow for the wagon or the men beside it. Jesper thought he heard faint noises a little way out to sea. He shaded his eyes with his hand from the glare of the afternoon sun. He noticed the wagon rolling along, seemingly upon the water and then entering into the fog bank. The men were in single file now; behind the drawn wagon. *My fever must be worse. This cannot be right. My eyes deceive me. I'm feeling weary now. Sleep, yes, just a short one.* He clawed his way up a nearby tree and settled onto a thick branch. As he dozed off, his limbs became heavy and his breathing shallower. Jesper did not realise he had not drunk any water since the previous day; he had become dehydrated from the fever and as time dragged on he grew ever more delirious.

During the night Jesper's fever became intolerable and he stumbled into the water to cool off. He wanted to quench his thirst, not through drinking the salty water, but by trying to soak it up; through his skin. He had become desperate. He started to swim further out. The water was cooler in the depths, but the effort became too much. He then turned over to float on his back and stared at the twinkling array of stars. He reached out to touch them, but nothing happened. *I wonder how many stars there are. I could coun…* The current however, had other ideas. It caressed his tired, hot body, enfolding and whispering; bending him to her will and then drew him towards the fog bank. He allowed the rhythm of the waves to lull him into a dreamless sleep as he entered the mysterious fog. A short while later a voice on the wind was heard.

"I know you; will I be alright now?"

Chapter 11

Show and Tell:

A short time before sunrise the knights lined up to perform their morning exercise and form's routine on the flattened grass area beside the camp; adjacent to the castle outer wall. Only thirteen performed this day, as Renny drew the short straw for guard duty. Commander Atesh improvised and performed out the front solo. They made sure this routine would be spectacular and memorable. They wanted to give the audience an excellent show, as well as ensuring the palace guards had a good eye full of their level of warrior skills and expertise. They hoped the guards would realise how they paled in comparison to them. Vanity was not a normal trait known to the knights, but after their encounter with Sergeant Philips the previous night and the uppity attitude of their Captain; it really did bring out the worst in the men. They were all in a mood for a bit of payback. This did not dismiss what a certain Sergeant would be in for later, when Captain Ballard went looking for a bit of fun.

The knights all wore black leather pants and soft leather leg hugging boots. These were knee high with extra grip on their soles that allowed flexibility and ease of movement. The women in the troupe chose decorum of modesty; they adorned black fitted singlet tops. The men however preferred to go as Mother Nature intended, naked from the waist up. They enjoyed showing off their bulging muscles and tight torso's. They all wore fingerless leather grip gloves for stabilisation; as they became one with the sword. A slip from a sweaty palm would mean certain death. Their form's dual rapier & scimitar swords were placed in a specially built wooden holder, a small distance behind them; away from the performance.

The routine started with a bow as a sign of respect for the Commander, who will lead the performance. Then they knelt and closed their eyes centring their mind and body; to be at peace. This allowed the body to work as one unit, each portion an extension of the whole; in complete and absolute harmony. They slowed and controlled their breathing in preparation for the warm up exercises. Then next the sparring drills and last the synchronised sword dancing. This commenced with single scimitars, then double swords and then pairs with Dual Rapier or Scimitars. The routines consisted of attacks /strikes, blocking or evading, retaliation and retraction. This would be performed backwards and forwards between the two knights sparring together; each set became quicker as Atesh indicated; to the head, neck, upper torso, abdomen and legs. There were angle strikes, upper, lower, inner and outer; stabbing and slashing. The arms and feet would beat out an automatic rhythm; an extension of their body; a synergistic relationship of movement, breathing and heartbeat. They commenced with the Dachi stance. Feet apart then as they moved one leg forward they would place their weight on this leg to accommodate the balance shift; always keeping in mind to maintain their centre. Then as they retracted, the weight would shift to the back leg. The dance became more complicated as they introduced the Hippo's, Saltus and Tripudio; spins, rotations, bending, twists, leaps and pirouettes.

As the routine was half way through its performance, a unit of the King's Personal Regiment was heading home from a scouting mission. They slowed to a halt and sat upon their tired, sweaty horses and watched with fascination and awe. Each of the soldiers' eyes was glued to the spectacular display. The soundless precision was expertly timed. Often the soldiers and the crowd that had gathered outside the castle and on the battlements, would either gasp or hold their breath in fear; waiting in anticipation of a wrong move. The word had spread like a raging fire throughout the village and castle; the knights were performing their dance forms. All knew this was something extraordinary to see. The 'Pace Knights' were well known for this, The Commander's first unit, especially so. The crowd's eyes became dilated or squeezed shut, hands grabbed the person next to them, as the knight's swords whizzed past their opponent's heads and bodies. The soldiers in attendance would shake their heads in amazement; they wondered how those sharp, shinning swords missed.

Faster and faster they twirled and leapt, slashed and fought. Prince Marcus the Commander of the King's Regiment and his army was glued to the knight out in front, commanding the performance. She was the most exquisite creature he had ever laid his eyes upon. She was majestic and line perfect in all her form's execution. Atesh's tight black leather leggings and singlet top were saturated from the workout and this seemed to enhance her trim, taught, feminine body. Her long golden coloured hair flowed in unison with her body movements; the tri-coloured braids twirled and soared to a blur of flames; kissing the left side of her face. Just when the crowd thought it was over, the performers lined up in two straight lines. They replaced their scimitars into their wooden holders and removed their long swords. They held these swords above their heads and touched the ones opposite making a pointed arch. Atesh also placed her sword above her head and it burst into a blue flame. It started with the handle grip and snaked up towards the tip; becoming brighter with intensity and heat. She pointed this flaming brand at the knight's arch and one by one, the swords held high ignited. This startled the crowd and most took an involuntary step back. A collective gasp was echoed from the entire crowd and the soldiers watching; but Atesh was not near to finished. The words 'Ferrum- Attollo- Flamma' were spoken. The swords all left the hands of the knights and floated up above their heads and infused together into a flaming orb. The knights then stood at attention. The orb had risen to a height that illuminated the entire castle, village and nearby country-side. The orb spun and twirled, which allowed the flames to reach out in all directions; finger tips stretching out to touch the stars. It then split into three smaller orbs and then separated every few seconds, first to six, then nine, then twelve and thirteen at the last count. Flames emanated from the smaller orbs as they transformed back into the swords and returned to the hands of the knights.

All but one was extinguished. Atesh twirled her flamed sword on the palm of her hand as she spoke the word, 'Pontifex'. The knights responded to this command by crossing their swords in front of their bodies; linking each to the other next to him. This produced a shining sword bridge. A blue flame shot out from Atesh's twirling sword. This slowly wrapped its wispy tendrils around, to completely engulf her. She leapt into the air and landed with gentle exactitude upon the first pair of crossed swords. The silence from the watching crowd was now deafening. They held their breath, as Atesh then somersaulted all the way along the metal bridge, a show of flamed blue flashing brilliance. Her hands and feet caressed each and every sword beneath her. There was no movement from the knights or their swords to indicate a weight had descended onto them. It was as if a feather had floated across to the end of the bridge. Atesh threw her arms up high, bounced into the air and performed the rare triple somersault. She landed smooth and intact at the end of the knights, without a trace of disturbed ground. The blue flame slowly ebbed away, working its way from her head down her torso, to the ground. All the knights placed their swords away then bowed to each other and then to their Commander, who replied in kind.

Atesh then turned and bowed to the crowd. A collective exhale of breath was heard. White knuckles released their grips from the arms of their neighbour and shoulders held tight slumped in relief. The cooling down exercises ensued with slow and steady movements, stretching all the hard worked muscles. The performance concluded as they turned to face their Academy Standard, flying majestic and proud in the morning breeze. Right hand placed across their chest in silent salute. With heads held high, they recited as one, their 'Pace Knight's pledge. Commander Atesh then dismissed the unit for breakfast and a soak in the stream. The entire village erupted in roaring, ear piercing applause. They clapped, whistled and called out for more. What ensured the spectacle was even more breathtaking was the timing of the sun, as it rose from behind the mountains and trees; giving an eerie and magical aura to the whole display.

Up in the castle two pairs of eyes watched in admiration and wonder. King Gareth and Wizard Master Thaddeus stood captivated; speechless. On the battlement standing amongst his men, Captain Kyle also witnessed the display with wonderment and lust. His piercing chocolate infused eyes were spellbound; not just by the display; but by the Commander's prowess.

It was only after all the excitement and noise quietened down, Atesh noticed another group watching. The soldiers from the King's regiment had all turned their horses inwards to the display and continued to watch the knights in quiet amazement. She bowed out of respect and received a standing ovation which was not an easy task, considering they sat upon their mighty war steeds. But each of the soldiers stood up in their stirrups, clapped and whistled. Atesh beamed with joy. She scanned the unit, acknowledging their applause with a head nod.

Then she noticed the Commander in the front. Her heart missed a beat as their eyes locked. Her cheeks flamed with heat. He looked not just at her; but into her soul. He had dark, piercing blue eyes with golden flecks, framed with sand coloured wavy hair that hung past his shoulders. Her heart beat and breathing increased; making her feel slightly light headed. His smile was adorable and genuine; for a larger than life, ruggedly handsome soldier. She did not even take notice of the blond curly hair, fetching young Captain beside him. The Knights' Healer Jenner discerned this most gorgeous specimen of man flesh; as they also locked eyes and smiled.

Commander Marcus watched Atesh as he motioned to his men to move out. They were indeed in need of some breakfast and a wash. The dust and grime had stuck to them for days and it had become near to intolerable. Captain Aiden his second in command, threw a questioning look to the commander. He knew his cousin well. Something was up. Marcus smiled at his second and touched his heart with his hand and closed his eyes. No more needed to be spoken. Aiden burst out with laughter; he had never known Marcus to be smitten at all. But he was bitten by the bug, yes! He was for the first time; mad, crazy, full blown, head over heels, caught and ensnared by the web; of love at first sight. Marcus was twenty two years old and the first born to King Gareth and his wife Anna, who had died soon after his birth. His father later re-married Brianna Freymore who treated

Marcus as her own. He knew one day the weight of the kingdom would fall to his shoulders. To find the one woman that would set his heart on fire had been a bone of contention between father and son. Marcus refused an arranged marriage; he totally felt appalled by the notion of marrying a stranger for the country. He had been betrothed as a child to his cousin Liera. He met her once, she a babe, he was four. He remembered the love he felt for her as he watched her giggling at him. Her tiny stumpy fingers had reached out to grasp his thumb as he peered into her crib. She was killed not long after, many years ago and his heart went cold. It would now not accept anything; but real love. So he waited.

After a light breakfast the knight's camp was packed and the men spread out up and down the stream. They looked for any further clues to Jesper's whereabouts. They searched the bushes and sandy edges for miles. Atesh and Ballard decided to traverse the stream to the other side and explore the undulating hills beside the ocean cliffs. They had noticed unusual tracks and wished to investigate.

"Ach, I dinna think this is a sound idea Lassie." Ciaran poked his head out for a brief moment from under her hood.

They were about to travel up a steep hill to look at the valley below when a voice in their heads yelled out, "*STOP.*" Well this grabbed their attention and they did as they were bid.

"Please do not come over the rise, you will be in danger. I will come over and talk to you, little humans. Go back to the far tree line and wait for me. I am Queen Mia of the Fire Ants from deep within the land's crust. I wish only to talk, no harm will come to you; I give my word."

Ballard and Atesh returned to the tree line and whispered amongst themselves. They felt unsure and nervous. Knowing how large the fire ants had been, it was a well-known fact, a Queen would be by far; larger. As they watched with anticipation and trepidation, they both ensured their weapons were at the ready, though Atesh sensed they must remain sheathed. They both became aware of the rhythmical ground vibrations and tree limbs shivering in the non-existent breeze, sending leaves cascading around them before the Queen crested the rise of the hill. All other small animals and birds were silent, hidden from view.

"My grandfather used to say Atesh. 'Well that's enough to put the fear of the ancients up ye skirts, laddie'. I never understood him to now. Smart man I think."

Atesh smiled at the thought. Nodded then stiffened her posture as the Queen ambled in sight towards them.

She was the largest creature they had ever seen or encountered. Ballard was considered a man that would not blend too easy into a crowd; an enormous tree of a man. This majestic creature eclipsed him a hundred times over. As she neared half way to them the Queen laid her abdomen down so she could manoeuvre her face up close to theirs. Atesh thought her heart would explode through her chest, could her eyes widen any further. Ballard was in the same bind.

"It is nice to meet the two of you. Do not be surprised. We may be mere creatures, but we do know about the world at large. We can admire valour and honesty when we see it. I am Mia. We; my family and race have followed your trail since we became homeless, as the earth shook and spewed its temper onto us. I knew you would lead us away from danger and back to the mountains where it may be safe for us to make our new home."

"Queen Mia, how is it you speak our language and knew to follow us?"

"We are sentient beings my dear, or rather I and my immediate family have nature magic. What you call innate magic, intrinsic to this world. Mine is with language and foresight, though the earth shake was not seen till it was upon us, that...I find vexing and unusual."

"Why did your ants attack us at Janlin village?"

"Well, that is one reason I wished to speak with you. I must apologise for that horrid display. It was two young bucks trying to prove themselves and become my daughter's mate. She was not interested in either, so they took it out on you. I'm afraid." She looked closer at Atesh with her large black eyes. "Do you know what happened to the earth, why it destroyed our home?"

"We had only the slightest warning ourselves. Master Elias Freymore contacted me and urged us to move on, that we were in imminent danger. I am sorry, I have no answers either."

"Ah…so Elias is still at the compound. I remember he and Thaddeus were always up to no good. You know, they saved my life when I was a young, foolish child. I wanted to experience the world, to explore…so many years ago. So then you are indeed, 'The Pace Knights'. I have chosen well."

"I am Commander Atesh and this is Captain Ballard. The quivering movement you see under my hood is Ciaran; a dragonelle." A small puff of smoke meandered its way up from the hood. "You know the Masters then? Thaddeus is the wizard in residence here at Beaumont Castle, and it is he we are to seek out."

"Yes, I thought I felt his signature, this is tremendous news." Mia turned her head to Ballard. "You are a long way from home young Prince. There are not many of your kind in this here Kingdom."

"Prince…did you say?" Atesh looked at Ballard who shrugged his shoulders and gave a cheeky smile. "We have some talking to do, old boy." Atesh punched his arm.

Ballard bowed his head in respect. He did not feel the thump Atesh gave to him. He had always told her she punched like a girl. "Yes Queen Mia, I am here to stay. The knights are my family now and someone had to bring this little rabbit up the right way."

"Atesh…I have heard whispers of your name on the wind. I can sense you have a lot of innate magic. If I am not mistaken, you may become a powerful wizard in the future. Is this why you have been sent to see Thaddeus? He is the best wizard trainer there is, you know. Well I shall not keep you here any longer or your unit will come looking for you. I do so look forward to meeting you both again, some time."

"Before I take my leave I would like to give this gift for the injured knight at Janlin. I watched from afar and was dismayed by it. Though, I do believe you and your unit handled the situation well. I hold no animosity for the deaths of those two young bucks. You had every right to defend yourselves." From around her neck Mia removed a small portion of her jewelled necklace. It was woven in gold braids with a blue crystal attached. "This will assist his innate essence to heal his broken body."

"Thank you, your highness that is kind of you."

"Please my friends call me Mia. Now to the utmost urgent of matters, the reason I had sought you out. May I ask a boon? It is rather large, but necessary I'm afraid?" Mia shifted her weight a bit so she could whisper. "We need to pass by the Beaumont Castle and Village to make our way to the Northern Mountains. Our size makes it impossible to trespass in silence, unseen. We do not wish to fight. We have lost many in the disaster, but we still number in the thousands. Would you be able to keep all the two legs inside the walls until we pass through their land in peace? I can control my species only so much. They are tired, sad and hungry. Survival instinct is a powerful motivator, so if the little humans come out to fight. The blood lust will take over and I will not be able to keep any in the village safe."

"It would be our pleasure to do this for you Mia. I'm sure Thaddeus would agree."

Ballard nodded in agreement to his commander. "Yes, there is no need for shedding of more blood. We will do our best, but can you give us a little time to secure the castle gate? Then we will place our standard on top of the battlements to give you the sign…all is clear."

"Thank you both." Queen Mia backed up and rose to her full height and wandered back to the others.

In their minds a quiet voice held them spellbound. *"Oh, Atesh and Ballard please keep the two legs quiet as possible. It will be safer if they don't draw attention as we pass by. Then they heard Mia's laughter. Fancy that, Elias and Thaddeus up to their old tricks again."*

Atesh was stunned and speechless at the information Mia had given her. *The crafty old bugger, Master Elias when I see you next…*

Atesh and Ballard retreated back to camp and waited till all the scouting parties had returned. They were quieter than usual and a bit paler for the experience. They sat around the last remnants of their fire pit and proceeded to explain what they had been up to. The Knights listened, unable to move a muscle. They dissected every word spoken, some shook their heads and a few eyes darted around, with a look of abject horror. They shivered with the thought that thousands of those fire ants had been close, all this time. That their queen was larger than the castle wall as Ballard explained, with his eyes opened wide in trepidation. Ballard did however; leave out a couple of the most personal bits that he and Atesh would no doubt thrash out later. A plan was formulated. An important component would be careful and precision timing. Atesh thought it best to inform Master Thaddeus, as they may need his assistance. Atesh meditated for a few minutes then spoke mind to mind with Master Thaddeus.

"Master Thaddeus can you hear me?"

"Atesh, why yes my dear girl. Are you about ready to come on in?"

"Yes sir, but we have a…well…rather a large problem; we may need your help with."

"What is the problem, Atesh?"

"It is Mia, sir, the Fire Ant Queen; an old acquaintance of yours. She requests permission for her colony to transgress on the King's land. They wish to pass Beaumont Castle and village on their way to the northern mountains. Their previous home was destroyed when the earth shook and exploded. The problem is we need to keep the village shut down and quiet while they pass. There will be thousands of those ants, like we fought at Janlin Village and Mia is taller than this castle's outer wall, sir. She wants no trouble. Do we have your permission to execute a plan to assist her?"

"Mia is here? Oh my dear of course. I would dearly like to see her; so I will be down in short order. Tell any guard that gets in your way that I have ordered you to do this. I wonder that she remembers me."

Atesh felt she should add a bit of spice to this tale; after all he deserved it. *"Oh she does sir. She told us a few of your infamous tales."*

"Oh my, she did that?" Laughter could be heard as his voice faded.

"Right then, Master Thaddeus has granted our request; we have some work to do. Are we ready knights?"

"Yes sir," They all shouted in unison, then burst out in laughter as they cantered off towards the castle village.

Chapter 12

Beaumont Castle:

They cantered all the way up to the Beaumont Village outer wooden gates. The Knight's beautifully decorated 'Ashmourne Academy, *Pace Alastriona*' Standard flew in the breeze and appeared to wave to the crowds that had assembled to greet them. The guard on duty saluted with his fist to his chest and raised the gate. The knights entered, lined up in formation and as one they dismounted without misplacing a pebble or dust particle. A collective gasp had escaped the crowd as they witnessed a single actioned, unified dismount. It was a display of poetry in motion; they were quick, efficient and silent.

Atesh strode with firm and precise movements to the gate's guardsman. She leaned across and whispered into his ear. He clasped a hand to his mouth, paled and leant on the stone wall to his rear for support; he then gathered his wits and walked forcefully into the guard house. A short time later two young cadet guards raced through the streets; sweat beading on their brows as they attended to their respected tasks. One was sent to inform Commander Marcus he was urgently required at the village entrance, with his men. The second was sent to inform Captain Beaumont an unsolicited army was to pass by the walls and should they obey the knight's request.

Ballard had Ciaran lead their war horses to the inner palace gates to await the Palace Horse Master. He sat atop of Kayne and directed the war horses in an assertive manner.

"Giddy up now lads and lassies, there's to be no slacking off; in double lines now, that's it, tallyho and all." Then he laughed out loud to no one in particular.

The guards were astounded when all fourteen horses walked up to the inner gates in line. They looked around the horses even under them, but no soldiers were near. A voice was then heard from atop the lead horse.

"Would ye mind opening them big gates so we can go about our business here, there's a good laddie?"

The guards shrugged their shoulders, shook their heads in wonder and opened the gates. The horses sauntered in and stood outside the soldier's barracks and waited.

Meanwhile back at the outer gate. Atesh had ordered all the crowd back inside the village and then proceeded to shut the portcullis and large wooden gates. The village was now in lock down. Some in the crowd became anxious and spoke aloud, questioning as to what was occurring. Ballard and the knights spoke quiet though firm to small groups in the crowd and asked them to return to their homes and remain there until it was safe to leave. They explained an army would be passing by soon and they requested no intrusion. Atesh had raced up onto the battlements and ordered the guards to remain on watch, but to make no sound and to place their arms down. They were not to draw attention to the village by acting aggressively or engage the army that was to pass by; at any cost. Once all the villagers were safe in their homes and all was settled; Ballard raised the Knight's standard up onto the battlement and waited.

"What is this army that we are hiding from Commander?"

"Be patient a little longer guardsman, you will see for yourself. Believe me when I say, we cannot fight this army; nor do we have need to. We have guaranteed their safety to pass without incident and that is what we shall do."

Atesh stood tall and resolved. Ballard as determined beside her. Eight of the knights stood in front of the gates; baring any access to the outside. The remainder were on the battlements spread out between the palace guards. The noise was heard before the sight that froze the palace guards to their posts. The guard that asked the question turned and looked at Atesh; new respect glowed from his face. He then turned to watch the show unfolding before him. Shear minded terror emanated from his soul, at the sight. The flesh eating fire ants had commenced their walk onto the main grounds beside the stream. Their long thick spiked legs weighed down by the enlarged abdomens sloshed through the water like one would a puddle. They marched two abreast and kept a good pace for their size. There were hundreds upon hundreds, if not more that kept appearing; from beyond the hills.

Atesh and Ballard turned around at the sound of many loud boots marching double time, alongside rhythmical clanging of metal. They jumped with little effort down onto the pavement and stood at the head of their knights; arms crossed.

"Right on cue, Captain Fancy Pants…he is like a bad wart that shows up when it is not wanted."

Atesh nodded and smiled at Ballard's assessment. She knew full well this was trouble indeed.

"Why are the gates closed and guarded Commander Atesh? This is my village and 'I' say when to shut the gates or not."

"The Village is in lock down for a short period Captain to allow a large army to pass by unhindered. This is my order Captain and it stays."

"Open the gates at once by order of the palace guards. If there is an army outside then we will meet them. They do not have leave I take it to trespass on our land? We will turn them back and send them packing."

"Captain keep your voice down, we do not want to give ourselves undue attention. The gates stay closed. They have permission for safe passage. Believe me, you do not want to mess with this army Captain; so BACK-OFF."

"I have given no permission, nor have I word from my father. You are a liar and a coward. Ha, you are supposed to be the famous Knights, all show I think; yes, cowards the lot of you." Captain Kyle pointed to all those standing before him. "What would you know about war and fighting? You commander, are a girl trying to be a soldier…pathetic. Girls are only good for one thing; so come over here little Commander and I will show you what a real man looks like." His screeching became more hysterical. "Move out of the way or open the gates. If you do not comply with my order I will order my men to force you." Captain Kyle believed he showed up Atesh for what she was, a silly girl and he the shining star of the day.

Villages poked their heads out from their homes and shops, some even ventured out to watch the showdown.

Ballard and the other knights had their fists clenched though they remained at attention and still. Their faces were transformed into masks of anger and determination. If writing would be on their foreheads; it would have spelt four letters, 'KILL'.

"I have no intention of playing a game of masculinity with you Captain. We will not be moved. Nor are these gates to open; till it is safe to do so. You are willing to risk all the lives in the village; for your ego? This army was the most formidable we had ever encountered and we have made a pact with their leader to allow them to pass. Master Thaddeus has granted this boon."

From up on the battlement, the guard in charge on duty spoke to his Captain. "Sir I would listen to the Commander, sir. She has the right of it, sir. Knows what she is talking about. We cannot win against this army."

Kyle looked at the battlement, his face creased into a sneer. "Guard present your-self."

The guard walked in a swift gait down to his superior, though he was still a bit unsteady on his legs, after what he had witnessed. As he saluted his Captain, Kyle whipped out his sword and plunged it into the young guard's abdomen. He then pushed him off his embedded bloody sword with his boot. The guard crumpled into a heap on the ground and proceeded to bleed profusely. His fellow guards were horrified that their captain attacked one of their own, unarmed, saluting and for speaking the truth.

"See how your cowardice infects my men. Now Commander, I mean business. Move or we will cut you down like the pathetic sewer scum you are."

Atesh nodded to Jenner to see if she could assist the guard. She and two of his colleagues carried him away to the side of the standoff. In a quiet but authoritative tone Atesh once more, reiterated her stance. "We are not moving Captain. Again I ask you to back off."

Kyle raised his hand and screeched to his unit, "Archers fire on the cowards."

Not one of his men fired. Kyle was in a hysterical state with his over-inflated ego embellishing the blood lust coursing through his veins; he did not see the gargantuan ant body with its head arced down to rest on the outer wall; to his right. The large eyes stared at the men and events below. His men however did notice and they replaced all their weapons and stepped back away from their captain.

Kyle turned around at his soldiers; he yelled and screamed, called them cowards and other ear splitting insults. He grabbed a spear from the guard closest to him and with all his might as he turned back to Atesh, threw the spear to kill her.

Atesh held out her hand as her eyes sparkled with blue fire. The air seemed to thicken around her and time slowed down. The spear aimed true, bearing towards her heart. As it approached, she caught it; rotated the implement of death and placed the tip onto the ground. Time resumed as normal again. She stared at Kyle and dared him with her eyes to make another move.

Kyle was now blind with fury and unreasonable. He ran at Atesh with his sword unsheathed, his eyes were narrowed, lips turned up in a sneer; wanting to slice her into small pieces. Atesh in three quick movements, pole drove the flat end of the spear up under his chin to thrust his head back with force. She then aimed and propelled the spear once into his abdomen and reversing the spear head she swiped his legs out from under him. Kyle landed in a crumpled heap on his back. Dazed and bruised, but otherwise unhurt. Her left foot stood hard on his right arm and dislodged his sword. The tip of the spear was pressed firm under his chin.

The guards parted and Commander Marcus and Captain Aiden from the King's Personal Regiment ran through. Master Thaddeus had also appeared on the battlements, looked down at the occurrence; sighed, tuttered and shook his head.

"Commander what is going on here?" Marcus was trying hard not to smile at his brother's predicament? "Why is Captain Kyle ummm…lying prone, at the end of your spear?"

"You may receive a statement from me later Commander. In the meantime this poor excuse for a human, needs removing from my sight; before I end his miserable life." Atesh was flushed with rage and fury.

Ballard smiled and stepped forward, he knew by the look on Atesh's face she needed to calm down. "Commander Marcus, I am Captain Ballard, this officer attacked and wounded one of his own men without provocation and then tried twice to kill our Commander. We are under direct orders from Master Thaddeus. Captain Kyle was endangering this whole village; if you would join us on the battlements, we can explain further sir."

"Marcus." He looked up to see his grandfather standing there, beside an enormous creature with intelligent, understanding eyes. "What Captain Ballard says is true. Your brother needs to answer to your father for his lack of judgement and abhorrent crimes."

Marcus ordered four of his men to escort his brother to the King. "Do not let him out of your sight. Please explain to father what has transpired here." Marcus turned to gaze upon his brother's unit, "The rest of you men, best if you go back to your posts."

Kyle was dragged away kicking and screaming all the way to the castle. He yelled obscenities and cussed at anyone in hearing range.

The four officers, Commanders' Atesh and Marcus; Captains' Ballard and Aiden all strode up to the battlements and greeted Master Thaddeus. Atesh and Ballard bowed to the strange creature that had rested her head now upon the top of the stone pier.

Master Thaddeus performed the introductions. "Queen Mia may I present Commander Marcus Beaumont and his Captain, Aiden Beaumont. Men this is Queen Mia of the Fire Ants. They bowed and looked up at her with admiration and a little fear. They then stared out over the fields. Their hearts seem to miss a beat in unison, as thousands of the largest creatures they had ever seen, passed by quick and quiet; towards the far mountains.

"This is the army that my brother wanted to attack?" Marcus bowed his head, shaking it in despair. "I apologise Your Majesty, if this incident has caused you any affront."

Mia turned her face towards Marcus. "Ahhh…The King in waiting…you will make a fine and just ruler young Marcus. Do not worry; I had every faith in Atesh and her knights. After all…they fought and beat two of my young bucks. I am ashamed to say they too had big egos. Be careful there, young prince. Your brother is dangerous, now he has lost face amongst his men."

Marcus turned to look at Atesh; she smiled and shrugged her shoulders.

Mia then directed her gaze to Ballard. "Nice to see you again Captain. You have done an exceptional job with your ummm…little rabbit."

Atesh's cheeks warmed up and turned the brightest red. *I think we are even now. You tattle tale.*

Ballard beamed and stood tall.

"I knew your ancestors Ballard." Mia closed her eyes for a moment remembering times of her youth. "They went by the nick names, Blue and Grey; isn't that right Thaddeus?"

Thaddeus head twisted slow and fixed his gaze upon Ballard, though he remained silent…thinking…brooding on the past.

"Yes, they were as big as you. Blue, the elder one was always interested in the unusual, loved to play war games, obsessed really; a sweet cheeky boy. He went on to be a good and strong King, your great grandfather perhaps. Grey the younger by such a short period of time was more serious. He loved logic and philosophy. Still he enjoyed the mischievous side of life as well. Yes, they were also twins, both lots identical in features, undistinguishable. It was often said, much to my amusement; if you cut one the other one bled. The four of them together certainly gave the academy some headaches, but oh, the adventures we had, eh Thad?"

Thaddeus nodded and gave a cheeky grin.

"My dear, dear Thaddeus, it is so wonderful to see you after all this time. I have missed you and Elias. I would like to give these four young rising stars a gift." Out from under her breast plate she handed

Thaddeus five small fire gems; the rarest in Cerahya. They are found only in the deepest recesses of the land. "Please wear these at all times, they will keep you safe and assist with your inner magic. Now this one is a special, extra gift for Atesh." She handed Thaddeus a clear sliver of a diamond like jewel. "It is one of my tears, I shed when my mother died." She looked with sadness at Atesh. "This will keep you safe in the darkest of times; it will help you to remember and remain true to yourself. I will give Thaddeus instructions on how you should wear this."

"There is one left over Mia?"

"Oh yes, I near forgot, that is for the dear little dragonelle, Ciaran. This may help him overcome some of his fears, be the man he is supposed to be. Dragons are supposed to fly and breathe fire you know."

Thaddeus gave Mia the biggest head hug and tears rolled down his cheeks. "Will we meet again Mia?"

"I guarantee it dear Thad; we have an alliance now between this Kingdom and mine. With the sliver in place Atesh may reach me from anywhere in this world. I must be off now; we have a long walk ahead of us. Bye now dear friends." As she turned to leave, Thaddeus was given the explicit instructions in his mind on how to implant Atesh with the sliver. Atesh watched with concern as Mia's parting words in Master Thaddeus mind made him reel and hold on to the stone to balance himself. *Take care of that granddaughter won't you now, dear Thad. She will become more powerful than you can imagine. Teach her well for she will need to control her powers to defeat your foes.*

"What do you mean granddaughter, which one do you refer to Mia?"

"Oh Thaddeus, the one standing not ten feet away from you, can you not tell? Your missing granddaughter has come home at last. Do the sums dear man. She has the birth mark. I can feel her essence, your blood signature echoes loud and clear to me."

"I do not feel it. Are you sure Mia?"

"Yes Thad, the block will be removed at her turning, beware of the power."

It was many more hours before the all clear could be given. The village reopened and the inhabitants went about their tasks as before, but some wondered what it was, that so worried the knights.

Back at the Palace, Thaddeus spoke in a sombre tone to the King. Gareth had gone rather pale at the thought of his son's consequences and stupidity. He had Kyle locked in his rooms at the moment and was unsure how to deal with this strange child. Kyle had screamed, ranted and needed to be dragged by the guards to his quarters. He was beyond reason; threatened all sorts of punishment to the cowards. Two guards were posted outside his rooms as his door was locked and all visitors barred.

Atesh and her men made their way to their billet. They gazed upon a splendid elongated two story stone building, what was now considered; the old barracks. The top floor the Accommodation Master explained was one of many such accommodation departments. There were two large suites for the officers and twenty beds situated on either side of the room. They were arranged in a dormitory style; with lockers and a table beside each bed. Garderobe's were up the left corridor with bathing facilities further along. Down stairs was an open lounge area, large enough to sit one hundred soldiers. A fireplace graced each wall, ensuring a cosy, warm environment. Tapestries of battle scenes decorated the walls and over the fireplaces were displayed the many strange and wondrous ancient weapons of years past. The dining room was of equal size with a horseshoe shaped table arrangement. The kitchens were located out the back, attached by a covered walkway. In the far corner was a large office to be utilised by the Commanding officer for coordination. The building was only occupied when visiting dignitary's guards required housing or a group of trainees came through. More than not it stayed near to empty.

A larger more up to date building stood beside this one and was occupied by both the King's personal regiment and village garrison. A single story square building squatted in between the two. Inside was a series of bathing pools. A small round well of sorts held the steaming hot bubbling spring water that spewed forth from beneath the earth's surface. Each hour the water cascaded down special built brick aquaducts to the first two pools. Another connecting channel with cool river water met this heated water and the resultant mixture became a soothing warm bath. The water then circulated through to the next pool. The third one held fresh cool water only. The steam from the spring water was bellowed into two steam rooms. The first where the soldiers could sit and scrape off excess dirt prior to entering the pools and the second to relax and sit on wooden benches arranged around the walls. Here they could enjoy an array of intoxicating herbed aromas placed on the hot steam infused rocks and forget about their worries for a while. The workers who maintained these areas were dedicated and diligent, though the work was hot and the hours long. Another set of aqua-ducts travelled beside the outer wall leading down into the village bathing houses.

The knights grabbed their saddle-bags and settled their war steeds into the stables. It was a known fact that only the riders of such creatures should go near them. Many a groom had lost a finger or been tossed out of a stable, by a battle hardened war horse.

Atesh led her merry band up into the accommodation area. They had quietened down after the morning's events.

Atesh in her suite was down on her knees looking for Ciaran. "Come on old man, you can chase rodents later; stop mucking around." As she spun on her knees, she noticed a pair of large shining, though well-worn pair of boots standing in front of her. She worked her way up, drinking in the scene before her; slow and steady. *Oh my*, the sturdy legs led to muscled abs, bulging out of the white linen shirt. Then, *oh damn*, large shoulders covered with loose, sand coloured wavy hair. Atesh held her breath as she digested and stored all this information within her mind. She now stared straight up into dark sky blue eyes with sparkling gold flecks. *Wow! What amazing eyes and dreamy smile.* She returned to reality and jumped up onto her feet, exhaled and brushed off her black leather trousers and thrust out her trembling arm for a greeting. Marcus obliged and took her forearm in the Academy greeting of friendship. A strange tingling was felt. A peaceful feeling of belonging passed through them both. They stood stunned for a moment, staring, lost in each other's eyes.

"Sorry to interrupt you…ummm whatever you were doing; but the Barkeep Ben at the Anvil Inn has put on a lunch for us all. He has become your biggest fan, though he would never admit that to me of course. May I enquire as to what you were doing, talking to yourself on the floor?"

"Oh, I was trying to find Ciaran; he has run amok, looking in all the nooks and crannies for little rodents to play with."

"What may I ask…or should I, is a Ciaran? I noticed Queen Mia mentioned that name too this morning. You seem to make acquaintances from some rather unusual creatures."

A movement scooted out from under the bed and scrambled up onto Marcus's leg. Marcus stood still. His eyes widened with anticipation, after witnessing Atesh's friend this morning, the Queen of the Fire Ants. He dare not look down at whatever had climbed up onto his shirt. Ciaran moved higher so he could see Marcus's face. Then with a bow of his head, he announced himself.

"Commander Marcus…I be Ciaran; this lassie's dragonelle at ye service sir."

Marcus lowered his eyes and looked down to see the sweetest face on the smallest dragon he had ever seen. He threw his head back and laughed with such gusto, he almost dislodged the wee critter. "Well I never. May I touch you kind sir?"

"Oh lassie, dis here one has manners . Of course ye may sir. I do however; prefer a scratch behind my ears." Ciaran presented to purrrrr with satisfaction ; but Atesh knew otherwise . He was informing her that here was a good catch.

"We will discuss this later, old boy."

"Oh before I forget, the Livery Master was wondering when your wagon and supplies will be arriving. He likes to keep everything in order and maintained."

"We carry only what we need Commander, there are no wagons or anything to worry about thank you."

"Please…call me Marcus. I saw your camp down by the creek, you had tents and a kitchen set up. Where is all that equipment?"

"All our requirements are carried with us at all times. We have no use for wagons or extra pack horses. Atesh then glanced with innocent intent towards her saddle-bags."

Marcus stood for a minute then went and lifted the saddle-bag, which was as light as a feather. He looked at Atesh who was trying to stifle a laugh. He then looked at the bags again when it dawned on him. "Of course, you are from the Academy of Magic, you sneaky things. You have bottomless, magic saddlebags."

Atesh's face was a picture of purity, batting her eyelashes in rapid succession.

"Ha ha, that won't work with me; I have sisters you know. Any chance you could have two sent to me as a favour. One for Aiden, his eighteenth birthday is next week and for myself please…oh mighty Atesh." He knelt down on both knees and pleaded with his hands, as he bowed to the floor.

Ballard had walked in on this display and watched on, speechless.

"Of course, oh King in waiting. How could I refuse such a heart-felt request?"

Both laughing they turned and there was Ballard. Arms folded across his chest with the strangest look on his face.

"Don't ask Ballard."

"I know better than too by now, Atesh."

As they walked to the Inn Atesh spoke to Marcus. "It's a secret you know. Please keep it quiet; unless Master Thaddeus can talk Elias into making them for your Regiment."

Chapter 13

All in a Day's Work:

"Some of my men would like to join in the festivities if you don't mind Atesh."

"Sure Marcus, we can wait here while you gather them." She then turned to the knights, "Men go on ahead and start without us, we won't be far behind you; Ballard and I will stay and wait for Commander Marcus and his unit."

The knights all turned in accord to look at their Commander. Each adorned a roguish smirk upon their faces.

"What? Go on with you...shoo."

Atesh had been told the grounds of the Beaumont Palace had a grand reputation, well known in all areas of the Kingdom. As in the tales told, every inch was beyond astounding. They were designed in such a way that it simulated an optical illusion of breathtaking beauty that meandered on forever into the distance. Over to the left of an out building was a striking solo monument. It was covered with an array of tri-coloured roses that dangled off the white-washed stone walls. Being curious, Ballard and Atesh wandered over for a closer look. They found the varied array of scents intoxicating, almost to the point of giddiness. It was then they noticed the glint of a head stone peeking out from the greenery and fallen coloured petals; a peaceful surrounding, to lie at the end of one's days.

All Ballard observed was the first name 'Anna,' engraved on the head stone. He gasped and placed one hand over his heart. His face had lost some of its previous colour; in fact, he went a shade paler than usual. In measured movements, he sank down to his knees. Tears cascaded without permission down his cheeks, though he attempted to wipe them away, lest anyone see. Atesh stood back and watched in silence, not understanding the significance of all this. Marcus soon joined Atesh and watched with furrowed brows. Atesh touched Marcus on the sleeve and ushered him away to give Ballard his privacy. They walked a way down the road and discussed nothing in particular. Marcus kept turning back to watch Ballard, he felt an uneasiness in his stomach with this scene.

"May I enquire as to whose grave lies there Marcus?"

"That Atesh belongs to the late Queen Anna Beaumont. She wanted to be buried within her favourite place, the rose garden. She was my father's first wife…and my mother; she died not long after giving birth to me."

"Oh…I am sorry Marcus, I didn't know. So Captain Kyle is only a half-brother?"

"Yes, after a couple of years my father re-married to Master Freymore's daughter Brianna. They are also distant kin. You know, someone's ancestor was kin to someone else, keep the first three blood-lines in the family. I have known Brianna for most of my life. She is the only mother I remember. Of course she treats me as her own. I have now two half-sisters and two half-brothers…So Atesh," Marcus was eager to change the subject, "you were saying before that, at oath time all the knights take the surname Ashmourne and you relinquish your previous name?"

"Yes, that's correct, or one can choose to hyphenate their name. Mind you, there are still a lot of folk who do not possess a last name; they are known by their given name and the village of their birth or the profession of their father. That is why we are called by our first names only; we are all equal in this respect. Knights are not granted the status because of who they are, but what we can contribute. There is no distinction between rich, poor, scholar or royal blood. What makes you a knight is what is inside you. Here, this is what counts." Atesh placed her hand onto Marcus's chest over his heart. She was sure it had missed a beat. "Of course there is one criterion that is at the core of who we are and what we do; an essential requirement. It is the foundation for which the training can build upon. All candidates must have a moderate amount of innate magic; for the oath to be binding and to activate various implements that assist us. This makes us all one big family; actually there are one thousand of us at the moment."

"That is astounding; we are not taught much about your side of things; though I ask mainly for my younger brother, Israe. His dreams are to be a knight. In fact, if he knew you were here, he would walk on water to return sooner from his trip to Tyral. He talks non-stop about the imaginary creatures he will slay. He even has his own back sheath with two wooden swords. He slashes and prances around the castle killing bags of potatoes, mother's plants, anything that doesn't move too fast; annoying everyone."

They both chuckled at the thought. Ballard and the regiment soldiers now joined the walk down to the Inn.

"Seems so peaceful here Marcus, do most of the villagers work for the Castle?"

"Yes Atesh, it was easier to house them all here with their families close by, then to have them commute daily by wagon. They are happier, we enjoy their company and it is friendlier somehow. We know the royal houses serve the people, as much as they serve us. We come to understand their needs and in return we earn their trust and support."

"That is an altruistic ideal Marcus, one that will stand you in good stead for the future. Perhaps others should adopt this philosophy."

Ballard had walked up behind them. His eyes and cheeks were somewhat ruddy, his demeanor quieter, but everyone made sure not to mention this fact. There were however, some questioning looks between the soldiers. Marcus then relayed the conversation to his men about the knights and why they only use a first name.

"Well what about the ladies in the service. We noticed Commander that you have three in your unit, isn't that unusual?" One of the soldiers queried.

"Yes and no. We have been set on this course of change for a few years now. Being the first female Captain and then the Supreme Commander, the Masters' thought…why not go a bit further and introduce more females into the Knight's domain. However, we are the first unit to trial three females at the same time, most are scattered singularly throughout the battalions. We found the girls joined for different purposes. Some wanted to be fighters, others had the call for healing and then a select few like Jenner, wanted to learn both. Stranger still as this sounds, a few wanted to be attached to a unit as a soldier and a science acolyte, each to their own. Innate magic has a way of deciding what we shall become. As far as names go, yes we are called by our first names too. As an officer, it is easier if I answer to Sir or Commander or Atesh. Lady Atesh seems so…ummm…feminine."

Ballard burst out laughing; "Did you say…Lady Atesh, oh I need a drink."

The regiment soldiers seeing the humour of it all joined in the frivolity. Marcus shook his head and wondered what in all Sofala he was getting mixed up in.

Atesh narrowed her eyes at Ballard and thumped his arm with her closed fist. He never even twitched a muscle, only laughed all the harder.

Shaking her hand from the sensation she had thumped a steel plated tree, Atesh continued. "If you think about it men…it stops any confusion. When I call out to the boys, well more than not; they all answer; no matter what their gender. We are all the same, treated no different in most respects. We know that we don't have the strength of a man or a tree, like Ballard here, but we take advantage of our smaller stature with some added ingenuity." She fluttered her eyes at Ballard, to the soldier's amusement and his embarrassment.

From near the back of the crowd a voice asked what they all had wanted to know. "Commander what was your previous name before you took your oath?"

"Well I didn't have a first or family name at all. I was a foundling, a stray rabbit and the Academy itself adopted me when I was a young child. So they named me Atesh, meaning fire. My hair was redder in those days."

"I have never heard of an academy adopting a child before?"

"It was unusual, or so I am told Marcus."

"Well if I remember correctly, she was named for her feistiness, not the colour of her hair." As Ballard explained further he demonstrated a small Atesh to the crowd. "She was a wee little rabbit, no taller than my knees, hands on hips, face all screwed up tight with concentration. She would try and keep trying at whatever task she set herself, till she mastered it. Woe betides anyone who got in her way. The finger would point, her foot would tap, her lips pouted at you and then you knew to back off."

"And your previous name Captain Ballard, someone yelled out."

"Greymont was my last name." He turned and locked eyes with Marcus.

"Ballard, what name did you say?" Marcus whispered as he now saw Ballard for the first time. "My mother was Princess Anna Greymont from the Southern Island, before she married my father. What was she to you?"

"She…was my older sister, Marcus."

All in the immediate area stood stock still and looked up at Ballard. Their first Queen had been this Captain's sister? Atesh and the regiment soldiers' eyes darted between the two large men. They were assessing the resemblance now; it was easy to see, once you really opened your eyes. After the initial shock was over, Atesh hooked her arm into Marcus's.

"Well, Sir King in waiting, you have not only gained an uncle, but thirteen more family members; we must celebrate." And she gestured with a bow and then proceeded to laugh.

Ballard led the way into the inn with a smile on his face. Atesh followed with Marcus close behind her; still in a sort of daze. They had moved quick and silent towards the back room when a step past the entrance to this area, Ballard stopped short. Atesh could not arrest her forward motion and she ploughed into his back. It was unfortunate that Marcus then performed the same manoeuvre. Atesh was caught between the two hulking men. Berend yelled out from the end of the room when he saw the predicament the Commander was in.

"Boys…we have a Commander sandwich on our hands."

Riotous laughter broke out with spilling of drinks as mugs were thumped upon the table.

"Move…you big lump." Atesh tried to push away from his back. "Why did you stop like that?"

All Ballard did was take a further step in and pointed for Atesh to see…and no further explanation was required.

"What in all Sofala is going on here, Bear?" She thumped the enormous back still standing in close proximity to her face, "oh…sorry Ballard."

He half turned and glared down at his Commander.

Some of the knights fell about now; crying with stitches cramping their sides. Vykter could contain his mirth no longer, he inhaled whilst drinking and ended up snorting his ale, it bubbled and flew to the ceiling; to the amusement of all. On the middle of the table was Renny, trussed up on a chair with a piece of cloth wedged into his mouth. Bear shrugged his shoulders and looked over and pointed an accusing finger at a little creature trying his hardest to hide under Vykter's collar.

"Ach lassie it be horrid; jist horrid I tell ye."

Atesh shut her eyes and sighed. She wandered over closer to the table. "Renny, were you trying to sing again?"

His head nodded left then right, no. Then a sort of shoulder shrug…and a head movement forward, in the affirmative.

The men all nodded in agreement.

Atesh massaged her temples and then ran her fingers through her hair in utter exasperation. "If the men untie you…will you promise not to sing again until we are so drunk, it won't bother anyone?"

Renny's head bobbed yes, eyes reddened and pleading.

"Alright Bear undo the man and Renny…geeze wipe your nose man, you are drooling snot everywhere…ewww."

Berend stood and saluted, though he missed his forehead. His hand managed to go as high as his nose. "Yes Sir, Commander Sandwich, anything you squeeze, umm…please sir."

That set the men off again. They laughed and snortled all the harder.

From the door way echoed a collective gasp. There was a neat stacked and packed bunch of regiment soldiers all half in or out of the small entrance behind Marcus, wanting to witness this event.

Atesh turned around with eyes narrowed and motioned to Ballard. "Well invite your friends in then."

Ballard locked eyes with Marcus and whispered ever so quietly to him as he walked past. "Temper…I told you, not the colour of her hair; it was for the temper."

Introductions were performed by Captain Ballard and Commander Marcus and the regiment soldiers squished in between the knights. Marcus made sure he was seated at the head of the table in between Atesh and Ballard. Aiden had placed himself next to Jenner; Captain Skip pushed his way in next to Ryna, all was right with the world for this small moment. Ale kept coming in as each took a turn to retrieve the jugs. Commander Marcus stood up and shushed the rowdy crowd. He had something to say.

"I would like to toast the arrival of, the Ashmourne Academy Knights…and my thanks to each and every one of you, for saving our village and all who live here today." He raised his mug and they all responded in kind. "Secondly, I would like to welcome an uncle I have never known. Ballard welcome to the family." Mugs again were raised, but the knights all looked to Atesh with questioning eyes.

"It appears men, the late Queen Anna, who was mother to Commander Marcus here, was also Ballard's elder sister. Yes, we have been rubbing noses with royalty." Atesh bowed to her Captain.

The Knights all stood up, bowed and raised their mugs, then drank to his health. Merriment continued on for a few hours, but Atesh only ever sipped at her mug. She didn't like the feeling of ever being out of control. The knights and the regiment soldiers acted like old friends, kindred in heart and spirit. As time flew by they became rowdier than ever. Ben and his team brought out the best array of foods to eat, which certainly helped quieten down the noise somewhat for a while. After the feasting Wyart, Chale, Vykter and Renny decided to share their recent adventures with the crowd and added extra wild gestures and embellished the scenes to excess. First to be insulted was Berend and they each performed the latrine jiggle. Then it was Ballard's turn and how his near death experience had changed this poor man forever. Captain Gizzards was reborn. They re-enacted the dramatic scenes at the bridge and how a dragon that will remain nameless clung to the Commander's head as she was carried away downstream. Vykter came up behind Wyart and tried to straddle his head.

"It was like this." They both ended up in a heap on the floor laughing.

"Oh the best was at Janlin village." Renny grabbed Wyart; they twirled and threw ale into the air from between their legs to simulate the original ant challenge. They stomped around the room beating at their enlarged puffed out chests. Marcus and his men laughed so hard, a couple fell off their seats. "Thus, this ends the tale of Kerwin and the stinky pinkie." Nothing was sacred with these stories and since the men found out Captain Kyle was only their host's half-brother, well he was the next casualty.

Renny gave an outstanding performance of Captain fancy pants. One arm flapping in exasperation as he strode around the room, the other stroking his non-existent beard. "I'm sure I felt a hair there yesterday. What happened to it? Who stole it from me…hmmmm?" He strode over to one of the soldiers and pulled out a long blonde curly hair from his head. He proceeded to stick it to his chin with some spit. "Ahhh is this it? Well it will have to do." He introduced himself with an over exaggerated bow to Vykter, playing the infamous Commander Ballard and thrust out his hand mere inches from his face. "What did you say? You are not he?" Then proceeded to wipe his hand on the nearest soldier's head to remove the filth he had obviously contracted by the handshake with the imposter. He then waddled over to Chale and bowed. He performed a little head toss, eyes wide with astonishment ; he screeched . "A girl, nay it cannot be so, a girl? You cannot be he, the master of all." Wyart then came up behind Chale and started spraying ale infused words at Renny. "I am the Dragon Master and I spit on you, Captain Fancy Pants."

This brought the house down with screams of laughter, snorts, belches and cries of stomach cramps. Even Ben the Barkeep slid down the side wall to land in a heap of shaking jelly.

Ciaran rolled over onto his back, his stumpy legs thrashed wild, as his body convulsed in laughter. There was near perfect cadence between the ale infused belching from his mouth and his smoke rings pulsating from his nostrils. "Stop…I beg you all. I canna take any more."

Marcus watched as Atesh's cheeks reddened. He memorised every inch of her wondrous face. His heart pounded fierce within his chest. Adoration and admiration was foremost in his mind. He thought she was exquisite. *Is this what love feels like?*

This was the perfect opportunity Atesh thought to get some air. She rose to go and gather more ale. Ballard shaking his head and wiping the tears from his eyes stood to accompany her and calm himself down. They both leaned on the front bar and waited for their ale jugs. They talked in hushed tones with their backs to the patrons in the main common room. Atesh spun around to meet the two palace guards who had thought to sneak up on them, with their swords drawn. Ballard half turned, but stopped short when he felt the pointy end of a long sword on the side of his neck.

"What is the meaning of this?" Ballard asked the unknown assailants.

"We told you last night scum. We don't want your type in our village causing a ruckus; and here we are again the next afternoon. You dare to return with your whore."

Atesh's eyes had widened at this suggestion. "What did you call me?"

"We do not abide by whores peddling their wares and spreading their filthy diseases here in this village."

Atesh turned her head a little and whispered to Ballard. "I look like a whore?"

He shook his head no, with fervent ferocity. "So I assume we have here the one and only, Sergeant Philips."

"Ha…well that you remember me scum, but you do not like to obey orders. You are both under arrest by order of the palace guards."

"Arrest on what charge Sergeant?" Atesh enquired, as polite as her temper would allow.

"One for disobeying a direct order and two; no whores allowed in this here village."

"I think you have made a mistake sir."

"Well, there be no mistake missy. Our Captain issued specific orders last night. If ever we were to see this man and his companions in this establishment again; we were to arrest them on the spot; put you in the lock up and throw away the key. He was very specific, that if you gave us any trouble, we were to run you through and dump your rotting carcasses in the pits"

Atesh closed her eyes, released a large sigh and with her right hand behind her back, touched the oath ring on her middle finger with her thumb. Ballard shifted his hand so his ring activation would not alert their captors to the next event. Silence was immediate from the back room. The men stood up in tempo when their rings' illuminated to a fiery red glow. The knights' demeanour changed from frivolity to serious intent. With haste and little noise they strode with purpose to the outer main common room. Marcus and his men followed with narrowed eyes, furrowed brows and questioning looks. They noticed the rings shone for a brief moment then returned to their usual state. He wondered what it meant. Marcus had a twist in his guts. He felt all was about to become another event. Ryna explained to the Master at arms, Captain Skip that this meant the Commander was in need of assistance. Skip had taken an instant liking to this lady knight. In fact, he like his two fellow officers was besotted.

The Knights stood at the entrance to the common room and drew their swords from their back sheathes, in a quiet and efficient manner.

Meanwhile; Sergeant Philips whistled for his unit to stand behind him. They had been within the castle proper or manning the outer walls in the far distance all morning and had just completed their shifts. These twelve guards had no idea or cared who they were messing with. They had not witnessed the morning's events at all. The bar-keep Ben stood still, eyes narrowed in disgust. He was not worried about the knights. He knew all too well what they could do. Marcus however, decided he needed to see what was happening and intervene before blood was spilt. He pushed his way through with Captains' Aiden and Skip behind him.

"Sergeant Philips what goes on here?"

"Commander Marcus, we were apprehending a couple of undesirables. This large one was warned last night to never enter this village again and yet, he returns, this time with his whore. There is a writ against one such as this, applying her trade here sir. Captain Kyle's orders were specific, sir. If they were to return they must be arrested by any means necessary."

Marcus felt the rage build up inside of him. He took a deep breath, stood tall, regal and commanding. "Is this how my brother teaches you to arrest now Sergeant?"

"Sir, Captain Kyle said he had received information that this man and his companions were dangerous. He described these two in detail. Mercenaries and outlaws and he placed the death penalty over their heads; so any force was deemed appropriate."

"The death penalty, what nonsense is this? Since when do we not bring any accused before the King for justice and sentencing? Your Captain has overstepped his office. Sergeant I am ordering you and your fellow officer to remove your weapons and sheath them; stand down, NOW!"

"B-but sir, we are under orders from our Captain."

"Sergeant, your Captain answers to 'ME'. I am the Commander and your next King, are you really going to disobey and argue with me?"

Captains' Aiden and Skip, plus the other regiment soldiers stood behind their Commander. Near the entrance to the outer room halted the knights with scimitars drawn.

Sergeant Philips looked up. His eyes widened as he gaped at the armed men. "SIR… following you are his companions so armed."

All the palace guards drew their weapons and a standoff began to unfold.

Commander Marcus drew his sword and rested the tip upon the chest of Sergeant Philips. He was not in the mood for playing this game. "Now…I said, stand down and sheath your swords, or I will slice you open Sergeant; from navel to nose…. Palace guards place your weapons away and step back."

The regiment soldiers then surrounded the palace guards with their weapons drawn.

Sergeant Philips seemed reluctant, but at last he complied. His face was screwed up into a sneer, baring his teeth. Then with as much venom as he could muster, he spat on the floor beside the Commander. "Your father will hear about this abuse of your power."

Looking at the remnants of the mucus beside his boots, Marcus felt his stomach turn. "Nothing would give me more pleasure than to see you discuss this with my father. However, before you make a further fool of yourself, would you like to know who you have been accosting in the most cowardly of fashion and accusing of some trumped up charge; by my pathetic specimen of a brother?"

"You know this low life sir?"

"Philips, this large low life as you call him is Captain Ballard Greymont of the '*Pace Knights*', my uncle a Prince of the realm. The lady you have insulted is Supreme Commander Atesh, of the '*Pace Knights*'. Those men at the rear who are ready to tear you limb from limb are the Commander's first Battalion from Ashmourne Island."

"No, you have been misinformed sir. That cannot be so. Captain Kyle assured us he had information on these miscreants. We were given strict orders sir."

"Your orders were wrong, Philips. Do you have something to say to them now?"

Philips shook his head, folded his arms and spat on the floor in front of Ballard. "Captain Kyle would never do wrong by us or this village sir."

Ballard eyes widened, his hands clenched to ashen in anger. He fixed his gaze upon Marcus. Not asking, but demanding and received a nod.

Marcus turned to his men with a smirk upon his face, "Commander Atesh would you please accompany me into the back room; Jenner and Reyna, you two as well."

Atesh winked at the girls and nodded for them to comply, but she stood firm. Blue flames emanated from her eyes and finger tips.

"Men weapons at the ready. Place a perimeter around the common room, ensure no knives or swords are used." He turned to Aiden. "Once this is over, I want Philips and the other guard in the lock up." Marcus turned to leave the room and heard a crash from behind.

The guard at the initial assault sailed past him and out into the street. He was covered in ale and remnants of an ale jug. All the other patrons who had witnessed this affair scattered , preferring the safety of the exterior of the inn with their mugs still in hand . Ballard quick as lightning punched Sergeant Philips with all his bent up fury. He flew out the entrance of the inn taking two guards with him and landed next to the previous victim. Marcus turned an accusing eye on Atesh who had a smug smile on her face and a broken ale jug at her feet.

Marcus shook his head, "Definitely … not named for hair colour." He beckoned her with one finger to follow him as Berend yelled out,

"Bar fight."

The knights sheathed their weapons, flexed their hands and roared with fury as they bolted for the guards, then it was one great big melee. Broken furniture splintering could be heard, it vibrated throughout the inn. Curdled screams, grunts and cussing resonated from men as thumping and crushing sounds were muffled. Marcus and Aiden secured the outer back room. Ballard's emotional day and pent up anger finally had its release.

Marcus gave Ben a handful of gold coins for the damage to his inn, but he was reluctant to take them. Marcus however insisted. "You may not have much of an inn left after the knight's get through with those pathetic, brainless cowards."

"Oh sir, my Inn will now be famous . I can boast we had the first major bar fight with the Academy Knights . I am however , embarrassed and sad at what Commander Atesh had to endure. She was cool and calm the whole time . But then 'wham' oh … can she punch sir. Never have I seen a lady with such power behind such a delicate body. She is one of a kind sir."

Marcus's eyes sparkled. "Oh that she is Ben … that she is."

Marcus and Aiden snuck a peak out through the doorway to assess the situation; they noticed Ballard with a guard in a head lock, while he downed a jug of ale with his other hand.

"Definitely related sir," Aiden stood tall, but with an angst longing on his face. "May I?"

"Oh … of course, give one for me as well. Oh, the pain of command. I miss all the fun; go man go."

Aiden ran and landed on top of a guard that had jumped on the back of Ballard. Interrupting a man and his drink was an abomination. The regiment noticed their Captain in the midst of the skirmish. He gave as well as he received. Bets started up and a few decided what the heck and they joined the fracas as well.

"Marcus, I told you before we do not distinguish between men and women. Why do you not allow us to fight?" Atesh stood arms crossed with blue sparks radiating out from her eyes.

"Well, here in this town we do not allow ladies that kind of behaviour. If you were to get hurt, do you think the alliance between the Academy and the King would stay intact? I don't want to chance it thank you…Oh and by the way." Marcus gave a wink and a smile. "Great thump back there. I'm glad you don't punch like a girl." Marcus ducked as a jug whizzed past his head, he backed up and laughed at the sight and made sure the lady knights remained out of danger. If truth be told, they would have fared better than his men.

A large crowd gathered to watch the fight from out in the street, when additional village garrison guards arrived. A runner had informed them assistance was required by the officers inside. But, upon seeing whom they were tussling with, they decided it best to stay outside and perform crowd control.

Ben was now outside the inn taking bets, all odds in his favour of course. The bar remained opened via the side door. Drinks flowed out as fast as his staff could pour them. He placed a hand on his son's shoulder; his pocket's bulging with coin. "Oh I hope these knights stay around a while, Binji my lad. We will become the richest Inn-Keep's in all Sofala and famous ta-boot. Fancy the Ashmourne Knights, the saviours of this village having their first altercation here at my inn."

Chapter 14

Never a Dull Moment:

Thaddeus paced his room in long ground eating strides. *"Elias can we talk…are you alone?"*

"Yes I am in my office, what is happening Thaddeus? You sound distressed."

"I am sorry to say, we have lost one of your knights. Jesper and his war steed have disappeared in mysterious circumstances; much like the others. He was fishing in a nearby stream, down from the Castle. Atesh and the knights are devastated."

"Oh dear me, I cannot make sense of all this. Why one of Atesh's men? On the surface, there appears no pattern that I can see. Was there a witness to this event; this creature Thad?"

"No Elias, but on a closer inspection the knights found Jesper's smashed pipes. Then tangled in the bushes nearby was a piece of unusual black fur and an enormous paw print embedded in the river sand. Ciaran mentioned there was an abhorrent magic odour lingering about, though I am not entirely sure what he meant by that."

"Perhaps he means Black Magic Thad; dragons are very sensitive to that sort of energy. I was wondering…is it all connected do you think? There are the disappearances increasing in volume, then the creatures breaking out through the northern boundary and now the earth shakes? Do they not say; bad tidings come in threes?"

"Come now Elias, you know that is superstitious clap-trap."

"The problem is Thad; we have no idea what this is all about. Could it possibly be a High Wizard or other type of magic user attempting ancient magic or perhaps a necromancer from the other side of the world; we may never know who it

is. Some wizards may still be alive from eons past. Remember; there are places we have no longer access to."

"Elias do you think…is it possible…there may be a way across that ocean chasm and vortex? We know from history that there is life and many lands on the other side of the world. Who is to say there are not powerful wizards or dark magicians with a vendetta over there? After all, many of the ancestral races left for lands on the other side millennia ago, before the cataclysmic event."

"I will do a search here in the Academy archives. If I recall, we had some ancient tomes somewhere discussing how the great divide was formed. But that was so long ago they may have turned to dust by now Thad. Anything else happen…I get the feeling you have more news, eh dear brother?"

"Well yes some astounding news. Atesh and Ballard have met Mia. She is now Queen of the Fire Ants and has made an alliance with them." Thaddeus sat down in his chair by the open fire and placed his hand to his forehead.

"You have spoken with Mia…oh how splendid Thad, has she grown at all?"

"Well, she is now taller than the outer castle wall Elias."

"Oh my, that is larger than her mother. What pray tell did the King say?"

"Speak! Ha…he could not, his mouth hung to far ajar."

The brothers both stopped talking to calm their laughter down.

"I have a question to ask you, though I must insist on an honest answer Elias."

"Certainly, I will not lie to you dear brother."

"Did you know…that Atesh…was my missing granddaughter Liera?"

"What did you say Thad…" Elias placed his hand over his aching heart, *"Did I hear you correct? Who told you this?"*

"Mia…you know she has strange powers. Did you know…Elias?"

"How is this possible? In all the years living so close to her, I have felt no family innate signature. No Thaddeus, of course I didn't know. But, then seeing how powerful she is becoming, it does make sense, I suppose."

"Tell me about how she came to be at the Academy please, Elias."

"Of course Thad, though you are aware of the bare bones of the event; it is not a story I like to recount."

After a lengthy discussion Thaddeus sat back in his chair by the roaring fire and shook his head. His hands exhibited a slight tremor. *Oh my goodness, what that poor girl has gone through. I wonder what had happened to her in the years between being abducted from Tyral and found on*

Ashmourne Island. Thaddeus poured himself a strong drink as a few more tears cascaded down his now sodden cheeks. He remembered the night as if it was yesterday, some fourteen, no near fifteen years ago. He walked into his office and pulled out his life journal and read the notes that broke his heart.

I stood transfixed by the flickering fire within this study at Beaumont Castle. I was unable to move or utter a sound; as a vision had taken me unbidden. An incident was unfolding many miles away on the island of Tyral; one very personal and heart wrenching. Tears welled in my eyes, but only a solitary tear escaped and cascaded down my left cheek. Consequences, I realised would be bound within future events, thus were the nature or curse of these visions. The events would be profound and unknowing; this I felt in the very core of my soul.

On the third floor of Wilmont Castle-Tyral, a struggle transpired. The nanny had awoken to the sounds of soft splintering wood. A large creature, part panther with luminescent wings folded against its muscled body had broken into the royal nursery and made its way to where the young Princess Liera slept. Prince Aiden was asleep in a crib nearby. The nanny stumbled out of bed snatched a piece of the broken window frame and thrust it at the creature's back. Large hairy paws grabbed her and held tight. The nanny let out a blood-curdling scream; before being crushed to death and discarded. The resultant noise echoed loud along the moist stone walls, late into the sleeping hours, throughout the castle. The few souls that were still awake stopped and turned their heads to listen; eyes widened, breaths held, as a macabre growl silenced the human cry. The castle soldiers on duty whipped their heads around towards the sound. Their legs stiff from standing still, groaned as they were willed to move into swift action. They leapt the stairs two at a time towards the upper floors that housed the quarters of the royal family.

Duchess Lysanna lounged in her favourite chair. Eyes closed, whilst her chest rose and fell to a peaceful rhythm; she dozed beside a blazing fire. An unfamiliar sound drew her out from that place between reality and dream state. She sat up alert, her heart beat forceful and resonated within her ears. Taking quick shallow breaths, a cold shiver emanated down her spine, her neck hairs stood up in unison. She ran from her sitting room, nightdress held up to her knees, as she headed towards the nursery. The soldiers and Lysanna arrived together; breathless. They opened the door and witnessed a large black beast, with luminescent wings. It sprung out of the broken shuttered window, into the moonless night. Clutched in its front paw was the three year old Princess Liera; her pale limp limb's swung wild and unruly, her head lolled uncontrollable. They found the nanny lying beside the small bed, tuffs of black fur matted in her bloodied fingers. She had been fearless to the end, in defence of her charges.

Lysanna fell upon her knees and looked around the room with tear streaked rose coloured cheeks. Her hand's trembled as she wrapped them tight around her waist. Curled in upon herself; she rocked back and forth. The only sound in the stillness was the broken heart of a grieving mother. I would never forget the look of utter despair on my daughter's face as she descended onto the floor. The silent sounds of her grieving heart. Nor the smile on the creature's distorted lips, as it admired the fine catch lodged within its gigantic paw; just before it disappeared into the darkness of the night sky. I remembered many others throughout the known lands had similar experiences; cries could be heard on the whisper of the wind, as parents discovered a child missing or partners their loved one vanished. These disappearances had been a part of life for so long; it was difficult to remember when they first commenced. The victims came from all walks of life. There was no logical pattern that I could see rich, poor, farmer, bard, scholar, even creatures; domestic and wild. No one was immune. Hunters went out and trackers were paid substantial amounts, but to no avail. The Duke would spend many years searching in vain for his daughter. His guilt was profound, as he blamed himself for not being home to protect his family. A cold shiver woke Thaddeus up from his past musings.

The King Gareth Beaumont had been informed there was a riot at the Anvil Inn. The village guards and regiment soldiers were in attendance and required further assistance. He did not understand how this had happened. He summoned his two personal guards; Hector and Vector. They were brothers in their late twenties. Their appearance was unusual and foreign from the local inhabitants of Sofala. They exhibited large, wide foreheads, chiselled facial features, ebony coloured eyes, darkened skin tones and many long black beaded hair plaits tied back at the nape of their thick necks. They were descendants of the local volcanic island true blood stock, a secret society that had maintained a long held tradition. They had the privilege of being the personal guards to the High King since the first; many thousands of years ago. Their bodies were the circumference of a thick tamboo tree and a head taller than Marcus or Gareth. To say they resembled a small giant from the ancient fables would be close to accurate. They were large of frame and limb and carried heavy maces; though they ran with lightness and grace.

The three found their horses readied and raced off together towards the inn. Gareth decided the quickest and safest route was the secret road. This was built underneath the outer wall in the castle grounds and it was wide enough that horses could easily ride two abreast and high enough for a carriage. This was initially built for escape during war time or to sneak up on an invading adversary. At a certain point along the wall, the King placed his palm against a rectangle stone embossed with a dragon and anvil. This portion of the wall groaned and dust wafted up as the stone work rearranged itself to open a short distance behind the Anvil Inn. Having heard the melee out the front, the three men strode in unison through the back exit. Standing at the entrance to the main common area was an engrossed Commander Marcus. Gareth flanked by his guards walked up to Marcus. Atesh watched with amusement as this tall, broad shouldered stranger placed a black gloved hand on the Commander's left shoulder and gave it a squeeze. Marcus's posture straightened up immediately until he glanced at the fingers on his shoulder and his head dropped. He turned around as his facial features turned ashen, horror showing in his widened eyes and bowed his head.

"What may I ask in all Sofala is happening here son?"

Marcus explained as quick and succinct as possible.

The King listened and absorbed all the relevant information. He nodded in approval and smiled. The King stuck his head out for a moment and retracted it as a piece of broken furniture whizzed by. "Well…looks like you have this in hand son. By the way, who seems to be the victors?"

"Need you enquire Sir?" He pointed towards Ballard and his knights.

He handed over four gold coins to Marcus. "Place my bet down will you. I want that huge mountain man to be the last one standing." Who is he by the way…damn…will you look at the size of him? One of the knights, I gather."

"Sir that was mother's younger brother Captain Ballard of the 'Pace Knights'."

"What! No…Ballard has turned into that gigantic tree of a man?" Gareth's eyes sparkled as he made a whistling sound; he was full of astonishment and admiration. "Which one is Commander Atesh? Gareth again leant out to scan the melee."

"Sir…father, she is the knight behind us with the golden hair and blue flaming eyes, that would like to rip me to pieces for leaving her out of the entertainment in there." He turned and gestured with his head towards the side table.

"So Atesh is a female-I-see." He looked deep into his son's eyes and noticed the extra sparkle and wide smile that adorned his face. "So…this is why you have decided to abstain from the merriment; to watch their honour?" He slapped Marcus on the back and turned to leave. Gareth noticed the forlorn looks of his bodyguards. "It would be no contest men. Come on now; lift those lips up, before you step on them." As he passed Atesh he glanced her way. One eyebrow and the corner of his mouth were raised in mischievous thought and then he continued on without a…by-your-leave. At the back door he turned around for a moment and locked eyes with Atesh. She smiled and bowed her head. Gareth returned the gesture in kind and nodded to himself all the way back to his horse. He looked to the sky, arms stretched out wide. "Finally…thank you."

Although the palace guards outnumbered the knights two to one, they were all spent, each one down and out for the count.

Marcus cupped his hands around his mouth and yelled out from the back, "Tis to be the last man standing." This echoed across the room and outside in the street.

Ballard jumped up on the bar with Berend next to him and they performed the wildest, primordial call ever heard in these here parts.

This was answered by screams of glee from both the knights and the regiment soldiers. Teams no longer existed. There were no more sides; it was dog eat dog. The last man standing takes home the pot of gold. Marcus knew this was his father's way of acknowledging and sanctioning the previous altercation and the need to release any pent up anger and frustration with the fighting men. For a King, he had a way of understanding his soldiers like no other royal before him. Ben was ecstatic and continued to collect bets and sell ale and mead, watered down of course; but no one knew or cared. Some of the local lads joined in and bedlam was the word. Marcus and the three ladies stood and watched from safety. They cried out, hooted, winced, and laughed.

"Well at least we won't need to practice fighting drills today." Marcus spluttered as a piece of broken clay jug skimmed by his face. "I think a retreat is in order." They returned to the back room to await the final outcome. It was quite some time before a deafening silence enveloped the front room. Moments later a war cry was heard. This signified a winner; a lone survivor.

"That's Ballard; I know that victory cry anywhere." Atesh jumped up and thumped her arm into the air with a loud, "whoop."

Not one stick of furniture was left whole. There were bodies in all sorts of weird and not so wonderful positions. Berend was hanging upside down from the banister, an empty mug still clutched in his right hand. Renny his head was somehow wedged between the spokes of the broken candelabra. Vykter was spread eagled, half in and out of the front, now non-existent window. Chale, Skip, and Aiden along with the rest of the men were mixed together; bodies, limbs, heads, all needed to be sorted out and unravelled. The regiment soldiers held up well, though most still came off second best. The worst injuries by far were the palace posers; they would be laid low for days to come. Atesh had wondered where Ciaran had got to when she heard a familiar hiccough from behind the bar. There the little dragonelle lay on his back, his stumpy legs splayed, his eyes rolled up as he blew smoke rings with his ale infused burps.

Marcus, Atesh, Ryna and Ben assisted Jenner with the unravelling process of the knights and soldiers. Jenner was certain to have her hands full with healing tonight. Cold water was required to assist in the rousing of the men prior to escorting them to the back room. Renny however, necessitated the assistance of the local blacksmith for extrication of his head from the tight twisted metal. How this feat was performed in the first place had all the rescuers stumped, though their laughter would erupt without warning often through the evening when they looked Renny's way. The local lads were attended to by their mates, with lots of back slapping and laughter. The other patrons jostled each other through the front entrance to view the state of the fighters within. Tales would be told of certain feats of ingenuity for days to come. The palace guards were dragged to one side and lay in a heap of bloodied and bruised bodies, except for the two that started this debacle. Sergeant Philips and his minion were thrown in the lock up.

It was a long and arduous walk back to the barracks later that evening. Atesh was not sure who held who up, as they struggled up the stairs to the accommodation billets. The men threw themselves down on their beds and stayed in whatever position they landed.

Atesh gave them all a kiss on the forehead goodnight. "Thanks for protecting my honour men." She staggered off to her room and was asleep before her head hit the bed. She cuddled up to a drunken dragonelle. Ciaran smoke plumes burst forth every now and again, as he belched ale infused odour.

Marcus watched this from the end of the dormitory. He was beyond any doubt, smitten. *She was one in a million, yes sir, one in a million.*

Back at the palace, Master Thaddeus Freymore waited in the King's sitting room. He stood in front of the open fire and gazed into its myriad of flicking colours, mesmerised. The flames seemed to caress his soul. It sent his mind into that realm of wizard space and time, the in-between; a place of safety for thoughts and deep reflection. He wondered how life became so messed up. He went over the information Elias divulged; and yet, he still found it hard to comprehend what must have happened to the little girl, his grand-daughter to be found in such a state. He shuddered to think. He now understood what drove her to be so committed; to be the best; but also to keep love at a distance. *How do you fix a wounded body and mind?*

It was while Thaddeus's mind wandered into this faraway place, Gareth bounced in the door, whistling. He saw his father in law and yelled out. "We must celebrate! I have good news. At last, it has happened." He rambled on for a bit until he noticed the tear stained face and reddened eyes on Thaddeus. He ceased his yammering and stared.

"Thaddeus, what has happened?"

"First Gareth, what are we to celebrate?"

"Marcus is in love. I saw it in his eyes, his face and he is radiant."

"Thaddeus closed his eyes, for he knew what was to come. "Who is the lucky lady Gareth?"

"Thaddeus," The King's eyes narrowed, the smile disappeared. "I have a bad feeling about this, what is wrong?"

"Gareth who is the lady Marcus is in love with?"

"It is Atesh the Commander of the Knights."

Thaddeus sat down hard in the chair behind him and placed a hand to his face; tears welled and threatened to spill over down his cheeks unchecked.

Gareth kneeled before him; hands on Thaddeus knees. "Please tell me what is wrong; I have only ever seen you cry once, all those years ago."

"Gareth you need to sit, I have a tale to tell you, though I need your absolute silence on this."

Gareth sat stunned for a long while. "All this time, she was so close?"

"I am afraid she will be more powerful than both Elias and I together."

"But that is not a bad thing…is it Thad?"

"Gareth she may be long lived or even immortal, once her powers turn in a week's time. Or…the turning may kill her."

Gareth paled at the thought.

"But the problem I see mostly is Atesh herself. She has never let anyone get near her except her unit; they are her family. I told you she was a foundling and that she was undernourished and lived in a hollowed out tree. But when they finally found her and took her to the infirmary, the healers were in a rage. She had survived with two broken and partly healed hips, breaks in her pelvis and burn marks all over her body with strange animal claw rakes on her back." Thaddeus paused for a moment, his lips quivered and tears again fell unchecked down his cheeks, they moistened his face as they fell. "The healers believed by the marks she had sustained that she had been tortured…She still has all the scars over her poor body. She walked with a brace for two years, but still every day she performed her exercises and forms; it was her therapy. She even nursed her familiar, Ciaran back to health, he had terrible injuries too."

"What creature would do something like this Thad…to a little helpless babe?"

"She has no memory thank goodness; for if ever it came back. I don't know what would happen to her mind, or worse; what would she do."

Gareth poured them both a large drink. "Well she has shown her mettle. Let's see how it plays out. If this is as you say, she may very well keep her distance from Marcus."

Chapter 15

True Lies:

Meanwhile, Captain Danurel and two units of knights set up camp close to the north east mountain border. The men knew this area well as they had each taken their turn with boundary duty as part of their cadetship, but this time the atmosphere felt different. The looks between the knights spoke of silent misgivings; an unsettling feel overtook them about this venture. The men all stayed on alert whilst attending their duties and watched for any movement around the camp perimeters; their weapons within reach at all times. There was no question as to why the men all felt on edge and wary. Quiet murmurs of Commander Atesh's report had filtered down throughout the ranks of the entire academy, prior to their departure. She had noted the villagers' concerns regarding recent episodes of creatures poaching close to their homes. The farmers had described in detail the physical, sickening evidence of what had been fierce, unbridled blood lust in attacks on their domestic pets and ranging herds. They implied it was no ordinary predator assailing their animals. The alarming unknown cries at night would send the bravest man's bowels to water. Captain Danurel expressed his utter contempt for this type of fear mongering and seditious behaviour. He had stated not once, but often on the journey to this posting, how the Supreme Commander exaggerated her report for her own self-importance.

Master Elias believed Atesh of course, he witnessed their arrival home after their altercation with the red eyed wolves and felt sure these creatures may have ventured from behind the northern mountain boundary. Yet, the most vexing problems were the crystals. They still indicated; the magical barrier remained intact. He felt a closer and more detailed inspection was indeed warranted. Master Elias instructed the knights to assess the eastern side of the mountain range for any possible weakness; such as a newly formed fissure or other such breach. The older knights all knew the boundary history. By the time the two units arrived at their destination, even the younger men had heard it many times around the camp fire at night. It was near two hundred years ago, after many incursions from unusual and ferocious creatures, the Academy's High Wizards, at the behest of the reigning King, had raised the earth up; into one continuous high mountain range. It stretched from the eastern seaboard through to the west, segregating the last portion of the north from the rest of Sofala. Then to indicate the ongoing effectiveness of the mountain's integrity, the academy placed a series of wizard enhanced crystal beacons along the entire southern side. It had taken the life of all the high wizards involved. They were spent, exhausted; the power required was too grand. This was their ultimate sacrifice; legacy to their King and country. It was after this tragic event and the fact that no thanks was ever received that the academy voted to never again give fealty to a reigning monarch. They would be an independent entity with their own warrior unit, trained to keep the peace and monitor their own side of the boundary. Thus the modern day, '*Pace Alastriona Knights*' came to be.

The sheer cliffs became a natural barrier that for the past one hundred and eighty five years had been effective in securing rogue creatures behind it, away from the Sofalan population. Master Elias knew it was only a matter of time before the natural weather patterns would wear down the mountain and a possible breach would occur. After the white season, the melting snow would often cascade down the sheer cliffs creating wondrous cataracts. The water would then surge through the snake like streams amid the bracken, rocks and forests beside the uplifted base; to engorge the mighty Meder billabong. This catchment area would channel the flow into two river systems. The largest meandered down the midline of Sofala called the

Jangly River. The second smaller stream wandered further west past the Beaumont Castle. Its nickname was, the Tiddler.

Captain Danurel was bored and fed up with what he considered as the 'leftovers.' Posts Commander Atesh was not delegated. He despised the men for selecting a young foolish girl over him to lead the elite knights and take command of the primary unit of the first battalion. Danurel was often found to be muttering into his ale. "I should be the Supreme Commander. It should have been mine. I worked long and hard for the position and some young upstart, smiles at the men and they cave in; weak minded fools." His mug was thrown out to the left and right, spilling ale, as he spoke to no one in particular. "I know she must have cheated in the magic competition; I have way more innate power than she. I was better at forms, but they chose her in the ballot. Huh…maybe that was rigged too." Danurel treated these men he commanded with disdain. *They deserved to be treated like the flea bidden dogs they were.* He yelled, cussed, threw objects and had them work nonstop; from morning till dark. He was not going to get his hands dirty on some irrelevant, pathetic, no job. He sat each day outside his tent sipping his ale and dreamed away his allotted time. He fantasised how he was the master, the lord of his own domain.

The men disliked Danurel and tried their hardest to keep out of his way. They would cringe when the forms roster was posted and his partner for the next day was announced. It often ended with the knight wounded, mostly shallow slices, but on occasion it had been known to be severe and life threatening. The Captain would explode in a rage; with abuse on how inept they had been and purposely tried to make him look bad. In reality, he was not alert and poor at co-ordinating times with another. The men joked about him being off the mark, always just behind everyone else's rhythm. They all witnessed how he drank till all hours of the night and this did not help to ensure his movements the following morning to be agile and smooth. Their knights' code was sorely being tested.

During the night Danurel awoke and sat bolt upright on his cot. An uninvited guest was in his tent. He wiped his eyes and blinked the sleep from them. He tried to draw his sword hidden under the blankets, but found he was now unable to move at all. The intruder crouched down on the ground and looked up into Danurel's eyes.

The words he heard were spoken in a quiet tone so as not to alert the guards. "My name is Mason and I work for a powerful Wizard Master. I have it on good authority that you Captain, are not happy at the Ashmourne Compound and feel thwarted in your rise to command, is this true? Please nod your head, yes or no."

Danurel watched Mason, not answering the question, his mind a muddle.

"If you promise to be civil, I will allow you to speak. If you try and warn the guards, you will be dead before a word is spoken. Do you understand me, Captain?"

This time Danurel nodded in the affirmative.

"Fine then, now answer the question please Captain. Are you happy with your lot in life at the Academy?"

"Before I answer you, I would like to know what it is you want with me."

Mason thought on this for a few seconds and stared into Danurel eyes. "My Master searches for a special person to become his apprentice. My sources inform me that you may fit the criteria. He is not affiliated with the Wizard's Academy, but has worked on his own for close to two hundred years. He needs assistance with his work and has charged me with finding a suitable candidate. Are you up for the challenge?"

"Well to answer your first question. No I am not content where I am. My power grows daily, I can feel it, but they hold me back; bypass and ignore me at the Academy. They do not appreciate what I have to offer."

"Yes I have heard this Captain."

"What do I gain from being an apprentice? What is in it for me?"

"When the time is right you will inherit all his work and gain High Wizard status and all that goes with it; power, riches and long life. This is his agreement for the right candidate."

Danurel wondered if this may be a trap. "Explain how he has remained outside the Academy. I was led to believe all High Wizards must be affiliated with them and their codes. What work does he perform that he needs an apprentice? How can I gain power to be a wizard of that calibre?"

"Some of these questions only the master can answer. What I can tell you is that he has travelled to many strange and wondrous lands and has acquired knowledge and powers far beyond anything they have seen here. You forget, I said he was a High Wizard Master and can perform powerful magic. If you desire knowledge, power and riches and yes, even revenge; then I am offering you this opportunity and more. So what is it to be captain?"

"Mason…I would be honoured to accept your gracious offer."

"That is wonderful news Captain. There will be a trial period of course to gauge your aptitude. Though from what I have heard of your tale, I would think it be, but a mere formality. I will inform the Master…now we need to make arrangements for your departure. I will return in two days with travel arrangements. Oh, ease off the ale; you will need a clear head for a while."

"Now before you depart Mason. What is it…you do?"

"I am the Master's assistant. I perform whatever duty he requires of me. I will be there to assist and guide you, the best I can." The next minute he was gone, as though he had never been.

The Captain could move again. He stood and looked around his tent; maybe he had dreamed the whole affair. He moved something on the ground with his foot. He glanced down and picked up the object. It was a clear crystal. Once held, it sent images into his mind of a sunny and beautiful island. It had white sandy beaches, lush green grassed areas, a forest towards the rear and smiling worker's ploughing a field. A large multi-towered castle arose from the middle of the island where the sun reflected off the tiny sparkles, embedded within the stone walls. Mason stood out the front, he bowed and the images faded.

So not a dream, Danurel rubbed his hands together in excitement. *This is going to be wonderful…me a High Wizard.* He returned to his cot and dreamed once again, being the master of all.

The next morning the men noticed the Captain's disposition had changed. He smiled and greeted the knights with apparent sincerity. This unnerved the men more so. They began to whisper amongst themselves. Silent looks passed between them. They were in fact waiting for the cracks to appear, the resultant implosion. For many days they had not moved camp. The knights all knew their orders and realised early on their captain was not up to the task. This did not bode well with the men at all. They took their duty, their oaths with grave, honest intent.

The next day with little fore-warning, Danurel sent one complete unit of men further to the west for five days. They were to assess the boundary at the base, log any unusual creature activity and visit farms, small villages and outposts near to the border. They were then to travel to the Meder Billabong and down through the Jangly river crossover. This would normally take two weeks if completed as Master Elias required. To accomplish this task in five days was irresponsible. It could not be a thorough assessment. The men were at least glad to be away from Danurel and would perform their duties to the best of their abilities. The second group he kept close by, practicing their forms and armed combat skills.

Two days after the first visit, Mason visited the Captain in his tent and handed over a small square object. This was to be placed into the ale barrel that afternoon and the effects would render all the men who drank from it unconscious. Then he could be transported away in secret.

What Danurel did not know, was that the entire unit would also be conveyed along as well, with the aid of the gatherers. The Master would have a new apprentice and a whole knight unit to utilise. Mason wrung his hands together; he was so pleased with himself for this coup. *What an accomplishment, fifteen knights and a stooge…ah apprentice.*

Meanwhile, Danurel considered different scenarios on why he was distributing ale to all the men; when a brilliant idea dawned on him. *Yes, yes of course…it shall be my day of birth celebration. They are not to know it is not, so they must drink a toast to me at dinner, each and every one of them. I am so devious, I surprise even myself.*

The cook for this unit was Thomas a quiet, nervous type of fellow. He was from the academy kitchens, on loan for this mission. He could however, handle a weapon if required. He preferred to be invisible, so when Captain Danurel came over to his fires to discuss the evening's meal, he near stopped breathing. He showed him the two small barrels of ale that were left and what food supplies he had.

"That looks adequate. I will send you an assistant. I want the finest celebration dinner you can muster; do you hear me cook?"

"Y-yes sir, I am honoured sir, to do this for you, sir."

"I would like to try the ale now, to make sure it is to my liking. Go and fetch me my tankard from the tent will you, that's a good lad."

So while Thomas ran like his pants were on fire, Danurel dropped the cube into the first ale barrel. When Thomas returned, Captain Danurel poured a sample of ale into his mug and strode back to his tent pretending to drink, but instead he tipped the fluid out where no one would notice.

That night a splendid meal was had by all; Thomas outdid himself and shone with exuberance. The ale was poured out for the entire unit, even the guards; they had to wish their Captain a happy day. It was an order. The men drank as heartily as ever, for they believed tomorrow the Captain would revert back to his horrid, unreasonable self.

Only one man did not drink more than a sip. It was the horse handler Jett. He had felt quite ill for some days. He walked off into the bushes to check on his charges and fell asleep amongst a thick group of vegetation, under long spindly weeds. The rest of the unit gradually fell asleep around the fire pits. Even the knights on duty were out to it and dropped in a heap at their guard post.

Mason arrived out of thin air to consult with Danurel.

He found the Captain kicking the knights as they lay on the ground. "I wish I could see their faces tomorrow." He roared with laughter.

"Captain there was one small detail, I may have left out. I see now, it should not be a problem for you."

"What might that be Mason?" Danurel narrowed his eyes to mere slits, as he looked now with disquiet etched onto his face.

"Well we will be taking this unit with us to the island; the Master has use for them."

"How do you expect to do that? They are all unconscious. What could you possibly want with these idiots?" *Am I being double crossed here?*

"We have our own ways to transport cargo; do not worry about the details now. But to show you my good will. I shall share a secret with you." Mason leant over and whispered to Danurel.

When he finished talking Danurel was speechless. He paled first at the thought and the information he had been given. He sat down heavily on the log beside the fire pit and tried to digest it all. He looked around at the men from his unit and then looked at Mason. A small crease in the side of his mouth appeared and then this grew larger until he threw his head back and laughed, till tears ran down his cheeks. He glanced at Mason once more. "Really…are you saying this is true? Never would I have imagined this. Oh, this is too good."

Abi and his gatherers then received the nod from Mason and they swooped down and carried away all the men and horses they could find. Danurel was starry eyed when he saw these winged creatures. He watched in wonderment and anticipation. He clapped and laughed with hysterical fervour as each creature took off with a soldier or warhorse.

Mason beside him smiled with glee. *Yes, he had chosen well for the Master.* When the deed was completed, Mason turned to Danurel. "Are you ready to leave Master Dan?"

He turned to look at Mason. "Master Dan…I do like the sound of that." Then he surveyed the camp site. Took a deep breath and closed his eyes. "Yes Mason, I believe I am." With that they disappeared and all turned eerie and quiet.

Chapter 16

Some Secrets Revealed:

The next morning at sunrise Commander Atesh, Jenner, Ryna and Captain Ballard performed their exercises and forms, though at a slower pace than the previous day. The knights emerged one at a time from their ale infused slumber and either sat down and watched their comrades or crawled to a nearby bush and deposited a technicolour yawn.

Atesh wondered how Ballard's constitution held up to this punishment. *Maybe he has hollow legs…well; he is built like a tree.* Atesh looked around and noted her little friend was absent. *"Ciaran are you up and about yet?"*

A small plume of smoke wafted out from her bedroom window.

Well I guess that answered that question.

To Atesh's surprise Marcus and Aiden watched while they leant on the arena boundary fence. Marcus looked in fine form, standing straight and tall. His arms rested on the top paling, while the golden flecks in his eyes sparkled; as the sun rose to kiss them good morning. But Aiden, he leaned further into the fence. His head hung lower and his face looked pale with a greenish tinge. On one side a large dark purple bruise had formed from his right cheek bone and radiated down his jaw line. The right eye was bloodshot and his left eye, normally blue and sparkling, lacked its lustre.

Ouch that much have hurt. Atesh screwed up her face at the thought of the fist used to cause such damage. Noticing that Jenner watched Aiden from the corner of her eye; Atesh decided to call forms to a halt earlier than usual. "We will do our cool down now that will be enough for today. I think someone is needed elsewhere." She winked at Jenner and observed her cheeks turn a tomato red. *Well at least I'm not the only one that turns her cheeks aflame.*

Once cool down was completed they all strode over to the water trough and took a turn at dunking their head. Atesh often wore a black sleeveless under shirt, but this morning with her muddled mind, she had worn her white shear undergarment. She hadn't thought about consequences till after she glanced down and noticed the wet shirt had clung to her skin. Not only had it revealed her curvaceous figure, but also showed her raised scar lines that marred her torso. At times she forgot about them, until a suitor would pursue her. Then the scars would stand up and yell 'look at me,' of course she ran in the opposite direction.

Atesh glanced up to see if Marcus had noticed; he stared ahead at nothing, off in dream land she hoped. *That is a relief.*

Ballard ever the noble gent stood in front of Marcus and blocked the view of his Commander, in her compromising outfit. He glared with murderous intent at his nephew.

Marcus never blinked; he assumed the pose of one with his mind off in deep thought. He had in fact noticed Atesh's attire or more to the point, lack of it and it took all of his will power to ignore it. *If I die now I shall be a happy man.* He snapped out of his internal musings, raised his eyes to meet Ballard's and smiled. "Are you ready for breakfast Ballard? I am starved. We will be honoured if you all would accompany us and take this meal within our dining hall. The cooks have excelled themselves today with berry porridge, extra crispy bacon, large goose eggs, beef sausages, gravy, biscuits and fresh baked bread, all hot from the ovens. Oh and their amazing tomato and spiced onion relish. It's to die for."

Marcus announced these foods out loud, to gauge the knights' response. Some of the men groaned, turned a darker shade of green and held their hands over their mouths as they raced past Atesh for the bushes; to become one with nature.

Atesh threw her head back and laughed as she ran all the way to the barracks to bathe and redress. Her usual attire would be worn.

Black leather trousers, white cotton long sleeve shirt and black knee high boots. She decided to leave her hair out and tied her side braid with a red ribbon. She felt lightness to her steps today, something different in the air. As she dressed her fingers caressed her scar lines. *Why won't they disappear?* They still ached at times, as did her hips. She always knew when it was about to rain. Ballard often called her a human weather forecaster. *Master Freymore said to look forward not back. Not an easy task some days.* Atesh noticed from the corner of her eye, her pillow moving as if alive.

"Hey…Ciaran are you partaking in breakfast today?"

"Ach no thank ye lassie…I might keep ma head under this wee pillow; if ye dinna mind."

"I will come by later to make sure you are alright."

A hiccough and a plume of smoke leaked its way out from under the covering. "Ach, ma heed; the drums needs to cease."

Seeing that everyone was ready and waiting, Atesh bounced down the stairs; a grin parted her lips and her eyes sparkled with blue intensity. Ballard gave her a wink and a smirk, which she ignored.

The morning moved along at a rapid pace. Atesh and the men, who could stand assisted Ben with re-establishing his inn. New furniture arrived from Mere Town around mid-morning with compliments from the King. Ale flowed free to all workers, but most settled for herbal tea or water. The splintered wood from the broken furniture was carried back to the castle grounds for a bon fire that evening.

"What is our agenda for this afternoon Marcus? We are at your disposal sir."

"We have a meeting with the King and Master Thaddeus, which I suspect will take a while. Then Atesh, I was hoping for a favour."

"Oh and what might that be sir?"

"Well…the men and I would like to learn the knights' exercises and forms."

Atesh and Ballard looked at each other. Ballard raised his eyebrow, indicating…your decision boss; Atesh shrugged her shoulders and smiled.

"May I enquire as to why, Marcus?"

"Well, our performance yesterday was dismal. I noticed the difference between the knights and my men in skill and stamina, there is a vast gap."

"I am sure we can accommodate you Marcus, but I am only willing to teach the King's personal regiment at the moment. Time and permission would be required from the academy for anything more. It takes a lot of constant dedicated practice. So we shall start with exercises to build up muscle and flexibility and work from there. Is that agreeable?"

"Yes absolutely Atesh. I have one hundred and fifty in my regiment. So we can start with the officers and then we can incorporate the rest of the men. Perhaps one day we can integrate a version of this within the soldier's general training."

"Small steps Marcus, let us see how we go with this group first. Have the officers watch the evening service, then all your men to watch the morning routine. We can work out the specifics this afternoon in my office, if you like."

"Oh…I near forgot. Tomorrow I have been charged with escorting Queen Brianna and the family from the harbour back here to the castle. They are docking in at Mere Town around noon. Would you and a few of your knights like to accompany us?"

"So how many are a few Marcus?

"Four to six will be fine, add a bit of colour to our poor looking group."

"Sure, it would be a pleasure."

"Great, well come along Aiden, we must not tarry any longer. We shall meet you at the command room this afternoon, unless of course you would like to deal with the village guards?"

"No thank you. They have a better chance of staying in one piece if you administer their justice Marcus, best of luck."

"Oh Atesh, before we head off. I was wondering about a games tournament tonight at the fire pit. Thaddeus has a couple of the older games of chances we could borrow. Say… your two best players against ours. Then the final match for the ultimate, 'Game Master' of Beaumont Castle."

"Yes, we accept your challenge sir." Atesh smiled and nodded in reverence.

Commander Marcus and Captain Aiden strode away in rhythm to the castle.

Atesh and Ballard wandered back through the castle grounds.

"Are you up for it, old boy?"

"Of course; you know we are unbeatable. Though I am not that old you know; I have a weathered look…maturity." Ballard patted his face and smiled.

"Yes, much like cheese that is left to age. Crumbly and worn on the outside, but soft and gooey on the inside…oh and with a pungent odour to match."

"You are getting cheekier you know, hmmm…perhaps you are not too old to go across my knee."

"I am boss remember, you're my slave. Not the other way around."

"Ha, ha, slave is it now. Oh…I must have erred in raising you somehow." Ballard feigned a wounded heart.

"Come on my brave weathered warrior. I would like to check on Kayne, do you want to tag along?"

"Changing the subject are we now, good move. Certainly, I feel sort of strange not attending to Caesar. It's unnatural, don't you think?"

"Yes I agree. How else do you create that special bond; to be one with your steed?"

Ballard gave Atesh a friendly push on her arms. "Ooh…you get to meet the father this afternoon and the mother tomorrow. Watch out, they will have you wedded before you can blink."

"What do you mean wedded? To whom are you referring…not Marcus? He is to be the next High King silly. I am a commoner, worse a foundling with no parents or ancestry to speak of. Get a grip man." Atesh shoved him back and laughed at the absurdity of it all.

"Ballard's face turned serious. I know a man in love when I see it Atesh. He is smitten, caught in the web, bitten by the bug. So either encourage him or end his misery."

Atesh stood stunned for a minute. She was frozen to the spot with eyes widened. "I have not said, nor done anything inappropriate, have I? I…um…what should I do?"

"Atesh you are so much more than a commoner. You are the Supreme Commander of the greatest warriors in Sofala. You are indeed his match in every way and act with more courage and honour than a lot of royal brats, I once knew. Please never belittle yourself for being a foundling. You are my daughter in my eyes and that must count for something; right?"

Atesh looked up at Ballard; a single tear ran down her cheek. "Thank you Pappy." She snuggled in for a big man cuddle. "I love you too, you know old cheese ." Atesh turned to walk away from the stables. "I think I will check on Ciaran. See you after." She sauntered up to her room and closed the door behind her. Her mind going over all the conversations she had ever had with Marcus. *Is it true? Was I too friendly ? Did I lead him on? What if he takes one, close look at me and is appalled . If I can never accept how I look, then how can I expect anyone else to want, or love me? No, I will put a stop to this now before it gets out of hand. I shall not encourage him; it's the best way.*

Ballard shook his head as he strolled up to the stables. With a curry comb in hand, he started his usual daily pampering session. Ballard spoke of all manner of subjects to his best friend and often Caesar nodded his head in agreement. "Women are a mystery to me Caesar. Do you think us poor souls will ever work them out? They are such complex creatures."

Atesh met Ballard later down in the sitting room and they walked in silence to the castle. Atesh had composed herself and acted like nothing had been spoken about. They were met at the entrance to the command centre by Aiden and Marcus and escorted into the large room. Atesh noticed the beautiful carved wooden table that extended the length of the room. Lying on top was a large map of this side of the known world before the great divide. The walls were decorated with all manner of weaponry; old and new. Standing up from the two comfortable chairs next to the open fire was Gareth Beaumont and Master Thaddeus Freymore.

Marcus performed the introductions. " The Supreme Commander of the *'Pace Knights'* Atesh Ashmourne , I would like to introduce the High King, Gareth Beaumont."

Atesh went down on one knee with head bowed.

"Please Atesh." Gareth moved forward as she rose and shook her arm in the academy manner, but held on a little longer than felt comfortable and stared in her eyes. Atesh could feel her cheeks warm and flame.

"Sire" pulling away his father's gaze. " This is Captain Ballard of the *'Pace Knights'* First Battalion."

Ballard also knelt down on one knee. As he rose, Gareth stepped up close and pulled him into a man hug.

"I cannot believe it. Look how you have grown. Bigger than your father I'll bet. All these years and you never visited? You do know you will always be family Ballard?"

Gareth turned to look at Atesh with a cheeky smile on his face, a similar feature to his son. He placed his arm around Ballard's shoulder. "You know Commander, this little monkey ran away from home when he was no more than seven years old and stowed away on his father's ship. They had brought Anna, his elder sister over to Sofala to marry me. He found his way to the academy and begged them to accept him. His father always described him as knight crazy, much like our young Israe. It must be in the blood...I am glad you found your place in this world Ballard. Having two older brothers and two older sisters must have been a trial for any man."

Marcus coughed to interrupt his father's tales. "I believe we are all acquainted with Master Thaddeus Freymore." They all bowed their head to the Wizard Master. "Right then, so let's have a look at what you have here for us sire."

Atesh felt awkward the whole session. She felt three sets of eye's boring into her. She studied the map with extra thoroughness, as she was afraid if she looked up; she would meet one or more set of those eyes. "Sire, can we indicate where all the abductions have taken place. What or who was taken and denote in a different way...say with a cross where the other creature sightings have occurred. There may be a pattern." Atesh pointed to each different part of the map.

"Very sound strategy." Master Thaddeus nodded as he surveyed the map.

"We need more information Father, perhaps a trip around the north west side to account for abductions and sightings. We could travel as far as the North Mede village and then split into two groups and spread out on either side of the Meder River. We should meet back down at the river junction." Marcus pointed at the map where the river then separates into two smaller streams. The first headed east to the Meder billabong and Jangly river system, the second where the Meder River narrows into a smaller stream and runs down past the Beaumont castle. "We should stick close by the river, as the mountain ranges can be treacherous this time of year; snow will be appearing on the high peaks. This may take around five to six days. I also believe Atesh, your new friends may be there somewhere."

Thaddeus weighed into the conversation. "I can contact Elias at the academy and gather information from the east side and mark the map from here."

Gareth tapped the map with his finger. "My brother, Morgan arrives tomorrow. He can fill in for the island of Tyral and the Waste Lands."

Atesh looked up at the men that surrounded her. "What about the south west of Sofala and the other lands? Have you thought of the Southern Lands and Chain Islands? There are the villages on the volcanic islands along the Archipelagos as well?"

The chattering stopped and they all looked to Atesh and then down at the map. It had finally dawned on them, recognition as to the huge task to gather information from all over the known lands. Gareth leaned over and looked at the lands outside his immediate Kingdom.

"Well, we will need to send messages to your father Ballard; he rules the Chain Islands and Southern Lands. The pirates we leave alone unless they trouble us, though I will send a message to their Chieftain Cedric."

A commotion was heard outside the room in the corridor. All heads turned as a guard knocked and excused himself. "Sire, a soldier from Janlin Village, says he needs to speak to Commander Marcus about an urgent matter."

Marcus strode out the room and left the door slightly ajar. In the corridor was one of his soldiers sent to relieve the men stationed at the Janlin village.

"What is it Sergeant? What is so important?"

The soldier's face was ashen; his hands shook in an uncontrollable tremor. "They're all gone sir. No one was there…except a soldier that had been spread over some of the town. It was gruesome, sir. Not eaten, but looks like he was dropped from a great height. He held in one hand this, his knife and attached to it was the black fur and a large grey claw. All the livestock gone as well, it…it was a ghost town, sir. We decided to lock it up and return." The soldier handed the items to Marcus.

"Give the men the night off and tell them to keep this to themselves. I will address the entire group tomorrow, thank you." He looked into the eyes of a man that had been shaken to his very core. "Look, take the men down to the Anvil Inn and have a drink and calm down."

Marcus returned to the meeting as he held something in his hands. Atesh had overheard the conversation and stood stock still and glanced at Marcus, his hands and then turned to Ballard.

"The men at Janlin village are missing, presumed abducted by the flying creatures. One soldier looks like he had tried to break free, but was too high up and died after he fell. He held this in his hand." Marcus carefully laid the knife, claw and black fur on the table.

Ballard took one look at the knife and picked it up. "This belonged to Captain Tredenick. He would have died fighting, that much I know."

"I am sorry Ballard, was he a friend of yours?"

"We worked together many years ago Marcus. He and his men at Janlin assisted us in recent times with the two rogue fire ants."

Gareth and Thaddeus were speechless. Never had they seen such an enormous claw.

"Sire, we must depart the morning after tomorrow. We cannot adjourn the information gathering till after the celebration; we cannot delay further."

Resignation firmly etched into his features and with crossed arms, King Gareth would not relent. "Marcus, we must not make haste. We need careful planning and there is a lot of ground to cover. No…you leave as scheduled, in seven days."

"I agree with your father Marcus, there is much to do in the meantime, patience please." Thaddeus implored. "Atesh, I would like to see you for a few moments in my rooms when we finish here."

Atesh nodded to Master Thaddeus, but wondered what he had to discuss in private.

They finalised routes and message arrangements, then all left to go their separate ways. Ballard headed off with Marcus and Aiden to organise stores and duties for the impending journey. Then arrange for the regiments new exercise routines. Gareth strode off towards his office. Master Thaddeus and Atesh walked in silence to his apartment.

"Please take a seat by the fire. Would you like a drink my dear?"

"No thank you Master Thaddeus. What would you like to speak to me about?"

"Well Atesh, we…that is my brother and I…believe your eighteenth birthday is sooner than you believe. Elias has watched your powers grow and was concerned that the time of your turning was at hand. I concur with his assessment. That is why Elias sanctioned the second mission, so you could have some tutorage with me. We thought we would have a bit more time together before you set off on your fact finding mission. But this is paramount what we must discuss here, now."

"What has you concerned so with my turning?"

"On an eighteenth birthday Atesh, as you know, all magical beings will experience a maturity to their inner essence. A burst, if you will that shows your true, ultimate potential. Most humans with some form of innate magic will feel energised or a slight tingling throughout their body. A few, who exhibit a bit more than the average innate essence, may experience a severe headache or pains .You however , have already displayed far more power for your age than the average acolyte wizard. Elias and I are in agreeance. We believe that on your turning, your power will manifest into an extreme level of higher magic. You will become a powerful wizard, perhaps the most powerful to inhabit this known world. For some unexplained reason within you is a convergence of inherited magical essence, never before seen?"

Atesh sat and looked at her hands as she twisted one of her rings; she closed her eyes and asked the pertinent question. "So what does this actually mean? What aren't you saying?"

"Well my dear." Master Thaddeus moved forward and held her hands. "It means at your turning, I can see only two scenario outcomes. It all has to do with the amount of power you generate and how strong your will is. The first scenario is that, it may be so extreme it will overwhelm your body and ummm…vaporise you. The second scenario is that, you may be able to control the amount of energy you build-up within your body and find a way to safely release the excess. If you can achieve this, you will become a powerful magic conduit. The consequence I am sad to say may be immortality; or the least, very long lived."

Atesh opened her eyes and stared in abject horror. "What sort of a choice is that?"

"None, I am afraid. You are a natural, born with this in your blood makeup. Unlike most wizards, you will have no need for words, incantations, a staff/wand or fancy hand movements. Your magic will work through your thoughts and emotions. Pure raw power, untamed and I am afraid; untrained at the moment."

Atesh placed her hands to her face and shook her head.

"All I can do between now and when this blessed event occurs, is encourage you to practice control with centring yourself. I can show you some extra breathing techniques and one important ritual for the day on question; to release any pent up energy. I must stress this last part Atesh! If you find the power is starting to overwhelm your body; you must release it, or die."

"How soon…when do you believe this will happen?"

"We believe you will have no more than five days, till your turning."

"Five days. How will I know when this begins? What should I look for? What if it occurs later while I am away and the date was wrong?" Tears streamed down to moisten her flushed cheeks.

"Atesh, believe in these old men, the date is not wrong. You must believe in yourself and learn to control the power or it will be fatal. Now my dear, once the turning has completed and we can assess how powerful you are; I can go through and teach you the wizard trials. Show you how to harness the power, control it and calm it down. But, I will say I have never known anyone that will be like you…in all truth; I don't know what to expect. I can say for certain you will not change; you will still be yourself, but not age as others do. Our father was considered among the most powerful of his time and he was a long lived wizard, over eight hundred years old. But from what we have read in his journals, you will have many times his power. He may have lived longer, but for the raising of the northern boundary and the energy for the crystal barrier that extinguished his life force. Both Elias and I…we are over two hundred years old. None of us changed or turned into monsters. You will learn, adapt, and perhaps perform great feats."

"You seem to have aged, how long will you live for?"

"This is a slow aging glamour Atesh. How would it look if I appeared younger than my children?"

He de-cloaked his illusion spell and there before her stood a man about the same age as Ballard. "I have quite a few more years left, the same as Elias."

Atesh was speechless. "So you do this on purpose to fool people?"

"Well I wouldn't put it as harsh as that, it is for the best."

"It will be different for me though right?" She grew pale and light headed. Thaddeus knelt in front of her chair and she fell into his arms. They stayed like that for a while, till the shock had worn off a bit.

"How can I ever marry, have children, watch them grow old and die, over and over; how do you do that?"

"It is difficult; I have been married only once; to a mortal. Both my girls have some power in them, but refused the academy. They wanted a family, not magic. But no matter, they will both live quite a while longer than their husbands. Marcus and Ballard have a great deal of innate magic, they will live long lives. Israe, I am afraid may be similar to you. He will be the next one to watch. But you know, I would not have traded one single moment I had with my beautiful wife Liera. She died too young. A freak accident took her away from me; she fell and hit her head. It was not that hard mind you, but she never regained consciousness. Loving her felt like loving a whole life time…you too will find that. My granddaughter was even named after her before she disappeared. Elias is married to the academy so to speak , he took over after our father died. Our younger brother Jimmie, he became an adventurer with his best friend Gil. They set sail one day and never returned. Life still goes on my dear."

Atesh wiped the tears that threatened to cascade down her face.

"The afternoon before, you and I will take a short trip to my sanctuary; there we will have peace and quiet to meditate and prepare. I will be with you the whole time. So, take the night off; perform your duties tomorrow and come and find me in the afternoon. We will go through your centring lessons, alright."

"Why me Master Thaddeus, I am a nobody, without family, or known ancestry. How did this come to be in my makeup?"

"One can never choose what they are given by an ancestor Atesh; even I cannot answer that one."

"Thank you for your honesty and help Master Thaddeus." Atesh turned to leave then stopped. "One little thing before I leave. When you said immortal that is from age and disease right? What if I am stabbed or attacked by a creature, can I die then?"

"Well that is an interesting thought…I will consult some of the old tomes within my library and Elias of course on this matter. I cannot say for sure Atesh, maybe we have to wait and see."

Atesh walked out with her head held high; composed. In the corridor though, out of sight, she wilted and leant up against the wall for support. She gathered her thoughts, wiped her eyes and walked with firm resolve, back to her quarters.

Atesh did not realise Marcus had been at the other end of the corridor talking to a guard when he saw Atesh exit Master Thaddeus' apartment. He watched with concern, his brows furrowed and arms crossed.

Atesh detoured at the last minute to the stables. She felt comforted when she was with Ciaran and Kayne. As she wandered in, the fresh smell of hay and horse dander welcomed her. Binji the stable boy from the anvil inn was paying a visit and laughed aloud at the antics of Ciaran, whilst he fed Kayne and Caesar carrots.

"Well good afternoon boys. Having some fun are we? No one called me to join?"

"Aye lass, this here laddie be spoiling us a wee bit."

"I am in need of some fresh air; I can drop you home if you like Binji. Give your mates something to talk about eh."

"Oh Commander, that would be swell, thank you."

They trotted out the inner castle gates and cantered slowly down the roadway to the inn. Ciaran had sat on Binji's head and whooped aloud to all they passed. This drew the young ones out from all manner of hiding places. Ciaran threw sweets down to them as they ran alongside Kayne. They then all gathered around, as Atesh assisted Binji to dismount. He was the hero amongst his peers now.

Ciaran bounced up onto Kayne's mane; he was in fine form and loved to act up when a young crowd was nearby. "I am the King of the beasts; hear me roar." Only a small squeak, a mouse would be ashamed of exited his mouth. "Hmmm…well maybe not today. But I am hungry, so I will roast you all before I devour you." Ciaran huffed and puffed till his face went red and blotchy, then blew with all his might. Different coloured smoke spirals flowed out from his nostrils and chased the boys around the immediate area; to their squeals and laughter of delight. Some of the adults stopped and watched the little theatrics; they laughed and clapped at the hilarity of it all. When the vapour dissipated the young lad's fell exhausted to the ground.

Atesh smiled to herself. *So young and innocent, was I ever, really like that?*

Atesh and Ciaran continued on with a wave good bye and exited the village. Once outside, Kayne's strides grew long and rapid, his hooves skimmed over the ground. They rode as one, a majestic symmetry of movement and beauty.

A short way behind, Marcus followed on his pure white ceremonial horse called Cider; she was regal and formal in her movements. Marcus had felt distress emanate from Atesh and it tore at his heart. He didn't understand the deep connection he had with the Commander. But he would not fight it either.

Kayne came to a halt down by the stream, quite a way from the castle walls. Atesh sat down crossed legged on the carpet of sweet smelling grasses and tried to centre herself. Her mind was in a jumble. All her life dreams shattered in one afternoon. She then drew her legs up to her chest; encircled them with her arms and laid her head on her knees, while tears flowed unchecked. She spoke in a quiet tone to Ciaran.

"What should I do?"

"Well lassie, do nae keen. There be no decision to make. You must learn to control this here power and deal with life, one day at a time. You do realise that I am long lived, most sentient beings are. So we will be together for a long time, eh? That's good at least…oh I believe we have company lassie. That handsome king to be is sitting a ways off. He is concerned for you."

"Yes, Ballard already gave me a lecture today. Seems Marcus thinks he is smitten with me. But I am so confused right now."

"Well lass…this part be simple. Do ye or don't ye have feelings for the laddie?"

"That's just it, when I am around him; I feel alive. My heart beats so fast, I may explode. He is so dreamy; his eyes look right into your soul. But then, he is so darn stuffy, no sense of humour, always proper. And don't forget he is to be the next High King. I am nothing, a foundling; now…I am to be an immortal wizard. Who wants to be saddled with that little gem?"

"Why don't ye find out, because here the laddie comes?"

"May I intrude on your quiet moment of solitude; I also find this place refreshing."

Atesh turned her head up to gaze into his golden flecked, sparkling eyes. "Sure Marcus, but I am not in a bright mood at the moment . I would go so far as to say, I am poor company."

"That's fine; we can at least enjoy the stream sounds together."

They sat there beside each other not a word spoken, but both longing for what they may never have. Ciaran spotted a dragon fly whizz pass his nose at great speed. He jumped off Atesh's shoulder and performed strange hopping movements to snag his prey. Both Atesh and Marcus roared with laughter. Ciaran puffed rings of smoke at them as he continued his launch and hop to catch the tormented insect.

"Atesh may I ask you a question?"

"I suppose, but depends on the question as to whether I will answer you or not."

"Fair enough…are you attracted to me at all? I know I am not a handsome man like my brother Kyle. But I feel alive around you, whole."

Atesh turned her head to look at his serious face, hands clamped tight around his legs, also pulled up to his chest.

"Why would you ask me that Marcus? Whether yes or no, you are to be the next High King, ruler of all this known land and must surely court within your station?"

"Well my father married for love both times. Though they were distant kin; he was perchance lucky. I promised myself, I would do the same. I refused long ago to have an arranged marriage…You have been the only one that has taken my breath away, stolen my heart. I know it is right"

"I am not the right one for you Marcus, believe me."

"I wondered, thought that I would enquire, if you could…ever one day, love me; not the station or the crown, me; the man?"

Atesh bowed her head and stared at her feet, she did not trust herself to speak again. Tears rolled down her cheeks unchecked. Her fists clenched ashen.

Marcus nodded his head with painful resignation; his heart broken. He didn't understand why she would not say more. As he walked away, on the wind he heard a faint whisper.

"I already do love you."

He stood still for the briefest moment, not quite believing what he had heard, though his heart knew alright. It pounded through his chest with force, as he walked back to his horse. A smile spread across his face.

Chapter 17

The New Apprentice:

The transfer from the northern border camp to the island of mist-wick was quick and painless for Captain Danurel; unlike the knights that would arrive soon. He was taken to his suite by Mason. It was three stories of pure luxury.

"Welcome to Castle Grey on the invisible island of Mist-Wick, Master Dan." Mason opened his arms wide and spun in a circle; a large grin adorned his face. "Please take your time and explore. You will notice the rooms are much larger on the inside than they appear from the outside, a little perk living with a high wizard. If you need me, just holler out; I will hear you, though I shall return soon with some supper."

Danurel felt amazed at his new destiny. He surveyed each area and noted all. There was a private bathing room and garderobe where all the spouts were automated and plumbed. In the main bedroom was the largest four poster bed he had ever seen and all the robes were filled with clothes for all occasions. Two other guest rooms were similar in style. The enormous windows looked out over the right side of the island, with its lush bush land that led down to the ocean. The next level up held a large sitting room with an open fire place with the usual adornments of couches spread out. Then off to one side was a reading room; stacked with all manner of books, which then led into an even larger office. This whole floor opened out onto a large open terrace. *This would be perfect for entertaining.*

He climbed up the elaborate carved wooden staircase to the third level. This held the most exciting room of all; his work area. Tables and a few chairs only graced this room, so far. His mind spun with all the possibilities to his new life, as he sauntered down to the bottom level. He walked out onto the intimate balcony, off his bedroom and gazed at the moon. It was full, bright and smiled down on him. He was high up on one of the castle towers. He watched the waves as they glistened with the moonlight's reflection and pounded against the island rocks. He wondered why he could not see the fog that surrounded the island that kept all intruders away. He felt invigorated with the sea air filling his lung and inhaled deeply. *I had not realised how that whole academy of incompetent fool's, sucked the life out of me. I intend on revenge someday, but I will bide my time and learn all. This was a solemn oath; I pledge to you lady moon.* A knock at his door woke him from his musing.

Mason announced himself and entered. "Your supper Master Dan; I am sure you didn't eat too much at the other feast tonight." A cheeky grin adorned his face.

"Thank you Mason, this is more than I ever dreamed. It is real, right?"

"Oh yes sir, this is all real. The Master would see you at breakfast. I will come and wake you in time."

Dan thought he would rest a while after his splendid meal; he was not really in a sleep mood at all. The next moment, Mason had opened the curtains and the sun streamed in.

"The Master will be at breakfast in short order. I will return and escort you."

Mason walked spritely for a mature gent; he escorted Dan down many flights of stairs to the ground floor and out onto the large shaded deck. The Master sat facing the ocean, his back to his guest until he heard their boots on the stone decking. He turned around and smiled as he watched Danurel walk straight and enthusiastically up to him arm out-stretched for a hand shake.

Master Grey grabbed the forearm as they do at the academy, whilst he watched Danurel's face. "Welcome, welcome dear boy. I have looked forward to this day for quite some time."

Danurel stared up at the master. He had paled somewhat, his eyes widened in apprehension. "Th…Thank you Master…it is an honour and a pleasure."

The two men locked eyes; Master Grey wondered what had frightened this poor fellow. Yes, he was rather a large man. Tall by any standard and maintained his physique. He still practiced his forms, when he remembered. All the men in his family were solid built. His hair and beard, he had trimmed from its long and unruly state. Maybe it was his eyes; yes they were black now and endless when you looked into them; so he had been informed. The best thing he ever did though was to change his name; he was now invisible to the outside world. "Is there something wrong Danurel?" An innocent expression adorned his face, whilst he raised one eyebrow in a questioning manner. "You look like you have seen a ghost."

"No sir, perhaps a bit over whelmed. I am…I cannot wait to commence my training Master."

"Well then, sit dear boy and have some wonderful breakfast. Share the morning peace and quiet with me."

They sat in silence until Mason delivered the most amazing breakfast; they then started with small talk, mainly about the island. Dan soon relaxed as he was determined to enjoy the experience. His shock however was still there, held in the recesses of his mind. As the inhabitants of the island awoke to the morning; noises and smells, both familiar and unknown, assaulted his senses.

"Has Mason explained what we do here, our purpose?"

"No Master, Sir. We really didn't have that much time."

"Please Dan call me Master Grey, that's the name I prefer, an old nickname of sorts."

He placed down his mug and sat forward toward Dan. "Well we perform quite a few functions here, but we will get to that in time. I can promise you this; you will accomplish great feats and have wonderous adventures. You will learn of magic from ancient times and become more powerful and richer than you ever dreamed possible. There is so much to do and accomplish. What I will tell you is that a small part of our function here is to make the war strategy board game, called 'Chances'."

"You…make board games?" Dan almost felt let down, his heart skipped a beat. He gave up a life of fighting for this? He tilted his head forward a bit in thought, closed his eyes and placed his thumb and forefinger to his nose. It did not take him long though. He jerked his head up with a questioning look. "You are the Game Master?"

"Indeed I am Danurel." He looked deep into the young man's eyes.

"But sir, why do you need an apprentice if you make games and why the strange flying creatures?"

Master Grey leaned in further, to be closer to Dan. "You have seen and played the latest games Dan?"

"Yes sir, I have."

Did you ever wonder how I create the game pieces, the unusual creatures and how they all move, be interactive, eh?" He leant so close now to Dan that his breath was felt on the side of his face and heard…one of the secrets to the game.

Dan felt frozen in time; his breath squeezed out of his lungs. The world he had known imploded . He looked into Master Grey's piercing black eyes. There was silence again; while Dan digested the information he had been given . *So that is why there were so many weird creatures behind the northern boundary, the left over's, it had to be.* "H…how do you…"

"All in good time my dear boy; we have all the time in the world. So are you in or out?"

"Oh Master Grey, I am definitely in, no doubts at all. I am over-whelmed and amazed at your brilliance."

"Did Mason explain about the consequences once you start your training? Do not forget, the breaking of your blood oath from the academy? Don't look so concerned Dan, we are not into necromancy in our day to day activities but, we do dabble in ancient magic, long ago rejected by the academy. Once you commence there is no going back."

Dan looked at his ring that was fused to his finger on his right hand. "I had forgotten about the oath; I must admit. But what are you referring to? Surely with your great magic we can get around the consequences. It's not like my finger will drop off or anything like that ?"

"Well…I am afraid that is exactly what will occur. Dan there is nothing I can do about it. We must all suffer to attain our freedom."

Dan looked ill now; he stared at his finger with abject horror. "H…ow…how long will it take sir?"

"Well it will be different for each oath breaker; the ring will get tighter and tighter, eventually cutting off the blood supply. Then the ring and your finger will disintegrate to nothing. We can administer pain relief for you, but the fever and deliriums that accompany this event are not pleasant."

"Can you not cut the finger off before it all starts?"

"The magic will not allow that to happen. I am sorry dear boy, but this is the penalty that you must pay for your dreams." The Master leaned over and patted Danurel's hand. "It will turn out fine in the end, I promise. We all get what we deserve." *Oh Mason what have you given me to work with? He is not only a kiss-ass, but a lily-liver as well; no backbone.*

Dan looked down at the large calloused hand that patted his own and noticed one of the master's fingers missing.

The day seemed rather long and Danurel kept looking down at his hand. Mason showed him around the inside of the castle. He introduced Mistress Maisey and her new assistant who had a rather blank, no one at home look about him. In fact most of the workers seemed the same way. They worked hard, spoke little to each other, but when addressed, they were polite and eager to please. The grounds were extensive with some strange creatures wondering around. Mason introduced him to the leader of the Gatherers Abi, then to the Troldwite leader, Kroll. He explained the areas not to venture alone, as some of the Troldwites could not be trusted. There were a few outer building that were off bounds, with no explanations given.

"Where may I ask are the knights held Mason?"

"Master Dan, don't be concerning your-self about them now. They are being taken care of." Mason sniggered, as he licked his lips.

This sent a shudder up through Dan's spine. *What if I had said no to the master? I would be creature food now too.* As they walked around the perimeter of the island, Dan noticed a small old wooden cross near the edge to one of the cliffs. It had fresh flowers at its base. He decided later he would ask Mason about that, he did not want to push his luck with being too nosey today. Mason then showed him the many floors and rooms within the castle. Ground floor held the servants' quarters and two kitchens. A large dining room, sitting room, library and many other doors, they did not investigate. Then there were four distinct tower suites. Dan had the right side one. The Master had the largest overlooking the front and left side of the island. Mason had one on the left back and a guest suite in the rear tower. Two other towers were not mentioned.

"You may explore anywhere you like within the castle, but the Master's suite of course and the lower levels. They are too dangerous to venture down without a guide."

"Lower levels? Mason how many levels are there?"

"Oh it goes down into the bowels of the dirt Master Dan; very extensive. The Master will escort you the first time and explain what all the rooms are for. I believe you will need to practice some of your spells in the safety of these rooms; they are enhanced with high magic for that wizard learning, you will be doing."

A short time after dinner, Mason knocked on the door. "Excuse me sir, but the Master has a small job for us to do."

They arrived at the top of the stairs to the Master's internal workshop, knocked and entered.

"Ah good, would you mind going and seeing what is making the racket with the mist alarm. Something or someone has approached uninvited? Take the small skiff from the underground pier. Thanks boys." Master Grey turned back to scribbling in his journal.

Danurel and Mason wound their way down to the pier that was found beneath the castle foundations. A sailor manning the skiff awaited them. They exited a large cavernous area, to the open sea. They bobbed on the gentle rhythmical waves till they saw a man on his back, barely holding onto a large branch or piece of wood. He appeared to be asleep, but as they drew closer; they could see he was scant alive.

Dan held a lantern high to get a closer look at the half submerged figure and gasped. "What in all the ancients is he doing here? Quick now, help me drag him aboard."

"You know this man, Master Dan?"

"He is one of Commander Atesh's knights; they should be in the west at Beaumont Castle by now. He has been wounded and is burning up."

Opening his eyes, Jesper looked up at Danurel and smiled. "I know you…will I be alright now?" He closed his eyes in relief and the darkness enveloped him again.

"Yes Jesper we will look after you." Dan smiled a wicked grin, sniggered and then looked over at Mason, shrugged his shoulders and lifted his eye brows, "What?"

"Ah, this must be the soldier Abi lost in the northern woods. He assumed the wolves had dragged him off to be eaten. He will be pleased to know he was not a complete failure to the Master."

"You attacked Commander Atesh's unit over near the Beaumont Castle. What was Abi thinking? Have you any idea who you will be dealing with now? He was not just any soldier, but a knight from the first battalion; the Supreme Commander's handpicked warriors. Atesh will be like a dog with a bone, she never gives up. This is not good, not good at all." Dan shook his head in disbelief.

"Well you see this is another reason why I picked you Master Dan, inside information. Do not worry, no one will ever find us here. We are invisible to the world; all they see is the fog bank, no one dares enter on purpose."

Dan looked at the confidence on Mason's face and relaxed. "Fine then, though I would like to have seen Atesh's face when one of her own went missing, it would have been priceless. Shame she is so darn gorgeous, watching her perform the forms makes you lust; oh, and her eyes drink you in, caress you and you become lost. But, if you get too close, go the next step, wham…she spits you out like pig's swill. She spurned me you know, led me on being friendly and all. She was the Master's pet. So they gave her the Supreme Commander's position over me. A girl, ha! Now who has the better deal my dear?" He laughed out loud all the way back to the pier.

Chapter 18

Boys to Men:

Marcus returned from the stables, his heart had pounded with ardour within his chest; all the way back to the castle. *I know I heard that! There is hope after all.* He decided to borrow the old war games for the tournament tonight. This gave him the excuse to visit his grandfather and have a little chat. He strode up the stairs two at a time; his long muscled legs straddled them with ease. He arrived at his destination, then knocked on the door and entered as he was bid.

"Ah, my dear boy, what brings you to see this old codger, on a glorious afternoon?"

"Grandfather…I need to know, what is the problem with Atesh? I feel her hurt and confusion in my soul. Why was she upset after seeing you this afternoon? Now, before you try and weasel your way out of this. I saw her leave here. I implore you, please tell me the truth."

"Come and sit here by the fire lad and have a drink with me and tell me why you are so interested in what we discussed. Why, is it that important to you?"

"I feel unsettled when she is not happy. When we touch, it's like, small bolts of lightning going up my arm and running through my body. She feels the same; I saw it in her eyes. I feel alive when I am near her. I want to protect her. I am sure; I am in love with Atesh. She is the one I choose for my wife. I will have no other…ever; I know this in my heart and soul."

"Oh my, you do have it bad. You feel it that deep, this connection?" *That is interesting.* "What if I told you; she is not the one for you Marcus?"

"Atesh told me that same thing; but, her posture and her eyes told me different. Why is she not the one, what can be so wrong. I know she is not of the blood line, but why should that matter. Look what she has accomplished. Everyone loves her and her men respect and worship her. They will do anything to protect her. Please, I beg you?"

"Oh Marcus, it is not for any of those reasons I say this to you. I think your father had better be here to help me explain this to you. Wait a moment and we will ask him to join us"

Thaddeus walked to the door and asked the guard to transfer a message to the King. "While we are waiting, I have news of your brother's condition. It seems Kyle has been consorting with the less than fine establishments down in Mere Town. He has a very advanced stage of bad blood."

Marcus looked at Thaddeus with questioning eyes, confusion.

"The pox, dear boy, it may have reached his brain; he is going, no gone insane. That may be the cause of his erratic behaviour. Or he is just plain mad, you know the wiring all twisted. Perchance our three royal bloodlines have been too close for too long. We have decided to place him at the Hospice in Mere Town. He is in a secure area; a special suite set up, where he will receive all the right care he needs. This is sad indeed. Such a bright boy, he didn't need to go to those lengths to find a lady. I don't understand him."

"Well I didn't know he was doing that grandfather, but I had heard he used to get a bit rough with some of the local girls; though they all refused to lay charges. Maybe that's why he went down to Mere Town. Who would dare speak out against him from a whore house?"

A knock on the door announced King Gareth; he strode in his usual strong, confident manner; devouring the floor as he walked. "Ahhh, the two schemers, what are you men up to this time, eh?" Gareth sat down in the third chair in between the two men; where a drink of fine wine was poured for him. He looked left and then right meeting the two faces and threw down the mug of wine in one go. "Oh this is going to be a doosey…I can feel it."

"Gareth, your son has asked a question. One I feel better answered by you sire."

"Oh it is one of those 'sire' type questions, is it?"

"Father, I wish permission to court and wed Commander Atesh. She is my one; my soul mate. What is the problem that is placed in our way? Grandfather will not tell me. Atesh will not tell me. Please can you tell me?"

"Well son, how does Atesh feel about you, surely she has a say in all this too."

"She told me she was not the right one for me; yet her eyes tell me different. Every time they meet, she sees into my soul. She sees me the man, not the prince or the commander. I know she feels the same way. I feel like I have come home when I am around her. But I know there is a heavy burden she carries; a barricade I cannot penetrate. I am feeling uneasy, what is wrong that you are not telling me?"

Gareth and Thaddeus looked at each other for a long minute and nodded.

"Alright son, so be it."

"Thaddeus stood up and paced while he spoke to Marcus. "Atesh will experience her turning in five days' time. Like we all went through, if you remember. You had bit of a rough time, as you have a good deal of innate magic within you Marcus."

"Yes I remember, not that pleasant. So…."

"Elias and I believe as Atesh has displayed so much power already for a natural that the turning will…have one of two effects on her. It may actually be so powerful that it will kill her, or it will turn her into a very powerful being."

"How powerful, what are you saying?" He turned his eyes to Gareth.

"Son, she will be the most powerful being in this known land."

"But, surely that is not a bad outcome, is it father?"

"Son, a person that powerful may…well…become…immortal."

"You mean immortal, like forever, nothing can kill her…can this be true? And the other outcome, how can you prevent this from happening? Can you help her with any of this grandfather?"

"Yes, I will be guiding her in lessons and the ritual to release extra energy; this is why we did not want her going on a mission till after the event. We will go to my sanctuary the afternoon prior and stay there till it is over; one way or the other."

Marcus sat quiet for a moment, "So this was why she was upset this afternoon. Why she wants to keep me at arm's length. She will not turn into a monster…anything unnatural."

"No nothing strange, just very powerful."

"Well then, where is the problem?"

Gareth and Thaddeus both shook their heads at Marcus.

Gareth closed his eyes, his hand rested on the side of his face. "You do have it bad son, you can certainly pick them."

"Are you positive on the date, in five days' time?"

"Yes Marcus absolutely positive."

"As a foundling, how can you be so sure of her day of birth?" Marcus stared at Thaddeus.

"Elias and I have discussed it at length; trust in us Marcus, the date is correct."

Marcus saw a look though brief, pass between the two men. He stood and walked to the window, glanced at the soldiers below, gathering the wood for the bon fire tonight. "Strange isn't it that both Aiden and Atesh turn eighteen on the same day?" He turned slow and fixed his eyes on his father. He felt the bile rising from the pit of his stomach; all his muscles tightened. His fists were clenched at his sides.

"How long have you both known?"

"What do you refer to son?"

"Father, do not treat me as a fool. Is Atesh…my missing cousin?"

Gareth closed his eyes for a moment and steeled himself to answer this awkward question. "Yes, Thaddeus and I believe this to be so."

"That is why she will be so powerful, with your blood line and history running through her veins, eh Grandfather."

"I am afraid that may be part of the case Marcus."

"Does she know?"

"No! She must not be given any more information that could jeopardise her mental state at the moment. Any further revelations and she may not be able to concentrate at the crucial moment. Remember, this may kill her. There is a fifty-fifty chance. I have never assisted anyone this powerful before. But I promise you…I will do my utmost to bring her back safe."

Marcus looked ashen; he felt all the blood drain out of his face, leaving it cold and lifeless. "What about Aiden. Does he have a lot of innate power? I know he often looks at Atesh with a strange expression on his face. I wonder what he senses."

"He is the same as most of your kin; he will feel a bit unusual on the day, nothing he cannot handle. Israe is the only other with a lot more power, sending him to the academy soon will be for his best chance. He will be a great wizard-knight like Atesh."

"So son, do you still feel the same about Atesh, now you are aware of the barriers you must face?"

"Nothing has changed at all for me, except now I will turn grey on the night of the celebration. But I give my oath; I will not say a word. So father, what do you say to my courting and wedding Atesh after all this drama is over with?"

"Well son, I can see you have made up your mind. Let's agree to see how this all turns out first. Then, only if she is willing, I will agree to discuss it further. That is all I am willing to give at this point in time."

"Agreed father," Marcus smiled; his whole face now illuminated the room. He bowed to both men and went to walk out the room, before the door he turned straight and confident.

"Grandfather, may I borrow the older versions of chances. We have challenged the knights to a tournament tonight, for the title of 'Game Master of the Beaumont Castle' at the bonfire. Please, both of you join us for a drink later when you have time."

"Certainly Marcus, the games are in my office next door on the top shelf, help yourself. Yes, we may see you later, thank you."

After Marcus had departed, packages arrived from the village jeweller to Master Thaddeus. The stones given by Queen Mia had been set and completed as requested.

"Perfect time too, I believe this arm band may help keep Atesh safe. The tear sliver, I will imbed tomorrow, as Mia instructed."

"Oh please." Gareth held up his hand. "Do not tell me where you intend to place it. My mind can conjure up all sorts of scenarios, without your help." They chuckled at what might be.

"You are a bad influence of me sire. Well at least we have a good excuse to visit the bonfire for a drink or two, don't you think?" Thaddeus patted the packages.

"Oh children, I wish we could somehow cushion the blow of life's lessons on them Thad; I feel a heartbreak coming on."

"Yes Gareth, I fear Marcus forgets she is a knight; first and foremost. That is her life and what ever happened to her as a child has had a great impact on her psychological wellbeing. Elias informs me she has spurned all the men that dare to get too close. Her exterior persona is a far cry from the interior."

"I noticed she is focused, perhaps to the point of obsession. Maybe she needs love to heal?"

Thaddeus nodded, but stroked his close shaven beard in thought.

Gareth reached for the wine jug, "I believe another drink is in order. If my darling wife does not arrive home soon, I fear I may become a drunkard. She has a way of calming the demons in my mind. Take this last hour for instance. That was certainly an awkward moment. I must confess…I don't do awkward well, especially with my family."

"Yes, Marcus took it rather well. Fancy him putting all the pieces together so quick. He is a logical thinker, perhaps one day a great strategist and a smart King; eh Gareth?"

"We can only hope. Oh nice wine by the way, is it a special vintage, Thaddeus?"

"Oh, of that I am not sure. The wine was a present from the Wine Guild. A merchant of some note; a Master Briens I believe; left a few cases for the knights. They sent one over for you; it's in your office and another for me. Apparently Atesh and her men saved his caravan and family last week from a creature attack."

"Great, here is a toast to Atesh, the knights and family."

"Agreed Sire, to our extraordinary family"

After Marcus had left his grandfather's rooms, he wandered back to his suite. He muddled through all the discussions; everything he had been told. *Well I can understand now, why she could not give me a direct answer, the poor thing. If only I could comfort her.* He placed the two old games on the wooden writing table in his drawing room to await the tournament tonight. He then wandered into his bed chamber. There beside his bed were two large wooden crates. On closer inspection the Ashmourne academy emblem had been stamped into the top of each. A scrolled parchment written in fine script was addressed to him. Master Elias had written a detailed explanation of the items enclosed. Inside there were two, gold threaded, double stitched saddlebags. Both with the King's crest embroidered on the right side and their individual initials on the left bags. One was a birthday gift as requested by Marcus for his cousin. The second was a special thank you to Marcus, from Atesh and Ballard. A full Commander 's travel kit was placed within each right side bag. A list of contents was also attached . These were the gifts from the first battalion . There were also two small jewellery boxes from Master Elias Freymore. He was very fond of his great nephews. Atesh can explain how to activate these presents and recharge them.

A second message explained, as a reward to the King's first regiment, for dedication to their duty and assisting the knights in their time of need; the soldiers will each receive a knight's saddle bag and travel kit. One hundred and fifty in all and they should arrive within the next few days. Marcus sat down heavy in the chair opposite his bed; he read the message twice to ensure it was real. *Now this has placed me in a dilemma. I hate waiting to open gifts. Worse, I can never wait to give them either. Oh...that will mean I cannot use mine till Aiden receives his, no! This just won't do. I must find him and give him the choice.*

Marcus raced outside and found Aiden talking with Ballard and the Knights. "Ballard, do you mind if I borrow Aiden for a moment?"

"No, of course I don't mind Marcus, I was thinking of looking for Atesh anyway."

Marcus held Aiden by the arm and guided him away from the crowd. "Aiden I have a dilemma that I need your assistance with."

Aiden narrowed his eyes, arms crossed ready. "Yes sir. How may I assist?"

"Well…say you knew someone's gift arrived early, prior to their celebration day. Should they receive it early or wait till the appropriate day?"

Aiden put on a most serious face. "Well Commander, it would depend on two things. First…if it was too good to keep as a secret and if I didn't hand it over, I would bust my buttons. And secondly, if and only if, I got to play with the item as well; then it is cause for an early consideration. Are any of these the case?" Aiden turned his frown into a smug , cheeky smile . He knew his cousin would be tormented by this dilemma.

"Well Aiden I would have to say yes, to both conditions."

"Well Marcus all I can recommend is…" and he bolted for the castle as fast as his legs would carry him, before Marcus could utter a word. Aiden yelled as he kept on running. "I'll race you to your rooms."

Marcus having longer legs than Aiden, soon caught up as they entered the castle. They took the stairs two at a time striding as fast as possible. They pushed, shoved and laughed up the corridor till they reached Marcus's suite.

The guards chuckled at the antics when there was a scramble for the door lever. "Boys will be boys." One whispered to the other.

Aiden's neck was by this time, firmly ensconced under his Commander's armpit. His teeth bared ready to chomp his way free, as his finger's scrambled to unlock the door first.

Gareth and Thaddeus both popped their heads out into the corridor when they heard the commotion and what felt like a heard of wild beasts thundering past their room. Two of their own streaked past like the wind, with the wildest looks on their faces. They followed at a quiet distance, eager to see what had the boys in such a dither.

Once they managed to push their way inside, Marcus made Aiden sit in his drawing room and close his eyes. A difficult feat since he would not stop fidgeting. Marcus strode into his bed chamber. He noticed his father and Thaddeus at the opened entrance, as they leant on the walls watching. The King's two personal guards peeked over their heads through the door as well.

"Right then, happy eighteenth birthday cousin, you may open your eyes now."

On the floor in front of Aiden were two parcels; one small jewellery box atop a large wooden crate. He used his knife to pry open the crate and gasped when he looked at the contents. His eyes widened as his hands were careful to unveil the prize; a beautiful set of black saddle bags, golden stitched with the King's emblem on one bag and his initials on the other. Gasps also came from the four faces at the door.

"Is that what I think it is?" Gareth moved in closer to inspect.

Aiden looked at his uncle, then the others with raised eyebrows. Marcus portrayed innocence, whilst a large grin adorned Thaddeus's face.

Aiden was confused. "Am I missing something? They are the most beautiful saddle bags I have ever seen but…"

"Aiden dear boy, have a closer look. They are made at the Ashmourne academy."

Gareth knelt down in front and looked over the fine saddler work. "If I may, Aiden watch this." He opened the buckle on one of the bags and placed his hand inside. His arm continued to be eaten up by the gaping maw that was once a saddle bag; it disappeared up to his shoulder.

Aiden jumped up, "What…how…where did your arm go sire?"

Gareth, Thaddeus and Marcus chortled so hard, tears welled within their eyes.

Thaddeus bent over to relieve his side spasm. "This is one of the best kept secrets of the academy, son. It is a knight's magic saddle bag. All you ever wanted to carry will fit in on this side where your initials are embedded. The other side is for your military kit."

Gareth opened the other side and pulled out a short letter and a list of interesting items stored within. "OH MY, packed already with an all-inclusive Commander's kit. And a bottomless shoulder bag for short journeys."

"Did you never wonder where the knights' supplies were kept Aiden, when we saw no wagons at their camp? All in their saddle bags everything, tents, kitchen, bedrolls, and extra swords…the works."

"Wow, this is the best present ever, thank you Marcus. Oh and I must thank Atesh and the knights for the kit, the letter explains this was their contribution to my gift."

Aiden explored like a child, both sides with *'oohs' and 'ahh's,'* as he found all sorts of interesting items stored within.

Marcus returned from his room and announced to all. "Have a look at what I also received."

Aiden *whooped* as well. "This is indeed a great day."

"There is one more present to open from great Uncle Elias."

Marcus handed the small jewellery box to Aiden. Inside was a ring with a perfect eight sided, translucent, channel setting crystal.

"This is amazing. Is it like the ones the first battalion wears?"

Thaddeus gave it a quizzical look. "Oh Aiden you are certainly in the favour of my brother Elias. I can feel this ring will enhance your innate magic, with strength and agility, plus a few other little surprises. You have family and friends who love you dearly. A lucky young man indeed."

"How does it work grandfather? Do I have to wait till my turning, before I can use this?"

"No my boy, Atesh can show you how to use this, activate it and recharge it."

"Damn wish someone would love me that much." Gareth leaned over to Thaddeus with a cheeky grin and whispered in his ear. "Bit of a hint to be sure."

"Well Aiden, did I make the correct decision."

A big cousin hug ensued. "You are the best."

"Actually sire all your first regiment will be given a set of knights' saddlebags with a standard military kit. Not as spiffy as ours, but magical all the same. They are a gift from Uncle Elias and his men."

Gareth stared at Marcus, "You jest, surely?"

"No it's true, they will arrive within the week…isn't that some-thing?"

The boys repacked their bags and headed out into the corridor to show them off.

All in the vicinity heard a '*whoop*' from the King's sitting room. His head popped out into the corridor. "I have saddle bags too."

Thaddeus clapped his hands together in applause. "See Gareth, you are loved, almost as much."

Everyone was beaming with delight. Marcus watched Thaddeus smile and nod his head. He knew being from the academy he would already have one hidden somewhere. *That sneaky old codger, I wonder what else he has hidden?*

Chapter 19

Games under Foot:

Marcus, Aiden and the other officers all watched the knights working through their evening routines. Ballard always led these evening sessions and he had explained it was a schedule made of exercises; to strengthen, stretch and enhance flexibility. They would then perform the centering skills; being one with the self and with the sword. This allowed the weapon to become an extension of the arm; not a separate entity. Slow methodical movements, elegant and peaceful were executed, all in harmony with the world. They recited their pledge and bowed in remembrance of the fallen.

Ballard strode over and enlightened the curious onlookers. "The evening sessions quieten the body's rhythms down, so you can sleep. But it keeps your preparedness on a slow burn, ready to ignite at any given moment. The exercise routines you will see and learn in the morning will promote activity. They limber up your muscles and remove the night's stiffness and cobwebs. The forms will ensure your feet and swords work in tune with the body. It is a holistic approach to being a soldier. We were taught at the academy that to be an effective weapon you require the mind, body and soul to be as one; a synergistic effect." Ballard noticed Marcus and the officers' furrowed brows, confused. "That means each of the three areas: the mind, the body and the soul as a separate entity, cannot defeat an enemy alone. You must have all the parts working in harmony together, to be as strong as you can be."

They each thought about it for a moment and all came to same conclusion.

"Of course Ballard, we cannot defeat an enemy with our strategy alone or a mindless sword swing or merely wanting them to die. Yes, we must make sure it all works together."

"Correct Marcus, but we go a bit further and ingrain it all into the unconscious mind. What our professors called the psyche and in doing so, it becomes natural instinct. We can therefore perform it faster, with absolute precision." Ballard then utilised his legs and arm gestures in slow motion; emphasising each movement. "You will find after a while when you spar or fight an enemy, the feet movements come naturally and balance can be easily adjusted. It is the dance of life."

Marcus addressed his officers. "In the morning you will observe the routine and then divide into groups with a knight to supervise each. Aiden has the teams organised and Atesh will lead the training. Then before lunch some of us will head to Mere Town for escort duty. The rest shall stay and practice, till our return. Now, I believe we have a bonfire to start and then the *'Game Master'* battles begin."

Atesh came over to join the officers' discussion. "I see someone could not wait to hand over the birthday gifts. Did you like the added touches Aiden?"

"Oh indeed Atesh, I am speechless." He gave her a big hug; they both felt a cold breeze rush up their spines. As they parted they both shivered and stared at each other. "Weird right, you felt that too, Atesh?"

"Yes, like someone walked over my grave, my old tutor used to say; eerie."

"Have we met before Atesh, like years ago or something?"

"No, this is my first trip to the west, why?"

"I had a feeling almost like déjà vu."

"Oh Aiden, I thought you were interested in Jenner? I um…you are a nice fellow, but you see my life is with the knights."

"Oh no, Atesh you misunderstand my intentions. Yes, Jenner is definitely special. You wouldn't happen to know if she has mentioned me at all." Aiden looked down and away, as he scuffed his boots in the stones.

"Well…as a matter of fact she has and I can tell you…definitely interested. She is generous to a fault, a brave knight and skilled healer. She has an inner light, I have seldom seen before on anyone; a rare gem Aiden."

"Thank you for that Atesh. Forget what I said before, alright."

"Sure thing…oh tonight we will practice the activation for your ring, after the game of course when we give you boys here at Beaumont a thrashing."

Ballard smiled as the two departed. "I don't believe I was once that young."

Marcus laughed and slapped Ballard on the back then returned to the castle.

The bonfire roared, the flames licked the timber in an aggressive embrace as the soldiers and their guests either sat or stood around its edges. They warmed themselves from the cool evening air. A large trestle table was set up with the older strategy board games *'Chances'* organised; one at either end. A spit roast was being devoured by all, with ale and fine wine from Master Briens. King Gareth and Master Thaddeus also joined in the festivities.

"The last night of freedom before the hoard returns tomorrow, eh Thaddeus. Let's have a toast to freedom."

"To freedom Gareth," they all raised their mugs and skulled their drinks.

Gareth then took hold of Marcus and Ballard by the arms and ushered them away from the fire.

With their heads together, Atesh thought it reminded her of a gaggle of geese, gossiping together. After a moment Atesh noted Ballard with his head bowed. Gareth placed his long, tree limb sized arm around his kin's shoulders and spoke in soft tones. *I wonder what they are talking about.*

"Sorry to tell you this tonight Ballard, but it is important the two of you be aware of what has transpired."

"A whole battalion Gareth; I cannot understand why Captain Danurel would do this?"

"Well at least one small piece of the puzzle has been worked out."

"What do you mean father?"

"Well, we now know there is a Master Wizard behind all the abductions. He uses the panther creatures' to do his dirty work; why? I cannot tell you. But in all honesty, these creatures would need to be fed. From what Elias indicated, he believes there are quite a number of them."

Ballard bowed his head and screwed his face up. "Oh, Gareth that is not right. They are to be creature food? It is enough to curdle one's stomach."

"Now this is important. Not a soul is to be informed of this, till after the celebrations. I want your word; both of you."

"But Gareth, Atesh is the Supreme Commander, not me."

"Ballard, Atesh will be leaving the day after tomorrow on a journey with Master Thaddeus and it is imperative she not be told." Gareth went on to explain his reason, in full detail.

Ballard blanched and held his head in his hands. He understood now and agreed. He pulled himself together and the three walked back to refill their mugs. Ballard eyed the set-out before him. "Right, what do we have here? Gee ancient games there Marcus; a blue and white board and a black and red board. How do you want to do this?"

Gareth mixed up four infantry men then he held two colours behind his back as did Thaddeus. Atesh picked a hand, Marcus then Ballard; Aiden had the one left over.

"It looks like, Ballard against Marcus on one board and then Aiden against Atesh on the other; the winners will then play for the crown. Not mine of course, but I am sure we can make another." Gareth decided he would explain the rules to the observers. "There are ten squares across and ten down on the game board. Each square has an alternate colour and you can only move your army on the same colour. You have ten infantry soldiers; five with swords, standing on their colour in the third row, another five with lancers lined up behind on the second row. They can move one square at a time. On the first row of the board at each end is a castle with an archer; the archer can only shoot in a straight line. Then beside each castle there is a knight seated on his war steed. They can move only two squares in any direction. Beside them are a wizard and his staff weapon. The staff blasts can go in all directions, even diagonal. The one queen can move in any direction. Her main role is to safe-guard the king. Then last, the weakest link with no magical powers is the king. He can move one space only in any direction. He must be protected at all costs. The objective of the game is to wipe out your opponent and catch or kill the king. Now each player has one move at a time and so on. The first will be an exhibition game. So Atesh and Aiden would you like to show us all how to play this ancient game for the crowd."

Atesh let Aiden win this pre match game, but she strung it out to twenty moves. The crowds closed in for the real tournament and Gareth moderated their game. Thaddeus moderated the one between Ballard and Marcus. Atesh won her game against Aiden this time in five moves. He was stunned, as never had he seen it played so aggressive.

Ballard and Marcus were working hard to beat each other, they seemed evenly matched. Atesh watched from the side lines, but did not want to see too much, she preferred to work out the opponent's strategy for herself. Marcus performed an unusual tactic and sacrificed his queen, so when Ballard thought he had the king barricaded in a corner; Marcus swooped down and killed Ballard's king with his wizard's blast.

"That was a terrific move Marcus. I must remember that sneaky trick for the future. Well played." Ballard slapped Marcus on the back as he stood up and bowed to the crowd.

Gareth stood and beckoned all. "Well this is the championship round, drinks first then we will have the best of three games."

While Marcus and Aiden set the board pieces to play. Thaddeus and Gareth showed Atesh the jewellery that had arrived.

"They are magnificent, all of them."

"I will present them to you all tomorrow morning after forms, if that is suitable Atesh?"

Atesh bowed her head in acknowledgement.

Gareth called for order. "Let the games begin; who shall be the *'Game Master'* of this here castle?"

Game one Atesh won in eight moves. Game two Marcus won in twenty moves, it was becoming serious. Ballard knew Atesh allowed Marcus to win; he had seen her many times deploy this tactic. Giving the opponent a win makes them a bit too sure of themselves and then wham, she wipes them off the board. The third game was half way through and it was near even. Marcus stared with ferocious intent at the pieces before him. Atesh was relaxed and had a smile on her face; Ballard knew it, now she was going in for the kill.

A rumble sounded from the distance. It was loud enough in tone that all in attendance turned and looked beyond the castle walls to the high mountains. The ground beneath their feet vibrated for a moment and then settled. The animals, night-birds and the sounds of life, all became eerily silent. Atesh thought it felt like every living creature in the known world was holding its breath. She stood and moved away from the table. Her wide eyes were fixated on the ground beneath her feet. All the hairs' on her arms stood erect; as a sense of foreboding slammed into her mind. With no further warning the ground groaned, shrieked and shook sideways. It then rose up a few feet and reversed to suck down with aggressive momentum. People, food and mugs of ale were thrown in all directions. Cracks opened up beneath some of the crowd as they began to run; pushing each other in a frenzy of fear and need for survival. The ground became hostile. Small pockets of steam opened and vented to great heights, spewing hot vapour onto those nearby.

The game was tossed up in the air and the pieces scattered. They however, returned to the game's hessian and leather box container which was studded with small crystal jewels and settled into their allocated places. The lid closed, then all disappeared from sight back to their safe haven in Master Thaddeus's study. One large crack opened wide and a village resident screamed as he tumbled into the chasm before it closed. Those within the castle ran outside to utter chaos. Small pieces of its foundations dislodged and pelted those sheltering in its shadow. Only some smaller outhouses fell inward in a heap.

Aiden yelled out to his grandfather. Gareth and Thaddeus spun around at the same time. Gareth grabbed hold of Thad's arm and pointed to Aiden. They ran as fast as possible to see a fierce drama unfolding before their eyes. When they drew near, Gareth stopped and froze for a moment and stared. Aiden and Ballard were holding onto a pair of legs. Pain and fear etched into their faces. Their bodies were soaked from the strain of holding on. Arms stressed to near bursting. Their boot heels dug into the ground were now shifting against their will. Forward slow and steady; inch by inch. Atesh was face down, arms extended as she lay half inside an open rent. She held on to Marcus with her right hand. He in turn held onto Binji with his left, both dangling precariously inside the crater. Her left hand held Ben from the inn. He in turn held onto Captain Skip. Atesh's eyes were blood shot, her brow cascading beads of perspiration, her face set in a grimace. She looked to be concentrating to the point of exhaustion. Thaddeus could see the inevitable and yelled to Gareth.

"Atesh is keeping the fissure open, but she is near the end of her ability."

Ciaran sat on her shoulder lending all his power to her as well.

Gareth lay down and with some of the soldiers assisting; they formed two human chains, one on the left of Atesh and one on the right. They then inched forward on their bellies, reached in and grabbed the dangling men. This released Atesh of their heavy burden. Slow and methodically they dragged them up the side of the crevice, careful not to cause a jerking movement, which may result in the loss of the either Skip or Binji. Then they emerged over the top of the crater to safety. Marcus, Binji, Ben and Skip all collapsed in a heap on the hard cold ground.

Thaddeus had lent Atesh the extra power she needed to sustain her effort. She was also dragged back onto solid ground and Thaddeus indicated to her she could let go now. "Let the fissure close up Atesh."

"I don't know how to let go. I have tried."

"Listen to my voice Atesh. I will tell you how to do this." He spoke quiet into her mind, getting her to relax her arms and thoughts.

It seemed to work as the earth shook and started to close. Ciaran was so excited and exhausted he let go of her shoulder and over balanced and fell into the closing earth.

"Noooooooooooooooooo," Atesh screamed with the last of her energy, as a flash of white light engulfed her and the surroundings.

Marcus scrambled over to Atesh and pulled her into a close embrace as she drifted off into darkness. Ballard lay flat on his back and closed his eyes, tears welled within them. Aiden hit Ballard on the arm and pointed. They sat up and stared at his grandfather. Thaddeus glowed white and within his hands he held the little dragonelle.

Gareth and the entire crowd clapped and whistled. "Now Thad that's what I call, taking a bow."

Chapter 20

No pain...No gain:

Atesh awoke early the next morning. She remembered the darkness had enveloped her, yet she felt a strange calmness. She looked down and upon her chest was a snoring and smoke snorting dragonelle. She went to bring her hand up to give Ciaran a cuddle, but found it was wedged under a sleeping mass of sand coloured, wavy hair. Atesh lifted her head slow and steady; turning it left and then right. She noticed dark forms lying all over the floor. Ballard was splayed out on her desk chair, with his legs hooked over the side of the arm rest. Bear was on top of the desk curled up into a ball. *Oh that must be uncomfortable.* The stale smell of ale infused breath wafted up to her nose in rhythmical bursts from the men. She smiled to herself and went back to sleep.

As the morning dew was lit from the ascending sun, the men arose. They groaned, stretched and grumbled about their unusual sleeping arrangements. Marcus awoke to see a pair of enchanting blue eyes staring at him.

"Good morning sleeping beauty. Hope you are up to meeting the hoard today?"

"Good morning Marcus…men. Umm…thank you for keeping your eyes on me last night. How did?" and she nodded toward Ciaran.

"Grandfather caught him with his white light trick; a close call though."

Ballard was awake and full of voice. "Alright men, out now so the Commander can have a bit of privacy; yes that means you too, lover boy." He laughed as he exited the room and shut the door; leaving Marcus behind.

"I wanted to say thank you for saving all our lives last night. It was a courageous and noble thing you did." Marcus bowed and gently picked up her hand. He held it enclosed within his own. With eyes closed he bought the back of her hand up to his lips and caressed it with a kiss.

This sent a warm feeling throughout Atesh's body and her eyes sparkled as they stared back at him. His smile was infectious and genuine. Yes, she knew deep within her soul. He was the one man she could truly love forever. *If only.*

No more needed to be said. Their eyes expressed what was in both their hearts. Marcus turned and left the room. He had much to do this day and Atesh wondered how he would concentrate; she watched as his aura burst into flame the moment his lip's touched her skin. *Or so it seemed.*

The knights performed their usual morning routine, watched by the entire First Regiment of the King's Guard. They stood surrounding the group and looked entranced as they observed up close; the precision movements. King Gareth and Master Thaddeus seated within the royal private dining suite, high up in the castle, watched the performance as well.

"I have decided Thad that I am going to learn these exercises and forms. I sit around too much. All I do all day is paperwork. Last night gave me a great deal of concern; I don't feel we have seen the last of these strange happenings."

"I agree and shall join you. It has been too long since I stopped doing my exercises from the academy. Do you realise Gareth that today is a momentous occasion? Never has this been allowed before, knights' teaching their tactics to others; outsiders if I may be so bold. Then to top it off, the academy giving your regiment a set of magic saddle bags each. It is unheard of."

"Maybe your dear brother has another agenda?"

"Very astute of you Gareth, I thought the same myself yesterday. So I asked Elias straight out. Well…apparently Atesh made a suggestion a while ago prior to coming here and he has mulled it over and decided it may be a grand idea."

"Don't leave a man in suspense. What devious plans have you evil twins and your young apprentice have up your sleeve for my kingdom, eh?"

"Right, now picture this if you will Gareth. Let me finish before you say a word. The knights and the first regiment soldiers join together, so there is only one elite army within Sofala. We build a campus here. The *Kingdom Knights'*, oh that name was my suggestion by the way, will be split in two. One half stationed here and the other half at Ashmourne Island. Of course a subgroup would be the palace/village guards, perhaps those who have little innate essence. You may not be aware Gareth that you need a certain amount of magic to activate the knights' oath rings. Oh, there would be tutors, healers, all manner of maintenance staff of course. I mean a smaller version of Ashmourne academy. That would ease the burden on them and ensure the whole realm can be covered from the north to south, east and west with the best fighting force."

Gareth furrowed his brow and pursed his lips.

"Gareth most of your men cannot read or write. Think of the possibilities, they rotate between Ashmourne and here, the two elite armies joining forces. We will need to discuss terms of allegiance. As you know Ashmourne territories have always been independent of the Kingdom. Elias must have assurances that would never change. We cannot have any powerful wizards under sway from the royal line. I am sure you understand this, but perhaps now is the time for some minor changes, perchance a partnership of sorts. The other advantages outweigh that one glitch. This would swell your village bringing families, sharing the financial burden with the academy."

"So…what does the academy get out of this, so far it seems all my way and I am not that naive, Thad?"

"The academy is stretched to the limit with their resources and the amount of people they are required to protect. They need the co-operation of all the magic users to keep this kingdom safe. One thousand elite knights have been reduced by fifteen in one swift diabolical action. It is quite evident that the number of knights left is not near enough for future needs. The final straw was that Elias has had a sense of foreboding, something is coming and we need to be prepared for it. We need to take his prophetic abilities seriously, he has never been wrong."

"Yes I too fear for the future Thad and I can see the possibilities."

"Gareth the east side of Sofala has been isolated from the rest of the kingdom for thousands of years. Elias and I are not getting any younger. New blood will breed new ideas, but we need the underlying ideals to stay the same. That is our army will be peace-makers, we do not go out and start war, we look after the people. They must come first. There is of course another reason to do this." Thaddeus walked over to the observation deck, looked down and smiled. There below were two different kinds of soldiers working in harmony, learning off each other.

Gareth smiled with one eye raised, "Of course, you sneaky old buzzards."

They both laughed at the ingenuity of it all.

"Yes, they would need a Wizard Master, one of my bloodline to administer the campus, one that was powerful, a brilliant tactician that everybody respects and loves…including Marcus. Who said you cannot have your cake and eat it too, huh?"

"Damn fine idea and of course, she is family after all. Yes, I believe negotiations should commence. I will need to know specifics, numbers and financial considerations. I had better look at the mining and crop situation. See how the treasury is doing. Wow, this will be a huge undertaking and will take time."

"There is one other consideration I believe would be beneficial, a suggestion only Gareth."

He turned to once again look at Thad. "Oh I knew this was too easy."

"I believe we need to build a warrior unit with naval specific qualifications, a third subsection of knights. To explore, travel past the great divide and make new alliances. Have the fastest ships and best weaponries' in the whole world."

"Oh you mean to conquer and divide…no thank you Thaddeus."

"No, I mean to be prepared to go to places we have never been. The old tomes describe many lands on the other side of the world. What if they decide to find us first? We were not around when the great wars were fought, the land sundered. It was bloody, fierce and horrifying for all involved, which was why the academy first included their own fighting force, a warrior unit to keep us all safe for the future. Then near two hundred years ago the first of the creatures appeared and the raising of the northern borders. I was around back then. We decided to change the fighting force to be an army of magically enhanced peace keepers, but the best fighters we could train, thus the forms were designed and added to the exercises."

"Made your point; Yes I will take this all under consideration. But, I would like to discuss this part with Marcus first. What if they on the other side of the great divide are behind all the disappearances…the creatures?"

"Worse still Gareth, what if it is happening to them as well. Their people disappearing and they believe we are at fault. They may arrive here first, looking for answers."

"Oh," a pained expression adorned his face. He sat down hard on his seat, hand up to his head. "Yes what if they do? I wonder…is this the future Elias has envisioned for us?"

At breakfast the regiment soldiers were full of questions. They were very eager to begin their (TL), torture lessons as a few called it. Ballard and Aiden designated the groups, there was fourteen groups with one knight per group; Atesh would be out the front co-ordinating. Ballard had unit one with Marcus, Aiden, Gareth, Captain Skip and Archery Master Olyver Reece, Gareth and Thaddeus when they could spare the time. The remaining thirteen groups would have four officers in each and they were spread out in two rows, the first row of eight arced out and spaced; in between them the second line of six were placed. This allowed Atesh a view of them all.

Atesh explained that they would learn the specific words or phrases of the academy. "Where they originated I cannot tell you, but know, they are old and have always been used at Ashmourne. We will go through each section slow and then you practice for two hours then break. Today some of us are on escort duty. The rest will continue with their practicing. Tonight believe me you will feel tight and a bit sore; the worst day will be tomorrow. You will master each section before we continue on, this will take time. So be patient, remember most of the knights here with you have been performing these manoeuvres for many years. I have been working these forms since I was six years old; so twelve years, eight days a week. Ballard well, he has been going fifty years or more."

"What!" A commotion from the back of the group was heard.

"Making sure you had not dosed off, Captain."

The entire crowd sniggered. They were well aware by now, the bantering the two officers pursued.

"I know you all want to get to the good part, but for now we must see how you go with the exercises. We need to find those hidden muscles and shock them into action, strengthen them, stretch them and get the blood pumping around your body. You will learn how to centre your mind, body and soul. This will assist with balance in any position you find yourself, in the heat of a battle. Last, you will learn how your body moves. Look at the limits, strength, and improve your posture. Captain Ballard over to you to organise the teams then we will begin."

Captains' Ballard and Aiden coordinated the groups and set them up as per previous discussion.

"They are all yours now to torture, Commander." Ballard bowed with exaggerated arm movements and lady like hand flick.

Atesh rolled her eyes up at him then resumed her position out the front; she commenced on the exercises . "We always begin with the preparation; this should take around ten minutes." Atesh went through the exercises with thoroughness, explaining, showing and then having the team leaders perform them and then the men. They commenced at the feet and worked their way up every muscle. Every motion all joints could perform, stretching, working and moving. They discussed the breathing and centring; the mind control. The gentle jog around the oval was the last portion shaking their arms and rotating their shoulders to release any tension.

The regiment soldiers were beaded in perspiration, clothes saturated and faces flushed. The knight team leaders looked like they had been to a picnic; smiled at their groups.

"This will be your practice for the next two days, a short break between sessions. While I am away this afternoon, Vykter will coordinate. Any questions before we have a short break and then we restart again?"

There were a few moans from within the groups, but most held a grudging admiration for their knight team leaders. After the next two sets of exercises the men all took a long break.

King Gareth and Master Thaddeus presented to the outstanding few, their awards from Queen Mia of the fire ants. Marcus, Ballard and Aiden each received a ring with a fire stone embedded. As they were placed on their left hand middle finger each of them gasped, eyes widened in shock as the fire stone connected with their innate essence.

Ballard went down to his knees and became quite pale. He arose in short order and shook his head. "Wow that had a kick."

Gareth hesitated to place the beautifully carved arm bracelet on Atesh. It was a dragon that wove around the top of her arm with the fire stone as the dragon's eye. He handed it to Thaddeus to do the honours. "All yours, oh mighty Wizard, I'll stand back here."

"Atesh take a deep breath, looks like you may get a tickle."

Once placed up onto her arm the eye ignited and glowed red. It then connected with her inner essence and she bit her bottom lip. Perspiration dripped from her brow to dampen her widened eyes and then she too sank to her knees shaking all over. "A tickle you said Master Thaddeus, a tickle? By the ancients…I am on fire."

"Last but not least is Ciaran. Where is the little Dragonelle?"

"I be hiding sire. If it be all the sames to you, I will wave aside my here present."

"Oh, sorry Ciaran, but Mia insisted you must have this."

Atesh received the gold neck band with the red channel setting jewel embedded and placed it gently around Ciaran's neck. It looked magnificent. When she clasped it together the seam disappeared.

Ciaran yelped, jumped off Ballard's shoulder into the air and let out a puff of smoke which actually had some flame to it. "Did ye see that lass, I had flame, oh my word?"

Gareth eyed them all. "Well that was an interesting presentation. The last thing we must do is say a few words for the merchant guard that died last night here at the castle. There was no family to grieve for him, so we shall honour his life.

Chapter 21

Betha:

Commander Marcus, twelve of his men and eight knights made for a stunning welcoming party to the King's flag ship. On the way they took a slight detour to be shown some of the popular sites of Mere Town. They then stopped off at the hospice to visit Knight Kerwin. Marcus presented to him a necklace from Queen Mia. This gave Kerwin hope for a speedier recovery, to return home to his wife and soon to be, newborn child. The guard of honour then raced off down to the docks in time to watch the pride of the fleet arrive; in all her majestic glory. The large Galleon was known for the dragon figure-head that adorned her bow; it seemed to warn intruders to stay clear. The Dragon's Breath was a four mastered square rig; the royal multi-decked naval vessel. The sailors were all efficient and professional with Admiral Atien calling orders, as they slowed to a stop; beside the main pier. Marcus and Aiden dismounted and assisted their family to disembark and make their way to the two awaiting carriages. One was for Queen Brianna, her twin daughters, son and her sister Duchess Lysanna. The larger carriage was for their ladies-in-waiting and their entire luggage.

Atesh, Ballard and the knights dismounted in a seamless cadence to the gasps of the sailors on the deck; they whispered to each other and pointed. The knights' uniforms shone out from the red and grey of the king's regiment colours. Atesh and her knights had on their black leather pants, knee length black boots, white long sleeve shirt, purple tunic and gold coloured belt which shone in the sunlight. They held onto the two spare horses, one for Duke Morgan Beaumont and the other for his son, Prince Fynton. Atesh could see a young boy fidgeting, a desperate look upon his face. He was trying to free his hand grasped within his mother's firm hand. Atesh smiled at him and beckoned him over. He managed to break free and bolted over to her. Eyes widened to near breaking point.

"Are you a knight, my lady?"

"Yes, Prince Israe, I am."

"How do you know my name?"

Atesh leant over and whispered into his ear. He jumped back and took a deep breath in. Atesh laughed at the sight, she was sure the young man would explode. "Israe, would you like to sit up on Kayne; my war steed?"

"Oh yes please, that would be splendid Commander. I have my own back sheath with swords, did you know?"

"Yes, I have heard there was a warrior within the castle, killing potato monsters."

Israe stuck out his chest. "Oh and I slay green, garden goblins and wart-men, with the occasional dragon and troll too."

"Well you must show me sometime. I have never been up against a…wart-man, he sounds horrid."

So while the adults were discussing family. Israe, Atesh and Ballard had a merry time, talking soldiers. Specifically the best ways to kill wart-men and trolls found in the vegetable garden, back at the castle. Israe jumped up onto Kayne's back then let out an, '*oh*' as Ciaran peaked out from within the saddle bag.

"Hello Mr Dragon, sir. Are you friend or foe?"

"Ach I be definitely a friend, Master Knight."

"Then sir, may I pat you?"

"Why of course laddie, since ye asked so nice." Ciaran jumped up onto the young man's lap and cooed as he was patted.

"His name is Ciaran, a dragonelle."

Marcus sauntered around the horses. "Well well, what's this eh Israe? I had a feeling I would find you here."

"Look Marcus I have a dragonelle on my lap. Can I get one for my own, do you think?"

"I don't know; that is something you will have to discuss with father."

Duke Morgan and Fynton walked around to where the horses were held, they were given a brief introduction to Atesh and Ballard. Then all mounted up.

"Marcus, can I please ride with Atesh and Ciaran; please?"

Once again Atesh could feel eyes boring into her head. *What is it with this family and their eyeballing?* Atesh nodded that it was fine and jumped up behind Israe.

Marcus informed his mother; that Israe would ride with the escort ,she was a bit apprehensive, but agreed.

The knights were on point and rear duty. So Atesh and Ballard led the procession away towards Beaumont castle. Then Jenner and Ryna with Marcus, Aiden, Fynton and Morgan either side of the carriages…the regiment rode in-between. Hagan, Sage, Berend and Wyart brought up the rear.

At about the half way point Atesh placed her arm up to stop the convoy. She dismounted and placed her hand upon the earth. She had her eyes closed and turned her head a little to the right. The breeze bought with it a faint odour from an unusual source and it was becoming stronger. Her eyes opened sparkling with blue flames. She remounted and whispered into Ballard's ear. His head whipped around to the north east direction.

Commander Marcus and his uncle, Duke Morgan cantered up to point. They noticed both Atesh and Ballard in discussion, whilst they gazed up towards the north eastern side of the mountain range.

"What's going on Atesh?"

"Marcus everyone needs to move over to the trees , *now* ." She pointed over to their left, but kept her head firmly in place. "Oh and be as quiet as you can…please."

Marcus noticed her eyes flaming . Her hand's blanched tight on the reins and her brows were furrowed . He did not blink or hesitate , but signalled for everyone to move on over to the left. "Uncle Morgan, please follow me and I will explain."

"Ballard we must bunch them in tight, and then we can activate the rings. We will need to blend in; believe me, you do not want to mess with what is coming our way."

Ballard raced over and started to organise the regiment soldiers and carriages into a tight formation. All regiment horses that were agitated had their eyes blindfolded with any cloth they could find. Ciaran spoke to the animals in their mind and reassured them. Atesh activated her Commander ring which flashed red and all the knights raced to her side. They were given directions to spread out and completely encircle the group. Then she would activate the blending spell. As she inspected the size of the containment field and the placement of her men, she heard noises emanating from the first carriage. A woman's voice was loud and distressed. She jumped down and assisted Israe to dismount; he opened the first carriage and jumped inside. A large smile adorned his face.

"I am sorry for the inconvenience Highness, but safety is paramount. Please remain seated within the carriage and be completely silent. We have a foe we dare not encounter headed our way; being out of its path is our only option." *I am sure; I've had this scenario before, not too long ago.*

"No! I will not be quiet young lady. I am your Queen and I command you to keep going. If we come across a foe, then you will fight for me."

Atesh didn't have time for tantrums from uppity royals. "I am not your young lady, Highness. Nor are you my Queen, though I will accord you every politeness. *I can muster.* We will be staying here till I say we move. If you want to survive this encounter, you will do as I say."

"Can you not see my sister does not feel well? The sea voyage has upset her so."

"I am truly sorry for this, perhaps sips of water to ease your stomach; I can have our healer come over to you. But we must stay here and be quiet…please." Atesh shook her head and held the bridge of her nose between her fingers. "You may keep the windows of the carriage open, if you all promise not a word; no matter what you see or hear…is that a deal?"

"Where is Marcus? He's in charge here, not you? What does he say about this?"

Atesh leaned over to the Queen and whispered into her ear; Brianna's eyes widened then looked down and nodded. Atesh departed and shut the wooden door. She stood outside the carriage and still could hear their raised voices.

Royalty, why are they so loud?

"Brie, what did she say to you…who is she?"

Israe jumped up to face his kin, "Aunt Lysanna that is the Supreme Commander of the Ashmourne knights."

"Oh…a female Commander that is a first. She is so young too. I wonder why they are here."

"Lysanna," Queen Brianna leaned over and held her sister's hand. "The Commander told me I am with child…that is why I am unwell. Also, there are enormous, fierce creatures headed our way." Brianna glanced down and held her stomach. "I cannot ask my subjects to fight wild creatures and die for me, if we can avoid it. Gareth would not want that at all. I was being silly before."

All in the carriage stared at Brianna, not sure whether to laugh or cry at the news they were given. This child, they all knew was precious, wanted and needed. They would definitely comply with the Commander's orders. The second carriage was quiet. The ladies held on to each other and had their eyes closed.

"Marcus, I don't have all my knights here, so we could use the assistance of anyone who has a decent amount of innate essence. If they could be placed in-between my knights to close the gaps on the perimeter, it would greatly assist us. They have to concentrate on being unseen that is all, when the time comes. Place yourself and Aiden beside the carriages to comfort your family and touch your ring with your mind as we showed you this morning and then, think of lending us the power."

"What did you mean unseen?"

"That information, I am not allowed to say…except that we have a way of being undetected for a period of time. But, I cannot cover sounds. It is part of our oath, we cannot discuss this with you, please trust me."

Everyone was in place and Atesh held up her hand to indicate silence. She activated her Commander's ring and all the knights concentrated, some with eyes closed, others with faces screwed up and furrowed. It was mere moments later that the earth beneath their feet started to vibrate. It had many rhythmical beats that became louder as it approached. Dust floated above the trees ahead of them. Every so often a deeper sound reverberated off all the surrounding trees, sending their leaves cascading down to the ground in clumps. Concentration became an effort. Perspiration beaded on brows. Heart rates increased in cadence with their short rapid breaths. Muscles in trembling limbs tightened, as fear became etched into the knights and soldiers faces; overtaking their previous calmed exterior. However, the younger occupants of the first carriage leant towards the opened window, craning their necks to see the spectacle.

A stampede of gigantic wild, fanged dogs and boars with razor tusks raced down the roadway. They were chased by a large pack of over-sized, grey horned, red eyed wolves. Followed close behind were two enormous brown bears and some unusual six legged, striped horses. They all had eyes widened, fear written on their faces and their coats were lathered from running. The creatures' flight produced ear splitting noises that pulsated throughout all in close proximity. The stench and dust produced was over whelming, but past they ran. They turned right, down the roadway and headed for the ragged cliffs beside the sea; never seeing the group that blended into the trees.

Atesh waited for the terror that had these creatures stampeding. She heard the intake of many breaths when eight large, black hairy legs walked past with short rapid steps. It was as enormous ebony coloured Arachnopod, with a wide fire red stripe down its back, dragging along by its rear pincers, two oversized scorpioids. They had been partially wrapped in webs and on their backs; they carried large white egg mounds. A few minutes later the other booming sound was upon them. This pounding sent everything not pinned down bouncing off the ground a short way in quick repetition. As the wagons rattled, the ladies within became unbalanced and frightened. They held on tight to each other and the seating. Israe of course, was in his element. Most of his body was hanging out the window, held onto by his terrified sisters; a wide grin split his face from one ear to the other.

All Atesh could see was the first portion of eight hairy legs with razor sharp spikes sticking out from all sides. *What now? I don't like this.*

Atesh and Ballard looked up as the sky above darkened as it became partially blocked from view. The knights and regiment soldiers faces' blanched; their eyes wide in terror as a shadow descended over the entire area they were hiding in. The legs stopped moving and both Atesh and Ballard heard a voice in their minds.

"Are you the little Commander, I have heard so much about?"

"I am Atesh, my lady." Atesh bowed her head to the creature.

"Is that the prince from the Southern Islands beside you, as your second?"

"Yes my lady, this is Captain Ballard."

Ballard bowed his head in reverence to the creature before him.

"Mia sends greetings to you both; I can feel her fire stone upon a few of you. That is good, a rare gift for two legs. I shall not harm anyone here. I am travelling past, moving my husband and new offspring off shore for a while and taking some travelling food with us. There is great evil at work in the north. Putrid, ugly, unnatural creatures roam unchecked, spreading their foulness. We shall return once this is sorted out."

A gigantic round black body lay down and a crater formed under her weight, this dispelled a plume of fine red dust over the entire group. Betha's head turned to look at the two knights. Her pincers were three times the size of a horse, they continually grated and gnashed. One of her many eyes came in close to Atesh. *"Ah yes, I can see you now. There is a quivering being under your collar too. He has a frail constitution that one."*

The sounds, odour and the thought of what those sharp cutters could do to his wee body unnerved Ciaran to the point of fainting. Atesh could feel his energy slip and placed her hand on her collar to reassure her little dragonelle, that he was in no danger.

"You two are as Mia described. You did well in hiding this group. My husband may not have so understood if he had seen you. All Queens of the ancient species are sentient beings and my gift is to see true as Mia's is to have visions. So your invisibility blending does not work on me. You see we, like Mia are the original inhabitants of this world; have been since the beginning of time. Those

abominations in the north must be dealt with Atesh; I feel them, see them for what they are. I believe you are the only one that can do this. I have held a gift for you as well." She opened her cavernous mouth and with three rows of sharpened teeth pulled out from between her front leg spikes a small rod of amber coloured wood and placed it down beside Kayne.

"This piece of angel wood I give of my own free will. You see Atesh; one cannot remove by force these branches from the most ancient and magical of trees. It must be given without guile for the good of this world. So I say unto you. Fashion your wizard staff from this and all the blessed powers will be yours. We will meet again someday Atesh, be safe and be well. If you need advice call me. I will hear you, now that I know your signature. Learn from those mischievous wizard twins, they will not steer you wrong. Though I cannot guarantee they will not get you into all sorts of weird situations."

Betha drew back her lips and showed her teeth. Then a strange sound burst from her enormous cavernous maw. Her body shuddered in small rhythmical movements sending bits of putrid food stuff forth, over all those within reach. The men within the escort stared horrified, as bits of blood, bone and offal sprayed outwards. The occupants within the carriages ducked for cover.

"My name is Betha, Queen of the Arachnopods and I take my leave of you now. Good bye and best of luck, Commander, Captain and wee beasty."

"Thank you, my lady for your understanding and kindness, I will do my best."

"Oh before I take my leave Atesh that is one tiny two legs to keep an eye on." Betha turned her head to look at Israe. She grinned at his innocence, hanging half out of the carriage with a genuine smile. *"He will be a handful; perchance a grand knight and a powerful high wizard one day."*

Atesh looked behind her to young Israe and nodded to him.

Betha raised her oversized body and all watched, as the largest creature alive in the known world, strode past them. A loud splash was then heard and droplets of water fell from the sky. Betha had jumped into the ocean to the right, past the group's safe haven, to follow her family to the islands; way out in the endless sea.

Atesh deactivated her ring and slumped forward with her body drenched in dampness. Ballard reached out to her and held her steady in the saddle. Ciaran crawled out from under her collar and back into the saddle bag, still shaking and exhausted.

Atesh gathered all her strength and dismounted to sit on the ground and pick up the piece of the most beautiful amber coloured wood she had ever seen. It emanated energy and as she held it, it connected to her innate essence. *Oh no, another tickle* and she grimaced and bit her bottom lip, hard enough to break the skin.

Ballard slumped down beside her; they both had the majority of the effort, as they worked in harmony to encircle the group.

Most of the men were unlucky enough to have spider clag spray them. They jumped off their horses and tried to brush the horrid smelling bits off. Some had bits stuck in their hair. They performed little jigs and pirouettes, arms flung this way and that with accompanied, *oohs* and *ewwws*. Marcus leaned over and plucked a piece of bone with sinew attached, from the head of the Duke. His uncle seemed less than amused.

"Oh look, I have a partial leg bone. Anyone have its foot?"

"I have a jawbone Marcus; gee…I am not sure what creature it's from?"

"Oh by the ancients Aiden…that is some jawbone. Look at the size of those teeth?"

The soldiers and knights all stopped, looked at each other with wild grins; then a mad scramble ensued. The aim was to find and bring home a trophy from their near death experience. They found all sorts of odd pieces of carcass, that they had initially flung from their bodies. The ladies were now quiet; they looked on at their escorts' glee, with narrowed eyes and pressed pouting lips. It was clear to Israe, his mother was not pleased. The Queen had hold of the back of his trousers, as he tried to inch further out the window to join in the fun. They held perfume sprayed kerchiefs up to cover their mouths and noses from the horrid stench; emanating from the soldiers, their carriages, Israe and surrounds. When Marcus thought the men had enough tension release, he applied order back into the guard and arranged the group once more for travel. Marcus wandered over to the two seated and exhausted looking knights.

"May I enquire as to what just transpired Atesh? You made another friend, eh?"

She looked up at Marcus and giggled. He had not realised that whilst talking he was quite animated with his hands. He was flinging the leg bone hither and thither, sending small bits of offal in all directions.

"I shall debrief you on our way back to the castle, if…you have finished playing with your supper."

He looked down at his hands, but all he could muster was a devious, eye twinkling, broad grin. When they had recovered, he assisted both of them onto their horses. "Geeze, you are a lump Ballard."

Atesh signalled for them to move onward at a slow pace. Although the men looked and smelled atrocious, they each carried their trophies with honour.

Chapter 22

Clagged:

The guards on the outer gate at Beaumont village stood to attention as the Queen's procession passed. Atesh realised they must look a sight covered in red dust, sweat, sea water and gizzards. She smiled to herself as she thought of the extra apparel the escorts wore. They displayed their trophies with fortitude and pride. She noticed as they rode by the facial expressions of the guards and villagers change; of course it may be the horrid stench that accompanied them; a lasting effect from the giant spider laugh.

King Gareth and Master Thaddeus were waiting at the castle main entrance when the party emerged through the inner gates. The carriages rolled up to the two men. They immediately took a step back and eyed the entire escort with frowns and twitching noses. The men had lined up beside and behind the carriages and they looked beyond words. Human, horse sweat and an aberrant odour overwhelmed the welcoming party. Marcus dismounted and handed his reins to the stable attendant. He bowed to his father and assisted his family to exit their carriage. The women looked up at the two scowling men whilst they held firm, their kerchiefs to their faces. They walked passed in silence with heads held high. Duke Morgan, Captains' Fynton and Aiden bowed as they bolted in after them. Marcus was prevented from moving a step. A booming voice spoke just-one-word.

"Marcus!"

Marcus turned to look his father in the eyes. "Yes sir, how may I assist you?" His eyes left Gareth's for Thaddeus, as he flicked a piece of gizzard off his trousers.

Gareth for the moment was silenced. He followed the flung glob onto the ground and blanched when he recognised it. It was a bit of eyeball sinew; attached to a scull fragment. He swallowed his bile as it roared up from his stomach and tried to exit; in a most un-king like fashion. His eyes then roamed over the men and horses before him. They widened when he spied the leg bone sticking out from the back of his son's saddle. Gareth's face warmed up, his breathing quickened as his chest wall pounded in rhythm with his overextended heart. His hands clenched by his side as his left eye twitched when he spied all the soldiers standing up straight and proud. Attached to their uniforms were all sorts of skeletal parts, some with the tissues and rotten meat parcels still connected. He stared at the one with a partial rib cage atop his head with a feather sticking out the side.

"Explain Commander, what happened to a simple escort duty and the state of my family and men? And what in all of Sofala is on…that soldier's head?"

"I think Grandfather may be able to explain better to you what happens when Betha laughs." He turned and dismissed his men with a smile then strode past into the castle. A cheeky grin radiated from his face as he thought about his father's facial expression and beetroot red cheeks.

Thaddeus had his hand over his mouth hiding his widened smile till he could no longer contain himself. Tears welled up in his eyes and he roared with laughter.

Atesh, Ballard and the knights watched in awe from the stables, they felt it would be safer there, out of Gareth's reach.

"Thaddeus what in all blazes is a…Betha…is that a…a leg bone sticking out from my son's saddle?"

The elderly wizard was beside himself. He held onto an attendant's shoulder to steady his shuddering body, he was laughing so hard. "Oh my," was all he uttered for a minute. "They have all been *Clagged*, oh my." And he roared again, now bent over holding his side.

"Do I get no sense from anyone today?" Gareth placed a hand to his head and moaned to no-one in particular.

"Gareth my boy, come with me and I will explain over a strong drink; you are going to need it. We must not venture near the ladies; believe me in times like this, it is best to stay clear." He placed his arm around Gareth's shoulder and escorted the distressed King to the family sitting room.

"You are having me on now, aren't you Thad?" Gareth swallowed his drink in one guzzle.

"Oh no, not at all," He laughed at the shocked expression on Gareth's face.

"So they met on their way from Mere Town, a spider called Betha and she covered them in what you called, Clag?"

"No, not any spider Gareth. Betha is an ancient arachnopod, the Queen of them all. She is the oldest known creature to inhabit our fair land. Remember how huge Mia appeared? We saw her from up here. Well imagine something three sizes larger with eight razor sharp hairy legs; pincers the length of three horses and six eyes; two large with four smaller, two above and two below. Then imagine what was caught between her many rows of teeth. There be thousands of years' worth of bone and animal flesh. She is a sentient being, so we will need to find out what transpired. But I am betting Atesh had a conversation with her and she laughed, caking all around her in rotting, decayed bits of bone and gore. What we wizards named clag. I have seen it before. Yes…and I too have been clagged, my boy. Terribly hard to rid oneself of the memory, let alone the stench. She is actually a friend and ally of Mia's."

"I cannot imagine a creature so large Thad. How frightened must they have all been? I am a dead man…not my fault, but…." He clasped his hands over his head. "Yes sir, a dead man."

"Well they arrived in one piece and that is saying something. It is rare for Betha to travel alone and never this far west. Her companion is known as Red Jack; he is smaller, but has a mean, nasty temperament when he gets upset. You can tell him from afar from his red stripe down his back. I wonder if that's what caused the earth to shake last night? Betha moving through the lands beneath us, it's very possible." Thaddeus leant forward and patted Gareth on the shoulder. "Here have yourself another mug dear boy; you will need the courage to face your wife later on."

"What of the men, why were they wearing those…those things?"

"Trophies Gareth; imagine for a moment what must have gone on out there? Your family and men all came through unscathed in a manner of speaking. Smelly yes, but alive. They may have all ended up as a tasty morsel. This may have been their way of unwinding, making sense of it all. You should commend Marcus, not condemn him. Let them have their spoils. They deserve it."

Atesh asked Jenner to whip up a concoction for the knights to rid them of the odour. She then sent some to the regiment's quarters and over to the palace for King's family. After they had all bathed and adorned fresh clothes. Atesh walked down stairs to the lounge area. Awaiting her were the men from the exercise yard who witnessed their arrival. She left the story up to Berend and Wyart to tell, of their escort adventure. The men were all fascinated with the trophies, but banished them outside. The knights knowing their Commander shook their heads and laughed.

"Well if I don't return this afternoon, I expect you may find me in the lock up. I am off to explain to the King." Atesh bowed to them all and turned to walk out.

"Wait up there Atesh; I will accompany you into the pit."

"Thanks Ballard, nice of you to place your head on the block with me." Laughing they strode over to the castle, heads held high, shoulders straight and tall.

They were led into the sitting room where Marcus was standing on the balcony overlooking the countryside, lost in thought. Gareth and Thaddeus had departed to see the family. He turned around when he heard the door open.

"Thank you for the powder, it certainly worked well Atesh."

"I am really sorry about all that Marcus." Atesh couldn't remove the sight from her mind and she sniggered.

"Yes we looked a sight. Father will be arriving in short order, and then you may hear how loud a King can get. Would you two like a cup of courage with me?"

"That would be nice, thank you."

The three sat down and shared some fine wine, awaiting their fate.

"Marcus I am glad she didn't sneeze, it was just a small laugh."

Marcus screwed up his nose and shuddered at the thought. Ballard spurted his wine out as he burst into laughter. Then the three of them cackled away, in-between discussing different scenarios that could have befallen them, all disgusting or repellent.

"You know Marcus, the wizard's call what happened to us as being *Clagged*, don't let the men know or we will have another nick name to contend with."

Gareth strode in and sat down opposite the three officers. He eyed each one. "I wish to thank you three for bringing my family home safe. It was a shock to see their state upon arrival. But after what Thaddeus and Brianna told me, you are lucky to have met Betha and Red Jack and live to tell your tale. Israe hasn't stop talking of the whole affair…but, the truth please. Was she really…that big?"

"Father the outer castle wall would fit under her abdomen. The stampede that preceded her was a collection of many strange wild creatures…what did she call it Atesh?"

"I believe it was their travelling food."

"It is almost un-comprehendible. If I hadn't seen Mia, I don't know that I would have believed you all."

Gareth turned to Atesh. "The Queen would like a word with you. Then Thaddeus would like some of your time."

Feeling dismissed, Atesh left for the Queen's quarters. Upon entering, Brianna was seated next to a fire and had more colour in her cheeks.

"You sent for me your highness?"

"Commander, please come and sit with me. I would like to apologise for my behaviour today. I am not usually like that. I have been moody of late and the sea voyage had upset my stomach. I was miserable and took it out on you my dear. Please accept my apology."

Atesh nodded to her.

"I also wish to thank you for keeping us safe. Gareth explained what you must have gone through to keep us all hidden and at the same time talk to Betha. I must say, I have never been so scared in all my life. Her size was amazing, but yet she appeared regal in a way. That is until she laughed; ewww the smell of that waste." She leaned over closer to Atesh. "Did you mean what you told me and are you certain?"

"I am absolutely certain."

"Will we live through the birth Atesh; that worries me, with my history and age?"

"I believe Jenner is our best healer at the academy. Perhaps the King can make some sort of request to Master Elias to borrow her for a while. I am not one to see the future. So I cannot tell how it will all go. But I need to tell you something else about your pregnancy and I am not sure how to say this."

"Oh is it good or bad…oh now I am worried, Atesh what have you sensed."

"Well my lady, you are having more than one baby. I could hear three distinct loud heart beats."

"Did you say three? Brianna placed her hand up to her mouth and laughed. "Oh dear what will Gareth say?"

"I am sure he will be happy."

"Now…on an entirely different subject, I was going to ask; do you have a dress for Aiden's birthday celebration? It would be the least I can do for you."

"No my lady, I shall not be attending the celebration. I am required to be elsewhere; I have another matter to attend to."

"Oh, that is no good. Maybe I can speak to Gareth on your behalf. Aiden would be devastated; he is so taken with you and the knights."

"The knights will be attending. It is…that I am unable; I am sorry."

Queen Brianna looked at Atesh with questioning eyes, then an understanding illuminated behind them. Her mind was working on all sorts of possibilities. *I wonder what she is up to. Her look…those eyes…hmmm.*

"If you will excuse me my lady, Master Thaddeus awaits me." Atesh bowed and left.

She wanted to escape the interrogation, so she headed towards Master Thaddeus's apartment. Her shoulders slumped in relief.

"Ah my dear girl, come in. Chatting with more of your ancient friends, I hear; please tell me all."

Atesh reiterated the blending, the stampede, conversation and the resultant clagging.

"Oh…she laughed at that comment. Oh my, we must have left an impression on her. I am sorry Atesh." His eyes twinkled and he roared with mirth. "That was the funniest sight I have ever beheld, when the men all stood to attention before the King wearing their trophies. I swear he had no colour left in his face, the eyeball flick was priceless. I thought my innards would burst, never have I laughed so hard. Well I have had my fun for the year, now back to business. Will you please bring the branch of angel-wood over later? I am eager to see such a wonderous item. Now to a most pressing matter, we must address the tear issue Atesh. After supper tonight we shall perform the implant. Mia gave me explicit instructions; so do not worry."

"Master Thaddeus, did Brianna say anything to you about my conversation with her?"

"No, I have not seen her as yet; I was waiting till she had rested. I let her husband be the target for a while. Why, is there a problem?"

Atesh told Thaddeus of the pregnancy. That she had heard three strong heart beats and a softer echo of sorts, she couldn't understand. "I believe my powers are emerging faster than expected Master, it is unnerving to say the least."

"Well…we leave tomorrow at lunch time for my retreat Atesh. Pack for overnight. Say your goodbyes in the morning and return here. Now triplets you say; my…my…my…oh, this will be a first for my line. Though that echo as you call it disturbs me, another do you think? One fading away perhaps," Thaddeus shook his head as he stroked his beard. "They will have innate magic, yes?"

"I believe so, but I cannot tell to what strength."

"Another cluster…that is interesting."

"Cluster, what does that mean?"

"Oh, it happens every now and again throughout our ancestry. The last time was the group Elias and I were born into. There were seven of us with a great deal of innate magic; prior to that it was in my grandfather's time. Seems they are becoming closer. It could be described as a group of individuals born in and around a short time frame with powerful innate magic. Most become Higher Wizards; Masters of the elements. Perhaps the blood lines from the first three wizards are converging. Well, we can look into that later. The other concern I have, is the fact Betha had decided to leave. What evil do you think she was talking about?" Thaddeus started to pace, which he often did when thinking or agitated. "I must discuss this with my brother." He stopped and turned to Atesh. "Thank you for all you have done for the family Atesh. You are a blessing in disguise." Thaddeus reached out and pulled Atesh into a hug, something she had never experienced before from a Wizard Master.

A smile lit up her face akin to a lantern, it felt warm and comforting. "That's an odd expression, Master. Betha also used that term, blessing." It was a deflection tactic from her apparent embarrassment.

"It's from ancient times Atesh. I read it once and it resonated with me. Habits are hard to break sometimes. They would refer to events in our environment and everyday lives as the behaviour or blessings of a particular divine being or God. A good mood or approval meant crops grew, babies were born healthy, everyone was happy. A God in a bad mood meant, there may be fire, flood or disease. Some were more loving than others. There was one for all the seasons we have, as well as mother moon and father sun. It was endless and each area believed they had the only true ones. There must be an all mighty power somewhere; even if it is within us, or around us, in the earth we tread or the air we breathe. I have never given up hope of finding the answer. But the internal wars have stopped for more than a millennium and that is a good thing too."

"I wonder what the belief system is on the other side of the world, Master. Perhaps one day we can discover this."

"Maybe we should let sleeping children lie. We have no idea what they have evolved into since their departure, still an interesting area for research."

The afternoon was spent with the regiment soldiers and their workouts. They were progressing well. Atesh beckoned Ballard in to her office after one of the breaks and shut the door. "Ballard I wanted to thank you for everything you have taught me and supported me with. You have been the only father I have ever known, a best friend and mentor to me and I respect and love you as my only family, well apart from Ciaran."

Ballard sat and narrowed his eyes and raised his eyebrow. "I feel the same way you know. Where is this leading Atesh? What is going on with you?"

"Tonight I will be having Mia's tear embedded in my body and tomorrow at lunch time…I will be leaving with Master Thaddeus for a couple of days. You are to take my place."

He sat back. "So it is happening soon then, your turning."

"How…how did you know?"

"Well I am not blind Atesh and I know you. Your powers have been growing. You are going to be extraordinary and powerful, I can feel it. Plus, Mia let the cat out of the bag remember. So what day will this happen?"

"It will be tomorrow night or the next day."

"When are you going to tell the men?"

"Tonight around a fire pit like we used to talk that is what I would like to remember."

"What do you mean…remember? You will be back the next day, eyes glowing blue flames."

"Thaddeus told me I have a fifty percent change of not coming back at all. But I cannot tell them that."

"It's alright I can handle the men while you are away. I have faith in you. I always have." He stood up to leave; his eyes had begun to brim with tears. A single droplet cascaded down his cheek and he did not want Atesh to see how upset he had become.

Atesh knew full well what was going on; after all, she had grown up with Ballard too. She rushed up to him and threw herself into an embrace. A father-daughter type one. She held him tight. Ballard rested his head on top of hers. "You are dripping on me old cheese; perhaps you have sprung a leak."

"It will be alright you know. Master Thaddeus will be there beside you the whole way. And don't forget, we will be here sending you our love and support. All of us poor, pathetic souls, who are unfortunately, crazy in love with their Commander." They parted and both laughed whilst wiping their faces with their sleeves at the thought of grown men bunched up around the fire pit, crying like babies.

"Please look after Ciaran for me; he cannot venture to the sanctuary with us."

"Come back to us little rabbit, we will be waiting."

Atesh nodded.

Later that evening Atesh entered Master Thaddeus' apartment with Jenner. She was placed in a state of unawareness and dreams while Thaddeus embedded the tear above her heart. Jenner was on hand to heal the wound and ensure no evidence was detectable. When Atesh awoke, she felt refreshed and reinvigorated. As she walked back to the fire pit, Atesh looked up to see all the Beaumont men watching her from the balcony. *Creepy,* Atesh waved and indicated drinks were being served and they were all invited. A *"thank-you"* echoed in her mind. *Strange, I wonder which one said that.*

The Duke and the three younger men sauntered over for a short time to have a drink and to formally meet all the knights. Duke Morgan was the spitting image of his brother Gareth, though one year younger. He smiled more than Gareth and had a wicked sense of humour. Atesh noticed Marcus observing the interaction between them all. Marcus turned a fiendish smile to Atesh and mouthed the word, *Clagged.*

Atesh felt her face go warm and she shook her head and pleaded with her eyes, not to say a word. *No, please don't try and have a sense of humour, now of all times. We have been a bad influence on the King in waiting.*

Duke Morgan had his arms around Ballard's shoulders. "You have grown into a grand looking lad Ballard, your sister would have been proud. Well we had better return to the family. Thank you for your hospitality and of course, our excitement today. Come along Marcus we may need your protection."

Phew, saved by a whisker. Atesh stood and shook the Duke's hand as it was thrust at her. He then held it between both his hands and spoke in a quiet tone.

"Atesh, if there is anything I can ever do for you. I mean, you saved my family today. How can I ever repay that?" He looked into her blue sparkling eyes and a shiver ran up his spine. "Have we met before, you look familiar, but I cannot place when?"

"No I don't believe we have sir. This was my first chance to travel over to the west coast."

He bowed, then let go and turned quickly and walked away, lest he break down. Her sparkling eyes reminded him of his little daughter who was taken away before she had the chance to shine. Fate was cruel that day.

Chapter 23

Preparations:

The morning forms saw not only the knights, but the regiment officers and some of the senior soldiers performing the exercises. They then sat out and watched the knights complete their sword dance. Although they were all eager to execute these manoeuvres, they realised, since commencing the exercises that it will take quite a while to be proficient. Atesh noticed the King's family watching from high up in the castle. They, like any other seeing this for the first time, were awe struck; mesmerised by the sword dance. Duke Morgan watched Atesh with different eyes; a frown often accompanied his stare.

After breakfast Ballard again led the exercises; though this time, Atesh gave a short speech first.

"You have practiced your exercises and performed well. Over the next few days you will combine what you have learnt with the next portion of your training. This will allow you to understand about balance and centering your body. This builds up the muscles you have been preparing; the basic movements for the battle dance. It will involve attacks, strikes, blocking, evading, retaliation and retraction. There will be angle strikes to the upper, lower, inner and outer portions of the body, with stabbing and slashing movements." Atesh allowed her hands to guide them visually through the movements. "Wooden swords will be used only." She looked at them with a smile, "No we don't want to lose limbs today, now do we?"

"You will commence with the Dachi stance. That is, stand with your feet apart then as you move one leg forward, you shift your weight onto this leg. This will accommodate the balance shift. Some may use right, others left leg; always keeping in mind to maintain your centre and back straight. Then as you retract, the weight would shift to the back leg. I will now leave you in Captain Ballard's hands, as I am off on a short mission." A brief pause ensued while she gathered herself, "Best of luck to you all; and thank you." Atesh bowed to all the men on the field, saluted with her right arm across her chest. She stood still as all the men bowed to her in kind and saluted back. She saw pride and admiration staring back at her; enough to choke the hardest soldier.

Atesh walked in a vigorous manner over to the castle and headed for Master Thaddeus' apartment. Here she went through some meditation exercises before they departed. They left in silence before the sun was high in the sky. Atesh knew there would be a couple of eyes watching her leave. She glanced up at the castle. There Marcus and Ballard with Ciaran on his shoulder stood together upon the balcony, outside of the royal sitting area, not a word was spoken.

Atesh and Master Thaddeus cantered away down the covered laneway between the wooden arches; where climbing roses adorned the entire structure. As the breeze rustled the leaves and the mornings became crisper, it sent the last of the petals raining down onto the ground. This produced not only an array of vibrant colours; but a gentle assault upon one's senses. After many miles of this structure they exited into the open where the midday sun beamed with mild strength. Both sides of the roadway were wrapped in acres of fruit orchards, cattle grazing and crops. Even the undulating hills were swathed in rows of grape vines. The palace grounds were picturesque and vast.

Thaddeus explained the geography of the area as they rode. "The outer wall extended as far back as the black mountains in the distance. The battlements were divided into sections and soldiers regularly walked these; always someone on duty. Many of the villagers work these fields and were paid well. Taxes of course were paid annually from all areas; even as far as Tyral and the Southern Lands. For although these areas ran independently; a Vassal King, Chieftain or a

Fief Lord still owed their allegiance to Gareth the High King of this part of the known world. Of course this money is used to improve the communities and pays for the regiment soldier training, naval protection and kingdom wide, military forces."

"If there has been peace for so long Master, why do we have a need for a large military force?"

"Well Atesh, there are always local and political skirmishes between towns and yes; even kingdoms. There are roaming bandits to contend with. Then there's the monitoring of the western side of the northern border and now and again rogue pirates, or slavers give us indigestion. Healthy finances also mean the crown can assist when environmental disasters occur like floods, famine, disease or erupting volcanoes." Master Thaddeus became quite animated with his hands. "They learnt a hard lesson after many long years of peace. The Kings became complacent; let their military run down. Then one day out of the blue an invasion occurred from an unknown source of formidable soldiers. They were not of the Sofalan Kingdom; it was told they were at least two feet taller than our soldiers with bulging muscles and unusual metal weapons to match. It was only when the magicians of that time assisted the King's pathetic army did they overcome the opposing force. The lessons of ancient times had been forgotten, banished to become stories to tell children. So the High King decreed from that date on, the military for the entire kingdom must be as strong as finances could afford. That is the way it has been now for hundreds of years."

"How did they pass the great divide or did they come from the other direction, the endless ocean?"

"Yes a good question Atesh, one I cannot answer. We know that eventually the endless ocean must lead to land if what they say about the world being a sphere is correct and science would suggest it is. In times past they were not literate in the sciences as we are today, thus the name the endless ocean. If the invaders came from the other side of the world, the time it would have taken to sail that way, must have been many months or even years. We have sent out many a ship ourselves, but none ever returned. Before the great divide and the catastrophic event we know there were lands to the east of the

Archipelagos. Now that way is barred to us, so we are content within our own kingdom. We do not bother whoever is out there and we hope we go unnoticed to them."

"For many thousands of years my ancestors had maintained a hospice and education centre for healing on Ashmourne Island. Then they decided to expand their teaching to incorporate all forms of innate magic, high wizard training for all the sciences and research into new technology to enhance our way of life with crystal power. They envisaged one day they would create a special unit of magic enhanced warriors. They would have integrity and honesty as its core ideals and peace as its mission; so after the raising of the northern boundary, the *'Pace Alastriona'* came to be. We incorporated all our usual exercise routines and sword work and added soldier drills and magic items, with great success I might add. The Wizard Master was adamant that all high magic users would continue to remain independent of the High King's fealty. We feared that if a king could use, or manipulate us to overcome friend or foe, then that would be paramount to slavery. Imagine the power an unstable king could wield? We therefore only give council to royalty unless we are invaded again. Then any action taken is of course at the discretion of the Master of Ashmourne."

"Since the first Wizard Master Eldred Ashmourne, only a direct descendant may govern the academy and the lands, similar to Gavin's bloodline. Although we do not use the title of king to rule, the Master is a King none the less. It was bestowed on Eldred though he preferred his descendant's heirs be Wizard Masters. Every generation we have produced one to fit the bill. The children are still princesses and princes with all the trappings. The land titles held encompass the island of Ashmourne and all the eastern side of Sofala from the midline border of the Jangly/Meder river system east. It starts at the north behind the boundary to the southern tip of Sofala. There is also a parcel of land, well mostly mountain, on the western side, known as the Sanctuary that is my own slice of heaven as well. Oh there are many small islands in the Burning Sea including the sacred islands near to the great divide."

"Master you are a Freymore, how is it you are a direct descendant of Master Ashmourne?"

"Well Atesh, Master Eldred Ashmourne produced only females and the eldest daughter married a local healer named Skye Freymore and that is my lineage. I am the only one so far in my immediate family to have produced children. So it may fall to one of my descendants to carry on the governing line of Ashmourne."

"How is the Master selected if there are many children?"

"For some reason our line does not produce many children and when we do, males are rare. Perhaps because finding love has been difficult for us, we need to find the one that is the other half of our soul. Settling for second best never produces children. It is the most powerful high wizard in that family that takes on the responsibility. That is the way it has always been and shall always be. Elias and I are the same in power and strength. Although I was the elder, born by a few minutes, I wanted to have a family and peace to teach and perform my research. Elias loved the academy with a passion, so I stepped back for him. Now I feel Israe may be the next Academy Master, Gareth will not claim him for the throne, I will see to that."

That afternoon they headed north-west towards the ocean and the looming mountain range. Atesh loved the smell of the sea air; it made her feel alive. They ventured ever closer to the Black Mountains where in due course a large cavernous opening in the mountain rock could be seen. Entering this area, Atesh noticed that it tunnelled under the mountain for quite a way; wide enough that two horses could ride side by side. Within this area were many archways leading off to the left and right; into the darkness. It wasn't dank or musty, not the usual moisture laden, mossy walls that would be found underground. As they rode along, glowing crystals within the passageway walls would light the way ahead, they winked out as they passed the next crystal. Atesh looked at Thaddeus with a questioning furrowed brow.

"Yes, the crystals are magical, attuned to movement, a natural phenomenon, if you please. Well...I may have fiddled a little with them. There are many tunnels, as you have noticed. They lead to other areas on this estate. Amazing when you think on it, what magic and nature can achieve. Oh...one even leads to the castle via an underground roadway, built many years previous; we can explore them some other time if you like?"

They exited into a sight of majestic beauty. Atesh gasped and Thaddeus laughed at her open mouth and wide eyed stare. For before her, rested a hidden village with lush green carpeted grounds and blossoming trees exploding with colour and rich fragrance. A cacophony of bird sounds could be heard echoing off the rock walls from within the tree limbs. All the buildings were built and blended into the side of the mountains. It was completely enclosed; surrounded by the black glistening rock. At the far end was a castle. Only the front portion was visible, the rest lay deep within the rock. To the right of this structure was a thundering waterfall that led to a large clear sandy reservoir. A water wheel was found further along the stream; this enabled the water to keep moving as it meandered through and across the centre of the entire area. They crossed a delicately carved wooden bridge and rode up to the castle entrance.

"Atesh if you look to the right down a ways, there is an archway that leads to farming lands, cattle grazing, sheep, pigs, fowls and other food crops. My family has owned this parcel of land for many generations, gifted by the tribal chiefs to Eldred for saving their people. Here, over time we have all contributed to the build and what you see today, *The Sanctuary*. It is impenetrable; and self-reliant. The opening is closed magically at sun set and re-opens at dawn. There are retired knights and a few soldiers on duty throughout the front area of the mountain, unseen from the outside, so if ever we need to protect ourselves, we have ample warning. The mountain range goes for miles in all directions; we even have an ocean cove and jetty where we fish and a vessel moored if required."

"I don't see any wood forests; how do you heat all this area?"

"We have wood cutters up in the north end. We also utilise a thermal spring in a large cavern. This revealed it was once an active fire mountain, now thankfully slumbering; so the mountain maintains its own warm environment. We vent the steam and heat from this spring. Between a bit of magic, crystal power and engineering, we devised a method by strategically placing air shafts up through the mountain. This allows the outside sea air to descend and forces the steam the spring produces, along the larger shafts. This then heats the forges, homes, workshops and kitchens. We have a large dining hall where we all sit together and we eat as one big happy family. How about a quick tour before we get down to business. I am sure you would then like to freshen up and we will meet back in my study."

Back at the Beaumont castle, King Gareth joined the men as they worked hard with their routines and later all walked stiff and sore towards the bathing rooms. A few of the knights were still quite frisky and laughed and mimicked the soldiers as they walked awkward after their gruelling sessions. Gareth turned and watched. He was not amused. Putting on a brave face himself, all he wanted was to soak forever in a hot bath.

"Captain Ballard seeing as some of your men has energy to spare. Would you do me the favour of collecting the wood for the fire pit tonight? A large bonfire would be nice, if you don't mind." *That will teach them to be haughty, laugh at us will they?*

The knights set off in an ordered, slow rhythmical run into the forest, axes slung over their shoulders. They let loose with a loud bawdy song as they ran, to pose all the more and heard groans from the soldiers behind.

"Away we go a wand 'ring through hills an dales an cricks.

To find a bonny lassie wid, good teeth, great curves, big…"

Gareth shook his head in amazement at the knights' stamina. He nodded as he strode by the workers, assembling the large marquees. Inside men were setting the trestle tables and placing numerous bales of hay around for seating; all in preparation for the birthday celebration tomorrow.

Brianna now fully rested went in search of her husband, they needed a talk. She had fallen to sleep early and noticed Gareth kept close, hovering around, when he wasn't outside trying to keep up with the younger soldiers. She had not spoken to him of her news as yet, though she held all others to secrecy. She found him in the sitting room beside the fire, paperwork in his hand, eyes closed. He looked exhausted. She stood and watched his chest rise and fall in the rhythmical dance of life. Her eyes and facial expression said it all. Yes, even after nineteen years of marriage she was still in awe and deeply in love with her husband. Her brows furrowed for a moment. *What will he say to this news?*

As if sensing her presence Gareth opened his eyes to find his wife staring at him with a cheeky smile upon her face. He raised one eyebrow and gestured to her to sit beside him. She manoeuvred closer, then sat upon his knees and placed her arms around his neck. He made sure she did not see him wince, his muscles screamed at him after the day of torture on the field; with those inhuman knights.

"I love you, Gareth."

"I am wildly in love with you Brie. How are you feeling now? You worried me, being so pale yesterday."

"I am fine, we all are thank you; the girls are back to their old selves and Israe is… well he is, what he is." She laughed for a moment and then her face turned serious. "I need to talk with you."

"Oh…what sort of talk? A husband talk, a father talk or, is it…a sire talk?"

"The first kind, my love; can we adjourn to our apartment for some privacy?"

Brianna sat on the edge of the bed, Gareth snuggled up beside her.

"Alright, let me have it, what can this husband do for you?"

"Well Gareth…I…am with child."

Gareth sat upright and stared at her. "After so many years, are you sure, Brie?"

"Yes, a reliable source informed me yesterday…but there is more." Her hand's blanched as she wrung them tight beside her. "I am…not having just one."

"What! Twins again, that is amazing."

"Gareth, no…I am not having twins." She held up three fingers.

Gareth went pale and shook his head. "Oh you are having a joke with me, right?"

"Apparently not, it is two boys and a girl to be exact."

"How…who, oh my, two boys you say and a girl."

"Atesh told me yesterday and father says that it would be correct."

"Tell me what I drank that night and I promise to never drink that again. Oh, I don't know whether to laugh or cry. It is wonderful news, but…will you be alright."

"Atesh said I should ask Uncle Elias to borrow healer Jenner for the duration. Can you do that for me please?"

"Certainly, I am sure Elias will do this for us and I think one young nephew will be thrilled."

"We must celebrate; this is the best news possible for us."

"Please can we wait a few more weeks, in case I lose them like last time?"

"Of course, perchance a wise move. But, there is also something, I must tell you." He held her hands tight and looked into her eyes. Gareth then told Brie what transpired while she was away. "I am sorry my love, placing Kyle in the hospice was all I could think to do. Thaddeus spoke of bad blood, the pox, but they can't be sure if this is so, or if it is something else." They both allowed themselves time to grieve for their wayward son.

After some time Gareth spoke of the preparations for the coming celebration. "Are you still up to this Brie?"

"Yes, Aiden is like one of our own. By the way where did Commander Atesh and my father go? I saw their horses saddled."

"I believe they have gone up to the Sanctuary for a few days."

"Why now, when it is Aiden's turning tomorrow, what if we need him?"

"It was important my love."

"Why go to the sanctuary? He does not take outsiders there. Please tell me what is going on?"

"Wizard stuff, you know how he is."

"Hmmm…Maybe when they return, we can have a formal dinner. I would love to see Atesh out of that uniform into a beautiful dress, she would look elegant. Strange thing is, she reminds me of my grandmother when she was a young lady; such likeness. Father has her painting up at the sanctuary, the same tri-coloured hair, though she braided it up and around her head. Those piercing blue eyes that seem to be like fire. I saw the way Marcus and Aiden look at her. Does she have them both eating out of her hands?"

"Oh no, Aiden is smitten with healer Jenner. Marcus well…yes he does have it bad, I'm afraid. But we will see."

"Who might be her family Gareth? Are they related somehow to this bloodline?"

"She was a foundling I am told Brie, perhaps enquire with your father when he returns."

Brianna narrowed her eyes. Her thoughts ran all different scenarios through her mind and left the conversation at that. *Wizard stuff my bloomers, what is that old codger up to?*

That evening Ballard and Marcus sat around the fire pit after all the others had retired. As the moon reached its peak; full in all its glory. It signalled the start to the new day; the first day of the cold, white season. Both men turned their heads and gazed to the north. The castle crystal lights had dimmed to an eerie glow, casting shadows upon the faded walls and flapping canvas. Out the back, the kitchens remained in full swing. They roasted, basted and stuffed all in preparation for the large feast in a few hours. The cooking odours wafted throughout the castle grounds and caused all awake to stop, lift their noses higher and inhale deep. Stomach growls were heard from afar as guards stood watch, torment apparent.

Marcus threw a stick into the fire and watched the ember sparks dance away into the night, he turned to Ballard and broke the silence. "Can you tell me about Atesh? How is it she was found at the academy with no family to claim her?"

"Perhaps you need to ask Atesh, not me, Marcus."

"No, I need to hear it from you. The one that found her, please Ballard, I implore you."

Seeing the anguish in the eyes of his nephew he relented. After a deep breath he began the story.

"Well…Vykter, Berend and I had been at the academy since we were kids. The three of us stuck together with everything we did. During forms this particular week, Master Elias placed us at the back of the knights. This was a huge honour; it meant now, we no longer were juniors. One morning I noticed, during our routine Master Elias standing on a balcony above in the tower, his eyes searched behind me and he smiled. In my head, his voice told me not to turn around; as a young child was watching from the bushes. As you know we turn quite a bit with the forms. So each time I glanced back, I saw this small waif of a child performing our routines, with odd sorts of movements. I had never noticed her before, but she must have been watching for a number of days, week's maybe; to understand it all. After the forms the three of us searched all through the forest beside the parade ground, but could not find a trace of her.

"The next day was the same. So we decided to make small wooden swords and left food out for her. These disappeared and again we could not find a trace. This went on for a week. Master Elias said she used the swords well. He was surprised and delighted. Then two days in a row she didn't show. I was summoned to his office and given instructions to use the hounds to find the girl, Elias had a bad feeling, something was wrong." Ballard got up and paced back and forth before he continued. "It took some time, but hidden behind some bushes at the far end of the forest was a hollowed out tree bole and inside laid an unconscious girl curled up beside a miniature dragon creature. We rushed them to the healers; they felt feverish and looked ashen. I can tell you they worked hard to save both their lives. The Master Healer cornered us the next morning and asked how we came by them. Well we couldn't tell him much at all. Then a few days later Master Elias summoned me to his office.

"The poor mite was malnourished, all skin and bone. She was covered in layers of mud, dried blood and grime." Ballard then described her injuries to Marcus as Master Elias had explained them. "She remembers nothing at all. On her threadbare shift was basted a little rabbit, so this became her nickname. I was asked if I would assist in raising the child, as every time I visited she held onto my hand and cried when I had to go. They re-broke her hips and straightened her legs. They healed her internal injuries, they believed caused by a fall from a great height. The…burns had left deep scarring. The healers' say from a hot implement dragged across her abdomen many times Marcus."

Marcus had paled by this statement. "Oh! She was a child, who would…why?" He held his head between his hands.

"It was apparent by the evidence, she had been tied up. We had thought perhaps slavers or pirates. It took many painful sessions to remove all the threads of rope that were imbedded into her ankles and wrists. She later had tattoos placed around her wrists to camouflage the scarring. She was placed into special leg splints which lasted for a couple of years. We were given a double suite at the compound and I became her surrogate father. Vykter and Berend took turns as well; they were her favourite uncles so to speak. Master Elias and the healers oversaw her daily health needs and education. Atesh does not know this but, Master Elias believes all her injuries were not human made, he would not elaborate on this and I did not press him…."

Ballard placed his hand on his nephew's shoulder. "Marcus she is not only scarred physically, but in her mind as well. She believes that her parents rejected her for something she did or didn't do and to hurt her in such a horrific manner. A punishment so no-one would ever want her. She must be flawed somehow. Her scars remind her each and every day that no-one will want to be close, she is an abomination. I have tried to teach her about love, friendship and family, by supporting, guiding and understanding her. Though I am not old enough to be her father that is how she sees me. She poured all her hurt and anguish into her studies. She needed to be the best to show the world she was alive and worthy."

"How did she perform the routines with broken bones and all that damage?"

"Apart from sheer will power, some of her bones had healed, but they were crooked. She improvised the moves, ingenious the way she did them. Perhaps the energy required to do the forms was the reason she became so ill and near died."

"Ballard, maybe she needs someone to really love her; to be patient, kind and understanding to heal. Not a father figure, a partner equal in all sense. You and the men have performed an unbelievable feat. Atesh is an amazing lady. She is compassionate, honest and funny; a brilliant knight and Commander."

"That may be true Marcus; though for your sake, I do hope she gives you the chance to find out."

"Ballard there is something now I wish to tell you, but I must have your oath to say not a word until Master Thaddeus says so: agreed?"

Ballard raised his eyebrows and looked deep into Marcus's golden flecked, blue eyes. He took a deep breath and whispered, "Agreed."

"Grandfather spoke to me yesterday. He believes he and Elias have worked out Atesh's identity. That was why she was taken to the Sanctuary; for peace and safety to all."

Ballard stood up and looked down at his nephew. "WHAT, is that you say?"

"Sit down please, Uncle."

"Who is she Marcus?"

"Atesh is Liera Beaumont, my cousin and Aiden's twin sister."

Ballard was speechless. He stared at Marcus and then turned his gaze upon the fire. "So the story of Aiden's sister dying at age three was false?"

"Well… they assumed of course. She had been carried off by a flying panther creature, after it had killed their nanny. Uncle Morgan searched for years, but there was never a trace. It was Queen Mia that informed grandfather; she told him, she felt his family's innate signature in her. Her lineage has some powerful wizards Ballard and Israe may in the future be similar in power."

"Oh dear ancient ones, her family are here and they didn't recognise her? Do you think they suspect Marcus?"

"I have watched Uncle Morgan and he has an expression I am unable to read on his face when he watches her. Aiden has a connection I am betting, but doesn't realise what it is. But I cannot say if they suspect what is in front of their noses."

"If Atesh was abducted as a three year old and we found her as a five or six year old, where had she been all this time, Marcus?"

They both sat quiet and wondered at all the pieces of the puzzle.

Chapter 24

The Turnings:

After breakfast Marcus and Ballard scheduled volunteers to perform sword demonstrations and wrestling matches to entertain the crowd later in the day. They watched as the Circus and Carnival folk rolled in. They arrived in wonderous, colourful, wooden caravan homes; pulled by their majestic dapple grey Clydesdale horses. Smoke emanated from their chimneys and potted plants bloomed from their window boxes. Music and children's laughter were all around, as they supervised the setting up of the acrobatic, ball juggling and fire breathing Jesters. There were also mystical palm and crystal readers, a puppet theatre, men walking on stilts, wire-walkers, tumblers and a singing bard; full of grand tales and bawdy songs. The Kings men arranged the archery shoots, horse racing and spear throwing arenas; these were placed behind and away from the main marquee.

The castle attendants rushed about like scattered roaches, as visitors and dignitaries arrived around midday, in their gilded carriages; all requiring attention. Master Elias sent his apologies; he was closely monitoring the north east boundary. He had sent four knight battalions to find the breach and if possible, seal it. The watch at Beaumont Castle was doubled for the next twenty four hours and the knights elected to have their turn on sentry duty as well. So Marcus decided that there would be one knight and one regiment soldier for each area around the castle; with four hour rotations. That way all were able to enjoy a portion of the celebrations.

Master Thaddeus had calculated a time chart; indicating how each day was separated into twenty four hourly segments. He utilised the positions of the sun and shade during the day and the moon and stars at night. He marked out hour intervals within a drawn circle, indicating their world. Full sun was midday-1200 hours and full moon was at 2400 hours. He then designed a metal sand device that would take exactly one hour to empty. This was the most difficult part, gathering the correct density of sand granules for the precision he required. After many tries he found the clean white sand from Tyral emptied to the accuracy he desired. Then, when his apparatus rotated it would recommence the hourly countdown . It was one of his first inventions. The castle chimer would ring the time bell for each hour as indicted by the sand device and time chart.

Then Thaddeus worked out, there were eight days to a week and then twelve weeks per season. There was also the in-between times, a period of eight days when the season would change from one to the other. This occurred four times within the year. The first season was Red, this was the hot, dry time; the days were long and humid. Yellow season was next; these days were comfortable to work in. Tree leaves turned from orange to yellow and blossoms began to fall to the ground as the nights became cooler. White season was the cold time; when rain, wind and snow filtered down from the sky, filling dams and rivers. The last season was the time of rebirth, the green season. All creatures and vegetation would bud and blossom with regrowth, while the farm animals would give birth to their next generation. This cycle would recommence again each year. So essentially fifty two weeks per year.

The afternoon festivities arrived all too soon. King Gareth, Duke Morgan and Prince Fynton watched the sword fighting demonstrations. It commenced as a round robin and the victor played the next and so on. Ballard wiped the floor with all opponents that came before, now he was sparing with Marcus. Those not in the know would say the men were evenly matched, but there was one who watched with a smirk on his face. He had arrived not a half hour earlier with an escort of ten men. He stood large, tall and regal. He was a head and a bit taller than Gareth, long blond hair that was now greying in places, with piercing raptor blue eyes. His presence spoke power and authority.

"He is playing with your son Gareth, putting on a show for the audience; he could have taken him many strokes ago."

"Yes, you are right there Angus, the people like to see their Prince give a good show. By the looks of his beaded brow and damp shirt, he is trying his hardest."

"Yes Gareth, but look at the opponent. A big fella, but moves with such grace and lightness…one of the knights, I gather. Not even a bead of perspiration on him, what amazing stamina. Who is he? I would like to poach him for sure."

Gareth had a mischievous grin adorning his face. "I will introduce you when they finish if you like."

Not long after, Marcus was flipped onto his back and disarmed. Ballard placed his foot on Marcus's chest and raised his sword, indicating victory. A round of applause ensued. He bowed to the crowd and assisted his opponent up off the ground.

Marcus and Ballard wandered over to grab a mug of ale when Gareth and the larger gent came up behind them. Marcus turned around. He was introduced to his maternal Grandfather, King Angus Greymont of the Southern Islands. Ballard stood frozen to the spot, not wanting to breathe or move, his eyes closed tight, spoke volumes. How he wished he could be invisible right now. A smile broke out on Angus and he gave his grandson a bear hug.

"You have become quite a good sized lad, your mother would have been proud. Now my boy, would you do this old man a favour and introduce me to your excellent opponent."

Marcus had paled and wasn't sure what to say. "Umm…Sir, this is Captain Ballard of the Ashmourne Knights' First Battalion."

Ballard turned and looked directly into his father's eyes.

Angus recognised only the eyes on the young man standing before him; and involuntarily took a step back. He then thrust out his hand as a good will gesture. Ballard looked at Gareth and then Marcus. Took one longer, hard look at Angus, then turned and strode away.

"Well Gareth, fancy that. Not even recognising my own son." He shook his head in chastisement of his own ignorance . "Though , it went better than I envisaged it."

"Angus, go after him, make amends. We all need to work together on our problem tomorrow. Come on, it has been what…twenty years or more; too long to hold a grudge. He is a superb knight, dedicated, honest and second only to the Supreme Commander; whom he raised and mentored. He needs to know you care."

Angus watched as Marcus sat beside his son talking in hushed tones. He grabbed two mugs and sauntered over to the fire pit and sat down on the other side of Ballard. He noticed movement close by as the knights congregated behind their Captain. Marcus stood and walked over to the small group. He reassured them their Captain was in no danger. That it was a father and son moment.

"Time to make amends son. I must admit I did not recognise you out there. The boy has certainly become that which he so desperately yearned to be, a great knight. So have all your dreams come true then?"

"I am happy and content if that's what you mean sir."

"You ran away remember. I did not force you to go."

"I had no choice, what was I to you? Did you know I even existed, the youngest son? I was invisible to you. You never said two words to me in all the years I lived with you."

"I am sorry son. I was a lone parent, we do the best we know how, it was never perfect and I had such responsibilities. We try to be everywhere, always giving, making decisions. It doesn't always work out. I never blamed you for your mother not surviving the birth, if that is what you thought."

Ballard hung his head, his voice breaking. "I needed to know you cared. A hug, one simple hug was all I ever wanted. Why now? Why wait all these years to see me, or was this an inconvenient coincidence?"

"I understand your hostilities. I am here for the treaty, to form an alliance to assist with this abduction problem we are all having. We have felt this too in our lands. I had hoped to see you on my way home, so this has been a fortunate event. Let's start slow perhaps." He put out his hand again and this time Ballard looked at the hand, then grasped it. "You have grown up my son, into a fine young man. I am proud of you."

Marcus and the knights were not far away, pleased with the outcome.

"So Commander Marcus, that large tree of a man is the Southern King, our Captain's father? What are the women folk like, if all the men look like giants?"

"Well Vykter that I am not too sure about, but my mother was average height, slim with golden eyes and blonde wavy hair down past her waist. I hear she was a real beauty, intelligent and feisty. Gee I missed out on her best bits eh!"

They all laughed and slapped each other on the back, but stayed close by in position, all the same.

As the evening progressed, Ballard and the knights performed one of their sword dance routines. All the spectators were mesmerised, as the knights, twirled, slashed and fought to a rhythm, no one else could hear. Co-ordinated by Ballard, he was exceptional. His red flaming sword looked like an extension of his body and they were one, the perfect synergistic relationship. The crowd roared and gasped when swords passed by their opponent by a whisker. Angus stood and stared at the spectacle, never seeing or believing this was possible. He turned to Gareth as it concluded his eyes wide in wonder and amazement.

"Yes Angus, they are truly that good. You should see their Commander. Wow and when those two perform together, it is out of this world I can tell you."

"When is he returning?"

"Oh, Commander Atesh is a she Angus and what a beauty. She has all the men eating out of her hands."

"A female Supreme Commander…my son is second…to a woman!?"

"Not just any woman, a magically powerful and competent Commander. Your son mentored her from a child. That alone, you should be proud of."

"Are they an item, Gareth?"

"Gosh no more like a, father and daughter relationship. They are close, a strong bond; but not in that way. Marcus is the one bitten by the love bug."

Gareth and Angus turned to the main marquee when they saw Marcus running towards it. Aiden had collapsed feeling unwell. Duke Morgan and Prince Fynton were beside him talking quiet.

"Aiden practice your breathing as Grandfather taught you, it will not last long. Concentrate on my words." Marcus held his arm and talked him through the technique.

Aiden's face blanched, his hair line was beaded with perspiration. Droplets cascaded down to moisten his reddened cheeks and dampen his shirt. Ballard and Jenner were summoned and soon rushed over to Aiden. Jenner closed her eyes as she placed the clear crystal on his forehead. It burst into colour; blue flames swirled within the jewel. She gasped and sat back hard on the ground. She looked up at Ballard with Marcus, Morgan and Gareth staring down at her with furrowed brows.

"He is channeling extra power from elsewhere. I have never seen this happen before. He needs to relax and terminate the bond or it may consume him. What is going on here?"

"Jenner he needs to terminate this link. Believe me it will not end well if he does not. I will explain later, I promise." Marcus then turned to his father and ushered him out of the tent.

"Father he is channeling power from Atesh, somehow they have connected. He will die if he does not sever the link. I wish grandfather were here."

"I am sure he has his hands full now Marcus. Let us hope he sees this and have Atesh break the bond first."

The immediate family surrounded Aiden, worry etched in all their faces. Ballard looked at Marcus and raised an eyebrow. Marcus nodded ever so slight back. Ballard then walked over to Gareth.

"Sire you must tell Aiden, so he can break the bond. I know Atesh and she may be struggling with the enormity of the power, let alone a link to her twin, please...I implore you."

Gareth looked deeply into Ballard's eyes and saw only concern and a great deal of love and fear. "So you are aware then who Atesh is?"

"Marcus had confided in me, yes sir."

Gareth then looked at Marcus and Aiden. "So be it."

Gareth asked for the tent to be vacated except for family and the attending knights. He then sat down beside Aiden and spoke loud enough for all in the immediate vicinity to hear. "Aiden you have accidently channeled into another turning tonight. You must break this bond now, relax your mind and concentrate; visualise cutting a piece of rope. Jenner please stay beside him and assist, he must visualise severing the connection." Gareth then spoke to the family kneeling around Aiden's bed. "Morgan the other person turning eighteen tonight has an enormous amount of innate magic, so much that she will become not only a higher wizard in time; but the most powerful in the known world. Aiden has accidently tapped into this. It is understandable and confirms our suspicions. Morgan please sit down for me, I have something to tell you brother."

Gareth told Morgan and the family what they had learnt about Atesh, but wanted confirmation by her turning before saying anything.

"So you are saying, Gareth that this Commander Atesh is our daughter Liera, Aiden's twin sister. How…how can that be? We looked all over. There was never a word, a hint. You are telling us we have been this close without knowing our own daughter?"

"It is true, I am afraid. Ballard can explain how she came to be at the academy as a young child."

Lysanna placed her hands up to her face covering the tears that welled and escaped down her reddened cheeks. Brianna sat in thought; a smile lifted one side of her mouth as she gazed, nodding at her husband.

Morgan placed his arm around his wife's shoulders. He looked up at Ballard. "This is correct, Captain?"

"Yes sir, I believe this to be true."

Jenner overheard and stared at Aiden wide eyed, then Duke Morgan and Captain Ballard. Jenner looked back to her patient. "Marcus, Ballard I need your assistance quick."

Aiden's eyes had turned up and his breathing became shallow. They continually spoke words of encouragement, imploring him to sever the tie. Aiden arched his back and let out an almighty scream, blue sparks shot out from his eyes, as a seizure took hold of him. He was turning dusky around the mouth, white foamy fluid trickled down from one side to pool next to his chin. They held on to him tight as he went rigid and all his muscles contracted into abnormal positions. Marcus moved his hand towards Aiden's mouth. Jenner reached out in one swift motion and grabbed his hand.

"Marcus you will lose fingers if you place them near his mouth. He may clamp down hard and there is nothing you can do to open his mouth when he is in this tight state. You must wait till the muscles loosen."

Marcus looked at his fingers then Aiden's mouth and shuddered.

Jenner placed a clear crystal on his forehead and spoke quiet words over him. Then with the assistance of Marcus and Ballard they turned him over onto his side, with his head tilted back, so he could breathe. In time his body relaxed. Colour crept back around his lips.

Outside a commotion occurred. Ballard rushed outside to witness the brightest blue flame shooting up into the sky; it then exploded into a thousand tiny stars, way off into the north. The crowd clapped and whistled for the spectacular event was mind boggling. Outside the tent the knights and regiment soldiers had gathered. After the display with the blue flame had ended, they bowed to the north and saluted with their right arm across their chest.

Ciaran sat on Vykter's shoulder, tiny crystal tears dropped onto his shirt and tinkled as they fell to the ground. "That be the most beautiful sign I ever seen. The lassie will return tomorrow, ye will see."

"How do you know that?" A unison of voices enquired.

"Well I did hear a *woo-hoo* in my head. That was the extra power the lassie finally let go lads. Oh, she will be a powerful one now; that be for sure."

Aiden awoke some time later holding Jenner's hand. He breathed easier and colour had returned to his face. When he opened his eyes the blue now contained sparkle like flashes. He smiled but did not let go of her hand.

Up at the Sanctuary, Atesh lay flat on the grass next to the water pond. She was saturated and exhausted from the effort of the turning. Master Thaddeus found Atesh's turning far more powerful than he could ever have imagined. Worse still, Aiden had tapped into her power with his, thus opening a two way valve. With the magic travelling back and forth between the two, it seemed to expand in size and ferocity. Thaddeus had no choice, he had to join with them and assist in the release of this almighty force. An explosion of this magnitude would be catastrophic for the whole kingdom. He instructed Atesh on talking Aiden into severing the link first. While ever that bond was intact Atesh was unable to discharge the extra build-up of power and it threatened to consume not only herself, but Aiden and perhaps incinerate the entire west coast of Sofala as well. Then together Thaddeus and Atesh released the built up power into the night sky.

"Well that certainly was a first for me, my dear. Though Elias and I turned together, I don't remember being linked to that extreme."

"I am afraid that some of the extra power filtered through into Aiden. We connected so strong, it scared me. He was also afraid and hung on near too long. I could feel Jenner on the other side encouraging him to sever the link. I am concerned as he has a lot of that power now; do you think he will be alright?

"Yes we shall soon see how he fares when we return. There is another matter I must speak with you about, though it is all connected with this blessed event. I suspected, but I needed confirmation before I spoke my mind to you. Well Atesh, I believe now that I have witnessed this turning; I know your lineage. You are…Aiden's twin sister, Liera."

"How can this be? I was a foundling. It is not possible Master Thaddeus."

"Well…you see, Liera was abducted by a flying Black Panther creature as a three year old and never seen again. The family all assumed she had perished. The scars on your body were from creature marks, not human made Atesh. My brother Elias could not tell you this before. He felt it best you didn't know this gruesome detail of your childhood. He could not understand how you came by these. Your family did not desert you Atesh as you believed. They had tried to find you for years. You…are…my lost granddaughter ." Thaddeus choked up at this point.

Atesh had placed her trembling hand to her mouth, her eyes wide, misted with tears. "Did you know when I first came to the castle? Did Master Elias know who I was all this time?"

"No we had no idea. It was Mia who first enlightened me to your identity. She felt the family's innate signature. Now that you have had your turning, I can also feel the block lifted. I would like to know who placed that on you. Only another High Wizard could have performed that spell."

"I remember nothing before the academy, I'm sorry Master."

"Well no matter, we must return first thing in the morning to assist Aiden. Both of you require tutorage now. We have a lot of discussions to attend as well. This has been a big revelation, for us all. I am glad to have found you; my family is once again complete." He moved forward and gave Atesh a wonderful warm hug.

A short while later Atesh sat next to the running stream. A warm cup of tea in one hand the other fiddled with the grass next to her knees; tears continued to cascade from her eyes. "All those years thinking I was not wanted, I was ugly, unlovable. Now you tell me I had a family that looked for me for years. Where was I Master? Why can I not remember? You tell me that…creature that abducted Jesper was the same one that took me away as a child?

"Yes it does seem that is so Atesh. Not many of us remember what happened to us as a child, so do not be too hard on your-self. The best outcome has been achieved, if you look at it. You somehow escaped and are now the Supreme Commander of the greatest warriors in this kingdom. You have an extended family that loves you and if I am not mistaken, a young man whose heart you have stolen."

Chapter 25

The Alliance:

After a good night's rest Aiden was up and about as usual. He felt full of energy and vigour, though his muscles were quite a bit tender. There was an inner excitement he could not explain, let-alone contain. He met his father in the corridor and a quick word was spoken. They would meet with Thaddeus and Atesh upon their return and discuss what had transpired the previous evening. After breakfast with the family, he bounded outside to see the men when King Angus beckoned him over to the stables.

"I present a small gift to you my lad, for your eighteenth birth-day."

A beautiful black foal was led out to the yard. He stood tall and majestic for one so young.

"You do know, we breed the best horses in the kingdom, don't you?"

"Oh Uncle Angus, can this be true? He is mine? What do you call him?"

"We have left that privilege up to you laddie; he will make a fine war-steed, no doubt."

Aiden moved slowly up to the foal. He spoke quiet and touched him with gentleness on his withers. He felt the little shivers go down the foal's spine. Then he moved up to stroke his face. Their eyes met and both felt a two way energy transference.

"You are so handsome little man, what shall I name you?"

"My mother calls me Donal; I will be a great warrior someday. I will make you proud my prince."

Aiden stepped back with widened eyes and then turned to Angus. "Uncle, the foal spoke to me in my mind."

"Well that doesn't surprise me lad, after your show last night. What did the little fella have to say to you?"

"Well, he said his mother called him Donal, so that is what I shall name him."

Angus walked away chuckling to himself. Aiden stayed and walked the foal over to the grassed area. While he gave him a brush down, Aiden seemed to be discussing something profound, using wild hand gestures. The foal oddly enough, nodded in all the appropriate places. There was even a show of small white teeth; his top lip turned up could be interpreted as a smile. It looked quite amusing to anyone that passed by.

Gareth, Marcus and Ballard sauntered over. "Oh, someone has his own pet to play with, eh Angus."

"Yes apparently they can communicate; they will be good friends, I feel."

Marcus and Ballard walked off a way and stared out to the north in quiet contemplation.

"So Gareth what is happening with those two? What is their problem?"

"Oh Angus, one is pining for his soul-mate to return. The other a guardian worried about his charge."

"Care to explain that eh?"

"How about we discuss this over a brandy and a cigar; they were a special delivery from the islands. You know Angus, for a few minutes. I feel everything is right in the world; or so it seems." They watched the men for a while before retiring to the King's sitting room.

The men were back to preparations for the northern trip, checking supplies, rostering the soldiers and ensuring all horses were fit and battle ready. The new saddle bags had arrived and were placed ready for the unit's horses, but the regiment soldiers would not find out till tomorrow. Marcus wanted to witness their expressions in person.

That afternoon the exercise and battle routines continued; this time Ballard increased the speed. This the men found exciting, challenging and enjoyable. When they completed a few sets of these, they walked away stiff, sore and bruised. As they strode past the stables, Kayne was being led inside. Ballard, Marcus and Aiden whipped their heads around to see Atesh leaning by the entrance to their accommodation, a large smile upon her face. Ciaran dove off Ballard's shoulder, he hopped and partly flew into her open arms; he cooed and snorted smoke, to the laughter of all. Master Thaddeus' black cape swung behind him as he disappeared into the castle.

All the men rushed at her, big hugs and slaps ensued. Ballard, Aiden and Marcus stood back and waited for the melee to be over. The men gave her three cheers. They then went to organise a celebration inside.

Ballard strode up and gave Atesh a big mountain man hug; she buried her head in his shoulder and hugged back. She wiped the tears from her eyes.

Aiden went up and also gave her a hug, whispering into her ear. "Can you come up and see me after. We need to talk…alone?" Atesh nodded and held him tight.

Last was Marcus, the others scattered and left them alone. "Atesh may we sit for a moment?" He held her hand and led her over to the fire pit, which was smouldering. "I, um…am so relieved to see you are well. Last night must have been frightening for you. We here certainly had a time of it. I know Atesh about your turning excitement, father told me. This doesn't change how I feel. I wanted you to know. Oh dear…I am not saying this right, am I?"

Atesh smiled at him. Their eyes met and no further words needed to be spoken. Atesh stood and Marcus thought he had lost the moment. She turned to face him and threw her arms around his neck and gave him a gentle and passionate kiss. His return kiss was fuelled by intense heat. When they finally parted breathless; Marcus whispered into her ear.

"Will you m…."

Atesh placed her finger upon his lips. He pulled her down to sit on his lap. They continued with their passionate embrace, intimate words without speech. Atesh disengaged herself and stared into Marcus' blue, gold flecked eyes. She saw the depth of his feelings for her and it frightened her, to her core.

I am a knight. This is who I am. I cannot give up my calling, even for love. Can I? What if I do live forever, how can I love and have a family and watch them grow old before my eyes and die. I don't know if I am strong enough for that, over and over never-ending. "Marcus, there are some things you need to know about me, but now is not the time or place. Let us see how all this turns out."

"Agreed, but I know there is nothing you can say that will change my mind."

From behind them, the men all vying for a better view were squished between the wooden window frames and the door entrance; parts of bodies were hanging out of the accommodation building. A lot of pushing and shoving had occurred until they were stacked, racked and packed in tight. There was a rousing applause and woof whistles from all the knights and soldiers. Both Marcus and Atesh felt their cheeks heat up. Atesh buried her head into Marcus's shoulder and sniggered.

"I hope my face is not the colour of fresh beetroot like yours Marcus."

"It sure is, oh powerful one."

"Oh we are never going to hear the end of this Marcus; prepare thy-self."

They both laughed and joined the party inside.

Master Thaddeus entered the sitting area to find Gareth, Angus and Morgan all having a brandy and cigar. "May this old man join you?"

Gareth jumped up. "Oh Thaddeus it is good to have you return. Please sit and tell us how you endured up at Sanctuary."

Thaddeus eyed them all. "It went well enough, thankyou sire."

Gareth got the hint and changed the subject. Morgan sat quiet and bored his eyes into the side of Thaddeus' head; he wanted a conversation, but now was not the time.

Thaddeus turned to Angus and placed out his hand in a friendship gesture, "I am not sure, have we met sir?"

"Sorry Thaddeus I assumed…this is Angus Greymont; King of the Southern Islands."

"Ballard's father, yes, yes, I can see the resemblance…Oh my goodness. I did meet you many years ago, now that I remember." Thaddeus eyes glazed over for a minute remembering days gone by. "Ah yes in the old academy days, my brother and I had all sorts of adventures with the southern twins, we called them Blue and Grey. Blue would have been your grandfather perhaps. Yes, he returned to the islands to be King. Grey however found himself at the wrong end of my father's ire. He disappeared with our youngest brother Jimmie, on a sea adventure."

"Yes Master Thaddeus that is correct, they were never heard from again. I often wondered where they could have ended up."

"Yes, it was a mystery eh, Angus. Oh is there anyone yet to arrive?"

"Only one Thaddeus and he should be here any time now."

As if on cue, a runner from the gate carried a message to Gareth.

"Well, looks like Cedric has just arrived with his entourage."

The men all wandered down to the castle entrance to meet with the Pirate King, or Chieftain as he liked to be called. There had been an alliance for many years now between them all. Their families were all intermingled. A nightmare to work out, if one dared to try.

Cantering through the gates were ten golden Palominos with beautiful blonde manes gently waving in the breeze. The leader of this party was a tall battle worn gent, of similar build to the Greymont's, with dark brown undulating hair that rested past his shoulders. Many strange and alluring decorations dangled from his left ear lobe. He glanced around with eyes a deep chocolate with golden flecks, tightly trimmed moustache and beard. He had a twinkle of mischief to his eyes and was ready with a generous smile. Behind him sat two similar featured, though much younger soldiers and then more battled hardened warriors to be sure, in all sorts of unusual and colourful garb. The one item they all had in common were their cutlasses. Each adorned with different coloured jewels.

"Cedric welcome to my home. Your suite is ready and the unit has quarters with the knights, if that is acceptable to you all?"

"Most gracious of you Gareth," He bowed his head in respect. "Thank you that will be fine with us." He dismissed his soldiers and they were shown to their quarters. Cedric walked beside Angus Greymont.

"Nice to see you old boy, how are Elara and all the grandchildren?"

"Ha old boy, I am younger than you, remember cousin." He slapped Angus on the back. "They are doing well and we must all visit, once this drama is finished with. You know, I lost a whole crew. The ship we found dead in the water, no-one on board. My niece Captain Charlie, a mighty fine Captain at that; all disappeared. I thought foul play at first, but the sails were ripped to shreds with enormous claw marks, such bad business this."

"Charlie? Oh you mean Charmaine. So she eventually conned you into giving her, her own ship; the shrewdest pirate to roam the unforgiving seas. So she is lost too? I am sorry cousin that's not good at all."

A large banquet was prepared for all the family and guests. The knights, regiment soldiers and southern guards were introduced to the pirate warriors; they were quite a mixed bag of muscle.

Ballard vacated his suite and bunked in with the men, he felt it was appropriate for Jenner and Ryna to have his room, now there were so many unknown men within the dormitory. After all, he had explained to them. "Pirates never really change their ways, always on the lookout for what they can steal or plunder. They can be ruthless cutthroats when there was booty or women involved." Ballard knew another sister was married to Cedric's eldest son. And there be two younger cousins bunking in with them now, though he had never met these kin.

The Commanders, Captains and Kings were sequestered into the war/briefing room for discussions. They stood at the balcony prior to taking their seats and watched the knights and soldiers below continue their usual routines of self-inflicted pain on the field. They were led by Vykter this afternoon. The remaining visitors sat to the back of the field and watched. Some tried to emulate the movements and fell flat on their faces, to the raucous laughter of all.

Cedric shook his head. "Well that was embarrassing."

"Do not concern yourself too much Cedric. You should have seen us last week; all black and blue I tell you. Some of us will never walk properly again or bear children I fear."

Laughter broke out amongst them all, which relieved the tension in the room. In the briefing room Gareth placed a large, detailed map upon the table and all areas were marked as previously discussed.

"A list of the type of abductions still failed to find a common denominator: it seemed at first glance, random." Thaddeus indicated all the marked areas.

"There is a plan to look at areas where we have no immediate intelligence. Tomorrow Marcus and a combined group will depart for North Mede and travel down both east and west sides of the Meder River. In the meantime another unit will be sent to the southwest to gather information. Any assistance with volunteers would be helpful." Gareth looked at the group gathered around the table.

Cedric was happy to send out a few vessels to search all surrounding islands in the fire seas. Angus would send out units of soldiers throughout the Southern-lands. His naval vessels would also sweep the islands south of the Archipelagos. The northern islands were inhabited by local native tribes and it was rumoured mercenaries with cannibalistic tendencies hid within this area. That would be a battle for another time. The eastern sea from the Archipelagos was forbidden, as it was too near the great divide. Duke Morgan would combine with Gareth's army to search Tyral and the south west of Sofala. Admiral Atien and his fleet would circumnavigate Sofala. Elias was investigating the eastern side of Sofala and any islands in close proximity. In the end an agreement was written up between all parties to share the responsibilities and finances for the investigation of all the areas in the vast kingdom. They would form an integrated army when the time arose to combat whatever or whoever was behind these abductions. Prince Marcus was elected to lead this coalition with Commander Atesh as his second.

Marcus explained to all in the room that Atesh had other allies and only she would be the go between. Cedric and Angus however objected; they felt there should be only one leader and negotiator. They were then enlightened with the stories of the relevant Queens and their armies by Marcus and Gareth. With horror etched on their faces they retracted their objections and looked at Atesh with awe and something akin to respect. Atesh would coordinate with Queens' Mia and Betha.

Atesh looked over at Ballard who pinched his fingers around his nose bridge, his head bowed. He looked fed up with this business. The conversation and debate raged on over the same topics, again and again. She wondered if all the talk had led to naught, as most had no basis or actual facts; it was all pure conjecture.

That night the knights performed their evening routine and as usual the newcomers were wide eyed and speechless. They had wondered what all the exercises were about, now they knew. One of the soldiers explained to the warriors, they should wait and see the morning routine that would blow their minds.

Chapter 26

The Cube:

Master Thaddeus strode with purpose after the meeting up to his apartment. For a man of his age he had a spring to his step; an attendant chased him and handed over a small package.

"This arrived yesterday sir, it appeared on my desk for you."

"Thank you young man," *Oh, it is smaller than I imagined. This cannot be the new game?* He sat on his favourite chair beside the fire; when a shiver went up his spine; all hairs stood up on end. *Oh the cold season certainly lives up to its name, especially within these stone walled castles. Why does the chill never seem to leave your bones?* He un-wrapped the package and found he held a small cube with ancient wizard script decorating the entire surface. He removed the golden ribbon that held the cylindrical parchment and read the letter.

> Dear Honoured Customer,
> The cube yours to open, stand back and prepare.
> Follow the script, be precise; be very aware.
> It is more than before, one player is all.
> To command the large army of Morphids and Tors
> Just think of your move, the creatures will know.
> They are fierce battle ready and blood lust will flow.
> It is time to play now, the Game Master's hand.
> It is yours against mine; this battle be grand.

Good luck to you all, who will challenge me thus.
Take a bow, battle hard and enjoy this I trust.
The time limits set, two hours no more.
Then return to the Master, the next to explore.
Place your order, be quick, take a chance; heed the call.
Own the one of its kind the best game of them all.

Thaddeus stared at the writing and the cube. *My goodness what have we here? I have never heard of Morphids and Tors. Well I must get the fellows here tonight for the exhibition game. Oh, how exciting.* He asked the corridor guard to send messages to Commanders' Marcus and Atesh, Captains' Ballard and Aiden and Prince Fynton. *Let the old men sit and pollute their lungs. We young ones will have a game.* Thad laughed to himself.

After dinner the five young soldiers met in Thaddeus' apartment.

"Well, what is the exciting news grandfather? Come on spill it before you burst."

"Am I that transparent, eh Aiden, Alright then?" He went into the office and brought out the cube and letter. He read it out aloud to them.

"It gives you a time limit? How can you win a battle in such short a time?"

"It must be an example Atesh. It sounds like there is only the one game made, so this will start the bidding wars going. Seeing that I am a preferred customer with a go-between to remain anonymous, I always have had the first choice to accept. Let's have a game, shall we? Right, I will need all your strategic brains; this will be us against the Game Master, the ultimate challenge." Thaddeus was excitable to the extreme, as his body seemed to be agitated, fidgety and strung taut.

"The instructions to open are specific; so we had better stand back. I am not sure how vast this will be."

Thaddeus placed his fingers on the cube as instructed. The odour of faint lavender emanated from within the tiny structure. It then sprang out of his hands, much to the surprise and excitement of all. It twirled, jiggled and emitted a high pitch resonance, before it opened up before them. At first it was the size of a journal, and then it doubled in size every other second. The growth ceased when the game became the dimensions of four substantial banquet tables lashed together. Any larger and it would not have fitted into the room.

There before the onlookers materialised a peaceful sun drenched country side. It floated mere inches below chest height, above the wooden, mat covered flooring. In the midst of this scenery, a majestic looking crystal infused castle sat, with elegance and grace; bound by a wide, deep moat. Then the nearby scenery blossomed to life with a plateau of lush emerald carpet. This led to a mixed terrain of undulating, wild flowered covered hills and fauna infused forest to the rear. The tree branches swayed as a gentle rhythmical breeze touched and caressed them. Small coloured butterflies and honey thrushes flittered around the wild flowers and leaves giving a burst of extra colour to the already mind exploding canvas before them.

In stark contrast to the accord of the land, a broad stream roared into existence, sundering in two, the peace and harmonic land of the first minutes of the cube's creation. It rushed headlong into a rock infused thunderous band of white water rapids, cascading down step after step, till eventually it forced its way out into the coastal foam. The sea calmed the tumultuous beat of the river water, as it cascaded away to mist over, a mile or so from the shoreline. The waves then returned, ebbed and flowed as it lapped upon the white sandy beaches and pebbled shores.

The six were mesmerised at first; all speechless.

"Thaddeus you can feel a breeze as if it were real. Look at the butterflies moving in the flow. How can this be?"

"I am as stunned as you Atesh. The Game Master has outdone himself this time. What powerful and unusual environmental magic this all is. Quite unnerving if you think on it."

As the characters appeared in units of around fifty or more, all six players stepped back further. There were infantry in the front row. Their armoury differed as much as their appearances and weaponry. Some held spears with broad points or javelins of varied lengths, battle-axes, knives and scimitars or long kopis swords. Each carried a round shield with forearm straps. To both left and right flanks were the long bowmen. The cavalry were placed next at the rear; they included a row with lancers and the rest with swords. There were two large trebuchets behind the army, assembled with hurling stones and hard clay fire bombs that could be thrown with the lever and sling attachments. They hurled around 200 pounds of stone per 300 yards. Then creatures held ropes ending with enlarged grappling hooks and ladders that would reach up the side of the castle walls.

Two multi masted galleys appeared on the seaside close to the beach, with fierce looking sailors standing ready with ropes curled around their waists. Four large slings anchored to the decks perched on the port side. Large stones with glass embedded on one side were stacked to each side, ready for placement into the rubber slings.

There were few actual humans among the offensive force. Although most of the warriors were strange and intense looking creatures, they all showed a depth of battle expertise, precision and hardness. All wore armour of hardened leather, chain mail shirts with long sleeves and bronzed breast plates. The cavalry creatures were six legged, with lengthy brown matted wavy hair that hung below their stomachs. Manes and tails were long and white. The forehead was parted by two horns that curled around their elongated ears. Such strange abominations Atesh had never seen before. The men seemed to be the officers sitting on their proud creatures to the back of the army, with a wizard in a white robe that carried a wooden staff.

The Game Master's intricate patterned insignia flew for all to see atop the castle turrets which then sprang to life. Again the players, most of them similar type creatures. There were archers some spread around the battlements, others hidden next to the archer slits within the walls. Standing beside each archer were sword fighters; to repel ladders or climbing creatures. A wizard could be seen standing ready with his hands raised and the tip of his staff sparking light. They had fire, pitch and boiling water prepared to pour over the side or through spouts and soldiers to man the mangonels. The metal portcullis was down and the draw bridge that would normally span the deep, gloom filled moat was raised.

"Is that all they have to defend the castle Master Thaddeus?"

"Oh no Ballard, the rest I would think is a surprise; remember...you never know what your enemy has hidden from you."

The Commanding General turned to Master Thaddeus and bowed his head. Thaddeus returned the gesture. In his mind he heard the voice strong and true.

"Ready when you are sir. How would you like us to proceed?

Thaddeus turned from his Commander still silent with awe.

"All right my dear fellow players; we must storm the castle, any ideas?"

Atesh nodded. "We need to spread out and coordinate to hit them at the same time along differing points. But we need to keep the heads of the infantry covered with their shields, groups perhaps locked together like a turtle."

"Ballard, Marcus, boys, what say you?"

"Yes, I agree with Atesh, hit them at different points, see where their weaknesses are."

Marcus nodded his head. "Yes, I agree with Atesh and Ballard too."

Fynton knelt down to eye the scenery from a different level. "We need to somehow transport our army over to the castle with as little hassle as possible; so I would have a bridge for the men to run across the river."

Aiden pointed to the man standing stock still, hands raised as if summoning an evil. "I am concerned about their wizard. If we get too close without knowing what he is capable of doing. They could all be fried before we know it."

"Good point Aiden…all sound strategies and worthy of note; I will give the directions." Thaddeus spoke to the General and gave the instructions.

The General nodded in agreement and sounded a deep resonating horn to inspire and provoke the army into their battle chant. The creatures stomped their feet and thumped their weapons on dented shields in time with the drummer; off to the rear. Then the rhythm sped up, till it whipped them into frenzy. The creatures' hearts raced, blood pumped wild within their legs as they smashed them into the ground with tempo ferocity. Their loud grunts and screams echoed around the game and gave the six watchers the shivers.

Marcus wandered around the board looking at it from all sides. "This is going to be a blood bath." He gave an involuntary shudder. "That moat looks deep and I swear there was something moving in it. How do we get them across that moat and up to the castle alive?"

Thaddeus then asked the General about their wizard's skills.

"He may have whatever skills you desire sir."

"I would like him to freeze the water on the moat, so the men can traverse it with wooden planks."

"So be it." The wizard complied with ease.

"How about that little gem, eh Aiden, Marcus?"

The castle sent down flaming arrows, some struck their targets, but most the metal shields kept the arrows at bay. Trebuchets from the attacking army pounded the castle with enormous rocks; hitting a target or two and causing untold damage to the walls. The castle responded in kind; large boulders whistled through the air to land amongst the infantry.

Thaddeus rubbed his hands together . "There is nothing better than a good old fashioned castle storming. This is the ultimate strategy game at its best."

The archers sent a volley of flamed arrows over the castle wall, then a set of black arrows. These often took soldiers unaware and caused untold casualties. Around the sides the warriors with the ropes and grappling hooks attempted to snag them on the battlements. The castle soldiers were running around like ants here and there; many orders were yelled out, often contradicting the one before, they seemed to be missing a solid Commander.

A couple of the Morphids scrambled up the castle walls only to be shot by arrows upon reaching the top. If the arrow didn't kill them, the fall was certain to.

The group noticed when a Morphid soldier was killed on either side; they reappeared on a distant hill to sit, watch and wait for the conclusion in silence.

The castle soldiers' poured flaming oil and pitch over the side to cascade down the stone walls. This killed many of the infantry soldiers; though they were muscle bound they tended to move slower than a human. They however kept attacking; the thought of death did not deter them. Thaddeus had the wizard use fire to break the drawbridge ropes then with the white wizard fire he melted the steel portcullis. Once the bridge came thundering down, the cavalry moved in with great speed. Arrows rained down and their wizard started blasting them with his glow sticks. The infantry were entrenched deep in battle lust as they fought hand to hand. The enemy did not work as a team like the attacking side; it seemed every soldier battled alone. Once again a Commander, good communication lines and unity were missing. It became difficult to tell friend from foe, they all looked the same.

Thaddeus conferred with Atesh, and then spoke with the General. *"While the main kill zone is underway at the front Commander; can you have a few Morphids go around the side or back? Have them scale the wall, try and attack from other sides, perhaps catch them unaware."*

The General sent a handful of the Morphids around to the side of the castle. One of them managed to make it up over the top and killed quite a few before he was taken out by an axe to the back. He reappeared up on the hill and sat and watched the battle with the others. The castle was being overrun; the opposing side seemed to be winning this battle. After a while the creature with the axe wedged firm within his back removed from his pocket a small set of wooden pipes and started to play a mournful battle tune. This seemed to resonate with the ones on the hill and they hung their heads and wept. The castle battle turned into a melee, blood lust was in fever pitch and the creatures hacked and slashed all in their path. The sailors now sent their rocks hurtling through the air from their ship into the opposite side of the castle, eliciting a lot of damage to the walls, battlements and casualties.

Then the creature on the hill with the pipes began to play; a battle song to give heart to those still fighting. The next one was a soft heartfelt, love song. A mournful ballad one played for a lost love, or one that could never be. Often played to quieten a rowdy inn, to have the men remember, reflect on perhaps what they had and now lost. Atesh and Ballard started to sing along without realising what they were doing, knowing the words off by heart. They sang through the chorus harmonising, to the sniggers from the others in the room.

Atesh's warning itch then started. She shook her head trying to dislodge the feeling; after all they were only playing a game. The warning signals within her body were on full alert, the hairs on her arms stood up on end and a spine chilling thought screamed at her from the partitioned corners of her mind. Atesh stopped singing and whipped her head around to look at the piper. She then moved in closer and stared at him. She noticed the way the creature held the pipes with his head slightly tilted to the left. His fingers though large and cumbersome moved like fluid over the pipe holes, with the little finger stuck up in the air.

Atesh held her breath; she felt it difficult to breathe at all. Her heart sounded loud in her ears and pounded with fervour through her chest wall. Her eyes widened in shock and horror. Atesh's body began to tremble as her hand went to her mouth. She watched as the Morphid had his eyes closed and played the love melody from his soul.

The creature was hideous, not human at all. It had a large protruding forehead and horns stuck out much like the Tors, from behind the large ears. A thick mat of springy hair covered the muscled body parts not clothed. Yet the music was pure angelic. She looked up at Ballard who was still intent on the game, singing along to the song. Atesh stared hard at Ballard; he turned as he felt her eyes boring into his head . He stopped singing when he noticed how ashen she had become, how wide her eyes were. He followed her gaze as they again looked at the creature playing the pipes. This time he listened and heard the tune played and realised what he had been doing. His hand clutched at his chest. His face grimaced as his heart resounded , threatening to explode out of its containment.

Thaddeus and the others noticed the quietness of their fellow players. "What was that song? Played so beautiful for such a creature don't you…"

To the astonishment of the others, Atesh and Ballard had backed away from the game. Ballard was bent over, grasping at his chest, his colour pallid.

"Oh Ballard, *No…No…*It cannot be." Her dinner curdled and threatened to rise and expose itself.

"It is a coincidence Atesh, how could it be more?" Ballard stepped closer and he too studied the pipe playing Morphid. He turned from ashen to green and went down to his knees. "By all the ancients, what foul magic is this?"

Atesh with hand over her mouth turned and dashed. She ran as fast as her legs would carry her out the main door. Ballard was right behind her, yelling for her to come back. She ran all the way outside to the grassed area and collapsed onto her knees on the cold damp ground. She rocked back and forth with her hands held up to her face, as the tears streamed down unchecked to saturate her shirt.

Ballard caught up with her and knelt down beside; he placed his arm around and drew her in close.

Atesh leaned into his shoulder, "No…No…No why Ballard?"

Tears welled in his eyes as he held her tight. Ballard looked up to the sky and whispered to the night moon. "Oh my little rabbit what had they done to you, to Jesper?"

Marcus, Aiden, Fynton and Master Thaddeus all came rushing out soon after. The two hours had completed and the game stopped. The General saluted to Master Thaddeus and it all disappeared right before their eyes.

They stood and watched, wondering what was wrong.

Marcus knelt down next to Atesh and Ballard. "Please come back inside, the game time has finished."

Marcus and Aiden assisted them back inside Thaddeus' room and they sat down by the fire. Atesh had curled up into a ball next to Ballard; she didn't want to let him go. Thaddeus poured some fine chilled wine into mugs and handed one to Atesh. She thanked him, but her hands shook so violently, she had trouble holding it.

"Ballard we are all wondering what was wrong? One moment we are all enjoying a grand old battle and the next, you both run for the hills."

Ballard swallowed hard and steeled himself to answer. "Thaddeus as you know we lost Jesper the first night we camped here. He was… we assumed abducted by the flying panther creature. Well…Jesper was our resident artist and musician. He played the wooden pipes. We found his broken, down by the stream beside a large paw print. But he always carried two sets. The second tune that creature played tonight was a song…that…Jesper made up while we travelled here to the castle. He named it…a ballad for Atesh. No-one else knew this song, but our battalion; it was our unit's secret. Jesper you see, loved Atesh, but knew he could never be the one for her. Though she told him she did love him as she loved all her men in the unit. The service was her life. He only completed it on the way from Janlin the few days before we arrived at the castle here. So we only had the time between then and here to learn the words. The men loved it so much, he played it every night as a good night theme. It was how every knight felt about our Commander."

Everyone was silent; Thaddeus had his head bowed and his hand running through his hair. "Are you absolutely sure of this Ballard?"

"Yes sir, all of us sang the words around the fire every night before he was taken. He had driven us mad humming it and penning the words during the trip. Then we all sang it to Atesh. It was our way of saying how she carries…a piece of our heart within hers and so it became our good night anthem. So she would never forget and sleep well knowing how we all felt. But that is not all. The way the creature held the pipes and played was the exact same as Jesper. He had a peculiar way of holding his head and always the little finger stuck up at an angle. That was Jesper, I have no doubt."

"I think we need more wine grandfather, lots more."

"Superb idea Aiden, be a good lad and grab another, no make that a few more bottles for us please."

"Grandfather, how long have the abductions been going on for?"

"Marcus for so many years, it is hard to remember. Perhaps over one hundred and seventy years. It used to be one person now and again and then it increased of late. Now whole…oh…my, oh my! Whole groups of soldiers have been abducted."

"Taken for a war game grandfather? Why would someone transform men for a game? What kind of sick, twisted mind would do this? A Wizard Master does not have need for money do they? Can they not conjure anything they desire?"

"Marcus, this is not as straight forward as it seems. This is old, dark forbidden magic that should never be practiced. Where did he learn such things?" Thaddeus bent down and grasped her hands. "Oh Atesh, I am so sorry my dear."

All six of them had tears cascading down their faces; Marcus lifted his head and stared wide eyed at Atesh, then his grandfather. He had a realisation of what his grandfather meant.

Thaddeus looked at Marcus and shook his head indicating not to say a word. He walked to the door and asked the guard to take a message to the King that it was urgent. They required his presence as well as Duke Morgan, Kings' Angus and Cedric.

After everything Atesh had been through, this felt like the final straw. She shook so violent, her teeth chattered. Marcus moved to the other side of Atesh, she was once again sandwiched between the two big men in her life, she felt warm and comforted. Marcus stroked her hair and whispered words into her ear. Her shaking subsided to a mere tremor.

Gareth and the other nobles arrived a short time later. They became concerned when they entered the room to dead silence and red eyes all around.

"I believe we have been summoned. What's been going on here Thaddeus?"

"Gareth, sires' please take a seat, I will explain." Thaddeus stood with clasped hands; he related their story and what they had discovered.

Gareth, like the others was speechless as they each digested the information.

Cedric stood up and walked over to the balcony and looked out. "Oh my beautiful Charlie, turned into a hideous creature? What would possess someone to even think of doing this? It is too horrid to contemplate."

"Creatures…creatures, you say?" Morgan turned up his nose in disgust and kept shaking his head. He looked at Atesh who seemed to shrink further between the two men.

Thaddeus noticed this exchange and needed to act quickly, less his son-in-law lose his entire daughter's respect. Thaddeus pulled Gareth aside to speak in private. "Gareth you need to disperse the group, now they have the important information. Atesh needs time to come to terms with this. Remember…she was taken by these creatures too, maybe her injuries are from trying to transform her, I do not know."

Gareth bowed his head. He realised the consequences of this night would be far reaching and if not handled well, could be damaging too many near and far. "Right, Captains' Ballard and Aiden, you need to explain to your men what we have discovered. Morgan, Cedric and Angus I will leave this up to you, how you wish to deal with this information. Thaddeus I would like you to stay here and see to your guest for a while. Marcus I will see you in my rooms in short order."

The royalty all departed to their suites in quiet contemplation.

Thaddeus spoke in a gentle, calming manner to reassure Atesh. He insisted she practice her deep breathing techniques and centring skills.

Her mind needed to focus, to be strong. She felt cleaved; her heart reached out for the family she knew would now turn away from her; again she was denied. She noticed the look of horror on Duke Morgan's face. Then the sneer appeared; as he turned to focus his eyes upon her. *Does he think I am a monster too; my own father? He has shown his true colours.*

Atesh opened her eyes sometime later feeling refreshed. She realised she had been overwhelmed. Now her mind stood firm in its resolve. Determined to reclaim her strength, she locked the hurt, rejection and weakness behind a partition of bricks and mortar in the far recesses of her mind. She would once again be the Supreme Commander, an elite fighter, not some snivelling teen. Ballard often informed her she was too hard on herself and perhaps; she was her own worst enemy; well…*so be it*. This was how she overcame her adversity as a child, it would work again now.

"Atesh did you hear what I said?"

"Sorry, I was zoned out for a bit."

"Leave your staff behind, it is safe here. Go on your fact finding mission and when you return, we will begin the higher magic control lessons. Examine with care what sort of raw powers you have without spells and incantations. Then, on your return you will need to meditate and craft your staff with a design from your innate essence, one that will hold a wizard's crystal within it."

Atesh furrowed her brows, "Why again do I need a staff and crystal?"

"Well Atesh, there are always consequences when you use your own energy force to perform magic feats; now you have completed the turning. Utilising a crystal will lesson that effect to practically nothing. Be careful how much you use whilst away on your journey. Chanel the energy needs through your rings and or amulet. Aiden must do the same, now that he has been given some of your power. The ring Elias has given him can now be utilised to its full potential."

"I understand, thank you for all your assistance Master Thaddeus."

"Grandfather now, remember lass."

"Are you sure…I mean absolutely sure?"

"Oh, without a doubt, I could not feel your signature before. I am certain now there was a block placed on you, covering your energy signature from me. Since your turning, it has broken away. You are definitely my kin. I am very proud of what you have accomplished Atesh, the proudest grandfather in the world."

Thaddeus moved forward and enveloped Atesh within his arms. His warmth and energy surged through every portion of her body. She sighed with contentment for the first time.

"Oh there is one more thing you must do, an unpleasant task, I am afraid."

"Oh no, can it not wait till I return?"

"No, I am sorry, you must be formally acknowledged by not only your immediate family, but also by King Gareth. He must bestow your title back to you and amend the royal records."

"I shall keep my name please and Ballard will still be acknowledged as my Guardian. He raised me; he was and still is the only father I want. You saw the look Duke Morgan gave me. Please grant me this grandfather."

"I shall speak with Gareth on your behalf. Since you have pledged yourself to the knights, I cannot see why it will be too much of a drama. Now, my dear, can I escort you to your other family, I believe they await you by the fire pit."

"No thank you grandfather. Though I feel a bit unsteady, I would like to do this myself. So I will see you after forms in the morning before we depart."

Chapter 27

Bricks and Mortar:

Aiden and Ballard had walked over to the fire pit and reignited it; Ballard sat there and activated his Captain's ring. A red light shone for a brief minute then one by one the knights appeared in silence; some with furrowed brows. The regiment soldiers also followed, they were aware now what the red signal meant. They all sat around the fire and waited for their Captains to speak.

Ballard explained the situation to them and what Master Thaddeus deduced from it all. He then gave clear details why Commander Atesh was not the one to break the news to the men about their discovery and why she was so traumatised. He described how her true identity had been recently uncovered. How she was taken as an infant by the same flying creature as Jesper and somehow escaped captivity three years later. He informed them how Berend, Vykter and he first found Atesh in the academy grounds gravely ill snuggled next to a dying Ciaran. She has no memory of any of the events. He told of her injuries. They were horrified by all this news. They all hung their heads. Most had tears cascading from their eyes and Ciaran's crystal tears shattered; as they crashed to the earthen floor. Renny bolted over to the bushes and threw up. He knelt down; hands tightly wrapped around his waist and howled; he knew he would never see his mate Jesper again.

Berend walked over and brought Renny back to the fire, he spoke quiet words to him as he kept his arm around his shoulders. Yes, they gave Renny a hard time. But when the chips were down, they were there for each other. They were family after all. The knights knew that the meaning of family had many and varied interpretations. For them it meant a group of close knit men and women that experience adventure and tragedy together. They mind each other's backs. Look out of one another. Unity is strength.

Once outside in the corridor Atesh called to Ciaran to come and collect her. Ciaran took off like an arrow; a dragonelle on a mission. He ran fast with hops and bounces to the castle entrance. This was not lost on any of the men; they turned and looked around waiting for their Commander to appear. Ciaran found Atesh as she walked slow and clambered up onto her shoulder, cooing and petting her. This felt like home to her and a large smile broke free. They eventually walked up to the fire pit where all the knights and the regiment soldiers were huddled around it, to gather some warmth from the cool night breeze. Once their Commander came in view, they all paused and saluted; arms across their chest to their hearts. They stood tall and proud; though some had fierce, damp eyed looks adorning their faces.

Ballard and Aiden soon broke into large cheeky grins and bowed from the waist. The men all picked up on this and performed the same gesture. A couple even curtsied. Atesh stood transfixed and looked at each and every one directly into their eyes. Loyalty, love, trust respect and sadness were expressed in their return gaze. This almost brought tears to her eyes again, but she breathed deep and returned the veneration in kind; with an exaggerated arm flick.

A loud shout from one of the men broke the awkward silence. "Whose turn is it for drinks? The anvil inn waits for no man. Is anyone up for this?"

Atesh turned to Vykter and noticed his mischievous grin. Now she knew her moment of tenderness was over; it was back to business. All cards were on the table, she was aware now she would be in for some serious ribbing. *Oh it is good to be amongst family again, they mean so much to me, yes; these are my true family.*

Ballard nodded in agreement. "Sounds good to me men, I could use a jug or two or three…perhaps four."

Atesh, Ballard and Aiden led the way with the noisy rabble behind them. Ben the bar-keep was always pleased to see the group and ushered them into the room at the rear; which he now kept empty for their use. He joined them and listened as the men discussed recent events. He gleaned that the Commander; Atesh was in fact the missing Princess.

"This keeps getting better." Ben was so overwhelmed with this news that he shouted food and drinks for them all. Atesh and the knights were his heroes.

After a few drinks Vykter stood up and proposed a toast to their Commander. "Supremeo Commander Sir, Oh Mighty Wizardness, Highness and Princess of our hearts; we salute you for finding our friend. Geeze, this is a bit too much of a mouthful. Can you not shorten your title for us; Oh brave, glorious and magnanimous one?" He curtsied with embellished movements and near toppled into Renny. "Oh and please do not turn me into a toad or something gooey." He went down on his knees bowing and pursing his lips at her boots.

Atesh sat stunned for a minute; her eyes glowed with blue flames and then with her own pert expression, spoke so all could hear. "Thank you for that wondrous introduction , 'Oh Infamous Gastronomous ' of the First Battalion. Please I am the same person I was last week alright? Well maybe a little more powerful that is all. No I am all out of gooey tonight Vykter, you are safe for now."

The men all laughed as Vykter stood up and bowed repeatedly as he backed up all the way outside.

Ballard nudged Berend. "Would you mind ensuring he does not fall into the thunder box? We don't want to lose our cook now do we, it is a long drop and I do not think our food will ever taste the same."

"That is an odd expression for an outhouse Captain, a thunder box."

"Well, you see Ben that is what our unit call all pits and garde-robes now, since one bright spark that shall remain nameless; right eh, Renny. Decided to see what happens if you place a burning branch down one…Boom! The gases build up in them you see; highly flammable."

Ben, Marcus and his soldiers stood speechless, eyes widened with the thought.

"So shall it be named from now on," Ben laughed all the harder.

"Will we ever get Jesper back Commander, like he was before?"

Atesh gave Renny a look somewhere between sympathy and worry. "I don't know. Of that it was Jesper, I am sure, but then it wasn't, like a part of him, his soul was missing; it was surreal. Let us hope and put all our energies into positive thinking now. We need him back to make our family whole again."

All agreed with this and again raised their glasses in a silent salute to their mate and comrade.

"Umm…while we are on this subject Atesh and calmed down. There is something else you all should know."

Atesh and the men turned to Ballard who had risen out of his chair; he stood tall, and serious.

"Alright Ballard spill it, this sounds like an ominous…umm."

"Well, Master Elias had informed Gareth and Master Thaddeus that a whole battalion sent to the northern border to investigate the breach had been…." Ballard stumbled at this moment and looked around at all the faces around the table.

"Had all been what?" Atesh stood now and faced her second in command.

"They had all been abducted by flying panthers, the same as Jesper and Badges."

"What? A whole battalion was taken?"

All were stunned to silence once again. Heads bowed in quiet contemplation of this tragic news.

"How did this happen? Who was? Oh no….Do not say it; Captain Pathetic led that investigation? How could he allow this to happen?" Anger infused her whole being and blue sparks emitted from her eyes; raced around the room. Her hands' had balled into taut blanched fists. "I hope they choked on his sorry, spineless…."

"Calm down Atesh please; you are scaring the children." Ballard knew he had to diffuse Atesh or someone may get hurt, if she lost control.

They all felt the crackle of energy flowing around them as her power built up. The hairs on some of the men sitting closer to Atesh started to stand up on end; they looked on in awe and fright. Atesh scanned the room and settled back down; she drew long deep breaths and held her power in check.

"Oops, sorry men, I am not used to all this power yet. I apologise; I didn't mean to scare you all. It's that poor excuse for a man, riles me so. Please continue Ballard, sorry to have interrupted you."

"Right then, Captain Pathetic did not get taken as the rest of his men did, he…co-orchestrated the whole affair."

Atesh held her hand to her heart. "How would they know this Ballard?"

"A witness explained how he collaborated with a wizard and as the panther creatures flew down and grabbed his men, he was seen to be laughing hysterical and clapping with glee. The men had been rendered unconscious during the evening, by a potion placed in their drink. They had been celebrating Dan's birthday and all the men, yes even those on duty were ordered to raise a mug to their captain."

"It's nowhere near his birthday that lying son of a motherless dung beetle. Who was the witness Ballard?"

"Jett the horse handler Atesh; he had been unwell and didn't partake in the festivities. He had curled up and fell asleep under some spiked bushes. The noise woke him and he stayed sheltered and watched. They for whatever reason had missed him. The second unit was sent off on a mission miles away the previous day. All was planned in advance."

"All those men missing and their horses; Ballard do you suppose they were the pieces in the board game, the knights turned into all the Morphids and the war steeds as the Tors?"

"Very possible Atesh, at least some of them if that is what's going on. But for the life of me, I don't understand why someone would go to such extremes for a game."

"Do you have any memories of the time when you were abducted Atesh?"

Atesh sat back down and looked over to Aiden. "No, I remember nothing at all; I was too young; they would not want a babe for a game. I am wondering why I was taken at all. I was told no ransom was ever received."

Atesh turned to Ciaran who sat perched on Ben's shoulder. "How did we meet Ciaran?"

"I be not knowing that Lassie. All I recall is that ye have been with me since before; nothing else."

"How can this happen when we have such powerful wizards around us, with Master Elias and his brother, do they not know anything?"

"Ryna that is a good question, but from what I have heard they know as much as we do. Though I believe the magic used is ancient and forbidden. The only clue we have is the premonition Master Elias had prior to our travels here. It was a sort of warning to me, though at the time, it didn't mean anything."

"Tell us the words Commander, maybe we can put all our big 'eds together and work somethin out."

"Alright, Berend, it was in this rhyme.

Watch your back brave one, the game is in play.
Find the answer, the truth; the spell to decay.
Seek the mountain that's blind and sways to a beat.
Use the dance you have learned; this time to defeat.
Find a tear from afar, the tool you shall be.
Hide inside for the strength; your mind must be free."

They all sat going through the verse. Fingers flashed up and down as they counted off the number of items to remember. Lips moved, going over the wording again and again, but no words were spoken. Silence was deafening except for the whirring of their brains. Their eyes would often roam around the room staring at unseen objects. Faces creased with lips drawn up like sour lemons. Then a head would emerge, eyes brighten up as a thought registered. Mouths would open wide enough to swallow a hairy intruder when an idea came along.

"The first line mentions the game. Well…we know what the game refers to now. We know a dark powerful wizard be behind all this, but maybe not so smart if he wants Captain Dim-Wit working for him. So then, find the answers and truth to the spell? Perchance find out his secret for morphing. Didn't ye say Atesh; it was ancient, forbidden magic. Well the academy would know about such tomes that contain this sort of thing."

"True Berend, we have Master Elias and the acolytes working on finding that information, but so far all the ancient tomes from the locked library vault are too fragile to read. The first one fell to dust in his hands."

Ballard pondered on the portion that was not magical. "What is a blind mountain?"

"I have no idea Ballard and how can it be swaying? Full of trees perhaps?"

"Well that would cause a mountain to look like it's moving in the breeze. But then again; it seems too easy, doesn't it?"

"Sounds like you are going to fight this Wizard or Danurel or both Commander?"

"I am afraid so Ben; I look forward to meeting Captain Numb-Nuts, but a powerful dark wizard; not so much. The tear we all know came from Queen Mia, so I suppose I am going to be the bait."

"Oh no, I don't think so." Ballard was adamant about this.

"Well Ballard I have a horrid feeling. I will be returning to the Game Master somehow and if my mind has to be free, then sounds to me I may become a Morphid too." Atesh shivered all over.

"Won't this tear protect you from being turned into…a Morphid? How will we know where you are, to rescue you? You could be anywhere on this side of the known world. A wizard that powerful can perform all sorts of magic and illusions."

"I am hoping Vykter; the tear will keep my wits intact. I can then contact Masters' Thaddeus or Elias with the details. As far as morphing goes, I have no idea. Geeze they were ugly right? I cannot imagine myself looking as they do…ughhhhh. Talk about having a bad hair day: I would need to brush my face too."

The tension in the room mellowed and they all laughed. This brought a fierce cacophony of snorting and ideas from the men for the best ways, the most unique patterns and identification of different body parts to shave hair on a Morphid.

"There is something else we have forgotten about?"

All turned to look at Aiden.

"How do the creatures from behind the northern boundary fit into the picture? Or do they? Why are they breaching the boundary after all this time? They do not appear to be normal animals. From what we have seen and heard about, some are mixed in species. Are they his experiments gone awry?"

"Yes and what about the ancient creatures we have seen; Betha moving off Sofala."

"And what is causing the land shakes, the rents to appear spewing out steaming hot vapour?"

"All good questions Aiden, Jenner and Wyart, I believe it is all in some way connected. It seems inconceivable it is all coincidence. Why, how, is beyond me at the moment; I cannot connect the dots."

"Maybe Atesh, after our investigation in the north, it will assist with these confounding questions."

"Well Aiden, let us hope so."

"It could be misdirection."

"What did you say Ballard?"

"Atesh, it could be a case of simple misdirection, a war strategy. Remember the game of chances; clever really. Keep us busy running around capturing and killing those creatures that breach the boundary; whilst the wizard is left alone to pillage and abduct whomever he likes. The focus is not on the Game Master. The land shakes; maybe this is how he forces a breach in the boundary, it is, but a thought."

Ben commented as he bent to clean up the empty ale jugs. "What about the fact that nature is alive here on Sofala. Remember we all have some portion of innate magic in us. What if it she is trying to re-order her world, getting rid of the dark magic that is smothering her?"

"Ben that is a plausible idea too; I never conceived that the land would revolt against such evil magic, but it is a real possibility. It would explain Betha moving away."

"Ballard your idea also has merit. So what if he is playing a game within real life, using war strategies. But nature is also mixed up in this and is railing against dark energies interfering with her order in life. Are we not taught at the academy that life is a continuous cycle? We are born, live and we die. But what the Game Master is doing halts the living and dying process for maybe hundreds, if not thousands of humans and animals. Nature's order is out of balance. If we don't stop this chaos who knows what may occur? Well we are going to have to outplay him. Maybe do a sneaky, Marcus manoeuvre; like he pulled on you at the game night Ballard, what do you say men?"

Marcus stood and raised his mug. "We must out manoeuvre the Game Master. Play the best darn game of strategy we can. Who is up for the game of our lives?"

A unanimous shout, *AYE*, was echoed throughout the anvil inn.

Chapter 28

Reality Check:

Danurel had been working long hours, reading ancient texts and all manner of wizardry scrolls. He was however, becoming bored with this sedentary life. He stood outside on his balcony surveying the hazy surroundings and allowed the warm sea breeze to transport him into a dreamlike daze. Far to the west a bright blue light stirred him from this state, as it speared up into the night's sky. He continued to watch in fascination as it exploded into a myriad of exquisite glistening clusters.

"Such power," Mason had walked up beside Dan and watched in awe. They were both mesmerised by the intensity and brilliance.

Turning to Mason, "What do you suppose that was all about?"

"I have no idea Master Dan, perhaps a fireworks display. If this is so, the fire magisters have outdone themselves. That was near the west coast, I believe. To see the spectacle all this way on the east coast is impressive, I must say." Mason turned to Master Dan with a smile adorning his facial features. "Maybe the King is having a shin-ding and of course, our invitation was lost."

"Oh no Mason, was it not pigeon pie we ate for tea last night...oops."

Mason rubbed his chest. "Yes that's right. I wondered what gave me indigestion this morning. Velum never cooks up too well does it. I will have to talk with Miss Maisie about more seasoning for '*Pidgeon-a-la- invitation*'."

They both laughed at their attempt of humour, a rare sight to be seen.

"Mason, I need to escape this daily grind; do something physical. Can I not assist the Master with any of his projects?"

"Why don't you enquire Master Dan? I am sure he would like your enthusiasm."

As Mason left Danurel star gazing out on the balcony, he strode back to his rooms; one hand caressing his chin stubble in thought. *That raw magic display and energy release was extraordinary. I would not be surprised if that was a rare turning event. I am astounded Master Dan did not feel the waves of power. Maybe he has not the essence to make a Wizard after all. We must take care. This bodes ill for us. I shall need to inform Master Grey.*

The next morning, Danurel walked up the steps to Master Grey's study. He felt nervous, but taking deep breaths calmed his thumping heart. He unclenched his fists and knocked on the wooden door and entered as requested. He noticed the Master leaning over a vast game board of serenity and beauty.

"Ah, yes dear boy, good timing, come and see the latest game version. It is unfortunate, but we have to tweak it. I am afraid the castle creatures require a stronger leader, any ideas?"

Danurel circled the board. He looked at it from all angles. He was impressed with the reality of this one. The creatures were all lined up for inspection.

"Well it does look like the opposing forces have a formidable looking leader. Your client was not happy, I gather?"

"Oh, no to the contrary, he was immensely content. In fact he loved what he called, the old fashioned war game. However, he did mention about the castle creatures; they appeared to have little to no order. Running around like ants on a picnic; was how the client phrased it. Once we remedy this situation, he would be delighted to purchase this one off game."

Dan had an evil sneer on his face, he almost felt ashamed; but his devious side won out. "Why don't you place the officer from the opposing force within the castle and find a strong leader for those on the field. I could…maybe, suggest someone. Though it would take some cunning and deviousness, if you are up for it; that is?"

"Oh! Was that a challenge I hear, my young apprentice. I do like the way you think; reminds me of myself at your age…hmmm. Alright give me the name."

"I thought of Commander Atesh from the academy. I know I have beaten her many times in simulation games, but then, not many have bested me."

"Now we do not want anyone too good Danurel; remember they are not supposed to win the game. Atesh…Atesh the name is not familiar to me."

"Atesh is the Supreme Commander of the 'Pace Knights'. A female to be precise, but she would be recognised right away in Sofala."

"That may not be so, my dear boy."

"What do you mean?"

"You haven't got an evil mind, have you Danurel."

"Oh, I thought I was performing quite well."

"Move up closer, look at the creatures on the field waiting for battle."

"Yes ugly ones aren't they? How did you think of that design?"

"Have a good hard look at them young Dan." Master Grey was beside himself with mirth; his black eyes twinkled, as he roared with laughter.

Dan looked closer still; he inspected each and every one of the Morphids and screwed up his face. "Ewwww they are disgusting."

"Yes Dan, they are. So you noticed nothing unusual…nothing familiar; nothing at all?"

"Familiar? No way sir; I bet their breath would melt the enemies faces' right off, no need for weapons."

"Oh Dan, they were your fellow knights; morphed into creatures by an ancient spell."

Dan stood frozen to the spot, his mouth agape and eyes widened. He placed one hand against the wall to steady his nerves and felt his heart miss a few beats. "What did you just say Master? Did I hear you correct?"

"Oh yes Dan." Master Grey sat down hard on his chair and continued to laugh till tears formed in his eyes. "Each and every one was from your battalion we bought back from the northern borders; plus a few extras we had picked up on the way from the west."

Oh no Jesper? "Do they know sir? Can they speak?"

"No, only the General speaks and only to the one that plays the game. As for knowing; no they have lost most of their memories except what I choose to leave intact. I removed a portion of their soul and placed it away for safe keeping. It allows them to live, but not so to speak, for as long as the game exists."

"So, not creature food then Master?"

"Only the ones that do not Morph, they become expendable."

"If we abduct Atesh, will she end up like these creatures?"

"Yes, Dan, if that is what you wish."

Danurel's eyes darted to the game board; he looked once more upon the creatures. "What if I could persuade her to join us?"

"Do you think there is a chance?"

"I am not sure, but I would like to try, if I may?"

Master Grey looked deep into Dan's eyes and understood without words. "Then you shall have that chance. We may then need to look for another leader."

"Now I almost forgot, why the visit, anything special?"

"I would like to assist more Master. Books are boring me to tears. I would like some fresh air, a task…anything."

"Yes, well I suppose it is time. I will have Mason make arrangements for the next part of your training. You must undertake a journey, a time for reflection; a sort of self-discovery, inner learning for you. This will lead you to find the one crystal that resonates with your innate essence, to be placed into your wizard staff. The northern mountains will be the most ideal place to look, I would think. On your return, you can commence more complex spells and incantations. I have many old scrolls to show you and of course you can practice them in the underground work room. I will even show you the gem room; the special accommodation cells and perhaps in time the secret to the morphing. If you are ready, that is. You will leave in the morning, so be up bright and early. In the meantime, why don't you ask Mason to accompany you around the island? Get some fresh air in your lungs and stretch your legs; open your mind to the next phase of learning. By the way, I have been meaning to ask you, how is your hand feeling? Has the ring felt different yet?"

"Yes, it has started to warm up quite a bit and feels tighter. I suppose that is also giving me the jitters, trying to keep my mind off the inevitable."

"I have summoned Mason, he will arrive shortly, be careful; remember there are some nasty creatures on the outer perimeter." *That is a trifle odd, what am I missing here? His oath reversal should have affected him more by now. Unless he is either acting or be not as powerful as we had believed. Well this next step will show what he is made of. Yes, perhaps the perfect stooge. Oh well, maybe this Commander Atesh will make a better apprentice.*

Chapter 29

Northern Mission:

Commander Atesh's knights were ready to be escorted to the north-east boundary, by Commander Marcus and a group of sixteen regiment soldiers. They had hoped to venture forth around midmorning after the re-naming and acknowledgement ceremony. It was around this time of day when Atesh strode out of the castle; quiet and subdued. Captain Ballard was two strides behind her. It was obvious to all she passed by, that she was not impressed with the morning's events. The men knew she dreaded confronting her biological parents and would rather wrestle a sabre-toothed bear. The northern expedition waited outside in the main courtyard. The knights, their war steeds and the regiment soldiers, with their shiny new magical saddle bags all stood at attention, awaiting their Commanders and the signal to mount up. There would be thirty warriors in all, ready to take on a new adventure and find information leading to the whereabouts of the dark wizard. As Atesh approached, every second soldier bowed with exaggerated arm movements, the alternate men curtsied, noses pointed to the air, lips in a pert pout.

Renny then raced up and set himself down on all fours beside Kayne; Atesh's powerful war horse. "Would you like a step up your ladyship, to reach your wonderful steed?"

The men held fast their stony faces even as Renny's falsetto voice cracked and grated on all their ears. Atesh stared around as Ballard tried hard not to break into laughter; tears welled within his eyes from the restraint. Eventually it became too much and a loud snort escaped.

Atesh returned an evil grin; a blue glint sparkled in her eyes. She bowed back to the men in gracious reply, then jumped in an unsympathetic manner onto Renny's back and leapt up onto Kayne. Renny was flattened to the ground face down compressed into the dirt; such was the bounce Atesh performed on his exposed back. Laughter burst forth from all the men as Renny was dragged up and assisted onto his horse. He spat dust and other unmentionables from his mouth as he wiped his eyes and face on his uniform sleeve.

Marcus and Aiden witnessed this event from the upper balcony and roared with laughter all the way to the entrance. It was unfortunate that castles tend to echo loud noises out towards the open windows; especially ones that sat along the stone walled corridors. As they strode out the door together, their body language embellished the mannerisms of seriousness and down to business; though now and again a snigger would escape their lips.

Atesh glared at these two supposed mature officers, while her lips turned up in a fierce snarl.

Marcus looked around wide eyed and made an exaggerated gulp; he leant over to Ballard; "Definitely not named for the hair colour."

They both knew they skated on thin ice, but enjoyed this frivolity while it lasted. The group exited the castle grounds without delay in silence, then arced left around the outer gates and travelled the main road to the North Mede castle and village. Plumes of dust powder were kicked up behind the cantering war horses, as they dislodged small particles from the well-worn dirt road. The horses seemed eager to be on the move again as they tossed their heads, pulled on their halters or bridles and some pranced around showing off to one another. Such was the cadence of man and beast that the energy and excitement from the mounts transferred to their riders. The men had large smiles brightening their faces; a slight forward posture was all that was required for the horses to surge forward and increase the pace.

The knights noticed the continual change to the country side with each mile north they progressed. The lands to the right of the road revealed many farmlets with low jagged stoned walls as their only defendable perimeter. There were orchards with an array of coloured fruit trees, bearing late season oranges and early white season lemons, limes and apples. To the left leading up to the outer castle ground wall were patches of stringy wild grasses and low thready bushes. Many small insects buzzed around the men and called out challenges for a race. It wasn't often such splendid and speeding horses went past them. Ciaran missed out on viewing the natural beauty of the surrounds and the opportunity to chase those annoying insects. He had decided early on he would snuggle up warm and cosy in Atesh's saddle bag. Loud snoring and the occasional puff of smoke was all that was seen of this little beasty.

Further north could be seen miles of lush green forests that swayed gentle with the mountain breezes. They were dwarfed by the multi-hued mountain ranges with sky reaching peaks; that glistened white from the latest dusting of snow. The Beaumont castle grounds to their left extended to the base of the Black Mountains in the far distance and the hardened dirt road kept parallel to the outer boundary stone wall. This ancient and foreboding wall could tell many tales, of travellers past. Of strange and wondrous creatures that lurk in the darkening hours. Of soldiers on battlement duty, as they pounded the lonely miles from one post to the next; with thoughts of a warm hearth, a cool mug of ale or a secret rendezvous with a sweet heart. It now watched in silent wonder as this group of energetic young soldiers moved towards a future of unknown certainty.

Marcus decided a midday break was warranted, as they had pushed their horses hard for the first leg of this journey and all now required a rest and refreshment. As they neared the area for their respite, the air temperature was noticeably cooler. The bitter wind picked up in ferocious eddies that whipped around unprotected heads and tangled hair into wild webbed snarls. The more experienced local soldiers wore their hair back; tied at the nape of their neck.

Ballard thought it was a grand idea for his men to adopt such a fashion too. They had reached the junction where the Meder River collected into a proud and majestic inland tarn. It then divided in two; one meandering stream continuing south past Beaumont Castle and the other headed east and up towards the mountains, to later branch into the Jangly River.

The tarn was turquoise closer to shore; with many insect infused lily pads growing in clusters. The water darkened as it showed more depth towards the middle; it was framed by white, sun bleached sandy borders. The grasses were sweet and green and the air smelt fresh, though invigorating and chilly. The men were ordered to dismount, rest, eat and lead their steeds down to the water's edge. They would need to be watched as too much green grass would render the horses with bouts of colic; a disaster for an expedition such as this.

Atesh wandered around to gather some warmth into her limbs, she felt agitated and restless. All her arm hairs stood up on end and her sixth sense screamed at her; as her eyes darted, to and fro.

"Men…we should not linger here, I don't like this."

"What's the problem Atesh? Not more friends I hope. Please tell me this is not so?"

Atesh was not amused. "Marcus I am sorry to disappoint you, but there is something not right here. Listen for a moment, hear that…nothing. No birds or frogs, it's too quiet; eerie and plain creepy."

Ballard strode up beside the water and fixed his raptor type glare to it. He walked in silence to where the men sat and watered their horses. In a calmed manner he approached them. "Please move your horses away from the water's edge and keep as quiet as you can. Use a bucket with gentle movements only for watering."

A few of the men were competing at stone jumping further along the shoreline; they wanted to see who had the most skips along the water before the pebble sunk. Then they would challenge the knights.

Ballard grabbed the soldier's arm as he swung it back for his turn. "Do not disturb the water any more men."

They looked at this Captain as if he had sprouted horns. "Sir, this is a well -known waterhole to spend the hot red season days . Respectively sir, there is no danger here."

Ballard turned his focus upon them. "Men humour me, alright."
"Yes sir."

The soldiers ambled back up to the main camp site where Vykter had rations ready for them all; bread, cheese and fresh picked apples. One of the regiment soldiers scoffed at the Captain's irrational fears.

He whistled as he refilled the bucket with water from the lake's edge. No one noticed when the whistling had ceased. A second soldier later went in search of the first. He found the bucket upended on the sand beside the water. He detected a red slick that bubbled up and formed not far from the shore. The soldier yelled out to the Commanders to attend. It was unfortunate that in circumstances such as this that he turned his back to the water. The next instant he felt something sharp had grabbed his right leg and lifted it into the air; this sent him face first into the sand, arms splayed out in front. He was then dragged effortlessly, backwards into the water. He now screamed for help and dug his fingers into the wet sand to hang on.

Marcus and Ballard reached him in a few strides and grabbed an arm each. They anchored their feet, with heels first into the unforgiving sand. They were now all being dragged to the water line. A large reptile with many rows of large pointed teeth had latched onto this unsuspecting soldier's leather boot. The rest of the group having heard the shouts ran behind Atesh and Aiden with swords out and arrows notched.

They all let fly with their arrows, but as they had learnt from past experiences, these bounced off the creature's scaled exterior. Four of the knights held their sliding comrades and battled with all their strength to keep them all from entering the lake feet first.

A blood curdled yell, a form of challenge erupted from Berend, as he ran and jumped on top of the creature and buried his long and short knives into the nape of its neck. The creature released his prey and arced up into the air and flipped over backwards into the water. Berend still hung on as it started its frequent roll over's, taking Bear out into the deeper water. Bear could be seen at intervals taking large breaths as they resurfaced. His eyes had glazed over; he was deep in crazed blood frenzy, as he kept thrusting his instruments of death into the creature. There was such anger built up within Berend, he had finally snapped after losing Jesper, his fellow knights and friends to such abominations. The force of his knife thrusts chipped off pieces of the reptile's outer scales, others buried deep into its soft flesh.

Atesh sighted her arrow straight and true. Vykter, Renny, Wyart and Chale next to her followed suit; they all aimed for the eyes or neck.

On the next resurfacing they fired in unison, each shot seemed to have penetrated their chosen target. The exhausted pair submerged beneath the churned up bloody water, then silence enveloped the horrified group on the shoreline. There was no sound and no wave movement. All stood and waited what seemed like forever. Silent words of encouragement were spoken by the men, willing Bear to make it out. The water rippled and Berend's head finally broke free and he swam with sluggish movements toward the water's edge. His knife clenched tight within his teeth. An arrow stuck out from his shoulder. Prolific bleeding cascaded down his arm to drip from his fingers. Atesh yelled for him to hurry up and pointed. A pair of yellow eyes, large snout and a serrated fin had surfaced not far behind him. Arrows arced out to reach the new creature, but it was shrewd and submerged. Berend finally made it to shore, although exhausted. He had the wildest, cheeky grin on his face, satisfaction with the sating of his lust written all over it. Renny and Wyart ran over and hauled him up the grass to safety. They all breathed a sigh of relief.

"Who the bloody hell shot me, Wyart?"

"Could have been anyone of us, you were moving so much."

As they retreated back up to the camp-site a large splash was heard from behind them. Atesh and Ballard whipped their heads around, swords unsheathed in an instant. There before them emerged from the water an enormous reptile, mouth open wide enough to swallow a man whole. It has risen up on its two hind legs and walked like a man. The front appendages reached out with webbed paws. It grasped at the air propelling itself along with an unsightly gait. The regiment soldiers stood frozen, never before had they encountered the likes of this horror.

The knights however had met previous unusual foes, so they set about to bring this monstrosity down. Many arrows sped towards it and lodged into the yellow eyes and softened areas of its face. This caused the creature to throw back its head and scream; such an unnatural sound, high pitched and furious. A few of the regiment soldiers felt brave now and charged at it with their swords drawn. Two were swatted away like flies, they landed in the water. Large claw marks adorned their bodies where they had been raked by the fetid claws.

Three more harried the creature, but their swords skimmed off its rough, tough hide.

Atesh looked on in horror. "Damn bravado. Get back, get back now you men; you will only get yourselves killed. Knights, we will use the flaming ultima arrows if you please; archers ready on my signal. Marcus can you hold your men at bay." Atesh raised her arm. "Fire, aim for the soft spots."

The creature advanced at a run now, arms flailing wild, it hit out at any movement. The arrows that struck true burst into fierce flaming orbs. Burnt and blackened areas under its eyes developed. The eyes now sagged as they melted sending out small plumes of smoke with the stench of putrid over cooked meat. The creature was now beyond anger.

"Men short knives are needed…Ballard when you are ready."

Berend, Ryna and Ballard sent their knives spinning towards its opened maw and exposed throat. They stuck firm; two inside the roof of the creature's mouth and one deep into the throat. The creature swayed on its feet then fell to the ground, thrashing for a while. Atesh and Ballard ended its agony with their scimitars.

The soldiers dragged the creature up onto the grassed area to inspect it. It was a strange looking reptile. Like most the knights had previously encountered, it was a combination of a few known species, only larger and more ferocious.

"Ciaran have you seen one like this before?"

"Aye Lassie in dem ancient tomes back in the academy library, there be a similar creature, but not so large. They have not been seen for thousands of years."

"Why would the Game Master make a creature such as this?"

"Oh, I be not knowing that Lassie. Perhaps dem creatures are breeding in dem wilds and makin dere own wee monsters."

Atesh turned to Marcus who sat staring at the monstrosity. "Marcus you need to warn your father about this. I have a bad feeling about the northern border."

"I will send the mortally wounded men back with an escort and inform father of another casualty."

"Don't look at me. Not on your life Commander. Mine is a mere scratch. Jenner will fix it, won't you oh, mighty healer?"

"Berend that is more than a flesh wound, but yes I will do my best for you seeing as you asked so nice."

Atesh just shook her head, she knew from experience it was useless to try and get Berend to see reason.

Ballard turned to all the men, "We must be more aware now. Expect the unexpected, and never go anywhere alone."

Marcus turned to Atesh. "What was that you used on the flaming arrows that burns so fierce on contact? It had an unusual smell."

"Oh, that is a small added feature we call Ultima fire. The last resort and it is extremely volatile. We only carry a small container within our packs. It is very sticky and explosive. The ingredients are a well-kept secret, one I cannot share with you Marcus. Though what I will say is…there are only two ways to put it out. Never use water that only enhances the ingredients and makes it worse. Use sand, lots of sand. Once you flame it-*whoosh*, burnt offerings."

"And should I even ask about the second way to put it out?"

Atesh leant over and whispered in his ear.

Marcus's eyes widened and he wore a lopsided grin. He looked down to his trousers. "Really…this is true?"

"Yes, Ballard can vouch to what I say. We watched a young acolyte messing around with it when the inevitable happened. All the senior wizards ran over, lifted their gowns and put out the fire. It was the funniest scene we ever observed."

Chapter 30

Dilemmas:

Marcus and Atesh pushed the unit on, so they could reach safety before sunset. They decided to set up camp at the Inlet, a cavernous maw within the *Table Top Mountain Range*. They would be required to traverse this to reach the North Mede Castle. The entrance loomed before them mysterious and bleak. It appeared as a large wound, gouged out of the mountain side. A dark and encompassing tunnel lay beyond the opening; it beckoned them into the unknown. As they entered this passageway, crystals within the stone walls illuminated the way ahead. Atesh noted this was very similar to the sanctuary pass. The channel of bed-rock led them through a gentle ascent. It was wide enough for four horses abreast or even a wagon to navigate through. The air was stilled underground; it smelt musty, though cool; so they meandered along till they reached their destination for the night. The group remained quiet, they all knew that rock echoed noises and after the morning's excitement, they did not wish to alert any other creatures to their presence.

By evening they arrived at their campsite; in a well provisioned, opened cavernous area. It was obvious to Atesh as she scanned around that it was used often this time of year. Wooden stalls were erected to the left side of the rock-wall for horses and other stock. A large fire pit, set off centre was encircled by elaborate carved stone seats; these looked inviting for a cold white season's night. To one side lay weathered logs stacked and piled. A fresh, trickling waterfall and pond in an alcove could be seen off to the right and a large cooking area fitted out in another. Designated pit and wash areas were shown to the knights to the far left back corner and sleeping quarters with clean straw bunks with another fire place were through an archway to the right.

"Ahhh reminds me of home."

"Maybe yours Captain Ballard, but I prefer being greeted by a bevy of beautiful buxom women and the smell of ale and cider smoke, wafting along the wooden rafters. Now that's home."

"Well Bear, a man cannot argue with that eh, Marcus?"

"I am keeping out of this one. I'm in enough strife as it is." He turned to gaze in Atesh's direction.

Vykter was in a great mood singing away in his tenor voice, as he prepared the evening's meal. Ryna was assigned kitchen duties this night, so all the men knew the meal would have a feminine touch and taste superb, but no one would ever mention this to Vykter. They were content with his cooking as long as Renny stayed away from the food preparation.

After supper the atmosphere in the cavern turned quiet and eerie. The flickering fire tormented all within the vicinity by creating shadows that danced along the stone walls and arcing crown. This ignited one's imagination; add the dampness that crept under their clothes, it set some of the men's hairs to stand on end. It was no wonder the guards on watch were often seen to startle at the slightest sound.

Ballard and Aiden were over to the far left, brushing and fussing over their war steeds when Ciaran skittled over to the big man and clambered up his clothes to sit on his shoulder.

"Laddie, may I have a wee word wid ye?"

"Sure, of course Ciaran, What is troubling you?"

"Well...I been thinking with all that's been happening and what ye and the lassie have seen, that maybe..."

"That maybe what, come on puff it out."

"Well, maybe I be one too."

"I am not following you, one what Ciaran?"

"You knows, a Morphid creature...like them others."

"Oh by the ancients, why would you think that?"

"Well simple logic; why can I not fly laddie? I have tried. Vykter has been throwing me, but I crash every time. I cannot breathe fire, only puffs of smoke more than not, now and again a tiny burst of flame. More from something I ate me thinks and…Have you ever seen another like me around?"

"Oh, I see what you mean. Hmmmm…Hop over on Caesar's back and I will check you out. See if there are any similarities with the Morphids."

"Oh thank ye so much laddie."

Caesar turned his head around to eyeball Ballard; he rolled his eyes, let out a large sigh and shook his head and mane in exasperation. *I am definitely too old for this rot.* Kayne in the next stall rolled his top lip up and laughed at Caesar. "Boys hush now." Ballard placed his finger to his lips.

While Ciaran was readying himself for this inspection, Ballard's eyes glimmered with mischief; his fingers restless, flexing them in and out of his palms. "Right, let's start with your head shall we?" Ballard checked his eyes, rubbed his weather worn hands over Ciaran's elongated head. He poked his large fingers in his ears and wiggled them around and then looked under his snout and in his mouth tapping on his wee teeth.

Aiden noticed this unusual event and wandered over closer. He leaned on a post nearby to give a second opinion if required.

"Well next I will check your body." Ballard ran his fingers expertly over the small dragon like body. He checked under each wing which he pulled this way and that, stretched them to their limits, then felt down his tail.

"Please no butt poking laddie?"

"Would I do that to you?" Ballard's face was now serious; his brows were furrowed and posture upright. "Right, I need you on your back now Ciaran. I must check your belly."

Ciaran hopped over onto his back. His little stubby legs stuck out and straight up like a dead roach. Aiden covered his mouth to stifle his laughter as he watched. Ballard again rubbed his fingers over his belly and his legs. Without a moment's hesitation an evil smirk adorned his face and he commenced tickling Ciaran under his forearms, wild and unrelenting. Ballard knew this was Ciaran's one weakness. He was terribly ticklish. Ciaran roared with laughter, blew smoke rings and kicked his tiny legs. He wriggled and squirmed to be free of the relentless attack. Ballard and Aiden also laughed so hard they had tears rolling down their cheeks.

"Please stop laddie, I canna take anymore." He continued to roar and snort with mirth.

Ballard at last conceded and conferred his findings with Aiden. There was lots of head nodding by the pair and Ciaran watched them with a worried look.

"Well Ciaran, we are of the opinion that you are…too damn ugly and ticklish to be a Morphid. Nope it is definite; you are a Dragonelle, perhaps with a few mental problems; but nothing more."

"Ye are sure? Ye mean it Ballard?"

"Yep, pretty darn sure, but we could test you some more if you like." He flexed his fingers ready for more tickles. Ciaran jumped over on to Ballard's shoulder and gave him a big dragonelle smooch on the cheek and scampered away back to Atesh and snuggled into her neck.

Atesh felt his little heart racing and he puffed with small rapid breaths. "Are you alright Ciaran? What was that all about?"

"Aye, I be fine now lassie. More than fine thanks, tis somethin between the big laddie and me."

Aiden and Ballard resumed their horse grooming, odd little laughs and snorts would often escape their lips. Atesh and Marcus looked at each other, shrugged their shoulders and continued their conversation. She would however, question them later that was for sure.

Atesh turned to Marcus with a serious look. "What do you think we will find up near the Northern Border?"

"Honestly, I don't know. I hope it's no more of those Gnasherdiles."

Atesh spurted out her drink, spraying it over herself. "What's a Gnasherdile?"

"Those reptile creatures we encountered today; nasty, smelly critters."

"Oh, so you are naming them now?"

"Well I thought seeing they be a new variety; I could do that."

"Will you be gracing us with this naming vice of yours for all the new species we stumble upon?"

"Well, it is a lot safer than your vice, Atesh."

"What! I don't have a vice sir, I will let you know."

"Oh, so making friends with the most ferocious man eating monstrosities ever to grace this fair land is not a vice? I mean, let's be honest Atesh. Betha was so large she blocked out the sun for goodness sake and what did you do? Oh, you decided to sit and chatter. And how many damn eyes did she have staring at us? While the rest of the escort shook in their boots and stained their britches."

"I would say, not quite a vice, more of a little inconvenience." Atesh rocked back and forth as she laughed and held her nose to make a point to Marcus.

Marcus looked at her in horror. This gesture held odoriferous recollections, ones he hoped to forget. His body however failed him at this point; his face warmed to fire up his cheeks and glowed like a beacon.

"Why are you blushing oh, *King to be*?"

"Am not, it is a little warm, sitting by the fire."

"Well then sir, let us drink to your vices and my ummm…inconveniences with finding new and unusual friends."

They touched mugs and skulled their warmed spiced tea.

"Atesh, I shudder to think what creature you may find to be your next friend. A two headed monster bee, a blood sucking beetle, a sabre-toothed roach or a slimy one eyed serpent. I am honest to goodness concerned for you."

"I will try and behave, for you, kind sir. Now I must check on the men before I retire." She jumped up and strode away towards the perimeter. She had hoped by exiting quickly, she would stall Marcus from broaching another delicate subject.

Ciaran had soon recovered from his exhausting Morphid inspection. He scampered again over to the animal pens and climbed up onto the stall railing and watched as Ballard pampered his steed. He sat quiet and watched as the big man's gaze often fell over to the two Commanders. Ciaran jumped onto Ballard's shoulder which brought him out of his day dream like state.

"Geeze, you startled me, ol' man, you feeling alright now?"

"Aye laddie, I be fine now thanks to ye." He made his way carefully around to the front of the white linen shirt and ventured up close to Ballard's face.

"What's this about then eh?" Ballard leaned his head and shoulders back to look into Ciaran's grey, almost colourless eyes.

"I have another wee question to ask ye?"

"Fire away then. Oops sorry poor choice of words. I do beg your pardon."

In a quiet whisper, "Why haven't ye told her?"

"What are you talking about now?"

"Ye know full well what I be talking about laddie."

"I am not discussing this with you Ciaran, so leave it be."

"Why not laddie, why is it you nae tell her how ye feel?"

"If I do that I might lose her, you know that. She loves Marcus not me. I am only a substitute father to her; nothing more."

"But ye love her right?"

Ballard's face paled and he rubbed a hand through his wild hair. "I always have. Since the first moment I saw her. A tiny wee thing, all scrawny covered in dirt. Remember, I was a kid myself then too. But…losing her friendship and respect will hurt more than losing her to Marcus. The problem is…I am not sure what kind of love it is? I don't understand it. Is it a father's love for his charge or a deep friendship and comrade love? Or is it a love that can never be, the everlasting kind? I am very protective of her, or is it jealousy? Though, I know in my soul, I want her to be happy more than anything else in my life and Marcus is a fine young man. I am very naive on affairs of the heart; so I am very confused right now."

"I am sorry laddie, truly I am. I cannot know the difference either. The lassie holds my heart and soul; she is my best friend that is my love I have for her. Very deep and spiritual, I suppose."

Little did they know Atesh had completed her rounds and had wormed her way into the next stall without anyone noticing; hiding from Marcus was her idea. She sat there quiet next to Kayne and could not help but overhear the private conversation between Ciaran and Ballard. Oh, how she wished she was somewhere else right now. She drew her knees up to her chest, placed her head face down into them. Her hand was over her mouth. *What a dilemma I am in now. What do I do? Life used to be so simple, now it is all mixed up.* Kayne sensing her unsettled distress lay down beside her and nuzzled his head under her arms. Atesh snuggled into his warm body and pretended to be asleep lest anyone notice her. She waited till the area was clear before she emerged and retired to her bedroll.

Chapter 31

The Plateau & Ridgeways:

The next morning after forms, when they set off for the plateau; the men were quieter than usual. A sense of foreboding had overcome them. The darkened tunnel felt like it was closing in on them, as mile after mile they ascended up through the mountain range. The usual road that circumnavigated around the mountain range would be impassable for weeks at a time after a good snow fall. It was lucky this season didn't last more than twelve weeks, though this passageway through, allowed supplies to be continued to the north; no matter what the weather threw at them.

The air in the tunnel whistled along the small upright tube-ways that were punctured within the rock's crown. Fresh cool air would circulate through those breaches from the outside world. At times though, when the tunnel walls seemed closer, it still smelt stale. A combination of mineral and dank dirt odour assaulted their noses. Their shuffling movements, hoof beats and voices echoed loud along the dark rock-walls. The men often looked back to see if there were more feet than there should have been, it was an unnerving experience. The illuminating crystals embedded at irregular intervals sparkled into life as the first person passed it by, sending forth a brilliant array of colours. They displayed unusual shapes and patterns all around the tunnel and then winked out of existence. This left the mind to conjure all manner of strange creatures, lurking behind; watching and following. Perhaps they were licking their lips with thoughts of a quick meal or gruesome death for the intruders in the darkness. It played on their minds like a canker.

By midday they emerged onto a large plateau. The bright sun saw them squint and shade their eyes for a while. A campsite was maintained here all year round by the North Mede guards, but as they approached this area, it was noticeable; all was quiet and vacant. The embers in the fire-pit were cold and lifeless. Marcus and Aiden were concerned and looked around for any signs of life. Worry etched in their faces as they ordered camp to be established. Atesh and Ballard had wandered over to the far edge of the plateau that overlooked North Mede Castle, the port and village. They lay down on their bellies and shimmied as close to the edge as safely practical. Here they could view below unseen. Ballard pulled out of his belt a tube apparatus and as he gazed below, he gasped. He handed Atesh the narrow black cylinder with the clear crystal implanted at the end. This allowed all who peeked through it, to see the distance, enlarged; up close. She placed her eye on the end of the tube and scanned around, then with horror etched on her face, stared up towards Ballard.

"You have got to be kidding me, right?"

Marcus and Aiden noticed the other Commanders' strange behaviour and wandered over. "What are you two doing? And what in all Sofala is that contraption you are holding?"

"Better look from this prone position Marcus. This is a sort of distance seeing spectrum. There is a special crystal lens cut and curved in the end of this tube. It magnifies the distance, so it appears closer. Look through the cylinder with one eye and close the other."

Atesh slapped Marcus on the shoulder and laughed at his antics. "No silly don't close the eye you are to look with."

Marcus held this tube up to his eye and whistled. "Wow this is fabulous." He then aimed it down upon the village and castle. His posture stiffened, brow furrowed and lips turned up into an ugly sneer. He turned to the others. Without a word he handed the spectrum to Aiden and pointed down for him to observe the events below. Marcus placed his forehead on the ground in exasperation. "When is this going to end?"

Aiden was also ashen faced and speechless.

"I am afraid this may be only the beginning Marcus." Atesh pointed at the distance. "Notice the northern boundary. The crystals on the poles are lifeless, some are missing altogether. The boundary is no longer in-effect."

"What did you say?" The three men seemed to echo in chorus. Then they all turned to stare out to the distant mountain range and shivered as though the future that lay before them was now uncertain.

Aiden broke the silent musings. "Atesh, what is that covering the village?"

"If I had to guess Aiden, I would say some sort of webbing."

"But…they are coloured?"

"Yes, quite spectacular. But I am certain they are webs of some kind. They are either huge or a great many creatures made them. Some sort of Arachnopod to cover such a vast high area."

"What do you think Marcus, Ballard? Should I reach out to a mutual friend of ours to ascertain what we may encounter? I would not be too quick to go up against any of Betha's relatives; if you get my drift."

Ballard stared at Atesh, "Sound idea Atesh, I was thinking on similar lines. Imagine Betha's wrath if we killed her kin? Oh, I feel sick, thinking about it."

Marcus paled at the thought, "Oh no that would not do at all. Being clagged is one thing; being *THE* clag is quite another." As he sat back from the edge of the plateau, Marcus turned to his officers. "Let's go and make a plan. We are now officially on a rescue mission. There is no point information gathering. We must warn the King. He can recall all the villagers and outlying farmers to move into the towns for safety."

Atesh contacted Thaddeus and relayed all they had seen. Then she concentrated on finding Betha across the sea; she meditated and used her amulet and rings as a conduit for her power.

"Betha, this is Atesh. May I speak with you?"

"Oh, my dear what an unexpected surprise, your powers have indeed grown. What seems to be the problem, little one?"

Atesh discussed what they had seen from the plateau and their dilemma.

"Yes, I see why you would be concerned for your villagers. I will contact you when I discover what is happening up there. The Northern Border worries me now the protective barrier is breached. This has never happened before. You are a special lady Atesh. No other two legs would concern themselves about my kin, very considerate indeed and I thank you."

That evening all men stayed on full alert and watches were set on the township for any signs of activity; be it creature or man.

Later that night a voice startled Atesh as she sat by the fire-pit.

"Atesh this is Thaddeus. Are you all safe at the moment?"

"Yes sir, we are still on the plateau."

"I have spoken with Gareth at length and he has recommended you use the old Ridge-way tunnels. There are many, unused for eons, so take care and make as little noise as possible. We are not sure how stable the tunnels would be after so long. You only need to traverse two. One to the harbour and the other turns off and heads beneath the castle. They intersect a few lengths from the castle outer wall. Marcus should remember how to access these from the plateau. Once beneath the castle, there are secret passageways between the old and new walls. It has been added on and changed many times over the years. Access to the main common rooms will be by a loose brick with an embedded dragon crest, located behind some of the fire places. Turn the brick outward and a small lever can be manipulated. Once inside the room there will be sconces placed on the walls beside the fireplaces, one will lever down. The best area to enter would be the main dining hall and then you can walk around unhindered and find the people. Gareth believes there is a tunnel that should go from the castle under the village to the main civic hall. Maybe some have taken refuge there as well. Please my dear, be careful there are passageways that have not been traversed in thousands of years and we have no knowledge of where they lead."

"Would not the residing Lord and his family know about these tunnels?"

"It is possible, but Gareth is not sure what his cousin knows of the building. Best of luck and be safe."

Throughout the night a dusting of bone jarring cold sleet cascaded down upon the north. It lay upon the webs, caught within their sticky tendrils, the droplets sent out an array of spectacular colours; yet at the same time it was eerie in the full moonlight. It was rather a breathtaking sight if it had not been so deadly a circumstance. The only movement seen was that of a predatory night bird. It had been caught in a web after it chased oversized insects; attracted to the illumination. The observers indicated for the Commanders to come over and view this event. The bird struggled with all its might which only made its plight worse, tangling ever more so. The vibrations alerted the owners and a mad dash by six hairy spider creatures fought each other for the thrashing prey. Vicious was an understatement. They had the usual eight legs and large gnashing pincers. What concerned Atesh and the observers were the coloured and evenly striped, protruding spikes. They marked the full length of their spines with an eye situated on each spike. They were large enough to swallow this bird of prey whole.

"I don't believe these are naturally occurring inhabitants Marcus? Bird spiders do not look like these."

"Damn it all Atesh, they are ugly. They have a face only a mother could love. This wizard sure has a weird imagination."

"Or perchance, he has a perverse sense of humour?"

All turned to Ballard as he spoke with his nose wrinkled, shaking his head.

"Well Marcus, almighty *Royal name-myster*, what would you call these beauties?"

"I guess…Arachnoeyespikes sounds good to me."

"Oh someone shoot me now and put me out of my misery, please?" Ballard placed his head upon the rock and simulated banging it up and down. "Are you serious?"

Atesh fell onto her back and rolled on the hard ground and laughed till her side cramped. "Eye-spikes…?" Atesh was set off again. Laughing and crying at the same time.

Marcus didn't understand her behaviour at all; he was serious about naming these creatures. His face warmed up and he stalked off after Ballard, whose shoulders shuddered as he walked.

Atesh settled down and joined the men at the fire-pit. Ballard tried to hand a steaming mug of nettle tea to her, but noticed how she sat upright; her eyes glazed and staring.

"Atesh, it is Betha my dear. Those creatures at North-Mede, they are not of this place. Wizard made I am afraid, abominations to our species. They were hounded from the northern forests by Troldwites; a nasty combination of rock troll and ancient dark mountain dwarves."

"Why would these troll creatures chase them? Do they eat spiders?"

"Not usually on their menu, only if there is nothing else around. The spiders were herded, one could say and pursued down from the mountain straight into this village. The inhabitants fled for their lives into the surrounding mountains and ran straight into an extensive ambush, laid by these cunning hunters. The Troldwites are carnivorous and now the boundary is open, most of their accessible food has started to move down into the main areas of Sofala beyond their reach. So they too came looking for food; two legs are a rare delicacy. Well after the village was deserted the arachnoids laid claim to it. They will not give this up without a fight. It is a safe haven for them while ever the two legs are on the Troldwites menu. I believe there are still a few inhabitants trapped within the Castle. The arachnoids are waiting to pounce and try two legs themselves. See what all the fuss is about. So my dear speed and stealth is essential if you wish to recover the villagers. I really hold no sway over these abominations. Their Queen was adamant, they will fight to the death if need be, so beware. Their needle like fangs and spine spikes are toxic, quite fatal if you are bitten or stung. But their weaknesses are their many eyes, the back of their throats, between their front legs and a small patch before the rear stinger. Keep safe and call me again if you need me. I have a feeling we will all be required at the end; to beat this wizard. The ancients, all manner of creatures and two legs must join together; for the battle to end them all."

"Thank you for all this information Betha, we shall do our best. I will keep in touch."

The horses and most of the large gear were left behind on the plateau, guarded by a couple of the regiment soldiers. Each man to journey below placed their immediate needs into a side or back pack. Weapons were checked, sharpened and sheathed. They then assembled and in silence commenced their rescue mission. Atesh and Marcus led the way throughout the ridge-way tunnel heading to the North Mede Castle. This particular passageway has not been utilised for years, yet the crystals within the walls; still illuminated their way as they passed. This they thought was a great mystery in itself.

"I am wondering how long these crystals last Marcus?"

"Atesh, I have no idea, but I do know where magic is concerned, anything can happen and everything is possible."

Atesh noticed the walls were now saturated with embedded crystals in all shapes, colours and sizes. There were also white and yellow veins crisscrossing in all directions of the passage way walls and would burst alive in a splendid, sun like colour.

Marcus cautioned all behind him, "Be-careful men, no naked flame where you see the yellow veins in the walls. They will ignite and I would dare say bring the mountain down on top of us all."

The air became dank the deeper they travelled and a peculiar odour wafted more often out of the many angled narrow passage ways that deviated to the left and right of the main. This gave all in the group the jitters with nerves tightened to near breaking point. The temperature remained stable, though cold and they often huddled within their jackets for warmth. Their breath could be seen rising, like a mist as it cooled afore their faces. Noses and ears unprotected became reddened and unfeeling. Their armoury clinked as they strode along at a good solid pace until Atesh stopped the group and ensured all were tied more securely to lessen their noise.

"We do not know what lay up ahead, so quietness may be our only advantage."

They all agreed with this assessment as they looked around with silent thoughts.

Ciaran who had been in disgrace again over his apple raid in Vykter's kitchen kit; his favourite food in the world; was hidden under Atesh's cloak. He popped his head out. "Lassie, we are not alone down here. There be old magic I be smelling, take great care; I do not ken what it be."

"What do you mean old magic, like at the stream?"

"Ach nae…this be older, like ancient. T'is giving me the creepiness." He again buried his head under the jacket, but this didn't stop his small body shaking every so often.

Atesh turned to the men behind. "We need to bunch up more men and be extra quiet, no talking alright?"

Although the cold musty air seeped into their very beings, their edginess made them perspire and breathe deeper. They continued to wind their way down the mountain range. Descending at each turn or so they thought, but it was very deceptive; they were in fact going in both directions. After what felt like hours of continual movement they stopped for a much desired break in a large opened cavernous area. A fire-pit was set in the centre, but had not been utilised in quite some time. A wood pile was found to one side, so they lit a fire and the men all sat around and warmed their aching bodies.

Ballard, Atesh, Marcus and Aiden decided to wander around the perimeter. Drawings old and dulled from many years of dampness and neglect, adorned the walls surrounding this cavern. It depicted amongst other scenes a great battle scene with large creatures; part man, and part amphibian descending from strange seafaring long-ships. They attacked a small village. Three tall men in long black wizard robes held their hands outstretched, lightening was sent from their fingertips towards the strange entities and their ships.

"It is obvious the Wizards won the battle, as the next picture, though faded showed a celebration feast and…Ballard? What in all Sofala is that? Oh I see…" Atesh turned her head sideways, then further upside down. "Interesting I must say…Is that even possible?"

"Come away from that Atesh you don't need to get strange ideas into that head of yours."

"Spoil-sport Marcus, the ancient inhabitants were an inventive race, I must say."

Ballard noticed another panorama on the adjacent wall. This one was of a serpent with long sharp-edged fangs and piercing green eyes, stalking two trolls in and out a cave. He turned to the others with widened eyes. "You don't suppose either of these depictions are the odours we have smelt and seem surrounded by, do you? The serpent or the…umm trolls?"

"I thought trolls were fairy-tales, meant to scare kids into behaving?"

"Oh nae lassie, they existed thousands of years ago, when all manner of magic creatures lived here on Sofala."

"Yes Ciaran, but they do not exist anymore, except what our friend creates, do they?"

"Ach nae, dem tomes I read at the academy believe they all left when dem fancy ones did overnight, *poof like*…gone."

"That is so strange; I wonder why and where they went?"

"Well, not strange at all. To be precise they left for the other side of the world of course; to live in peace, as they wished to." A deep commanding voice spoke from within a darkened side tunnel.

Ciaran hid while the others turned their head's slowly. Fear etched on their blanched faces and widened unblinking eyes.

Chapter 32

Eggcitement:

"Mason this is the third cave we have been in and I have found nothing. The so called gems here are useless."

Mason sighed. "Everything takes time Master Dan. Why don't you meditate tonight when we stop for camp and see if anything calls to you?"

"Well we may as well keep searching while we are in this flee-bidden dark hole." Dan flicked his hand at the Troldwite leader. "Lead the way Kroll." Dan then leant down to Mason. "By the ancients, these creatures stink enough to melt one's face." Dan held his nose between his fingers, whilst he screwed his lips up.

Mason stifled a snort behind his hand. Subtlety was not one of Dan's best features. He in fact pulled such a face; it had the semblance of a withered old hag. Mason hadn't had this much fun since, well in many hundreds of years. *Can this day get any better?*

"Oh geeze Mason, what is that stuff under their fingernails? Ewwww-why can't they at least wash after they have eaten…whoever?" *Stinking lizard's gizzards.*

Mason now could not contain his mirth. He roared with laughter as Kroll the leader of the Troldwites turned and sneered at Master Dan. Kroll and a few of his creatures then lumbered down the main tunnel of this cave system, halfway along the northern boundary ranges. This entrance was spotted after a massive earth shake and rock slide the month before. A few of the stronger workers who had the job of carting the crystals back up to the exit; ran along behind the

Troldwites. The rest stayed close to the entrance of the cave as they stacked the dug up gems into the cart for Master Grey.

Danurel was not a patient man at the best of times and this business of crystal finding was another boring and tedious task. One he felt beneath his genius and social standing. He sauntered along after Mason, the workers and the creatures; down yet another dark, dank reeking passageway. Dan had limited vision in these darkened areas unlike his escort, only his oath ring shone for illumination. Mumbling to himself, but loud enough for the walls to echo his sentiments to any who would listen, he stumbled over a small rock and his feet became entangled. His fingers splayed and scrambled at the pebbled wall, then air as he pirouetted to land in an un-wizard like heap of tangled arms, legs and robe. He bit the dirt with a squeal that would have made a pig blush.

Kroll and his team sniggered as they sped up ahead. They had hoped to lose the pathetic two legged specimen. That was one; they would even reject to eat.

As Dan straightened up and dusted down his clothes and wiped his grime encrusted face on his sleeves, he noticed a glistening off in a small side passage. Without thought about anyone else, he hastened in an awkward limping fashion after this glowing trinket. He found it was not a single gem, but a vein of shiny treasure, enlarging as he followed its trail. The tunnel became smaller as the further he wandered along. It twisted left, right, up and down. At one point he was required to jump down a vertical shaft. Still he scrambled onward entranced by the thought of wealth. At last it opened into a large cavern with elongated rock spikes, dripping a milky substance that pooled into small deep tarns.

There were many alcoves and other passageways leading from this area with the same rich sparkling vein, all ready to explore. After a couple of hours he was so turned around he wasn't sure which way he had originally entered from. He sat down for a rest and started lobbing stones into the largest murky water pond. He was hungry, tired and thirsty. Pure frustration had built up and showed in the increased aggressive manner of his arm thrusts.

Bored with this game, he turned and noticed a small tunnel off the ground to his right. *Why didn't I notice this one before?*

A glint caught his eye, a portion of a shiny white gem half buried in the wall called to him. "Ahhh there you are my beauty." A short way inside this tunnel was at last; his prize.

Danurel scraped with his knife, but needed to crawl further along to reach around the gem. His body had little spare room to manoeuvre his knife. So he twisted, swore and dug with his fingers. All the while, his knees down to his feet hung outside the tunnel, a few hands spaces off the ground. Perspiration cascaded from his brow down his face in large droplets. They sloshed against his squinting eyes, the salty fluid stinging without mercy. Wiping them was out of the question. He must persevere and endure this pain to reap the reward he deserved. He was determined more than ever, this was his golden moment; his treasure.

As the large white gem started to dislodge, a pain sharp and intense shot up his left leg, he was tugged from behind back out of the tunnel. He could not reach his sword as it lay trapped beneath his body and in all the confusion, he dropped his knife. He yelled, screamed and kicked out with all his fury. He was dragged out into the cavern with one final tug. There surrounding him was a group of white lizards with wide opened maws, showing him their two sets of sharp, pointed teeth. They had long snouts, thick set scaly bodies and six legs. Their long blue tongues had partial splits dividing the first meaty portion, this poked out of their mouths in rapid succession as they hissed. Their slashing tails curled upwards adorned with blue and white striped edging spikes.

Dan looked at the abominations in silent revulsion. His heart raced and his face flamed with heat. "No! The treasure is mine. You will not stop me. I deserve this." He slashed and hacked at the creatures with his sword. For each one he killed or maimed another would rise out of the murky water and take its place. Others attacked their own injured, ripping, hissing and growling as they tore giant hunks out of the hides in a feeding frenzy. Dan was surrounded on three sides as he scrambled up against the cave wall and looked on in disgust and horror. He screamed for Mason and Kroll and hoped they were nearby to assist. He knew the hungry creatures would soon turn their attention back to their original quarry.

A noise of hurried foot falls echoed throughout the cavern as Mason and the Troldwites raced in from the opposite passageway. Swords slashed, teeth gnashed as fire balls arced into the mob of frenzied, ferocious lizard creatures. It did not take long for all the creatures to be either dead or dispersed; much to Dan's relief. Kroll and his team gathered a few each to take back for their supper. Dan silent and breathing deep short breaths could say nothing, but stare in disbelief.

"Mason, wha…wha…in blazes be those creatures?"

"I have no idea Master Dan, but we became worried when you disappeared and have been searching for you. The commotion echoed loud throughout the passageways and Kroll led us here."

Dan closed his eyes for a moment to gather his thoughts, and then having his breath back, ran over to the small hole in the cave wall and scampered in. After finding his knife he resumed the excavation of his prize. "Mason, look what I found. I did it. The one crystal that resonated with my essence; isn't she a beauty?" Dan handed it over with tenderness.

Mason held the crystal within his hands for a brief appraisal. "Yes, I can see you fought hard to win your prize, Master Dan."

"Great, then we can depart this dirt ridden, creature infested and rancid dung heap. I am so over this."

"Certainly sir, we must however keep moving along the boundary to collect all Master Grey's requirements. Only then may we return home." *For a knight Dan has been acting rather precious.*

A loud rumble caught them all off guard, the walls vibrated with sound movement. Rocks and debris from the ceiling began to tumble down onto the exploration party. White lizard creatures emerged from small water ponds and burrows to scramble down in frantic abandonment, to one of the passageways to their right.

"Quick Kroll, lead us to the surface before we get caught in a cave in. Master Dan please can you follow the Troldwites and I will bring up the rear."

After they exited into the fresh air and into the early evening light, a large plume of dust exploded out from the tunnel. A massive rock fall now blocked this entrance. Two of the workers did not return to the surface, they were lost in the cave-in.

As they sat around a camp fire that night, Dan polished his crystal with meticulous care. Mason watched with much curiosity.

"May I have another look sir, now you have cleaned your gem?"

"I suppose so Mason, but be-careful."

"Oh, I will sir. Extra careful I will be." The crystal was the most exquisite milky white colour he had ever seen. It seemed shaped to fit a staff to perfection. It even had an inner glow that troubled his inquisitive mind. Using his third eye, he examined it in more detail and depth. As he first suspected, all is not what it seemed.

Dan did not realise that Mason was equal to Master Grey in wizardry and power. Honour and a life-debt were at the core of Mason's foundation. So he chose to serve his friend and accompany him back to Sofala from the other side of the known world.

"Thank you Master Dan, it has given me an idea of how powerful a wizard you will become. Yes, I am certain you deserve this reward." Mason walked off into the bush for some solitary time, a smirk adorned his face. Now and again a small quiet chuckle escaped his lips. *I wonder what Master Grey will say when he sees this gem. Oh, he will be beside himself. Any wonder those lizard creatures fought us so hard, trying to protect what was theirs. An egg…he fought those creatures for an egg. Oh, this is too much.* He slipped down onto his knees. One hand around his waist, the other plastered firm on his mouth. He tried to hold his breath and not make a noise as tears trickled down his cheeks. *What will happen when he places it into his staff and activates a spell…, he will be covered in fried lizard gizzards?* A large snort and spurt escaped his lips, it could not be helped.

"Are you alright over there Mason?"

"Y—y-yes sir, I ummm…had a bad egg." He snorted again whilst stifling a laugh. "A belly-ache, nothing more; no needs to worry." Mason was now rolling on the ground in agony.

The next morning the two remaining slaves packed all the gear ready to move along the mountainous border. "It is a shame we lost two men back in that cave-in. Master Grey will not be too happy.

Perhaps Master Dan we should go through to the other side of this range?"

"Oh did we lose some of the slaves? Are you sure they didn't take off with some of the gems here. I am sure we had more yesterday."

"They were not slaves Master Dan, but paid workers and trustworthy. I can assure you, they did not run off."

"Well no mind I am sure we can find more to replace them. So how do we traverse this mountain? There are no known roads through and the wards are in place to keep the mountain intact."

"Oh we have our ways Master Dan, but the problems are with all the earth shakes, some of the routes no longer exist, whilst other new ones have opened up. I fear the mining of the border mountain range may be causing these little hiccoughs. I am troubled though, we have not seen a wild creature yet on this side of the border. I wonder where they are."

"Oh that is why the escort…well that is easy to answer Mason. They are in Sofala creating mayhem, murder and misery. That was why I was sent to the north in the first place, to find the breaches and close them."

"Oh goodness me that would be devastating for the farmers and villages…that is very interesting."

"So you know about the creatures here then?"

"Yes Dan, some are from the Master's failed experiments. Others are wild bred; nature finds a way you know. Believe me the word fierce for some, be an understatement."

"Oh, so what Commander Atesh said was true then, huh…I thought she exaggerated her report for her own self-importance."

"No I am sure she was accurate in her assessment from what you have told me of her. They are territorial, cannibalistic and often quite mad. You see, at one time the Master decided to meld two or three different creatures into one species. Well it didn't always work out for the best. So, if he could not control them, he transported them here to the wilds."

"Why does he do this?"

"He is trying to create a combination of certain attributes. When melded together they will form a creature that is fierce, warrior trained and will take orders, much like the ones that existed in ancient times. It all has to do with creating a…ummm better game. We must keep moving along this way for one more day, then through a secret passageway."

"Well that was amazing Mason. I would never have considered looking behind the waterfall for an entrance through the boundary."

"It was naturally occurring, we of course made slight adjustments, extended it here and there. It is concealed with magic as best we can. Kroll we will make camp here beside the stream."

A Troldwite out scouting the perimeter ran up to Mason and reported that a camp of two legs was a little way further down. They had small ones tied up and their Commander was yelling strange words, waving his sword around and then flapping his arms like a bird.

"Master Dan, there is an unusual camp we must investigate downstream. I am intrigued as to its purpose; care to join?"

"Lead the way Mason, what is the problem though?"

"Well let's go and find out, shall we." Mason placed a protection ward around the party as they neared the strange camp. They were hidden by the many trees and they stood still and listened. Dan soon became agitated and excited.

"Mason did you hear what they said? They abducted those two youngsters from the King's palace and will exchange them for Commander Atesh. Oh…such intrigue. She does get under your skin. But to have upset that raving loony, strutting around like a peacock on heat; she must be in fine form."

"Yes, this could work in our favour Master Dan. If this is the Commander, Master Grey spoke to me about, then this would be a coup for us both; easy pickings."

"What about this Commander Marcus he is bent out of shape with and wants to ahhh castrate. A bit drastic-don't you think? I wonder what lady they have fought over. Oh wait a minute…they must both be from the Beaumont Castle, no, surely not Atesh. Well that would explain the oddball behaviour of this poor sucker and the need to kill his rival with as much pain as possible. That name Marcus." Danurel placed his fist up to his forehead and hit it a few times to try and jog his memory. "I am sure he is the Prince. Yes, the heir to the throne."

"Well, we could do with another Commander for the game if Atesh turns, so we take him along as well. We can have Abi here at the right time and his group can transport them to the Island. We shall make a trade with them."

"Trade Mason, what have we got to trade?"

"Why Master Dan…their lives of course."

Dan sniggered behind his hand. "Well sir, lead the way, oh Mason the evil genius."

Chapter 33

Escape from Mere Town:

Prince Kyle Beaumont listened as his guardians discussed the local occurrences. The news had spread like a raging fire. The Northern Boundary's magical border was no longer in effect. He watched disorder through the window within his special suite at the Mere Town Hospice. This was his prison now for daring to challenge Commander Atesh. *After all, I was only doing my job; protecting my village.* The window seat was his place of refuge, a view to the world outside. He knew his father would order all the citizens that resided in the outer lying districts to seek safe refuge, within the nearest town. The Beaumont Village, Mere Town, Janlin and Ashmourne Village amongst others, would now be in the midst of ordered chaos; as hundreds of men, women, children and their cherished animals descended on these places of refuge.

In Mere Town, barriers were erected or reinforced. Soldiers were stationed on watch day and night. Gates closed at dusk and didn't reopen till dawn the next day. Overcrowding with makeshift tent communities sprung up in all parklands and wherever a spare plot of ground was found. Inns were filled to capacity and dusty, flea-infested barns accommodated the overflow.

Tempers frayed as the days wore on. Farmers became loud with their concerns for their crops or livestock left behind. Too much ale was consumed due to idleness, gambling and boredom. Soon fights and scuffles broke out between the townies and the country folk. A gang of young thieves terrorised the newest in town. They felt it was their duty to relieve the purse of any that came near to their patrolled streets and for a certain amount, they would ensure their safety. The town guards were over worked often outnumbered keeping law and order. Desertion for some seemed to be their only recourse. It did not help that the local council was vexed on maintaining their town disease free with hygiene, fresh food and clean water supplied to all.

Kyle watched with interest as the hospice became a bottleneck of squabbling, sick and anger infused people. They were lined up to be seen by the healers all hours of the day and night. Dysentery raged through-out the parts of the town with the most over inhabited population. The clean water supply had been contaminated by the dumping of human refuse. If a clean latrine pit was not handy, then some of the rougher characters would either lift up their skirts and squat or drop the trousers; even in the middle of the street. The rain would then wash this filth down into the stream from which their water supply originated. The inhabitants of the more affluent parts of town were horrified at the stench and often sent their maids to the markets with a perfumed kerchief up to their face. The lady of the house would never consider stepping outside their front door; the air they would have to breathe may be contaminated, diseased. Able bodied men were eventually rounded up and indentured, to dig wells and latrine pits, to ease the spread of the disease.

Kyle felt it in his bones, freedom would be soon. They would find a way; his loyal men. They would not see their Captain languish away from society forever; he had faith in them. He only had to bide his time and behave like a model in-patient.

Whilst all this confusion was going on, a Sergeant Philips visited his former Captain. Only one guard was on duty this day, the other sent off on an errand. He was new to this position and had not yet been fully briefed. The army Sergeant was polite and he was from the regiment after all; so his papers informed the guard. He therefore thought nothing of bending the rules and allowed Prince Kyle this one visitor.

After a short period of time a shout from Sergeant Philips called the guard into the room. The prince lay unmoving on the floor. As the young man knelt down to see what was wrong, Kyle stuck him through the heart with a knife hidden up his sleeve. The young guard was dead before he hit the flooring. The sneer on Kyle's face and the aggressive manner he drove the knife in, showed his inner most feelings. He was incensed at this incarceration; an honourable and loyal son to the King. Philips and Prince Kyle fled in silence to awaiting horses; hidden in an alley close by. There were at least a dozen men hanging around; watching for trouble. They were his most loyal followers, all recently sacked as guards by his older brother; Commander high and mighty Marcus. Others had joined Philip's troop for injustice to the prince. Still more were paid mercenaries. They rode swift and unobtrusive through the back roads to the brothel district, where Kyle owned a pleasant run establishment. They hid their horses and made their way to his private chambers to celebrate and plan an act of revenge on Commanders Marcus and Atesh. She above all, caused his public humiliation and confinement.

Kyle and Philips sequestered themselves into a small antechamber; here they brainstormed different scenarios. One plan came to Kyle unbidden and he jumped up excited, from his seat, as if stung by a bee.

"I have it Philips, I really do."

"Well sir, the suspense is killing me. Please tell, what is this devious plan?"

Kyle looked down his nose at Philips; "Devious my good fellow, how so?"

"The look on your face sir, your eyes have not sparkled so bright for a long time, it is good to see sir."

"We can dispense with the sir when we are alone Philips, we are friends, are we not?"

"Yes sir…I mean Prince Kyle."

"Right, now listen to this masterpiece." Kyle outlined his most ingenious plot ever.

Philips sat back and whistled. "Wow that is cunning. Do you really think we can pull this off?"

"I am sure we can, with stealth and planning."

"You wouldn't really hurt him, would you; after all, he is an innocent?"

"Oh, do not go soft on me now man, but of course not. It is all in the game you see. I cannot wait to see the look on that whore's face when she is outplayed. I will enjoy this outcome. Remember, tell the men she is mine to dispense with." Kyle's face creased up at one side and the artery in his neck protruded; it pulsed strong and rapid. His eyes squinted to mere slits as he thumped the wooden drink table. "I will have my revenge Philips. I will be remembered for ridding Sofala of that pathetic pretender and his whore. . . One day I will be King. I know it; I feel it." Kyle stood up tall and proud as he looked down his nose again at Philips. "When all the power is mine, you my friend will be my Chief Advisor and body guard."

Philips sat stunned, his hands wrung in anticipation. "Chief advisor, I do like the sound of that my prince. Shall we inform the men?"

"Well perhaps the first bit. We do not want them knowing too much now; enough to comply with my wishes?"

Over the next couple of nights the gang of the *Sofalan Liberators*, as they called themselves; made their way to the village of Beaumont. They rode in a few at a time, so as not to raise any suspicion. They hid in an underground bunker that Kyle knew had been abandoned for eons. It was hidden beneath a stable at the far end of a back street. Some of the men rode north east; up deep into the mountains and set up a base camp. Prince Kyle and Philips kept a look out for the right moment to carry out the next section of their plan.

Their vigil paid off sooner than they expected. One afternoon that week, at the rear of the Beaumont castle main grounds, young Prince Israe and his friend Binji, the bar-keep's son were playing knights. They fought together back and forward with their home made wooden swords. Being the same age of around eight summers, their imaginations were far greater than their sword skills, for they bruised each other more than they connected. They laughed and struck poses, killed pretend dragons and other menacing creatures. One guard was on duty to watch over these energetic and enthusiastic youngsters and he kept score for them as well. The ultimate winner and slayer of the most creatures would receive a double helping of the cook's apple pie.

These were made especially for the weekly bouts and most times it ended in a tie.

Kyle and Philips snuck up behind the guard and Kyle ran him through with his sword. Philips had placed a hand over the mid-aged gent's mouth to ensure no cries of alarm were uttered. Once he slumped to the ground, Philips and a handful of men grabbed the unknowing boys, tied their hands and placed gags in their mouths. Though the boys struggled with valour, it was in vain. The men performing their job were fierce and battle hardened mercenaries. Israe was hit hard on the head and he crumpled unconscious. He was then thrown over a soldier's shoulder as they sprinted for their horses. Binji ceased struggling and his eyes widened in fear for his friend. They rode off at a fast pace though they kept the noise to a minimum. With the influx of Sofalan inhabitants through the main gates, no one noticed these men leave. They travelled up into the mountains via dirt tracks and headed for their base camp. Binji was beyond frightened. He was only allowed to hang on to the horse with his legs. A few fingers clung on desperate, to bits of horse mane as a large soldier was seated behind him. His friend Israe was lying straddled over the front of another's saddle. His head shifted up and down with the horse's movement and his tied arms swung wild.

The first night in the mountains a makeshift camp was set up. The two boys were bundled next to the fire pit, their ankles tied now as well. Binji repositioned himself and leant over his friend where slight moans escaped his mouth. A large purple bruise was now visible on the side of his head. Late the following day they reached base camp and the rest of the gang. The camp consisted of a small rock alcove with an overhang. Large wildrid trees with their think canopy of limbs and leaves surrounded the cleared area in front of the opening. This sheltered and maintained their privacy from any trespassers. A small creek meandered nearby, with trout a-plenty and cool refreshing mountain water to consume.

Kyle strutted around the camp with crazed purpose, he muttered to himself often. The first parts of his plan were executed with proficiency; so he now felt invincible. Philips however would often glance at the boys, trussed up like animals. He was not happy with the harming of these innocents. The only larger thought that kept him quiet was the promise of power, influence and wealth. He ensured they were given food and fluids, though he noticed Israe was slow to respond. Binji's hands were untied at these times to assist his friend the young prince, as best he could.

The following night two mercenaries arrived at the camp, they had abducted a local villager between them. He was blindfolded and arms tied behind his back. His mission was to deliver a message back to King Gareth in person. This was placed in a small satchel and slung over his shoulder. The blindfold was kept in place whilst he was in the camp, though his hands were untied while he was given food and a warm drink. His hands shook so fierce he had trouble holding onto the mug. Kyle sat next to the young man and spoke in a gentle manner. He was there only to complete a small errand and then he would be released unharmed. This calmed the young villager enough that he consumed the tea; unfortunately this also had a potion that rendered him unconscious.

The young man awoke late the next afternoon beside the main roadway to North Mede. To show Kyle meant business, the soldiers had removed four of his fingers with little finesse. A light dirty bandage was laced around the stumps to stop him bleeding to death; too soon. The stumps oozed slow, ebbing away his life force. Only time and the assistance of a healer may save his life now. A saddled horse was tied to a bush nearby for his use. The young villager made the journey to the front gates of Beaumont castle before he collapsed off his mount, in a dead faint. In his hand was clutched the satchel with the personal message for the King; covered in dried blood and dirt. One guard ran all the way to the inner gates with the message, another summoned the healer.

Gareth opened this message with trembling hands. He had the look of a man who had little sleep of late. His face was ashen and unshaven, his eyes glazed and bloodshot with darkness beneath. Thaddeus ran into his office and noticed Gareth blanched further and sat back in his chair with a leaden posture. He handed the note to Thad.

"Why…who are these people? What is…*the Sofalan Liberators?* They want Commander Atesh in exchange for releasing my son and young Binji? It doesn't make sense. Marcus is to deliver her on a specific day and place. I don't like this at all."

"Gareth, I have other news. I came to inform you that Kyle had escaped from his confinement. I have received a missive a few moments ago. I am sorry; there was an influx of inhabitants to Mere Town after your decree. The town is in disarray. Guards deserting and the water supply have been contaminated. The sick are lining up, more each hour. The hospice cannot cope with the number of patients. They are in need of assistance as soon as possible. That this news comes around the same time; bodes ill."

"Thad, are you trying to say…you believe this is Kyle's doing? But Israe is his kin?"

"Yes, I do consider this a possible scenario. A young guard was killed in a rather aggressive manner during his escape. I cannot say if he will harm either of the boys. His mind is in fragments. I have no idea what he may be thinking, but Atesh he despises above all others. The guards spoke about Kyle's murmurings; always Atesh and revenge. This may be his way of ridding Sofala of the people he detests. Atesh and Marcus would be at the top of his list. My informants tell me there were quite a number of unusual mercenary type men hanging around Mere-Town of late."

"Where are Atesh and Marcus now, do you know Thad?"

"Gareth, they are on their way to rescue the inhabitants of North Mede from large coloured Arachnoids. They are not natural, but wizard made, and have taken over the entire area."

"Thad, they have given us seven days to comply with their wishes. What am I to do? What do we know of the messenger? Can he inform us of anything? Where the boys may be held?"

"He is being cared for by your Healer, but he may not survive the night."

"What happened to the messenger?"

"They were none too gentle with this lad. They'd cut four fingers off to show you they mean business. It was not performed hygienically or with care, as you can imagine; quite barbaric. He was naught, but a villager; abducted, blindfolded and mutilated. He has lost a lot of blood. But worse for him; they covered his hands with filth ridden wrappings. He is now delirious and feverish; ill humours have spread throughout his body."

"Oh no, another innocent victim pays for my son's treachery; what of his family?"

"They are with him now, Gareth."

"Can you reach Atesh, Thad?"

"Certainly, I will give it my best. What is your message Gareth?"

"Save the villagers and then bring my son and his friend back safe. Tell them to…do what they must." Gareth placed his head between his trembling hands. "What am I going to tell Brie, Thad?"

"Be gentle; tell her the boys are all right. Remember, we do not want to risk this pregnancy."

Meanwhile up at Kyle's camp, Philips informed the men that a time frame of seven days was given to the King; for the exchange to take place. A group made up of soldiers and mercenaries would meet Marcus and Atesh, at the designated location. There they would be blindfolded and led back to the camp. Philips could see this news caused tension and division within the ranks. The group of *liberators* were not in the best of moods. Waiting seven days in the rugged mountains in the white cold season was not their idea of fun. Mercenaries preferred to be busy, fighting battles, killing and maiming; not babysitting a crazy prince and his unusual ideals. The old palace guards met this time frame as a challenge, they idolised Prince Kyle and would not hear any dissent from the outsiders.

As sleet cascaded down each evening, it wet everything in its path. Thus, the makeshift shelters, kept no warmth in. Their bedding, equipment, clothes and wood were sodden from one day to the next. The length of daylight hours shortened, with frequent cool breezes that would eddy around the camp. This movement whipped up and dislodged chunks of ice from the laden tree branches onto the unsuspecting guards with regular occurrence. The two lads still trussed up, lay huddled together beneath a small rock overhang next to their small fire-pit, which produced more smoke than heat. Though miserable and afraid, they watched with a glint of delight, the soaking the guards received; however never a sound did they utter.

Kyle strutted around the camp with glee and enthusiasm. Nothing would dampen his spirits, not even these blinding unforgiving headaches. He was a free man, controlled his own small fierce army and slept in a warm, dry and cosy alcove. He was their Prince, saviour and way of becoming wealthy men, after all.

Philips was concerned with the mutterings from the outsiders. The last thing he wanted was some kind of mutiny or desertion. He continued to watch all happenings within the camp and discussed the group's tension with his prince.

"Father always said a busy man never has time to grumble. Perhaps this time he was right. So Philips, we need to ensure the men are not idle. You will deal with this for me, won't you Captain?"

"Captain…you are promoting me, sir?"

"Think it is about time, don't you?"

"Thank you sir, I…I am honoured." Philips had the men rotate on guard duty; day and night. They scoured the forest for dry wood, gathered water and fish, killed and cooked game and pandered to Kyle's every need. They set up an area to practice their hand to hand combat, sword fights and knife throwing. They were all aware the magical border had failed; they did not want any surprises; creatures sneaking up in the night to have them as their supper. Philips realised the only reason the mercenaries stayed around and did not kill them all in their sleep was because of the riches they were promised. They believed this prince was mad enough to keep to this agreement. Philips knew better, Kyle would dispense with these men as soon as he had accomplished his goal.

On the evening of the fourth night in the mountain camp, Prince Kyle and Philips sat around the open fire-pit discussing their plot in the finest detail. It was an especially large blaze tonight. A find of a fallen tree dry and seasoned gave them warmth for the first time. One of the Mercenaries struck up a tune and others joined in. Ale was consumed and all was bright in the world. A voice unknown startled the men. Swords were whipped out as they stood to face the intruders.

"Well, well, well. What have we here Mason?" Two strangers became visible as they sauntered closer to the fire-pit.

"Men to me, to me…Intruders…protect your Prince."

"Don't worry about your men Prince Kyle; they are safe for the moment as are you."

"You know who I am? What we are? Are you not afraid? And yet you still sneak up on us?"

"You are no threat to us Prince. What you suggest is laughable."

"Who are you? What do you want?"

"My name is Master Dan; my companion here is Master Mason. What we want my dear Prince is the same as you are after. We want Commander Atesh and you have given us the perfect scenario to access her."

"No, No, No, she's mine. I have waited and prepared…men kill them. This is my camp, my army, my rules. How dare you speak to me like…like, I am some commoner."

"Sorry to disappoint, but I am afraid she will be ours Prince."

"Please sit down Prince Kyle. Master Dan will explain it all to you. In the end you will see it is for the best."

"We, that is, Mason and I would like to discuss a trade of sorts."

"What could I possibly want from you that I would trade my most prized possession? She is mine, my revenge not yours, my glory, my crown."

Kyle was becoming quite unreasonable and agitated. Philips looked on in horror. He was concerned the prince would get them all killed.

"Why Prince, I think you will find this exchange most agreeable." Master Dan looked down with contempt written all over his face. He had turned his lip up in a sneer. "Your lives for Atesh; is that simple enough for you?"

"You are having a jest with me right? You are two masters of nothing, against my army. Ha…you are dead men." With a flick of his wrist and hand to his captain; "Philips, fix this problem for me, that's a good man."

Captain Philips sat frozen, his face ashen and his eyes wider than the moon up above.

"He understands well enough Prince Kyle; take a look over to the right. Yes that's it. Now scan the perimeter and tell me what you see?"

"Where are my men?" Kyle's voice pitched to a high falsetto. He stared at the creatures' illuminated by the fire light that surrounded the camp. They were grotesque and he blanched and shook with fear and rage. "What in all the lands are those things?"

Mason smiled to the mad prince. "These wonderful creatures are Troldwites. My army Prince Kyle and they have, but one fault. Can you hazard a guess what that could be?"

Kyle nodded his head, he was unable to speak. Their odour took his breath. He placed a kerchief up to his face.

"No? Well they have an exhausting appetite for two legs; man flesh. Raw or cooked they are not fussy. So you see you would be wise to take our offer. Now for the last time Prince Kyle will you agree to an exchange?"

"Yes…No…That coward is mine; Leave me alone, you are giving me a headache."

"Yes Masters the prince will concede." Philips was aghast at Kyle's behaviour.

Master Dan and Mason looked at each other. Dan shook his head in wonder and bewilderment.

"Oh, there is one condition."

Kyle looked up and stared through Master Dan, his rocked back and forth, his mind was jumbled, his hands wrung in a constant motion.

"Atesh is not to be harmed at all. Not one hair on her head is to be out of place. *YOU HEAR ME?* We will be watching you. So mark my words, any change to this plan and the deal is off."

Philips had snapped out of his despair to take charge. "Wh…What do you want with the likes of her anyway? Doesn't look like your type, she being a whore and all."

Master Dan kept his cool exterior, but on the inside he seethed. He raised his eyebrows and nodded to Mason. Mason clicked his fingers and held one finger up to the sky. Philips rose into the air, his hands clutching at his throat. His face was turning blue as he struggled to breathe. Philips eyes bulged from sheer fright; his legs dangled and kicked out into the air. Soon his body went pale and limp. Mason timed it perfect, not enough to kill Philips, but certainly gave the men around the fire something to think about. He released his grip and Philips fell back to the ground. Unable to arrest his fall, he smacked like a clap of thunder, next to Prince Kyle. With an evil sneer Master Dan and Mason bowed and all the intruders disappeared, as if they had never been.

The guards soon reappeared confused and dazed.

Kyle kicked Philips as he lay on the ground unmoving. "Get up, get up you lazy pig. Did you see what they said to me? How could you let them sneak up on us like that. Why didn't you do something? Get up I say." Kyle strutted around the camp site. He mumbled and spoke to the sky. Arms gesturing wild and exaggerated, his movements became ever more so erratic. He stormed over to one of the guards, screamed and pointed to him. "This is your fault. You told them where to find me. I know you did." He walked closer, "Tell me why…why you would do that?"

The guard looked around, imploring with his widened eyes for assistance from anyone nearby. He was at a loss, not understanding why he had been singled out.

"You betrayed us all." Without another thought, Kyle lunged with his knife and skewered the guard with a fatal blow.

A voice on the wind eddied around Kyle's head. "Remember we are watching you."

Kyle threw his toothpick onto the ground, covered his ears and screeched in a falsetto pitch. He ran into his cave and hid under his blankets, shaking and mumbling to himself. He did not want to hear the voices of the night ghosts and their smelly, human eating creatures.

Chapter 34

Barron:

"Who may I ask is trespassing in ma hallways, loud enough to wake them dead?"

"We…umm…apologise for disturbing you sir, but we are on a mission for the King."

"Which King would that be, wee warrior?"

"King Gareth Beaumont, sir."

"And again, I ask. Who might you be?"

"I am Commander Atesh of the *Pace Knights* from the Ashmourne academy. Beside me is Captain Ballard and Prince Marcus Beaumont, Commander of the King's Regiment then Captain Aiden Beaumont." They all bowed in deference to the large, bright green emerald eyes; glaring back at them from the darkness.

"May we know whom we are addressing sir?"

"My name is Barron. I am Lord of this mountain, protector of the mines, master of his own destiny and story; I might add. I was sanctioned by the First King; Wizard Master, Gavin Beaumont."

Marcus shook his head in confusion. "King Gavin Beaumont? No, not possible…he lived many thousands of years ago."

"Yes that is correct young Prince; I am long lived, perhaps immortal and have roamed these hallways for all that time."

Atesh's grin near split her face as she fidgeted with eagerness. "May we look upon your face, sir?"

Both Ballard and Aiden wide eyed, shook their heads, nooooo. Marcus placed his fingers up to the bridge of his nose, head down and shaking it as he mumbled under his breath. "Is this my torment for waiting to find true love?"

"Many who do are frightened, but then again…they are to be my meal; so that is expected I suppose. It has been a long time since I have had a pleasant conversation with young distinguished guests. So I shall grant this request." Barron slid out of the darkness, silent for one such as him. When he entered the cavern and rose up to his full height, his head grazed the roof.

The four officers took an involuntary step back and arched their heads to look up at this enormous reptile. He had two sizeable elongated pointed fangs. Barron's surface was covered in multi coloured gems and iridescent crystals, which gave off eerie shapes upon the cave walls from the fire light. Marcus turned to Atesh with a raised eyebrow and a *see I told you so* expression on his face. Atesh shrugged her shoulders; her eyes wide with glee sparkled with small blue flames as she bestowed a cheeky smile back. Atesh then turned towards the men around the fire-pit. She beckoned them with her hands to rise, but she placed a finger to her lips to indicate silence as they gave a collective gasp and then rose in accord. The commander's ring had not indicated an enemy and after what they had previously encountered, anything Atesh had to do with was possible.

"You are a magnificent creature Barron. Are you magic made or natural occurring?"

"I suppose Commander, I am both. I was born a creature of the wild then formed into what you see today, for a specific purpose by the first King; but that was so long ago for me. Please sit and I will lower my head for you. Do you know the story of the first three and of the prophecy foretold by the last tribal seer?"

"No I do not believe I have heard this story or anything of a prophecy."

"I must ask then Commander. Are you one of two? Would this strapping young Captain be your other self?"

"If you mean, is Aiden my twin brother, then yes, I believe that is correct."

"You believe? Do you not know your own kin?"

"We were not brought up together. It is a long story Barron."

"Well, never mind, you have found each other now."

"Why is that relevant Barron?"

"Ah my dear it means the prophecy is in play…it has awoken from its slumber to complete its mission. There are perilous times ahead. Sit, sit and I will explain." Barron looked up to see the mass of men, inching slow and steady towards him; so he beckoned them to come closer. "Do not fear me young warriors, I have slaked my appetite for today." His forked tongue darted out a few times over their heads in quick succession.

The soldiers now feared they would be this creature's next meal; they in unison all stopped their forward motion and reversed their steps one at a time, as their wide eyes darted between the looming creature and their Commander.

Barron roared with laughter. "I am jesting with you fine men, come now I give you my word, I shall not harm you. I am a historian of some note, a fine story-teller I have been told. Come a tale awaits you." His crystal body clinked as it motioned with his continued merriment at his own joke.

Atesh introduced the men to Barron. "These are the Knights of the First Battalion and the King's Personal Regiment soldiers at your service, sir."

"Nice to eat you…oops… I mean meet you all. I have not had an audience for an oration in a long time."

Atesh furrowed her brow at Barron's lack of sensitivity. *Why are all these ancients so…so…eccentric?*

The men all sat down in trepidation in front of the enormous, fierce looking creature while he cleared his throat and began his story.

"Now if you are unaware, their speech back in the first age was basic and not educated as we here today. So please excuse me if I explain this part of our history in my own unique way." He cleared his throat a few more times, "huhum…huhum…" the vibrations within the cavern sent shingle raining down upon the audiences' heads.

"Back in the ancient times there were many creatures cohabitating, magical and non-magical, both good and evil; as is always the case. Some lived above ground, some below and a few even lived within the tree-tops. The tribal elder that ruled this great land was a mighty prophet/seer that would sit for hours; sometimes days and gaze into the flickering fire. His eyes would glaze over. He neither ate nor drank whilst in this state, but would mumble to himself in a language no-one else understood. After one of these sessions he awoke quite agitated and excited. He called a council of the surrounding elders and wise inhabitants from all over this land we now call Sofala, in the world known as Cerahya. For in those days there were no names for the land they dwelt on. No-one owned what nature provided. The inhabitants were defined by either the way they lived or by their ancestor's trade and some, they just existed. He informed the council of a vision he had seen, one that would have a profound impact to their lives and future.

"In a time not far away, an enormous dark cloud will form over the entire north west land. So large in fact; the sky grows dim as the sun retreats in fear. The inner portion of this cloud will spin at a high speed around itself, developing a long tube that stretches from the sky to the ground. It has a large black, endless void within the centre. It is called a whirlwind. It creates such violent ferocity that it breaks free the trees from the ground and throws them without due care onto the surrounds; crushing all in its path. If the inhabitants do not find shelter below ground or in caves, they shall be in grave danger; such is the destructive force of this power." Barron had the men enthralled. They sat quiet listening. Not a murmur was heard from any of them. Then Barron shouted, "*BANG!*" All in the cavern listening jumped in fright and gazed around with guarded discernment. Barron grinned at his own story telling abilities; a mischievous glint twinkled in his eyes as his large head moved around focusing on one man, then another. "Then…as the cloud dissipated and the land stilled to silence, the sun again shall show his face. Three humans will be thrown out from this unusual wind formation and dumped upon this land. They be three potent magic users, what we now call Wizard Masters or Higher Magicians, carried here from another place amongst the stars."

Barron lowered his head so his face sat closer to the men. "They were told to make them welcome and to revere these unusual beings. For in the near and far future, they would save them in times of their most dire needs." Barron then spoke in hushed tones. "In a measure close to pass, an invading force of unusual, enormous, cannibalistic creatures from a realm far away, was at that moment on its way to conquer and destroy all those living on this fruitful land. Without the newcomer's magical assistance, none would survive the onslaught."

Barron looked around, his manner was relaxed and a smile adorned his face. Which in itself, with his large fangs showing and his top lip turned up would scare the wits out of the bravest of men. But, instead it showed he had the entire group once again; spell bound. They all gazed at him with awe and pride. He was in his element and felt privileged to be the one to explain the history of this great kingdom.

"These men would be known as the *First Three*. They'll eventually take up the veneer of rule. Be wise, trustworthy and mighty. This new beginning, the second age would be a beneficial alliance. Lailoken explained they would teach the local inhabitants many new ways of living; no longer dwelling in burrows or in tree branches. They'll be taught how to build houses, to grow crops, to fashion weapons for defence, to speak, read and write the strange language they brought with them. The wizards in turn would be taught the lore of the land; to understand and respect nature's harmonious relationship with the inhabitants. They would gain knowledge of herbal remedies and ancient healing methods. Then lastly they would be taught how to harness crystal and gem magic; found beneath all the mountains on Sofala. Although many local inhabitants were born with innate magical abilities, they were not all powerful and what power they did have was limited by their understanding and knowledge of the underlying principles of magic. Some races such as the tree-dwellers or what we now call Elves, felt that sharing their knowledge and skills would do more harm than good. So any information they discovered was kept to themselves. They alone felt superior to all other races, including man.

"As is the way in life, change always brings about dissent from those who preferred things the way they were; tradition and routines. Lailoken explained to the elders, this change was not a bad thing. Still disagreements and arguments happened and some of the rare and magical inhabitants decided to move to the other side of the known land to live as they please. Peace and prosperity would then reign on

Sofala for many years. Of course, now and again there would be small skirmishes or feuds over territories and political rivals and yes, sometimes inhabitants from other lands would try to invade or extend their kingdoms.

"After the first part of the prophecy was shown to the elders, Lailoken instilled fear with his last oration. He warned the elders that this next event must be remembered down through time, or humanity may be doomed. Foreknowledge will be the only way to survive the environmental catastrophe. It will be an era of uncertainty for all the inhabitants. The time frame for this event Lailoken did not know. For it was in the far future. The animals will know when this event will occur as they will run in fear to the highest lands. The birds will stop singing. Nature will be silent. This is the first and only warning sign Sofala will have. But Lailoken understood to combat the impending catastrophic event the first three wizards would need to amalgamate their magic and then enhance their colossal power with certain rare crystals. This was the knowledge they must find and learn to harness before the inevitable occurs." Barron once again lowered his voice, so all listening had to lean forward further to hear the important information. He was playing to the best audience he had ever entertained and loved every minute of it.

"A magical event on the other side of the world causes a calamitous trigger point to the east off Sofala, deep within the ocean. Lailoken explained to his audience. In the future magic will be formidable and used without accountability or rigorous, conscious thought. As with all things, when using large amounts of this type of raw power, for every action performed; there must be an equal and opposite reaction. It is the law of balance within nature. We now know at this time in our lives, having learnt hard lesson that there will always be consequences when we transgress beyond our learning, ignorance is no excuse. Combine those two flaws and together we find ourselves with a tragedy of epic proportions. Whatever transpired on the other side of the world, its impact will be profound for us here. He told them; 'take me not lightly when I say this'. For the side effects of their arrogance and stupidity will cause a gaping chasm to open up within the vast ocean floor, from the northern ice fields all the way down through to near the southern lands of Cerahya, east of the archipelago islands. The seabed will move and push up on either side of this rent, creating a row of differing sized underground fire mountains and apertures. The land of Sofala and the nearby islands will shake with tremendous force. Fissures will form allowing vents of hot steam to billow out swallowing whole villages. The many volcanic mountains located within the chain islands will perform their traditional songs together in harmony; breathing fire and lung burning thick, black smoke. The force exerted will send spewing, flaming ash and rocks miles into the sky, and then rain down on all known life. This shall set alight forests, homes and the surrounding sea." Barron noticed frowning faces and creased brows. He took a breath. "Do we have a question?"

"Sir, how can the sea burn like you say?"

"Oh my…you have never been taught about gases?" Barron looked to Atesh.

"It is not a subject required for warrior or soldier training Barron. That is for wizards, the science students and the seafarers, I believe. Would you explain for the men please, it will be useful for them to know?"

" I shall do my best Commander…Well young warriors, the sea burns when large pockets of gas escape their confines and leak up through cracks in the surface of the world and catch alight. The bubbles of this gas smell like the yellow mixture the magicians use for making, sparkling sky flyers, wiz poppers and the like." Barron noticed he was losing them again. "Oh I know…Imagine the odour emanating from the latrine pits after an army of men had spicy meatballs the night before, or…you were all locked in a tiny room together after a hard week of exercise with no change of clothes or water to wash, then one of the men decided to let off some pent up intestinal steam." He now could see the men's eyes widen and their faces screw up with the thought of the offending odour. It was strange thought Barron, how they all turned to one soldier in particular, stared him down and moved a little distance away.

Atesh noticed their behaviour and placed her hand up to her face to hide a giggle at poor Renny's predicament. His face had turned the colour of a fresh beet from the garden.

"Right you get it now? That nasal flaring, pungent smell is the gas we all produce. Some unfortunates have it worse than others. Yes even myself, though I will not admit to it, if asked of course." Barron did his best impression of turning his nose up in the air.

"In large quantities it can be rather explosive and in confined spaces, such as digging a tunnel, if you are unfortunate enough to hit a pocket of this gas, the bubbles will kill silently and with speed. Oh, the mere thought of it turns my nasal hairs rigid. Right…now how does it get to be underground? That I am sure one day some intelligent wizard will work out. But, my own thoughts are that all beings produce this gas after eating and digesting foods. It stands to reason then maybe it was trapped in the land from whatever creatures inhabited the world in the time before the first two leg's age. Maybe from their latrine pits or their rotting carcases buried for millions of years. We also know now that volcanic islands are all inhabited at some stage and they rise and fall within the ocean's floor. This of course depends on the power of the fire mountain's breath. We know also that this land we live on moves and groans at times and could cause fissures to open, expelling air. Though at this point, I am wildly gestulating at how the gas bubbles end up in pockets within the oceans.

"Anyway I digress. Right…now; where was I? Oh yes…Lailoken scaring the bloomers off the elders that is if they wore them of course. The day will turn to twilight, as a destructive rolling dust cloud blocks out the rays of the sun. Then when the land quietens the people breathe a sigh of relief, for the wizards would have done their magic and saved this land from being torn asunder. But alas, there is a consequence when interfering with nature and the water surrounding the east lands will be sucked out into the far distance, leaving only the muddy sea floor, bare as far as the eye can see. The inhabitants Lailoken stressed must follow the creatures and race away from the coast up to the highest mountains and inland to escape the next incident. For what had disappeared will be sent hurtling back, as an enormous high wall of furious water, pounding and destroying all in its path. It will wash over the lower lying areas for many miles inland at a thunderous pace, eating and destroying all in its path. Many of the smaller islands will disappear forever beneath the waves.

"Well it all happened as the Seer Lailoken foretold. Three young wizards did fall from the sky, from a tear in the fabric of space and time. A Master Beaumont, Ashmourne and Greymont landed unceremoniously on the beach north of this mountain. These young wizards had an experiment literally blow up in their faces. They were a sight, I am told. Blackened all over, hair fizzled and matted, clothes holed and smoking, with eyes widened in fear and confusion. They were greeted with open arms and soon became quite famous amongst the inhabitants. Master Beaumont married the seer's eldest daughter Liera. Master Greymont married the youngest daughter Frayne and Master Ashmourne married the daughter of the local healer, Miriam. They all produced healthy offspring; as to returning to their own world? I cannot say what they thought. Master Gavin Beaumont was elected as the First ruler and worked hard to keep the peace and became High King of the entire known world. The three were in fact all related and royal by birth, so it was only fitting they would rule this world someday if they so wished. Gavin named this land we live on Sofala and ruled the Western Kingdom and the Island of Tyral. Jimmie Greymont ruled the islands and the southern lands, while Eldred Ashmourne moved to an uninhabited island off the east coast of Sofala. He was not interested in ruling, but set up a hospice and magic school. He was later coaxed into ruling the eastern side of Sofala, but refused the title of King, he chose instead to remain a Wizard Master.

"The three wizards were of a decent age when the second calamity occurred around eight hundred years old, I believe. They aged slower than the regular inhabitants, though it was not known if this was because of the different environment they had come from or their unusual magical abilities. And as Lailoken told, forewarned is foreknowledge and all of the inhabitants were saved by evacuating as the first signs appeared. The three wizards worked for many years to safely combine their powers, then enhance this force with crystals and they indeed stopped the chasm from splitting this world completely in two, destroying all life. The power exerted by the three is what brought them to near the end of their days. Of course there are always remnants to such use of higher magic…but that tale is for another time.

"That is why; it is a place to this day that no sailor in his right mind will sail near. Many have tried to traverse these areas over time and none have ever survived, or even returned from such an adventure. The underground volcanoes are still active, surrounded by wide vents that expel the gas bubbles seen rising out of the ocean. Around this hive of activity, whirligigs form and drag down any or all who venture near. I have also heard of the group known as the guardians and a creature that watches these areas and attacks any who approach. It has many long tentacles, one large eye and a huge opening maw with many rows of sharp teeth. The remnants of that disastrous event will live on forever. There never will be a way now to traverse the sea to the other side of the world from the east side of Sofala. I was told once, there were many islands and other lands accessed before the split, lands with unusual wondrous creatures. But also a race of dark wizards that had as their assistants' insect hybrids. They use human slaves with innate power to do their menial tasks. Oh and of course there are the descendants of those that once inhabited Sofala. For the last few thousand years this part of the known world survived on its own; under the reign of the Beaumont High Kings. For many years sailors and adventurers tried to traverse to the other side of the world from the west side of Sofala. They would sail for many months with only the waves as their companions, hence the name the endless sea. Then a couple of lucky lads found land. An arid desert leading to an enormous mountain range thousands of feet high, stretching from one end to the other, to this day, no man has been able to negotiate this mass.

"The first three being wise and thoughtful of the future, wrote what they could down in tomes and journals. They introduced all to charcoal and coloured inks made from plants and sand. Quills made from animal feathers, books made of velum, paper from trees and reeds, hides from animal skins and scrolls from reeds and certain barks. They taught us how to make weapons, how to treat leather for boots and clothes. There were new crops harvested such as rice, wheat and cotton. All found wild in the forests.

"The prophecy was meant to slumber for many thousands of years and would awaken when the known world would once again be in crisis. It was spoken, a child would be born. Not any; but one of two. This person would have a concentrated mixture of all the rarest and potent ancient bloodlines. They will become the most powerful wizard of all times and fight for truth and honour with blue fire. There is a rhyme about some specifics of the prophecy, but it does not contain all the information. Most of what was spoken was lost, handed down not in writing, but as prophecy used to be remembered; by visions from a seer. Does that answer your question commander?"

"Well yes and no, I suppose Barron. Would you happen to remember the prophecy by chance, or where we may find a copy?"

"Perhaps in time I may remember some more, but the old tomes are still in the First Castle's vault I believe; in the ancient library down below ground. They are in a hideaway behind the wall tapestry depicting the coronation of the First King, Gavin Beaumont. Now… tell me my dear, what has got your King's bloomers in such a knot, to send you here into this old roadway; through my chambers?"

"Well Barron we're on a fact finding mission to the northern boundary. Our initial parameters were to find any clues to the location of a Wizard Master who has been performing ancient, forbidden magic. Then locate any problems with the western side of the boundary. We have been experiencing unusual vicious creatures from behind this border; terrorising throughout Sofala. But we cannot find where they have breached. We were wondering if there was a connection between the two nuisances. Then whilst up on the plateau, we noticed the boundary was no longer intact, the crystals have ceased to glow."

Marcus then took over the discussion. "Now…we find the North-Mede castle and village covered in rainbow webs, from large territorial and aggressive Arachnoids. We are concerned for the welfare of the North-Mede inhabitants."

"Well, that could explain why there are strange creatures down in my hallways, smelling wrong. I believe they are called Troldwites, a mixture of mountain/rock trolls and ancient dark dwarves. Nasty creatures, messy; taste not to my liking."

"Father told us this secret way to the underground chambers of the castle and to the docks. We had hoped to rescue the villages and lead them to safety."

"Well there be no wizards here in these hallways I am sure, but there has been a lot of noise and movement in the lower levels. Be careful of those Troldwites, they be formidable opponents. I have missed a lot of happenings since few of your kind grace my hallways nowadays. I am sorry I cannot be of more help to you." Barron's eyes moved closer to Atesh. "I feel Queen Mia's magic; most notable within your aura Commander. You have met this ancient being…yes?"

It was at this moment Ciaran poked his head out of Atesh's coat pocket. He looked up at Barron. A puff of smoke wafted out from his snout. Eyes rolled up and he passed out into a dead faint. Atesh gasped as she caught him before he hit the ground.

"Oh my, did I scare the wee poppet; fragile eh? What is it, by the way? I cannot say I know this creature type."

"This is Ciaran, a dragonelle and yes, he gets a bit anxious. I am sure he will be fine."

"Hmmmm…I have never heard of a dragonelle, but then again, never seen a Troldwite before now either."

"To your previous question Barron, yes, we have met Queen Mia of the fire ants. She is a gracious leader. We have also met Queen Betha of the Arachnopods, as she was departing for other lands."

"That is not good news to hear. Leaving Sofala with Red Jack I suppose; bad temper that one. Well I will not hold you up any more. You have my permission of course to travel my hallways whenever you like. But, before you leave me, I have a small gift for you Commander." Barron pulled out a gleaming, smooth eight sided diamond like crystal with a graceful though diminutive, inner sky blue sapphire in hue from his chest. "Take good care of this rare treasure, for this is the only one of its kind anywhere on this world. I have been its keeper for many thousands of years, awaiting you, my dear. This is for your staff, may it serve you well." He then bowed his head and dropped the crystal into Atesh's open hand.

Like the other gifts she had received from the ancients, it attached itself to her innate essence. The searing pain buckled her knees. Her eyes widened and clouded over with magical focus. She inhaled long deep breaths and concentrated on her inner strength to remain conscious. *Great another tickle, oh this one is a doosey. I should be accustomed to these by now.*

"From this reaction Commander, you will indeed be one powerful wizard. Who did you say was your tutor?"

"I didn't say, but Master Thaddeus Freymore has offered to teach me." Atesh managed to croak out between clenched teeth.

"One of the twins…oh my…my;" Barron burst into laughter, so loud this time the cavern walls shook. It sent small pebbles and dust particles raining down on the soldiers again. "They were the most excitable pair of young wizards; always off on adventures. Such mischief, I wondered if Sofala would survive them. Now if I remember it was, let me see… ahhh yes, it was Master Eldred Ashmourne's eldest daughter that married a Freymore. They were local inhabitants and were powerful with innate healing. Oh, they were exciting times. Best of luck to you Commander, Thaddeus will not steer you wrong but…"

"Yes Betha explained the '*but*' to us thank-you Barron."

"Oh no, so you have had the pleasure of a clagging? Oh this day keeps getting better. I wish I had seen that!" Barron lifted his head as far as it would go and roared with mirth; this time spittle flew from his elongated fangs. But the men having seen this reaction before, dived for cover out of the gloop's way.

"It was no pleasure; I can assure you Barron. I will never till the end of my days, live that down in my father's eyes…never."

"Oh, please do tell laddie."

"We had been on a simple errand, to escort the Queen and her family back from Mere Town to Beaumont Castle, when we met Betha and her travelling companions. The Commander here felt it was a grand time for a chit-chat while the rest of the escort all looked on in horror. Then Betha laughed and sprayed us all in her disgusting partial digestive remnants. What I now know is called clag. Well you can imagine my father's reaction when we rolled up to the castle. Master Thaddeus standing beside the King was beside himself with laughter; I thought he may have a heart turn. He had to hold onto another to keep from falling over. Father stood there in his regal best outfit, nose twitching at our odour and watched as I flicked an eyeball from my trousers onto the ground near his shiny boots. Well I was in bit of a mood myself. The stink, horrid, I tell you…horrid. He turned the brightest shade of green, I have ever seen. He then gaped in horror at his personal regiment as they stood wearing their hard won trophies. Bones with and without putrid attached decaying meat, ligaments, hair or entrails; positioned in all manner of places upon their person, with proud smiles adorning their faces. The final straw came when he spied a soldier wearing a partial pelvis on his head like a well-worn helmet, one foot skeleton sticking upright, its fur waving in the breeze."

"Oh please…no more. I beg you. My crystals will crack with the pressure." Barron's head rocked back and forth he laughed so hard. Diamond like tears rolled down his cheeks and clinked as they fell to the hard ground before dissolving.

The men all covered their heads, lest more rocks pelt them from above as they backed away further from the thrashing, spurting serpent. They now caught on to the conversation and the word *clagging*. With mischief written all over their faces, they whispered and planned some future event; a special treat for their Commanders.

Atesh noticed their heads together in quiet conversation and raised her eyebrow at the men; her eyes sparkled with blue flashes, daring them to say one word on the subject. Once all had calmed down, they said their goodbyes and once more moved along. Atesh placed the gem in her coat pocket where she felt its warm embrace next to her semi-conscious Ciaran. A puff of smoke would occasionally arc its way up out of his enclosure, but venturing out would not be on his agenda for some time.

Chapter 35

The Mountain Rescue:

Atesh and Marcus led the group further into the mountain range. It continued to amaze the men how the ancient crystals that illuminated the old passageways created such spine-chilling, sinister, ghostly shapes onto the cave walls as they passed by. This kept their minds on alert. They knew now that formidable creatures inhabited areas somewhere in the bowels of this terrain and there was a real possibility of an encounter, with one or more of them; at some time.

After what seemed like hours of walking, they turned down into a steep right hand bend. Atesh felt the cold shiver of impending doom race up her spine; she stopped and raised her head. She inhaled the air and then placed her arm out to halt Marcus' forward motion. An odour reached out to them all. It wafted around, unusual and retched. The men stopped, creased their noses and unsheathed their weapons; slow and quiet. They all moved forward, silent in measured paces, till they could see the beginnings of another large cavern opening. Atesh noted four side tunnels that led away; two towards the left and two to the right. Sitting around the fire-pit in the centre, were large hairy, thick set creatures. Not quite trolls like the cave drawings, but similar. They spoke to each other in a combination of human speak and a primitive tongue of grunts and gestures.

The men noticed the pile of bones; picked bleach clean, lying to one side. They appeared to be human bones, adult in size and shape. Noises and voices emanated from one of the right side tunnels.

A man's loud voice begged for mercy and then screamed. "NO, NO, NO."

A creature dragged him out feet first to the main cavern, his hands grasping for any object to arrest his forward movement. It was clear their intention for this man. He was stripped naked. Arms and legs then tied to a long pole. They started to build up the fire, ready for their roast, a-la-two leg.

Atesh hoped they did not intend for this man to be roasted alive. She knew there would not be much time to save him, so she held up three fingers. Archers notched their arrows, swords and knives unsheathed and ready. The heartbeat of the men pounded within their ears and raced throughout their bodies in unison. They were eager for some action, to rescue this unfortunate gent and give a bit of payback. Atesh was within a moment of racing out from the passageway, when they heard the clatter of heavy armed feet in the tunnel behind them. The group would be caught between the two; front and rear. Atesh whipped her head around searching. Close to the right of her position was an alcove; a dead end portion of a tunnel. She indicated for all to move silently into this area. So they squeezed, racked, packed and stacked themselves within; not an easy task by any means. Atesh had hoped the group's odour would be masked by the creatures' lack of a sense of smell that was, if their own apparent lack of hygiene was any indication.

"Geeze, by the ancients Ciaran, these critters reek. Maybe they should change their fragrance."

"What was it ye told me Queen Brianna had on her dresser ... 'Eau-de-Garderoben' some fancy new perfume? I hate ta think where that originated lassie ...hmmmmm. Maybe we's could bottle this here stink and sell it at dem markets, 'Eau-de-Critter', hahaha..."

"Oh no, you are bad Ciaran...but still..."

Silence was imperative now. Atesh and Ballard activated their rings and they blended into the surroundings. A large group of the creatures marched past without noticing anything unusual. They continued on their way through this cavern and down the left sided passageway. Two of the creatures, the last in this group however stopped for a moment, they were in the heat of an argument. They pushed and shoved each other; one came within a hair's breadth from both Atesh and Ballard. Their eyes widened in fear of discovery as drips of perspiration cascaded down their cheeks. A voice yelled out from within the cavern and the most aggressive creature ran off. Then the last one shook his head as he placed his back against the wall and reached down to adjust his armour. The two knights moved apart; Atesh a little to the left and Ballard to the right. The Troldwite fell through this small gap into the group of soldiers behind without uttering a sound.

The knights dispensed with this creature quick and with minimal fuss. As they were packed in so tight, the creature's life blood ebbed away all over the group. This created a most putrid, sticky stench. Then out from the deafening silence, an unexpected audible high pitched bugle was heard. All men knew what this meant. The clenching of one's butt cheeks, holding in desperation, the most annoying and often offensive act the body could perform; the elusive intestinal punctuation. They all craned their heads to eyeball each other. Eyes creased in frowns as tears welled up, faces twitched, hands if they were free reached up to hold their noses. The air was becoming staler by this stage; if not toxic. Add the odour of the dead creature; the confined space was not a pleasant place to be in. Ballard went red in the face holding in a snort. Atesh placed her hand up to her mouth to stifle a laugh. For as she turned around, she observed knights and soldiers crammed on the shoulders of others, arms and legs spread in all directions. Renny's head was under Berend's armpit with both hands over his mouth, to stop himself from gagging. Marcus and Aiden were covered in the green blood from the dead Troldwite and sweat dripped from the men above them down onto the unfortunates below. Their grimacing facial expressions and teeth baring sneers conveyed how they felt about this predicament.

Atesh and Ballard heaved a sigh of relief when they unshielded the group and moved out into the passage. The men pushed and shoved albeit in a quiet manner to get out of the alcove and breathe some fresher air. Although the air in this passageway was creature foul, what they experienced within the confined space was beyond words.

"Damn, my dead granny would smell sweeter than that begotten space and she has been tits up for the past ten years. Alright who in this ancient forsaken place is the bugler?" Berend held his knife up in an alarming manner.

Marcus was also not amused; he flicked off the creature's blood and entrails he was covered in.

"Shhh, men keep it down." Atesh received a look from Marcus that defied words. She knew she had pushed her luck once too often with his high and mightiness. Atesh walked over to Jenner and whispered ever so quietly into her ear. "Could you please hand out a sip of your special elixir? I think we could do with it now, if you don't mind."

Jenner nodded her understanding. As she handed it out, she explained to the soldiers it was a restorative to calm their tempers and give them a burst of energy. The knights had used this on previous occasions and rather enjoyed the kick it gave them. But, later they knew the effects would wear off and a nasty headache would result.

Marcus and Atesh organised the men in two groups; swords in front and archers behind. She strode up to Renny and indicated for him to bring up the rear. He nodded and they understood each other very well. She kept him as far away from Berend as possible.

As they readied themselves for battle, Berend glanced behind and noticed Renny had an alarming smirk upon his face and this concerned him enough that he was determined to keep an extra eye on him. *He was the bugler for sure.*

There were around ten of the creatures in the centre around the fire-pit, though more were sure to be found where the prisoners were held. The archers sent their arrows in first and dispensed with three of the creatures. Their hides were thick and hairy so many of the arrows glanced off them. The soldiers followed up with their swift sword work, whilst Atesh and Aiden untied the mid-aged gent from the roasting stick. He trembled and cried out when he saw Marcus.

"Marten is that you?"

"Sir, you received our message. Thank you, oh thank you sir."

"What message Marten? We are on a fact finding mission. We only noticed North Mede from atop the plateau. So we journeyed through the old tunnels to see if we could rescue any villagers trapped."

"Many of the villagers are here, sir. The men are in a cave to the right and the women are down that tunnel somewhere." He pointed ahead.

"What about my kin, Lord Stewart and his family?"

"I believe they are still within the castle, sir. I have not seen them at all, after he told me to lead the townsfolk to the mines. He ordered me to leave them, sir."

"You did well Marten. How many are alive here with you?"

"I lost count sir, after we found it was a trap by these creatures. Folk ran every which way. It was total chaos." Marten looked around at the remnants of some of the town's people, the bleached bones piled up in the corners of the cavern. "They ate some of us, sir. Never have I seen anything so gruesome; the screams, the smell." He started to cry. "I could not save them. I tried and that was why I was next. I was too outspoken for their liking. I tried…" He fell to his knees and covered his face with his hands and sobbed.

Marcus sat with Marten for a few moments and placed his arm around the previous Mayor of North Mede. "Right men, let's find our people. The right tunnel first. Archers cover the left and right, knights the centre."

There were a dozen creatures caught off guard and dispensed with no difficulty. Surprise and fuelled anger at the senseless carnage were the keys to success. They unlocked the bars to the cages and one hundred and sixty men, boys and elderly stumbled out. They had not been fed or given much water in days; many had become quite frail.

Atesh scanned the area. "We must keep moving on Marcus. We don't know how many of these creatures are about."

"Marten, which way lead to the old docks? We need to get you out into the fresh air."

"Down the main tunnel there is a secret passageway on the left. It looks like a dead end. Opened only by the hand of the royal family, that will lead you to the secret inlet around the point from the docks. But what about our women folk sir?"

"We will find them on the way, don't worry. Oh and please go and put your clothes back on, that's a good man." Marcus looked around at all the strained faces. "Now remember stay as quiet as possible and do not lag behind. We will get you out to safety. We have the *Pace Knights* with us here, as well as some of my own regiment. So the best is at your disposal."

They moved along swift and quiet. The villagers assisted by each other, kept up out of pure fear. About an hour down that tunnel they came to another large cavern opening. There were about twenty troll creatures milling around a fire. Moans could be heard from a short distance to the right.

A large creature stood and strode over with aggressive tendencies towards a smaller one in the dark back corner. A fight ensued and the small creature was tossed into the fire, his back broken. Screams now radiated out from this corner, female human sounds.

"I believe we have found the women, Atesh."

"Oh I am sure we have Marcus, now let's get some real payback."

The formation was the same and they attacked with fervour, slashing, hacking, arrows loosened. Atesh even let fly with some blue fire-balls from her finger tips. These were effective, though the creatures' burning haired bodies were not pleasant to smell. The male villagers picked up anything they could wield and set forth to attack the creatures as well, such was their anger. Atesh and four of the knights crept down the right passageway. Four creatures were making so much noise they did not seem to notice a fight was going on. Beneath them were women tied to rings face down on the floor. They were in the throes of vicious physical assaults. The troll creatures died before they registered what had happened. Berend took the head off one with a single stroke. The others fared no better. They were thrown over to the side. The women were set free and they assisted the ones that were lying near death, battered and bruised. Some walked over to the creatures' dead bodies and kicked and spat on them, a small token of taking their honour back. The women milled around one woman. She lay with eyes opened in shock as she died. She had been staked ready for the next meal. They closed her eyes and covered her naked body.

"These creatures are way past disgusting. We need to rid the world of them all Atesh." Ballard spun around when Atesh did not answer.

Atesh had zoned out. She stared down at a woman tied to pickets on the ground. A burning fire pole was resting next to her body, still clutched in the creature's hand. The creature lay dead from partial decapitation and deep sword wounds. Atesh covered in its green blood and gore. The woman had burn marks from the flaming brand dragged across her abdomen, in long stokes. A large sharpened stake stood up against the cave wall next to her ready for the spitting.

The thought of this entire scene made Ballard shudder. Then it dawned on him. *Oh no, the fire branding marks, the pieces of rope embedded in her wrists and ankles, the fractures. Oh geeze Atesh, I am so sorry you had to witness this.* Bile raced up Ballard's throat. He swallowed hard, wiped his swords clean as he walked over to Atesh. Her eyes were glazed over, blue sparks emanated from them. He placed his arm around her shoulders and drew her to him. She hugged him back then turned and walked away.

Marcus and Aiden watched the interaction with curiosity, and then they strode over to Ballard.

"What is wrong, what did she see Ballard?"

He pointed behind him and then in a quiet voice so only the two could hear. "I believe she saw a childhood memory. This is what she went through as a wee one Marcus. Can you deal with that?"

Marcus stared with wide eyes. Aiden faulted, bent over and emptied his stomach.

Ballard steadied him by the shoulders. "We will never understand what she went through as a child. We can only offer her our love and understanding." Ballard then strode away as he wiped his eyes on his dirt and blood stained sleeve. Ballard's voice could be heard issuing orders, for all the women to be huddled together supported by their men. The knights would take point and the regiment soldiers to be the rear guard.

Atesh noticed Renny standing next to a creature still with an element of life left. It sneered and growled at him. Renny thought it was funny and poked him with relentless fervour with his scimitar and a long red-hot pole. It was unusual behaviour for a knight. It was not their way to torment an enemy. Quick, clean kills is what Atesh always advocated. The men also watched in horror and despair. Atesh strode over and stared Renny in the eyes. She pointed her finger at the Troldwite and a burst of intense blue-fire shot into the creature. He vaporised, leaving a small smudge of ash behind. She raised an eyebrow at Renny, but said naught. He re-joined his group seething with anger, when he faced away from the men.

Berend noticed all. *So is this the real Renny now? Is there more to him than what he portrays. Hmmmm…Not such a bumbling idiot after all, perchance he is more dangerous than we thought?*

Atesh noticed Berend's furrowed brow as he observed Renny's change in disposition. She nodded ever so slightly to him. Berend understood all too well. He will shadow and be alert. Now he had his orders. The group set off down the passage-way to hope and freedom.

Chapter 36

The Ways that Time Forgot:

It took most of the night to traverse the passageways and find the hidden tunnel. Many of the rescued villagers were weak and required assistance to keep moving forward. Water and small pieces of bread and cheese were passed around, to ease the gnawing cramps from days of neglect; too much and their stomachs would reject it. They emerged from the claustrophobic tunnel to an opening surrounded by briar bushes . Large thorned fingers seized torn clothes and wove into matted hair or marked raw skin. Marcus and his group tried their best to heave aside the virtually alive vegetation . To cut through it may alert others to the location of this hidden passageway . After a short intense struggle a worn , but light hearted group stood at a sandy inlet and all breathed in the fresh brackish air. The North -Mede inhabitants spread out and fell asleep in small groups ; nestled within the warmth of the sand . No encouragement was needed . Exhaustion and the sense of freedom overwhelmed their tired bodies , watched over by the knights and their comrades in arms. A sea fog was soon rolling in, which would shroud the moon and the twinkling night stars; bringing dampness , an eerie look to the surrounds and a bone chilling cool breeze. Marcus felt it was too risky to light any fires or continue to move the group onward. A plan had to be devised.

Aiden, Ballard and a dozen of the strongest swimmers had the new task of retrieving boats from the cove around the other side of the headland. There were many small skiffs that could hold up to five people each at a squeeze; beached on the sand there. Two larger merchant vessels and traders bobbed up and down with the current. They would require some sea faring knowledge or even better, expert sailors to manage. Marten was sure sailors were still on board those ships, waiting to load or unload their cargo.

The water was ice cold as the fourteen brave men climbed over sharp rocks and swam around the point to the sheltered dock area. They became economical in time and spent energy. To be efficient, they had to be resourceful. They tied a few skiffs together and dragged them back or rowed all the unmanned vessels they could find, without calling attention to themselves. Ballard was unsure if any of the troll creatures were in the caves near the docks and didn't want a confrontation. Two manned merchant ships out in the middle of the harbour were commandeered. One Captain refused to weigh anchor until he had assurance his employer was one of the rescued and that there would be payment at the other end. Transporting people was not a lucrative business. Time was money.

The other was a self-employed carrier, an obnoxious privateer and was only interested in profit. Or as Aiden thought, raiding the village after the creatures had left. Aiden then wondered if he was a rogue pirate, acting as a merchant. It did not bother this Captain that lives were at stake or creatures had taken possession of North Mede. Aiden used all his diplomacy skills he could think of. When that failed and he was threatened with being thrown overboard in small pieces. The crew arced up and mutinied, the first mate subdued the deviant Captain and the crew was eager to sail the vessel for a rescue mission. They realised all was not right in town and were concerned for fellow sailors on shore -leave and friends . They were refused permission to leave the ship on pain of death. The first mate resumed the Captain's position and the crew heaved to and set sail. The captain was thrown in the brig and would be handed over to the sheriff at Mere Town.

By early sunrise a fleet of mismatched boats had been anchored close to the secret inlet. Marten would lead the flotilla down the coast to be intercepted by the Kingdom's Naval Galleys already en-route. There was one strong rower per skiff. The weakest, elderly and young were secreted below in the holds within the larger vessels. Four regiment soldiers accompanied the flotilla and with the assistance of volunteer sailors, they took it in turns in transferring to a skiff as relief rowers. They all kept together and maintained the pace for the slowest vessel. One kingdom galley would drop anchor and wait around the cove to transport those left behind within the castle.

Once the flotilla was on their way, Marcus, Atesh and the rescue party again wove their way back into the tunnels beneath the mountain. Onwards they trudged, toward the North Mede castle via another set of secret underground roadways.

Marcus became animated with information sharing of his supposed knowledge of the tunnels. "This one should lead to the caves beneath the castle foundations. I am told ancient steps carved into the rock ascend up through hidden doorways and tunnels, often ending in the basement of village structures. Others they say lead through into the tangled web of sewers and waterways; some even into the inner walls of the older portions of the castle."

Atesh had been quiet, her eyes dulled. Marcus noted her sparkle was absent. He surmised the last twenty-four hours had been trying for her and perhaps this was her way of coping with the horrors she had witnessed and memories that had resurfaced. However, he could not have been more wrong. Atesh was focused not on the past, but on the future ; on revenge . She made a vow to herself , to wipe those abominations from the face of the world . Atesh was also trying to work out how she could beat this Wizard . Find where he lived and free all the game players . It was maddening.

The key is the game , but what exactly is the game he is playing ? It is not the board game; I know that in my soul. It is something far bigger. What are we missing? How do you beat someone that has had hundreds of years' experience with practice and knowledge in magic? What is Dan's role in all this? Why did he collaborate with this man of mystery? What did he offer that was so good to break a solemn vow?

Atesh moved in an automated fashion. The men stopped for a break and some breakfast in a small cavern. This sudden cessation of movement meant she almost ploughed into Ballard's back. He turned at the last minute and grabbed her by the shoulders. He instinctively knew she was elsewhere that morning. Atesh whipped her head up and her focus returned.

"Sorry Ballard I was zoned out for a bit."

"Yes, I worked that out a while ago. I kept alert for us both; we don't want another sandwich situation now, do we?"

Sniggers could be heard from a few of the bravest knights, but as Atesh turned her glare onto the men. Only serious faces looked back, *Cunning men, oh real cunning.*

Atesh walked over to the neat wood pile the men had gathered together for a fire. The men that swam still had the shivers even after their walk and needed to warm up their cold bodies. She aimed a finger at it and a streak of blue light flew into the wood and it burst into flame. She turned with an evil, one sided grin on her face and blew her smoking finger out. Her stare was directed at Berend and Vykter who both decided to hide behind other bodies, lest she turn her finger their way and reduce them to ash. The rest of the men's eyes widened in astonishment and perhaps a bit of fear, sat quiet.

"Well that was a neat trick, no need for flint eh?"

"I thought I would give it a whirl Ballard. Thaddeus did say to practice different skills to see what I can and cannot do."

Standing very close and personal so only Atesh could hear. "I agree with the theory behind this Atesh, but scaring the men is not the way to go about this. Back off, and think this through."

"Sorry Ballard, You are right, my anger got the best of me. It won't happen again...well. . .I will try and behave. Is that alright for now?"

"Sure, practice on the enemy from now on, agreed?"

"Agreed...hey Aiden can you conjure up fire? Give it a go; see what you are made of brother dear?"

Aiden looked at Marcus for permission.

"Granted Aiden, but be-careful."

"Remember to channel it through your ring, like this." Atesh pointed her finger at the wall on the far side of the small cavern where small bracken lay in a pile. The timber burst into flame. Then she withdrew the flame and it snuffed out.

Aiden aimed his hand and thought fire with all his might. A brilliant purple flame streaked out from his fingers and impacted with the wood. It exploded, sending flaming shards of wood splinters flying in all directions. "Wow! Did I do that?"

"Yes, but ease off a bit. Do not concentrate so hard. You are more powerful than you realise. Remember you have some of my excess power within you now, as well as your own innate power. Start with thinking about a lesser fire. Restrain the power, trickle a small amount of energy out at a time."

"Is that why my flame was purple? Your blue and my red combined?"

"That is a possibility; we should discuss this with grandfather later."

Aiden practiced and realised the most difficult part was pulling back the power that wanted to escape. This became a trial for him and soon his head ached and his vision became blurred.

Jenner rummaged around in her healer's kit. "Here drink this tea. It is my special brew of chamomile, honey, lemongrass and a few other herbs. You will feel better soon. Take it slow. If you over do it, there are severe consequences and the least of them is being burnt out."

They packed up and moved out once more, the Commanders out in front, leading the way. The men lagged behind enough to keep their distance from the two fire makers. They bunched up together and whispered amongst themselves. Devious plans were in the making. Atesh and Aiden may be all powerful, but when it came to getting even or underhanded trickery, Berend and Vykter were the best. Although they did take the praise for Atesh and some of her most memorable beauties; she was an eager apprentice when younger.

"*Aiden can you hear me when I speak into your mind?* "

"*Yes loud and clear, oh mighty blue spark.*"

"*Me too Atesh,*" Marcus smiled.

"*Me three,*" Ballard raised his hand.

"*Aye Lassie, I also as you know.*"

"*What…the four of you?*"

"*You have no need to shout, we are close by you know.*"

"Sorry Marcus, I didn't realise…have you been able to hear me before."

"No this is the first for me."

"Me Too Atesh," Ballard nodded with furrowed brow. *"Though I always knew when you and Ciaran were conversing, it felt weird, like hairs on my neck would stand up."*

Atesh then looked to Aiden.

"I have heard whispers all my life, sometimes clear, other times like bees buzzing in my ears. I never told anyone, but now it was like you were shouting from a mountain top."

"Geeze, I will have to practice aiming my thoughts at individuals. I wonder who else can hear me. Oh my…what if that Wizard Master listened when I spoke to Master Thaddeus?"

"Atesh I do not think so, unless he knew about your powers. I am sure grandfather would have been aware and placed a block on eaves-droppers."

"Oh, I hope so Marcus for all our sakes. I do need lessons on all these powers. I will be extra-careful from now on…I wonder if the men can hear me."

Atesh turned to the men following and looked at them with curiosity. "What are you fellows up to eh? You all look guilty of having your hand caught in a cookie jar."

They all feigned innocence which gave Atesh more to be con-cerned about.

No good I bet. I will have to watch you sneaky buggers closer.

"I have a small experiment I need your assistance with, if you don't mind."

"As long as it doesn't involve fire, we are here, but to serve you. Oh most exalted and glorious Wizard-ness."

"Oh Renny shut it, no it does not involve fire, but just for you I can make an exception."

The men all took a step back, away from Renny and he was left standing alone, to fend for himself.

"Right, I want you all to be still, calm your breathing and listen for my words in your mind. I would like to know who can hear me."

Atesh steadied her mind and spoke to the men. *"I know you are up to no good. I will be watching you. The first one to step out of line will be fed to the spiders, head first, got it."*

Berend, Vykter, Jenner, Wyart and Sage sniggered. The rest looked blank.

"Can you speak back to me…concentrate in your mind?" Unfortunately the five all spoke at once.

"Yes whoa there, I get it. I can hear you, but it's all at once, sounds like insects buzzing. So you five have more powerful innate abilities than the others. This is good, maybe we can utilise this. After all this is over, we will practice and have a good communication network going."

They walked for what felt like hours again, time seemed to stand still under the mountain without the sun or moon to tell the time. They found the entrance that would lead them to the lower ridge-way. However, it took some time before they found the hidden lever. It was buried behind some old tree roots. The door was made of ancient packed clay, rock and crystal, obvious from a time before the first three arrived. It took some force and removal of debris to open. This passageway would lead to their ultimate goal, the caves and tunnels beneath the North-Mede Village and Castle. The passage wound in all directions, till after some time Atesh and Marcus were not sure which way they were headed.

"Are you sure this is the right secret passageway, Marcus?"

"Yes, pretty sure, but I was only a child when Grandfather explained this to me."

They once again felt turned around, the corner almost looped upon itself. The ancient gems that illuminated the many previous passageways were now sparse and they often stumbled into the depths of darkness. Atesh summoned her blue bright light and Ballard shone his ring for the men to follow.

Atesh noticed the men once again bunched up, but more so; concern etched into their faces. *Big sooks, knights and regiment soldiers acting like frightened girls.*

Atesh turned to Ballard and nodded her head for him to look behind. He turned and placed his hands on his hips. "Well now look at my brave men." He then looked up above them, stepped back and stared in horror. "Geeze what in all…"

The men pivoted, heads swivelled upwards, swords drawn. Their eyes darted left and right.

Atesh and Ballard bent over, hands on their knees, laughing so hard they had tears welling in their eyes. Ciaran sniggered with puffs of smoke emanating from Atesh's pouch. Marcus and Aiden stood in amusement at the games these professionals play on each other, yet somehow they manage to muster and be the best at the right time.

Berend and the men sneered at their Commanders. "That's two we now owe yea."

"Come along wee kiddies the nasty creatures await."

Chapter 37

This Way to the Cave-in

A cavern loomed up ahead of them. Atesh and Ballard extinguished their lights and they crept along in silence with scimitars unsheathed. The cavern was immense, with a high vaulted ceiling. From the entrance they all stood and stared. The only noise was the intake of gasps from the men. For before them all stood hundreds of enormous, green, illuminated mounds; the height of an average man and four arms in circumference. Not only were they covering the entire floor, but hundreds more were suspended from the ceiling in a web like netting. Veins of white and yellow surrounded their exterior shells; in a crisscrossed pattern. The continuous drip of water from the glistening damp ceiling pooled beside the structures, adding to the eerie glow.

"Perhaps this portion of the cave system lies below a water course from the village or a stream." Atesh glanced over at Marcus and raised an eyebrow.

"Don't look at me like that. This I would have remembered if told to me."

Ballard doffed his gloves and reached out and touched the cavern wall. Thick green slime caked his fingers. "Hey Atesh, look at this stuff, it is sticking to my fingers; it smells and feels like hog glue."

"Don't touch it if you can help it men…Geeze what a damn awful stink." Atesh glanced around the perimeter of the cavern. "It looks like we have to exit from the other side of this cavern. So we need to watch our step. Do not be too noisy as you make your way over." Atesh pointed in the direction she wished the men to traverse.

The men fanned out, still with weapons in readiness. After what they have seen they could not be sure one of the mounds would crack open; or their mamma should return home.

"I don't know what they are, but I have a bad feeling they may hatch into something we do not want to fight. *Again,* so please men, do not wake the babes."

Ciaran sat on Ballard's shoulder; he was as taken with the sights as all the others.

"Ciaran have you seen these before?"

"Ach, nae lassie, they be a mystery to me as well."

"Wow, they are so beautiful." Renny stood mesmerised.

"Renny, please do not touch."

Berend was right beside him and pulled his hand away from the mound. "I will break ye hand, then head, if ye try that again; hear me boy?"

Renny looked around at Berend and smiled. Saluted then walked off.

Marcus and Atesh led them weaving throughout the maze of mounds. Marcus deviated to the right and inspected a few of them a bit closer.

"Hey Atesh, come look at this."

Atesh stepped slowly and quiet. She made her way over to where Marcus stood. They noticed one had been smashed by a rock when it dislodged from the ceiling. The left side was caved in. She had to admit the type of creature that could have laid these intrigued her. Her innate warning device was screaming at her to run and not look back. All the hairs on her arms stood up, but still she ignored this. Curiosity had taken a hold. Atesh knelt down to examine the finding while Marcus wandered to the other side. *Yes, they were definitely eggs, but the shells were like stone. How huge must its mother be?* The skeleton of a creature near to fully formed lay amongst the partly disintegrated mound; it was the length of a small man's body. It appeared a cross between a wild boar and a strange long faced dog. It had an elongated proboscis with a small curved mouth. Above and on either side of the mouth were two arched tusks with pointed tips about two hands in length. There were four holes, vacant of any substance, where eyes should have been, two on either side of the head. There were large elongated ear cartilages, a long curved spine with spiked nodules extending upward. Tuffs of matted brown fur lay in clumps some attached to the bones; others beside in the green gloop. Four long legs with elongated flat feet lay apart from the main skeleton. The large extended tail with protruding spikes was splintered underneath debris.

The men also found the idea of these creatures fascinating. Vykter, Aiden and Ballard set about counting the mounds. The mixture of this creature gave Atesh the shivers.

"Oh burning dragon balls." Marcus had stepped into something that squished under his left foot. It had stuck hard. Try as he might he could not raise his leg.

"Was that our royal perfect-ness taking a dragon's name in vain?"

"I'm sure; I don't know what you mean Commander. You must be mistaken. Delusional from this odour I think; hearing things."

Atesh laughed and rose up silent beside the mound. This took Marcus by surprise and he fell backwards, landing not so delicately on his royal behind.

"Men?" Atesh glared around at her fellow knights. Her eyes sparkled blue. They all stood up to attention. They had listened to the Commanders' conversation and understood what was required of them. They complied with smirks trying to break through their straight facial expressions. Ballard led the chorus, with a nod.

"The Supreme Commander of the first battalion is never wrong, nor is she ever mistaken. Sir, Commander Marcus."

"See Marcus the men…" Atesh looked around her. "Where in blazes are you now?"

"Oh mighty Commander, the most wonderful, exalted, astonishing, marvellous and remarkable pain in my rear end I have ever met, if you must know; I am down here."

Atesh walked around and found Marcus sitting and covered from head to toe in a mess of green luminescent gloop. A stunning smile adorned her face as she peered down at the stricken prince. He looked about as unroyal as one could become, without trying. He held his hand out, eyes pleaded for assistance. He knew full well, that not only was his foot stuck to the ground, but now so was his behind. Atesh grabbed hold of his arms and heaved with all her might. Instead of pulling Marcus up, she overbalanced when her feet slid out from beneath her. She released his hands and her arms splayed out as she crashed with full force; backwards. Down into the grime laden cavern floor, with an almighty thump and splash. The men had snuck up on the two bantering Commanders and when they spied their predicament, they all roared with laughter. Ciaran almost toppled off Ballard's shoulder, he snortled so hard. It took four men each to peel them off the glue like substance.

Turning a shade of bright red, his cheeks aflame, Marcus wiped and scraped his feet and britches and strode over to Atesh. His eyes squinted in quiet rage.

Atesh had used her magic to wipe off the sticky substance and stood looking the picture of innocence. With an exaggerated bow, Atesh battered her eyelids as Marcus approached. "Come…your green gobliness and check this out."

His look was dangerous, hands clenched, body rigid, steam may have even poured out of his ears, if that was possible. Atesh showed him the skeleton creature she had found. His disposition transformed in moments. His face blanched and eyes widened.

"By all the ancients." Marcus looked around at the number of mounds in the cavern. "There are hundreds of these flying sticky flops. Can you imagine if they attacked towns in Sofala, they could devastate this kingdom? I dread to think how large a full grown creature would be."

"Flying w…ha…t?" Atesh could not contain her mirth. She placed a hand up to cover her mouth; her laughter hidden as best she could. There was no hiding the tears that welled within her eyes and spilled over to trickle down to stain her cheeks. She tried to mask her heaving shoulders that moved in harmony to her smothered laughter sounds. Try as she might, the more she struggled to stop the worse it became. There was no way she could be Commander like, at this moment.

The men all realised that to join in the laughter may mean a quick death by his Royalness. Hushed sniggers and snorts were barely audible. Ballard and Aiden leant over and examined the creature and shook their heads in wonderment; mixed with abject horror.

"We need to move out of here Atesh; this bodes ill in my bones."

Atesh nodded in agreement, to Ballard's suggestion. She had not fully contained herself to speak. The men manoeuvred themselves to view the creature's skeleton as they walked past. Most turned up their noses and pulled an array of facial expressions. Their heads darted around to ensure no other mound had started to crack open with all their noise.

A loud distant deep rumble interrupted the moment.

"Geeze, I hope that wasn't mother returning…Darlings' Mamma's home, is that supper I be smelling, my wee poppits?"

"Vykter that's not funny at all." Ballard gave him a shove, "But yes a good point…past time we went men, gear up."

A long grating, high pitched squeal sent all the adventurers bending over in agony; hands pressed firmly against their ears. It was not a sound one wants to hear when traversing underground; that of a rock being forced against another under enormous pressure and speed. Next a tremor shook the ground. The men unbalanced into each other, as it vibrated to and fro. Then silence once again enveloped the cavern. They all looked to each other and breathed a sigh of relief. Small trickles of dirt began cascading from the roof at regular intervals. Atesh and Ballard glanced up.

Atesh shoved Ballard. But like the mountainous tree that he was, it felt nothing more than a feather touching his skin. "O-oh…Ballard, men go…this may be only a lu…"

Another tremor started, before the earth vented its full anger. The ground twisted and moved at a rapid and deliberate pace. It began to rise up and down, ebbing and flowing with the rhythm of the damaged earth's energy release. Standing became difficult as the men rode the ground waves and were thrown about, often landing into a mound. Atesh and Marcus were flung backwards as small vents began to appear in the floor and steam burst forth. It sprayed any near in boiling vapour. Ballard glanced around and yelled for all to withdraw back to the tunnel, they had minutes before exited. It was the closest passageway. Two regiment soldiers were in full flight mode and could not stop their forward movement in time. A vent opened up in front of them, spewing hot steam and molten rock into the air. The last anyone heard were short blood curdled screams. The stench of sulphur and burning flesh began to permeate throughout the cavern. This caused some to stop and empty their last meal. A large rent in the ceiling brought rocks, debris, egg mounds and muddy water crashing down. Creature foetuses, formed and half formed sprayed in all directions. The centrifugal force below the cavern floor wrenched the ground apart, revealing a chasm that ran from one end of the cavern through the middle to the other side. This was effective in cutting off Atesh and Marcus from the rest of the group.

Atesh yelled out to her Captain. She pointed back to the passage-way. "Go Ballard, get the men to safety and meet us at the docks."

Atesh and Marcus turned and ran for their lives to the other passageway entrance on the far side of the cavern. The knights and regiment soldiers all moved as fast as possible. They ducked and weaved, dodging falling rocks, broken egg mounds, scattered partly formed creatures; back the way they had come. The ground rose beneath Vykter and he fell head first into a cracked egg. It sliced and gouged his flesh down his body from his right cheek through to his thigh bone. Aiden grabbed him and together they limped over to the exit. The noise again became deafening as the chasm widened and swallowed mounds.

Berend ran behind Renny. The ground beneath Berend gave way and he started to fall. His arms grappled in the air, hoping to find some amount of unyielding form to hold onto. He pulled out his dagger and thrust it with all his might into the solid ground ahead and hung on with both hands for dear life. "Renny, Renny! Give me ye hand."

"Sure, grab hold Bear."

Berend reached up and grabbed hold of his hand. He still held onto the dagger dug deep in the earth with his other. His legs were dangling in mid-air. Renny bent over and looked Berend in the eyes.

"So sorry ol' boy, but it be payback time. You pathetic excuse for a knight; you and your precious Commander make me sick...and well...I do have my orders you know." He peeled Berend's fingers apart so they would let go as he kicked dirt in his face. Then stamped on his hand, again and again which forced him to let go of the knife. Berend fell backwards down into the void soundless, as dust and steam billowed out, choking off the breathable air.

The cavern was breaking apart. Renny looked around and ran off into the darkness. Berend meanwhile had landed on a small shelf not far down the shaft. Ryna and Captain Skip Stein observed the exchange as they sheltered beside an egg. Once Renny ran off they lunged together over to the opening and peered down, coughing and wheezing.

"Berend can you hear me?"

"I am here, just need ye hand thanks Ryna. Think I have busted me insides."

"Skip lay down and reached in and assisted Berend up and over the lip of the rent. Ballard and Chale ran back over and grabbed hold of Berend and carried him to the exit and safety. Ciaran sat huddled under Ballard's shirt; he had been pelted with debris and tiny hot steaming rocks. The roof was falling in at a rapid rate, large boulders and buckets of rubble and mud were tossed around like leaves in a breeze. Ryna and Skip held hands and ran for the exit. Ryna tripped on rocks that had fallen in front of her, taking Skip down with her. They scrambled up and took off again.

"Come on you two hurry up, there is not much time"

"On our way Capt…"

The roof caved in right on top of them. All the men near the exit with arms stretched out to grab hold of the pair were blown back by the force of earth exploding into the cavern. Another loud explosion was heard as the floor gave way into the widening crevice. The men all lay stunned from the blast and now were covered in dust and debris. Only the whites of their eyes could be seen.

Meanwhile, as Atesh and Marcus reached the other side, they were flung and slammed with an almighty force into the ground by an explosion of falling earth, rubble and rocks. They were buried where they lay.

Atesh felt her spirit lift up into the void and scatter into a million stars. She sensed all, she could see all. Her mind was in confusion, everywhere yet nowhere. Of her physical body she had no awareness. *Is this what it's like to die?* She travelled beyond and within. There were moments of darkness, yet it was peaceful and comforting. Then an explosion of radiance was all around her. She was free to travel the world, the universe, unlimited and energising. Her spirit gathered together slow and graceful. Atesh's thoughts assembled once more. She remembered all she had seen in the last few weeks. New friends she had made.

Without the sensation of movement, she had travelled. She watched Betha and Red Jack as their children climbed all over them, playing on an island way out to sea. They looked happy and content. Betha stopped and looked to the sky. Next she found Mia and her daughter creating a new home with their subjects. They were deep inside the mountain range to the far right of Beaumont Castle. She too stopped and stared at the sky. *Can they see me, or just sensing my energy?* Atesh's soul pieces kept moving. Next she witnessed Master Thaddeus at the Beaumont Castle, striding down the corridor conversing with King Gareth. In midstride he clutched his chest and leant up against the wall. He turned his face up to the ceiling. Tears formed in his eyes. Master Elias at the Ashmourne academy was delivering a lecture. He stopped midsentence, his eyes glazed over. His students looked on in concern. Even a cold shiver passed over a Wizard leaning over a game board. He wrapped his cloak closer around his body and walked onto the balcony and looked out to sea. Atesh knew he was important to her, he looked familiar, but she did not remember why.

She travelled and searched for Ballard, Ciaran, Aiden and her men. There in the dark passageway they sat; hands held tired and wounded heads. They coughed and breathed deep, dislodging the dust and debris from their faces. Ballard held Ciaran against his chest. The small dragonelle was bleeding from lacerations and abrasions. He trembled and whimpered. Ballard and Ciaran both glanced upward through the dust and smoky haze. A single tear cascaded down Ballard's dirt encrusted cheek, creating a track for others to follow. Ciaran shed crystal tears, his bottom lip quivered. Atesh looked around, surveying the men. *Were there not more, how many survived?* She concentrated harder. Where were Ryna, Skip and Renny? Some of the other regiment men were also missing. Berend was held down by Aiden and Chale. He was crying, angry, upset over something. Vykter lay wounded with Jenner beside him using a crystal to stem his bleeding. *So few, left.*

A voice called to her, it was distant though compelling. Marcus, yes where was he?

Another voice deep, resonating and powerful interrupted her musing. Back ye go wean. This is nae ye place. You must learn to travels the right path lassie, it is too dangerous to be scattered so. Her spirit was slammed back into her body. The pain was immense as she opened her eyes and drew in a deep breath.

"I thought…I had lost you." Marcus cradled Atesh in his lap stroking her hair. He was covered in dust, mud, green goo and dried blood. He wiped his face with the back of his blackened sleeve. Drew in a deep breath and settled his thumping heart. He brought the water skin to her lips. "Here have a sip, not too much or you will send it back at me."

"Where are we?"

"We made it to the passageway by a small margin, then blown further down by an explosion. I believe the cavern has been completely destroyed."

Atesh tried to sit, but dizziness over took her. "My head pounds terrible." She held on to his hand and fixed her blurred gaze onto it, then up to his smudged face. "What have you done to your hands Marcus? They are all bloody, the nails torn."

"Oh nothing, do not worry about it."

"Are your cheeks wet and smudged for a reason? Were you…?" Atesh turned her head. She noticed many rocks, large and small had been dislodged. There were scratch and drag marks in the dirt. "You dug me out of that rubble, with your bare hands?"

"What was I supposed to do? Don't you get it yet? You drive me crazy, confound me, confuse me; yet…you are the love of my life. I knew you were in danger and then you were gone. I couldn't sense you anymore."

Atesh turned her head away. She felt many emotions racing throughout her mind and body. Love, embarrassment, relief, awe and confusion amongst others; tears welled in her eyes and her cheeks felt warm.

Marcus knew he was treading on delicate ground. He took a deep breath and steadied his thoughts and then with a smug look on his face. "Well of course, it was the noble thing to do."

"Oh, don't make me laugh, it hurts too much."

"I need you in my life Atesh. I was taught; to rule was to be alone. To give your all to the people, to forget what you want and marry for the Kingdom. In my soul, I knew there had to be more. So I steeled my heart and waited. I knew one day my father would win this battle and have it his way. Then I saw you out on the paddock performing your forms and you turned my world upside down. Have you never heard of love at first sight, the bonding?"

"Oh now you are getting all mushy. Do you have a head injury too?"

"Perhaps I do."

"You must explain this bonding to me some-time please."

"It is from an old fable, from times long forgotten. Grandfather told it to me as a child, maybe later after we have rested. I wonder how they fared over the other side. Do you think they made it?"

"Marcus, all is not well over there. I think we lost a few."

"How would you know that?"

"Can I explain it to you later, I am so tired. I will try to communicate with them after a while, alright?"

Atesh closed her eyes, but she was not asleep. She thought of all Marcus had said to her. Yes, she believed in love at first sight and felt that connection when they shook hands. *That spark of lightening, was he the one? Yes he takes my breath away, those dreamy eyes, his soft lips; his compassion for his people, so honourable and straight down the line. His poor sense of humour makes me laugh and cry at the same time. But what of my oath to the academy and my independence? Oh geeze what would Ballard think? What would Gareth say about the time I was missing? Would Marcus be disgusted about my scarred body? It is so complicated. Why can't I have it all; love and a career? The men can, so why can't women too. I want to be a wizard and help those in need. I feel scattered; pulled in many directions.*

Marcus sat against the passage way wall. He cuddled Atesh closer, to keep her warm and safe. He looked at the rocks and debris that blocked the entrance to the cavern. Then he looked intently at this sleeping beauty and in a quiet voice, so as not to disturb her. "I thought for a moment…I had lost you. Oh, you are going to be a handful my lady." He closed his eyes and rested. A smile of contentment stretched across his face. His cheeks flamed rosy red as he kissed the top of his beauty's head.

Chapter 38

The Wrong Road:

Atesh and Marcus walked at a slow and steady pace down the tunnel. Many areas had not been used in countless years. These passageways were so ancient that natural lace curtains hung from ceiling to floor. No spiders were around to claim their adornment, but still they glistened with tiny crystals when illuminated by Atesh's ring.

"I know there is nothing alive in this webbing, but it still makes me feel like things are crawling over me."

"Yes I agree they give me the creeps."

"You're not afraid; almighty *King in waiting Sir*, are you?"

"Glad to see you are back to your old self Atesh."

They once again reached a vast cavernous area. This time to their relief it was uninhabited. The only noise came from a natural spring to one side. The fresh, cool, mineral scented water seeped out from between moss covered crevices. It cascaded down small rock-falls and settled beneath; in a circular tarn. Aged stairs etched from weathered rock led down from the main floor to the pond.

"This looks ideal, but too good to be true.... Do you sense any danger Atesh?"

"Seems fine to me, I am going in for a swim, try and remove some of this grime."

"I will stand guard and you for me, alright?"

The water was cool, and refreshing. After a mighty scrub and relaxing soak, they set about making a fire in the once used fire pit. Their meal was the usual soldier rations and Atesh shared her unit's secret energy bar. It was full of fruit, oats, corn, honey and nuts all dried and cooked together with Vykter's special ingredients. Atesh tried to reach out to Ballard, Aiden or Ciaran, but her head pounded severe and black spots flickered in her eyes. Atesh thought of a solution to relieve her pain. She retrieved from her kit, a large silver flask.

"Would you like some zinger juice Marcus?"

"May I enquire as to what is in this concoction?"

"I have no idea. Each year the first year science students compete for the best concoction. They must go up against the previous year's winner. The students this year at the academy have been experimenting with different herbs, berries, honey and potatoes and this was their third attempt. They reckon it's the best yet…one sip will send you to the stars."

The fluid was amber in colour and they each took sip. The warmth spread throughout their bodies; rapid and intense.

"Wow Atesh, that is…smooth."

"Hu…um, told you Marcus. Want some more?"

They became quite merry after a few more sips. Hours seemed to pass by, talking, bantering, and getting to know each other. After a while Atesh stood and walked down to the water pond and sat on the cooling sand and stared into the gentle rippling water. Marcus followed and sat down beside.

"Tell me the story of the bonding please."

"Well the way grandfather tells it. It occurred long ago, in times well forgotten. They say it is only a bedtime story, but once it was reality. There was a race of beings known as the tree dwellers, or the longer lived or more common; the elves of the Northern Silverra.

They were a race of tall, lithe, well educated, regal beings. They lived in harmony with all nature and were powerful in innate magic. Though long lived they had the curse of bearing few children, perhaps one every hundred years, if not less. Every life to them was precious. They joined together with a partner, but once in that life-time and only to their *one*, the bonded. So if anything happened to their life partner they would live alone for the rest of their days. The bonding was said to be so powerful nothing would come in between the two. Not war or distance or class status. For in this Elven society they were class distinctive. High Elves were of Royal blood. High middle was the Counsellors and Masters in Education, Arts and Magic. Then lower middle class was made up of the best warriors; the King's personal guards. The lower races were the labourers, woodsman, hunters, farmers and regular soldiers. The bonding is magic from nature's spirit. It has an ability to pair the right people together; it selects them. Once the two feel each other's innate energy signature, no other suitor will do. They are hooked forever to search out and find the source of the pull. Often as not, when they meet and touch hands a tingling will travel up their arms, the recognition phase. Their love is eternal, even extending to the here-after and the next life."

"What happened to them?"

"I don't know neither did grandfather. But he believes they either moved to the other side of the known world or disappeared as their numbers dwindled."

"Oh that was sad, but yet beautiful at the same time. They believed in the hereafter and more than one life? I would like to learn more of this nature's spirit. Are there any old tomes that have this written lore?"

"There are still ruins left from that time in the very north of Sofala, buried amongst the forest and jungle. Maybe one day we could search for old relics or tomes of that era."

"That would be nice. I would very much like that."

"You are shivering, come closer and let me warm you. What about another drink to warm the soul."

"Do you think Marcus-we are like-the bonded elves?"

"Part of me thinks this may be so. You felt it too, when we touched for the first time. I knew from the moment I saw you. I know we are descendent from the three first wizards, but we also have local blood mixed in as well. What if we had a small portion of elven blood in us? Why is it I cannot get you out of my head? You confound me, confuse me. Make me laugh, comforted and strong. I want no other, Atesh. It feels like, I have waited my whole life for you."

Marcus leaned over and kissed Atesh with soft, yet unbridled passion. She responded in kind. For the smallest time, Atesh forgot about her body image, her worries and allowed her-self to be loved, wanted and needed.

When they woke many hours later, Atesh and Marcus were entwined beneath their rugs beside the water-fall. Atesh nudged Marcus awake.

"Oh… good morning my beautiful dove."

"Marcus…did we?"

"Certainly not, what do you take me for?" Marcus made a poor showing of looking offended. Then a cheeky grin overtook his facial features. "I have never taken advantage of a woman after a few drinks…Well not until last night any-way." His eyes shone like the stars.

"Oh no…I…we…you…" Atesh placed her hands up to her face, took a deep breath and strengthened her resolve. "Come on lump get up, we have to get moving."

Marcus could not contain his smile as they walked along the creepy tunnel. Nothing was going to bother him today.

Atesh however, was embarrassed and walked with her head down, cheeks flaming hot. *Did he see…did he touch the scars? He must be laughing at me right now. Why did I let myself go, idiot?*

They came to a crossroad. There were indents, strange markings partly covered by years of moss, webbing and dust in the rock straight ahead, but no tunnel. There was however a passageway to the left and one leading off to the right.

"Which way do we go now Marcus?"

"I don't know, I have not been told of this intersection. I am sure of it."

"Let's have a break for a bit, maybe something will trigger a memory."

Marcus started to laugh. Atesh looked at him, stricken to the core. She turned and walked away and slumped down beside the far cave wall.

Marcus was now confused. He wandered over and sat down beside her.

"What did I say to make you upset?"

"Was I that hideous last night that you mock me today?"

"Oh no, you misunderstood. They were good memories, fun memories. I love you more today, than I did yesterday, if that is even possible. Everything was beyond perfect. Why would I laugh at you?"

"You would have noticed my repulsive scars, didn't that bother you?"

"No, they didn't bother me at all? Ummm…I mean what scars?"

Atesh glowered at him. "You were my…my…"

"First…yes…and second, third….Sorry, I realised too late, I'm afraid. Like I said, you were beyond perfect. Here…let me dry your eyes, no more tears. You be mine now, don't you realise?"

"Do I have a say in this at all?"

"I will have to think on that. What's it worth to me?"

Atesh stood up. "Oh men, you give them a bite of the apple and they want the whole orchard. I am going to have some severe words with those students when I get back to the academy. Zinger juice, huh…more like inebriated gypsy juice."

Marcus roared with laughter then held his head. "Oh that was not a good idea. I think hammer head is a good name for it."

Little did they know, faces peered out from the walls; watching and listening. They blended into the cave's dusty interior and then disappeared.

"I've got it; I think I know which way to go." Atesh moved over to the far back wall where no passage-way stood.

"That is a dead end Atesh. Are you able to read the inscriptions there? I have never seen the likes of this writing before."

"Do you remember Marcus, I told you about a gypsy who read my palms. At the time it didn't make a lot of sense. But, she knew things. She told me of a strange event that would occur in my near future. One day I will have a decision to make where there appears to be none. One hand will want to go right, the other left. But, if I combine them together, I will find my way in the dark…Don't you see?"

"Well I can understand the left and right tunnels, but ahead; there is only a wall."

"Look at the markings, Marcus. Doesn't that look like faded indents for two hands in the wall? So if I place my hands over them like this." A loud click was heard and the wall gave way with a groan. Dust billowed out as the air escaped. "Here Marcus, help me push."

They both placed their shoulders against the partial shifting rock and an opening appeared before them. It was wide enough for them to squeeze through and then the swinging rock slammed shut, cutting off any hope of an exit. Another plume of dust escaped into the surrounding air and covered the pair.

Atesh wiped her eyes and spat out remnants of the air particles. "Of course, there is more of this rotten, dank-smelling filth to cover us in. Oh, I will be happy to see the light of day, to breathe clean fresh mountain air once more, pfft, pfft…ugh."

Marcus sniggered as he too wiped the grime from his eyes. "You would never make a dwarf, you know. They carved most of these passageways before they left, eons ago."

"My dear magnificent, dirt encrusted one. I have no aspirations of becoming a dwarf thank you. I like fresh air, sunshine, the beach and clean, warm sand."

"I am magnificent? Is this true?"

"Oh someone save me. Is that the only word you heard? Men are so…so…"

"Well I did hear something about sand too." Marcus battered his eyelids at Atesh. A wide grin near split his face, then he pursed his lips for a kiss.

Atesh was mortified; she knew she would never hear the end of this. Whispering profanities and curses she turned and walked away. *I suppose he thinks that is funny, no idea about women or humour at all. Oh I have my work cut out here, but why me?* She could hear Marcus sniggering at his own joke, not far behind her.

They walked on through a laden crystal illuminated passageway, down three flights of stone carved stairs and then out into another enormous cavern. It was filled to the brim with gold coins, jewels, gems, crystals and statues. One small passage way wound its way through the treasury.

"Can you believe this, all this time? I wonder who owns it Marcus."

"Maybe it is a dragon's hoard. I heard they love jewels and gold. Geeze, we better get out of here. Do not touch a thing Atesh. I have read they memorise every piece they collect."

"They don't exist anymore silly."

"Really Atesh…after what we have encountered. You want to make a wager on that statement."

"Well you might be right. I retract that comment sir."

They walked through the shining hoard then up more steps. They climbed for what seemed like hours, till the muscles in their legs screamed at them. On the last landing they walked around a corner to be confronted by an opening half way up the back wall.

"Oh you are kidding me Atesh. Well after you *Commander Zinger*."

"Oh no this is all yours *Commander Hammer head*; oh honourable and noble one…huh."

Do you want to try the men again Atesh, or maybe Grandfather before we go into the creepy tunnel?

"Sure, my legs could do with a break. Nothing; it is like, there is a block. I can't find my way through. The pain in my head has eased quite a bit though. Maybe I did extend myself too much when I tripped around the country side."

"Well you were warned, if I remember."

"It was not like I did it on purpose. It just happened."

"Alright then we should continue on. I shall be the hero seeing as, I am magnificent and all but, will you save me if I get stuck?"

"Depends what it is worth to me? I suppose I could always use my blue fire and turn you into ash."

"Alright you win, I shall behave."

Marcus did not have a lot of room left inside the tunnel; he was after all almost as large as Ballard. Atesh being lithe of frame traversed this area without any difficulties.

"You do have a cute royal behind, sir. I can say this now and you cannot turn around and accost me."

"Well my lady, I can give it a damn good try, if you like."

They laughed and joked all the way through till the end. Marcus crawled out first and then helped Atesh. They found themselves in an open area the length of the Beaumont Castle, though not as wide. On each side sat stone carved crypts. They were adorned with worn sculptures on the lids of those laid to rest, some decorated with crystals and jewels. Faded names were etched into the front panels and above these, carved into the walls lay inlets or shelves with partly clad, decayed skeletons.

"Marcus these are the ancient catacombs, did you know they were here?"

"The site of the ancient Kings' burial chambers has been lost for many generations. This is a wondrous find Atesh. These should be our ancestors."

Atesh and Marcus walked silent as possible, so as not to disturb. They noticed three enormous crypts, decorated with plated gold and blue crystals. The middle one had a gold filigree circlet embedded in it.

"Wow, do you think that is the resting place of King Gavin, Atesh?"

"Well it certainly looks regal enough. I reckon you be right."

"Ach, of course ye be right laddie."

They both stood still, breath held with trepidation.

"Oh Atesh not another of your friends, please tell me this is not so?"

A clearing of one's throat was heard directly behind them.

Chapter 39

The Ancient Catacombs:

They both turned in unison, to look behind. They let out a sigh of relief when no creature sat there waiting to devour them. Instead a tall, larger than life spectre loomed over them. He was a giant of a man, with broad shoulders. Upon his head sat a gold and jewel circlet, surrounded by long flaxen wavy hair that cascaded down his back. His facial features were intense, though he had a generous smile. His beard was trimmed close to his chin and he wore a high necked, long sleeve gown. It was translucent and flowing; though no breeze was felt. He oozed a commanding presence as an illuminating glow surrounded him, sinister and eerie. Atesh and Marcus stared with eyes widened, mouths opened, but no sounds came forth.

"Ach, lost for words are we now. You haven't stopped ye incessant yapping for many an hour. Did we ask ye to disturb our eternal rest?"

Atesh and Marcus looked at each other and then bowed.

Marcus lifted his face to eye the ghost King. "Sire, we apologise for the intrusion into your chamber. We were cut off from our group due to a cave in and became lost. We are on a rescue mission to North Mede."

"Well ye both display courtesy that is a change for such wee sprites." The spirit of the first king looked around. "What be the penalty for this here transgression, my fine fellows?" His grin sent shivers down the two Commanders' backs. Murmurs and voices were heard all around, increasing in volume, but there was no sign of any other.

"String-em up by dere toes."

"Hang draw and quarter dem."

"Boil em in oil."

"Spikes under dem finger nails."

"Off with dere heads."

"Bury dem in an ant-hill wid honey hair."

"Oh sire a skinning it be. Tis been a long time, since we heard dem musical tones of desperate screams."

Atesh eased closer to Marcus. She looked around, her face ashen. A mild tremor ran throughout her body as hundreds of spectres began to appear, surrounding the pair. With one hand up to her throat, she looked up at Marcus as he frowned down to her. "Boil them in oil? Off with their heads? Skinning? Who are these people?"

"Nor bad choices, I must admit." The king stroked his iridescent beard. "Did ye see them their faces," Fierce laughter echoed throughout the chamber and resonated off the encrusted walls and decomposing skeletons. "We haven't had dis much fun since…well never." Again laughter erupted.

Atesh now became infuriated. Being taunted by ancient kings and kin was unroyal, discourteous and boorish. Blue flames danced from her eyes. "If you have finished playing at our expense, may we continue on through your hall sire?"

King Gavin ignored Atesh. He floated forward and looked at Marcus. "What be the problem here young prince that ye need to move below ground, through the ancient ways?"

"You know, who I am sire?"

"Ach of course, did ye nae think I ken me own descendant's innate energy? So answer de question laddie."

"We were told to use the old Ridgeway by my father King Gareth, as there are creatures that have surrounded the North Mede Village."

"Oh I see, but ye have missed the ridgeways and stumbled into yon ancient passages."

"I am ashamed to say sir we did not know all this existed here. The location of your resting place has been lost for many generations."

The King threw his arms up. His sleeves stayed in place, held up by the air it seemed. "Well I should have known it; no one calls in for a spot of tea, no one sends missives anymore. We be all alone here amusing ourselves." Sniggers were heard all around.

"Who or what are we, sire."

Gavin turned his piercing pale blue eyes to Atesh.

"Well wean, do ye think I am here alone, twiddling my thumbs, navel gazing all the long day?"

Atesh directed her gaze at the king. *What did he call me? That was the same name in the void.* "I do not know what to think, to be honest."

"Ach, we have us here an honest voice lads. How did ye ken to open de secret door if ye did not know we was here, hmmm? What be your name lassie?"

Apparitions appeared, closing in one at a time, surrounding the pair tighter.

"It was a guess, instinct. I am Atesh Ashmourne, sire, the Commander of the *Pace Knights*."

The King burst out laughing. "That is a fancy title for a wee lass. It be an oxymoron if ever I heard one. Ye my lass, be a walking contradiction."

Atesh felt her cheeks warm with heat. With her arms crossed. She met the King's gaze. Her eyes once again blazed with blue flames. "How so sire?"

"Oh and a feisty one too, well lassie; ye are a knight of peace is that not so?"

"Yes, that is correct."

"Well a knight be a warrior, a fighter, a war-maker. Not a peace-maker, what idiot put that group together?"

"Master Freymore was no idiot, sire. We maintain the peace by being the best at what we do. You may have been the *First King*, but your manners remain offensive."

Atesh's eyes sparkled. Marcus touched her arm to settle her down. The ghost sat back on an invisible throne. Two more ghosts appeared either side of him similar in features.

"Eldred...I believe this one be yours, but yet, there be something about ye energy that confounds me lass."

The three faces enlarged and moved toward Atesh. She moved closer to Marcus and held onto his hand for moral support.

"Tell me young prince, what be the creatures dat have invaded the village above here?"

"Coloured Arachnopods with eyes on numerous back spikes, large and vicious. They have covered the village and castle in their webbing. We have reason to believe they are not natural, but dark-Wizard made."

"Well, that be interesting. And ye think, ye little group," he held up two fingers. "Can save the day?"

"Of course we can, that is what we train for."

"Eldred can ye nae tame your progeny?"

"Sire, if I beg ye pardon; she be nae all mine. She has your signature in spades sire. Look at her stance, her colouring. Who does she remind ye of?" Eldred held up his hand to hide his sniggering face. " There be others too."

"What. Mine? Did ye not say Commander your name be Ashmourne?"

Marcus felt he should defend Atesh here. "Sire, if I may explain. When the knights take their oath, they relinquish their given name and take on Ashmourne, so all are equal in status."

"Then what be your family name Commander?"

"Well that is complicated sire. I was a foundling and adopted by the academy at age five years. So I have always been known as Ashmourne."

"Do ye know who your real parents be, Commander?"

"The academy's my family sire."

"Eldred what do ye sense, can ye at least tell me, what dis fire-cat will not."

"Yes, I believe I can shed light on this here subject." He bent forward and pulled free a hair from Atesh's head.

Atesh narrowed her eyes at Eldred, but kept silent.

Then he rolled the hair around in his fingers, 'umming and ah-hing'. "Right then: first, I believe her family name would be Beaumont, in some-way a close kin to the king. Her mother I sense be a Freymore, from the line of me eldest lass, so indeed an Ashmourne.

One or more ancestors be from Jimmies line. I sense great wizards throughout all dem lines. Then two other words come to mind for ye, sire."

Master Eldred Ashmourne leaned over and whispered into King Gavin's ear.

"Ach nae, you be having me on now; after all this here time?"

"Afraid so sire; that be why the signatures be so confusing."

The three ghosts once again sat forward on their thrones and gazed at Atesh with intense scrutiny.

"Tell me then young Commander of the peace warriors; are you perhaps…one of two?"

"If you mean am I a twin? Yes, I believe that to be so."

"Then tell us, how did ye become a foundling?"

"I was abducted as a baby from my home and somehow escaped my captors after a few years and the academy found me and raised me as an unknown."

"Yes, well that explains it all; can ye be any more nebulous?"

"Sire, I was a young child, when things went astray. I remember nothing."

"Do ye know your future Commander?"

"I have been informed sire. I must thank you all, for giving me this curse."

King Gavin sat back on his throne and looked down at Atesh with eyes widened and furrowed brows. "So ye are telling us, ye have had your turning. And the prophecy has again awoken and be in play?"

"Yes sire, it has begun." Atesh burst forth into blue flame.

Marcus stood still and stared; he dared not breathe or move.

The flame ebbed and disappeared. "Most powerful wizard ever, blah, blah saves the world. Oh…and be immortal. I think that covers the basics."

"I can see ye are not pleased. I can understand that. Nice theatrics though. Right then, so ye have our blood in ye veins, the three of us. Plus, if I be not mistaken a couple of other mixes in there too. Which are what Eldred?"

"Prophet Lailoken comes through loud and strong and one other…'High Elven' I believe. Now dat be the darndest thing, I have ever seen."

Atesh shook her head in disbelief. She looked at Marcus with tears in her eyes. He placed his arm around her waist and pulled her to him.

"Well then, what be this I see? Young Commanders, do we have another situation here? Are ye two by any way…hand fasted?"

Marcus nodded affirmative. Atesh furrowed her brow and shook her head in denial.

"Ach goodness, make up ye minds. Well…be it…aye or nae?"

"Again sire it is complicated. But, yes as children we were promised to each other with our parent's blessing."

Atesh looked at Marcus with accusing eyes.

"Ye didn't know dis information Commander?"

"No sire. I did not."

"Well ye do look a bit too familiar with one another. Have ye two…ummm been together as…like husband and wife?"

Again Marcus nodded in the affirmative. Atesh stared down at the floor.

Three ghosts from behind the group floated up and spoke to the king.

"They did what? Where? That be true?"

Gavin turned to look at Marcus, a smile adorned his face; "Down by de waterfall, eh."

Atesh wanted to shrink up now and die *rotten zinger juice.*

"Right Jimmie would ye do me the honour…" Jimmie nodded and faded from view. King Gavin Beaumont stood tall or rather floated tall. He looked around at all the royal faces before him. "I wish to announce that these two love bids, our kin will be wedded by me, in short order."

Cheers and laughter was heard all around.

"Married, do I have a say in this at all?"

"No, Commander, ye do not. In my day ye would already be considered married. There will be no blemish on dis here family, do ye hear me, both of ye. But I will ask ye one question and I will want an honest answer."

"Do ye lassie love this here young prince?"

"Yes sire, with all my heart, but…"

"There is no room for buts." Gavin turned to Marcus. "Do ye laddie love this here wee fire-cat?"

"Yes sire, more than life itself."

"Well then, there is no problem I can see."

"Umm…sire if I may interject. I can feel an energy spike around these two, an unusual phenomenon; rarely seen. I believe we be witnessing a bonding in play."

"A bonding of what Eldred, what be this you speak of?"

"Lailoken explained it to me once. It be through his line, that both these young ones have the ancient and mystical *Royal Elven* blood line running through dem veins. As ye all know this old and revered race be known as the long lived. They only ever marry their one true soul mate. It be known as the bonding. Once they find each other they will never part, it be love at first sight, never ending, from one life to the next and so on. It seems stronger in Marcus. But it be there in both, none the less."

Noises and curses were heard emanating from the king's tomb. Jimmie finally emerged and handed King Gavin two rings.

"Perfect, thanks be to you. Gather closer my kin, as your direct ancestor and first King of Sofala; I believe these two adventurers have completed the conditions for marriage. That be, ye have had the blessings of both parents in a hand fasting ceremony . Ye have consented to be together as man and wife, witnessed by some peepers who should have known better. And an apparent bonding has taken place prior to walking these halls. Evident in the giving and receiving of each other's hearts already. So I say to ye both. Love well, stay true to each other and live each day to the fullest. Now do ye Prince Marcus Beaumont take this wee fire-cat to be ye wife? To love, nurture, protect and toss over ye knee when she misbehaves?"

"I do sire." Marcus struggled to keep a straight face.

"Do ye Commander Atesh Beaumont-Ashmourne; take this handsome prince who happens to look like an ancient ancestor when he was in his prime, to be ye husband. To love, honour, obey and promise not to flame him to ash when the mood strikes ye?"

Atesh mumbled something under her breath, her head looking at the floor.

"I cannot hear ye, wee fire-cat?"

"I will not obey. I am my own person sire, but yes, I promise the other stuff."

"Well that will have to be enough then, one cannot ask for miracles now, can we?"

I give ye both a ring to remember this hour, this solemn promise and these ancient old wizards, whose blood ye both share. Ye have given some meaning to our endless time here. For we, be ye ancestors, ye kin. We witness this joining and rejoice. You may kiss the bride now."

Marcus leant over and kissed Atesh, tender and loving. Atesh felt enraptured in his embrace.

"Alright that be enough smooching…really? Ye can kiss for that long? Fantastic stamina these two have. I must say…Break it up now, split…I command thee. Oh look they came up for air at last. Now if ye two ken compose yourselves for a few minutes we must place the rings." King Gavin floated over to Marcus. "Kneel laddie and wear this ring with pride." The ring was placed on his left thumb. It was made of white stone, a dragon depicted around the rim with a red gem for its eye. "Atesh if you please." She also knelt and a ring with the same adornment, but more delicate was placed on her left thumb.

The first three Wizards stood together in their gowns of flowing light. With arms raised they spoke an incantation. The rings warmed up then attached to their innate energies. Marcus bent over and drew in a deep breath. Atesh slumped to her knees, her eyes glazed over. Her breath came quick and forceful. *Oh great, no more please, enough with the tickles.*

"Ye will indeed surpass us in power Atesh. Learn well from your mentors. We wish ye all the best in the trials yet to come."

Atesh looked at her ring; she then lifted her sleeve and noted the same pattern on her armband.

Gavin stared at her arm. "Well, I'll be lassie, blood does shine through, it seems."

Marcus stood grinning, admiring their rings. "Thank you for the honour and our ceremony. These are magnificent sire. I cannot place this white stone used. They are so smooth."

"Oh they be not of stone, my lad, but bone from my skeleton. It was a waste laying there. The rubies be from my crown."

Atesh forced a smile, even though bile raced up her throat from her stomach. *Keep it down.*

"Well sire that is certainly original, thank you again. Could you please direct us to the castle and perhaps the old library? Barron told us we may find a copy of the prophecy there."

"That old crystal still around, that be marvellous. Yes, I will have some of ye kin guide ye."

"Oh, out of curiosity sire. Who may I ask owns all the gold and jewels we wandered through before? Is it a dragon's hoard?"

"Oh I had forgotten about that. Well laddie that be the Beaumont treasury. Let's say, my wedding gift to the both of ye. I have no use for it now. Remember, this ancient passage way is for family only. We do not need to have everyone traipsing down here for a how-d-do. Atesh when ye have been trained , all ye will need to do be think of the treasury room or this here room and ye can be here in moments . But do not try it before hand or ye may end up arriving inside a rock. I will lift the magic block over the passageways for Marcus and your signature only, you may bring another with you, say your mentor when you are ready."

"Yes sire I shall be mindful and thank you for the ring and cere-mony."

"Atesh, if I may speak to ye in private. I have a boon to ask of ye?"

Marcus was then surrounded by a bevy of ghostly female ances-tors all giving him advice on women; he couldn't see Atesh and Gavin speaking.

Atesh and Marcus walked surrounded by many spectres, some jostling for a closer position. Questions were fired at them, about the times, the fashions, what was everyone up to. They came to a rock face and all, but one said a final farewell and faded from view. The last ghost to leave was a tall regal lady with red curling hair that cascaded down to her knees.

"I am Liera Beaumont, King Gavin's wife and ancestor to ye both . I be so proud to have met ye and witnessed that ceremony. My father was the Prophet Lailoken. I am afraid; I be the wild-cat of the family, the red hair you see. You are much like I be as a youngster Atesh. It was my attitude that took Gavin's eye. He does like it you know, bit of feistiness in women . I think he enjoys the challenge , the game . I be sorry the prophecy has caught you up in this. My father worried about the future and the consequences of the mixed blood. But now I think he can rest in peace . Having met ye both , I can see ye are from honourable families. Atesh you will do well in whatever nature throws at you. Remember nature can be fickle, but she must have balance for life to continue to survive here. Please do not forget us here and visit as often as you like. I would love to hear all about the outside world and your adventures . Open this doorway the same as the first time, then turn right, till you find an intersection , then right again. Left will lead from the castle down to the docks. The right passage way will lead to the ancient library under the castle and up the stairs to the inner workings of the castle, the secret passageways . The throne room can be accessed through the old fire place . Find the brick with ancient script and push ." Liera started to fade , but as her face was last to disappear, she smiled. "Yes Atesh, what ye suspect be correct, but he was too proud to say." Then she was gone.

"What was she referring to my darling wife?"

"Oh, I will darling wife you…you…oh I could spit fire."

"You didn't want to marry me?" Marcus looked wounded. He placed his hand on his heart. "Yes barely beating."

Atesh punched him hard on the arm. "Move over *Sir Lump*…wink, wink at the waterfall. I have a door to open."

"So is this our first married fight?"

"What! Are you crazy?"

"Well I thought if it was…maybe we could make up, before we go on."

"Focus, please Marcus."

"So we are looking for a hand indent again, right."

"Oh, I am so lucky to have married such a marvel as you."

"This is going to be a long day, I can feel it. Come on then my fire-cat, let's move it along."

It was a short walk to the intersection and they stopped for a drink and snack.

"Marcus…I am happy to be your wife, it was…"

"Yes I know, taken out of your hands, no choice."

"Well something like that, but also…I…I never thought I deserved to be loved, with the way I look."

"You so deserve to be loved. We will have to work on your self-esteem and acceptance. One day at a time."

"I meant every word I said back there."

"Me too wifey, what did Queen Liera mean?"

"Oh nothing much, when I was travelling, while under the rubble. I was in the wrong realm and someone directed me back to this one and into my body. I suspected it was King Gavin when he called me wean. But I wasn't sure."

"What does that word mean?"

"Ciaran used it when I was small, so I think it means young one."

"Strange words some of the older ones speak."

"Yes, I have heard Master Freymore at the academy come out with a few and then correct himself. Maybe it is from their time…I should try and contact Ballard, see how they are faring. I am concerned at what I saw, but it was strange, like a dream."

Atesh sat and concentrated. Ballard responded straight away. He told her they had lost Ryna and Skip, two of the guards and Renny was missing after trying to kill Berend. A few more were injured and they had made their way slow and weary back to the sandy cove for the night. They would be at the docks tomorrow. Atesh informed them of their adventures, but left out the marriage news. That was to be told in person.

Atesh cuddled into Marcus as she retold Ballard's tale. Sadness crept into their hearts.

"This Game Master has a lot to answer for Atesh. How many good people have to die for his whim?"

"Too many so far is all I know. What was with Renny? Whose orders do you think?"

Atesh eyes then glazed over. She was unresponsive, so Marcus sat and held her while she communicated with another.

When Atesh came to, she stood up on shaky legs and placed her hand against the wall. She bowed her head to steady her pounding heart.

"What is it Atesh? You have gone pale."

Tears welled within her eyes as she looked up at Marcus' concerned face. "That was grandfather. Marcus we have new orders from your father."

"Please, what has upset you so?"

Atesh turned to face her husband. "Kyle had escaped the hospice and kidnapped Israe and Binji. They killed two guards and mortally wounded a villager for no other reason than to carry a message to your father."

"What was the message?"

"They want me in exchange for the boys' lives. We have only a few days to reach them before the deadline is up. You are to accompany me to a place they designate, then the exchange will take place and you shall escort the boys back to safety."

"The King's orders Atesh, what did he say?"

"To rescue the villages, do what has to be done. Bring the boys home safe."

"No, No, No, you know what Kyle will do if he has you?"

"The boys are innocents, Marcus. I will do what I am trained to do. You know this."

"Israe is our kin, how could he do this?"

"We will work on a plan. We have a few days, alright. First we rescue the trapped. Then we must make our way to the plateau. Then to the rendezvous."

"Fine, but I shall not leave you without a fight. I told you. You belong to me now and forever."

Atesh stood on her toes, she threw her arms around his neck and they melded once again in their love.

Chapter 40

North Mede:

Atesh and Marcus entered the ancient library. The large brilliant cut gems dangled from the ceiling. They burst into radiance, illuminating the interior of the unexpected; neither dusty nor dank hidden room. They looked around for the tapestry that Barron had described.

"Here it is Atesh, it is still like new. How in all Sofala is that possible? Look at the intricate stitching, such majestic work."

The relevant scrolls were hidden in the open vault behind; as they had been told. Many were sealed with magical wards. These they were warned not to touch, much less open them. The one to the far right was the ancient prophecy with a string of plaited grass enfolded around it. Marcus placed it in leather wrappings to read at a later time.

"Come on oh mighty, sir wonderous snail, we have got to move along."

"Good idea, my heart's delight, not only beautiful, but smart as well. I have got it all." Marcus placed his hand to his heart and sighed.

"Oh you do push your luck dear husband. You know I could vaporise you with one finger tip, poooof."

Marcus sidled up to Atesh and enveloped her in his large muscular arms from behind. "You wouldn't do that too little ol' me, would you sweet pie, apple dumpling, sugar snap?"

"Oh you are a rogue; stop it before I get a toothache." Atesh giggled at the big man's playfulness. *Maybe I am bringing his royal pain in my butt, out of his stuffy shell.* "I could spend a life time down here going through these old tomes and journals; so many of them, all in pristine condition."

They again climbed rock carved steps to a platform and a dark cob-webbed corridor. Lighting the gloomy hallway with her Commander's ring, they soon found the old fire place and the brick. They pushed on the brick and shoved with all their might against the ancient escape hatch. As they entered the throne room what sounded like humming ceased. It was a group of inhabitants' speaking in low tones.

They stopped and stared at the two dusty and webbed covered intruders. A middle aged woman with a regal bearing, wearing a green jewelled gown, stepped forward.

"Who might I ask, be you?"

"Gwen is that you?" Marcus had bent over and was dusting off his shirt and pants.

"Marcus … Marcus , oh I didn't think anyone would come ." She bolted over and threw her arms around him , near knocking him to the ground.

"Oh, sorry my dear and you are?"

"I am Commander Atesh of the *Pace Knights* my lady, at your service."

"Oh…a girl Commander, is this so, Marcus?"

"Yes Gwen, the Commander's First Battalion are all nearby."

"That is fabulous, how many are there of you my dear?"

"Only the two at the minute, but others are on their way to the cove as we speak."

"Two…only two, have you not seen what we are up against Marcus?"

"Yes dear Gwen we have seen your foe. It is a long story, for perhaps another time. Where is Padric?"

"He went out for the last of the villagers and is over due to be back. We have been gathering them here, a few at a time. We can crawl around under the webs. But I fear something is wrong."

"Well, we had better go and find him then."

"Oh Marcus, please do not leave us alone, what if you don't return?"

"I will go Marcus, if someone can come along and direct me."

"Mother, I will go with the Commander."

"Sean well met, that would be splendid." Marcus performed the introductions albeit brief.

"Right, Sean let's be on our way then."

"We often go out during the day, but now and again we have had to go at night. It is more dangerous then, as the spiders are awake and on full alert. Father went to the last hall to gather anyone left…Are you really the Commander of the knights. That is so amazing. I mean being a girl and all."

"Do you always talk so much Sean? And yes, I am the real deal and I will let you in on a secret…I am a wizard as well."

"Wow! Will you marry me?"

"I am afraid I am spoken for, sorry." Atesh let out a small giggle.

"Dash it all."

"Come on my amorous fellow, mind on the job now."

"My sister Salandra wants to marry Marcus, she has been sweet on him since she was small."

"Oh? Well, that should be interesting?"

"What do you mean, Commander?"

"Please, call me Atesh alright. Marcus is already betrothed."

"No, we would have been told."

"Well I have it on good authority, it is true."

"Hope she is a stunner like you."

"Oh that she is Sean that she is."

"Ready? We open this outer door and start crawling as low as possible. If you touch a web then stay as still as you can. If the spiders do not investigate, then we keep going, if you see the web vibrate; hide."

"Lead the way Master Sean."

"Oh I forgot one thing. If they get real close, do not look at them; their eyes will target you."

"Right got it, stay low, go slow, don't touch, no peeking."

"Wow, were there many to compete with for your Commandership?"

"Oh, so you don't want to make it to adulthood Sean?"

"Just messing with you, ease the tension you know."

Atesh and Sean snuck outside into the twilight; the moon woke and decided to shine with all her glory to compete with the darkening sky.

"Oh it couldn't be a moonless sky tonight, now could it?"

Atesh smiled at the young man. "Come on hero show me the way."

In some places they could crawl on all fours. In other areas they had to slide on their stomachs, heads turned sideways. Twice they saw shadows above them and they lay still under the cover of a roof overhang. When they spoke it was with hushed tones, barely an audible whisper.

"What is that smell Sean? Ewwww, turns my stomach?"

"That is the leftovers of their kill. They only suck out the blood then leave the dried husk to swell and bloat in the day's sunlight. At night at least we have had a dusting of snow now and again to ease the odour. Our white season has begun mild this year. Normally we are feet in snow from the beginning."

"So the pass is open then, we don't have to travel back through the tunnels?"

"I don't know, but I would believe that to be true."

Atesh tapped Sean on the leg and pointed to the right. A shadow of immense proportions was edging it way closer, but only a few feet off the ground. Atesh again pointed ahead. There to their left, was a wooden bench seat, wide enough for two lithe frames to fit under. They moved quick and quiet. Sean moved under first and pressed his body up against the side wall. Atesh positioned herself next to him, wedged together close and personal. She noticed a sly grin on the young man's face. As the shadow grew near they both placed their faces down to the ground. Atesh could feel the energy from the spider; hear the suctioning feet, on and off the webs. It leant down and surveyed the bench. All the eyes turned as one, searching for anything alive. The stench of the creature became overpowering. This made it difficult to hold one's breath. The spider satisfied there was no meal, wandered off. The hidden expelled their air and relaxed their shoulders. Perspiration saturated their foreheads and backs. Sean had a slight tremor to his body which Atesh ignored.

"That was too close Sean."

"They are becoming agitated. They don't come and investigate movement, unless it touches a web."

"Maybe they are hungry. Time we all left this place Sean."

"You may be right Commander."

"Call me Atesh remember Sean, after all we have been so close of late."

Sean's face shone bright red, his cheeks fired up like a typical young man sprung looking and thinking about what he should not.

"Right then, lead on, mighty warrior."

"Yes sir…Atesh."

Again they set off; this time they increased their speed.

"There is the hall. Oh no…It is surrounded by the spiders. Any wonder they can't return."

"That does present a problem. Any ideas as to how we get into that building Sean?"

"This end of town is the newest, so there are no tunnels or cellars."

"We need a diversion, perhaps a distraction." Atesh looked at Sean and grinned.

"Hey don't look at me. I need all my blood thanks. I am too young to be a dried out husk. You are older than me, almost ancient I gather."

"Are you always this cheeky too?"

"Only when I am so scared, I could piss my britches, begging your pardon."

"You would make one hell of a knight Sean. I can see you and Berend together; up to no good."

Pointing to the large building, "Which door do we use Sean?"

"There, the one in the middle. It has a small verandah and portico covering the door."

"Then that is how we shall enter. I will create a disturbance over to the far left and we make a run for it, alright."

"This should be good. I am going to see some Wizard stuff, yes."

Atesh's eyes glowed with blue sparks; she concentrated and held onto her amulet. She felt for the farthest area away from their destination in her mind and sent a blue beam of fire out to slice through the webbing. The spiders' all whipped their eyes in that direction, the vibrations indicating a catch. They took off in a volley of legs and raised spiked tails, racing and fighting each other to get to the far left corner of the village.

"Now Sean, go."

They both raced on all fours over to the door and barged inside. They were met by many blades, aimed inches from their faces.

"That's a fine hello father."

"Son, you could have been stuck like a pig. What are you doing out there?"

Standing up, the two rescuers dusted their clothes off and then wiped their sweat encrusted faces on blackened sleeves.

"Father, this is Commander Atesh of the *Pace Knights*. Marcus is at the castle with mother."

"About time he showed up."

"Commander well met, nice to have you in our wonderful village."

"Thank you sir, rather a fleshy welcome mat you have out."

"Yes, sorry about that, I would normally offer you a personal tour, but as you can see; we have a sticky situation here."

Oh damn, like father like son. "I must inform you sir, Commander Marcus and our group didn't know of your situation. We were on an information gathering expedition to the northern boundary. It was as we looked down from the mountain plateau that we spied the predicament below. Then as we travelled through the tunnels to reach you, we came across and rescued many villagers trapped in the caves by Troldwites."

"What do you mean trapped? What in the blazes is a Troldwite? Did not our messenger reach the King?"

"No sir, there was no message. Troldwites we can discuss once we are safe from this situation, sir. We need to be out of here as soon as possible. Those spiders are hungry and man is on the menu."

"Well Commander we do have a slight problem here, the reason for our initial delay. The man over in the corner we found wandering the local forests a few days prior to our invasion. We cannot get much sense out of him; something has turned his mind dizzy. He will not accompany us out of here and if we try to leave, he screams. This alerts the creatures no matter what we try and do. We do not wish to leave him behind, but I have others to think about too. The noise attracted the spiders and now, as you know we have been surround-ed."

The villagers were now gathered around Atesh, twenty in all. They seemed to speak all at once, till Lord Padric placed his hands in the air.

"My friends this is the Commander of the knights to assist us with our situation."

"Let me speak to this man you found and I will let you know what we will do. Please…we must keep the noise down."

Atesh and Lord Padric strode over to the far corner. Atesh scruti-nised the man as they drew closer. He muttered to himself, hands twisting together and legs agitated with a constant unsteady rhythm. Hair matted in tight ringlets, eyes widened in fear and confusion. His feet were bare, with long ragged toenails caked in all manner of vegetation. His odour smelt of a long time between baths, mixed with fear. Atesh walked closer and sat down before him, hands turned up, elbows rested on her knees. Padric stood back, watching in fascination and a little irritation.

Atesh concentrated on this man. She noted his apparent weight loss. The rags he wore for clothes hung loose, with a belt made of twisted vines to hold them in place. Many small abrasions covered his body, seen through the tears in the clothes. Dried mud and blood stuck in his hair matted with leaves, twigs and unknown small insects. He stopped muttering and turned towards Atesh; their eyes locked. Both knowing, yet working through lost memory. Flashes of pictures raced through Atesh's mind in and out of the dark forbidden places in the farthest reaches of her childhood. A name came unbidden to her.

"Fleet, come and sit awhile and tell me your story."

Recognition, stared down at Atesh. He shuffled over and sat in front of her.

Atesh placed her hands out in a gesture of friendship. Fleet grabbed hold gentle at first, then as tears welled in his eyes, the grip grew more determined.

"Fleet it is alright, you are now safe. I am here to take you home."

"Little happy is that you? It is your eyes, but…y…you are all grown up now."

"You know me?"

"Yes, it is you. The Master, he tells us you fell from the cliff, when the creature hurt you. We cried so much. We lost our heart, our song. You were our happiness."

"I was your happiness?"

"'Always smiling, skipping, picking flowers and blowing us kisses, hugs."

"I am a knight now Fleet. Yes I did fall, but kind people fixed me up. What has happened to you, how did you come to be wandering in the bush?"

Tears cascaded down his cheeks. He reached out to touch Atesh's face. "They take us from the field and we go with Master Dan and Mason and they bring those monsters. They dig in the mountains for the crystals for The Master…the monsters always want to eat us. Kroll growls at us, he tries to trip us up. We take out the bags of crystals and stack them in the wagon. Then they dig in wrong place and crash, big rocks come down, the ground shakes. The mountain was not pleased for us to be there. They ran when rocks tumble, they left me behind in the dark, I could not get through. They left me behind…alone; why?" He placed his hands up to his ears and rocked back and forward.

"It's alright; I am here now for you."

"I found my way out through another hole in the mountain. I climbed the trees at night; the noises, the screams, the creatures' fighting over their kill. It was so bad…so bad." His shaking became more violent.

Maybe that is how the large creatures are getting through the northern mountain.

"Fleet will you trust me? I will get you out of here. My men are waiting at the docks with boats. Will you come with me? But you must do exactly as I say. I promise I will not leave you behind."

"Yes little happy, you are all grown up now. Will you take me home? The others will be glad to see you too. The Master will smile again and Miss Maisey will not be sad."

Who are these people you speak of Fleet, where were we?

"Will you tell me later Fleet, about the Master and Miss Maisey?"

"Yes they will smile again. Little happy will come home with Fleet."

"Come along now, time we headed out."

Fleet followed along behind Atesh, quiet though he still trembled.

Lord Padric stared in disbelief and shook his head. "Do you have a plan Commander to get us out of here in one piece?"

"Yes Sir I do, if you will give me, but a moment to organise it." Atesh walked over to the window and looked through the wooden slats. She called to Ballard in her mind. *"Ballard can you hear me"*

"Yes Atesh, loud and clear"

"Me too," Marcus shouted in his mind.

"Me three," Aiden acknowledged.

"Aye lassie," Ciaran sniggered.

Dash it all, I need to get a handle on this privacy. "Marcus can you gather all within the castle and have them ready to move out when we return."

"Not a problem Atesh, we shall be ready."

"Ballard and Aiden can you lob some arrows over to the far left end of the village, create vibrations along the webs. Then when the spiders congregate use our flaming Ultima arrows. You know, burn them all from this world. We are at the other end of the village and will need to make a run for it back to the castle."

"Sure thing Atesh, give us a few minutes to get closer."

"Ach, lassie be careful they be nasty critters. They smell all wrong."

"I will Ciaran. Don't worry."

Atesh turned to the group. "A plan is in place. It is going to get noisy and a bit hot. So when I give the word. Go as fast as you can under the webbing back to the Castle."

The sound of a myriad of tiny suctioning feet racing around the village to the other end of the town resonated throughout the hall.

Screeching and fighting were heard as they attacked each other for the food they believed was tangled in their webs. The vibrations indicated a large catch or multiple casualties.

Atesh opened the door. "Right, go now and do not stop and please; do not touch the webs."

The villagers took off one after the other; led by Lord Padric. They crawled on all fours down the main thoroughfare, keeping as close to buildings and overhangs as possible. Atesh brought up the rear. Fleet was content now to follow in the other's wake. The main problem was the dust enveloping those behind the first few crawlers. Coughing and sneezing were hushed up with the use of necklet ties and shirts pulled up over their noses.

Atesh placed a magical barrier around herself and Fleet. "Fleet keep your head looking down to the ground, otherwise you will not be able to see for the dust and dirt they are kicking up in front."

Half way to the castle flamed arrows were seen arcing across the sky into the mass of spiders now racing around in confusion. They caught alight with ear splitting screams filling the night sky.

"Don't stop, keep going."

The first few in the group had stopped to stare at the melee. This caused the ones behind to bank up.

"Keep it up Ballard, burn those eyeballs to hell." Laughter and 'Woo hoo lassie', was all Atesh heard back.

The return trip though nerve wracking for the villagers was fast and furious. It was not long before they were all safe and sound back inside the castle. They did look a sight however. They were breathless, drenched in sweat, dust and ash. For the last ones in the cue, only eyes could be seen peering out from dust encrusted faces.

"Marcus well met lad, so glad to see you here."

"Well met cousin. I see the rescue party did well."

"It is fire and brimstone out there."

"We need to leave now, these Arachnoeyespikes are going to be peeved and hungry; especially the Queen." Marcus rolled his eyes as Atesh stifled a giggle. He strode over and opened the secret escape route.

"Well I be…I had no idea about this exit Marcus?"

"Oh don't worry; it was only a recent discovery."

Splintering wood and high pitched keening was heard emanating from beyond the throne room entry door. All heads whipped around to stare. Marcus waved the people onward up to the exit.

"It was past time to go now. Take it easy, one at a time, no pushing or panicking. We will all make it out. Watch your step down the spooky tunnel; this will lead you to the docks. The knights await you at the end of this passageway."

Lord Padric led the procession, his sword unsheathed ready to protect his family and people. He looked around for torches to light, but as with the previous ancient tunnels, crystals embedded in the cave walls illuminated bright as movement passed them. "Well this is a bonus…come along now. The sea waits for no man."

Sean stood guarding the rear of the line, closest to the entry doors. A loud thumping was heard behind him. He had turned forward to check on the moving line of villagers, when he was blasted face first onto the floor. The double locked wooden doors were smashed apart with a violent imploding force. As he began to rise, a large spiked tail swung into the room. The vibration of the sudden emergence of the enormous appendage caught Sean and flung him sideways across the floor. Fleet moved quicker than was thought possible. He had slammed into Sean as he tumbled and pushed him backwards out of harm's way. Fleet was speared by the barbarous poisonous dart and lifted into the air. With a hostile guttural scream, Atesh ran and leapt up at the back wall. Using her feet to push off she ascended above the appendage. She willed all her might into the blue flaming scimitar she held with both hands. Atesh lifted it high, and then swept down severing the creature's tail from its body. The spider retreated and screamed a high pitched wail in agony. The tail's detached portion twitched for a few moments and spewed rainbow coloured, foul smelling, burning liquid over the floor. Atesh and Sean ran over to Fleet. There was no way to pull the barbed spear from his body without further damage.

"Oh Fleet…thank you, but why…why would you do that?"

"I could see you are a good boy. I had to."

Atesh wiped his hair back from his bloodshot eyes. She cupped his face. "Fleet thank you so much. You are a brave man...I am sorry...I wasn't quick enough."

"Not your fault. Master would be smiling if he saw you now. Fleet...glad he helped little happ..." His eyes glazed over and he expelled his last breath.

"Damn it Fleet." Atesh punched the floor and bowed her head. Tears cascaded down her cheeks.

Simon pulled on her sleeve. "Come on Atesh, he is gone. We need to leave."

Atesh cut off the end of the tail section with the stinger. Wrapped it safe and stowed it in her shoulder bag.

"Ewww you are getting a trophy Atesh, really?"

"No Sean, my grandfather studies unusual items like this. It is a present for him. You know what Wizards are like, poking, prodding, and investigating the impossible."

"Well I have only met two. The King's Wizard Counsellor, a relative of a sort and now you today."

"Ah yes, he can be scary when he wants to be, eh."

"So you have met him too?"

Atesh turned to face Sean with a large smile on her face. "Oh of course, that is my grandfather."

"No wait...But that means...wait are you...wow. You sure you don't want to marry me Atesh. You can dump the other guy, right?"

"Come on lover boy, you don't want to be on the menu now, do you?"

They raced up the throne room into the tunnel and closed the fire place. They soon caught up with the rest of the group.

Marcus stood waiting with a wry grin on his face. "Nice of you two to accompany us, you worried me."

"I was fine. I had North Mede's most eligible bachelor for an escort."

Sean stood still, chest puffed out, shoulders straightened.

Marcus pulled Atesh to one side. One arm encircled her tiny waist. The other hand traced the outline of her face and lips. Then his fingers curled into her hair as he leant down and gave her a passionate kiss. She melted into his embrace. Their bodies were illuminated by a faint blue glow that encased them, swirling and sparking.

Sean now stood with eyes widened and mouth agape. He knew he should look away, but he was transfixed. He let out a big sigh, his heart a tiny bit broken.

"Someday I will have a love like that."

"Yes you will, my warrior boy." Atesh smiled at him and winked.

"Now young Sean, did you make a play for my wife, while my back was turned?"

"Wife…did you say wife, Marcus? Oh sir, I would never, if I knew…Oh cat's piss! Am I in deep trouble now, begging your pardon Commander?"

"We need to have a talk, man to man, if you will excuse us my dear."

"Certainly your wonderfulness, as long as you remember we are on a tight schedule; the plateau, the boys. *Be gentle Marcus.*"

As they neared the exit to the cove a commotion was heard up ahead. The villagers parted to either side of the passageway. Some of the women squealed as a small creature barrelled its way through legs or scrambled up and jumped from one head to another.

"Out of da way, Come on, move it along, nothing to see here. Where are ye lassie?"

"Back here Ciaran." Atesh took off like an arrow and they collided together with Atesh ending up on her back as usual. She laughed and cried to see her lifelong friend. Big dragon hugs ensued to an audience of shocked villagers who had never seen a dragonelle before.

"You see Sean, what I have to compete with. Not a level playing field I can tell you."

"Marcus you are a lucky man and my lips are sealed; I promise."

The knights had lined up outside the exit and saluted with their hands over their hearts when Atesh strode out. She looked at them all. So few left from when they commenced this adventure. Her eyes welled with tears, her heart swelled with pride. She saluted and bowed back to the men. Once all the villagers were safe on board the various vessels. They said their goodbyes. Berend had to be held down to stop him from jumping ship and joining his brothers in arms. Vykter had his body entwined in bandages and watched in silence. They would re-join the knights back at the Beaumont castle.

Sean gave Atesh a big cuddle as he spoke quietly into her ear.

"Best of luck to you Commander, he is the finest you know. But I don't want to be around when my sister finds out, not a pretty sight. If ever you change your mind, you know where I will be." He gave Atesh a cheeky grin and shrugged his shoulders, as he caught Marcus watching the exchange with a raised eyebrow and smirk on his face. They set sail back to Beaumont castle.

The knights set off for the plateau via the outside roadway which was winding, cold and steep. Once they became visible to the creatures in the village below they utilised the Commander's blending ring, till they reached the top. After a short break they all lined up along the edge of the plateau.

"Enough now, I have had enough of Wizard made creatures."

They fired with a deadly cadence into the village below. Their Ultima fire arrows arched with precision, burning the spiders, their webs and North Mede into history. Atesh was sure Lord Padric, his family and the villagers would see the destruction of their home from miles out to sea. This indeed was a sad day.

Farewell Fleet, you will be remembered and I vow, Dan will pay for what he did to you.

Chapter 41

The Exchange:

Once Atesh and the remaining group saddled their warhorses, they set off at a cracking pace down the mountain side, through the muddy pass and onward towards Beaumont village. They made a cold camp that night outside the entrance to the inner mountain pass. Retired early and set off again at sunrise straight after forms. Towards midday Marcus indicated a left turn at a small dirt track.

"This is the one Marcus?"

"It's the only one I know that leads up into those mountains Atesh. You will trail us at a distance soon, Ballard?"

"Yes Marcus, we don't want to risk the boys by our bravado. You do know we can move with stealth; when the need calls for it?"

"Sorry Ballard, I am a little anxious for them. I am still coming to terms with Kyle's behaviour. I find it…difficult to believe, I suppose."

Atesh rolled her eyes and huffed. "Oh I believe it alright. Though, after all we have been through in the last month…you become anxious now?"

Marcus stared at Atesh then threw his head back and roared with laughter.

"What are you laughing at Sir Green gloop?"

"Oh no, this one is all mine Commander Fire-cat." Marcus's shoulders shook in rhythm with his mirth; tears streamed down his face. The more he glanced at Atesh and her ferocious; 'I will kill you later look,' the harder he laughed.

"Care to share this joke with us. We could all do with a laugh too, you know."

"Ballard, oh I wish I could. It is priceless I tell you. But my life may end short if I do." Once he settled down, Marcus led the way to a camp area by a meandering stream some hours ahead. "We will set up camp here. I dare not go any further into the mountains. Then Atesh and I will continue on our own in the morning to the rendezvous area."

Atesh stared ahead into the horizon. Dust particles rose from the dirt track and danced around before vaporising into thin air. "We have company Ballard."

"Where, which direction Atesh I can't see anything."

Half an hour later, Wyart trotted into view and waved to his Commander. Ballard shook his head is resignation. Yet again, Atesh was right. Marcus stilled his mirth this time. Atesh's eyes blazed with blue sparks, threatening something worse than a quick death.

"The way ahead has seen a lot of movement of late Commander. I followed discreetly and with caution. There be a group of Mercenaries camped about half a day's ride, beside a large stream with their backs to the mountain ridge. Sentries patrolled all areas except the top of the ridge. Rather silly when you think of it. That would be the first place I would set a watch from. Anyway I found a safe hidden area from which to climb up to the top away from their sight. It is a bit steep in sections, but foot holds were available between the rocks. Once at the top, it is flat enough to lay prone and observe below and hear conversations . Their voices echoed off the rocks all around me. I observed them for a while . Prince Kyle is there as well as Sergeant Philips."

Wyart turned to Commander Marcus. "Sir, I am sorry, but your brother, he was acting unstable, talking to himself, arms gesturing wild. He screamed about ghosts and fierce creatures wanting to kill him. At one time, he pulled his sword out waving it around. The mercs were not happy at all. They gathered at one point down next to the river, the trees kept them hidden from the main camp. They jumped at any small sound, eyes darting around wide in constant fear, of what, I do not know. Their fingers were agitated, flexing and straightening around the pommel of their swords. I would think dangerous comes to mind. They muttered quite a bit in a low volume. I heard small bits of their conversation. They didn't want to bring their dissent to the attention of the prince. He had killed a couple of his men for no apparent reason. It did sound like they were organising to desert, but wanted their pay first. The Prince argued with Philips about Master's Dan and Mason and an exchange of some sort. Philips was scared and kept wringing his hands, but the Prince kept saying no, no, she is mine. They cannot take her. Philips wanted to pack up and leave, forget the whole affair. He seemed to be looking after the two young boys. They were tied up next to the fire pit. I fear a trap Commanders . Worse though was the damn awful odour that lingered around the camp, it was similar to those Troldwite creatures. Why would that be there as well?"

"Thank you Wyart, at least the boys are alive for now."

"Could Master Dan and Mason be Captain Danurel and the Game Master, Ballard?"

"It is possible Atesh, I suppose. But what sort of exchange? The talk of creatures does make sense with what we know of the game master. Though I feel our Prince fancy pants has got himself into a situation he may not survive from."

"Meaning what Ballard? You are the brains, me brawn remember?"

Ballard smiled and raised one eyebrow. "I don't believe we have to worry about finding where this game master hides. He will find us, or more to the point, find you."

Marcus stood and stared at Ballard. "Hang on a minute both of you. Are you suggesting all this was contrived by the Game Master? That he had the boys kidnapped to exchange for Atesh, why? And how did Kyle become mixed up in all this? I am sure he has his own agenda."

Atesh sat down on a log and pondered that question.

"Do you remember back to the last game grandfather played Marcus?"

"It is a bit hard to forget Atesh."

"Well he did make the comment back to the Game Master that the enemy army had no leadership within the castle. Now Captain Pain in my rear end is there and who does he despise for beating him to the Commander's position? Now it seems obvious. He failed to have Renny kill me on our latest mission, of that I have no doubt. So what if this is payback or revenge and a way to remove me from the Commandership. Give them a leader for their game."

"Well I am sorry Atesh; it would have been me they would kidnap then."

Atesh leant over and thumped Ballard on the arm. "Be serious now, do you think this is possible?"

"You may be onto something Atesh."

"Oh I know I am Marcus. I feel it. I think I will be returning to the game master. Well as you say, at least we don't have to worry about finding his hideout."

"I am not happy about this complication."

"Marcus there is nothing we can do about it. The boys will be safe that is the main objective for this mission."

"I don't have to like it Atesh."

"No you don't Marcus. But at least I can inform you where I am and this tear implanted will safe guard my mind, if I am morphed. But the Commander on the other side was not a creature, so maybe I won't be one either."

Marcus looked stricken. He stood and walked over to the forest, his hand up against a tree, head bowed. Ballard went after him. He placed his hand up to stop Atesh from accompanying him. She nodded and went back to the men to organise their camp.

"Marcus, what is it? What haven't you told me? I have two eyes you know and a few more years' experience with real life than you; so what gives?"

Marcus looked at his ring on his left thumb. He then looked at Ballard, his face ashen. "What if I lost her? I don't know if I could go on."

"Marcus what happened on the journey from the cave-in to the Village?"

"We…met our ancestors Ballard, even yours."

"What do you mean? They are dead, long gone."

"Oh you have that right. We found the lost ancient catacombs of the royal line and they haunt it that is for sure."

"You saw their ghosts?"

"Oh…not only saw them, spoke with, was tormented by and badgered. King Gavin can be quite scary you know. He towered over both of us. Boy, did Atesh give him a tongue lashing. Very brave that one, such fire and passion. Atesh and I were married by the First King and witnessed by generations of the royal line."

"Wait…what? Married? Why?"

"We had no choice. King Gavin demanded it."

"What do you mean no choice?" Ballard was raging on the inside. His cheeks and neck had turned scarlet, heated to fire hot.

"Gavin may be a ghost, but he is still a powerful wizard." He then showed Ballard his wedding band. We both have one, made especially by your direct ancestor, King Jimmie Greymont."

"Wow that is unusual. What is it made from? Attached to your essence is it?"

"Yes, the first three wizards performed some sort of incantation. It is made from King Gavin's skeleton."

"Oh! That is not right, gross." Ballard screwed up his face as he again looked at the masterpiece.

"You should have seen Atesh's face; green as grass when he told her."

"Why did they make you wed?"

"Well we had a bit too much of your academy's zinger juice and were spied on by some peeping spectres. In let's say a…compromising situation."

"Yes, well that would do it, if I remember anything about our ancient history and royal lore. You are lucky they didn't want to castrate you."

"Well they did talk about boiling us in oil; head lopping and skinning us alive. Oh and my favourite hanging by our toes over hot coals or something like that. But, get this; it was for disturbing their peace."

Ballard's, eyes widened. "Could they really do that?"

"I have no doubt, they could."

"Geeze…you do love her true, right?"

"Ballard I love her more than my own life, it is that deep gnawing in my guts that scares me. What if I lost her forever?"

"Remember she will be long lived, perhaps immortal. She will find a way back to you. I have no doubt. What does Atesh feel about all this?"

"Well you named her right. What a temper and a half. She stood up to the King and told him off. I have never been so scared and proud, but she couldn't deny what was in her heart. I just have to tell father now. I am not looking forward to that conversation at all."

"Well for what it's worth, congratulations. I know you two are a perfect match."

"Are you alright with this? I had wondered maybe…if you and Atesh were…"

"No, I am fine with this. I have had a lot of time for reflection on this journey and I truly love Atesh. I always have, but as a guardian should; a surrogate father. I realise that now. My love is deep, but not in a partner way, if you can understand that." *Geeze, what else am I going to say to him. It is too late now. So this is what a broken heart feels like.*

"Thank you Uncle."

"Ugh that sounds so old, enough of that alright?"

"Can we keep this quiet, till I inform father?"

"I suspect the men are aware something has changed between you two. Remember body language speaks aloud, to those who listen. I will speak with them and I promise they will keep this secret."

Atesh continued to watch the two men near the trees. She suspected what the conversation was about and decided to leave them to it. *I am sorry Ballard for breaking your heart. I do love you very much. But Marcus is my one. Please forgive me.*

Ciaran climbed out from under Ballard's collar. He looked at the men and scampered away back to Atesh. Small crystal tears cascaded down his eyes. He climbed up Atesh's trousers and shirt, then faced her for a moment; nodded his head then snuggled around her neck. While the men were in conversation she pulled out the scroll with the ancient prophecy. Her face blanched when she read the last line. '*But to win, play the game; may cleave her heart yet*'. She rolled it back up and stowed it away in her saddle bag. *It is just some words an old man wrote after a bad dream that is all. It has to be. I will not let it be true.*

The next morning Atesh and Marcus headed off together ahead of the knights. Ballard utilised his blending ring and stayed a short way back with the men.

By mid-afternoon the two Commanders were met by soldiers armed with every weapon conceivable. They were escorted to the meeting area. Upon entering the camp ground, they noticed Kyle sitting on a log beside the fire pit. The boys sat close by with hands and feet still bound. Israe yelled out to Marcus, but was cuffed on the back of the head by Kyle.

"Welcome Brother, nice of you to drop in."

"Kyle what is going on? How could you hurt our little brother so?"

"Oh Marcus you are always so dramatic. I would expect nothing less."

Atesh dismounted Kayne, "So what now Sir Kyle?"

"My name is Prince Kyle to you commoner."

Marcus started towards his brother, but Philips and two mercenaries stepped in front, swords pointed at his chest.

"You may untie the boy's brother and place them on the horses, they are free to go." Kyle flicked his hand towards Marcus.

Marcus walked over and assisted the boys to the horses. He placed them both on Kayne. "Are you alright Israe and Binji? What is that on the side of your head…bruising?"

"He was hurt real bad sir, I did the best I could for him."

"Thank you Binji, you are a good friend. Now off you go. Kayne please take them to safety." The war steed had accepted Marcus and allowed him to handle and issue orders. Apart from Atesh no other could usually ride or even get near her war steed. It was their nature and training. He understood that the boys were no danger to him and wheeled around and took them away.

"Tie the whore's hands and gag her mouth. I do not want to hear her voice. It irritates me so."

Atesh did not fight this, not while the boys' lives were at stake. They were still too close to be hurt.

"Oh and place this around her neck while you are at it." Kyle tossed Philips a gold neck-band. He smiled as he proceeded to place it none too gently on Atesh.

"What is that Kyle? What are you into?"

"A little precaution dear brother, it creates a barrier to her innate magic."

Atesh's eyes enlarged, her pupils dilated and she slumped to the ground.

"What have you done to her?"

"Nothing yet dear brother," Kyle nodded and Marcus was surrounded.

A mercenary lifted Atesh's head from the ground and placed a gleaming knife blade under her chin. A trickle of red blood dripped onto the dirt below.

"You fight me and she dies."

Marcus was out manoeuvred. He was then tied to a stake in the ground, arms behind his back. "This was not in your deal, Kyle?"

"Oh didn't I tell you brother? I changed the rules." He turned in circles, arms out wide and burst into laughter.

Ballard and his men watched from the top of the ridge, blended into the surroundings. He was about to order an assault on the camp when he saw a shimmer through the trees to the camp's left. They remained still and quiet.

"It is time I taught this whore who is the boss; who is the King. Tie her out."

Atesh semi-conscious was staked to pegs in the ground arms above her head. Marcus struggled with all his might against the ropes. He bit down on the gag, as he was beyond anger.

"Don't struggle dear brother, your turn will come. I cannot have you as a witness now, can I? You see, I remove you and I will be the next King." Kyle skipped over to Atesh with his knife in hand and knelt next to her. "Shame, you are one hell of a looker." He caressed her face, and then slapped her cheek hard. "Wake up! I want you to enjoy this with me." He slapped her harder. Finger-marks embedded in her soft cheeks. "I said, wake-up."

Atesh opened her glazed eyes.

"That's better. All the men are eager my dear. But as I am your King, I go first of course." He straddled her body and caressed her fine features.

"I don't believe that was our deal, Prince Kyle?" Master Dan and Mason walked into view.

"What deal? I don't know you? Go away. I am busy with my whore."

Mason clicked his fingers and all Kyle's men stood rigid; yet they could all still see and witness the events now playing out in front of them.

Dan sighed at the pathetic creature before him. "Kyle move away from the Commander, please."

"Why should I. I am your King and I will have you flayed for this interruption and insolence."

"Mason, could you teach this lunatic that we mean business."

Kyle was raised into the air, face flushed, then lips started to turn blue. His hands grabbed at his throat. Then an audible crack was heard and Kyle fell to the ground in a heap, eyes open; staring in disbelief and confusion.

"Thank you Mason." Master Dan walked over to Marcus and pulled away his gag. "You must be Commander Marcus. Is that correct?"

"Yes sir, that is correct. Who are you if I may ask?"

"I am Master Danurel, a former Captain of the *Pace Knights*. This is Mason."

Marcus eyed Dan. "Will you let us go free now?"

"Oh I am sorry Commander, but we have our orders, you see."

"Orders, may I enquire from whom?"

"Why, the Master of course."

Large creatures filed out from beneath the tree canopy to surround the camp.

Marcus looked around and narrowed his eyes. "These Troldwites are yours?"

"Oh so you have met my soldiers before Commander? Then you know I mean business. You will of course accompany us."

"Why do you want us?"

"Well Atesh for personal reasons and you Commander, for insurance."

Large flying panther creatures descended from the sky and scooped up all within the camp and flew off into the evening sky. Master Dan, Mason and the Troldwites shimmered and disappeared.

Ballard and his men lay motionless. They felt helpless, totally outnumbered and out outplayed. *This was not how it was supposed to go.*

Chapter 42

Never a Dull Moment:

After the area was vacated by all manner of horrid looking and odoriferous creatures; Ballard and his men continued to sit and stare. Their minds were frozen in shock. Ballard soon gathered his wits and sent Wyart and Chale out to scout for any unfriendlies left behind. When they returned, the all clear was given. Jenner was sent ahead to check out the boys and to administer healing to any injuries they may have sustained during their ordeal. The men then descended down into what was left of the camp. Prince Kyle's body was wrapped in one of the canvas tents and tied to a pack horse. His belongings were collected from the cave and packed alongside. Anything of worth was bagged and tagged; the rest was thrown onto the fire-pit and set ablaze. The men went about their work in quiet contemplation, though they often glanced at one another, a frown or a soft sounding curse would escape now and again. Ballard took a final look around and signalled to mount up and move out.

"We have special packages to deliver men." This was not a task he was looking forward to. He ran his fingers through his grimed covered hair and sighed. *At least the boys were safe and sound. But, not only did I lose two Commanders; one was the missing princess, recently returned to her family and the other the prince and heir to the Kingdom. Geeze, flaming goat turds. How am I going to explain that to Gareth? Oh, and by the way sire, some zillion year old pile of bones married Marcus and Atesh. I am a dead man. Perhaps I can plead insanity? Nope I am a dead man.* There had been so much drama over the last few months Ballard felt aged. He thought he would be old and grey before he reached thirty. *Small skirmishes and peace keeping that was our role. Look after the academy security, keep the peace between villages. Monitor the northern boundary on the eastern side of Sofala. How hard could that be? Monsters were never in the contract. Well…now we can add every type of crazed looking critter you can think of. A pay rise is in order. That is, if I am not swinging from the gallows.*

Ballard and the troops soon caught up with Israe and Binji. They had been waiting further down the track out of harm's way with Ciaran. Knight-healer Jenner had applied a special mixture to ease the burns around their small ankles and wrists. Ballard kept them all moving to be as far away as possible from this place of horror. He had not the opportunity to explain to the youngsters what had transpired at the camp. Though he realised they had seen the flying creatures; how could they not? The sheer size of the winged monsters would have made them quite obvious. The boys were distracted at the moment as they tried their hardest to console the little dragonelle. Ciaran had cried a mountain of crystal tears. He sniffed and snuffled as they petted and told him stories of all the creatures they had slain within the confines of the Beaumont castle, but the wee fellow remained inconsolable. Ciaran was heartbroken, separated again after such a short reunion. Atesh was his life, it's all he knew. Ciaran used his wings to fly-hop from Kayne's withers across to Ballard. This manoeuvre was a mixture of a hop, jump and flap. He stuck fast to the big man's shirt, looked up into the Captain's eyes then crawled into his saddle bag. Ballard let him be, he was better off sleeping his sadness away.

Ballard and Aiden pulled up on either side of the boys. "Are you doing, alright boys?"

"Yes Captain, we are fine now. Thank you for the rescue."

"It was our pleasure young Israe."

"Sir, what happened back at the camp? Where is Marcus and Atesh? They said nothing about hurting them. Kyle was not himself; it was like he didn't even know us." Tears welled within his eyes. "He scared me, kept talking and screaming to no-one."

"You are safe now Israe, do not worry anymore."

"Binji kept me alive, do you know? He looked after me when I had been hit on the head."

"You are a true friend Binji; I will make sure the King hears about your bravery."

"I was afraid he might die, but I told him he could not leave me alone there with those awful men. We are best friends, blood brothers sir."

"What do you mean by blood brothers Binji?"

Binji looked to Israe. "We made an oath to always be there for each other and sealed it with our blood, see." Both boys showed their palm scar from their binding oath.

Ballard looked on this with his serious Captain's face. "Well yes, I can see you meant business. It is good to have a best friend, one to look out for your back. You will both do well in the academy. I would be honoured to have you in my team after your training."

The boy's eyes lit up and sparkled. They spoke quietly with their heads together arranging their future with the knights.

Ballard turned to Aiden with a wide smile, "Isn't that the darndest thing you ever saw? Little knights in the making."

"They are cute, that is for sure. Shame such innocence has to see the harsh reality of life."

After a while the boys noticed one of the horses carrying a wrapped bundle.

"Who, who…is back there Aiden? Is it…Marcus, did they kill him?"

"No Israe, I am sorry, but that is Kyle. The others that came with those flying creatures killed him and they took Atesh and Marcus with them. Why, I cannot say."

The boys wept silent tears, their ordeal over for now.

Ciaran heard their sniffles and crawled out of the saddlebag and scrambled over to them. He patted and cooed with soft comforting words. They were in need of some distraction now. "Tell me again wee knights how ye killed those *tatomen* and the *green lettuce goblin*?" The boys and Ciaran were once again transported into the land of the kitchen monsters.

They travelled along at a steady pace back to the main road, stopping only long enough to rest the horses and have some refreshments. They continued on throughout the night using Ballard's ring for light. Aiden thought he might try a light as well, but ended up starting a brush fire. He was persuaded from trying again until his grandfather could train him. Once they turned off the dirt track the main outer wall extending from the Beaumont castle could be seen a way off to the right. Wyart was sent ahead to the wall sentry. A message was to be sent to the king informing him of the successful rescue mission of the boys and the group's expected arrival time. They travelled in formation with the boys surrounded on all sides. Ballard and Aiden were taking no chances with their safety.

They had ridden through the night and were tired, sore and bone weary from all their recent adventures. About mid-sun the following day, a plume of dust headed towards them. Wyart galloped like a madman. Ballard looked at Aiden with resignation written all over his face. He knew something was wrong. Ballard scowled at the way Wyart had ridden his horse. As Knights the first rule was to look after their warhorses as an extension of themselves. Breathless and saturated with perspiration, both man and steed was near to collapse.

"Sir, there is a farm house down the ways a bit and to the left, with the occupants perched on their roof. I didn't get too close, but they still chased us for a while." His breaths came in short bursts, shoulders heaving.

"You are not making any sense Wyart. Take slow deep breaths and tell me why there are farmers up on their roof and what in all Sofala was chasing you?"

"…Scorpioids sir, surrounding the farm house."

"Oh Damn, I knew we could not escape one lousy day without a critter poking its beak where it is not wanted. Right, how many and how big are they?"

"The largest was as high as Shiloh here, twice over sir. I saw five of differing sizes. The farmer's home be two story with a slanting roof. They were lucky or they would be in the creatures' bellies right now. They saw me and waved and yelled for help. It was when I waved back , the nasties came after me. They are fast with their tails up in the air, slashing."

"Why can we not have normal sized critters to fight anymore? How far is it to the castle Aiden?"

"Oh, I would guess about half a day's ride Ballard."

"It is too far to ride for aid. Right men, gather around. We have a family to rescue from a dare I say it, wizard made scorpioids. They are only the medium sized ones, but I am sure their mother must be nearby. Jenner and Ciaran you stay out here, hidden with the boys and if we look like losing, you go as fast as you can back to the castle." Ballard scanned the area with furrowed brows. *Where are Betha and Red Jack when you need them?*

"What is your other concern Ballard? I've seen that face before, in the tunnels."

"Aiden, what bothers me is…well these are underground dwellers. What has caused them to come out into the sunlight? What if something larger has chased them out of their home? And I have never known men to be on their menu, so they must be hungry or real angry."

"Maybe the earth shakes. It could have destroyed their home and they ran out a new opening from beyond the boundary."

"Yes, that is a thought too. By the ancients, we need that boundary back up. Do you think you could reach Thaddeus like Atesh, we need some answers; the best way to kill these creatures?"

"I will give it a go Ballard." Aiden concentrated while they rode along. Perspiration beaded on his forehead, dripped down his face to saturate his collar and shirt. *"Grandfather, can you hear me? It is Aiden."*

"Aiden, why dear boy this is marvellous, is it really you?"

"Grandfather , oh thank the ancients . We need some quick advice . Large scorpioids have surrounded a farm half a day's ride on the outskirts of the village. The farmer and his family are on the roof of their home . How do we kill the creatures to save these people?"

" Oh my, scorpioids, well I reckon fire would be the best way. Do the knights carry Ultima fire with them?"

"Yes, I believe they do. "

"That will do it. I am too far away to assist. Damn, I wish I could transport. What about Atesh's blue fire? Aiden did you hear me?"

"Yes I hear you; Atesh is not available to assist Grandfather. We have a lot to tell you. I have to go, a headache is coming on; Bye for now."

"Be safe my boy."

"Ballard, Grandfather said Ultima fire is our best chance."

"Sir we still have some fire arrows left and a few pots of the ingredients."

"Great Hagan, we go in using camouflage."

"Aiden are you alright to continue? You look a little pale."

"Yes I will be fine Ballard."

"Aiden you and four men go to the left and four with me to the right. Soak your arrows knights. Oh and Aiden watch out for mother dearest, she will get testy when her children start dying. They will have hard outer shells, so aim for the eyes or any soft spots you can see. Watch out for the tail spikes, they will carve you in two. If these are the game master's creations be careful of the blood spray; it may burn you. When we reach the farm house we will split up, this is when they will notice us. So until then, stay close to me and the knights; best of luck men and aim well."

They turned into the track leading into the farm. They could see slaughtered cows and sheep in the paddocks on both sides.

"Geeze, what a gory mess they make." Aiden was turning a little green.

"Not tasty enough? I suppose they want man meat, that doesn't seem right somehow. I would say; not a normal species."

"Ballard what is on their foreheads?"

"Geeze Aiden…horns on scorpioids? And look at their ends, stripes on their tails and I mean; two tails each. What is wrong with that blasted wizard? Hasn't he ever heard of normal? What was the man thinking?"

"Oh I can imagine what Marcus would say if he saw these."

"Oh no Aiden, don't tell him, please."

Sniggers were heard behind from the men. You could see their minds working on possible names Commander Marcus would call them; wagers would ensue.

Screams and shouting could be heard from the family upon the roof, they had pitchforks and shovels only for protection. There were four adults, two teenage boys and two younger girls.

"Are you ready men?"

"Yes sir, all the men repeated in unison."

"Let's go, camouflage on. Keep close now till we are at the house." As they progressed within firing range, Ballard gave the signal. "Fire when ready and keep it up."

The knights attacked with fury, confusing the creatures as flaming arrows arced out of the air, hitting their targets. They scattered in all directions often colliding with one another, slashing and stinging their own kind. The creatures lashed out to any movement; their sight not the best in the open sunlight. Their screams brought the mother racing to defend her children, as Ballard knew she would. The men kept as close as possible till the last minute, their arrows remaining true. The flames took hold of the creatures and burnt their exoskeletons down to the inner flesh. The stench was nauseating and smoke filled the surrounding farmyard.

Ballard vaulted up onto the porch roof from his horse and encouraged the farmers to work their way down towards him. Aiden and two of his men were now engaged with the mother. She was larger than four horses and vicious as can be. The Ultima tipped arrows hit under her neck as she arched back to scream; this set her aflame and tore through her body. She thrashed about and impaled Aiden's horse with one of her tail spikes, sending him flying through the air, to land beneath a tree. He was out cold for a short period of time. When he came to, the mother had zeroed in on him and headed screeching towards her prey. Aiden stood and concentrated on his ring, he excluded all noise and movement. He willed the energy circulating within his body to awaken and drew on a deep well of raw force. Warmth spread throughout his body and intensified as it circulated through his arms; red and blue flames shot out from his outstretched fingers towards the enormous creature as she closed in on him. The flames engulfed the creature and consumed her in seconds.

The scorpioid children still standing all shrieked in horror at their mother's demise. One turned with wild ferocity, its tails whipped around and missed Ballard by mere inches. He lifted his scimitar high above his head and bought it down with all his might, carving one of the tails in two. The noise that emanated from this scorpioid was a high pitched keening, loud and piercing. All the men in the vicinity held their hands to cover their ears. Ballard being too close to the sound fell to his knees with the pain. He maintained his weapon in readiness, so could only cover one ear. The creatures all turned at the sound and fled back toward the mountains.

The farmer and his family were eternally grateful. Their horses and wagon filled with their possessions were ready for travel, they had left it a little too late to leave for safety as instructed by the King, days earlier. They had them safe and secure within the enclosed barn. Ballard assisted the family down from the verandah and ensured they were ready for travel. He shook his head often as his right ear felt strange. His hearing was affected and a nasty headache pounded that side of his head. Dizziness near dropped him a few times if he turned his head too quick. He scanned around for Aiden, but could not locate him.

"Sir, Aiden is over by the tree."

"Yes, the family is free now."

Chale looked at his Captain. "Ummm…sir, are you alright? You seem a bit off your game."

"Sorry Hagan can you speak into my left ear. I have a damn buzzing in my right ear."

"Sir, it is Chale and you are bleeding from that right ear."

"What is wrong with my rear? Are my trousers torn or something?"

Chale sniggered, he thought if Berend was here they would have some fun, but the Captain must be hurt. He touched his ear and beckoned Ballard to do the same.

Ballard placed his hands up to his head and bright red blood trickled down his fingers. "Damn it all." *My blasted head is pounding and I am spinning like a whirly bird.* "I was looking for Aiden. Have you seen him?"

Chale spoke slowly up next to his Captain's left ear. "He is out cold sir, alive thank goodness."

"He used too much power eh. But wow he was good. Did you see that mother scorp disintegrate with the coloured flame, turned to ash in mere seconds? That boy has potential. Did we sustain any casualties?"

"A few minor burns and scrapes, sir. You were correct about their blood or whatever that yellow ooze was; it burnt through everything upon contact. We need to get Captain Aiden and yourself to Jenner sir."

"Oh I am fine Hagan; a slight headache is all, nothing to worry about."

"Sir, I am Chale not Hagan. Oh this is not good."

"Come on then let's get sleeping beauty seen to." *Gee I hope he will be alright, he better not die on us.*

They placed Aiden within the wagon while Jenner worked on him. The farmers sustained no injuries except their pride.

"He will be awake soon Captain. He will need to learn how to take it easy for a while. Now let me look at your head."

"I am fine Jenner, when we are home I will let you do your thing. I need to get these people to safety and I am over bugs and creatures."

"Well at least let me wrap your head up so the blood will clot." Jenner gave him some powders to help with his headache and dizziness.

Chapter 43

A Father's Fury:

Towards late evening as the moon hid behind the clouds, an exhausted ensemble arrived at the outer Beaumont castle gates. The village was shut down tight. The guards walking the ramparts looked down on the ragged group.

"Who goes there, identify yourselves. . .or we open fire."

Ballard noticed arrows knocked and aimed. He looked at Aiden and scowled. *Well that is a nice greeting.* "It is Captains' Ballard and Aiden with the remnants of the northern expedition. We are escorting a local farmer and his family, Prince Israe and young Binji back home."

The gates opened slowly with armed soldiers on either side.

"What's with the welcoming committee Sergeant, can you not see how bushed we are?"

"Precautions is all Captain, take no offense. We have been harassed by strange creatures throughout the nights and mercs trying to get a foot hold in the village."

"Can you please send a runner to the castle and inform the King we have arrived. Oh and also to Ben the Barkeep at the Anvil inn. His son is here safe and well, thanks."

The guards looked with mouths agape; some with furrowed brows at not only the state of the returned, but the number of men. It was half the number that departed less than two weeks prior. They scanned the faces for Commanders Marcus and Atesh. Ballard noticed and shook his head at the Sergeant.

"There are no more to come now Sergeant, you can re-shut the gates."

The farmers were shown down to an area they could camp for the night.

The men were met by King Gareth, Queen Brianna and Master Thaddeus at the entrance to the castle. Ben the barkeep ran all the way up from the village. He had arrived breathless with tears streaming down his cheeks. Brianna her belly enlarged had hold of her husband's arm so tight, her knuckles were bloodless. Ballard and Aiden dismounted and assisted the boys down and then handed Kayne's reins to the Stable Master. Israe stumbled into his father's embrace. Ben swept Binji up into a cuddle, both crying with relief and happiness.

"Ben will you and Binji come up tomorrow, we will need to talk. I believe the young man is in need of his family now. . .off you go."

"Thank you sire, thank you Captains and men." Ben bowed to the group and walked off home with his son.

Israe was handed over to his mother and with the assistance of their servants they retreated back into the castle. Israe waved at Ballard and the men.

"Men you are all dismissed, have a rest day tomorrow. Ballard and Aiden will you please join Thaddeus and myself. I believe we have some details to discuss." As Gareth turned to enter his castle, he noticed a body wrapped and tied to the last horse. He rounded on Ballard. "Who... is this?"

"I am sorry, it is Prince Kyle sire."

Gareth walked sombrely over to the body and laid his hands on the covering, "Oh Kyle why?" He wiped his misty eyes on his sleeve and turned to look at Thaddeus.

"Gareth I will deal with this, off you go and I will join you in short order."

"Thanks Thaddeus."

In the King's sitting room they were each handed a glass with brown liquid.

"What is this sire? The mug is transparent and smooth to touch."

"Oh that is the latest from your academy, it is called glass. Be careful it will shatter if dropped. I hear it's made from sands and intense fire. They are doing wondrous things with it. The drink is called Brandy from the pirate islands. It warms the blood, rather nice on a cool night and good for the constitution."

"Great, Aiden and I could use a bottle right now."

"Your reports can wait till tomorrow, but I need to know a few things, but let us wait for Thaddeus. I believe he needs some information too."

Two drinks later Thaddeus entered the room.

"Sorry gentlemen, did I miss anything?"

"No Thaddeus only a drink or two, but you can catch up."

"Right…now we are all here. Ballard, Aiden two things I need to know. First, where be Marcus and Atesh? Second, what happened to Kyle?

Ballard placed his hand up to his forehead and held it for a bit, his headache was worse. The bandage around his head was soaked with old dried blood; his ear at least had stopped oozing. Ballard started from when they arrived at the camp. He tried to explain what had occurred, but Gareth kept interrupting.

"Kyle did *WHAT*, to his brother and Atesh?"

"I have told you sire, he bound them each to a stake."

"But Ballard, Atesh is a powerful wizard in her own right. How could she let this happen?"

"Master Thaddeus, they agreed to do nothing to endanger the boys, so they waited till they were freed and on their way to us before they would act, but it didn't go as we planned."

"Grandfather, Kyle placed a golden collar around Atesh's neck and she slumped to the ground unconscious."

"Thaddeus what is this collar Aiden speaks of? Do you know of such a thing?"

"Where would Kyle get one of them…?" Thaddeus stroked his salt and pepper coloured beard, eyes deep in thought. "Yes Gareth, I have heard of them, though I know no one that has ever seen one, only vague references in ancient texts. They are called a Wizard's nemesis or nemi for short. It is a shield that prevents one from touching their power or innate essence. Used in ancient times for wizards who turned to using dark, forbidden magic; what we call necromancy? But never have I heard of it causing unconsciousness. I wonder if the tear was protecting her somehow. I will need to look into this. But yes, with that collar on Atesh would have no powers at all."

"Right, then you say, two other men a Master Dan and Master Mason appeared and argued with Kyle, over Atesh?"

"Yes Sire, Kyle had Atesh staked out on the ground and started to attack her even though she was bound and unresponsive. Marcus had murder in his eyes and struggled against the ropes, but a Mercenary held a knife to Atesh's neck and threatened to kill her if Marcus freed himself. It took all my will not to go and slice him in two, beg your pardon sir. Danurel was upset and said it was a part of their deal that she was not to be harmed. Kyle dismissed them, like he would a flea; he was not in his right mind."

"Then Mason killed him and abducted Marcus and Atesh and you could do nothing?"

"Gareth, Sire there were many Troldwites and winged Panther creatures surrounding the camp. We had only a handful of men left after the northern rescue. There was nothing we could do. Atesh knew somehow she would go back to the Game Master, now she has. Danurel said Marcus was insurance, but I do not know what for? They were flown away by the panther creatures toward the east. Then all the mercenaries, Kyle's men and the creatures vanished into thin air."

"This Master Dan was the former Captain Danurel, Elias warned us about. The Game Master's new apprentice, yes?"

"That is correct."

"This could be a good outcome Gareth."

Gareth stared at his father in law unbelieving of his last words.

"Well…" Thaddeus pointed his finger into the air. "We needed someone to tell us where this game master was hiding and Atesh may be able to, if she can beat the collar. She may be powerful enough given time. I do not believe this Wizard will harm either of them."

"How can you be sure of that Thaddeus? What if Marcus is turned into a Morphid creature?"

"If he is there only for insurance, it would be so Atesh complies with whatever the game master has planned. Remember, I won the rights to the one and only Morphid game. We should know when it arrives. But I must confer with Elias first, before I say anymore. Gareth you need to trust me on this."

"Fine…fine, let me know as soon as you have information." Gareth turned to the two Captains. They did indeed look exhausted. Ballard's dressing needed renewing.

"Thank you for all you have accomplished; Ballard and Aiden. Though, I didn't expect this."

"Umm… Gareth there is one more issue to bring up while we are here." Ballard poured himself another brandy and threw it down it one mouthful. His eyes bulged as the liquid burned, sliding down his gullet.

"Oh it's that bad eh, you need some courage. Well spit it out man. It cannot be any worse than what you have already told me."

Ballard looked with resignation to Aiden. Sat straight up in his seat and looked Gareth in the eyes. "Sire, Marcus and Atesh be now husband and wife."

Gareth stared at Ballard. He slammed his fist on the table, his knuckles were blanched. His face set in fiery anger. "What! How did this happen? He dared do this to me?"

As large as Ballard was, he felt as small as a mouse. *I knew it, I am a dead man, kill the messenger.*

Aiden and Thaddeus jumped with surprise that such an outburst occurred.

"Gareth calm down and let the man speak."

"Calm down…did you not hear what he said. How could Marcus marry without going through the proper protocols? My brother will have a fit. Oh the women, what will they do to me? I will never hear the end of this. Nag me forever they will. He is the next King; it must be a royal affair. They must ask me for permission. No, it will be annulled and he will marry who, when and where I say, that is the end of it; when he returns I will tell him so."

"Gareth will you stop yammering like an old woman and listen to Ballard."

Gareth looked at Thaddeus with flaming daggers and poured himself another drink. "Well then go on, how came this travesty to be?"

"We became separated with a cave-in. Marcus and Atesh ran to one side and the rest of us ran to safety at the other end of the cavern. We lost a few men in the calamity. You must have felt the earth shake down here?"

"Yes, Ballard we had quite a time of it ourselves. Go on."

"We had made plans prior that if for any reason we were separated we were to meet at the North Mede harbour. We made our way back through the old tunnels and swam around the point to the cove. Marcus and Atesh continued on the Ridgeway, but ended up lost and found themselves in the ancient passageways which landed them in the catacombs of the first Kings."

"What? They found the lost catacombs?"

"Yes sir, but in finding them, they disturbed the peaceful resting of the first three; King Gavin Beaumont, King Jimmie Greymont and Master Eldred Ashmourne and their royal lines. I was told they were not amused."

"Not amused, you are talking about men who have been dead for thousands of years."

"Yes Sire, dead they may be, but spectres they are and still powerful wizards even in the afterlife."

"No…you jest?"

"Never Gareth, they spoke with them and were threatened with all sorts of torture for disturbing their rest. You know ye ol, beheading, hot oil baths, being skinned alive was my favourite. Atesh even went so far as to give King Gavin a piece of her mind, for being rude and unroyal. His Royal boniness even named her a fire-cat, though Marcus felt he had taken a shine to her. It seems it was the first Queen Liera Atesh takes after; the red hair and feistiness."

Thaddeus sat back in his chair and roared with laughter. "Oh, what I wouldn't give to have seen that conversation."

Gareth was stunned into silence, sipping his brandy and shaking his head.

"King Gavin married them in front of all the other spectres. Jimmie Greymont made a special ring for each from Gavin's skeleton and then it was infused into their innate essence by an incantation from the three. They went by their ancient marriage protocols and it was witnessed by all their royal ancestors. They were even granted a wedding gift of the ancient Beaumont treasury. Marcus said it could fill this castle twice over, more than enough to build an academy here and stop poverty throughout the kingdom. That is all I was told sire. Marcus did say to keep it quiet till he could inform you and have a proper wedding here."

"The First King is still around, that is outrageous. Their rings made from his long dead bones. Oh, that is not right. Ye gads what were they thinking…now; the ancient treasury was a wedding gift you say?"

"Ballard, how did Atesh feel about being married?"

Ballard looked at Thaddeus, raised his eyebrows. "She was not impressed Master Thaddeus, she was not given the right to choose for herself, but she does love Marcus and could not deny what was in her heart."

"I want the truth now. Why did the King see fit to marry them? I know my ancient lore Ballard, so no getting around the issue at hand."

"Well sire, it was said they met all the criteria." Ballard looked at Aiden for assistance.

"How did they manage that?" Thaddeus held a smile behind his glass.

"From what I hear they were betrothed as children in front of their parents. They answered true about their feelings for each other. Both are of the royal blood line. There was something about bonding from an ancient elven gene and umm…."

"Yes ummm, what?"

"Sire, they were seen in…a…by a couple of peeping spectres." Ballard's hands were twisting and trying to assist him with the picture, but failing miserably.

"Oh, yes well that would do it." Gareth placed his hands on his face as he bent forward, shoulders heaving up and down. When he sat up he was laughing not crying. Peeping spooks, bet that gave them something to talk about for the next few hundred years."

"I believe Atesh blamed it on too much of the academy student's latest zinger juice."

"Well I can understand that. Each year it gets deadlier. Those science students are good at what they do. What was the bit about the bonding? Did Marcus say any more?

"No Master Thaddeus, we didn't have a lot of time to go into details, though he mentioned Lailoken's high elven bloodline and something about a prophecy."

"Thaddeus what is that bonding all about?"

"Gareth I will tell you about it when we have some more time, but it does answer a lot of questions for me. Prophecy you say, I don't suppose you have a copy?"

"I will have a look in their saddlebags, maybe Atesh found one."

"Well what is done now cannot be undone. That is for sure, so now to tell the wife, eh Thaddeus."

"Best of luck Gareth, I will be in my rooms if you need assistance. Better still, maybe we could escape to the sanctuary before she finds out."

"If nothing else, I will say good night to you three. Welcome home and good job up at North Mede and the boys rescue. The fleet with those from North Mede will dock in the harbour tomorrow.

Chapter 44

The King's Dilemma:

"Ballard can you call in and see me tomorrow? There is something I need to discuss with you."

"Certainly Master Thaddeus, was it something special?"

"I need clarification on a matter. In the meantime, can you see if you can find that prophecy?"

"Yes sir, if you will excuse us, a bath and bed is calling."

"Oh, of course, how silly of me; off you two go."

When they were outside, Aiden turned to Ballard. "What do you think Grandfather is up to?"

"I'm not sure, but if I find the prophecy, we will read it first."

The knights had finished with their evening unwinding exercises led by Hagan. Bathed and sat around the fire awaiting their captain. The regiment soldiers had disappeared into their dorm and loud snoring emanated from their rooms the next building over.

"I thought you all would be in dreamland by now?"

"The men and me, well we wanted to make sure you two were still with your heads on those shoulders like, sirs. How did the King take all the news?"

"As well as could be expected Hagan. The brandy helped calm him down. We must get some eh, Aiden?" A slight nudge almost sent Aiden barrelling across the room.

"Oh that is for sure."

"We will debrief in the morning after breakfast. Exercises as usual; but I don't expect forms. We'll see you men then. Oh and thank you for the last…well, since we left the academy. You have all made me proud to be your Captain and friend." Ballard saluted with his arm thumped across his chest, turned and headed upstairs.

The next morning Hagan again led the exercises. Ballard tried to perform, but kept leaning to one side and twice he fell flat on his backside. The men sniggered behind strange hand arrangements, to the amusement of any who watched. Ballard was perplexed at why his balance was off. He shook his head often; his right ear irritated him so. Jenner attended to him and explained he had damage to his inner ear. That it would take time to heal. He may be deaf on that side for a few days or weeks and yes, his balance would not be the same.

Aiden and Ballard went through the Commanders' saddlebags and found an old rolled parchment of vellum inside a casing of leather. They sat, unrolled it with care and read the intricate hand writing. It was called; The Last Prophecy.

In times yet to pass, in a world out of reach;
Three Masters of all will sunder a breach.
The test they will fail; the power be too grand.
Sucked into a vortex and thrown on new land.
In time they shall Reign, many wars to be fought.
Their bloodlines to mingle and peace will be sought.

When days start to cool; from the bleaching hot sun;
Two souls will be born; instead of just one.
Far in the west, three blood lines of old.
Will converge bright in one; the second behold.

The first will be strong, a friend to the King.
The second shall dance; the blue flame she will sing.
A struggle to live; her will shall be strong.
Her mantra, her soul shall not falter or wrong.

A leader of men, for peace she will fight.
The evil that chides, then steals in the night.
The ancients of old will know when they see;

The one that's foretold will set the world free.
Three gifts she shall find, to help with her quest;
But to win, play the game; may cleave her heart yet.

The Prophet Lailoken:

"I have never read a prophecy before Ballard where my sister and I are the major players…this alarms me to be spoken about; thousands of years before we were born."

"Yeah, I reckon it would be a bit unsettling. What do you suppose the last bit means?"

"I dread to think. Is she going to be a Morphid? Will someone die…that she loves?"

"That is the problem with these, they are so vague Aiden, and it could mean anything. We had better give it to Master Thaddeus. He can sort it out."

"Ah, gentlemen good to see you both this morning, do you perchance have any interesting news for me?"

"Yes grandfather, here is the Prophecy. Though Barron did tell us only a portion of it was ever found."

"You met Barron…you mean, *the Barron,* Forty foot tall reptile, large fangs made of crystal and gems from the ancient times?"

"Oh yes sir. Met him and listened to one of his tales of the first three wizards. He was an extraordinary story teller. The men adored him; he was so full of knowledge. He gave Atesh a gem. A translucent crystal of pure perfection, with a blue diamond within, it was spectacular. He said it was for her wizard's staff. It's in her saddlebag now, but it attached to her essence, so I dare not touch it…Well that makes three gifts then, Ballard."

"What do you mean Aiden?"

"It is in the prophecy, we read it. Oh and Grandfather, yes Barron did remember you and Uncle Elias. He near brought the cave roof down on us when he laughed. You two must have been quite mischievous; all the ancients tend to laugh when we mention your names."

Thaddeus felt his face heat up for the first time in many a year. Total humiliation, he blushed like a naughty boy caught with his hands in the cookie tin. "Well we were boys once too you know." He unrolled the parchment and placed it carefully on the table, after a few nods, ummm and arrhs, he looked up. "Well that is as clear as mud. Damn prophecies, why don't they say what they mean. I wonder which bit is missing, is it in the future or the past? So much of our history has been neglected or forgotten." He rerolled this old parchment up, to take to the King.

"Now to the matter at hand, I need to know; did Atesh experience something profound during the journey underground." He noticed blank looks from Ballard and Aiden. "What I mean to say is, did something happen to her that was traumatic. I felt her essence scattered and watch me at one time. It was like, my heart skipped a beat. If I didn't know any better I would have said…she sort of died."

"Well yes Thaddeus, for a while she did in a way. I believe she travelled when she was buried under rocks in the cave-in. Marcus dug her out with his bare hands. We felt her too, but then she was gone. I don't know everything that occurred; Ciaran thought she had died. Then he said, an ancient laddie found her and sent her back to her body. Does that make any sense to you?"

"Well if the ancient kings are still fooling around. King Gavin who was the strongest in magic may have found her and sent her packing. Crafty old character, though I would like to meet him some day."

"Ahhh not me thanks Master Thaddeus. I want to keep my head."

"Speaking of keeping our heads we had better go and see Uncle Gareth."

The three strode off towards the King's sitting room.

"I should have suspected the three of you were together, scheming as usual?"

"Never us, sire." Thaddeus looked a picture of innocence.

"I would like a detailed report from you two. Start from when you left here for the north." Gareth wrote in his journal every piece he could follow. He ran out of ink twice and bellowed for more. When they laid it out together in sequence, it seemed like one giant nightmare. Gareth sat and stared at Ballard. His mouth agape often, but n'ere a word was spoken. Ballard commenced at the bravery of Berend with the water reptiles and the death of the two regiment soldiers. The need for Marcus to name every new creature had the two story tellers burst into laughter at the questioning looks from the King and his Counsellor. When they discussed Barron, Gareth had both hands up to his head. But the coup de gras were the Troldwites and the rescue of the villagers.

"You mentioned these at the camp with the Game Masters' minions. Are they the same Ballard?"

"These may have been wild ones from behind the boundary. They chased the Arachnopods into the village and trapped the villagers in the nearby caves when they ran for their lives and tried to escape into the tunnels."

"And they are a combination of rock troll and some sort of ancient dark dwarf." Gareth placed his forehead on the table. "They eat people like we eat a boar on a spit, slow roasting over a fire with a sharp stake strategically placed. Oh, I am going to be sick." He had turned pale.

"Can we get you a drink Gareth to settle your stomach, some milk?"

"Where is the brandy? I may become a drunkard, if all this excitement continues for much longer. Please go on, just don't tell me there is a flaming talking tree in there somewhere or I may do a blood vessel."

"Not yet sire, but one can never tell what is around the corner."

Gareth narrowed his eyes at Ballard and received a shrug in return.

What the men in the King's study did not realise was Binji and Israe had snuck in earlier and secreted themselves behind some old furniture to the back of the room. They heard it all. They frequently had to place their hands over their mouths to either hold in their laughter or stop from throwing up.

Ballard and Aiden took it in turns to narrate the rest of their adventures.

Aiden found the unusual present for Thaddeus in her saddle bag and handed it over, ever so carefully. They all leaned in for an inspection. Gareth screwed up his face at the smell and Thaddeus was delighted and gleeful with his new toy. The men tried to skip over the killing of the spiders, but Gareth noticed their apprehension and demanded a full description. They then explained the only way to eradicate the threat was complete annihilation, so the castle and village were fired with Ultima arrows. North Mede was no more. Gareth stared at the two soldiers; he stood and paced the floor.

"Nothing left at all? Are you sure?"

"There may be some of the castle still standing, but the homes and creatures were gone. We are sorry sire, but there was no choice, no time. If they had gotten loose in Sofala…"

"Yes it is alright Ballard, I understand." He looked once again at the tail stinger Thaddeus was given and shivered." I just hope my cousin takes it well. He is a bit of a hot head at times. It was after all the first King's castle. I will have to compensate him, I fear. Perhaps finding the treasure will help here."

Ballard turned to Aiden with furrowed brows. *"I don't like the sound of this."*

Aiden met his eyes and nodded. *"I was thinking the same."*

Thaddeus was looking at them both with one eyebrow arched, *"Interesting development boys."*

Aiden continued the narration as Ballard watched Thaddeus stoking his beard, thinking. The next event was the rescue of the boys Israe and Binji. Once again Gareth wanted every minute detail. Then the last leg of the journey they discussed the scorpioid attack on the farmhouse and their fierce battle. Aiden sat proud when Ballard mentioned how he turned the mother into ash with blue and red fire, though he stated some training on reining back his powers would assist in reducing brush fires in the future.

"Right, now let me get this straight. All these events occurred while your unit was on a fact finding mission to the *Northern Border.*"

"That is correct sire."

"Remind me to *NEVER*…do that again…. In all my years, I have never heard of such mischief. How did any of you manage to survive at all?" He shook his head in wonder and abject horror." Gareth stared at Ballard for a minute, stood and paced his office floor again. This is a freak show… a nightmare. I am going to go down in history as the King of freaks. Is it alright now if I have a dizzy spit?"

Thaddeus burst out laughing; Ballard and Aiden sniggered with their heads down.

"Well it does sound a bit like overkill for such a simple task. Gareth let me make this a little easier for you to grasp."

"First, we need to understand the evolution of the strategy war game; called chances. The game emerged around two hundred years ago. It was a simple child's game, a single player against another, with static wood pieces and a board divided into ten by ten squares. These became more sophisticated over time, utilised by adults and the academy for strategy training. Being the first to create such a wonderous adult training tool, the Game Master became famous; though he always remained elusive.

"At around the same time the disappearances around the Kingdom commenced. A person or animal here or there went missing. No one took much notice. That was until the vanishings became more frequent and questions were asked. But of course no logical answers could be found. It was rumoured that pirates or slavers had found their way to our shores. We now understand after a few sightings that panther creatures from times long past, morphed into dragon-cat hybrids are performing these tasks for a High Wizard. It was also around this time that strange looking creatures started to inhabit the north and venture down into the population. And we all know how the mountain was raised to stem that…flow.

"Next the interactive pieces began to appear, the next evolutionary step; the wizard was learning, experimenting. He placed the abducted citizens in as the game pieces, only they are somehow altered to not know who they are; except the part they play. But this wasn't perfect. The games didn't have the wow factor he was looking for; the blood lust of real war. I cannot for one minute try and work out this man's ideals. Perhaps he started to believe in his own cleverness and wanted to pit his knowledge at war strategy against other wizards; a duel of sorts. Now as time passed he has learned the art of morphing a human. What he did with his failed experiments I hate to even contemplate. Now he is ready for the next version of his game. What is the idea behind all this, what is he up to. It cannot be for a mere game that is too simple and quite frankly mad. Honestly this part has me puzzled.

"Second point; we have creatures of mixed origins traversing through from the northern borders; terrorising the inhabitants again. Now, how are they getting through? I personally have a gut feeling; it could be a few coincidental events playing out. It may be that the earth shakes have caused fissures to open up. Why now does the land quake and groan? Was it the digging for crystals? What is so unique about them, they risk such catastrophic cave-ins? Is it possible that nature is railing against the intrusion and interference to her sense of balance? Is nature an actual sentient being? We are taught everything in life is weighed and measured on a spiritual or ethereal scale; existence requires uniformity; equilibrium. What this wizard is doing goes against basic humanity and the very essence to the laws of nature. Combine all what I have previously mentioned and we have a barrel rolling effect, one thing starts another and so on, the results are still the same.

"Last but not least, we now know an ancient prophecy is in play. It was written over three thousand years ago. And for some reason it had been forgotten. So was all this meant to be? Is it better not to know what is in it, or will it be a self-fulfilling prophecy? Once we read it, no matter we do or not do, we unconsciously make it happen, it all works out to be as it should? Does the game master know of it? Or is he ignorant akin to us and we are all stumbling along unknowing and unaware of our fate?"

They all sat at contemplated what Thaddeus had discussed.

"I feel grandfather he is becoming desperate, taking whole units of knights."

"Yes and as Aiden reiterated, this game master may be getting closer to his ultimate goal. If I was in his shoes, I would say; gathering and perfecting the ultimate weapon for perhaps, a war against another formidable foe."

"Well done my lads, Ballard and Aiden how clever of you. Yes...yes that is the best explanation yet. But who would he be fighting?"

Gareth turned to the three. "All I can say men is, this Wizard Master has a rather perverted sense of calling. He lacks an understanding of right from wrong."

"Pardon me Gareth what did you say?"

"Oh, which part? He lacks an understanding of right from wrong."

"No, did you say…he has a perverted sense of calling?"

"Yes, I believe I said that, why?"

"Oh nothing, it tweaked a memory of those exact words from many years ago. A strange saying; sorry please continue…"

Thaddeus's eyes glazed over for a minute he was elsewhere in his memory, back in the academy days.

Gareth continued to talk, not realising all eyes were on Thaddeus as he stared into space and another time. That is until the silence awoke Gareth from his ramblings.

"When you men are ready, we can decide and prioritise our next move. First though we need some food and a strong drink or two."

The two hideaways snuck out from behind the back cupboard and stretched their cramped muscles. "Let's grab some food from the kitchen and head into the old corridor behind the main walls. It is a bit dustier, but not so cramped. We can find an area to continue listening. Are you up for it Binji?"

"Yes sir, you bet I am."

"You don't have to call me sir, you know. You are as a brother to me Binji. I owe you a life debt."

"No sir, Israe, never, I did what any friend would have. We will be knights together. As close as Commander Atesh and Captain Ballard."

"I will ask father to give you an honorary title. Squire or Baron or oh, exalted one, perhaps the master of the bandaged head." They both sniggered at that, and then the giggling started till they were both on the floor bent over in agony. Tears streamed down their faces.

"Come on Israe, I don't want to miss this next bit."

A basket full of food and drink packed for a picnic. The kitchen maids were very accommodating. They were used to the boys going off on their hunting adventures, killing dragons, and other monsters. It was difficult to pull the wool over the kitchen master's eyes. He handed them both a clean blanket and two new candles each, flint and small holders with a wink. They entered through the back board of Israe's wardrobe. It pushed into the space between the walls for a quick escape. They squeezed through narrow corridors, up and down stairways and slid under natural curtains with small beady eyes watching their every move. They found their way to the area behind the royal dining room. A peep hole beside a vase of flowers confirmed their location. Voices were audible through the wall, though they had to concentrate to hear at times. They set their blankets down and proceeded to fill their stomachs and listen to the adults discussing topics, small boys should not be hearing.

"Right priorities as I see it. Please interrupt if you believe I have forgotten anything, or the order is out of skew."

"One; It is paramount to protect the people and the Kingdom."

"Two; Search out and destroy the creatures that transgress through the northern boundary and compromise our safety."

"Three; Maintain the kingdom running as normal as possible. That is commerce, trade, farming, fresh food and water. Sanitation, safe transport and extend the hospice services. Look at new ideas, inventions to assist the rapid expansion of the population in villages and towns."

"Four; Find and rescue the Royal Heir and Commander of the *Pace Knights.*"

They all nodded their heads in the affirmative.

"So Ballard you will be, 'The Commander' while Atesh is away. Aiden you are his second in command, Commander or General sounds good, whichever you prefer. Your roles will be to find and train enough of the right men for a new Knights/ Regiment-Battalion, an elite fighting force. To be stationed here at the future Ashmourne academy, Beaumont Campus. They are to be a combination of my regiment soldiers and your existing knights left here. Maybe Master Elias will allow you to poach a few from over at Ashmourne Island, but I know he has his hands full at the moment. You are aware of the requirements to be a knight that will not change. From what I have been told they will need a certain amount of innate essence. Master Thaddeus can assist with this, the right character; follow orders without balking or deviating. A good appetite for ale, terrific hand to hand fighter, can perform your daily torture routines without complaint and have a wicked sense of humour, is that about right Ballard?"

"Yes sir, pretty close."

"There is a need for a special unit to police this village and Meder Town. The regiment soldiers that do not have the requirements for the elite units can be utilised as guards on the battlements and for escort duty."

"I hear Gareth; young Simon from North Mede has a head for leadership. He is young and untried as yet, but he is not afraid to get his hands dirty. He may be of use."

"Good idea, thankyou Ballard. We also need to teach all the people how to defend themselves. All males over the age of thirteen to be trained in the Reserve army, females are welcomed if they wish, as well. Thaddeus please ask your dear brother to visit as soon as possible. We require his assistance and a quiet word.

"I will send a message for another allied council meeting. Thaddeus do you think you can contact Mia and Betha? Find out what they are willing to assist with. The navy will monitor the west coast line. I am sure that pirate Cedric can assist with monitoring the islands and northern east coast. Ahhh we need to keep those merchants hopping with purchasing and delivering supplies. I will meet with the guilds from Meder. I hear they have tripled their prices down there. That will not do."

"Double the guards along the wall, a fast horse for urgent messages. We are at war men, so the King's rule applies. That means all towns to be locked down at sunset and opened at sunrise. Any crime will be dealt with harsh penalties. All prisoners will be allocated work; no one will be in the lockups during the day. They are to have clean, dry cells and decent bedding and food. Uncooperative felons, murderers or other despicable crimes, will be punished by death or exiled outside the wall. My judgement will be final. Have I missed anything out?"

"Sire, do I not need Master Elias permission first?"

"Yes you are correct Ballard, Thaddeus would you do the honours tonight please. I will write up the proclamations and have them distributed throughout the towns."

"As for succession, we must appear to be strong; so Israe is next in line."

"I am sorry Gareth that will not do. Israe cannot be the next King."

"Why not, he is of my blood line."

"Gareth did you not hear what I said before. Israe will be like Atesh, a very powerful wizard and we will not allow him to take the throne. The temptation for corruption is too great. We do not rule as High King *EVER*."

Behind the wall, Israe's eyes had widened at this news. He smiled from ear to ear. Binji gave him a hug. Hands thumped the air above their heads.

"Can we block this from happening Thaddeus?"

Israe jumped and was about to shout out his indignation at that thought. Binji slapped his hand across Israe's mouth in time.

"Not with this sort of power. It is too dangerous. He needs to go to the academy for his own protection, to learn how to control what is to come."

"When will Israe start to show signs, Thaddeus?"

"Starts anytime, some as young as babes, others at puberty, then it is increased at his turning."

"Atesh said at least one of the new babes will be a male."

"Yes, I am hoping one is not too powerful as she could also feel their innate essence. I am hoping we do not have a cluster. It happens every two or three hundred years. A handful of high wizards are born. The problem with this family is we have bred too close; the three blood lines are concentrated now. But the main problem, I see is, they cannot rule for another 18 yrs. What if something happens to you in the mean time?"

"What is wrong with a female queen, one of the twins?"

"Beaumont has been the royal house since the first. I suppose she could keep her last name. Which one do I choose? Whom do I marry her off to?"

"What about Fynton? He is smart and a good leader."

"Yes, but he is heir to the Tyral duchy, then you would have to go home Aiden."

"But I cannot rule either sire. I have Atesh's power in me as well."

"Ballard, you have gone quiet, what about you?"

"What about me?"

"You are a prince with Beaumont blood in your veins. Do you want to be the next High King?"

"Not unless I am ordered to sir. You would have to adopt me, as I have older brothers that would contend for the throne."

"Would you marry one of my girls, Ballard?"

"I have sworn my oath to the academy sir. I have no desire to rule or be married."

"Think I would rather be turned into a Morphid."

"Me too Ballard, I know what you mean. Lucky I am too close in blood."

"Alright lads settle down before you give yourselves away, but thank goodness, I am too old."

"Are you alright Thaddeus?"

"Yes sire a bit tired, we need to continue this discussion some other time, enough tonight."

The boys slipped out the way they entered and ran around killing any creature they could find. The warm damper had his throat slit, the roast boar near decapitated. The potatoes sliced and diced. The cooks shooed them outside or dinner would be totally ruined. The cat saw them and bolted for safety, he out manoeuvred them again. They then snuck up and stabbed the gardener who they thought may be a goblin in disguise. The gardener pretended to fall to the ground and rolled around. Lettuce was flung in all directions.

"See green blood, Sir Binji. I told you he was a goblin." This brought raucous laughter echoing all around the exterior of the castle.

Thaddeus popped his head around the corner, *Ahhh, some dark fiends.* He stepped out in front of the boys and as they turned with surprise on their faces, he aimed his staff at them. They could not move, but they could utter sounds. He strode up to them. "So my dark evil fiends, you think we do not know you have come to kidnap the King's dinner and ransom it for treasure. Well…I am here to see you cannot; take that." Thaddeus tickled the boys without pause or mercy. They laughed so hard, it turned into squeals of delight and agony. Tears welled within their eyes. Then they all fell into a heap on the ground.

"Do I win now yon darkness? I want that cookie."

"Nay ye white wizard, we are imm…une to your…torturous behaviour."

Gareth watched from his balcony, a smile lit his face. He yelled down to Thaddeus. "Hang them by their toes. I hear they beheaded our supper that is murder in any court."

"Yes Sire, your will shall be done."

"Nooooo, Grandfather not the toes."

"I am afraid so, ye dark fiends."

The boys were rotated and hung upside down, their hair scraping along the ground. The boys spotted Ballard striding along the walkway. "Sir, Oh mighty Ballard, please help us, this white wizard has us at a disadvantage and we will pay handsomely for your favour."

Ballard stopped in midstride; he looked at the boys upside down and burst into mirth. "I cannot help ye dark fiends, it be the tar pit for ye now." He bowed and continued walking, though his shoulders shook as he continued to laugh at the boy's predicament.

"So do I get the cookie now fiends of darkness?"

"Alright you win this time grandfather, but be warned you are now a mark."

He let them down none too gentle and they lay on the grass and laughed till they were almost sick.

"Come along I think we all deserve a cookie and milk, what say you?"

"Yes please, sir"

Chapter 45

The Wizard's Nemi:

Atesh tried to rouse herself from that place between worlds. She floated in endless darkness. *This is not like before, where are the stars, my memories?*

"Ach are ye lost again wean. Ye be making a habit out of this."

"Lost yes, where am I this time? I feel nothing, an empty shell. Am I dead sire"

"Oh so ye worked it out, my fire-cat, nae not dead, but unable to touch ye innate essence; for the moment anyways. Some nasty fellow placed a nemi around ye neck. A wizard's nemesis, it be a golden collar to be precise."

"Why would they do that? My mind is scattered."

"Yes, ye essence raced through our resting place. Ye really do nor be wanting us to be at peace now; do ye?"

"Oh, I did not mean to disturb you again. Maybe my mind knew to call you for assistance sire."

"This time wean, I canna help ye; but maybe som advice could be parted to ye."

"Why can you not help me get back into my body?"

"The prophecy me dear, one cannot interfere with it. It must play oot as foretold."

"Oh piffle, some old crony wrote down a bad dream that is all. The future cannot be set in stone or we have no will of our own and that...I will not believe."

"Yes, well as it may be my fire-cat. It is this fire within you that will keep yer feet planted firmly on the ground and be a force ta reckon with that is for sure. Good blood lines ye see…Now listen to what I be telling ye and ye may be able to break through this here barrier…but remember small steps."

A gaggle of deep voices, close yet, far away at the same time surrounded her. The words were jumbled and patchy at best. She concentrated on those words as if willing herself to the light. Atesh realised she was unconscious and that someone was close by talking, but she had not yet broken through the nemi barrier. So patchy discussions was all she could understand. *I am taking the advice of a zillion year old dead king. I must have dust in my head.*

"I have never seen a reaction like this before…but…parchment."

"How long has it been…?"

"Over a month…still alive…skin and…"

"Should we bring…see her?"

"No he can do nothing…now…"

Then the void again, no sound, no light, no dreams. Strange wetness warmed her body. The sweet smell of rose petals infused her. Every now and again a rustling noise was heard and then silence and peace. There was only an echo of her thoughts in tune to the rhythmic beating of her heart. *I am alive, so where am I. What was the last thing I remember? …not again, the voices are back; leave me in peace, please!*

"Do you have the answer, Mast…?"

"Old writings…three reasons. I had forgotten…the first… overwhelming…innate…shut down."

"The sec…Master…"

"Block…after…tur…ing"

"The third is…stage…with its own…"

"…can either of the last two be true?"

"Have Maisie…"

"Mason…we must remove…or…permanent damage."

Mason removed the golden collar from around Atesh's neck. She took a deep breath and sighed, the first such movement in many weeks. Her eyelids fluttered as in a deep sleep.

"This is a good sign. When she is up and about send her to me. This Island is warded so do not fear. I don't think she is too powerful, if that collar reacted as it did. Danurel said her turning would not be till the first day of the red season on the mainland; so still a while away. We know he is not as powerful as he makes out. So I can see anyone with a fair amount of innate essence would beat him to the Commandership. Once she has her turning, things may be different."

"Maisie has been overseeing her care, Master Grey. I will ask her to sit and look after her while she wakens."

"Yes that is ideal; especially if…no….We will not consider the…if yet. Mason, keep Master Dan away will you. I am not sure of their relationship and I have a gut feeling, she and the prince are connected. He acts like a mournful puppy, when I viewed him through my sphere. Not the behaviour of a mere comrade in arms. I must talk with him soon. There was a familiar energy around him and it is bothering me. He is still kept well, yes?"

"Oh indeed Master as you instructed, he is after all the heir to the kingdom."

"Now this one is a mystery to me Mason. So young to be a Commander, yet she oozes presence, a fire; even in this state. Something is…I cannot put my finger on it."

"Master Dan was right in one aspect sir. She is a stunner."

"Oh that she is Mason; that she is."

Atesh awoke as the suns early morning rays peeped up over the eastern horizon. She tried to sit up, but her head swam in all directions. *Ugh I feel dizzy.*

"Good Morn dere Lassie, take it easy like. Ye have had a wee difficult time of late. Ye have been sicker than a landlubber on a boat. It will take time to get ye head now."

"Where am I?"

"Ye be here lass, n'ere you mind. I will go and fetch some tasty broth for ya. Do ye good to have someting in ye belly. Stay put mind, I will be back before ye know it."

Atesh looked up to see the sweet smiling face of a lady; her voice had a way of ensuring you did what you were told. It was obvious she had endured many years of servitude the way she fussed with the bed linen, straightening the covers, rearranging flowers; though from the size of her, Atesh thought she must be the head of the servants. Atesh turned her head slow from left to right, observing all she could see. She again tried to sit up and the world tilted. *Why do I not have any energy? I will close my eyes for a minute.* The next time she woke, the sun was in the midday sky. The sweet sound of the seabirds echoed as they dived in and out of the crystal blue ocean, trying to fill their bellies. A gentle breeze blew from an open doorway, rippling the curtains in a rhythmic and rather hypnotic motion. The lady from the morning sat beside Atesh, darning socks.

"Oh good, ye awake again lass. I will help ye to sit up now, a wee bit at a time."

"Did you say, I have been ill, or did I dream that? I am sorry, but I cannot remember your name?"

"It is Maisie to you lass. Oh my! Your eyes are stunning. Such blue I have only ever seen once before. So much like my little one, bless her poor soul."

Atesh placed her hands to her forehead. *What a head pound.*

"Here ye go lassie, have some broth. I kept it warm for ye on the fire. Ye need some energy, a bit low of fluids ye be."

"Thank you, that tastes wonderful." *Gee, never thought I would say that about hot water soup.*

"Ye have lost some weight and there be not much of ye ta start with."

"I do not recognise anything here. I smell sea air, hear the seabirds. Am I at the Ashmourne academy?"

"Nae lassie you be on Mist-Wick Island, recouping."

"Thank you Maisie." Atesh nodded off again.

Maisie looked at Atesh and smiled.

It took a few days before Atesh could sit up with her legs over the side of the bed. Today she decided to walk around unaided. *I must get my strength back. Now my memory has returned, thanks to you; old bony one. I must remember those mind exercises. I will have to act innocent, till I know what went on. Settle down now, get a grip; you can do this.* Atesh felt around her neck and the collar had been removed. *Now that had a zing to it, nasty piece of jewellery.*

"Well good morn lassie, nice to see ye stand for a wee bit. How about I help ye over to this here seat and ye can see outside a ways. I have someting to bring a colour to dem cheeks of yours."

"Good morning Miss Maisie. It does look a beautiful day and I do feel better."

"Here ye go, try some of this drink. I brought ye some fresh baked fruit bread as well."

"You spoil me. Are you trying to fatten me up?"

"Well ye are but skin and bone lass. Mind ye, most would have succumbed to dere illness before now, ye have a strong constitution in ye."

Atesh picked up the mug of hot drink; the steam emanated from the boiling fluid and filled the room with an enticing aroma. She placed her nose close to the mug and inhaled. Her eyes opened wide in surprise.

"Here now close dem eyes and then take a grand sniff like this."

Atesh followed Maisey's example. She then inhaled deeper and took a sip of the milky brown liquid. It was sweet and exotic, the warmth travelled throughout her body, caressing and stimulating it at the same time. "Oh this is delightful; I have never tasted anything like it before. May I enquire as to what it is called?"

"Of course, it be known as, de nectar of the ancients; what dem Islanders call, coffee. The best wake up drink, dis world can provide. Oh and I put a few drops only mind ye, of me own restorative juice. I make it me-self from them yamboo berries. They grow wild down by dat dere water."

Atesh repeated the process. "Oh my Lady that is…"

"Aye, dat it is lass. Villagers in the south of the Archipelago islands grow dem coffee beans. They roast dem over a fire like, crush dem, and then boil again, somethin like this. I added a titch of honey and milk from dem cows; perfection."

"Superb is the only word that comes to mind. My head seems clearer now; it has a liveliness to it."

"Too many of dem and ye will be runnin around dis here island like a headless chook. Now my dear, I be no lady as ye called me. I am de head cook and house keeper of dis here castle. I run a tight home here."

"Well Mistress Maisie you are my hero, definitely a Lady if ever I saw one."

"That be so sweet lass, thank ye, just call me Maisie."

"I am sorry for giving you extra work. I am sure you have other things you would rather be doing than tending to me. Was it yourself that washed me and well…other things?"

"Oh dat be fine dear, never you mind about all dat. I be happy to help. But dere was someting I was wondering, while I tended to you."

"The scars, is that what was bothering you?" Atesh placed her hands onto her belly; she winced when she touched fresh healed scars. *Oh no not more, wasn't there enough?*

"Oh dey be a frightful lot. What happened to ye to be hurt so bad, was it as a knight?"

"No Maisie, they happened when I was a child. The academy healers tried their best, but they took a long time to heal and then left awful scars."

"Oh my poor wee lass… as a child, do ye know how? I hope ye do nae mind me asking, jus the mother in me I suppose."

"They have been the bane of my entire life. I am not sure how they occurred. I have no memory of my early childhood. As soon as I was interested in a boy, they would rise up and shout for the world to hear. *'Hey look at me.'* Then I would back away."

"The right laddie would not worry about dem, let me tell you."

"So I have been told."

"How old were ye when ye went to dat academy? I hear lots of good and bad about it nowadays. I worked dere in dem kitchens as an apprentice, many long years ago."

"They found me as a five or six year old. They adopted me and I have lived there ever since."

"Well I never did hear of dat before. The academy adopting a foundling, dat be a first."

"Perhaps because of my injuries they felt pity. But for better or worse, that was my home. I owe them my life many times over. My injuries they say were extensive. Burns on my abdomen, deep lacerations, some say were claw marks. My hips and pelvis were broken and partly re-joined wrong, so they re-broke and straightened them and I wore metal braces on my legs for a few years to keep everything straight. I had damage to my ankles and wrists. I remember they kept pulling bits of yarn type material out from my skin for ages. It was a painful time, but I learnt to endure. I worked hard, trained hard and it eventually paid off. That is all I know of my childhood, pain and exercises. But also lots of love, support, encouragement and smiles."

"Oh lass, I dunno what to say to ye, what a difficult life ye have had. Well now it is my turn to spoil de likes of ye. Such a pretty one, don't ye be worrying about dem scars. Men is men, believe me, when they love ye, they neither will be noticing them at all."

Atesh had fresh tears well in her eyes and wiped them away on her night shirt. "I am sorry Maisie I get a bit emotional sometimes about it." *Marcus I miss you.*

Maisie leant over and gave Atesh a big cuddle. "They did right by ye lass, dat be for sure." She patted Atesh's legs as she stood .Right, now how about I spoil ye with some breakfast."

"I would love some, thank you."

"What be ye favourite dish?"

"Well I am not a big eater but, I do love bacon and banana on warm fire toasted bread."

"Well dat be strange, dat be my favourite too. I have never known me another, tis easy to fix then lass. I will be right back."

While Maisie went scurrying to the kitchen, ordering maids here and there, Atesh wandered to the bathing room and started to redress. After a short time she became unsteady on her feet and returned holding firm against the wall to the chair. *Gee my clothes are hanging on me like a rag doll, how long was I out to it for?*

She heard voices outside. The morning was coming alive with the call of the birds, animals and their young discussing the night's events. People were hurrying to start their chores. Strange creature noises, close and in the distance. *What do you have here, oh mighty Game Master. What unusual combinations will I find, hmmmmm…a centrapod with a goat's head perhaps…or a spotted cow with wings? You cannot be too bright if you picked Captain Prickle britches to be your apprentice .* Atesh walked over to the balcony slow and steady , and then sat on the carved wooden bench overlooking the extensive gardens . Below she spied three men performing the morning's exercises . *I can tell from here that Captain, no wait Master Pain in my rear, is there to the far right. He was always a beat behind everyone else. It is like he could not get his rhythm right. I wonder why they continue this routine, was Master of the game monsters an academy wizard?*

She watched with scrutiny their posture, alignment and movements. The man next to Dan was somewhat shorter than the average knight, he performed well. Next one closest to Atesh looked like an older version of Ballard or Marcus, he was built like a gigantic tree trunk. He had a huge muscular upper body, but with the grace and poise of many years practice with the forms. *That must be the Master, definitely academy trained. Wish I could focus better, to see their faces.*

The surroundings, even the vegetation was unfamiliar. Atesh noted where the sun arose. *So we are in the north of Sofala. She smelt the sea air and felt the breeze on her face, warm, blowing from the east, unusual for this time of year?* She sat with her back against the wall and concentrated on her breathing, eyes closed. *Relax, breathe, all will be fine. You can do this…Marcus will come and find me.*

"Oh dere you be dear, getting some fresh air, dat be good for ye. I will bring ye breakfast out here and we can sup together. Oh and I made a fresh batch of the nectar, would ye care for some?"

"That would be wonderful; Maisie who are the men down below us performing the academy exercises?"

"Oh that be the Master, Mason and young Master Dan."

"Why is Captain Danurel here, was he sick too?"

"Oh no, he be now apprentice to de Master. He has been here a wee while now, nasty business about the ring and all."

Atesh let that statement slip by; she understood well, what happens when you disregard your academy vows, *Serves him right, deserting sleaze bucket.* "I believe I could get rather fond of this nectar, Maisie."

"Ye be a nibbler right lass, little rabbit bites. Here then try one of me cookies."

Atesh smiled to herself with that comment. "That is what my foster father/guardian used to say."

Maisie almost choked on her steaming brew, she coughed and smiled back at Atesh.

"Brandy snaps my favourite. I do remember as a young child the smell of these baking over a fire grill. They would snap and pop as they baked. Then a pair of red mittens would scoop them up and place them on a tray surrounded with coloured daisies. I can still smell the daisies."

Maisie sat quiet for a moment; her face had gone ashen. She looked at the red mittens tucked neatly into her vast apron and as her breath quickened, her mind wandered to the past. "Well I must be off lassie, work to do, always someting to be doing. I will check on ye in a wee bit."

Maisie hurried out and met Mason headed up the stairs. He was heading for a refresh and change of clothes before breakfast.

"Are you feeling alright Maisie? You are looking a bit pale."

"Mason, I have had a most wonderous chat with da Commander. Can we speak in private please?"

"Certainly, follow me."

Maisie fidgeted, her legs trembled and her hands constantly wrung in her lap. Mason poured her a strong drink.

"Now what has you in such a tizzy? I have not seen you like this for some time?"

"Atesh said sometings this morning, Mason. Could she…is it possible she was alive all this time, our little rabbit?"

"Tell me more, you have peeked my interest."

"She has scars on her belly, nasty from burns, and other things. She was hurt terrible Mason. The poor wee thing, she was so young and alone. She talks about things, I knows only, I do them. I saw her mark where dat collar thing was. It be an ol one."

Mason sat and stared at Maisie, his mind working through all he knew. "How did she become a knight?"

"The men found her all broken; they took her in and cared for her. So she stayed, it became her home."

"Well that would make it rather interesting for the master's plans."

"Oh please Mason, do nae hurt our wee rabbit. If this be our little one, do me dis one favour?"

"I will talk to her and let you know what I decide. Now off you go and do not worry. If this is so, the Master has the final call and he will do what is right."

Mason strode over and knocked on Atesh's door and entered. Atesh was still on the balcony stretching her body. It had been too long without movement and she felt sick, her body ached and limbs shook. She slumped onto the seat in utter frustration.

"It will take time to regain your strength Commander. You were unconscious for quite some time."

"Maisie says the same, but I dislike being a burden to anyone, my pride you see."

"Oh Commander you are our guest, not a burden."

Atesh turned her blue eyes onto Mason. "Why am I here Mason? Why can I not remember how I came to be here?

"The Master will explain it all when you feel well enough to see him…perhaps tomorrow. In the meantime rest up and indulge in Maisey's wonderful cooking."

"Ahhh I see you have been introduced to the nectar, mind if I join you in a mug?"

"Please do Mason."

"Tell me Commander, what you can remember of your child-hood. Maisie has told me a small bit about you, but I am curious, how a lady so young could be…the Commander of the Knights?"

"I do not have a lot of memories. Flashes, images and dreams are all I have. I am told it was my inner strength, stubbornness, a fire in my belly as it was described to me once. That kept me going, pushing me on, showing the world I mattered, wanting acceptance."

"Yes I can see that."

"If you will excuse me Commander I will see you tomorrow."

"Thank you for your company, Mason"

The rest of the day flew like the wind. Atesh slept for large parts, ate small offerings and walked around her room when she could. *I hope Ballard and Marcus got the boys safely away. I wonder what they are doing now.* Atesh awoke in the small hours of the morning when the night still held sway over the world. All was quiet as she walked out onto the terrace. The gentle breeze soothed her restless spirit and she gazed towards the sea. She closed her eyes and concentrated on her breathing and focused on one person.

"Grandfather, Can you hear me?"

Chapter 46

Revelations:

After they departed for the day and chores completed, all their head's swam with what needed to be accomplished yesterday. Thaddeus sat in his chair beside the built up fire, he smiled to himself. Playing with the boys always made his life feel worthwhile. The thoughts of his childhood again triggered that earlier memory. He was transported to a place back in time, within the academy days as a young wizard. He had been summoned to the office of his father, Wizard Master Felix Freymore and head of the Academy. He stood outside the door waiting for the previous occupant to leave. Voices were raised. Inside Wizard Gil Greymont was defending his experiments and research within the older portions of the academy library. An area he knew was out of bounds. His father reiterated how many times he had been warned, to keep away from the old tomes, but it seemed to fall on deaf ears.

"You will not tell me why, I cannot research these old writings from an era of outstanding magic and mystics. The amazing magical creatures that lived here on Sofala must be somewhere, why did they leave? We lost so much…The tomes do not speak of magic that was black or evil, just different and unique."

"You would be better off to put your energy into something useful that would benefit our survival here and the future. Instead, you have a rather perverted sense of calling. You lack an understanding of right from wrong. Different you say? Experimenting with live creatures is not what we are about. Forget all this nonsense and move on."

"You are wrong Master Freymore; we can have so much more if we use the tomes. Can you not see that?"

"I can see I have no choice, but to ask you to leave this Academy for a while. What happened to you? Have some time away. See the world, find your place and make a choice. Come and see me in a few years' time and we will discuss your future."

"You are throwing me out…like that? I did nothing wrong!" He stormed past, tears streamed down his face. He stopped, turned and gave me a hug. "See you around Thad, say goodbye to Elias for me."

The last time I saw Gil and our brother Jimmie, they headed out to sea. Off on an adventure, to who knows where. That was around two hundred years ago. What are you up to old friend…is this you Gil; after all this time? What happened to our brother?

For the next month Ballard and Aiden ran from dawn till dusk. The two senior officers toured and inspected Meder's facilities each week. They organised the main battalions up at Beaumont then split the rest of the regiment soldiers into, policing and guard rotation between Mere Town, Beaumont village and the outer castle wall. The King's personal guard stayed the same. Simon headed up the regiment units with direct reporting to Aiden. Although younger than most serving under him, Simon had royal blood, the title of Count of North Mede, his father was after all the King's cousin and he had experience fighting creatures to add to his list of accomplishments. He was in fact, a natural born leader, now with a rank of Captain. The King had tossed around the idea of name changes within the officer's ranks. He had read some information in older journals in his extensive library that excited him, but then decided in retrospect to leave things as they were, till all this mess was finalised.

Knight Berend the Archery Master and Regiment Captain Reece, Master of the long bow headed up the archery lessons for both kingdom knights to be and the local reservists. Hagan the Master at arms; led the knives, staves, sword and axe practice. Vykter, Wyart and Chale assisted with hand to hand combat, spear throwing, stealth attack and defensive manoeuvres. Sage gave riding lessons and horse husbandry. Ballard felt it important to have Hunt Master Eamonn, show the kingdom knights how to move through the bush undetected. They were required to be effective and efficient at hunting and to track and scout humans as well as fauna . There would be four Kingdom Knight Battalions of twenty five men in each . At present they all worked as one team . They would be assessed on all areas and then eventually placed into one of the four groups . Ballard would not have a group, but may attach himself to the first on manoeuvres . Aiden was the Commander for group one. The composition of this most important group was a thorn in his side. It was not a decision to be taken lightly, to split up his original group or keep them together . He would have to consult with Master Elias on this aspect. The academy knights each took turns leading the morning and afternoon exercises and forms . There was still a lot of moaning and groaning after these sessions from the regiment soldiers , though the King was performing well and feeling fitter and Thaddeus was back to his usual academy perfection.

This was the eighth day of the week the one afternoon and night they allowed themselves to have a rest from their duties. So they sat around the fire-pits this evening and discussed all manner of trivial things. Ben the barkeep drove a small wagon up to the men. In the rear he hid a few kegs of his best unwatered ale.

"Oh Ben, you spoil us too much, you know."

"Commander what price can I place on my son's life eh. It's my pleasure men, as long as I can join you."

"Pull up a log Ben. We have a wild hog and a bull on the spit for supper."

Vykter sat down beside Ben after basting the spits. "Tis not a waste of ale as some of the men think . It makes the meat taste better ; tenderises and sweetens the meat." His face creased in mild anger as he swilled his mug. "I swear if one more of em pretty boy's call me teach…I will throw em head first in the pig swallow."

"Well Vykter at least you have the easy job. Ever taught lefties how to shoot a bow? Had us all it stitches they did. They killed more trees and hay bales than I have seen since we were kids eh Ballard, Sir, Prince, your Supreme Commandership."

"So funny Berend, you know I am a natural left hander, but I taught myself to work with both. Yes and I killed my number of trees, outhouses and food bins in my youth…Speaking of youths, how are the two dragon slayers going, Vykter?"

"They are both naturals, sir. With their weapons, no tato or pumpkin would stand a chance against em. Reckon the academy would be honoured to have em for knights."

"Actually they remind me of a young sapling and his sidekick from years ago."

"Oh Berend you never give up, do you? I might move them up into the knight's ranks for training; what do you think?"

"Fine wid me Commander." Vykter nodded to Ballard.

"Yes me too…sir sapling."

Ballard ignored the jibe from Berend, his oldest and dearest friend and pain in the rear. He turned to Sage, who he knew would make some sense tonight. "Sage, how are the boys with the horses?"

"Easy sir, there are no problems that I can see."

Chale sat down next to Ballard. "Sir if I may? This past month or so has been interesting and all, but the men want to know…when are we going after Atesh and Marcus?"

"While we are stuck here Chale as nursemaids, no offense Aiden and the powers that be are arguing over the same issues every day; we cannot move. Politics bores me to tears. Nothing is ever urgent. They go over the same information again and again."

"Sir, our units have killed fourteen groups of creatures and we have lost good men. We need to stop this blasted Game Wizard. Or whatever is creating these nasty critters. How many creature types are up his skirt?"

"Berend that is one question we cannot answer. No one has ever ventured up behind the boundary since it was raised, let alone ventured up his skirt." Ballard sat back and laughed at the thought.

"We need to plug dem holes and put up a strong magical barrier. Better still; why not eliminate them abominations all together."

"The academy is working on it Vykter. Where are they up to on this gem issue Jenner?"

"The crystals to be used for a barrier such as we require are rare. Finding them has been a difficult task Commander Ballard."

"Jenner do they not have a store of gems somewhere in a vault at the academy?"

"Yes sir, I believe so, but not the ones needed. I wonder if...Barron could assist us here."

"Jenner that certainly is an excellent idea, something to discuss with Master Elias when you see him next."

"Have we heard from Captain Barnacle and his crew, sir?"

"No Berend, it be Captain Barnwinkle."

Ballard rolled his eyes and sighed at the men. "Oh you are a barrel of laughs, real funny. It is Captain Barnett. No we haven't heard anything yet. Do not forget it is nearing the end of the cold, white season so the weather changes make the sea rough this time of year." *Will I ever live that day down? I had one ear wrapped up and deaf. I could swear Gareth said, Captain Barnacle. I am so glad the hearing is back. Embarrassing, so embarrassing. Between that and the lizard gizzard episode, I should hang my head in shame.* "The new green season will be upon us soon. Who wants the job of organising the harvest festival? What... don't all speak at once? So, we cancel it then for this year."

"Oh Commander, sir...you cannot cancel the festival. The dancing, music, drinking, the exquisite foods and women dressed in their finest. Do they jump the fire here sir?"

"Brock I am sorry to say they do not practice that in larger towns any more. They seem to keep to the old traditions in small country villages only. Seeing you know something of the festival. I thank you for offering your services. You will have the pleasure of working with Queen Brianna and Princess Rachelle."

"Ummm...I...Geeze, learn to shut your mouth man." Brock placed his hands over his head and shook it, chastising himself. "Yes sir, it will be your pleasure, sir."

Brock was near pushed off the log he sat on. The domino effect started at the other end with a shove to one's arm and it rolled on down the line.

"Ooh princess snooty you lucky fellow." Raucous laughter echoed throughout the night.

"Did I hear another volunteer? Do not be shy, speak up…no one? That is strange."

The men still heckled each other with shoves and slaps to their backs, but not a word was spoken. The fires in the makeshift town next to Beaumont Village were now lit for their evening meals and sent tendrils of smoke and sparks up into the night sky.

"It looks so peaceful and cosy down there by the creek. Do you think the dwellings will stay Ballard?"

"Ben, it may be peaceful at the moment, but some of those farmers are hotheads. They cannot hold their liquor. Any wonder with what they consume. That potato concoction they make, takes the hairs of your chest. Simon and his men are run into the ground some days, pulling men and packs of women off each other. I am glad you do not sell that gut rot in your ale house."

Berend sat up straight with a gleam in his eye. "Packs of women? You are kidding right, Commander? Point the way, eh boys. We can go and sort them out for ya."

"No we do not want an explosion of miniature knights running around next yellow season Bear, or an outbreak of the pox amongst you men. But, thank you for your gracious offer."

Ben pointed to the new external walls. "Commander is it true that Master Elias and the academy wizards made all these walls in one week?"

"That is correct Ben; they created stone blocks out of thin air. I suspect a quarry is stripped bare somewhere up north, they moved them into place, piece by piece. It was marvellous to watch. They created the large bath houses with huge furnaces for water heating and public garderobes. They channelled all the waste water back up to the gardens and orchards for fertiliser through an underground sewerage system. We did not realise that underneath us are a multitude of caves and natural water courses. They placed in lochs and gateways and a large pond that combines all this muck together. Man you should whiff it up close." Ballard screwed up his nose. "It is enough to make a man turn to the drink."

Chale went a dusky green. "Sir, are you telling us we are eating vegetables made from our dung?"

"Yes Chale you are one big pile of wallow…"

He stood and fled into the bushes, he ever had a weak stomach when it came to food.

A regiment soldier Traven leant forward with his brows creased. "Sir, what is with that wheelie thing up a ways in the river?"

"Oh that diverts a certain amount of fresh water going down stream, keeps it flowing. At selected times of the day; the water boys turn another smaller wheel, like the spokes on a carriage." Ballard knelt down and drew a picture in the dirt with a stick. "It changes the water course to arc into the narrow deep channels towards the farms. Do not forget we have had to more than triple our food production. They have done the same over at Ashmourne and at Mere Town. They keep it clean by running it through a series of pebbled areas, very ingenious those science students. There are so many new gadgets, new ways of doing things, have you noticed the glass for windows and drinking utensils . It has propelled us along so fast with technology ; our pea sized brains now have to catch up. I wonder if we will be replaced someday. When this is all finished with all these resources, it will be the foundations for the new academy here at Beaumont."

"Sir, what has Master Thaddeus been doing with his time? He is not seen about now."

"Oh Ben, I believe he has been in contact with Betha and Mia. They are negotiating till we hear from Atesh and he has been learning to move between places, through walls, rooms; just small distances. Some success, except for one time, he ended up in the ladies bath house. I am not sure who was shocked more."

"Why be he learning this?"

"Vykter, I believe he intends to visit the ancient catacombs; oh and the treasure room of course. There is a scroll he is after and hoping it is in that room; or close by."

"Nasty business that be; It would be best to leave em bones in peace."

"Yes we have all told him, but he has become obsessed with it. You know how Wizards can be, experimenting with strange ideas and searching out knowledge."

As if speaking of him, a shimmer appeared to the right of the fire-pits. The men stared, some stood up hands ready on their swords. Ballard sat and smiled, he knew what was coming. Two men appeared before them, both with their hair stuck up in the air.

"Wow that was intensive Thad, what a buzz."

"Yes sire, but ummm we need to fix ourselves a bit."

Gareth looked himself up and down. "Don't see the problem?"

"Your hair sire, it is sticking out like a bespoked wig."

"Oh, thanks." As he flicked his hair back down into place, a large grin adorned his face. He noticed Ballard and Aiden's relaxed posture, but some of the men stood ready to arms.

"Well that is a nice how d-do for your King. Was my hair that bad eh?"

"No sire, we did not know what was occurring?"

"Well Traven, Master Thaddeus here can now transport another. It has the most incredible feeling, tingling all over. You must try it Ballard and Aiden."

The officers looked at each other. Both shook their heads in unison.

"I believe we are fine as we are thank you. We do not fancy getting caught inside a wall or rock; though the bath house would be an adventure."

The King raised his eyebrow to that, but left it alone for the time being. He and his counsellor sat amongst the men and chatted with familiarity and ease. It was good to feel his old self again, even though he knew it was an illusion.

Aiden strode over to the soldiers preparing to exit for their night shift on the wall, along the Beaumont castle boundary. He wished them well and to inform those returning, food and ale waits.

Ballard, the King and some of the men were discussing long term academy arrangements when Sage cocked his head to the side, listening. He bolted upright and took off at a run to the other side of the castle. Ballard, Aiden, Gareth, Thaddeus and some others followed. They found Sage trying to catch a terrified and bloodied horse, one that had left only a short time previous with the wall's night shift. Once he had it under control and walked it into the light. They saw, claw marks raked down the side of its flanks, the saddle shredded. The horse was trembling. Its nostrils flared and a trickle of bright red blood oozed down to its lips. The eyes widened and breath ragged from sheer exhaustion and terror. Small tufts of black fur lay caught it the stirrups.

"Ballard, Aiden please saddle up a unit. Actually take some of the knights. Find out what the blazes has gone on. Are we under attack from creatures or…dare I say it. The game master is at it again?"

"Yes sire right away."

"Double the guard men, stay alert." Gareth and Thaddeus strode back to the castle. The King's temper rose with each step. "That is the last straw. Thaddeus he has to be stopped. How many more good men must we lose?"

"Wait for Ballard's report before we do anything rash now Gareth. We must wait for Atesh; we need confirmation on his location."

Ballard reported back later that evening, there was no sign of a struggle, other than the horse that returned in such a traumatic state. The men manning the wall had disappeared as well, so now another two units vanished without a trace. Abductions were the only explanation. They would search again in the daylight, but Ballard was sure they would find no other clue. Further units were mobilised and this time they were doubled. They were also given spears to strap to their saddle mounts with the sharp arrow heads pointing upwards. There was nothing else they could do for protection. Keep the fires burning along the wall and maintain communication between the sentries.

Thaddeus sat in front of his fireplace awake, thinking into the early hours of the morning. He watched the flickering dance of the flames, when a soft voice interrupted his internal musings, a whisper in his mind.

"Grandfather, are you there? Can you hear me?"

"Oh my dear girl, are you alright? It has been too long since we heard from you."

"Yes, I cannot speak long."

"Did you get the collar off?"

"Yes, they removed it, so I would wake."

"You do not sound alright, where are you? Can you tell me anything?"

"We are on an Island north east coast, beautiful and sunny, large castle nestled in the middle."

"Good that is good. Are you sure of the location?"

"Yes, I watched the sun rise and descend; positive."

"How is…"

The connection was broken. *I do hope she was careful.* Thaddeus walked swiftly down the main corridor and burst into the King's study. He knew Gareth would not be sleeping this night. Gareth looked up, dark rings shadowed under his eyes. He was pale and drawn from not only lack of sleep, but worry about his wife's condition, his missing heir, Atesh and his subjects' safety. It seemed to be closing in on him.

"She is alright. Atesh contacted me."

"What about my son Thaddeus, is he safe and well?"

"We spoke for only a moment, she sounded weak, tired. At least they have taken the collar off her. That is a good thing…we are now in business."

"So what did she say Thad?"

"She believes they are on an island off the north east coast."

"How can that be? It has been searched, by ship. The report says they found nothing to indicate an outpost, no island, or rock formation only white sandy beaches."

"Strange, I wonder why Atesh believes she is on an island, unless…"

"Unless what Thad?"

"Did the Captain mention a fog bank at all, an area he had to divert around? Remember we are talking about a powerful wizard here. Illusion may be at play."

"Yes, I believe he mentioned an area of thick fog, but this time of year it would not be unusual."

"I need to know if he felt he had to turn away from the area, a strange feeling of impending danger. It would have to be out from the northern boundary area and accessible to the mainland. I believe we may have found the Game Master's hideout. Ballard mentioned a vision my brother had before Atesh left for their original mission. It fits perfectly."

"What vision? First I heard of this, Thad."

"It is not something known to many. But Elias has prophetic visions at times. They are always in cryptic verse form, which I cannot remember verbatim. However there was a mountain that's blind and sways to a beat. How did we not think of this before?"

"Oh yes, I can see it now you mention it." Gareth placed his forehead on his desk in exasperation. "What are you talking about?"

"The sea has a beat. It ebbs and flows, yes? The sailors walk with a swaying motion when they walk on land, do they not? If the island is mountainous that is covered in illusion, say a thick bank of fog, it will be blind. No one sees out and no one can see in."

Chapter 47

The Return:

Master Grey fell asleep once again at his work bench. The rhythm of the island readying itself to slumber had a calming effect on the aged wizard. He often closed his eyes for a moment to wake refreshed the next morning. The island's creatures settled in for another night as small rodents took this opportunity to skittle across floors and cupboards, hunting out small crumbs and wholesome left over's. As delicate as they tried to be, the tiniest noise would rouse the sleeping giant. He woke with a start, rubbed his weary eyes and massaged his stiff neck. He wondered what had caused him to break his slumber; in the early hours of the morning. *What would leave you with a sense of wrongness? And the sudden chill down your spine.* He noticed the hairs on both arms standing rigid and his heart pounded loud and fierce. He placed his hands on his chest and breathed slow and steady to calm his rushing blood. The night air was temperate and serene, his doors to the balcony stood ajar as usual. There was no movement from outside, apart from the gentle sway of leaf and limb that may have alerted him so; *Perhaps a dream.*

He stood, stretched and wandered outside into the night. The moonlight shone with all her brilliance, illuminating water jewels as the waves ebbed and flowed, caressing the white shelled sand to and from the island. This time of the morning was peaceful. He looked over his estate below and then he noticed her. On a nearby balcony, lower down and to the right stood a mesmerising picture of splendour. A breathtaking scene unfolded before his eyes. A tall lithe feminine figure wearing a shear white flowing gown gazed out to sea. Her long wavy hair shone bright reflections from the moon, cascading down to the small of her back. *Oh dear Ancients ... take a breath damn you. Was she looking for him?*

Atesh turned and gazed up at the moon, and then her eyes locked with his for a moment, before she continued on into her room.

Now that was a picture of beauty. One I will not forget in a hurry. I can see why young prince, you pine so. As Master Grey walked back inside, his mind back to his work, he sat at his bench and read through his last journal page. *How am I supposed to work after witnessing that? I believe I need a drink.* A whirring sound started behind him, picking up in pace and pitch. That earlier feeling returned, erroneous and eerie. He slow and methodically stood and turned to face the noise. His countenance cold and clammy, his face drained of colour, his eyes widened, gaze fixed and brows creased in disbelief. He took a step backwards then sat down firm on his seat.

Master Grey was not at exercises this morning, as the sun rose over the horizon; its hue a translucent gold. Mason and Danurel continued their routine and performed alone. This was not an uncommon event and no more was thought about it. Later that morning, Mason entered the workroom to find the Master scribbling with furious endeavour in his journal. He continued to mumble to himself, often stopping to look at what he had written, then nod, chuckle and return back to his writing.

"Master would you like something to eat sir?" Mason noted his breakfast had gone untouched.

"Yes, yes thank you. But before you go, there is a surprising discovery I would like your opinion on. It is remarkable, wonderous and yet frightening; all at the same time."

Mason was intrigued. "Yes Master, how can I assist?"

"Come in, come in my friend...oh and would you mind shutting the door. Now watch this." Master Grey opened the game cube and watched Mason's reaction.

"Oh I didn't know you had made a new game, it is...?" Mason stood and stared at the setting before him. He circled the board that hovered a few feet off the ground. His head tilted left and then right. His finger's tapping on his lips, mind deep in thought.

"Wait for it."

The cube slammed shut, inches from his face with a sudden force and no warning. Mason stumbled back and unceremoniously landed on his backside. The whirring began, it started as a slow hum, then it became louder, faster and higher in pitch. It spun on one axis, opened and a different war setting appeared.

Mason manoeuvred up onto his knees, careful not to get too close. "How did you manage to do this Master? It is incredible and ingenious."

"Oh I didn't Mason, it is doing this itself."

"No…you jest?"

"It started early in the morning. It goes through a cycle of four settings, but always comes back to the second. I need to work out how to stop it from rotating, to pick one and have it stay for a game."

"It has become self-aware Master; it is making its own war game settings? Perhaps tell it which one you prefer."

"Could it be that simple? 'Cube', the third war game is the one we will play next."

The cube once again slammed shut, whirred, rotated and opened to the second game.

"Mason you are a…this is the second one again."

"This looks to be quite formidable Master."

"Yes it does. Well looks like the cube has made our minds up for us. The second one it is then. Come we will go have some nectar down in the garden. It is a wonderful day to be outside."

"Master, are you feeling alright? You stayed in here again last night. Did you get any sleep?"

"My usual, I suppose. Do not worry."

They strode off together downstairs and away from the locked workroom.

"What are your thoughts Mason?"

"Well Master…it worries me. If we cannot control it…I do not like it."

"Yes you may be correct Mason." He stroked his fine cropped beard, deep in thought. "Perhaps we have bitten off more than we can chew eh? One last blast, what do you say?"

"Certainly Master, this will test the armies to their maximum. We will know which ones then."

"I was thinking…I should send Abi out for a few more of those rugged beauties."

"Yes master, as always. Would you like Commander Atesh to see you today? I feel she is up to a visit."

"Yes, she is exquisite, isn't she Mason?"

Mason raised one eyebrow and smirked, "Master?"

"Oh sorry, I saw her last night out on the balcony in the moonlight. I will tell you it has been a long time since a woman took my breath away like she did."

Mason guided Atesh outside to enjoy lunch in the garden where a table was laid out for three. A short time later Master Dan wandered up and sat down.

"Atesh nice to see you again, it's been a while."

"Yes Captain, it has."

"Oh, I am Master Dan now."

"Master is it, how nice for you, Dan."

Mason could feel the animosity oozing from Atesh and the smugness from Master Dan. He sat in between the two parties and enjoyed this divergence.

"Not hungry Atesh. I seem to recall you always did eat like a bird. A little peck here, a little there…no wait, it was a rabbit, wasn't it."

Mason raised an eyebrow at this comment, but said naught.

"May I have some coffee please Mason; I have become rather fond of the nectar."

"Don't you want ale or a wine? Oh that's right, you do not indulge, too pure for that eh, Commander."

Atesh ignored the baiting.

"Commander, what do you think of our little home here?"

"Mason, I am not sure where here is. But it is beautiful and somewhat peaceful; although the insects can be annoying." Atesh stared at Danurel, eyes burning blue flames with loathing as she slapped her arm to simulate squashing a bug.

Mason burst out into laughter, "Touché Commander."

Danurel turned bright red, his cheeks felt like they would melt. He skulled his drink, slammed his mug on the table and left.

"Oh Mason, did I say something wrong?"

"I can see why you are the Supreme Commander and Master Dan was not. No class that one. You do not like him much, if at all. May I ask why?"

Atesh put one hand to her forehead. "Well…he is a poor loser, pathetic, a liar, self-indulgent and lazy. He has an overinflated belief in his abilities and is cruel to his men. Basically he is a poor excuse for a man and a knight. He has the morals of a dung beetle and the breath to match. That about sums it up."

Mason chuckled. He held on to his bouncing stomach. "Oh is that all?"

"I was just warming up." Atesh smiled now.

"Was he well liked at the academy? He believed he should have been Commander and you cheated."

"I do not listen to gossip. I do my job. I call it only as I see it. As for him being Commander; I beat him fair and square. His overinflated ego would not concede a female beat him. Never partner with him in form doubles, he is…how do you say…uncoordinated."

"Yes I worked that one out."

"Thank you for the company and lunch Mason."

"Thank you for the laugh, it has been a while. Shall we go and meet the Master?"

"Lead away Mason."

As Mason escorted Atesh through the Castle, past the kitchen with the mouth-watering smells of fresh baked bread, small flashes appeared to intrude into her mind. There were images, voices and smells from the dark recesses of her mind that pounded on the inside of her head, forcing its way through tiny cracks. *Do not do this to me now.*

"Are you alright Commander?"

"Yes, a bit of a headache that is all. I will be fine."

They passed Abi on the way through the corridor leading up the stairs to the Master's work room. Atesh stopped and moved over to place herself hard against the side wall. She stared at the enormous black shining panther with wings tucked by its sides and he stared back with those piercing yellow and ebony eyes. He bowed his head and stopped beside Atesh.

"Good day Mathter Mason."

"Good day to you Abi. May I introduce Commander Atesh? She is our guest here."

Abi sniffed the air close to Atesh; nithe to meet you again Commander. He sat and studied the Commander with deep intensity and curiosity. Mathter Mason?"

"Abi, I will talk to you after, for we now have a meeting with the Master."

Abi shook his head, in obvious concern, but continued on with his large strides.

Atesh turned her head to watch Abi. *I know that smell.*

They knocked and announced themselves as they entered the workroom. Atesh looked around with wonder; books lined most of the shelves around the room. There were jars with all manner of animal parts, unusual things that wizards love to keep, dissect and explore. It was ordered and unusually tidy for a wizard. The Master had his back to them, sitting at his desk putting the final touches to a drawing. Atesh noticed out of the corner of her eye the closed cube to one side on a bench. She ensured her face remained impassive, deception was paramount here. Her eyes roamed the wooden carvings on the bench, some unusual creatures she hoped to never meet sat there. Then she caught sight of a painting on the wall. It was drawn with obvious love and affection of a young child with a bunch of white daisies in her hand, smiling back at the artist. The eyes looked back at Atesh, cerulean blue and sparkling. She rubbed her arms as a cold shiver ran throughout her body. Her breathing became rapid. She only now realised, knowing and seeing the reality of a previous life are two different things. *I need to get out of here.* Mason watched Atesh as she stared at the painting. Her eyes darted around the room, confusion written all over her face.

"Sorry for my rudeness, Mason, I had to finish this. Now…welcome to my home A…" Master Grey got no further than that. As he turned and stood up, Atesh looked up into his face with his endless black eyes. Her hand went to her mouth. Her body trembled. She backed away slow and steady, step by step until the wall met her back. She shut her eyes and shook her head. The memories of her young childhood burst through. She was sitting on a lap watching Father Grey write in his journal, drawing pictures, teaching her letters, sounds, words. Racing and skipping through the fields as workers performed their daily chores. She picked flowers and always gave them one each. Fleet was always ready with arms wide as she raced towards him. She saw herself playing with gems and coloured crystals, picking out her favourite. Next she was eating warm brandy snaps with a smiling face and red mittens. She remembered her last moments on the island, the terror and pain. She looked down and touched her abdomen, falling, *falling*. Mason watched in fascination as Atesh turned ashen. She was frightened, confused and overwhelmed beyond measure. *No, no, no, no.*

"Commander what is wrong?" Master Grey narrowed his eyes, took a step forward and tilted his head, not understanding her distress.

Motionless Atesh's knees became jelly. She tried to speak as she stared again at the looming wizard in front of her. "Fath…Father Grey," her eyes rolled up and she slid down the wall into darkness.

Master Grey turned to Mason as he raced over to the Commander.

"What did she call me? Did I hear right?"

Mason shook his head. "Well…I'll be. I believe Master, our little rabbit has returned home."

Chapter 48

Memories:

Atesh awoke with a severe pounding behind her eyes. She opened them to see two men; one on either side of her, sitting towards the end of her bed. She sat bolt upright and scooted up as far back as possible, displacing feathered pillows. She winced with the movement as she placed her hand to steady her thumping forehead. Mason smiled at her. Master Grey though narrowed his eyes to mere dark slits, his brow furrowed. Atesh gazed with uncertainty, her hands busy fidgeting with the bed clothes. In that moment she ceased to be the outgoing, feisty Commander of the 'Pace Knights,' instead Atesh was replaced by a reserved, dazed and mortified young lady.

"We seem to be at a disadvantage here Commander. Do you remember your last words to me, before you so elegantly slid down the wall?"

"Yes sir."

"How is it that you call me so?"

Atesh looked down in dismay, unable to keep eye contact now. "Memories sir, the smell of the cooking as we passed the kitchen, stirred images from my past. Then I saw the old volumes on the shelves , the painting on the wall, the daisies and then I heard your voice. Not as they are now, but how they all used to be. All seemed to echo around in my head. Then you turned to face me. It was like one of my dreams, hit me in the face; became reality."

"The only child to call me that name, we believe died a long time ago, after an accident. Are you saying that you… are…this child?" His voice resounded throughout her head, loud and demanding.

"I…have no idea sir. I cannot understand what I saw and felt."

"Do you have injuries, scars that were acquired as a child?"

Atesh's face became ashen, she looked mortified. Her shoulders slumped.

"Well Commander, do you or do you not?"

"Yes sir, I do have many scars from old injuries, h…how would you know that?"

Master Grey turned and bellowed out into the corridor.

Miss Maisie came at a run. "Yes Master can I assist you?" She was ringing her hands with obvious agitation.

"Maisie dear, can you confirm for us please, if the Commander here has old injuries that may have been obtained as a youngster?"

Maisie's eyes lit up, hope sparkled. "Oh yes Master that be correct. Tis nasty burn scars all over her wee tummy dere. Ne'er have I seen such horrid doings on a beautiful body like the Commanders sir?"

"Thank you Maisie, we will not take up any more of your time."

Maisie curtsied and gave a questioning look to Mason as she turned to leave.

"If you are indeed our lost little one, Ashmourne Island is a long way for a wee bairn to wander; especially injured so. How did you manage that feat?"

"I have no memory of that time sir. Though I do have a recurring dream of crawling forever in a darkened tunnel, but I never seem to reach the end. I often wake smelling dank earth and feeling frightened."

"So you decided at what, six years of age to become a knight?"

"Sir, it wasn't like that at all. I am told I was found on the academy grounds, curled up in a hollowed out tree; quite ill. They healed me, adopted me and I stayed on. They were good to me, gave me a home, a guardian, a purpose. I belonged there; it was the right thing to do."

"The right thing to do that is interesting logic for one so little, don't you think. Now you are The Supreme Commander. A bit young aren't you for that role?"

"So I am informed sir." Atesh looked deep into those dark endless eyes. She shook her head to clear the blended memories swirling around in her mind.

"Is there something amiss Commander? The way you looked at me moments ago."

"My mind is a jumble of memories, flashes of…how you look so much like my guardian back at the academy." *So that be why I clung to Ballard when I was first found.* "The same small mannerisms, build and you have his questioning look."

"Oh a handsome man then." Master Grey and Mason chuckled. "And what be this knight's name that looked after you so well, to gain your absolute loyalty?"

"It was Captain Ballard sir."

Master Grey held his breath for a moment. "Ballard you say, an unusual name."

"It is a family name, I believe sir."

"Oh and what might be his last name prior to the knight's oath?"

"It was Greymont sir. Prince Ballard Greymont, the youngest son of King Angus of the Southern Isles."

Master Grey had paled. "I see." He stood up and headed for the door. "Please see me later on this afternoon when you have recovered." He turned to gaze at Atesh. "Welcome back home my dear."

"Mason, what did he mean by back home?

"Well Commander it would seem the little one we thought died, all those years ago was only lost to us. You are that child Atesh; our little rabbit."

Atesh knew this to be true in her heart, after all Master Thaddeus had outlined this scenario. Reality for her mind felt different. *Keep it together, you can do this. Don't give the game away, play it as the Master himself would play.* "Did I say something wrong Mason for the Master to leave?"

Mason sat still his mind, going over the entire conversation. "Do you feel up to a walk Atesh? Perhaps clear the cobwebs from your head. Wrong no nothing of the sort. We all have history, memories, family and secrets and sometimes they pop up when we least expect them to."

Ah, so an ancestor of Ballard's, it has to be. They look so alike it is uncanny; perhaps he is the one that went missing. Off on an adventure with grandfather's younger brother Jimmie. Interesting, I hit a nerve alright. "Will Captain Danurel be around outside?"

Mason smiled. "I cannot say if he will be. Why, did you want to see him?"

"Not if I can avoid it. Please Mason, do not say anything of what's transpired. His judgement would be never ending. Though if it happened we bumped into each other on our wanders; I would like to give him a message."

Mason's mouth turned up in a half smile. "I will see what I can do."

Mason and Atesh wandered outside. The sun was gentle as it beat down upon their bodies; the warm breeze carried the scent of the briny sea air, fresh cut hay and wild flowers. Every now and again one of the Island workers would look up from his task and take a peek at Atesh. She nodded and smiled back. One young man, whom looked more than he worked, she gave a wink to. He was mortified to have been caught, turned scarlet and buried his head into the load of hay he was carting. Atesh was feeling easier; her mind though raced with memories and what if, scenarios. She wanted to discuss what happened this morning with Mason. He for some reason made her feel at ease, whereas Master Grey did the opposite.

Out near the side edge of the island they spotted Maisie off in the distance. She was picking flowers, different coloured daisies for her earthen vase. Abi lazed down beside her, but his eyes remained alert. Mason kept walking, heading in that direction. Abi turned his piercing eyes to them, his nose twitching in annoyance as a bee was trying its hardest to land on him. Maisie then raised her head. She looked at Mason who nodded to her. She bounced up onto her feet and bolted towards them. For such a well-built lady she moved fast. With her arms flung out, she barrelled into Atesh and crushed her against her buxom body; her head buried into Atesh's neck, shedding an ocean of tears. Abi stood up and sauntered over to the unusual event. He then sat watching with interest.

"Now, now Maisie you will drown Atesh." Mason peeled her off Atesh and placed his arm around her waist and held her to him, patting her on her back.

"I be sorry Commander, I hoped for so many dem years that me wee rabbit would return home and now here ye be. Oh and such a beauty. It is a dream come true."

Tears welled in Atesh's eyes. *I was loved here amongst all this wrongness. Gee, I had it upside down for all those years, thinking I was not wanted.*

Maisie planted a large kiss on Atesh's cheek, wet as it was. "I will make dis wonderful dinner for you tonight, extra grand." She trotted off towards the castle, humming with the daisies clutched firm within her hands.

Abi walked up to Atesh and looked down at her. He then sat on his haunches so he could see her face to face. For the longest time he stared into her blue eyes. "You be not afraid of me?"

"Should I be?"

"Mosth are…little rabbit that be you? Yesth, Yesth."

Atesh patted Abi on the head; he rubbed his cheek on her arms. *That odour is the same…the black fur. I was sure I knew it. So Abi abducted Jesper and Badges.* Atesh then noticed a cross, the sun shining upon it with all its glory: up a ways. Her eyes glazed over and she strode towards it. Mason raced to catch up to her while Abi was seen to be jumping in circles; strange noises escaping his mouth. There, before Atesh stood her worst nightmare, she doubled over in pain, her breath became ragged, pupils dilated.

"Atesh take a breath, come on now. Listen to me, remember your training, breathe and relax. That's it."

"I can't stop the pain Mason, what…is…happening?"

"A suppressed memory nothing more, it will pass. The pain will ease; now keep doing your relaxation. Hear my voice. The pain is going. You are alright now. No one is hurting you."

Atesh felt her mind implode; a mighty tussle arose between the scared little girl from all those years ago and the Commander of the *Pace Knights. Relax that's it, you can do this…only a memory…so painful, burning… put it back in the drawer. Please stop, it hurts…Father Grey help me…breathe…Go away-I will not fall apart, not now. I am strong, I must win…breathe. Listen to Mason. It is only memories…breathe.* "Atesh calmed down, tears welled within her eyes. I am sorry Mason I don't know what came over me. It felt real, but somehow I knew it wasn't. Does that make sense to you?"

"Yes Atesh it does."

"Is this where I was hurt?" She knelt down in front of the white cross; a carving of a rabbit adorned the front. The tears now breached their borders and cascaded down her cheeks. "The cross was for me?"

Mason knelt down beside her. "Yes Atesh that is correct. It is not easy coming to terms with one's past, especially not face to face. Reality bites sometimes and for you, your memories became a reality again. I am sorry we could not save you from the hurt all those years ago. The torment we all went through after you disappeared was unbearable at times. For you see, you had grown into all our hearts. Yes, even Master Greys."

"Mason, I believed I was discarded, disfigured, maimed and left to the elements. I was a foundling with no past, but I was determined, I was going to have a future. Now all I had believed was wrong…you said you had grown to love me. Then how is it…I was here?

"Master Grey will answer all your questions in due time; as I am sure you will have a few."

Atesh wiped the tears away. She nodded to Mason and they started on their return journey back towards the castle. Atesh laughed as she watched Abi jumping around them like a huge kitten, this brought lightness back to Atesh's heart.

"I believe Atesh we have one excited kitty."

"Mason what is Abi?"

"All in good time my dear. Ahhh…here comes Master Dan."

Atesh looked in his direction with a glower upon her face. "Maybe we can have Abi eat Master Pig wallow."

Mason gave a small chuckle, hidden behind a pretend cough. He placed his hand in front of his mouth as Danurel had walked into hearing range by now. Dan increased his stride to a strut as he became close enough for Atesh to view his completed wizard's staff; with its gleaming white crystal firmly grasped by a delicately carved hand.

Mason eyed the staff, noting the intricate patterns and shape. He noticed Atesh's quizzical expression. Her head tilted left then right, her eyes narrowed as she concentrated on the strange sight before her. A frown transformed into a half smile as she gazed at the staff.

"Nice carving work Captain, didn't know you had it in you."

Dan let her insult slip as he gloated. "Thank you Atesh, it was part of my Wizard training, to fashion my staff and find a crystal that resonated with my superior innate essence."

Atesh choked on her spit as she tried to contain her mirth. "Since when did you get such power Dan?"

Danurel drew himself up straight and tall. "Well I am more powerful than you will ever be. You are only a girl, after all."

Atesh smiled and her eyes sparkled. "I cannot argue with the fact that I am indeed a girl, but one that beat you at our Commander trials; oh mighty one." She bowed before Dan. "But what's the deal with…"

"Atesh," Mason interrupted her before she could say any more. "Did you not say that you had a message for Master Dan, if we happened to come across his path?"

Atesh turned to gaze at Mason; he ever so gently shook his head 'No' back to her.

"Yes Mason you are right, I near forgot."

"What message Atesh?" Dan moved closer.

He happened to be one of these unfortunates who were so absorbed with their own ego and pettiness that he could never observe and read other people's body language. He was caught unaware as Atesh clenched her right fist and planted it with enormous force into his face. The impact sent him hurtling backwards to skid along the ground. His staff flew from his hand.

Atesh shook her fist to release the pain and tension. *He has a hard head, damn it all pickle britches.*

"Wow Atesh that is a good right hook you have there, for a slip of a girl." Mason bent over and roared with laughter.

Holding his sleeve up to his bloody nose, "What was that for? What have I ever done to you? You will indeed regret this mistake Atesh."

"What you did…you disabled my team with food poisoning whilst we were on a mission for Master Elias; putting us all in mortal danger. You ordered Renny, an honourable knight to turn against his companions and try and kill as many as he could; including me, his Commanding officer. He became a traitor…for what Danurel, your pathetic ego? Such behaviour is unacceptable for a knight, let alone an officer; you…disgust me!" Atesh seethed with rage and raw emotion. "Did you need to resort to assassination against my team, my family? When your personal vendetta alone was with me?"

"Well…you would be happy to see, I am no longer a prissy knight. I have found my place amongst likeminded fellows."

"Oh I believe you may be wrong there Dan." Atesh shook her head in resignation. *He cannot see it, poor pathetic fool.*

Mason creased his forehead at the news Atesh unveiled and Dan's response. *Like minded fellows; I do not think so? Atesh is right. Treachery and betrayal could undo everything we have worked for. An untrustworthy colleague is a liability Master Grey may not want? I have been misled into thinking Dan is more than he is. After all, even wizards have their own ethics. Though we may perform unpleasant yet, necessary tasks from time to time, in the end it is for the greater good. I must inform the Master and put precautions in place.* Mason then watched in surprise as Atesh bent down and recovered Dan's staff. *Unusual for this to occur, one's staff would naturally defend itself if touched by another. Oh my, he is indeed pathetic. Atesh had the right of it.*

Atesh inspected the handiwork of the intricate carvings upon the wooden staff as she calmed down her inner fire. She looked closer at the white crystal grasped within the delicate featured hand. She turned to Mason with a smile, one eyebrow rose again questioning. "Beautiful handiwork Dan, I commend you on this piece of artwork. Perhaps you have missed your calling."

"Yes it is rather exquisite; the jewel sets it off; perfect."

"Oh it is a…surprise package that is for sure."

An unusual noise behind gave the three cause for concern. Mason and Atesh turned to find Abi, on his back, legs in the air thrashing. A milky froth dribbled down from his mouth saturating his downy cheeks. His eyes watered forming elongated teardrops. His body was convulsing with rhythmical waves.

Dan was still sitting on the ground and looked on in horror. "What in all the ancients is happening to him Mason?"

"Well…I believe we are witnessing a first. Abi has found…a sense of humour. He appears to be laughing, Master Dan."

"Oh no Mason that cannot be good, I have seen what happens when large creatures laugh."

"Yes…I think Atesh, Master Dan it may be wise to be as far away as possible."

The noise turned into a deep rumble, it became louder, more urgent.

"Mason…we had better hit the deck."

Atesh and Mason dived for the ground; they had no time to escape the inevitable. Dan sat up to see what they were up to; he could not work it all out.

"Master Dan now would be a good time to lie back down."

"Oh you two are not right in the head. He just has a fur ball."

Mason threw up a barrier covering both Atesh and himself. He left Dan to place his own shield up if he wanted. Abi shuddered one final time and a loud, long, intense bugle erupted from his rear end. A plume of sulphuric coloured cloud sprang forth, volatile in nature and thick in substance. It covered all within the nearby surrounds. Danurel was enveloped in the odoriferous, putrid matter. Mason and Atesh sat up; both glanced at Dan and roared with riotous laughter. It was a sight they would not easily forget. Abi heaving and hiccoughing looked on with bewilderment.

"Abi settle down, or this event will be repeated. It may be best if you hid for a while from Master Dan. He doesn't look too pleased at the moment."

"I be thorry Mathter, it be an accident."

"Oh Abi it is fine, but I would run away now, if I were you."

Abi turned and darted away to safety amongst the trees, his tail sat firm between his legs while hiccoughs could still be heard.

"You are a dead cat Abi, when I find you."

"Oh Dan, calm down. It is not the worst, I have ever encountered. Get over it."

"Not the worst, not the worst! There is nothing on this land that could be worse than this goo."

"That Dan is incorrect. I know there is one thing that is more destructive to the nasal passages than this, believe me."

"More fantasy Atesh?"

"Oh no, Master Dan, I can assure you there is one thing worse. Have you… Atesh heard of a clagging then?"

"Heard of it Mason? I have indeed heard of it, saw it, wore it and smelt it."

"No; you are jesting with me?"

"I am not jesting Mason. I tell you…when Betha laughs you run for cover. But you had better be quick; because she covers everything in clag for miles, the stench would make the long dead brought back to life, smell like roses."

"True then, you met…the Betha…that is outstanding …Master Grey once spoke to me of this clagging event. How did you survive this encounter?"

"It went as well as could be expected, though we did keep out of Red Jack's way. Now…that one is scary." Atesh's eyes glazed over for a moment reminiscing. "She could do with some mouth wash; her breath ughhhhh…. King Gareth I can tell you was not impressed when we rolled up to the castle after the incident. He watched in horror as his son flicked an eyeball from his trousers and then went the best shade of green I have seen in a while. The men kept all their bone trophies and wore them with pride. Imagine Dan, pulling a thousand year old animal leg bone or partial jaw with decayed flesh still attached, from your hair. It was superb."

Mason had gone quiet, his eyes widened as Atesh spoke of her interlude with Betha. Dan sat glaring with intense hatred at Atesh.

"What oh wise Commander is this Betha you spout of? I have never heard of it."

"Master Dan, Betha is the largest of the Arachnopods ever to walk this world."

"Oh Mason, that is a fairy tale to frighten children."

"No Master Dan, she is the oldest of the ancient creatures, the Queen herself. Master Grey has spoken of her."

"Well, how large is she then Atesh?"

Atesh used her arms in exaggerated motions to demonstrate her tale. "Well Dan, as she walked past her body blocked out the sun; the day turned to night, I jest you not. So large in fact the King's castle could fit easily under her abdomen and just one of her six eyes was larger than my horse Kayne. Then when she strides along all her eight legs work in harmony. The ground vibrates and the royal carriages we were escorting moved up and down off the ground in time to this multi legged rhythm. Oh…oh and the best part was when she stampeded a large number of animals in front of her as her travelling food."

"And she happened to clag you all."

"Yes, oh mighty knowledgeable one, this is what occurs when she finds something amusing. In between her three rows of teeth there are thousands of years' worth of built up, old rotten food stuff that gets forced out when she laughs. The academy wizards call it being clagged. It is supposed to be an honour in their eyes. It took Jenner a while to fix a powerful potion to rid the men and those we escorted of the stench. It was an amazing experience that I hope never to forget or have repeated."

"Huh…you and your tales will get you in trouble one day Commander. Now Mason can you please clean me off?"

"Certainly Master Dan," Mason had a smile on his face that nothing could erase. "I would like to hear more to this tale later Atesh. Please do not leave me in suspense?"

Atesh nodded and smiled, "Dan did you join us for a reason or were you out strutting around to amuse yourself?"

"Oh that's right. Master Grey would like to see you Mason. I have been asked to escort Atesh around while you are away."

Mason turned to Dan and in passing. "Play nice now Master Dan, remember she is our guest."

Danurel glared at Atesh, his eyes mere slits. He grasped the staff with such force his knuckles blanched. "Wouldn't dream of doing anything else Mason."

His sneer sent shivers down Mason's spine. As he strode back to the castle, Mason's mind wandered back to all that occurred in the last short time. *She is unexpected, perhaps more powerful than we realise, fancy Atesh seeing the truth to Dan's crystal. Then of all things she experienced a Betha clagging. I wonder why Betha laughed. Oh this is intriguing, could she possibly be the one I saw and felt with the powerful turning on white season's eve? Master Grey did say as a child she was special. I wonder?*

Chapter 49

The Choice:

Danurel led Atesh around to the other side of the castle proper; they watched the farmers hard at work in the gardens and picking ripe fruit from the orchard.

"Dan, do you remember Fleet?"

"No not really, should I?"

"He was a mid-aged worker here and used to assist in the gem collecting trips."

"Hmmm, yes there was a worker like that, but he ran away."

"No Dan, you left him to die; trapped in the dark after a cave-in. Were you ever a true academy knight or have you been rotten to the core your whole life?"

"That is unfair Atesh. I was cheated from my destiny and you know it. How do you know this Fleet anyway?"

"We met up at North Mede . I held his hand while he died; a casualty of a wild creature attack. He spoke of a Master Dan, though, nothing nice comes to mind. I had no idea, it would be you."

Dan was not in the best of moods, his face still smarted and his ego had taken a punishing. "Come on I will show you some of the castle complex, follow me."

"Oh course, lead the way Oh Mighty Master."

"Enough with the wiseacre remarks Atesh. You know I could make you creature fodder."

"That Danurel will never happen; you heard Mason?"

Dan felt his face heat up, his cheeks turning a deep rose. "We will see Atesh."

Danurel led Atesh down three flights of stairs. Crystals illuminated their way as they passed by, and then winked out of existence as they reached the next. The lower they descended, the dustier the floors became. The air smelt dank, yet salty; it felt cool and eerie. They walked along a corridor where the walls seemed to be held together by patches of lichen. Oozing water droplets pooled along the base of the walls; creating indents and cracks.

"Where are we Dan? Is this below the castle, deep in the bowels of the earth? What could you possibly need to show me down here? Oh wait…I get it now. I am honoured that you would want to show me your home?" Atesh placed her hand over her heart.

"I see you are still trying to goad me…no Atesh, this is not where I live. These are Master Grey's work rooms. Authorised access only areas, get it?" Dan turned to stare at Atesh his mouth creased in a sneer, eyes reduced to slits. "This is one rule you must never break."

Atesh nodded that she understood and remained quiet; she sensed all was not right down here. The hairs on her arms stood up and objected to being exposed. She had an awful feeling in her bones. *What in all the ancients is down here?*

"Right then, here we are," gesturing to the left of the corridor. "These contain all the rooms we wizards work in. This one is my practice room, where I perform spells and incantation casting. The next few are old libraries. Then these ones are out of bounds."

"Why Dan, what is in there?"

"Don't know, don't want to know; it is always locked; warded. The Master's rooms they take up the rest of this side of the corridor. Down the other side are long term guest rooms. Well, more like cells I would think. This corridor leads to the lower floors, the jetty and store rooms."

"Guests down here, what sort of guests?"

"I am glad you asked that question Atesh. Come I will show you."

Danurel touched a panel on the far wall; it illuminated what the darkness had hidden. There were rows of large enclosures with thickened steel bars, to allow viewing into the rooms. "Now first up, we have his Royal Highness Samuel, from the Terra Mountain realm."

Atesh observed a chamber with a bed of straw tucked away in the right back corner. A trough with hay and grain was still half full. Fresh water trickled down the small indent in the back left hand wall landing into an earthenware dish. A small oval shaped opening up high near the ceiling, allowed a meagre amount of light to filter in. There was a dark recess to one side, which obviously led to another area. From this a creature moved forward into sight. He seemed to flow with majestic grace, toward his visitors.

"Samuel, this is Commander Atesh from the Ashmourne academy."

"It is nice to make your acquaintance, Commander Atesh."

Atesh bowed her head in acknowledgement, "Your highness."

"Samuel here is a Terracorn, a species that's part animal and part human."

Atesh couldn't help but stare. For, before her stood a being that oozed benevolence and humility. A four legged, long, tri-striped body; with a lustrous white, high arched tail equine. From the waist up though, he resembled a mid-aged man; like the centaurs of ancient fables. He had a muscled and sculptured chest, chiselled facial features with sand coloured wavy hair that cascaded down past his shoulders. A golden circlet sat regally around his forehead, while a nemi graced his neck.

"Thought provoking isn't it Atesh." Dan laughed at her silence, "Moving along now."

Atesh felt sick to her stomach to see such a wonderous creature locked away. She looked into Samuel's sand coloured eyes, as she turned to follow Dan.

He nodded in acknowledgement, her face said it all.

"Right, next few cells we have more creatures from the other side of the known world, but we can say hello another day." Dan left these in darkness. Atesh tried to peer in, but could not make out any shapes at all. He kept walking till he stopped before an extensive room. This one illuminated. "Now here my dear Atesh is Marina from the surrounding oceans." Atesh adjusted her eyesight and noticed a young lady, perhaps no older than herself seated at a writing table. She placed her ink quill down and glanced up, piercing them both with her iridescent, emerald eyes. Her hair moved as an extension of her body; thick, shiny and graceful. This enhanced the chocolate colouring with strands of red peeking through, weaving its way down to reach her knees.

"Oh I forgot to say, she does not communicate at all. Whether she is deaf, a bit touched or both. I am not sure."

"I am neither Commander. He is not too bright that one. It is nice to finally meet you Atesh. Welcome to the Island of Horrors." Marina stood and walked towards the bars. She did not want to give away her obvious secret.

Atesh smiled and nodded ever so slightly in acknowledgement; *"A pleasure to meet you too Marina."*

"I don't choose to speak to trivial little trough sniffers that are up to no good. Beware here Atesh, he is a sly one."

"Oh I know this only too well Marina, but thank you for the warning."

"What are you smiling at Atesh?"

"Nothing Dan," Atesh hid a snort behind her hand. "I am not allowed to smile? Is that against your regulations too?"

"You really are too weird Atesh…so as I was saying. She is from the Burning seas, much like Omni-blue who you shall meet another time."

"There are islands with inhabitants out there, within the wild waterways?"

"Oh sweet, innocent Atesh, of course there are, but this young lady is a shape-shifter; her family rule the Eastern Seas."

"A Selky, a real one, like from the old tales?"

"No…she is a Sea-Dragon Atesh; fierce and powerful."

"Oh yes, she looks fierce Dan. Now who is dreaming up stories?" Atesh's eyes widened and she glanced at Marina again. She was average height for a human female, feminine build, small waisted with a smile that was both genuine and beautiful. Yet she exuded strength and power. "Why is she here Dan? Why are any of these races here?"

"Don't know; don't care; like I said before. I do what I am told and I never ask questions that I don't want to know the answer to."

Marina once again spoke in Atesh's mind. *"I need to warn you Atesh. Do not react to the next guest he intends to show you. Can you act, how you say…indifferent. That slimy critter has set up a display for you. Do not allow him to best you."*

"Thank-you once again Marina, I will do my utmost."

"We will meet again, of that I am sure Atesh, best of luck."

Dan waved his hand at the next accommodation cell. For some reason he puffed out his chest and had a smug look upon his face. "Now, Atesh here is our prized guest. Apart from you that is. Here is our latest addition to this special corridor."

Atesh steeled herself, took a deep breath and calmed her racing heart. As she moved alongside Dan the cell illuminated. There sitting on the ground before the bars was Marcus. His shoulders slumped and head bowed. Atesh stopped breathing, her heart shuddered. "What is he doing here Danurel? He was supposed to escort the children back to their homes. What happened to the boys? What have you done Dan?"

"Unexpected eh Atesh, we needed a hostage so to speak."

Atesh displayed mild disinterest. "What do you think this will accomplish Dan? His father will tear Sofala apart to find his son and heir."

"Is that all you are worried about Atesh? Do you have no words for the dear prince here?"

Atesh looked into the eyes of her true love, friend and husband. Her face displayed no unusual emotion. "I am sorry Commander Marcus that you were caught up in all this. I will ask the Master to set things right."

Marcus played along as well. His face was expressionless as he looked deep into his beloved's eyes. "Thank you Commander Atesh. I do not understand what is happening. Why I am held a prisoner."

"You are a guest Commander, not a prisoner."

"Then why Captain, do I have chains upon my ankles and a gold band around my neck…if I am a guest?"

"I told you both before. It is Master Dan. I am no longer a Captain. Doesn't anyone around here listen to me? Master Grey will no doubt discuss your situation with you at some stage." Dan turned and glared at Atesh, he was becoming agitated. Atesh's response was not what he had expected. "So he is not your one and only Atesh?"

Atesh turned to Dan, furrowed her brows and feigned confusion. "Are you mad? He is a Prince, the heir to the throne of Sofala. I am a commoner without ancestry or a name."

"Well that confirms my suspicion of you."

"And what did your pea sized brain surmise, Dan?"

"That you cannot feel affection Atesh; you are a cold, calculating, heartless bitch. Now I understand why you rejected me. It wasn't me at all; it was to do with what is missing in you."

"Now you know my secret Dan. What is next on your list for this weird and not so wonderful tour?"

"Well played Atesh, keep it together now till you are away from him."

"I shall Marina, but know my heart is broken in two. I will return tonight. Can you please tell Marcus if you have a chance? With the nemi around his neck, I cannot speak to him."

"They should remove it once you have departed. It was all for show. Critter Stink's idea. But I will certainly speak to him. You are all he talks about. Has it bad, he does."

"There is one thing Dan…Why have you placed a Wizard's nemi around his neck? Commander Marcus has no powers, special magic."

"One cannot be too careful Atesh."

"Oh spare me your rhetoric Dan. You would be able to feel his innate essence if he were that powerful. Or is it perhaps you are bluffing here, trying to be something you are not?"

"You don't know what you are talking about. Master Grey has the utmost respect for my abilities, you will see."

That I highly doubt. Atesh followed Dan back up the stairway without a second glance back. Her mind was racing with possibilities, when and how to return to the guest quarters. *Oh geeze, grandfather and Gareth would be beside themselves. I need to make contact again tonight.*

A messenger found them as they reappeared from the stairwell. Master Grey requested Atesh's presence. Upon reaching his study, Dan was dismayed at his abrupt dismissal. He strode off in a worse mood, mumbling and cursing to himself as he entered the kitchens. He had a small respite from his dark thoughts as he barked orders at the servants.

Miss Maisie wandered through humming to herself. "Oh Master Dan have de lads here fixed ye up? Ye look to need som-ting to cheer ye?"

"Thank you Maisie, can you suggest something strong. I have an itch, I cannot scratch. A need to place my hands around a certain Commander's neck and squeeze." He demonstrated with his right hand, wringing it tight before her eyes.

"Oh Master Dan, nae be our young Atesh ye speak of?"

"She is so infuriating. Why does everyone treat her like royalty? She is after all a prisoner here."

"Oh sir, please do nae speak like dis here. Do nae let de Master hear ye."

Master Grey and Mason sat waiting for Atesh. "Come in lassie. Let me look at you. So long we believed we had lost you."

Atesh walked in closer. She had a slight tremor throughout her body. Memories returned unbidden with force and clarity. Tears welled within her eyes and she attempted to wipe them away with the back of her sleeve.

Master Grey stood, towering over her. He looked down and enveloped her in a hug. "Oh my wee rabbit; I never thought I would be able to do this again." She leaned against him and breathed in the familiar smells of a time gone by.

Mason smiled and he too had a lone tear cascade down his cheek.

Master Grey pulled back still holding on to her arms. "You have grown into a beautiful young lady, smart and talented I believe...I suppose you are wondering why you are here Atesh?"

"Well, yes sir."

"Do you know what we do here, what I am?"

"No sir."

"I am known as the Game Master. Mason here is my assistant."

"You are the maker of the strategy games?"

"Well yes, amongst other things. Have you seen the latest games? We had them upgraded to be as realistic as possible; to create interactivity."

"Yes, they are splendid to play."

"What we wanted Atesh, now I am not so sure I want to ask of you. But ask I must. We have pushed the boundaries on our next improvement Atesh. The games are now real battles played out in a place known as the Wizards' dimension."

"I do not understand sir?"

"Stand over here my dear and I will show you." Master Grey opened the cube that sat on his bench and the next game materialised taking up a small portion of the office space.

Atesh stared in amazement at this scene. She stayed calm and pretended she had never seen a similar game in recent times.

"Here Atesh look through this crystal devise; It enlarges the area to resemble reality."

There before her was displayed an island with sheer cliffs on three sides. High fierce waves battered against the rocks. To the front a tall tree jungle extended from the small white sandy beach to a black, gaseous marsh. A dry, sand and rubble encrusted creek bed then led to a high volcano that towered above the trees with lava flow tubes, some active others not. A castle tower was inserted on the edge of the back crater lip. Layers of large obsidian rocks lay strewn up the sides of the fire giant. The area reminded Atesh of a hot festering pimple ready to explode.

Master Grey muttered a few words of an ancient language, Atesh had never heard before. A ship materialised off the shore of the island. It was manned by sailors though lining the deck were many fierce looking creatures all standing still.

Atesh looked closer, her eyes widened, heart pounded as she recognised them. Yes they were the same. "This is amazing sir. Such scenery as I have never seen before. What is the mission here? A formidable army of…what are they exactly?"

"They are what we call Morphids, Atesh. The creatures they ride are known as Tors. The mission is to capture the crystal within the castle tower that sits on the peak of the volcano."

"But, is that not an active volcano sir? It is a suicide mission. What are the opposing forces? I cannot see them."

"Yes well that brings me to the dilemma we face. We are in need of a great Commander. The defending force is an unknown; the game has not revealed this information as yet. They will not however be Morphids. I do suspect fierce abnormal creature types."

"How does one command, is it with telepathy or speech?"

"No Atesh, you command from within."

Atesh turned to look at the two men standing close to her. It dawned on her what it is they were after. Her face blanched, abject horror written all over it. "You are in need of a Commander?"

"Yes, that be true."

"You want me to command these Morphids?"

"That was the general idea."

"How do you do this, with illusion?"

"No Atesh, we transform humans with an ancient spell into what you see before you."

"You want to transform me into a Morphid? That is why I am here?" Atesh looked closer at the Morphids standing on the ship; she turned to stare at the two smiling Wizards. She placed her hand to her mouth, tilted her head and then took a sharp intake of breath. "All those abductions, all those interactive games we played; were real people? You stole my knights, Jesper? You morphed innocent people...for a game?"

"That is what we do. It is brilliant is it not? Oh...but, so much more than a mere game. This is life at its most basic; survival of the fittest. It is pure, raw, brain and guts. We have bred the perfect soldier. Now they must be taught how to battle with the best leader and known strategist in the land." Master Grey flicked his hand in the air. "I owe this world nothing; we are all pawns in the game of life Atesh."

"Is that it...because you can? The man I remember was kind, not cruel. No...no, I do not believe this for a moment. You have a reason to justify this action. I know it."

"Do not make the mistake of thinking you know me Commander."

"Can it be reversed?"

"Never tried, never wanted to."

"You took me to command this army for you why? You want to change me into a hideous creature for all time? Haven't I been through enough?" Tears poured down her cheeks to soak her shirt. Her chest heaved with short intakes of breath. Her heart pounded so hard it felt like it may break through her skin. Blanched fists clutched the sides of her trousers, drenched with perspiration.

"Atesh we did not know who you were, when we brought you here. Danurel suggested you be the best one to assist with this game."

"Yes, I am sure he did the slimy serpent."

"Mason and I have spoken at length and have decided to offer you a choice."

"What choice could there possibly be?"

"Stay with us here and re-join the family you once had. Become my apprentice. Or be the Commander of the last and final game. The choice is yours?"

"If I do not become this Commander for you who would you have to take my place? No oh…no not Commander Marcus. Is that why he is here?"

"You know he is here?" Master Grey was not impressed, "How?"

"Dan showed me where you keep the overflow of guests down in their cells. Marcus was chained and collared."

Master Grey raised an eyebrow at Mason. "Yes, that is the backup plan. Marcus will take your place on the island. He is known as a formidable leader."

"But…he is the heir to the Kingdom."

"There will be others to take his place."

Atesh sank down to her knees. "You have Dan as your apprentice, why would you want me as well?"

"Atesh…I am sure you realise how inept Dan is. He misrepresented himself. You my dear are going to be a powerful wizard with training. I felt it when you were a babe and I feel it now. Mason has informed me you seemed to question the ahhh…crystal Dan imposed in his staff. Is this correct?"

"It is no surprise; he believes it is a crystal. Anyone with half a brain can see it is not. I hope I am not around when he activates a spell with it, the mess and smell would be too much to imagine…Why do you not have Dan be your Commander?"

"Because my dear, he has no chance of winning."

"You want the attackers to win?" *You have never been beaten in all the years. Why now? Why this game? Does this not defeat the purpose of all the games?*"

"This is the last one to be made, a parting gift, the only one of its kind. I need the battle to be as realistic as possible, to have substance, a supreme challenge for the client; them against the game."

That is an odd thing to say. What is going on here? "May I ask who the client is? Do they plan and suggest strategies as with the past games? What control does the Commander have in this one?"

"All relevant questions Atesh, first, we have no idea who the client is, never have known. It is not relevant to us. It is all dealt with by a third party. Your second question, you as Commander will have the final say in how you deploy your army. The client can make suggestions. You can however, communicate with them."

"Will I stay a Morphid forever?"

"One never knows what will happen if the 'Game' loses. It is a game of chance after all."

There, he said it again, the game, not the game master. "I have taken an oath at the academy, you would know this. I cannot forsake that, but, a Morphid?" Atesh shivered.

"We do not need an answer right away. Think about this carefully. We are offering you a chance for another life; One with power, riches with a family that loves you."

I do not want power or riches! "How long do I have to give you my answer?"

"We can give you twenty four hours. Planning, preparations and training must be undertaken prior to the game."

"If I agree to be your Commander, what happens to Commander Marcus?"

"He will go free of course."

"What of all the creatures, did you cause that too?"

"What creatures, what do you refer to?"

"There are ferocious, blended, strange looking creatures. They have found a way through the boundary and are terrorising Sofala."

"How is that possible, the boundary is sheer cliffs? The crystals along the ridges display if there is a breach, they enhance the security."

"The crystals are no longer in effect, some have even disappeared. The earth shakes may have created fissures and the creatures are escaping. That is what my men and I were doing in the Beaumont Kingdom in the first place, rescuing villagers. We have fought giant coloured spiders, trolls, reptiles, bears and wild dogs like creatures. Oh the list is endless."

"Well Atesh that certainly was not our doing. The creatures, well some experiments did not go to plan. Yes we placed them behind the boundary where they could be free to live and pose no danger to the inhabitants on Sofala. I would never sanction the removal of the barrier gems." Master Grey turned to look at Mason. "Will you be a good fellow and make some enquiries with Master Dan."

"Straight away sir," Mason shook his head. He strode off with anger written all over his face, lips pursed and fists clenched.

"So Atesh, is there anything I can say to persuade you to stay on with us here?"

"Sir I appreciate the offer, the choice, but I do not think I can place Marcus in that position. I need to think this all through."

"Why are you against Marcus taking your place?"

"Sir, you know who and what he is. He is needed for the King-dom."

"He is only a Beaumont Atesh; there would be many vying for the crown."

"How can you condemn your own kin to this fate?"

Master Grey stared at Atesh. "What do you mean by kin? The Beaumont's are no close kin of mine."

"Sir you must be my guardian Ballard's ancestor? You are too much alike not to be."

He sat staring and silent.

"Well Ballard's elder sister Anna, married King Gareth Beaumont and Marcus was their only son. His grandfather is King Angus Greymont of the Southern Isles."

"Gareth is married to Thaddeus Freymore's daughter, is he not?"

"Yes, that is correct now sir. But Brianna is his second wife. Anna the first died in childbirth. That would make Marcus a direct descendant to you…if I am correct."

"Makes no difference Atesh, I need a Commander with a great deal of abilities."

"Fine then, I will take the twenty four hours and decide."

"One more thing Atesh before you depart for the night and I would like an honest answer."

"Sir, why would I do anything different now?"

"Have you had your turning? Dan believes it is the first day of the red season, a little ways off."

"What do you believe sir?"

"I sense power, a great deal of power; yet untrained. You have a strange mix of bloodlines. I cannot put my finger on it; so the answer Atesh?"

A loud and aggressive knock interrupted the awkward moment.

"Yes, enter."

Master Dan entered with face flushed. The veins were protruding out from his uncovered neck and his fists clenched to blanching. "What has this liar being saying about me?"

"I will take my leave now sir." She exited without another thought and closed the door. *Phew that was close, not a bad performance. I would do well on a stage, perhaps a bard, or a story teller.* She smiled to herself for a moment and then remembered the previous conversation. *A Morphid, they wanted to mould me into a creature that is too horrid a thought*. Atesh freshened up for the evening. Maisie had promised to join her for dinner with a surprise menu. She walked out onto the balcony and watched the sun descend beyond the horizon to slumber. Beautiful hues of red and purples streaked across the sky. A light show before the moon rose to wake and watch over the night. Atesh noticed Master Grey from the corner of her eye; he too was outside surveying his land. A pain shot through her lower abdomen, she clutched her stomach and bent over to catch her breath. The other hand grabbed the railing and clung tight as the pain ebbed and flowed. Nausea threatened to overwhelm her. Atesh saw Master Grey watching her with curiosity and concern. *Damn too much excitement for one day.* As the pain subsided she stopped and stared at where her hand was placed. She sent her mind to the inner workings of her body *Oh no please dear ancients, do not do this to me now.*

Chapter 50

The Last Goodbye:

In the early hours of the morning when all were asleep and silence ruled the island. Atesh crept down to the lower levels of the castle. She was intent on not alerting the guards, so often times she had to blend into the surrounds with her ring or stand still with breath held within a dark walled recess. She noted the Morphids and Troldwites guarded certain stairways and entrances. They strode past armed with enlarged axes, cudgeons and all other styles of fearsome weapons. Otherwise most areas were free of danger. *Dan did say never to come down here alone, unescorted. Now I know why. Ewwww they smell.*

All manner of strange fairy-tale like creatures inhabited the cells in the bowels of the island. They were hidden away from the world and their previous lives. Atesh watched in awe and fascination as she walked soft and with purpose towards her ultimate goal. As she passed each cell, she counted the types of differing inhabitants discovered. They each looked up as she tiptoed by and nodded to her, or bowed their heads in reverence. *I wonder why they do that.* She responded in kind to each with a widened smile. She thought back to the academy lessons, how magical creatures inhabited Sofala before the ancestors landed literally on them. A smile adorned her face as she pictured old bony with sizzling robes and burnt eyebrows. *That is one event I would love to have witnessed.*

Atesh was drawn to the next cell by a small muscled man performing an exercise routine. He had a red braided moustache that grew to combine with his beard down to his waist. His hair slicked back in a tight braid accentuated his large shoulders and buffed arms. *I believe that is a rock dweller, a dwarf.* Atesh's eyes were then drawn to a strange light emitted from the cell two down. When she moved to stand before this one, a cluster of small lights flew into different directions. She counted twelve in all. She bowed her head and watched in amazement as the lights drew together and bowed as one back. She turned her head to get a better view and the lights copied her movement. Feeling a bit weird she moved along. The next room looked empty at first till out of the corner of her eye a shape emerged. It had blended into its surroundings. "Oh a chameleon, I wonder where it was found?"

There was a tree fairy asleep curled up on a leafy limb. Her companion sat and read beside her. He looked up and smiled. Atesh blew them a kiss, she didn't know why, but she felt it was the right thing to do. The last on this row of rooms she stopped and stared. The inhabitant turned and stared right back.

"You do know it is considered rude to stare Commander, even on this forsaken island."

"Oh I do apologise sir…I was taken aback, by surprise you see."

"Surprise…after viewing all those strange creatures before me; why would my appearance cause you alarm?"

"You are a tree dweller sir?"

"The correct name is Elf. Yes, I am a High Elf."

"I was alarmed to find one such as you here. I have only heard recently of your kind. That in fact your race was not mere children's stories, but reality and here…I find that reality behind bars."

"How did you learn of this, may I enquire Commander?"

"First sir please, I would like to know your name and why you are here?"

"Well my name is Orion, the second son of 'She' who is the 'Heart'. I am a historian by profession. Why am I here?. . .Well suffice to say curiosity led me to sticking my nose where it should not have been."

"Oh and how long have you been down here Orion?"

"Well Commander what is time to an elf. We live longer than humans and count our time by the stars, which you can see; I have no access to."

"Please sir, will you call me Atesh."

"Very well Atesh, the historian in me is keen to know how you became aware of our existence, for we do not live on this side of the known world."

"I was told by King Gavin Beaumont that I have Elven blood in my ancestry, through Lailoken the prophet."

"Oh I see…you mean…the King Gavin?"

"Yes sir, though it is a long story and yes he is as powerful as ever, bones and all."

"I would love to hear that story sometime Atesh. I will leave room in my journal for this."

"It is a deal Orion, may I call you that?"

"Well Atesh of course, seeing as you be some sort of distant relation. My ancestors also came from Lailoken's father's side." Orion paced his cell, hands grasped firmly behind his back. He turned and looked at Atesh; his deep blue eyes seemed to enter her soul.

"NO! Is it that time already? Are you…I mean do you know about?"

Atesh placed her fingers up to her lips. "Yes Orion the answer to your question is yes. Please…do not say any more; I beg of you."

"Oh dear, I have been in here too long, best of luck to you Atesh. I hope to see you again."

"I am sure you will Orion, good night." The next sections of rooms/cells were directly opposite the Masters Work area which was locked and warded. There were only three. The first two held enclosed salt water ponds. The second one, closest to Marcus, Atesh understood belong to Marina, the shape-changer. The first one however she was surprised to see was inhabited by a young man who paced his cell from one end to the other. Atesh dipped her head as he stopped and glanced her way. He walked with tentative steps, his pale sapphire eyes never leaving her face.

"Out for an evening stroll Commander?"

"Something like that, please call me Atesh, may I ask your name sir?"

"Certainly, ask away." Atesh raised one eyebrow. *Oh a cheeky one.*

"Care to enlighten me or do I need to guess?"

"Oh I do like games. I will give you two chances."

"Fine, now let me get a good look at you, hmmm." The inhabitant posed this way and that for Atesh. He flexed his upper torso, then other times misbehaving and suggestive. It took a lot of control for Atesh to stay her blushing. Though she would have to admit, she enjoyed his sense of humour. "Right, now…tall, lithe of frame, muscles…impressive. Long silvery-white coloured hair with a purple streak to one side. Tanned torso, cobalt legs covered in scale type short trousers, bare feet. You have a large inside pond, a table, no bed." Atesh sat down in front of the bars and stroked a pretend beard, thinking.

He mimicked her, laughing.

"I know—your name is Blue Mischief."

"No though not a bad try, only one guess left."

"Well it cannot be Danurel, fish face is already taken."

"Oh please, do not insult the fish."

They both sniggered at this.

"Mister Fabulous that's it right, it must be correct?"

"No, though I may change it to that."

"I give up, now will you tell me before morning dawns?"

"My name is Omni-blue from the Pearl City."

"Well, there you go and where dare I ask is this, Pearl City."

"Why in the endless ocean silly, where else would it be?"

"And what race might you be Omni-blue?"

"Race…I suppose you would call me a Merman, yes that would sum me up."

"More like a pain in the rear end if you ask me"

"Marina, sorry I hope we did not wake you?"

"No we are all awake at night here; it is the only time we get to talk with one another. Blue is insufferable at times."

Atesh burst into mirth. "I do need to cut our little interlude short however. I am on my way to see another."

"Oh yes, another time perhaps Atesh, It was nice to meet you, just the same."

Atesh moved past Marina's cell to stand in front of the last one. Her demeanour turned poignant as she watched Marcus walk up to the bars. "I didn't know you were here. I thought you were safe back at the castle."

"Hello to you too…no, they took me the same time as you."

"I don't remember much Marcus after we entered Kyle's camp." Atesh placed her hand to her neck. "Are the boys safe?"

"Yes they managed to escape. Kyle then changed the rules and had us both tied up. But the rescue party wasn't Ballard it was Dan, Mason and their minions. Then Dan had Kyle killed."

"Oh no…I am sorry Marcus."

"What do they want Atesh, why are we here?"

Tears now cascaded down her cheeks. "They…want a Commander for their army; Their next game." She whispered up close to the bars.

"But why do they want us?"

"They want a realistic battle with a Commander that has a chance of winning the game this time. Dan that piece of crab-crud told the Master we were the best leaders on Sofala. So the Master has given me a choice."

"What choice Atesh? Please tell me."

"They want me to be turned into a Morphid…a creature to command from the inside. If I refuse then they will have you as their back up plan." Atesh slid down the bars to sit on the floor. Marcus held her through the metal barriers and sat beside her; as close as he possibly could. She explained about the island, the Morphids and the new upgraded game.

"It is alright. I will do this for you. You can then go free."

"I don't think that is in the equation either. I cannot let you do this for me. You are the Heir to the Kingdom Marcus. I am supposed to protect you; remember?"

"I can order you to refuse."

"No you can't. The academy does not swear fealty to the crown."

"Then I can order you, as your husband."

"I told you, I would make a lousy wife."

"I am begging you, please Atesh…don't do this."

"My oath does not give me a choice Marcus, you know this."

"I do not want to lose you. I have only found you. Please…I love you too much to see you hurt. Let me do this for you?"

Atesh placed her head on the bars as they held each other tight. Foreheads joined by the smallest of touch. "I am so confused. I remember being here when I was young. I was happy. They were good to me. How could they have done all these horrid things?" Twinges started again in her stomach. Atesh placed her hand to quieten them down.

Marcus ever the observant one, noticed her hand placement, his eyes widened with a thought. "Atesh…are you…Is there anything else I should know, anything…to tell me?"

A voice in her mind gave a warning. "*Commander do not tell him. The torment will destroy him. You are both being watched. The wizards have a sphere that they view through. Be careful what you say aloud. I wish you luck.*"

"*Thank you Marina, you always seem to be saving my bacon. I will heed your advice.*"

"Only that I love you always and forever Marcus."

"And I love you with my whole heart." Marcus traced his fingers down the side of her tear streaked face. "*Remember me.*"

"I must go now Marcus. I will try and return again." She kissed her fingers and placed them on his quivering lips.

"I love you my fire-cat." They touched their wedding rings together and a blue light surrounded them.

Atesh wiped her eyes as she strode back along the corridor and snuck up the stairs. She noticed the tears from the other inhabitants as she walked by. They had all heard and felt her pain.

Master Grey and Mason sat back from their viewer and contemplated everything they saw.

"Mason what did they do? What sort of rings do they wear on their thumbs?"

Mason sat in thought and shook his head. "That Master I cannot answer."

"I think I will go down and have a talk with this young prince. Can you find Atesh and do the same. Find out about that ring and the other for me; the third reason the Nemi malfunctioned. If what I suspect is true, it may cause a problem with the morphing spell; one we have not encountered before." Master Grey strode down to the great cells. All the inhabitants that recently had been so active were now nowhere in sight as he walked past. He stood and watched Marcus sit cross legged on the floor, hands holding his head. "Commander Marcus I thought it was time I spoke with you."

Marcus looked up to see the Wizard Master walk through the bars like air. He pulled up a cushion and sat before him.

"So you are the one who has stolen Atesh's heart. I believe only a strong, loving man could have pulled that off."

Marcus wiped his tear streaked cheeks with the back of his sleeve and raised his head to look at Master Grey face to face. "What do you want Sir." He took a sharp intake of breath at what he saw.

"Yes I believe I look like a Captain Ballard is that correct?"

"Yes Sir, it is most uncanny."

"No not really. He is, as Atesh so cleverly worked out; a direct descendant to me."

"Then you are mine as well?"

"Yes, I believe we are kin. Though I did not realise the King had married one of Angus' children. No accounting for taste I suppose. So the Queen now is a Freymore, Yes?"

"That is correct. My mother died after my birth. Brianna is the daughter of Thaddeus, the Counsellor to the King."

"Ahhh yes Thaddeus and Elias the only decent wizards from that rotten academy."

"What do you have against the academy?"

"Nothing I care to discuss with you young man. Now may I see your left hand?"

Marcus held it out though he still had a slight tremor.

Master Grey studied the ring fused to his thumb. "Marvellous workmanship, I don't recognise the material used. How did you come by this ring?"

"It was given to me by King Gavin Beaumont, made by King Jimmie Greymont."

"Do not lie to me Marcus. Kin we may be, but you are still at my mercy and I have little patience for foolishness."

"I did not lie, it is the honest truth."

"Those men have been dead for millennia."

"You are telling me nothing new sir. They may be dead, nothing but dust and bones. But they have powerful magic and bad tempers as ghosts."

"No! You say you found the lost catacombs with the kings of old?"

"Stumbled across them, spoke with them and married by them."

"Yes, I had heard they were formidable in life, but to still be haunting as spectres, that is astounding."

"That is not a word I would have used, they almost scared us witless. Then Atesh stood up to Gavin and told him off. I have never been so proud. The rings are fashioned from the bones of King Gavin and magically fused."

"Oh I see. Yes I can imagine she would fire up when roused. As a child she would place her hands on her hips and stare me down. She was so cute…so bonded for life then."

"Yes that is correct sir…will you let Atesh leave, if I take her place?"

"She has not yet given me her answer."

"I beg of you sir, please do not turn her into a creature."

"Why would you sacrifice yourself, your future, the kingdom to take her place?"

He looked at Master Grey, ran his hands through his hair, as he breathed short shallow breaths. "I…love her and would do anything to see she is not harmed."

"Well maybe we can come up with an arrangement…let me think on it."

As Grey walked away, he smiled to himself. *That was easier than I expected. Yes, Marcus will do fine. He seems an honourable young man. You would be proud of him dear brother. Married by spectres eh, Dan you are indeed a fool.*

Meanwhile Mason knocked and entered Atesh's room. Her candles were burning down as she sat on a thick rug before the fire place, crying her heart out. Mason sat down beside her and placed his arm around her shoulder. "I am sorry it has come to this Atesh."

"Then why do this Mason? I don't understand."

"It is what we do, our life's work."

"Can you tell me why?"

"It is not for me to say. We are not evil as you may believe. It might not be the way you would accomplish this task, but it is our way." Mason needed to refocus her mind on other areas. "Tell me Atesh I was admiring your rings. I recognise the academy one's on your hand, but not the one on your thumb."

Atesh lifted her hand and caressed the ring with her fingertips; the red dragon eye glowed, though in her state of mind she did not notice.

Mason however did. He furrowed his brow and wondered again how strong her innate magic may be. "That is the finger for an ancient wedding band; if I am not mistaken."

Atesh nodded.

"So you are married to…the young prince…Commander?"

"Marcus, yes Mason."

"It looks fused to your skin how did this happen?"

"It is a long story Mason."

"Sunrise will be in a couple of hours. No point going back to bed now. How about I grab some of the ancient's nectar and you can tell me the story eh?"

Atesh recounted to Mason about finding the villagers and their terrifying tale with the wild Troldwites. Then the eggs found in the cavern and the type of creatures that they appeared to resemble. She was angry as she retold about the cave in and Renny's plot to murder his fellow knights. She explained about stumbling into the ancient corridors, though she gave no details of the actual catacomb's location. He roared with laughter at the Ghosts' antics. Then he looked perplexed by their forced marriage. He was sad about Fleet, amused by the coloured Arachnopod description and angry with Danurel for again lying and manipulating the truth.

"We are honourable men in our own way Atesh; we do not lie and cheat on each other. Someday they will see what we do is for the greater good."

Atesh looked at Mason. *He really believes this. They are not evil as we all thought, they are mad. How can they justify abducting innocents and morphing them into hideous creatures? Perhaps Dan was right, like minded.*

"Do you love this prince true?"

"Mason, I love him with my whole heart and soul, that was not the problem, it was…it became complicated, my oath, my life's work, my insecurities. I believed I was unlovable, thrown away because of the way I looked. I had no family, no history. I could not believe a prince of the realm, the heir to the throne wanted to marry someone like me; well below his station."

"But Atesh you are an exquisite beauty, can you not see that? We all can."

"It was the scars and marks on my body Mason. They always seemed to undermine my body image and self-esteem."

"May I see them, if it is not too intrusive Atesh?"

Atesh lifted her shirt to expose her abdomen and back. Mason leaned forward and touched the dark pink gathered skin. "Oh Atesh, I am so terribly sorry I let this happen to you. Oh my dear little one, please accept my apology?"

"It is not your fault Mason; if not for these…I would not be the Commander. They were my driving force; urging me on to do better, to matter, to be the best."

Mason pulled her into a hug. "You are the best Atesh. Our little rabbit has grown into a wonderous, young lady. Now then, how long have you two been married."

"We were married the week before we went to Kyle's camp; to rescue the boys."

"So it has been around three moons now."

"I suspect something like that."

"Well he is lucky to have you as his wife. Now I have taken up most of the early morning. Why don't you have a nap and I will send Maisie around in a while with some breakfast for you."

"Thank you for listening Mason."

Atesh tried to sleep, but her mind was in conflict. She placed her hand on her abdomen, closed her eyes and meditated. She reached for her grandfather, where a brief discussion ensued. All was in readiness. They will be in place within the week and ready to take on the Game Master with his island of freaks. Atesh arrived at Master Grey's study later that morning. Upon entering she strolled around the game, set out before her. She looked at it from all angles, noted where ambushes would most likely occur. She surveyed the volcano, where the lava flows were active, where the cold tubes lay. She stared at the marshes, the small though thick jungle, the sand and the obsidian rocks and shuddered. *I wonder what creatures we would encounter. What would I do?*

"Ah Atesh it is good to see you working out a strategy, eh?"

"I am digesting the layout and information gathering sir."

"So you have made your decision?"

"Yes sir…I will be your Commander. I will win this battle for you."

"Are you sure now?"

"Yes sir, I can do nothing else. One small detail has bothered me though."

"And what is that my dear."

"Why would you want me to win? What happens to me if and when I do?"

"I want the game to be as real as possible. No wizards, just brawn and brains. As to the outcome, we will have to wait and see. Now we have to organise the army and some training. Tell me, for this terrain; what types of creatures for infantry, archers and cavalry you would require. The Tors can also be reshaped to fit the terrain. I will give you two weeks to be a cohesive team; the island is not large so a limited amount of men and equipment is required. One-two hundred should do it."

They sat together making notes on supplies, weapons, types of multi layered armour and lines of command. Atesh sipped the tea offered while she paced around the island memorising all its peculiarities.

"You have my knights as Morphids sir…I would like them if possible. The Tors need to be able to withstand hot conditions.

Traverse the jungle, hot sand, bubbling bogs of tar and lava tubes, maybe climb smooth rock walls."

"Good thinking Atesh. There will be some knights I can give you and other soldiers, they are battle ready, so do not fear you will have to teach them those skills."

Atesh was feeling strange, her head pounded and her vision blurred. She sat down and the light faded as she looked up at Master Grey.

"Mason you can come in now, Atesh is out to it. We need to organise our battle team. Did you discover the information?"

"Yes sir I believe we have that third complication. What will you do about the long term plans?"

"I have a gentleman's understanding with Commander Marcus; all will be as it should."

"Have you made arrangements for the other two events Mason?"

"Yes Master, all is in preparation; we need only those you desire."

"Good man and our stooge?"

"Knows nothing, he will be kept busy. Shame Dan turned out to be a charlatan. He is all air and no substance. Though I would love to be around when he uses that staff."

"Yes Mason, it will be a mess to say the least; now my dear little rabbit...a Morphid to make."

Chapter 51

The Cube 11:

Raised voices echoed down the hallway mid-morning in the Beaumont Castle. King Gareth was in a mulish mood this day. Commanders Ballard and Aiden along with Master Thaddeus were objecting with augmented volumes of their own. Ballard's report of the missing wall guards had Gareth wanting to marshal his army this very day. Thaddeus was ever the voice of reason and as the King's Counsellor he often found it a difficult job; balancing Gareth's stubborn mettle with wisdom and politics.

"Let us make preparations Gareth. We send out pigeons to all our allies and co-ordinate a three pronged attack. We need to not only obliterate the wizard made creatures running wild throughout Sofala. We need to stop the Game Master and take Mist-Wick Island perhaps one route by sea; utilising our navy and Cedric's pirates. Secondly by land with the united force of the Kingdom's soldiers and the Ashmourne knights. Then have King Angus and his Southern Island unit, combine with a few academy wizards. They can stampede the creatures' roaming the west of Sofala back up through and behind the northern border. There Red Jack and his arachnopods, coupled with Mia and her ant soldiers can route them through to the east coast. There they will face the full force of the Kingdom's alliance."

"Fine then Thad, I will concede to this plan…if we can mobilise now; today!"

"Gareth we can organise and prepare but, can we not wait a while longer? There is no point to rushing in and having a slaughter. Atesh will contact us again…I am sure of it; we need to know the layout of the Island fortress."

"You three are conspiring against me. I realise what you are saying men. But we will have no soldiers left, the way those flying creatures keep abducting them." Gareth stood and paced his room. "Can this year get any worse, I wonder?"

"Gareth please do not bring down misfortune on us now. All will turn out as it should; you know this to be true."

"You are right Thad, it is just…I am fed up to my back molars with waiting, while my people suffer."

A few days later as dawn raised her head, Master Thaddeus did indeed hear from Atesh. She spoke a little longer and reassured him that Marcus was well. She agreed with the plan and told him that the game will be coming along in short order. She gave no specifics on the type of game, or her role. She conferred that they should mobilise now, as it will take many days at a fast pace to gather near the island for the final assault. She outlined the general plan for the castle and surrounds; the types of creatures they may find and the weapons they carried. Before she said goodbye, Atesh mentioned the one thing that bothered her the most.

"How did he say it Atesh?"

"I cannot remember his exact words Grandfather, but he inferred it was the player against the game, not the Game Master. What do you make of this?"

"Yes that is not a mistake one such as he would make; let me think on it. The connotations alone make me think; all is not right on that island."

Two days later, Master Thaddeus was handed a small square package. He rotated it between his fingers as his eyes glazed over, his face set like stone. When he blinked again, two men waited with arms crossed as they leaned against the stone wall.

"Oh good timing looks like we have the game men. Come we should open it in my office."

Gareth happened to be in the corridor and spied the three men with their heads together in deep conversation. "Aha-up to no good again? You three will turn me grey; you know this."

"The game has arrived this moment Gareth; we were discussing when to open it."

"Well, now of course; the war room is the largest."

"What if sire, there is a time frame and we start it by…opening it."

"Good point young Aiden, though last time there was a letter explaining this. So how about we open the letter and see what it says."

They strode in unison down the corridor to the war room, Thaddeus taking the lead. For a two hundred and something year old man, he was spritely on his pins. "Ready my battle compatriots?"

"Just get it over with Thad."

"Always in a hurry sire," Master Thaddeus opened the package and he placed the bright coloured cube ever so gently on the table. It was encased in an ancient golden tipped script. The exterior colours changed hues from reds to blues, then yellows to greens. This sequence then repeated countless times. The men remained silent, not even daring to move; lest it activated the opening sequence. The cube however, remained closed. There were no piercing sounds of alarm, to indicate a warning to the players. The men all let out a sigh of relief. Perspiration had beaded on Thaddeus' forehead. He wiped this with the back of his sleeve, then opened and read aloud the accompanying message with a slight trembling voice. It succinctly stated the following.

"Dear Honoured Customer,

Congratulations on your fine purchase. This game will be the only one of its kind. It may be opened at any time for perusal, though the game will not commence till the next new moon. Once you have played this game, there are three more options it will rotate through for your pleasure. Remember, time does not progress whilst in the game's phase; there is no day and night; it just is. The only limitations will be your imagination. The instructions are below as before.

Enjoy and battle hard, The Game Master."

Thaddeus stood back, furrowed his brow as he scratched at his greying, close shaven beard; snuggled around his jowl. "The new moon, that is in about two weeks and three days' time; if I am not mistaken."

"That seems about right Master Thaddeus." Ballard had a quick memory for facts.

"Now to the instructions," again Thaddeus read them aloud for all to hear.

"The Cube 11:

This game's the first challenge; inside you will see.
An island with jungle, sand creatures, blood fleas.
To place this in motion; these words you must say.
'Commander be here; set the battle to play'.
You've seen them before; the Morphids and Tors.
The ship's anchored ready; to set them ashore.
To win you must capture the base at the peak.
To kill all in sight and suffer through heat
No wizards this time, just brawn, brain and guts.
Battle hard, be prepared and enjoy this last thrust."

"In plain language please Thaddeus. I have never been good at deciphering wizard."

"Oh Gareth, it is sarcasm, not wizard." Thaddeus roared with laughter. "Come let us have some liquid courage and figure out what we are in for."

"Do you think Atesh will be the Commander, grandfather?"

"Aiden this may well be true. Why else was she taken to the island?"

Gareth sat back in his chair, closed his eyes and ran his fingers through his wavy locks. He then leant forward toward Thaddeus. One hand darted out to grab his arm; with widened eyes and a pallor to his cheeks. "He wouldn't, would he? Not Marcus?"

Thaddeus shook his head; shoulders slumped as he too sat back and sighed. "I cannot be sure, but I had hoped not."

"Tell me then Thad, what do you figure the challenge is about this time?"

"Well it is not the usual war strategy setting, which I find intriguing. He has up to date been pragmatic; going along the lines of our traditional logistical battles. This one is out of the box; so to speak. Different tactics need to be employed. We will require to do some research today on jungle fighting and if it is an island, there must be sand."

"What in all Sofala does he mean by…suffer through heat?"

They all looked at Ballard then each other and stared back into their drinks. Master Thaddeus swirled his mug, his drink sloshing about inside. He then stared at the fire place with its dampened down ashes. Every now and again a spark would ignite sending a small plume of smoke up into the chimney. Thaddeus sat up straight and looked at the message in his hand.

"Oh by the ancients…give me strength. What is wrong with that man's head?"

"Thad what is it? What have you worked out?"

"Gareth, the letter said; a base at the peak. An island with a peak has, but one structure that dominates it."

Ballard and Aiden sat forward on their seats. Gareth sat fidgeting with his mug between his knees.

"And…Thad do not leave us all in suspense man."

"It is an active volcano Gareth…blood and ashes. A heat filled, lava spewing, fire monster."

The colour had drained from all their faces. Gareth downed what was left of his ale.

Ballard stood up. "We need Eamonn and any soldiers from the Archipelagos to give us some clues as to what we can expect."

"Yes, yes…good idea. We must win at all costs this time. My instincts tell me this will be the final game from the Game Master."

"Why do you say this Master Thaddeus? We have to win our battle with him first."

"Well Ballard, Atesh was concerned by a slip of the tongue by the Game Master when we last spoke. He told her it would be the player against the game. That is an odd phrase to say when the Game Master always wanted the glory for his strategy prowess."

"What do you feel it means?"

"I am not sure at all, but it bodes ill in my bones."

"Grandfather, can…I mean…with the power of this dark wizard and the crystals with the ancient spells he has been manipulating. Can…it go awry. Become an entity, perhaps a sentient being; have its own innate essence?"

"Aiden, do you mean, can the game become alive and self-aware? Well, that is a possibility I suppose. With all the magic he must be applying to accomplish interactive pieces and taking the game out of our relative time space. He may have bitten off more than he can chew. Perhaps he is no longer in control of the game?" Thaddeus creased his brow. "That is a perilous situation to be in for the players within the game. If the attackers do not win, they may all vanish into thin air; lost forever in the dark and endless void, neither living nor dead." *Oh dear ancients! Gil if this is you; what have you done, you silly, arrogant fool.*

Ballard closed his eyes; a single tear cascaded down his cheeks. He opened his mouth to speak…but nothing would come forth. With his forehead leant against the wall his hands closed to tight fists. He vowed to himself and the ancients that he would do all in his power to retrieve Atesh, Marcus and free the others. "Right we have our objectives for the mission then; life and liberty. The last battalion wave will leave tomorrow before sunrise and make their way up to the border camp. With your permission sire, Aiden and I will depart with them. I am glad now we have staggered the main force when Atesh advised. The camps have been set up by the first group. These are utilised by the others as they reach them, saving time and resources. They will all be at the rendezvous point a day shy of two weeks. You are sure you can transport the leftovers from here to the main camp when the time is right Master Thaddeus?"

"Not a problem Ballard. I have still a couple of weeks to practice taking a group with me."

Ballard paled again and swallowed hard. "No offense sir, but I will be glad to move out tomorrow."

"Me too Ballard." Aiden shook his head to clear an image.

"Me three." Gareth piped up. "Oh wait I must remain till the last moment; dash it all. Who is left to secure this village Ballard?"

"Simon has control here with a handful of the Academy's senior students to assist the soldiers. Knight Jenner will also stay behind to assist the Queen."

Ballard turned to Master Thaddeus. "Do you know how the caverns and passageways are progressing with Master Elias and his team?"

"I believe Ballard they have the main areas completed ahead of schedule. The science acolytes are assisting with the supplies and furnishings for the accommodation. It is quite stable and the security is being organised. A stone guard has been placed there at the southern end of the tunnel. Camouflage has been placed at both ends and wards are in place."

"Did I miss something Thaddeus, what was that about caverns and Stonies?"

"Gareth, Elias and his team have tunnelled under and through the Northern Boundary on the east side of Sofala. They have created a cavern with areas sectioned off for soldiers: to practice their arms, large living quarters, bathing area, food preparation and food halls. There is another cavern with enclosures for all manner of animals and stables for the war steeds. The last I heard they were placing illumination crystals throughout the passage ways, and tunnelling ventilation and smoke shafts up through the roof. It will resemble a combination of the North Mede cavern and my Sanctuary entrance. A false entry will also be placed for security. The main cavern is where we shall all assemble away from prying eyes and danger from creatures that may venture too close. I gather the Game Master has all sorts of equipment at his disposal. It would not surprise me if he has a seeing crystal. I do hope Atesh is careful."

Gareth slouched; he continued to stare at nothing in particular. His mind was certainly not in the room at this moment, it was scattered; his heart was broken. Fatigue showed on his face and his normally vibrant eyes lacked lustre, cheeks drawn and pale.

"Come Gareth, you need some rest. Ballard and Aiden will organise the gathering of information for us. We shall meet back here tonight after supper."

Unbeknown to the group of despairing men; two young, would be knights, hid again in the cavity between the walls and listened with care to all that was discussed. Israe cried his heart out in silence and was comforted by his best friend Binji. They were determined to accompany the last soldiers 'leaving tomorrow for the northern border. Preparations must be accomplished in secret. When all had turned in for the night they would rendezvous and hide with their gear and weapons. They would stow away in a supply wagon. It would be too easy to be discovered if they rode their horses.

"We need to borrow knives, a sword each, crossbows and bolts and take our slings. Oh, and make a few of our special ball-poppers."

"Our what Israe? I don't recall a ball-popper."

"You know Binji the round bags we fashioned with the small spikes inside that scattered when it impacted on contact."

"Oh yes, so you are naming them now eh?" Binji gave Israe a shove.

"Seemed like a good idea. See what else we can…ummm borrow."

"Right, let's get to it then, *Sir Knight Israe.*"

"Brothers to the end, *Sir Knight Binji.*"

"Yes sir, to the end of time."

That evening a group of the finest minds at Beaumont castle assembled. A scribe sat at one end of the large table and was busy penning all the discussions. Master Thaddeus outlined the supposed battle site layout and then asked for input from the attendees. Although the letter did state you could open and peruse the battle site, he did not wish to tempt fate by doing so. There was King Gareth, and his two personal guards. Master Thaddeus, Commander Ballard,

Commander Aiden, Captain Simon, Hunt Master Eamonn and three soldiers from islands in the archipelagos. They talked through all the different terrain they may find on this island from, hot thermal springs and mud bogs, to thick jungle and swallowing-sand.

It was many hours later when the moon was at its peak that Ballard sat with Gareth, Master Thaddeus and Aiden.

"Ballard, did they really say; razor sharp rocks at the base of the 'Fire Mountain' and rivers of boiling lava that flow to the sea?"

Ballard nodded and leant over toward Aiden and gestured widely with his hands. "Oh what about the ape-like creatures swinging from the trees? They will take a man's head off as they fly by. Oh…oh and the howls from the unknown entity, that turn the bowels of brave men to water."

"Yes and smooth obsidian glass rocks that are un-climbable towards the apex. Burning pitch bombs that spew out, at frequent intervals and sand that can swallow a man whole in mere seconds."

"What in all the ancients are blood fleas and how big are they Master Thaddeus?"

"Now do not get all hysterical on me you two. Ballard and Aiden in the spare time we have, let us consider each problem and find a solution; a strategy. I cannot however, see how the Morphids and Tors as they were in the last game fight in such adverse conditions."

"Maybe Master Thaddeus, he has morphed them again into something different."

"Yes Ballard, after seeing his other creations, anything is possible. I feel that we need Eamonn at the battle site sire. He seems to have a good sense of strategy for the jungle and possible creatures that may be hunting our men, so to speak."

"Yes I concur with that Ballard, organise that for me will you. He can travel tomorrow with the last contingent."

"Think hard on strategy and solutions to possible dangers on your ride men and we will catch up in two weeks."

Chapter 52

Battle-lust:

A silent scream raced on the wind around Sofala. Atesh's body twisted and contorted; straining against the restraints that held her in place. Her hands arced forming tonic, inhuman angles. Her conscious mind was unaware of those attempting to transform her. Her unconscious mind railed against it and fought as hard as possible. The sound assaulted the senses of Masters' Thaddeus and Elias. Even Aiden felt cold from head to toe. He did not however comprehend what was occurring. He pulled his jacket around his body closer and shivered. The sound continued as the dark spell wove around Atesh's body. It reverberated through the magical bodies of the Ancients. Back on Mist-Wick Island, the creatures remained quiet. There was an ominous feel to the air this day. Those in the cells below the castle reeled and looked about in horror. Marina held her hands up to cover her face. This could not however conceal the cascading of crystal shaped tears that chimed as they scattered on the floor around her.

King Gavin Beaumont deep within the earth's catacombs placed his hand up to his skeletal head as he turned to his kin. "Aye, it has begun…" *Best of luck wee fire-cat; may all de ancients be with ye.*

"Just a little longer and we are through Mason."

"She will survive this, won't she Master Grey?"

"I hope so Mason. I too, am fond of our little rabbit. I think this will surprise her. A great design, even if I say so myself."

"Will it have any unforeseen complications Master?"

"Well you know magic is not an exact science so…I cannot say Mason; an interesting thought though."

Atesh awoke to find she was lying on a bunk in a roomy, dim lit cabin. From the room's motion, she realised she was aboard a ship; rocking to the rhythmic sway of the sea. Crashing waves could be heard outside indicating they were near land. As she sat up and forced her eyes to focus, her head pounded and her mouth was parched. *Oh no; I am a Morphid already? I don't remember how this could have happened. The last thing I remember was sitting discussing tactics with Master Grey, drinking tea. Oh! The rotten scoundrel, he drugged my tea. Did I have two weeks of training with the creatures? I must have. So it wasn't just a bad dream?* She looked at her hands, body and legs; they appeared normal. *I am me; how is this possible?* She wore her Commander's uniform. Padded garments and chain mail hung from a chair next to her bunk. As Atesh inspected them she noticed they had two long rents down the backs. *These are no good, they are ruined. Such beautiful work too.* She walked over in a stumbling gait to look at her reflection in the dresser. What she saw near stopped her heart. Her reflection showed she had indeed been morphed. She was a muscled monstrosity and what was that behind her. She pivoted and could only catch a small glance as the image moved with her. *No it cannot be…I have wings?* She concentrated and flexed her back muscles and there in the mirror opened a pair of snow white wings with tri-coloured stripes cascading down each one; the same shades as her hair braid. *Wow wings, now that is something…so why can I not see these changes when I look at myself? I still know who I am. Is it the tear, I wonder…thank-you Mia?*

She inspected her body in minute detail from the reflection. Many differing thoughts and emotions accosted her mind. *Ugh my nose is huge…tri-coloured hair? What finger's braided this disaster? I look unkempt. I wonder if my wings will support me ,a poor time to find out in the midst of battle. I can see it now, lifts off then splat, into the mouth of a mewling monstrosity. Geeze… thank you Master Grey and Mason. Well my scars are the least of my problem now . Funny how something like this, puts everything into perspective . Right then, to business. What armoury do I have?*

On the table laid out was her equipment. There was a black dual pouch containing a scimitar and a reeve blade. *Now how am I supposed to fit that on with these blasted wings? Oh I see they are specially made to fit between, ingenious.* Beside this was a scabbard with a dual edged sword and multiple sized throwing knives. The last item sent shivers down her spine. She stared at the oversized whip with sharpened bone and metal spikes all the way along. *Oh, I hate to think what we will be up against, if I have need of this.* She touched the fingerless gloves. *Get a look at the size of these.* And the black cape with red edging and a metal helmet with a nasty looking spike on the top. *I do hope I am the size of Ballard; at least I will be a formidable opponent. I must win this…all our lives depend on it.*

Atesh laid her hand on her lower abdomen, closed her eyes in silent meditation and concentrated. *All will be fine, please hang in there…believe in me.* A loud grunting voice was heard from outside her door. She opened it to find the Captain of the ship. *I thought the sailors were human?*

"We begin in short order sir, inspection in five minutes, if you please."

Atesh nodded. *I can understand grunt…that is new.* Atesh smiled to herself but caught this in the glass contraption. *Oh, never do that again…what a sight. I near scared myself to death. She gave a snort. Oh…by all the ancients, I snort too. What would Marcus say to me? Would he still pucker up to his beloved? She squeezed her lips ready for a kiss. Ugh…even I wouldn't want to touch lips looking like that. Oh no, damned pig's wallow…is that my breath? Maybe I can scare the enemy into giving up.* Atesh amused herself with this scenario for a moment, then blew Marcus a kiss and sent it on the wind. *Right…serious now, we have a battle to win. Steady your breathing, close your eyes and find your centre.*

Atesh dressed, though she had some time of it with the wings and her padded tunic. She took a deep breath and headed topside. There standing ready and waiting were two hundred and ten Morphids of all shapes and sizes. They were arranged in eight groups of twenty five. They had a Captain for each team; five were archers, ten infantry and ten cavalry soldiers. They all had the same equipment as she carried, plus their extra specialties . The ten left overs were the scouts ; four to traverse the exterior of the island and four to spread within the interior. They were to gather information on the terrain, traps, enemy weaponry and security. The last two were runners and messengers.

"Captain, what of the Tors the Master gave us for this battle?"

"Please follow me this way sir."

As they descended into the bowels of the ship, a strange cacophony of noises and smells assaulted her stomach and tied it in knots. As they approached, the Tors all stood up and awaited their orders. Atesh maintained a flat affect upon her face, the last thing she needed was any disorder. She was well aware of the ideals of unity and respect with the chain of command. She met each one, spoke words of encouragement whilst she assessed their strengths and weaknesses. There were soldier fire ants, some sort of centrapedes and scorpioids, all fierce and battle ready. *Good, good they can all handle heat.* They each wore special thickened leather armour with areas encased with metal scales. They were covered in spikes, hard and sharp and a reinforced saddle nestled in amongst these for the rider. There was one that stood out from the rest. This ant was by far the meanest looking creature. His saddle and all leather armour had red trimmings and he possessed a set of iridescent wings. *Ahhh my transport,* Atesh wondered at the magic it took to hold all these on one ship. *It must be like our academy saddle bags. I do love magic.* "Well done captain and thank you Tors." She nodded to all, turned and departed for the deck. "We now wait for the signal captain."

"The best of luck to you and your men, sir."

"Thank you Captain, I feel we may need it." Atesh looked at the island from their place a little off shore. Her mind was focused. "Any surprises I should be aware of Captain?"

"You have twenty five Morphids in reserve sir. They will take the place of the first ones killed or injured. That is all the game allows."

There it is again, this is the third time; what the game allows. Who is running this show I wonder? "I don't recall seeing them in the hold, where are they kept?"

"I am unaware of that information sir. I have been informed they will appear as the first re-emerge back on board this ship; after their demise."

A loud noise echoed throughout the ship. All on deck looked around to each other, and then stood to attention in harmonious cadence.

"What does that humming sound indicate Captain?"

"I believe sir the cube has been activated. We will appear to the game players in short order. As you mind speak they will hear and vice-versa."

"Is there a time limit to this game? Mason and the Master did not give me any instructions?"

"No sir, as far as I am aware the game player has the control of time. Remember there is no day or night in this realm. It will always be, at this hour. This is different from all other games made, the first and only one of its kind. The fight to end them all; I was told to remind you sir."

Oh so no pressure then. "Thank you Captain."

A bright light enveloped the ship and one by one the army of Morphids and Tors disappeared. They reappeared in team formations on the white sandy beach. Atesh was the last to be transported, arriving seated atop of her fire ant.

A familiar voice stated the following. "Commanders be here, set the battle to play."

The island with all its inhabitants came into view at a gradual pace. The wind began to blow soft, with the sea breeze. Birds wove in and about the island as they caught the air currents and the jungle trees swayed. The temperature rose to an uncomfortable, humid heat. Strange animal noises emanated from the interior of the island. Not one of her command flinched or battered an eyelid. The army was formed up ready for inspection.

Atesh turned her mighty steed to meet the shadowed faces peering down on her through a distorted glass sphere.

"Commander, are you ready to battle?"

"Yes sir, we are battle ready?"

"Atesh…is…is that you?"

"Yes sir, do I not look like me?"

"Unrecognisable I am afraid to say, my dear girl."

"Who else is there with you? I can only make out faint shapes."

"*Gareth, Ballard, Aiden and Eamonn are here. Do you feel alright? You do look fierce…hideous to be true, I must say. I am sorry for your pain my dear.*"

"*I feel no pain sir. Hideous you say? Do you not like my new hairdo? What about these beauties?*" Atesh extended her wings.

"*Oh Atesh they are stunning, I hope they will come in handy.*"

"*The strange thing is, I look at myself and I see me. But I look at my reflection in what the Captain called a mirror and I see the Morphid?*"

"*That is interesting? You remember nothing of the transformation then?*"

"*No, nothing at all. In fact I lost a couple of weeks I think.*"

"*Atesh, can anyone else hear our conversation?*"

"*No one on the island can hear our conversation. What about where you are ?*"

"*No I am the only one to hear. I shall be relaying messages both ways. Do not fear. I will say no more. Is Marcus there with you as a Morphid?*"

"*No, the Master promised me if I became the Commander, he would go free.*"

"*Oh that is good news. Gareth will be pleased. Thank you for your sacrifice my dear.*"

"*Sir when the battle begins can you please call me Commander; as I have a feeling the Masters will be watching.*"

"*Yes I expect they would. We cannot let them know we are on to them, good point.*"

"*Sir, do you have a game plan or any information to assist me? You should be able to see the entire island from up there.*"

"*Yes we have put together some information for you. I know you will have a plan as well. So how about we combine them and see what we come up with ? I believe we may also have a time lag. Our time will pass faster than yours . In fact time may be static where you are.*"

Atesh ordered the scouts to go about their mission . Gather information and return . There were two sent to the outer left of the island and two to traverse the right outside edge. Their tasks were to look for strategic weaknesses and a possible way to navigate up the external incline of the fire mountain . Then observe for any enemy ships in the surrounding waters . The remaining four were to spread through out the interior of the island . Find the best route to the mountain.'s base, assess for traps and ascertain the terrain. They were not to engage the enemy; stealth was the objective.

The army she set to routine errands. They placed a large tent inside the grassed area within the first line of trees for the command post. Areas were required to be cleared and set aside for fire-pits. Hammocks set up between trees off the ground for rest and enclosed areas nearby for their Tors . Guards were set on a rotation in all directions . Archers were to be placed in trees and traps to be set, to ensure a secure boundary. The men were to inspect their armoury and ensure they did not begin to rust with the salt air. The Captains would convene in one hour to hear and discuss battle tactics for their teams.

In the meantime Atesh sat and conferred with Master Thaddeus and his cohort. *"Grandfather, may I speak with you in private for a moment? I know they cannot hear me, but I still would like no-one else in the room."*

"Certainly give me a moment to clear them out. It is supper time for us anyway and that will give me the excuse to send them out for a bite to eat. Right… all is clear, what is the problem you wish to discuss with me?"

"Can you tell me if…I mean…is there a chance that being morphed…can it harm another?"

"Atesh, I am not sure what you mean?"

"Ummm, grandfather what I want to ask is…being a female can it cause any harm…"

"Oh my…I see and…would this be the case, Atesh?"

Atesh looked at the ground for a moment and nodded.

"WHAT? Did the Game Master know? "

"No, I don't believe so."

"Atesh I don't know what it may have done to one in this condition. Are you sure? I mean…positive about this?"

"Yes, I would have to say I believe this to be the case."

"Does Marcus know?"

"No, I couldn't find the words to say. You know what he is like. He would want to be the hero. My knight's oath prevents me from accepting his sacrifice, even for this It was my duty to safeguard him; my destiny to be here; not his."

"Oh my dear child, you truly do us all proud. We need to win at any cost, especially now. You must take extra care."

"I shall try."

Atesh knew that fighting through unknown vegetation was a danger in itself. That strategic ingenuity and simplicity were the key to success. Never take anything for granted. What concerned her and the Team Captains was the unforeseen enigma of the game being in charge. The Wizard, Game Master was at least predictable and kept to a strict routine of military battle strategy. After conferring with Master Thaddeus, Atesh was now aware of the specialised tactics of guerrilla warfare. This she felt was dirty fighting, but looking at the terrain and the secrecy of the enemy forces, she conceded this was the only way to fight this time. She must win at any cost. Although this game simulated reality in battle, she was glad that no actual soldier died. They disappeared from the game to reappear upon the original ship and await the outcome.

Only three of the four scouts returned from their interior observation mission. They were covered in large welts, from biting insects. Atesh noticed tiny score like marks upon their exposed arms and legs, something they would not normally take notice of, or worry about. But in this humid environment she knew fever could kill quickly and silent. It was unfortunate that one of the scouts later died from these insignificant wounds. Master Thaddeus suspected a poisonous plant was secreted amongst the ground foliage. As he crawled through, the poison would have slid under his skin with the tip of the plant spikes. His skin turned sallow and then gangrenous black. His face and then torso swelled up. He died an agonising slow death, till his organs imploded. Atesh noted he has traversed the right side of the interior. Any Morphid or Tor sent in that direction in future would need protective clothing, covering their entire body.

Eamonn suggested rubbing warm mud onto any exposed body parts. Then as it cooled it would dry solid and provide protection from the hot sun and biting insects. It had the added bonus of reducing blood fleas from attaching, thus reduce fevers, infection and death. Atesh then sent one team into the mud bogs to collect hessian bags of the thick black mud.

Two further teams were sent in to cut a path through the mid-height vegetation, beneath the tall trees, around their army's position. They needed to reduce the risk of a stealth attack by the enemy. Atesh requested they keep the noise as low as possible. And to set up pits/trenches with sharp stakes within and string rope vines along between trees with shells at either end. Any creature trespassing across the vine would send the shells knocking against each other and alert them to an enemy attack. All soldiers carried their weapons and shield at all times as well as a water pack. They were not to refill with any water found on the interior of the island, as it would likely be poisoned by the enemy.

Their plan was to surprise the enemy by striking in silence, run and feint a retreat with two combined infantry teams. Draw the enemy out and lead them into all manner of traps. A large group would be set up a short way within the jungle awaiting their smaller teams to run past. Then they would close ranks and attack in force. The fiercest Morphids would be concentrated in the middle, utilising the tight phalanx formation; with halberds, short javelins, multi-spiked spears and short swords. They would be flanked on either side by the centrapede cavalry, camouflaged and hidden throughout the high jungle bracken. Some of them would carry crossbows, others with scimitars or reeve swords. The use of convex shields would protect the riders against spears or other sharp thrown objects.

Archers would be placed in strategic positions up amongst the trees. Master Grey remade these Morphid archers for speed and durability. They carried think roped vines and grappling hooks in a back pack; as the first reasonable weight bearing branch of the tall jungle fenestrated trees, were some distance off the ground. They were competent with tree jumping or vine swinging from one tree to another. The fronds were thick with palm type leaves allowing a good environment for hiding unseen. They were not under any circumstance to climb on or jump to a tall evergreen tree. Thaddeus explained they were often rotten on the inside and would fall without notice.

Atesh sat on her mighty Tor, nestled in quiet solitude within a high branch of the large palm tree. *I am glad this is not in the realm of reality. There is no way a tree would normally hold such large creatures as we seem to be.* This was their first flight together. She realised that having wings was a disadvantage beneath a jungle canopy. Her wing spread was too large and she would become a target. Atesh took out her crystal enhanced spy glass. She noticed the tower was ringed by large grey rock type creatures that swayed back and forth on their four stumpy legs. "Is that a war dance? Or perchance the garderobe is occupied."

A slight vibration by the Tor beneath her, took Atesh by surprise.

"Was that you laughing, oh mighty steed?"

"Sorry sir, I could not help myself."

"May I ask your name?"

"You would be unable to pronounce it sir. I am afraid your tiny human tongue would be tangled; akin to those sand wrigglers. You may call me Van sir."

"Well Van who are you?"

"I was the General of Mia's royal guard."

"Oh, were you abducted or did Mia send you?"

"I volunteered. It was I that led the survivors past the two legs' castle, after our home blew apart. I was aware of your struggle within. We, our race, are forever in your debt. I therefore felt compelled to do this for you,for our queen and our existence . I am to be her consort after this game, as long as we win of course."

"Then I am honoured General Van to have you on my team. Do you also wear a tear? Is that how we can communicate?"

"Correct sir."

"Can you tell me Van? What are those rock creatures?"

"Nasty critters we call them Armadilly's sir. They are covered in a hard battle armoured coat. If they grab hold of you, there is no letting go. They will keep chomping with their second and third set of teeth and swallowing. They walk with fast short swaying type steps and near impossible to kill. I believe if you can push them over, upside down they are vulnerable. Their abdomen is soft and their back shell weight holds them thus. We used to challenge each other as younglings, who could spin them the fastest."

"Wow that would be a dangerous game Van?"

"We were young and foolish sir."

Scanning lower Atesh saw two upright lizard creatures darting between the large black boulders at the base of the mountain. Another similar in style, flew down from the tower and gave orders to those hiding. Spears were hoisted in rhythm with their raised, strangled gurgles. They were readying for an assault. Atesh observed the flaming lava flows were concentrated on the midline and right side of the fire crater. The lava tubes to the left were not active at all, some even disintegrated. The dry creek bed or so Atesh first believed, was in fact that mass of writhing sand worms Van spoke of. Every now and again one would untangle itself and wriggle out into the sun. Its many tiny appendages raced towards the jungle. It had one large eye. When it opened its mouth, row upon row of small sharp teeth were exposed. A loud whistle was heard, as a blazing fire ball raced through the air. It had been flung out from the tower's interior. It landed on top of the escaping sand creature. The screams of the target melded in with the yells and cheers erupting from the tower.

"Well…that wasn't nice. I guess they are perfecting their aim." Atesh turned her face up to the players. She explained what she saw from her advantage point. They decided it would be best if they go in for one major offensive to bring out all the enemy creatures. Then retreat and hope some follow them back into their traps.

Ballard noticed a few small openings half way up the outside of the sheer rock face on the left side of the island. *"It may be old tunnels or lava tubes. Create a diversion with a second attack. Keep the majority of the enemy busy while you and Van head for those caves."*

Atesh whirled around as she heard a clamour below. Through the trees she observed one, then more of her Morphids jumping about, clawing at their helmets.

Thaddeus looked on in concern. *"What is going on Commander?"*

"Sir I am unsure. General Van says to stay up here and be silent. I will do as he suggests."

A swarm of black flying insects appeared. They attacked the group digging the traps. They had crawled beneath the soldier's helmets and into their ears. One by one the Morphids slumped to the ground. Blood poured from their nose, eyes, ears and mouth. With the spy glass Atesh watched in horror, as swollen black slugs exited the Morphids. They slid out with the last of the frothy life essence. They had two sharp pointed stingers on their tail, two beady eyes and a forked tongue. They flew away at a slower pace and lower altitude. Engorged with whatever they ate inside the Morphids head, towards the right side of the island.

"Commander they are Earwiglarons. They burrow through the ear up into the brain. They gorge themselves on the living tissue. The digging vibrations must have attracted them as they live in the warm sand. Not often seen under the cool canopy of a jungle."

Atesh flew down with General Van and inspected the traps. The dead disappeared. "Well that is fifty five soldiers so far. The outer island scouts have also not returned." Atesh set the next group to completing this task, at a quieter and slower pace. She also had the two runners tear up cloth into small wads, to place underneath all helmets, to cover their ears. Hand signals will be utilised more often now. *This game is one big insect meal. We need to end this. The men will attack in short order, the first offensive sir."*

"Be careful Commander. Stay well back and watch the types of creatures and weaponry that is utilised."

Atesh knew the enemy were gearing up to attack, so this was the most opportune time to strike them while they were riled up enough to follow them back into the traps. The Morphid and Tors lined up on the sandy beach in their respective groups.

Atesh gave a heart-warming and stirring speech. "Men let the first battle begin, remember the plan and battle hard. Do me proud." *I wonder how many of these Morphids are my knights? If we win this, I can set you free.*

The first two partial teams commenced their assault. These consisted of six Morphid archers, three to the left and three to the right of the main force. Ten cavalry soldiers on fire-ants and scorpioids and ten infantry. They had crept up silent through the jungle to near the dry creek bed. The enemy lizards were gathering, preparing for their campaign. The Morphid soldiers threw exploding spike bombs. They soared over the rocks into the lizard's hastily made dugouts. They reacted swiftly, but with disorder. Some dashed out aflame, others missing body parts. The lizard officers, distinguished by their wings appeared. They grabbed at their own soldiers and hurled them forward, all the while yelling garbled orders. They sent their army out to counter the attack. There was so many of them oozing out from behind shadowed boulder trenches into the bright sunlight, it caused countless to become blinded, dazed and confused. They pushed and shoved each other vying for a place amongst the masses. Several fell into the writhing mass of entangled sand-mire worms. Others were dragged into the throng by a myriad of long tentacles . They were entwined in a twisting, snarling mesh and sank into the pit of horrors. Morphid bolts from their cross bows shot with deadly accuracy . Knives found their way into the eyes and throats of many lizards. They screamed loud in fury as they lumbered towards the Morphids and engaged them in a hand to hand bloody battle.

Atesh sat atop of General Van and both watched the battle with curiosity. They remained hidden from view. They were both distressed being out of the main fight. It was unnatural for them to be standing in safety while the Morphid and Tors fought for their lives, game or not. Atesh itched to be down there amongst them; leading them. She did not want these Morphids to die fighting up so close and personal. She signalled for stage two of the plan. One of the Captains sounded the horn. The Morphids disengaged themselves from the fight and ran for the trees. Spiked fire bombs rained down from the trees to allow the Morphids an avenue to freedom. The lizard creatures were however swift on their feet and hot on their heels. The lizard officers stopped and looked around. One pointed towards the mountain crater. They turned as one and fled back behind the boulders.

"What are the officers doing Van? Are they running away?"

"Cowards it would seem, Commander."

Fire balls from the mouth of the volcanic mountain began to rain down on the battle as the Morphids retreated to the jungle. These lava bombs were killing lizards and Morphids alike. The mountain did not seem to care to whom it targeted and devoured. The island shuddered and the ground twisted in anger. The Morphid and Tors left alive ran in an awkward manner. Often falling to the ground as the land swayed to and fro. They eventually bolted around the trap and into the trees.

"Perhaps Van, we have angered the game?"

"Anything is possible sir, maybe a little tantrum."

They both sniggered at that. "Interesting thought."

As the island quietened the Morphid army coalesced together and ran to meet the lizards beneath the canopy of the trees. The fiercest Morphids led in front, blood lust at its highest. The lizards did not expect to see a horde of aggressive Morphids, teeth bared racing towards them. Many were unnerved by this and broke from the group to retreat. It was unfortunate, but they were pushed back in by the sheer number forging forward. The lizard creatures were numerous and with two sets of arms bearing swords, they should have been a formidable opponent. Their only save was their thick, difficult to penetrate, hides. Their training had to be less than satisfactory. For no matter how large an opponent seemed, without discipline and weapon training they could not win.

With no word of warning, ape like creatures swarmed down from the trees. They jumped onto the backs of the Morphids and with their sharp razor like claws were able to partially decapitate them with one swipe. The Tors protected by their armoured spikes were scored, though some wings were ripped apart. Arrows and bolts rained down from the Morphid archers with deadly accuracy. They in turn often had to fight hand to hand with the ape creatures. The clanging of metal on claws reverberated throughout the trees. The officers now back in the tower sent fire balls racing through the first portion of the jungle which was the extent of their reaching arm. This only caused lizard soldiers near the back of the pack to die a horrid flaming death.

Atesh spun around atop of Van as she heard a grinding sound It became louder by the minute. Then out of the sand beneath the fighter's feet spewed a swarm of Earwiglarons, blood fleas and spiders. They all attacked with vicious intent. The Morphids and Tors had prepared well with wads of cloth placed firm against their ears and their uncovered body parts were encased in the dried mud concoction. No stinger or bite could penetrate this covering and the blood fleas could not attach. In frustration they turned their attention and appetite to the ape and lizard creatures. They now bore the brunt of this attack.

Atesh could not contain herself any longer. She and Van dived into the fray. She led the centrapede cavalry left standing. They squeezed the battle from both sides into a narrow corridor. They often turned the mangled melee into a particular direction. The Morphids would retreat a short way, then as the enemy followed they would spring their deadly traps. Fresh Morphid units were sent in to relieve those injured. Atesh using both her scimitar and reeve blade swung and sliced all within her reach. Her wings were useless here under the tree canopy. But joining the battle drove her army into fever pitched frenzy. The defenders started to retreat when all were beyond exhausted. Atesh signalled to follow suit. She did not want to overtax her surviving Morphids and at least it brought out of hiding the game's army and certainly showed their weaknesses.

"Commander was that smart to join in the battle?"

Atesh looked up at her Grandfather and smiled. *"Possibly not, but it did feel good. Sir they seem to have many more at arms then we do. This is not the usual is it?"*

"Commander, this was a concern for us here as well. It would seem the game is cheating, a poor loser, to win at any cost. That Commander makes this game very dangerous indeed, an unknown quantity. Rest up a bit then we go to the next part of the plan. Re-organise your soldiers and attack in force. While they are diverting the attention to the battle you and General Van sneak away to the left side of the island."

"Yes sir…do you have ideas as to how we get passed those armadilly creatures ? I do not like the thought of being eaten alive?"

"Never seen the likes before, perchance General Van can assist you there the best."

Master Grey and Mason watched the battle from the sphere on board their ship.

"Master…there is something odd going on?"

"Yes Mason, the game is losing and is pulling out all its dirty tricks. They are in fact cheating. Their army is leaderless, unlike ours. Atesh is wonderful, is she not?"

"Yes Master, one of a kind."

"She will win this game, of that I am now positive. I have to admit of being more than a little miffed. I do not like my good name sullied by that abomination. I have never cheated with a game in two centuries." He looked at Mason's sad face. "We will meet her again sometime Mason. Do not despair."

Atesh and Van snuck away a short time before her army set out on their second objective; the obliteration of the enemy and capture the tower on top of the volcano. The command she allocated to one of the surviving Captains. They consolidated their teams as they had only one hundred and six left of the original group and four of the reserves. So they had one hundred and ten Morphids and forty Tors. The rest sat on the ship and watched with trepidation. The Morphids all knew of Atesh's secret plan and all wished her success.

She and Van made good time, keeping near to the ground. She did not want ground vibrations to alert the enemy or be seen flying in the air. Atesh was content to sit upon General Van. She found her wings cumbersome and tended to slow down her reaction time. Her only injuries sustained were a few shallow score marks upon her flesh and slightly deeper ones to her wing membranes. So using them was a risk Atesh was not willing to risk at the moment; they may well fail or tear further. Her heart pumped wild within her chest as she noticed they edged closer to the cliffs.

Scanning over to the left, she pointed. "Van what do you make of that?"

"I am not sure Commander? Should we investigate or divert around?"

Atesh drew out her spy glass and swore to the ancients. "Van that is the two scouts, they look stuck in something. We need to check if they are still alive?"

They flew down and landed within the trees. Close by two Morphids stood upright. One sunk up to his chest, arms splayed out in sand; the other to his midriff. Atesh looked up to Thaddeus for advice.

"Commander, I am told it is a substance called sucking sand. The more they move the quicker they go under and drown. Find safe hard ground by using a stick to prod before you walk. It is normal in the desert countries."

"Thank you sir." Atesh pulled out a length of vine rope from her back pack. She called to the Morphid with his arms out of the sand. "We will hover above you. Grab the rope and tie it around your chest, under your arms and we will pull you out."

"Yes sir. It is too warm here. I have not much energy left sir."

"Come on grab the rope, slow movements." He did as command-ed and Van slowly rose up off the ground. Atesh had tied the other end to her pommel and she grabbed the rope and pulled with all her might. The sucking sound rose in volume as the Morphid alighted from the hungry sand trap. He was set down on the hard grassed area where he collapsed exhausted. Atesh threw him her water pack and next went after the second scout. "I am going to try and wrap this rope around your chest, do not move or we both will sink."

He nodded his understanding.

Atesh again tied her end to the saddle then flipped upside down and hung from Van by her feet entwined in one her stirrups. He hovered a small distance above the scout and Atesh with gentle movements, manoeuvred her hands under the sand and around his waist. She tied the rope as tight as she could. It was thick and indeed warm under the quagmire.

"Now General Van, gentle…that does it." Atesh's body jerked forward further into the sand. "Oh damn it and dragon balls. Pull now General, move us out. It is trying to suck me under as well." It was a great tug of war. Van was powerful and only hoped the rope held. They were both eventually pulled free with a loud, *'pop'*.

Atesh gave the two men instructions on how to stay alive and return to camp. They each tore cloth for their ears and the mud for their uncovered body parts was found in a bubbling pool not far away. After a short break Atesh and Van continued on their journey.

"Thank you Van for your assistance."

"Not many Commanders I have known would have risked all to save a mere scout. Or thank their mighty steed. You are indeed a true *Knight* and I am honoured to be here with you and call you friend."

"Thank you Van that means a lot to me; Yes, friends it is."

Atesh looked up to Thaddeus and the others and took a bow.

"Well done Commander. Though I will tell you we had a few heart stopping moments and groans, watching you. Then a couple of rolling eyes occurred…show off, was the word bandied around." Thaddeus laughed.

Once they reached the steep cliffs of the island's outer edge, they flew down to inspect the cave like structures. Two were too small for them to enter and then they noticed another one further on. It was a reasonable size and in direct line with the back of the main mountain. They flew in and Atesh dismounted, her weapon unsheathed. The tunnel was cool and unused so with care they continued on. Van decided he should go first as his eyesight was better underground in the dark. Atesh attached a rope and walked beside him. They walked at a steady pace with a slight incline. The ground was textured and uneven, yet smooth to the touch. Atesh could make out shapes in the tunnel now and again. Small crystals imbedded at irregular intervals within the walls illuminated the areas in front of them. She observed the unusual marks covering both sides of the walls.

"Those marks Commander are called step marks. They show the depth of the lava flow when this tube was active. We need to be careful that the actual fire flow is not a few feet behind the walls or below what we walk upon. If it feels spongy do not place your full weight upon it. In the past we had lost a whole soldier unit when they had walked on lava pads. These were cool to touch, but still soft in the middle. They broke with the slightest weight. They fell to their deaths into the active flowing lava."

After walking for a while in silence they noticed the air was thicker to breathe and the walls were not as cool. They in fact felt warm to touch.

"There must be a lava chamber nearby, Commander."

As they turned a sharp corner it opened into a vast cavern. The air vibrated with crystal power. Large clear, pink and yellow glass gems sparkled from the walls and ceilings; simulating the stars in the sky.

"What are these gems Van?"

"They are diamonds Commander, a rare jewel. We only ever see these inside a fire monster such as this. It is said they are sentient beings, so we do not touch them."

Atesh felt compelled. Her eyes glazed over and she reached out her hand to stroke one. It sparkled all the more and whispered to her.

"Welcome, she who is of the prophecy. We have a gift for you as you pass our home…to remember us by." The gem morphed into an elegant hand and within she held two exquisite diamonds, one pink and one blue. "We wish you and your little one's all the best my dear.

We do not approve of our island being used for such an evil purpose." This sentiment was echoed in whispers around the cavern.

Atesh held the gems and felt the love within. "Thank you ancient beings, these gifts will be treasured."

Van stood still and watched in awe. They wandered next through a narrow tunnel where old tree root systems still clung to the myriad of stones and rubble entwined within the walls. The atmosphere was stifling hot. The strange odour stung their eyes and throat. Atesh was startled by an explosion not too far beyond the wall she stood beside. She stepped over to the wall to listen further. But as she did, the location her foot touched disintegrated as she placed her weight upon it. She started to fall through the floor. Without hesitation she threw herself forward . Atesh then reached out with extended arms . She grasped with one hand the taught rope. With the other she tore at the floor's hard braid, infused shiny surface, vying for a decent grip. She held her breath as her hands tried to stall her plummet to a certain fiery death. It was only the quick thinking of Van that saved her life. He used his wings to propel his body forward. He dragged Atesh back up, out of the heat filled lava flow tube. She lay on the cool floor up the tunnel. her heart racing, ashen faced and drenched in perspiration. She drew in a deep breath. Van lay down beside her. His head bowed. Atesh placed her hand on his face and planted a kiss on his cheek and nodded to him a thank you. They both drank from their water packs and recuperated their energies before they moved on.

They came to the end of the tunnel and up ahead sat a large mass of twisted cooled lava. It extended from floor to ceiling.

"Ah that is our way out Commander. It is known as a *Lavacicle*. This goes to the surface."

Atesh sat again on Van and he traversed this rock formation with little effort. Near the exit Van peered out through the hole and found it was hidden by large yellow coloured boulders. A little way ahead was the tower surrounded by the Armadilly creatures. There was a fierce battle on the left side of the tower. The Morphids had taken the upper hand with the fight and had battled all the way up, close to the tower. While the occupants were concentrating on that offensive Atesh hoped they would ignore the back of the building. They raced to the tower wall. As they commenced the climb up the side, Van shuddered and fell backwards to the ground. Atesh was thrown clear. Hanging from his foot was an armadilly creature, munching away on Van's leg. He groaned in agony.

"Van, how do I get him off you?"

"Commander it is impossible. No one has ever succeeded. I am dead. Go now finish what we have started. May…I ask a boon…"

Atesh winced as the slurping sounds of being eaten alive made her stomach turn. Blood and bone fell from Van's leg; "Anything."

"Can you…end…please…?" Van turned his head to Atesh a tear ran down his face. He exposed his neck.

"Oh no, Van. Please how can you ask that of me? There must be a way to help you?"

"Please Commander…"

The crunching reached higher to the top of his leg now. Others waddled over to join in the feast.

Her face streaked with cascading tears and black mud. "I am so sorry Van. We will meet again after this is all over." She drew out her sword. With a clean stroke she plunged her scimitar into his neck severing the artery. His eyes glazed over and became vacant. A smile parted his lips. He then vanished.

The creatures upset they had missed on a meal headed for Atesh. She raced for the wall kicking them away as she started to climb the outside. A yell from behind, had her pivot her head to see an armadilly creature with its maw opened ready to grab her leg. A Morphid jumped into the air and landed on the monstrosity and they rolled away down the outside of the mountain. Atesh recognised him as one of the scouts she had rescued earlier from the sand pit. *Phew that was too close.* She used her wings to manoeuvre up the outside of the wall. Just as she neared the top her wing membrane tore. She scrambled to grasp hold onto any joint deep enough for her fingers to anchor. She used her one good wing left to keep herself upright. Looking back down, the armadilly were climbing on top of one another to try and reach her. With torn bleeding hands she dug deep into the wall grooves to heave her body up and over the lip of the tower.

With perspiration trickling down her face and chest heaving from the exertion, she raced down the steps into the courtyard. Atesh pulled herself up onto the dais where the blood gem was encased. Lizard officers raced out from their covered position and headed over to defend their prize. Atesh unsheathed her scimitar and roared with anger as she headed for the largest. She noticed out of the corner of her eyes, the other slimy lizard waited for her back to turn; so it could sneak up and attack in a cowardly fashion. She somersaulted over the head of the leader and sliced his head from his torso as she pivoted. *Yes I still got it; even as a gross Morphid.* The smaller one turned and ran away. Atesh smashed the outer glass partition and grasped the blood stone. A scream reverberated throughout the island. The volcano spewed lava, ash and steam high into the air. Then the game slammed shut.

Chapter 53

The Battle for Mist-Wick Island:

The witnesses to the end of the game sat still in horrified silence; as the game disappeared before their eyes. The players took a while to wake out of their morbid thoughts and all except Master Thaddeus rejoiced. He sat in quiet contemplation.

"Thad, what's wrong? Why are you not excited and celebrating our win?"

"Yes our win." Thaddeus stared ahead. "We did win, didn't we? Gareth, I believe we may have a problem."

"Why is that Thad?"

"It was too easy sire."

"You call all those critters too easy, Master Thaddeus?"

"I do Ballard. Indulge me if you will. Let us look at the bigger picture for a moment. The Game Master has always won the battles; not because of trickery or guile, but with strategic prowess, great battle scenarios and formidable opponents."

"I agree with your summation Master Thaddeus, but Atesh was the better strategist with this battle."

"No Ballard I disagree entirely. You are perhaps too young to…*OH MY* that's it."

"What is it? You have lost me Master Thaddeus."

"Aiden my dear boy, your idea about too much magic being utilised to produce such an extraordinary game, may be correct. The cube I believe has become self-aware; its own entity. It was not the game master we were up against; it was the game itself."

"How in all Sofala did you come to that conclusion Thad?"

"Well Gareth, think on the battle we just witnessed. Not the normal, thought provoking battle of games past. It was one of simplicity, dirty tricks and deviousness. Guerrilla warfare is not an honourable battle tactic. Then look at the defenders. Were they the usual, formidable, battle hardened and organised warriors? No, Atesh was pitted against a myriad of insect types, raw nature itself and lizards with a lack of self-discipline and leadership. It was infantile."

"Infantile, Master Thaddeus?"

"Yes Ballard, if my theory is correct. We played against an entity that has never been to battle before. A child that wanted to win by any means. It used sheer numbers to try and overwhelm its enemy. It in fact, cheated. When it was apparent that it lost the game, it threw a child's tantrum. The volcano exploded and it let out a high pitched scream. It slammed the game shut with anger and frustration, and then the cube disappeared. I do not believe for one moment this cube will bow out with grace. There will be a reckoning; mark my words."

"Well Thad, we shall have to worry about that when we capture the Game Master."

King Gareth, Master Thaddeus, Commanders' Ballard and Aiden set out to join and co-ordinate their various teams for the battle on Mist-Wick Island. King Gareth and Master Thaddeus were leading the main combined military force onto the island with Aiden's kingdom knights as the vanguard. Master Elias with his Ashmourne academy knights and wizards lay in wait for the stampede of abominations, headed their way; a little north of the island. To gather and herd the array of wizard creatures towards Master Elias, there was a need for the ancients to combine with allied forces. Queen Mia, her fire-ant soldiers and Red Jack the Arachnopod consort with his array of older children had commenced the round up in the north and south western regions a few days before. The eastern side was managed by King Angus of the Southern Islands and Prince Fynton of Tyral with their combined forces. They all had the creatures stampeding towards the north east coast.

The Pirate King Cedric and his main vessels set up a blockade not far off the north-eastern shore. They were assisted by the Kingdom naval ships. Together they also encircled the island of mist, so no creature or other inhabitant could escape. It was fortunate that over the past season Cedric's magisters had discovered a new weapon to be utilised aboard his ships. It consisted of long metal tubes infused with explosive yellow powder and ignited with barrels of steam under pressure, they called these the Chief's flame throwers. The creatures that escaped the academy wizards would be blasted to ash as they tried to enter the water.

Ballard and ten first battalion *Kingdom knights'* raced to the seaside to board the Royal flag ship, commanded by Admiral Atien Beaumont; a cousin to the King. They were to be transferred to the island in stealth; landing on the far side. Once there, they were required to find their way around to the underground jetty and hidden interior passages. Their tasks were to free Prince Marcus and the other prisoners in the lower third level cells and then assist with taking of the castle. Ballard knew the one problem with a plan such as this, was the unexpected entity of the enemy. *There's always a surprise.*

As soon as the naval vessel entered the mist, a loud ear piercing alarm sounded. This brought most on board down to their knees. Hands held up to their ears. The ship refused to respond to the helm, though the Admiral and the first mate fought it with all their might. The Dragon's Breath continued to change course on her own. All the sailors and Ballard's team could do was hope for the best. The further into the eerie vapour they went, the louder battle noises were heard, emanating from within the mist. Then without notice, silence enveloped them. The vessel slowed down with no warning; abrupt and harsh. The bow then dipped at an alarming angle. The stern rose up out of the water, tossing the men and anything not tied down forward into each other. Then she slammed back down washing the deck with seawater. The sailors shook their heads and scurried to the commands of their Admiral. Ballard and his men were entangled together and soaked.

"Berend, will you get your smelly foot out of my face man. Sweet lady of mercy that stinks"

"Sorry sir, but my face is stuck in a place you really don't want me to describe to ye. I shall have nightmares for a week."

Vykter and the rest of the men sniggered and untangled themselves, pushing and shoving each other.

A low groan of disaster was heard. The sailors' eyes went wide, their faces in a grimace. Atien braced himself and yelled out for all to hang on for dear life. The hull though built shallow on the draft, ground against the sand bed and rock. Her wood buckled in anger and splintered as they were tersely pitched starboard. The mist dissolved before their eyes and there above loomed Mist-Wick Island; they had been cast up onto the surrounding rock strewn beach.

Ballard picked himself up and looked over the side. "Well that is one way to get ashore without getting your feet wet." Ballard and his team departed and left the Admiral to assess the damage and assist any injured crew. The jetty was now within reach. As they clambered over the side and down the rope ladder, a terrified shout from the boy aloft in the crow's nest had them all craning their necks to look upwards. A large black winged creature heaved his package at the ship. A soldier and his steed had been scooped up from the battle field and the young man screamed all the way down; till they hit nearby.

Ballard winced and shook his head. *Ooooh by the ancients that would have hurt.*

The knights stood silent for a moment in recognition of the young man's bravery. As the knights reached the entrance to the underground chambers , the cave gave off an eerie , ominous feel; a cold shiver travelled up and down their spines. A dank rancid smell assaulted their noses as they scanned the area for creatures lurking in ambush . The knights kept close together as they wove their way up and down the stairways and long narrow passages . All the tunnels were illuminated by light crystals placed at intervals along the seeping walls. They kept to the left tunnels as instructed by Atesh . Ballard was glad he had a rough map by which to follow , as there were stairs and passageways going in all directions . It would be easy to get turned around and lost. They noted many rooms filled with all manner of stores; food, farming equipment , even a smith 's workroom and armoury . A *self-sufficient community*. They neared what Ballard had figured would be the stairway to the third level cells; beneath the castle proper and the royal prisoner. Voices echoed along the rock walls, they were heading their way. He motioned for the men to bunch up closer and press up against the wall. He activated his academy blending ring. With swords unsheathed they waited. Their beating pulses resounded in their ears. Their breaths came short and rapid. Adrenaline infused mind and soul. There were six distinct voices. As they came into view Ballard and his men stared in astonishment. This was not the enemy they sought, but a group of talking rodents. They were as tall as a man's thigh, exhibiting human traits. The three women wore long multi coloured dresses and bonnets . The males were dressed in brown trousers with suspenders, white tunics and boots. They stopped arguing as they saw the knights.

"Oh my." The female rodent in the lead placed her paw up to her heart. "Excuse me kind sir, could you please point the way out of here. I'm afraid we are a trifle lost…my husband here will never ask for directions; too proud you see."

"My dear, I have told you countless times. It is the journey that is the adventure; not the destination."

"Yes dearest, that is all well and good. Normally I would indulge you, but today there is a battle we must flee from. Have you seen the teeth on some of those creatures up there? Horrid, just horrid." She turned again toward Ballard. "Well sir, can you find it in your heart to assist us?"

"Certainly Madam." Ballard pointed his hand towards the way they had come from.

All the knights copied their Commander's hand gesture.

"Thank you so much gentlemen." They all bowed their heads, and then scurried past towards the jetty. "Quiet sort wasn't he. Unusual for a human, though for a moment I thought it was the Master. Near gave me a heart turn."

Ballard looked at his men with furrowed brow and a smirk on his face. "Not a word men. Do you hear me; not a word." *How were they able to see us, we were supposed to be invisible to all. Maybe in this damn castle our magic does not work.*

Sniggers were the only noises he heard. Berend held his hands up to his mouth to stop laughing. As tears rolled down his cheeks he snorted, covering the man in front in wet slimy boogifers.

"Berend get a grip man. Have you never seen a…talking ah, mouse before?"

"Well sir…can't say I have." Hysterics broke out though they kept it as quiet as possible.

"Oh and wipe that snot off Vykter's back. We don't want that getting in our dinner tonight."

The men went quiet at that and glared at Berend. They climbed the stairs two at a time till they reached about half way. Nature decided it was her time to perform her part in this fiasco. She moaned and groaned in apparent frustration. The foundations swayed. The floor buckled. Then the roof rained down rocks and rubble which sent the knights sprawling in all directions. A loud explosion up ahead sent dust and debris cascading down the stairs in a fierce storm. The knights hit the ground and covered their heads. In short order they unburied themselves and shook off all bits of dust and debris from their hair and clothing. They now crept over rocks and cell wreckage till they reached the landing to find the last two rooms destroyed and the passageway blocked. Ballard knew Marcus was in the last cell and he sprang forward to search through the mess. There was no body found. *Where could he be? I am sure this is the one he was in.*

A moaning was heard nearby, the knights dug and scraped furiously to unearth the person buried beneath the collapsed remnants. Ballard found that the body they dug out was of a young lady. He carried her out into the corridor, opened his water bag and gave her small sips and tried to wipe her face clear of dirt with the ends of his shirt. She looked up into Ballard's eyes and smiled. Ballard had never seen such amazing emerald green eyes in all his life. Her smiling face melted his heart. In a place such as this, he found his *one*. He was smitten. Even with the dust caking her features, his heart fluttered.

"You are safe now. Are you injured?"

When she tried to talk coughing occurred and tears welled up in her eyes. She held onto the sides of her chest as if in intense pain. She spoke to Ballard in his mind.

"I will be fine soon enough. I think my ribs may be broken. I can however selfheal in time. Thank you all for assisting me. Are you a friend of Marcus'?"

"You know the prince? Where can we find him? We were informed he was in this cell, but it's empty."

"He has been gone a few days now. The Masters' took him away when they left us here."

"What may I call you, my lady?"

"My name is Marina…you are Commander Ballard, yes?"

"How would you know that?"

"Atesh spoke of you and described her guardian to me. You seem like I imagined." So like him.

"Do you know another way out Marina? The earth shake has weakened the roof here and part of it has caved in."

"I am not sure, but we are below the water line here, as my bathing pool is tidal. If the outside wall is damaged this area will soon flood." Marina felt her powers again for the first time in many years. *Oh it feels good to be really alive.*

Ballard sent his men to investigate the other corridors and ascertain the integrity of the castle wall. It was not long before some of the men came racing back, fear etched on their ashen faces, eyes widened and beads of sweat gathered on furrowed brows.

"What is it Palin? What is the danger?"

"It be the largest critter I ever did see sir and it is right behind us."

The small male rodent came skittling past Ballard dragging his wife by the right paw. Her left paw was trying its hardest to keep her hat from flying off. The others were hot on their heels. "Run for your lives dear fellows, the Octonort is loose. We are all doomed; doomed I tell you. Hurry up my dear we must flee."

Ballard stared after the rodents as they raced up the steps. He knew the landing was blocked by the cave in. They were trapped. "What in all Sofala is an Octonort?"

"Only the meanest, mother lovin, fearsome beasty you could ever lay your beady eyes upon, my lad. It has eight rows of razor sharp, rot encrusted teeth. Oh and breath that will melt your face. A hundred long slimy tentacles that will suck the skin right off your body. Squirts a liquid that would burn through rock and they say it digests you slowly after it swallows you; over years. It was natural born, but wizards of old enhanced it powers. It was supposed to guard the great divide, keep the sailors away. But our beloved Master thought it would make a nice pet, now it has escaped its cage and is on the rampage."

Berend rolled his eyes. "Oh is that what the noise be about? Well no need for all the to-do then."

Debris smashed onto the ground and a sucking sound echoed along the corridor. A fetid stench enveloped them all as never before. This had Ballard whipping his head around towards the sinister resonance. A spine chilling coldness travelled up his back alerting the hair like projections to stand to attention. His heart thudded outward from his chest; short sharp intakes of breaths had blood racing throughout his body ready for action. Men came dashing out of another side corridor bloodied. Drawn swords were covered in a purple substance. The last knight securing their rear was grabbed around his ankles. This sent him sprawling onto the ground face first and dragged backwards. His sword clattered away from his hand. He clawed at the dirt and rocks to slow down his descent, all the while calling out for help. Ballard and Berend leapt to assist. Around the knight's ankles was twisted slimy pink tentacles. Ballard slashed into them and Berend pulled the quivering soldier away. A high pitch scream echoed from the depths of the cavern. Troldwites erupted from a lower corridor also racing for their lives and ran into the knights. A melee erupted. Knights fought hand to hand with the Troldwites, whilst the slimy creature grasped for whomever it could reach. Deep purple liquid oozed from the creature's cuts and yellow staining fluid squirted from round projectiles; on its plethora of tentacles. This burned anything organic it landed upon.

A Troldwite raced around near blinded. His fingers tearing at his face, as a yellow substance oozed down from his enlarged brow. The smell of burning fur and sulphur assaulted their senses. He bounced into the back of Ballard sending them both sprawling onto the ground. The Troldwite in a panic, clawed, growled and bit out at Ballard as they wrestled around. Ballard was splattered by small droplets of the acidic liquid, burning holes in his uniform and narrowly missing his face. He eventually placed his hand around the Troldwites neck and wrapped his feet around its body and drew his blade quick and sure across its throat. He held him till he stopped thrashing then rolled him off.

"We must bring the tunnel down or we are all lost Ballard."

"Agreed Marina that is all we can do for the moment, any ideas?"

"Have your men stand back here close to me; quick now."

"Men back to the landing now."

They all raced up and fought the Troldwites from the landing as they tried to approach.

Marina sat up. She closed her eyes and concentrated. She outstretched her hand to the cavern roof below the steps and a blaze of coloured rainbow light erupted from her fingers. The roof blew apart sending rock, debris and crystal shards raining down upon all below. She erected a shield around the knights. The cave-in was a success, though it now blocked off any hope of escape. They were trapped in between two rock-falls. The remaining Troldwites were caught under tons of rocks. The creature was heard screaming in anger and pain. It pounded on the wall trying to break through after its prey.

"Thank you Marina for saving our lives. How are we to exit this nightmare? If it keeps this up the whole castle may fall in on us."

Marina was pale and weakened after using her energy reserves. She pointed to her cell. *"Ballard if the wall is breached we can climb out from my tidal pool. I am afraid I do not have the energy left to do this. I wish you all the best."*

"What are you saying? I will not leave you behind. Come on now, show us the way."

He gazed at his team. "Men we are going for a swim."

"My dear fellow, what about us? We cannot swim. Will you not take us with you somehow?" Six pairs of eyes stared up at Ballard. Tears welled in the female's eyes.

Ballard looked down at the rodents, then at his men. They near all nodded affirmative. Ballard thought well they may not be all human, but as the weird and unusual was becoming the norm around them; they may as well be included. "We wouldn't think of leaving you kind folk behind. The men will be more than happy to carry you, so climb aboard."

"Oh thank you sir. Did you see how I kicked that critter? I threw some rocks too."

"Yes I did indeed. I will certainly tell the king of your bravery."

"Oh, did you hear that Mrs; I am brave."

"Now don't let it swell your head. You may well sink instead of float out of here, darling one."

Berend gave his Commander a pleading look and a shake of his head. Nooooo.

"Oh Berend would you do me the honour of carrying these brave…little folk?"

Bear grit his teeth in a forced smile. His eyes closed to mere slits then his lip curled up in a rhythmical quaver at the side. He was not pleased at all, but picked up the rodents and placed them on his shoulders. The others sat atop of Vykter and Palin.

"Let's hope that beasty does not take it into its head to come after us in the water. Let us be off then. I will assist Marina."

On the interior of the island the Troldwites were on full alert and met the Kingdom soldiers head on. The Gatherers, the winged panther creatures dived down from the sky to swoop and pick up man and steed, then throw them onto the rocks below, or pitch them into the water. Mercenaries also raced out from the castle into the fray and attacked the army without mercy. The few island workers left behind barricaded themselves inside their holding house. They were mainly elderly, peaceful men and women and hoped freedom was not far off. A few of the younger ones became excited, grabbed a fallen sword or knife and joined the fray. Creatures of all shape and sizes seemed to ooze out of the small depressions within the island. They had exited their cages when the magic holding the doors closed dissipated, as the alarm sounded.

King Gareth found himself in a difficult position trying to hold his own against an enormous bear type creature. It had two rows of sharpened fangs and a pointed horn that dripped blood from a previous fallen opponent. Its claws seem to be thicker than the norm and longer. Giving the bear an advantage of slashing from a distance. Sweat cascaded down Gareth's royal brow and stung his eyes; the salty fluid blurred his vision. Gareth's chest heaved with exhaustion as he swung his sword with all his might. But all he seemed to have accomplished was a few nicks on the side of the bear's face and chest. It became incensed and roared with its opened maw. Not far away two young lads sat perched high up in a willow tree, safely hidden by the mass of branches and green leaves. They watched in fear and trepidation as the King fought a losing battle. Tears pooled within their eyes.

"Come on Father, you can beat him, please." Israe held firm to Binji's arm.

They watched as the bear lunged at the puny human. Its claws raked and slashed. Teeth gnashed in anger and frustration ejected a bloody, mucousy drool that covered its jowls. Gareth met each swipe with his sword. Near exhaustion he held the sword with both hands now. Each meeting of metal and bone near unseated him, as his body twisted sideways with the extreme force. The bear's eyes were narrowed and fixated. He stood up high on his back legs and had only one objective on his mind, hatred mixed with blood lust. He was in the midst of a battle frenzy. He saw nothing else within his vision, only the target in front; he must eliminate. He swiped lower with his elongated serrated nails. They caught and dug deep into the horse's flesh. Then with enormous power it heaved the King's horse, shredding it as it slid along the serrated edge of the bony claws. This threw both horse and rider into the air. Gareth was covered in horse flesh, viscera blood and dirt as he tumbled off his steed and skidded along the ground. When he stopped he lay still, winded; the air knocked out of him for a moment. As the bear raced to his downed prey, Master Thaddeus turned and watched in horror.

"Oh No…No…No." He dashed as fast as his legs would carry him. "I don't think so." With such anger as he had never felt before, Thaddeus tossed his right arm forward and hurled a white, jagged lightning bolt at the bear. It severed the creature's head sending it hurtling sideways. The body and legs took a couple more steps with its forward motion before landing with such force; it dislodged a mound of dry dust, covering the area in a thick layer of fine red powder. Thad raced over and assisted Gareth to stand.

"Thanks for that Thad…I…am…spent…he was a formidable app…" the two men spun in urgency, as a loud noise was heard behind them.

A mercenary had also watched the battle from behind a tree stump. He grinned as the bear raced towards the King. Disappointment soon took over as the wizard arrived in time to save the sovereign. With anger and false pride, he crawled out from his hiding place and thought he could sneak up amongst the billowing dust and kill the King. As his arm rose up to stab down, his eyes widened in surprise. A cross bow bolt slammed into his neck. The ball popper attached to the end of the bolt shaft spewed forth a plethora of sharpened small spikes; impacting into the mercenary's head and imploding it from the inside. With a gurgled red foaming grunt he slumped to the ground, spraying bone, brain matter and blood. Gareth and Thad looked on in horror. Now covered in putrid gore they scanned for their rescuer. They looked up and in a tree nearby was Israe and Binji with their cross bows.

"Oh by the ancients, the boys are here…the little monsters." Gareth nodded his head in acknowledgement; a generous smile adorned his face. Pride swelled in his chest that gave him the extra energy he needed to continue and with Thaddeus they dove once again into the melee. Thaddeus was kept busy sending wizard fire bolts at the gatherers. He felt they were the biggest threat to their fighting men.

It took Aiden and two other soldiers working together to bring each Troldwite down. They all utilised the knights fighting dance steps and each gave thanks for the lessons. The vanguard followed his lead and dismounted to fight in small groups on foot. At times this may have seemed an ill-fated action, as the grassed grounds of the inner island became soaked with sweat, blood and gore. The soldiers slipped as they fought the muscled creatures, enhancing the enormity of the awkward situation, often bringing about their own demise. Aiden tiring of the dance of death with the abominations threw purple fire from his fingers and caught many creatures off guard; they turned into ash before his eyes. *Yes!* He then raced to assist his men with the dreaded mercenaries. These hated sub-humans battled using every dirty trick they could think of.

Aiden now clashed with an experienced warrior. He like his brethren was covered in an elaborate design, tattooed from his bald head to the tips of his fingers. His earlobes contained a handful of crystal studded piercings and scarring marred his bare torso. When their scuffle brought them up close and personal, Aiden noticed the chain of small finger like bones around his huge neck. It enhanced the wide spine-chilling grin the warrior wore, showing off his sharp pointed, fetid teeth and rancid breath. *Oh geeze these are the cannibals we had heard rumours about*. Aiden utilised the moves Atesh and her team taught him. He thrust and parried, keeping his centre, twisted and flexed his body as the opponent's sword slashed and lunged towards him. Metal clanged against metal, stroke for stroke. Then the unexpected handful of dirt and muck was thrown in Aiden's face; almost blinding him for a moment. Aiden listened for the swing, though his vision was hazy. He met this drive high with his right sword . With his left hand he had pulled out a dirk from inside the edge of his boot and stabbed the mercenary low in his abdomen and heaved it upward, spilling his life essence and entrails down his legs. The look of shock lasted, but a second before the enemy slumped to the ground. Aiden reversed his sword and drove it backwards . He had an eerie feeling another was behind him. He pivoted and kicked the mercenary off his sword, dead before he hit the ground.

The island was littered with bodies of friend, foe, human, steed and creature. The alliance gained the upper hand with some of the remaining Troldwites racing for their caves to escape beneath in the islands myriad of tunnels. Mia's soldier ants dived in the tunnels after them and hunted them down. Reinforcements arrived from aboard the Southern Island Kingdom ships. King Angus and his troops joined the fray. It wasn't long before they claimed a victory. The remaining mercenaries surrounded, threw down their weapons. All the creatures were subdued or destroyed. There was a short breath taken by those who survived this battle. Most slumped down where they stood. Chests heaving, heads bowed in sorrow for the fallen.

Then an eerie feeling surrounded those on the island. A gentle green misty breeze wove its way around the trees and over all the dead and dying bodies. A foreign, unfamiliar odour assaulted their senses. Master Thaddeus stood up, tasted the air with his tongue and scanned the surrounds. He drew his scimitars from their sheaths.

"Stand ready men. Foul magic is at work. Gareth beware. I have a bad feeling about this."

Chapter 54

The Un-dead:

Meanwhile up in the castle Atesh came to. She was splayed out face down on her bed. Her body ached in places she had not realised existed. With a groan she turned over only to come face to face with a pair of small, yellow sparkling eyeballs; mere inches from her nose. Soft feather like black fur encased a wide grinning mouth with the stubs of sharp canines. It sat and stared at Atesh.

"Oh my…hello little kitty, what are you doing here?"

Around its neck attached to a pink crystal band was a rolled up scroll. As Atesh sat up she held her head to stop the spinning and loud ringing in her ears. As she focused more on her surroundings, she realised the noise was originating from outside the castle, not from within her head. *Oh that was some trip. I feel ill. Boy they are noisy today out there. What is going on, a party?* Atesh advanced her fingers with temperate movements. Although it looked harmless she did not want to scare the fur ball and have it bite her. She unravelled the note.

My dearest Atesh,

I hope you can find it in your heart to forgive us for what we had done to you. We organised your spell to terminate the moment you completed the task upon the island. We had every confidence in your abilities. You will not see us again, for we are by now far away. We wish you all the best. Abi has given you this parting gift. One of his kittens, she has no name as yet, that is for you to decide. Yes, she will be able to converse as you teach her and her wings will not appear for some months. The Master, Maisie and I will miss you. You will be forever in our hearts.

Mason.

Damn it all, why couldn't you let me hate you? "Well, Miss Kitty, sounds like the battle outside has started without me. I should go join them…though I am not feeling myself yet, sort of strange. Anyway enough about me what shall I call you? What have you there? Oh yuck …an old stick. I am sure I can find you something nicer to teeth on." Atesh picked up the end of the misshapen and slobber covered piece of branch. The kitten bounced off the bed and hung on to the other end, making little growl noises. "Oh you are too cute, hmmm… Willow. Yes that is what I will call you. Alright have your stick."

The castle grounds gave a shudder; the first of many. Atesh held on to the bedpost to avoid being thrown to the floor. Willow froze and shook all over. Her tail placed firmly between her hind legs. Atesh placed her inside the bed covers. "Be a good girl and stay here where it's safe." There was silence for a moment then a high pitched scream pierced the quiet and a dissonance of noises began again. This time they rose in volume. Atesh could now make out sword strikes and the twang from arrows and cross bow bolts fired. Taking a deep breath she steeled herself, anchored her feet firm on the wooden floorboards as it swayed. Then she strapped on her back leather armoury sheath and leg knife belt. The two diamonds were secreted in her belt pouch around her waist. She touched them with fondness and tears erupted as she remembered Van. She shook her head to clear the memory. Then Atesh twisted in circles a few times, her head anchored against her right shoulder to see if the wings were still lodged within her back. *Where is that…what did the Captain call it…a mirror? Oh my head please stop spinning.* She wandered on unsteady legs into the bathing room and glanced at her reflection. *Oh thank the ancients; I am back to normal…Marcus? I must find him.*

Atesh dashed out the door and down the stairs towards the underground inner cells. As she passed the kitchen the stove fires were fading to coals. There were food scraps and bones scattered all over the floor and tables. All areas felt deserted. This sent an eerie feeling through her spine. All her arm hairs stood up on end. *"Marcus can you hear me. Please talk to me. I am coming."* *Why does he not answer me?* Atesh reached the landing that would lead her to the cells and work rooms. Taking caution she unsheathed her scimitar. The fire crystals imbedded in the walls came to life as she passed, thus illuminating her path. The first three cells were empty; their doors unlocked and opened. *That is odd where are the...*

The castle shuddered again, throwing Atesh hard against the side dank wall. Pieces of ceiling rock and dirt were breaking away and falling all around. Atesh waited till the castle foundations settled. *What is causing this to happen? The magic failing now Master Grey has left? Or is it nature getting her own back. Geeze, I had better hurry.* As she turned the corner a dull light emanated from the Master's workroom; the door ajar. Opening it further she stood wide eyed as she glanced around. This room was larger on the inside than it appeared. It was full with enlarged, hanging, translucent crystals. Inside swirled mist like tendrils. Wails seemed to resonate out from them, imploring Atesh to help and release them. She noted they were set in a uniformed pattern and there were some areas where crystals were missing. She tilted her head to look at the stones from all angles, her eyes narrowed as she placed her hand up to the one closest to her. Visions flooded her senses of faces twisted in agony.

"Who are you?"

"We are the missing soul portions of those that play. Save us please!"

"I shall tr..."

A voice urgent and threatening interrupted the conversation. "What are you doing here Atesh? This is out of bounds, forbidden to the likes of you." Dan pulled out his scimitar.

Atesh pulled her hand away and refocused her eyes. "Danurel what is all this?"

"This, creature fodder, is none of your business. How did you gain access to this area?"

"If you must know the door was ajar; so I stepped on through."

"I do not believe you. Remove yourself now from this area, before I force you."

"Don't make me laugh Dan. You-force-me? You will never be a Master of anything."

"We'll have it your way then." Dan lunged at Atesh with seething anger. His face creased up into a sneer.

Atesh raised her sword to meet Dan's thrust. His sheer forward force threw her off centre. She stumbled backwards and placed her right hand out to the ground to anchor herself. Dan feeling rather superior lunged repeatedly using a two handed technique. Atesh realised that deflecting from this angle would soon lead to her demise. He was placing ever increasing effort into his sword swipes. However, his quick breaths and shallow breathing were taking their toll. Sweat cascaded down into his eyes causing him to blink rapidly. He took a step back to wipe his face clear. Atesh taking advantage of the small reprieve sprang up onto her feet. They continued to fight back and forwards. Their swords clashing and grinding sending small sparks off into the darkness. Neither gaining any ground; Atesh bouncing on her feet, while Dan seemed heavy on his.

"Too much breakfast Dan, you seem a bit sluggish?"

"Goading will not help you today. You know I am better than you."

Maybe he is right; I am off my game today. I am still feeling awkward after the island.

Dan unleashed a fireball from his left hand, while he feigned an attack to the right.

Atesh spun out of the way as the heat past her body by a whisker. *Phew that was too close.*

He moved in sweeping his sword high above his head to swing it down and slice her from neck to knee.

Atesh could see what Dan was going to try. She had seen this manoeuvre before from him. *He is so predictable; roach remnant.* She pivoted to the left and back one step. Then as he had his sword raised high, she bounced on the balls of her feet and kicked out with all her might. Atesh caught him full in the chest, before he could affect his swing.

Dan went sprawling backwards into the dust, his sword flying from his hands. His head bent forward, his breath came out as a wheeze. One hand holding his painful ribs, he started casting a spell. Words silently spoken, lips moving rapidly, fingers outstretched.

"Oh before you turn me into a toad; did you notice the castle is quiet and empty? Don't tell me they left you behind. Did you not have berth on their next adventure?"

This news broke his concentration. "Another of your filthy lies Atesh?"

"No Dan, I mean where is everyone; Miss Maisie, Mason, Father Grey?"

"Whoa…wha…what did you call him?"

"Oh didn't Mason tell you? You have no idea who I am, do you? This is where I once called home." *Well true in one sense.*

"Your father that cannot be. All this time you, they…were acting ?" Dan turned , scooped up his sword and dashed off out the corridor and up the stairs two at a time. His face was set in a mask of horror, his chest heaving with the exertion.

Pathetic specimen of a man, Atesh , her left arm throbbing from Dan's assault felt a little worse for wear as she sauntered through the crystal room. This widened into an enormous rock cavern; dug deep beneath the castle foundations . Inside this area were all manner of game pieces ; humans in all shapes and sizes and animals, domestic and wild. Off to one side were Morphids and Tors . Some pieces lay busted others nothing remained , but a dust mound . Atesh backed out; tears welled within her eyes , now confused . *How am I going to break the curse if it wasn't winning the game?* As she re-emerged from the crystal room she spied Omni -blue in his cell sitting crossed legged watching in silence . Pounding footsteps echoed down the corridor , as Dan again raced towards Atesh.

Where does he get all this energy from? I am sure I broke some of his ribs. Maybe there is something more to him, I don't know about?

Dan rounded on her, his eyes ablaze in anger. "What have you done? They have all gone!"

"I have done naught Dan."

"You filthy miserable maggot; what lies did you tell about me? They promised to take me with them. This is your fault."

"I have said nothing Dan. Do not blame me for your inadequacies. You didn't measure up; simple logic."

"So why are you left then?"

"This was my choice. I am a Knight Dan; unlike you."

"No, no definitely you are to blame; you told them to leave me. No one is here now to save your pretty behind. You are all alone, without daddy dearest."

"I am never alone Dan." Atesh jumped back out of the way as Dan's sword sliced low towards her. She battered this away with her scimitar. "You always were a dirty fighter Dan."

Dan smirked and grunted at her as he withdrew his dirk from his boot. He now had two blades to fight with. They circled each other eyes staring into the soul of the other, waiting for the next move. The shifting of their feet against the grime strewn floor was wearing thin on Dan's nerves. His face twisted up first one side then the other. His eyes darting left to right.

Atesh centred her mind while side stepping, working out a strategy. *The staff is the answer.* Atesh noticed his staff was hooked in his belt now, hindering his movement, weighing him down on one side. "Dan give up on this foolishness. You know I am the better swordsman here. I can out manoeuvre you anytime. Remember … like I did at the Commander trials." Atesh continued to goad him; pushing him into hysteria. His face was turning redder by the minute. She nodded to Omni as he now stood up against the bars of his cell, looking on in concern. "Come on Dan, have you not got anything special for me? I thought you said you were a *Mighty Wizard*? It's obvious you learnt nothing? You really are a pathetic loser."

Dan was not amused. Something inside of him snapped. His eyes dilated as he hissed at Atesh. He pounced forward and resumed fighting with severe anger and fervent crazed passion. The air reverberated with the clanging of steel as Atesh was backed up past the doorway and into the corridor.

Atesh made it seem easy for Dan, as she continued to backup, eyes widened with apparent fear. She made sure to keep enough distance, so he could not lunge with his smaller knife and catch her in the midriff. *That's it keep coming churlish, milk curdler.*

Dan dropped his dirk and pulled out his staff with the hand grasping white crystal. He pointed it at Atesh and spoke words she didn't recognise. The crystal brightened with intensity, radiating enormous amounts of energy. It pulsated with a blinding light. Atesh turned her head and closed her eyes. Then a high pitched wrenching was heard.

"Now you die Atesh…good riddance." The extreme light exploded outwards enveloping all within its reach.

Atesh was thrown across the corridor to land at the feet of a cowering Omni-blue. She opened her eyes and shook her head. Looking up at Omni she nodded to him and indicated the floor. *" Get down now. I need to put up a shield."* *Remember Mason's instructions, concentrate* . She covered her face, focused her mind and grasped the blue hand reaching out from the cell. In the briefest moment Atesh erected a shield that enclosed both Omni and herself.

The crystal screeched and exploded. It covered Dan and the surrounding area in hot white slime mixed with bubbling blood and yellow creature innards. Dan was thrown back down the corridor. He pulled at his robe to dislodge the putrid smelling offal. Then stared in disbelief at his ruined staff; the crystal had disintegrated before his eyes. Atesh looked about and held her hand up to her nose. The odour was abhorrent . It took all her will power to not give up her last meal. Tears streamed down her cheeks as she looked at Dan's bewildered face and burst into laughter. She was joined by a giggling blue, writhing Merman.

"You really believed that was a crystal ? Dan , you are more stupid than even I could have imagined . It was an egg, you half-witted son of a motherless skink, a lizard egg."

"WHAT HAVE YOU DONE?!" Dan's voice was pitched in falsetto. He shook with rage and fear. "You…you swapped it on me. How could you?"

"No Dan, you were the fool from the beginning. Did you really believe you were powerful enough to be a wizard? They knew you were lying. You were used, baited and left behind to take the fall for everything the Game Master had perpetrated."

Dan threw down his staff in horror. He wiped the gore from his face on his dirt and blood encrusted sleeve and then raced at Atesh with his sword twirling between his hands.

Oh no not the twirling thing he does. Once again Atesh met him and the sword battle continued. This time Atesh utilised her sword dance routines to perfection. She was quick on her feet, efficient with her lunges, slices and parries. They twirled, danced and spun around each other. Although Atesh disliked Dan, she still couldn't bring herself to drive her sword home, into him. She nicked his arm, thigh and across his chest. Dan swiped low and wide with his scimitar trying to carve Atesh in two; she jumped over this manoeuvre and punched him in the face with her fist. Atesh broke his nose again as blood poured down his face. This seemed to incense him even more; if that was possible. Faster and faster Atesh pushed Dan till she had him backing up at a rapid pace in through the Master's room doorway and up against a hanging crystal.

Dan's sweat beaded now on his forehead and saturated his shirt along with his blood. He tried his hardest, but could not budge nor nick his opponent. Swirls of black smoke like tendrils raced out from within the hanging gems. Around the room they dashed; though they were still connected to the crystals; silent screams assaulted the fighter's ears. They then orbited Dan; howling at him; fingers reached out to touch his face, but not quite contacting. Dan swiped one hand at them, while still holding his sword out in front. Atesh stood back watching in awe. Then she felt the hairs on her neck stand up. She sensed a presence looming up behind her. Omni-blue shouted out, at the same time she saw a glint of steel racing towards her from a crystal' s reflection. Dan's face broke out into an evil grin, his eyes narrowed and a sneer curved up one side of his mouth .

Atesh pivoted and slowed the knife down that was headed her way. She grabbed the blade with her left hand and twisted it away from herself with an extra backwards thrust . With her right hand she brought her scimitar arcing around and sliced the cowardly intruder through the abdomen; almost splitting him in two. The knife meant for Atesh now headed for one of the larger crystals.

"Atesh noooooooooo…" Dan raced for the knife with his sword out stretched to intercept it. But as always, he was a beat behind the rest of the world. He miscalculated his timing and the knife struck the crystal and imbedded up to its hilt. It then imploded, sending forth a million pieces. It sprayed the room with gem stones as small as a grain of sand and others as long splinters of glistening rock. Dan took the full force of the blast and was sliced and shredded into oblivion.

Atesh was blown back with the immense force against the front wall of the room. She sat unconscious for a moment then slowly opened her eyes. Atesh realised when she tried to move, something was wrong. She was pinned by a large sharp shard of crystal, imbedded through her right shoulder into the rock wall behind. Now there was imminent danger as creaks and groans emanated from the other surrounding hanging gems. She threw up a protective shield as one by one they imploded causing a ripple effect that continued throughout the entire area. Atesh watched in fascination as thick wisps of black and white smoke circled the room. Some tendrils arced towards the ceiling, others raced into the large cavern area where the game pieces were held. The noise was loud and eerie, wails, screams and laughter echoed around and in-between the clinking of crystal. One piece had pierced an unusual yellow rock which had lain in dust on a shelf for eons. It teetered and fell smashing. A red light emanated from this one. A sigh in the air whispered, *thank ye* and streaked out into the corridor and away. Silence enveloped Atesh and the world around her darkened.

Atesh came out of the darkness to a voice calling her name.

Omni-Blue was yelling. "Atesh look beside you…for the love of the crustaceans. Please Atesh wake up…look beside you."

"I am sort of awake Omni." Atesh swivelled her head to the left which brought spasms of pain lancing through her body. "Oh no Renny is that you? You slimy gutter snake."

Renny had been almost divided in two when Atesh swung her sword around to catch the unknown coward; trying to kill her from behind. He was now glowing green and crawling towards her. The top half of his body dragged the bottom half by the few entrails still attached. It left a trail of blood, gore and filth streaking the ground behind.

The stench was over powering. Atesh started to gag. Bile rose up and down burning her throat. *Oh I am going to be sick. What did you eat last Renny? That is so disgusting.*

His purple finger nails dug into the rocky ground and broke as skin peeled off with the massive effort of this endeavour.

"Renny stop this. What do you think you are doing? You are dead, damn it. Act like it."

Renny turned his head up to Atesh; only the whites of his eyes were showing, glowing with that green tinge. His lips turned up into a snarl and he commenced gnashing his teeth, bloody drool dribbled down his chin.

Geeze I think I am in trouble now. "Grandfather are you outside the castle can you hear me?"

"Oh my dear girl you are here, that is good news."

"I am in a spot of bother, can you please help me. I am pinned against a wall and I am about to be attacked by a…a…I don't know what he is."

"Would it happen to be an un-dead?"

"That is a fair description…how did you know?"

"We have the same dilemma out here my dear; I will not be too long, hang on."

Atesh concentrated on removing the shard of crystal from her shoulder. She had tried to physically remove it with her left hand, but that didn't work. Then she tried with her mind. *Come on move a little at a time. That's it.* The pain sent spots before her eyes. It overwhelmed her and she again closed her eyes to the world. It was only a few moments later that another deep pain in her thigh woke her back into reality. Renny had crawled up close and personal and latched onto her thigh with his teeth.

"Damn it all, get off me." With her left hand she grabbed her scimitar. As she lifted it up, Renny's hand caught her wrist and wrestled her, digging his fingers into her arm. *"Grandfather please I need you now."* Atesh brought her right knee up and slammed her foot into his head. This dislodged him enough for Atesh to strike him with a fair amount of force. His head was thrown backwards onto his back then as he manoeuvred it forward again she sliced with her sword and sent his head hurtling to the other side of the room. She then heaved his body with both feet to join it. There were teeth marks now in her thigh and deep nail indents in her left arm. She placed her head back against the wall and closed her eyes for a moment. Her breaths became rapid as dizziness clouded her mind. Perspiration beaded on her forehead then cascaded down her cheeks to saturate her shirt. This added to the blood slowly dripping down her right side, creating a puddle next to her.

A strange tinkling sound emanated from many different areas of the room. She glanced around trying not to move her right shoulder. She even held her breath to listen. *What is that sound?* Then another scraping noise from the far end of the room started. *No it couldn't be.* Then she saw Renny again crawling towards her; one hand pulling the body forward assisted by the toes digging into the ground and pushing. The other hand held onto his head, teeth still gnashing. *Oh, by the ancients give me some peace.* Then rising up on his elbows was a crystallised Danurel; staring at her. He also inched forward on her right side. He was half formed; his legs were matting together in another part of the room. *This is just wrong. I cannot focus to use my innate powers. I feel so weak. I must be losing too much blood; so much for live forever; what a cruel joke.*

Omni-blue sat and stared in abject horror. Never had he seen such abhorrent events. "Atesh get up, can you move? Please…help, we need help down here." Omni smashed his fists into the cell bars. He tried to pry them open. "No…No…this is not right. Damn-it-all, open the doors…please open."

Both Renny and Dan crawled to either side of Atesh's legs. She moved to kick them away, but each time the movement brought severe pain from her shoulder throughout her body. Atesh's head was becoming foggier, spots continued to dance before her eyes. She realised shock was setting in. For a moment she lost concentration and her left hand loosened its grip on her sword. Dan's right hand pinned her left hand down. She woke to find his left hand had crawled up to her midriff. It was not yet connected to the rest of his upper torso and the shards of crystals cut and sliced their way up through her leather clothes. She stared at the sight before her, unable to move her upper body or limbs. Renny had thrown his torso across her legs. His head turned, vacant eyes looked at her. Teeth still gnashing as drool escaped between his blue lips. Dan's left hand kept working its way up her body till it threw itself around her neck and squeezed with all its might, all the while the shards sliced into her. Atesh struggled to breathe. She twisted her head, tried to bite his fingers, but that just cut her lips and face. *"Grandfather please I cannot hold on any longer. Marcus…I am…sorry. I have tried to get to you. I love y…"* Unable to inhale a breath she finally succumbed to the darkness.

Gareth and Master Thaddeus raced into the room, wizard lightning arcing from his fingertips. They wrestled the fingers from around her neck and threw it across the room with all the other pieces Gareth had collected and discarded. Thaddeus used his power to withdraw the crystal shard imbedded in her shoulder then stopped the haemorrhaging. They laid her flat and Thaddeus worked on her bruised, sliced and flattened windpipe. He lent over her and breathed life back into her body. He placed his hands on her chest and accessed ancient powers to restart her heart. Atesh drew in a large breath and opened her eyes.

"You gave me a fright my dear."

Atesh placed her hands up to her shoulder then throat. "Thank you Grandfather. I was so tired. I could no longer fight. What happened to my living forever bit?"

"You will need to first train with me for a while and pass the wizard's test. You do realise wizards are mainly men; well actually…they are all men. You will be the first female. Quite an achievement I must say. Then you will know how to heal yourself amongst other necessities."

"I don't have to wear robes or anything ridiculous?"

"You can wear whatever you like my dear."

Berend raced into the room with a handful of men. He surveyed the mess and walked over to where Renny's head sat and glared up at him, teeth grating. "So this is where you ran off to cowardly cur?" He lifted his sword and let his anger and blood lust take the better of him. "Now try and bite me, mewling scum." He carved the head neatly in two. The two halves rolled away from each other then returned upright to glare once again at him. "Bad business this is Master Thaddeus , though I do feel better for having vented my spleen on this foul gnat."

"Yes Berend you are correct, it is time to put these boys to rest." He engulfed them all in wizard fire and they turned to ash before their eyes.

Atesh stood on unsteady legs. "Omni-blue can you release the ward on his cell please?

"It is already done my dear."

"Gareth you are bleeding, are you alright?"

"Yes Thad, a shard nicked me while collecting Dan's bits and pieces."

"Grandfather we need to find Marcus. He will be down the hallway a bit."

All the men stopped and looked at Atesh. She eyed them with suspicion. "What…what is it?" She gazed at all their faces, one at a time. They spoke volumes to her. She sank down to her knees and let the darkness envelop her in its peace and comforting embrace.

Chapter 55

The Aftermath:

Ballard and his team had felt awkward with the King's instructions. No prisoners to be taken; no quarter to be given. The entire wizard made creatures to be eliminated on sight; to be hacked into pieces for the pyre. Any soldier that fell in battle was to be decapitated immediately. That was until they fought the enemy on the battlefield outside the castle. Ballard realised after joining the battle late with his knights that something was amiss. He had fought and killed the same man more than once. *How is this possible? I know he was dead.*

It was then he noticed the green mist and as it enclosed around the deceased soldiers, they would rise up with white staring eyes and re-join the fray. Some were missing limbs, oozing blood and entrails as they wandered, looking for their next victim. He watched in horror as some of the dead allied soldiers fought their own. Then he understood the instructions and ensured they all followed them to the letter. After the blood bath was over, he scanned the area. *What a mess.* Body parts littered the grounds.

Those lucky enough to have survived went on pyre duty. A duty always disliked by all was carried out with enthusiasm and speed. The enemy was stacked and fired on the far side of the island; the allied soldiers to the southern end. Creatures were piled down on the beach. The allied soldiers would normally be taken care of by their respective team members; as per their customs. However, due to the unusual circumstances, all the allied representatives agreed to forgo their usual burial rites and eliminate any further risk.

Chief Cedric of the island pirates was the last to concede. He was adamant his fallen comrades would be buried at sea. But as fortune would have it, as Cedric knelt beside one of his friends to say farewell; the dead man opened his eyes. He stumbled backwards as the pirate pulled a knife and with unseeing eyes rose up over him. His teeth were bared, lips curled up in a sneer, entrails dragging along the ground. It was only the quick action of King Angus that saved Cedric's life. He turned at the right moment and drew his sword and swung with all his might; decapitating the un-dead's head.

The Academy wizards and knights were laid out, side by side facing the diminishing sun to the west. Then as the sun's last breath touched the horizon their innate magical souls rose up and the bodies would vaporise into sparkling star dust and fade away. Master Elias and the remaining knights encircled them, giving a guard of honour. An academy wizard stood and watched over each funeral area, ready to incinerate any reanimated corpse.

Ballard heard a shout from outside the castle entrance and raced over to see what the fuss was about. As he reached this area, he stopped in midstride and stood with mouth agape, eyes widened. He watched in silence as people of differing ages and races; dressed in all manner of clothing, wandered out into the diminishing sunlight. Their expressions mirrored each other; utter bewilderment. They held one hand up to shade their eyes as the twilight brightness overwhelmed their senses. The leader of the horde, a tall lithe gent with shoulder length blond wavy hair, close trimmed moustache and beard, blue eyes and tanned skin stopped not far from Commander Ballard. He bent down on one knee, head bowed, all the others behind followed his lead.

"Please rise, do not pay homage to me my friends."

"Sir, we be returned from beyond."

"I am Commander Ballard. Who are you?"

The young man stood up and beckoned the others to follow suit. "You dinna knows who we are?" He fixed his eyes onto Ballard. "Ach I see…we be some of dem wee game pieces, sir. Ye have somehow broken down the spell and be setting us free from the in-between."

"You are the game pieces? All of you; there must be hundreds here?"

"Aye, laddie, but there be many more that be nae here. Some older ones have moved on to the hereafter. Others disappeared before the spell be broken. There be many of dem animals too. They be in cages underground, some snarling and snapping with the fear."

"Please wait here while I fetch the Kings' and the Academy Masters'." Ballard raced over to the officers' tent and asked his superiors to follow him, no questions.

"Ballard what is this surprise you have cooked up?"

"Sires, take a look over by the castle."

The Kings' Gareth, Angus and Cedric, Masters' Thaddeus and Elias, Commander Aiden and Admiral Beaumont strode out behind Ballard and peered around him.

"Oh dear ancients, who are all these people Ballard?"

"Gareth, these are the game pieces, the ones abducted. Atesh had banished the spell. Now their souls have joined with their bodies, back from wherever they have been."

"My word…it worked, how splendid."

"Yes Master Thaddeus but, which part? Beating the game or destroying the crystals …or was it the combination?

"A fine question my lad. One only Atesh can answer when she wakes."

"Ballard you will need to find them a place to stay and gather information on who they are and where they came from. Some do not look of the human race. Oh my, perhaps they are from the other side of the known world. Do not forget some of these good people have been missing for near two hundred years."

"Yes Master Thaddeus, I will get onto it straight away." Ballard strode away with a brisk skip to his step. *Atesh did it; I knew she would. Where are our knights then?*

He watched as Berend and his team organised the newcomers. The leader of the game players, the one who spoke for them initially stood on his own and stared at Masters' Thaddeus and Elias. He tilted his head a little this way and that. He rubbed at his neatly trimmed sun bleached beard and his fingers then stroked his hair back from his face.

Masters' Elias and Thaddeus turned as one, as if an unseen yoke had been pulled upon their necks. They stared back at the young man. In unison they walked guarded and slow over to him. "Jimmie is that you lad?"

"Aye that be correct."

"It is me Thad and this is Elias. Can you not remember us?"

"Ye be familiar, flashes of memory. I be nae sure."

"We are your older brothers, family."

"My brothers that does sound a tad familiar."

"Jimmie, it has been near two hundred years you have been gone. We may look older, but are still spritely, I can assure you. We were all wizards of the high order together at the academy. Though now we are in differing fields. I am purple for the Academy Master and Thaddeus here is blue for Royal Counsellor."

"That long I have been gone? Near to two hundred years away. What happened I be here? Is that why you all talk strange?"

"Yes speech patterns have changed. You will get used to it soon. We do not know why you are here with the game pieces. The last we heard, you went off sailing on an adventure with Gil."

"Gil, where is he, did he transform back as well?"

"We don't know what happened to him Jimmie, only time will tell."

"Welcome home dear brother."

The three took turns in huge man hugs. Then they sat down by one of the fires, wrapped a blanket around their brother laughing and crying together.

"Who or what is a Willow, Ballard?"

"Beats me Sire, but Atesh keeps asking for it; whatever…it…is." "

How about you send some men to search the castle, find her room and see if this *Willow'* can be found. By the way, how is your young lady doing now?"

"Well she is not my young lady sire." *Not yet anyway.* "But, Marina is healing rather swift now…she is something though, isn't she?"

"Oh yes dear boy, a special lady, to be sure." Thaddeus had walked into the middle of their conversation, turned and fixed his gaze upon the young lady asleep in the healers' tent. *She is a rare species indeed.*

"I cannot believe all these people had been abducted, missing for decades; some for over one hundred years. There are so many of them and with no previous memories. There are many races, not of this land. What troubles me the most is we have not had the knights returned or the pirate sailors? What of Marcus and the others in the cells below. Master Grey must have taken them all with him. Why do you suppose that is Master Thaddeus?"

"Ballard those are certainly interesting questions. Ones I cannot answer. I am sorry dear boy."

"I don't imagine you have seen Ciaran at all? Might he be with the two young stow-aways?"

"That is possible, though I cannot remember seeing him once the fighting started. I do hope he is not laying hurt somewhere."

Ballard went off to check on the men and to see how the arrangements for the sick, injured and confused were being handled. Vykter had many fires going. He had a team cooking up a storm for all the displaced persons, as well as the allied forces. Ballard then checked on the funeral pyres. They were well under way with the academy wizards in attendance to ensure the dead did not rise again and disturb the hard fought peace.

Berend strode over holding up a black hairy creature away from his body. It was making little muffled growl noises. "Sir I believe this may be a *Willow*. Here be a letter on Atesh's bedside table. The creature Abi that panther with wings, left this ball of fur for her, as a parting gift."

"What is it?"

"It be a kitten Ballard, with some nasty claws. It has a stick in its mouth that it seems not to want to part with."

"Why are you holding it by the tail man?"

"It be the only way to keep my arms intact sir."

"Here…pass it over. Willow that is a good little fur ball; how about I take you to your mamma."

Willow purred as she crawled up Ballard's shirt and snuggled around his neck. "She is so cute."

"Cute is not the word I would use for this creature sir. You do know what it will turn into, don't you?"

"I am sure Atesh will handle her Bear. The only problem is will Ciaran be jealous? That may become interesting."

"I have had the men looking all over for the lil mite sir. We haven't found him yet. We have searched all the places we can think of."

"Atesh will have a liver turn, if we cannot find him in one piece."

"I am sure sir, he will turn up."

"He has probably sequestered himself inside an apple bin. Oh…maybe he has found the ale stash?"

"Damn it all, why didn't I think of the ale bins? Good idea Commander. I shall take some men and sample…ummm I mean, check them out."

"Yes you do that Berend." Ballard walked away chuckling to himself.

Atesh came too and sat herself up, unsteady at first. Omni's smile lit up her face. She glanced around. Looking…searching. "Omni, thank you for saving my life today; I am in your debt."

"Let's call it even. You saved me from an egging, if I remember."

"Yes that was rather funny. Owww it hurts to laugh. What happened to Marcus and the others from the cells?"

"Master Grey and his team took them away when they departed days ago."

"Oh no, no, he…promised me. Marcus would go free…if I led the attacking team in the last game."

"Marcus handed me this letter for you as he was taken away. Never have I seen a man so forlorn."

"Thank you Omni. What will you do now?"

"Oh, now that I am no longer an errand boy, or a prisoner; I can wander off home. It has been quite a while since my capture. I think about ninety of your human years."

Atesh looked into his blood shot eyes. "Wow that long? You must have been a mere tadpole when you were abducted. Will you remember how to find your way home, all on your lonesome? You know…turn left at the big pink shell, then find the millionth sand grain and swim past two lobsters sitting on a barnacle sunken boat, gossiping."

"Oh so funny you are…not. Are you offering to accompany me?"

"I am sorry, but I am human silly."

"It has, strange as it may seem, been a pleasure to meet you Atesh. You will take care of yourself and find that beau of yours. I suppose if you ever need a friend to journey with…I am always available; for another adventure."

"I will consider it, oh mighty warrior. But how do I contact you; if you are from the ocean's depths? Oh and he is not my beau…he is my husband."

"Well that makes sense. Rotten luck for me…here…all you need to do is hold this tiny shell in your hand and think of me. Conjure in your mind, one who is handsome, gorgeous, fetching; you know…I will answer your call. We will be able to communicate." Omni placed the miniature mother of pearl shell on an azure leather braided cord around her neck.

"But Omni, I do not know how to talk fish…ummm merman."

"Glad to see you are back to yourself, two legs." They both laughed and hugged. Omni-Blue strode away to the water's edge and dived in.

Atesh opened the letter with shaky hands:

My Dearest Fire-Cat,

Forgive me for abandoning you, but this was the only way to keep you all safe. Yes, I figured it out; I made a deal with Master Grey that as soon as the game was completed, you would be returned unharmed. This Island, his lands beyond the Northern Boundary and all you find within, he has left to you. The paper work is on his desk and is in order. My signature was witness to this transaction.

I love you with all my heart and I could not live knowing that you would forever stay a Morphid. That sacrifice for me was too great. I am extremely proud of you and will miss you so. Except for the strange friends you tend to make.

My heart is broken. It hurts just thinking about not being with you. But I will keep up my end of the bargain.

Give my love to my family. Tell father I hope he understands what it is I must do. My half of the treasury, our wedding gift from the old spooks is now yours. Tell Israe to follow his dream and become a *Wizard Knight.* If this adventure has taught me anything, it is that life is too short to be unhappy. Follow your heart's desire and never settle for anything less. Do not forget me. Tell them…well you know the words better than I. Please do not try and find me, it will only cause

you further grief.

Master Grey will cover his tracks well, as you know. He, Mason and Maisie certainly have a love for you. You do have a way of getting into peoples' hearts; even one's as black as theirs.

You are my one and only, forever in this life and the next.

One day we will meet again.

> Your loving husband,

> Marcus.

Tears flowed unchecked down her cheeks. Her head bowed, she unfurled her fingers and watched as she allowed the letter to fall graceful from her hands onto the canvas floor. A shadow bent down and with large hands picked up the letter. Gareth stood before her. He read the letter and sunk to his knees beside Atesh.

"I am sorry sir. I tried to do the right thing. He outplayed me." "

So it is true. He is gone…my son and heir. I am told that you and Marcus were married?"

"Yes sir that is correct."

"I would like to hear about that some time…Were there any live witnesses, proof to this blessed event?"

"No sire, only those of the ancient line and the fused rings we wear."

"Right, that does make things a bit awkward. What does he mean he worked it out?"

Atesh entwined her fingers in agitation. "I am not sure sir."

Gareth stared at her for a moment, rose without saying another word. He left the letter beside Atesh and walked out of the healers' tent and into his own.

Ballard had stood quiet behind Gareth. He blanched when Gareth strode out. *Not a word, no thank you? How could he be so cold, after all she had been through?*

Atesh sat stunned. Her heart could not break any more, as there was only the smallest piece left. Enough to keep her body working. She placed her hands on her abdomen.

Ballard stared and knelt down, placing his course hands over hers. He smiled through his tears and nodded. "You will always have me in your life Atesh." Small kicks pounded at his hands. He looked down and smirked. Though you may get fat and ugly; I will still love you. We are family after all."

"Thank you grandpa, we love you too."

"But…I am too young and handsome to be a grandpa. Can you tell me, what is it to be…a boy or a girl?"

"Yes, it will be one of each popsy."

"True? That is wonderful." He enfolded Atesh within his massive tree trunk arms and whispered into her ear. "Reckon that will twist Gareth's bloomers when he finds out. How about a walk, get some fresh air. Come on you three."

Atesh rolled her eyes at him. "Remember keep this quiet for now, alright?"

They walked around the grounds surveying all that was happening. She gathered Willow to her shoulder, nodded at Master Elias and Thaddeus sitting beside a survivor and headed for the far end of the island. Ballard wandered off to find some hot tea for her.

Here, what seemed like the end of the world, she sat with her legs dangling over the cliff edge, breathing in the salty fresh air. Her arms wrapped around her middle. Her mind wandered with thoughts and quiet words of love for her two tiny babes.

"We love you too mamma."

Atesh laughed quietly to herself. *"Aware at your age, almost four and a half moon cycles that is amazing my little ones. Be well and grow."*

Her heart pounded loud in her ears as Mia's voice sounded in her head. She gazed up and woke from the daze she appeared to find herself in.

"I am sorry for your pain Atesh. The prophecy was millennia's in the making. It was as it should be what had to be, for you to be successful. You have performed well. Look at all the people you have saved. We, the ancients of Sofala, owe you a great debt."

"Then please bring Marcus back to me. Please…I have done everything that was asked of me. I beg you…grant me this one boon."

"Atesh you know if we could, we would. I am sorry dear one."

"Did Van and your soldiers find their way home?"

"Yes Atesh, they are all well. Van thinks the world of you."

Atesh looked at the sea and felt her heart missing not one, but two beats. *"Ciaran where are you? Speak to me. Are you hurt? Please do not leave me too…I need you."*

"Excuse me lassie, may I sit and speak with ye for a wee moment?"

Atesh looked up into dreamy deep blue eyes and shoulder length blond wavy hair. Atesh wiped her eyes on her sleeve and then her sweaty palms on her dirt and blood stained shirt. "Please have a seat, how can I help you?"

The lithe young man sat cross legged facing Atesh. "I want to say thank ye for saving all our lives. My brothers explained what you had gone through to break the Wizard's spell. Can ye…tell me about them crystals, were they all the same? I have no memory of being a gaming piece, as some of them others do."

"Brothers you say?" Atesh turned around and watched Masters' Thaddeus and Elias watching back intently. "Oh…are you Jimmie their younger brother?"

"Aye, that be sure."

"It is nice to finally meet you Uncle Jimmie. I am your kin too, Thaddeus is my grandfather."

Jimmie's eyes lit up and sparkled. He leant over and gave her an enormous hug. "Well then lass, I be doubly honoured to meet with ye."

As Atesh placed her head to his shoulder, her eyes caught the hint of a gold neckband with a red jewel under his shirt. The hairs on the back of her neck stood up and tingled all down her back. She withdrew from his embrace, her hands had tightened into fists and blanched with the effort she held them. Her stomach twisted and heaved. Bile rose up to burn her throat. Her breathing became rapid. She turned her head and looked into his eyes. "Jimmie what is around your…neck there?" He opened his shirt string and staring at Atesh was a gold collar with a channel setting fire stone within it. She bit the inside of her bottom lip. Then took a couple of deep breaths and steadied her trembling hands. "Jimmie oh my, where did you come by that neckband?"

"I awoke with this on. There be no join to remove it. Why…is it important Commander?"

"No, it is unique and beautiful that is all." *Oh please Mia no, no. Do not do this to me, breathe that's it, steady your voice, breathe.* "You were asking about the crystals in Master Grey's work room. The ummm…crystals were all large, hanging from the ceiling. They contained dark wisps of smoke inside them. They were all the same…except…there was one small yellow crystal, on a shelf covered in dust that fell and broke." *Oh no…that was you? All this time, you were not real.* "That is all I remember." *Take big breaths slow now.*

"Well thank ye again lass for all ye have done. My brothers tell me you have suffered losses in this madness; a loved one taken away and a bonded friend missing. I be sorry if I and the others were the cause of this sadness. I will leave ye be now. The other nice Commander be headed this way. I…hope our paths cross again soon." He turned to leave as Ballard strode over.

"Oh Jimmie ;" Atesh swallowed the lump rising in her throat. "Vykter has a barrel full of ripe apples, if you happen to be hungry. Let him know, I said it was fine for you to indulge."

"Aye that be awesome, thank ye lassie. I am rather famished. Ummm, how did ye know I adore apples?"

"Oh a guess, they are my favourite too. Perhaps it is a family trait."

Ballard nodded as Jimmie passed and looked at Atesh with furrowed brows. He had heard that last part of their conversation. Atesh leant into his arms and cried a thousand tears, her heart totally broken now. *How is this fair, I have lost them both?*

"What did he say to upset you so?"

"Nothing Ballard, he said nothing at all. You can call...off the search for Ciaran now alright."

Ballard swivelled his head around to look at the young man walking away. What are you saying Atesh? Do you mean to say that Jimmie was...no...are you sure?"

Atesh nodded her head. The tears would not cease and they continued to cascade down. Her shirt was saturated, eyes reddened and puffy. Her left fist pounded the grass beside her leg. "He has Mia's collar on. He woke up with it around his neck."

"Does he know?"

"No...I didn't have the heart to tell him."

Ballard leant into Atesh. Tears welled in the big man's eyes and spilled down his cheeks. "I am so sorry Atesh; I wish I could take some of this pain away for you." They both said goodbye to their little friend.

Mia again spoke into her mind. *"This was how it was meant to be Atesh. Without the neckband he would have vaporised into a wisp of pure energy and headed into the beyond."*

"You knew all this time why Ciaran was different Mia?"

"Yes that was my burden to bear; the curse of the foreseeing."

"You said nothing to me, no warning and no hint. Now I have lost my whole heart. It hurts so much, I can hardly breathe. What is left to give?"

"You will heal in time Atesh. I have faith in you. You know some come into our lives for a long time; others create the most impact only in passing. Marcus saw the real you. He gave you the strength to believe in yourself. Showed you what real love felt like, to open your heart to another; to feel. Yes, this meant that you may experience the pain as well as the euphoria. But isn't being loved, even for a moment; worth the heart ache? Ciaran taught you many vital things about friendship; of loyalty, honesty and integrity, a different sort of love, but no less intense or painful when it dissipates. You still have a father's love with Ballard. Your team adores you and respects you. They now will depend on your leadership to get them through the

the next few months. Yes, even those rogues that caused all this mess, they all loved you in various ways. You have been blessed indeed. For now you have two more to show you what unconditional love is all about. Oh and a tiny fur ball to keep you on your toes.... In time Atesh follow your heart and find that which is missing. I am here if ever you need me."

The breeze picked up and headed inland from the open seas. It eddied around Atesh and Ballard as they sat cuddled together in sorrow. A faint sound was audible on the wind. They both turned their heads, scanning towards the horizon. Dried smeared dirt, blood and tears stained down their cheeks.

"Don't forget me. I love you my fire-cat. Look after her uncle...don't forget me."

THE END

Glossary

Kingdoms, places
and relevant inhabitants:

Ashmourne Island: Attached to the lower east coast of Sofala; it houses the Academy of Magic. It is owned by the Freymore family, direct descendants of the first owner Wizard Master Eldred Ashmourne.

Ashe Castle: The original home of Wizard Master Eldred Ashmourne. Now is used as the academy of magic's education centre and home to his descendants.

Ashmourne town: Is a small town on east coast of Sofala, adjacent to the academy. All knights with families live within the town, as well as the academy's daily workers.

The Academy of Magic: (Also known as the Wizard's Compound): It is an education centre for all magical knowledge and learning. The Master of Ashmourne Island and the east side of Sofala is High Wizard Master Elias Freymore.

Knights of the '*Pace Alastriona*:' the academy's military arm, peace keepers.
Motto: Truth, Honour, Integrity and Peace through knowledge and wisdom.
Coat of Arms: Three gold circles for Truth, Honour and Integrity on a background of purple for Peace.
Oath:

1. To preserve the peace, uphold truth, honesty and integrity

2. To use the training, knowledge, wisdom and innate gift to benefit society and keep safe those less fortunate

3. To remember the fallen, and honour those that came before.

Total 1000 Knights (10 Battalions).

Supreme Commander Atesh: Is the eighteen year old first female Supreme Commander of the *Pace Knights*. War Horse is Kayne.

Ciaran (pronounced keer-in) Mascot to the first Battalion and best friend to Atesh. He is an ale drinking, apple gobbling, Dragonelle.

First Battalion: Primary unit.

Ballard: Captain; War Horse-Caesar.
Berend: Master of Archery, general arms (A.K.A the Bear).
Brock: General arms and archer
Chale: General arms and archer
Eythen: General arms and archer
Hagan: Lieutenant and the Master of arms.
Jenner: Healer, archer and general arms.
Jesper: Spear Master, musician; War Horse-Badges.
Kerwin: General arms. War Horse-Charlie
Palin: General arms
Renny: General arms, reserve from secondary unit.
Ryna: General arms.
Sage: Horse-Master, general arms.
Vykter: Cook, archer & general arms
Wyart: General arms; War Horse-Shiloh.

Others of interest:

Danurel: Captain of unit two; Store's master.

Freymore Felix: The Wizard Master of Ashmourne Academy prior to Elias. He was the father to the three Freymore boys (Thaddeus, Elias and Jimmie).

Freymore Jimmie: Wizard Master and youngest brother of Elias and Thaddeus Freymore. He went on a sea adventure two hundred years ago with his friend Gil, never heard from again.

Greymont Ballard (Blue): Heir to the Greymont kingdom two hundred years ago.

Greymont Gillard (Grey): Wizard Master sent on a sabbatical for failing to adhere to academy rules. He left Sofala for a sea adventure with Jimmie Freymore.

Jett: The horse handler for the second unit.

Thomas: Relief cook for the second unit.

Beaumont Castle:

The family home of the High King located on the west coast of Sofala.

Beaumont Royal family line: High Kings of the known world.

Gareth Beaumont: High King of the known world.

Anna Beaumont: First wife to King Gareth, mother to Prince Marcus-died in child birth.

Marcus Beaumont: Crown Prince and Commander of the Kings Military.

Brianna Beaumont: Current Queen and second wife to King Gareth Beaumont (Nee Freymore).

Kyle Beaumont: Prince and Captain of the village guards.

Rachelle Beaumont: Daughter to King Gareth and his second wife Brianna. She is twin to Alexandra.

Alexandra Beaumont: Daughter to King Gareth and his second wife Brianna Freymore second wife. She is twin to Rachelle.

Israe Beaumont: Youngest son of King Gareth.

Kings Personal regiment: (150 soldiers. Military 30,000 men stationed over Kingdom).

Marcus Beaumont: Commander of the Kingdom's army.

Aiden Beaumont: Captain

Atien Beaumont: The Admiral of the naval fleet:

Olyver Reece: Captain. **A**rchery Master

River Stein: Captain (AKA Skip**), **Master at Arms

Eamonn Long bow: Master Huntsman

Hector and Vector: High King's Personal body guards: Brothers in their late twenties. They were descendants of the local volcanic island true blood stock.

Thaddeus Freymore: Wizard Master, Councillor to the King. He is twin to Wizard Master Elias Freymore.

Beaumont Village: An expanding village within the walls of the castle grounds. Most of the workers and soldier's families live there.

Anvil Inn: An ale inn at the Beaumont village. Owned by Ben Aleman, the Barkeep.

Ben Aleman: Owner of the Anvil Inn.

Binji Alemanson: The young son of Ben the Barkeep. He works at the livery stables attached to the Inn. He is the best friend of Israe, youngest son of the King.

Beaumont village guards: They are the police force for the village.

Kyle Beaumont: Captain.

Philips: Sergeant.

Cerahya: The name of the world.

Gatlyn Town:

It is located on the east side of Sofala on the merchant route from Ashmourne Island to the Jangly River cross over. It is well known for its fine horse breeding studs.

Lord Lachlan Marshall: Mayor of this town.

Stella: Gypsy seer at the markets that tells Atesh some information of her future.

Jangly River: Is a long river system that runs from the northern border of Sofala right through the middle, dissecting the continent in two. It has two large wagon bridges, one north and one south; many smaller wooden bridges cross over for horses or pedestrians . It is the life blood of the farmlands and vineyards.

Janlin village: Small busy outpost that it a usual stop over for merchant caravans.

Tredenick: Captain of the village guards:

Mist -Wick   Island : It is Located off north east coast Sofala . It is surrounded by an impenetrable mist. It is around two miles from end to end.

Castle Grey: Master Grey's residence.

Wizard Master Grey: Known also as The Game Master: Has lived there for near 200 years.

Master Mason: Best friend to Master grey and assistant. He is a high wizard of unknown quality, rescued from slavery from the other side of the world.

Mistress Maisey: Head Cook in charge of running the house.

Master Danurel: Apprentice wizard, previously a Knight Captain of the second battalion.

Abi the abomination: The leader of the Gatherers.

Gatherers: A collection of panther creatures with wings they abduct as per the master's wishes. (A hybrid of a panther and a dragon).

Kroll: The Leader of the Troldwites.

Troldwites: A collection of creatures mutated together from dark mountain dwarves and rock trolls. They live in caves at the far end of Mist-Wick island and wild bred one's live behind the northern boundary.

Morphids: Humans changed into creatures for interactive war games using ancient forbidden magic.

Tors: Animals changed into creatures for war games.

Captives: The captives were special guests abducted by the minions of Master Grey. They were held for many years in cells beneath the castle.

Chameleon: A creature from the other side of the world that can blend into its environment.

Cluster of small Light creatures: Twelve bright light sentient beings that act as one consciousness.

Dwarf-Rock dweller: Was a small muscled man with a red braided moustache that grew to combine with his beard down to his waist. His hair slicked back in a tight braid accentuated his large shoulders and buffed arms.

Fleet: An elderly worker who was left for dead in a cave-in.

Marina: From an island in the fire seas near the great divide. She is a long lived sea Dragon shape-changer. Refuses to speak to her captors but will mind speaks to fellow prisoners and Atesh.

Omni-blue: Cheeky Merman from the Pearl City in the endless seas. Hair long silvery white with a purple streak to one side, cobalt coloured legs. He loves to play games.

Orion: Is the second son of 'She' who is the heart of the ancient Elven society. He is an Elven Historian who was abducted from the other side of the world.

Samuel: Is a Terracorn King. A four legged, long bodied, white tailed, tri-striped equine. From the waist up he was a buffed mid aged man with sand coloured hair and eyes and two horns curled on either side of his forehead.

Tree fairies: Small human type creatures with wings, they are very timid.

North-Mede Village: It is located on the north western side of Sofala, close to the northern boundary. It was the first area to be inhabited by the first three wizards. It became surrounded by coloured spider webs. Some of the inhabitants were trapped inside the castle and others escaped to the tunnels within the mountains to await a worse fate.

Lord Padric Faraday: He presides over North-Mede and cousin to the King

Lady Gwendolyn Faraday: Wife of lord Padric

Shaw Faraday: Disappeared from a hunting trip, assumed deceased.

Sean Faraday: Count of North-Mede. He becomes the Captain of the King's guards.

Salandra Faraday: Hoping to marry Marcus someday.

Sofala: The main continent in the known world.

Southern Lands & Chain Islands: Large continent to the south of Sofala. The chain islands are a group of smaller islands nearby. All ruled by King Angus Greymont.

Link castle: The ancestral home of Jimmie Greymont and his blood line.

Angus Greymont: Vassal King of the southern lands and the chain islands.

Rosalynn Greymont: Queen, died after giving birth to her youngest son Ballard. She was the pirate chieftain's half-sister from Volcanic Islands.

Conal Greymont: Future heir of the Southern Lands. Eldest son to King Angus

Anna Greymont:-Married to King Gareth Beaumont, died in childbirth.

Elara Greymont: Married to Chieftain Cedric's son Trent.

Bryce Greymont: Unmarried Captain in their Royal Navy.

Ballard Greymont: Captain of the *Pace Knights*; Unmarried.

The Island of Tyral: It is a medium sized island around one hundred miles long and fifty miles wide. It sits within two sea days off the west coast of Sofala.

Wilmont Castle: Home of the Dukes' family.

Duke Morgan Beaumont: Younger brother to Gareth. He presides over Tyral and the waste lands.

Duchess Lysanna Beaumont: Wife to Duke Morgan (Twin to Queen Brianna).

Prince Fynton (Fyn) Beaumont: Heir to the Tyral Duchy.

Prince Aiden Beaumont: Is the Captain of the High Kings personal regiment and second son of Morgan. He is Twin to Liera.

Princess Liera Beaumont: Daughter to Duke Morgan

The Volcanic islands : The volcanic islands are actually a group of archipelago islands of many differing shapes and sizes; off the east coast of Sofala.

King Cedric Blade: The Pirate chieftain (King) of the volcanic islands. Has ancestors mixed up with the first three wizard's line.

Trent: Heir to the pirate's throne. Commander of the fleet and Armed forces. He married King Angus Greymont's daughter, Elara.

Parker: Captain of the fleet and younger brother and identical twin to Darius.

Darius: Captain of the land army and twin to Parker.

Charmaine: Princess (Charlie)-daughter of Cedric. She was abducted along with her crew when she captained her own sea vessel.

The Ancients of Sofala:

Creatures from when time began. They are sentient beings are usually enormous in size and power.

Barron: Master of the North-Mede tunnels. A large jewelled snake, history buff and Story-teller.

Betha: Queen of the Arachnopods. She is the largest known creature to inhabit Sofala. She is so large she can block out the sun, when she walks the ground shakes. She has eight legs and six eyes. When she laughs all in the vicinity are covered in her clag (Pieces of food that have been stuck between her teeth for centuries).

Diamonds in the last game:

Red Jack: Betha's consort. He is smaller than she with a large red stripe down his back. He has a nasty disposition.

Mia: The queen of the fire ants. She has a gentle personality. Went on many adventures with the Freymore wizard twins as a princess. She is blessed with the for-seeing.

Van: The General of the Soldier fire-ants. He assists Atesh to win the last game and becomes Mia's consort.

Prophet Lailoken: The last prophet/seer and tribal elder.

The first three wizards: Wizard Masters' Gavin Beaumont, Eldred Ashmourne and Jimmie Greymont.

Strange wizard made creatures:

Ape like creatures: First appeared on the second cube game. Their sharp razor like claws was able to partially decapitate their prey with one swipe.

Arachnoeyespikes: Coloured spiders that have eyes on each of their spine spikes. They have sharp stingers on their tail and are aggressive and territorial. Their eyes turn as one. They inhabited North-Mede village.

Armadilly: Large grey rock type creatures that sway back and forth on their four stumpy legs. They are covered in a hard battle armoured coat. If they grab hold of you, there is no letting go. They will keep chomping with their second and third set of teeth and swallowing. They walk with fast short swaying type steps and near impossible to kill. Upside down they are vulnerable. Their abdomen is soft and their back shell weight holds them thus.

Blood fleas: Attach to exposed skin in the game Cube 11. They suck their host dry in minutes.

Centrapedes: Part of Atesh's cavalry. They are long and enlarged centipedes that can traverse heat and lava pools without any damage. They have one hundred shell encased legs. They can carry a morphid into battle.

Earwiglarons: They burrow through the ear up into the brain and gorge themselves on the living tissue. The digging vibrations attract them as they live in the warm sand. They crawl beneath soldier's helmets and into their ears. They have two sharp pointed stingers on their tail, two beady eyes and a forked tongue. They fly away at a slower pace and lower altitude once engorged with whatever they eat inside the head.

Flying sticky flops: These were found in a large cavern on the way to North-Mede. They were the length of a small man's body, a cross between a wild boar and a strange long faced dog. It had an elongated proboscis with a small curved mouth. Above and on either side of the mouth were two arched tusks with pointed tips about two hands in length. There were four eyes two on either side of the head. There were large elongated ear cartilages, a long curved spine with spiked nodules extending upward. Four long legs with elongated flat feet lay apart from the main skeleton. The large extended tail had protruding spikes.

Gatherers: A group of panther/ dragon flying creatures. They are able to comprehend simple messages and talk with a lisp. They work for The Game Master. Abi the abomination was the first and only one with granted a name. He rules the others.

Gnasherdiles: A large reptile that lives in the Meder Billabong with many rows of large pointed teeth. It has a pair of yellow eyes, large snout and a serrated fin. It can rise up on its two hind legs and walk like a man. The front appendages reach out with webbed paws grasping at the air propelling itself along with an unsightly gait.

Lizard creatures: The lizard creatures had two sets of arms bearing swords; they were a formidable opponent in the Cube 11 game. They did not wear protective armoury as their thick hides were difficult to penetrate. The officers had wings and ran away when their side started to lose.

Octonort: A mean and fearsome beast of the sea. It has eight rows of razor sharp rotting teeth and breath that will melt your face. A hundred long slimy pale pink tentacles that will suck the skin right off your body. Squirts a burning liquid that would burn through rock and it digests you very slowly after it swallows you; over years. It was natural born, but wizards of old enhanced it powers. It was supposed to guard the great divide, keep the sailors away. But the beloved Master thought it would make a nice pet.

Scorpioids: Enlarged scorpion creatures used as Tors in the Cube 11 game. Wild scorpioids also attacked a farmer and his family near the Beaumont Castle. They usually live underground or in caverns.

Stony: Large stone and crystal infused guards from the Ashmourne academy. They guard the bridge to the academy and have a dry sense of humour. They are intrigued by gossip.

Talking rodents: There were six talking rodents as tall as a man's thigh, exhibiting human traits. The three women wore long multi coloured dresses and bonnets. The males were dressed in brown trousers with suspenders, white tunics and boots. These were wizard made, but did not change back after the crystals were shattered.

Troldwites: A collection of creatures mutated together from dark mountain dwarves and rock trolls. They live in caves at the far end of Mist-Wick Island and wild ones inhabit behind the Northern Borders. They will eat any meat raw or cooked; they are vicious, without scruples and enjoy torturing their captives.

Willow: Is a gatherer kitten given to Atesh by Abi as a parting gift.

Glossary Ib:

Other relevant information:

A Wizards Nemesis: (Nemi), a collar that connects around a Wizard's neck and cuts them off from their innate magic.

An Ancient's tear: This is said to have magical qualities for the wearer. It must be inserted under the skin by a wizard.

Angel Wood: Is a branch from the Angel tree, a most ancient and magical tree. It cannot be removed by force and when it is given to another, it must be of the owner's free will and for use without guile. The one tree on Cerahya was lost millennia ago. Betha had a piece she gave to Atesh to fashion her wizard staff from.

Ball-poppers: Small hessian bags with spikes imbedded that exploded on impact. They are placed on the end of the cross bow bolt used by Prince Israe and Binji.

Bard: A teller of tales, a poet or singer. He goes from one town to another entertaining for his supper.

Bare Pear: When a drunkard usually pulls his trousers down and exposes his backside, a rude gesture.

Cannibals: A group of warriors that fight and eat their captives. They usually wear fingers as jewellery around their necks. They fought in the last battle on Mist-Wick Island. They have no body hair at all and are marked with many tattoos. The more kills the more tattoos.

Chances: It is a board game made by the Game Master that has evolved over the last two hundred years from static playing pieces to interactive game pieces. It is primarily a war strategy game, played mostly by those with innate magical abilities. The rules are; there are no rules.

Chief's Flame Thrower: It consists of long metal tubes infused with explosive yellow powder and ignited with barrels of steam under pressure. The flames would shoot out and blast the enemy to ash. This was bolted to Cedric's flagship and used to kill the wild creatures trying to escape Sofala.

Churlish-Milk Curdler: A cussing. It means an inbred person, with bad breath.

Glamour Spell: A spell higher magic users can accomplish, it involves changing ones outward appearance to look different, such as older or younger.

Guerrilla Warfare: It is a sneaky type of warfare. Small groups use sabotage, ambushes, raids, hit and run tactics. It is useful when fighting in bushes or unknown territories.

Hospice: A place where caring of the sick takes place. Wizard healers use crystal enhanced powers for all manner of extreme ailments.

Intestinal Bugle: The build-up of gas from digestion, then it is expelled from the rear end making a musical sound.

Last Man Standing: The last man to be still standing after a bar fight with no sides as the winner.

Lava Tubes: Within a volcano there are active lava flows and tunnels that are cold. The unused ones are made from the solidified lava flow, formerly occupied by flowing molten lava.

Lavacicle: a large mass of twisted cooled lava that sits from floor to ceiling.

Meder Billabong: Collection/Junction for the water from two main rivers, the Meder and Jangly running from the Northern Boundary they then split and run separately.

Meder River: The River that flows down from the Northern Boundary beside the North-Mede Town, this leads to the Meder billabong.

Mercenaries: Fierce warriors that battle for pay with no fealty towards anyone or any kingdom, only money.

Reeve Blade: Broad flat blade of medium length, used for cutting as the point is narrow and sharp. Used against those with chain mail or creatures with hard scales.

Scimitar blade: A double edged sword with a curved blade. Used primarily for horse warfare due their light weight. They are for slicing rather than stabbing.

Shallow on the draft: A nautical term, for a ship that can sail in shallow water. The bottom is flatter than a rough sea faring ship.

Step marks: These are unusual marks covering both sides of lava tunnel walls. They show the depth of the lava flow when this tube was active. One needs to be careful that the actual fire flow is not a few feet behind the walls or below what is walked upon. If it feels spongy do not place your full weight upon it.

Sucking Sand: It is soft sand found on islands and deserts. If stepped upon it pulls anything down into it. The more you move the quicker you submerge. It is warm and thick.

The Bonding: It is magic from nature's spirit. It has an ability to pair the right people together; it selects them. Once the two feel each other's innate energy signature, no other suitor will do. They are hooked forever to search out and find the source of the pull. Often as not, when they meet and touch hands a tingling will travel up their arms, the recognition phase. Their love is eternal, even extending to the next life and the hereafter. This occurs in the Elven races and their descendants only.

The Dragon's Breath: The Royal flag ship. A multi decked galleon that has a dragon figure adorning her bow.

The Great Divide: A magical event on the other side of the world causes a calamitous trigger point to the east off Sofala, deep within the ocean. A gaping chasm opens up within the vast ocean's floor, from the northern ice fields all the way down through to the southern lands of Cerahya, east of the archipelago islands. The seabed moved and pushed up on either side of this rent, creating a row of differing sized underground fire mountains and apertures. The underground volcanoes are still active, surrounded by wide vents that expel the gas bubbles seen rising out of the ocean. Around this hive of activity, whirligigs form and drag down any or all who venture near. There never will be a way now to traverse the sea to the other side of the world from the east side of Sofala. Thus it is known as the great divide.

The Northern Boundary: A large mountain range was raised up two hundred years ago from the East Coast through to the West Coast of Sofala to keep fierce creatures behind it away from the population.

The Pox: Also known as bad blood. It is transmitted by prostitutes, causes madness when it reaches the brain.

The Sanctuary: The ancestral hideaway of the Freymore's, a place of peace and tranquillity. It is located within the black mountains and is self-sufficient.

The Turning: The normal life span of an adult is around one hundred and twenty to one hundred and fifty years. Wizards live much longer lives depending on their innate power. The turning is when a young one becomes accepted as an adult. If one exhibits some innate power they may find this time difficult. Some exhibit mild upset such as headaches, aches and pains throughout their bodies. Others with more power can become quite unwell with intense pain as their powers are enhanced. There has been an occasion where a turning has resulted in death.

The un-dead: A Wizard spell of necromancy used to reanimate dead tissue or the dead to rise again. The only way to kill the un-dead is decapitation and burning.

Time is measured by the days, weeks and seasons: The weeks follow the lunar cycle. Eight days in a week = three lunar cycles, twelve weeks, or ninety six days in each season, Four seasons in a year. In between the seasons are eight days for change.

In total forty eight weeks of seasons and four weeks of in-between=fifty two weeks per year. The years are measured by the King sitting on the throne.

White Season (Cold and snow) and *Green Season* (Rebirth and new growth)

Red Season (Hot times), *Yellow Season* (Leaves turn colour and drop).

Zinger Juice: An alcoholic drink made by the science students at the academy using different herbs, vegetables berries and honey. It has a powerful kick.

Glossary II:

Ashmourne Academy of Magic-Exercise and Forms Techniques

Good day to you, I am Commander Atesh. The following are the exercises and form techniques I will be teaching today. At the end of the day you will feel tired and sore, there will be muscles not felt in a long while. Have a relaxing hot bath for tomorrow we will do this all again. Enjoy the journey and the end results.

The morning sessions: The exercise routines in the mornings will promote activity. It is a schedule made of exercises, to strengthen, stretch and enhance flexibility. Limber up your muscles and remove the night's stiffness and cobwebs. The forms will ensure your feet and swords work in tune with the body. They would then perform the centring skills, being one with the self and with the sword. This allowed the weapon to become an extension of the arm; not a separate entity.

It is a holistic approach to being a soldier. We were taught at the Academy that to be an effective weapon you require the mind, body and soul to be as one; a synergistic effect. It is the dance of life.

The evening sessions: The evening sessions quietens the body rhythms down, so you can sleep. It keeps your preparedness on a slow burn ready to ignite at any given moment. Slow methodical movements, elegant and peaceful are executed, all in harmony with the world. They recite their pledge and bow in remembrance of the fallen.

The exercises begin with the preparation; this should take around ten minutes.

Requiesce: This means to relax your mind and body. Then bow to the coordinator, as a mark of respect. They in turn will be acknowledged.

Cae-sar: We go down on our knees in one movement.

Inanem, animum: (In: An) Close your eyes. Empty your mind. Be one with your soul and be at peace. Take deep breaths in and out. A meditation form, this is good preparation also prior to any battle.

Aperi oculos animum Liberia: (Oculos: Lib) Open your eyes and your mind should feel free and light.

The next sets are the warm up exercises. They should take around an hour the most.

Exerceo: This is the grounding stage
(All exercises we start on the right side and perform ten movements then the left side ten movements unless otherwise stated. Remember smooth, light continuous movements).
Start from the feet and work up your body.

Lift foot and perform circle/rotation motion, right leg then left.

Raise foot up and down, keeping knees straight, right then left.

Raise knee up to chest; one side then the other.

Extend leg straight out from body, right then left.

Hands on hips and bend knees down bringing your body to heels these are the squats then stand keeping hands on hips, by ten times.

Hips we move back then rotate to the front by ten and reverse start at the front and rotate through to the back by ten. Remember stick that bottom out.

Now the buttock muscles, flex your knee up and circle across the body then back down right side then left. This requires some balance.

Stomach core muscles, now tighten and hold for a count of five then release for five. Repeat these five times. Don't forget to breathe in between, exhale at the point of tension

Rotate hips by placing hands on hips and rotate around to the right by ten the reverse and rotate around to the left by ten.

Raise, tighten and release shoulder muscles by ten.

The wrist and hand strengthening, hold both arms out in front of your body palms down. Make a fist; tighten arm and release when it burns. Repeat five times.

Pivot right wrist to the right by ten then to the left by ten. Repeat with the left wrist.

Gently move your head to the left shoulder and back, then right shoulder and back. Repeat this five times.

Place your chin down to your chest and hold it for five counts, then extend head back to nape of neck and hold for count of five.

Rotate right shoulder forwards by five, then backwards by five. Repeat with left shoulder.

Place left arm over the back of head and right hand grasps the elbow and gently pulls back to count of five then repeat with right arm.

Left arm to right shoulder, right hand on left elbow and pulls tension towards body to count of five then repeat with right arm.

Now shake your body all over to release any tension

Gentle jog around the area then have a break.

Repeat these exercises five more times.

Kihon: The preparation stage for basic moves with your sword. These should take around thirty minutes to work through. It will be a combination of sparring and drills, and combat skills. Always remember to centre your body throughout these exercises.

Stances are your feet positions
When attacking use front stance, weight forward on the front leg ensure your body posture is always centred. When blocking the weight transfers to the back foot. A centre stance is both feet apart

Start with head, upper-torso, abdomen and legs

Blocking

Evading

Attacking /strike

Follow up with your strike

Angle strikes, sides, upwards, downward and stabbing

Slashing

Strike and evade

Block and retaliation

Defend and finish

Strength in Tradition: This is where we use the shape of the sword to elegantly frame the body. They will carve through space, tell a story, show a battle mime from times gone by, or engage in a mock battle. Some like our intensive battle dances we call the frenetic hair splitters, are purely to give the audience a show, a thrill or heart turn. These will uplift the knights' spirits and teaches them concentration and fearlessness. This is the end result of years of training as a team, the perfect synergistic whole; our ultimate goal.

Longsword: This is used with basic walking steps. Forward, back, one foot crossed over the other to side step. Pivot on one foot, slow and steady rhythm. This is more effective with a two handed technique. They can reach further than other swords so opponents are at a greater distance.

Rapier: These are used to execute special steps with beats that are more erratic.

A staccato rhythm is where the timing becomes faster often disjointed and tighter. These are performed with one to four senior knights.

Dual Rapier: Again for the experienced fighter and sword dancer as they are using a coordination of both sides of the body, very disjointed and deadly.

Kopis: Dagger with an ornate handle, often used in conjunction with a longer sword; or as a throwing knife.

Scimitar: This is the preferred fighting and dance weapon of the *Pace Knights*. It has a curved blade for slashing rather than thrusting forward. The weight is forward on the steel and can be used one or two handed. It is tempered and balanced with a radius edge. It is often used in conjunction with a rapier and the one preferred for the cross-over dance routine.

About the Author

Kerry's love of life, literature and a deep hunger for learning has been at the core of her being. Growing up in rural N.S.W. as a third generation writer, her childhood was surrounded by animals, fiction characters, stories and verse.

Kerry's career in health; spanned thirty five years. She combined University knowledge with her vast clinical, educational and administrative skills. Together they melded into a long and distinguished multi-faceted Nursing academic career. It was on the poor souls in her lectures and workshops; she fine-tuned her wicked nurse's sense of humour.

Early retirement due to illness however, saw Kerry return to her passion for the fiction novel. She soon discovered the world of the Indie Author. It was only a matter of time; she embarked on reviewing, critical evaluating then mentoring, coaching and substantive editing. Finally she decided to write her own novel. The Tales of Cerahya was born. It will be a multi-novel, humour infused, action packed fantasy adventure.

It has been a journey of discovery and insight; infused with wonder, love and yes; at times frustration.

Kerry now resides in a quiet sea-side community in Tasmania, with the love of her life, husband Ken and their small fur baby Molly; who believes she is human. Here Kerry has the best of both worlds, country living and the beach. Her only nemesis remains, *'the spider'*

Thank You

I would like to thank you, the reader for taking the time to join me on my novel adventure.

If you have enjoyed this experience then please leave a review on the relevant author page from your place of purchase. If you feel there is some way I could improve an aspect for the next instalment please do not hesitate to leave questions, an area for discussion or a review on my webpage. I would really appreciate any and all constructive feedback.

Kerry Alexander-Hall.

You may find me on my Authors pages.

www.facebook.com/KAlexanderHall
Email: Kerryhall10@gmail.com

The Tales of Cerahya with Atesh, Ballard
and their crazy band of knights, will continue in

Book 2

This should go live 2017.